MYTHBORN I

RISE OF THE ADEPTS

Zach,
Hope you love
the story !

BY
V. LAKSHMAN

Author's Preface

MYTHBORN I
Rise of the Adepts

Cover art by Raymond Lei Jin and Na Sun
Map by Ralf Schemmann, Raymond Lei Jin

Certificate of Copyright Registration:
TXu 1-887-058

ISBN-13: 978-1-64058-053-4

Dawn's Light Media
Noble Sun Press
SillanPaceBrown Publishing, LLC

Author's Preface

For more information on Mythborn, please go to:
www.mythbornmedia.com
or
www.dawnslightmedia.com

For more information on SillanPaceBrown authors and
projects, please go to:
www.sillanpacebrown.com

Dedication

This book is dedicated to the thousands who've followed me Facebook, Twitter, and elsewhere in the online community, to my amazing editors, and to my friends and family.

I'm grateful for your faith, guidance, and unending support.

Author's Preface

NOTE TO READER

Please FOLLOW and LIKE us on:

Note to reader: We hope you enjoy

Mythborn I: Rise of the Adepts

If you'd like to learn more about Mythborn, please go to:

www.mythbornmedia.com
or
www.dawnslightmedia.com

Look for the rest of the Mythborn saga here:

- *Mythborn 1: Rise of the Adepts*

- *Mythborn 2: Bane of the Warforged*

- *Mythborn 3: Dark Ascension*

- *Mythborn 4: Arcadia Lost (Q4, 2018)*

- *Mythborn 5: Genesis (Q1, 2019)*

CONTENTS

Author's Preface

Author's Preface

AUTHOR'S PREFACE

Mythborn is about an assassin-in-training, a boy named Arek who begins to realize that a mission with his master may in fact be designed to sacrifice him to demons.

In fact, several powerful forces *are* angling for his death, and ghostly hints from an untrustworthy source only serve to create further confusion. When he gets separated from his mentor and sole protector and cast into a sea of potentially deadly strangers, he plumbs the depths of his own nature to find out whether or not he can survive. To make matters go from worse to worst, he has only eight days to find out.

The exploration of the villain's arc is what most interests me, and (I hope) entertains you. The story may seem to start off like every other fantasy novel, but don't be fooled. I'm using things that look familiar to open up something truly different!

If you stick with it, you'll see a world unfold unlike anything you've read before, with dwarven assassins, ultra-lethal combat, and no simple clichés; a place where death is only the beginning; where gods of our own making walk amongst us.

I hope you'll enjoy reading *Mythborn I: Rise of the Adepts*, the first book of the Mythborn series, as much as I enjoyed writing it.

And yes, there will definitely be a video game!

Thank you all!

V. Lakshman

February 2018

Author's Preface

Mythborn I: Rise of the Adepts

"Any sufficiently advanced technology is indistinguishable from magic."
—Arthur C. Clarke

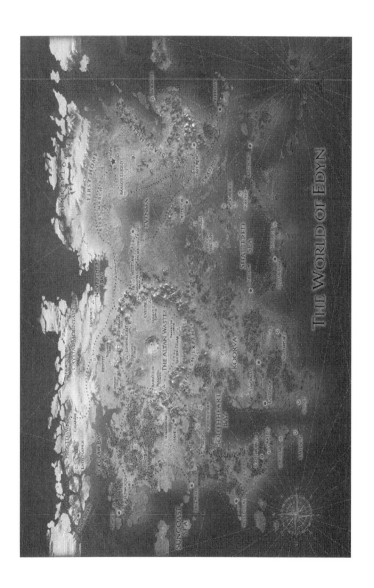

Author's Preface

FLASHBACK: SOVEREIGN'S FALL

"Winning my war was never about who was right.
It's about who is left."
—General Valarius Galadine

T he final battle lasted for days, leaving the ash slopes littered with the dead and those who still did not know enough to accept their fate. King Mikal Galadine stepped his horse forward carefully, mindful of those who had fallen in his name. New lines creased his face, and his shoulders slumped with the weariness of a man who had labored far too long at the task of war.

Have only four years gone by? He looked around, grimacing at the thought. *Feels like forty. And now one final duty.* He motioned to his king's mark, Captain Davyd Dreys.

"Milord?" The man grunted as he maneuvered his horse to stand by the king's.

Mikal fingered his leather reins, his calloused thumb smoothing the same worn spot he rubbed whenever his conscience complained. He looked up, his gray eyes narrowing at the sight of crows wheeling in slow circles above. "You know what they call a flock of crows?"

The king's mark was silent, his eyes tracking from his king's face to scan the skies, then the battlefield. Mikal knew the man wasn't going to answer. Davyd just knew him too well. There wasn't any need, so Mikal finished anyway.

"A murder," said the king. "A murder of crows." He looked down at his hands before taking a deep breath. "It seems appropriate for what comes next." When there was still no reply the king glanced sidelong at his second and flatly said, "You don't agree."

"It's not my place, sire. Those who've lost children to rift horrors will sing your praises."

Mikal shrugged, his nostrils flared, and another breath whistled out. "You know I don't care about that."

"I do," Davyd said, "and you're a righteous man." He looked over at the king and smiled. "If you're worried about my willingness—"

The king quickly shook his head and said, "No, not at all."

"Duty is seldom easy, milord." Davyd met his eyes and smiled. "We agreed this would ensure peace."

Mikal nodded. What would Davyd say if he knew the carnage he was about to unleash extended to the families, too? He met the king's mark's trusting gaze and said softly, "Bring the men forward."

"At once, sire." Davyd turned his horse and cantered back to the lines, barking commands at the assembled soldiers.

The ground shuddered. Mikal's horse whinnied, then stepped to the left, its senses attuned to the minor rifts occasionally snapping into and out of existence around them. The king had been told to expect small quakes, by-products of the magic allowing a space between their world and the demon plane to open. The tremors would pass now that the true Gate was closed.

He gave his horse a few pats on the neck to reassure it, and then turned his attention back to the slope before him and the ragtag band of men and women descending. They stumbled along slowly, supporting each other, with barely the energy to breathe, much less walk. Hundreds had gone up to do battle with the demon-queen Lilyth, but barely twenty staggered down from that final struggle, their black uniforms gray with soot.

Yet they had succeeded and the demon-queen was dead, buried in the volcano's smoking pit. Lilyth had destroyed vast stretches of the land in her quest to subjugate and rule, and much work remained to bring back what her forces had ravaged. The army of mages had bought new hope for the land, but Mikal reminded himself it had been their arrogance which had begun this damned war in the first place.

So many signs had been missed and so many mistakes made. His fingers let go of the reins and tightened instead on the hilt of his blade, *Anzani*. Mistakes had indeed been made, but some debts must be paid in blood. A younger Mikal Galadine might have dwelt on regrets and allowed them to change his heart, but thinking about the children of Edyn taken from their homes deadened most of his remaining doubt. *Davyd is right,* he thought. *Duty is never easy.*

The survivors came down the last rise. At their lead was Mikal's friend Duncan, who raised his hand in greeting. The king could see the effort it cost him.

"Rai'stahn has pulled the dragon-knights back. We were successful. Lilyth is no more." Duncan lowered his pale eyes, his tone becoming more intimate. "Mikal, I'm sorry about your brother . . . no sign of him after he opened the Gate. We tried—"

The king brushed off the concern and said, "Whatever was left of him died years ago. We do what we must."

Duncan turned his attention to the people behind him. Mikal felt a strange detachment settle over him like a cold cloak, stealing whatever joy today's victory had grudgingly lent his heart. Instead, a cold hardening—a kind of crude mental shield—was forged, separating him from the moment. *No point in dragging this out,* he told himself.

"Your leave to move to shelter? Sonya is especially drained." Despite his immense weariness, a slight smile touched Duncan's lips as he turned back to the king. His leaden arms moved automatically to support his wife as she tottered beside him on unsteady feet. "She's the only reason we survived."

At Duncan's touch, Sonya leaned into the comfort of his embrace, but Mikal noticed her eyes never left his own.

They were clear and resolute, as if she already knew things were not going to end well. He shook off her gaze, turning instead to address his friend.

"A moment," King Galadine said, holding up a gauntleted hand. His king's mark cantered forward and handed him a scroll. After he'd backed away, the king undid the black ribbon and unrolled the parchment.

Consternation ran across Duncan's face. "Your Majesty?"

Mikal looked down at the parchment and began to read:

"On this day, the twentieth of Peraat, I, King Mikal Petracles Galadine, proclaim the Way of Making a danger to our lands. It shall no longer be practiced in Edyn. Those who continue to adhere to and follow its teachings shall be put to death. Those who exhibit the Talent shall be sacrificed for the greater good."

The king met his friend's confused gaze.

"Never again shall we find ourselves under the yoke of the Way." A breath passed, and in that instant the two knew each other's hearts. Then Mikal bellowed, "Archers, forward!"

The king's mark repeated the command and one hundred archers moved forward in lines on either side of the king.

Duncan looked about in alarm. "What are you doing?"

"I sacrificed my brother for the safety of this land, Archmage. Why would I spare you?"

Duncan dropped all pretense of mannered speech and exclaimed, "We fought side by side! Now you're going to kill us?"

"No, you're a casualty of war." The king turned and nodded.

Bows bent and released, their strings thrumming as deadly shafts sped to their targets. Having defeated Lilyth, few mages had any strength left to defend themselves. Arrows pursued those who tried to flee, ripping through flesh and finding vital organs. Most died where they stood.

Sonya screamed, diving at her husband, who still hadn't moved. Mikal watched as she caught hold of his chest, placing herself in the way of coming death. In a moment the sound of bowstrings stopped. Only she and Duncan remained.

Duncan looked around in shock. "You . . . they defended you with their lives." He looked up numbly. "They had children, families . . ."

"No," the king said.

His answer caught the archmage off guard. The king's dead gaze never shifted as he watched the sickening realization wash over Duncan's features.

"You killed them, too?"

Mikal remained silent, his eyes searching the blasted landscape for an answer. Then he looked back at his friend and said, "Every time magic is used, rifts open and children disappear. I can't let this continue."

Duncan shook his head, "You slaughtered our families?" He paused for a moment, his eyes wide in shock, then added, "Why have we been spared?"

The king motioned with his hand and a runner come forward with Valor, the fabled bow of House Galadine.

"You haven't, for I share the burden of my law." He grasped the weapon, rune-carved and ancient. Its black wood seemed to soak up the little light left. "Hold each other. I will make it quick."

Sonya stepped forward, her hands protectively over her belly and said, "You'll be killing three of us."

It was plainly said, sweeping aside royal formalities, speaking directly to Mikal the man, instead of a king who sat in judgment.

His gaze fell to her stomach, her meaning clear. Slowly, his chin dropped to his chest. He could feel himself crumbling inside, every part of him physically echoing the grief washing through him. He sat for a moment in silence, then answered her from under his helm, his voice sounding hollow even to himself.

"It is the worst thing I have ever done," he said, even as he slowly nocked an arrow. "But not the worst I will ever do."

As he began to draw the bow, Davyd's hand closed on his forearm, firm but not threatening.

The king's mark looked torn, his eyes darting back to the two and then to the king's face. "Mikal . . . did you, did we…"

King Galadine shrugged off his hand and said, "You forget yourself, King's Mark." To his satisfaction, Davyd's gaze dropped and he backed away.

"How will you live with yourself?" demanded Sonya, pulling his eyes back to her face.

The king took a deep breath, then raised himself and met her incredulous stare without flinching. "Make no mistake, my lady. I never said I would."

Neither answered, but the battlefield replied with the moans of the dying and the caterwauling song of a murder of crows. Mikal watched as they turned to each other. Though no words were exchanged he could hear, knowing these were their last moments made them gasp and hug each other tightly.

Their embrace lasted only a moment before Duncan met Mikal's eyes and said, "Nothing dies." It was an age-old adage, warning of the ghosts injustice always raised.

Now was the time.

The king's grip tightened, but he said nothing. He sighted down the shaft, his hands steady, and slowly drew back. Valor groaned, as if the runebow knew its purpose and ached for release. Then its twang-thrum echoed across the battlefield, the sound scattering the black-winged thieves, their bellies full with the flesh of men. Two bodies fell, pierced by one arrow.

The king looked down, drew a shuddering breath, then turned back to his handiwork. His eyes remained hard, like the granite rocks surrounding him, and just as dead.

I have become something . . . less, he thought, *something beneath apathy.*

Darker times, though, were still to come . . .

Flashback: Sovereign's Fall

PART I

Flashback: Sovereign's Fall

THE LORE FATHER

In combat, make every intention
to kill your opponent.
Every cut, every strike, every breath,
must feed victory.
—Kensei Tsao, The Lens of Blades

ou know he might not survive."

Y Lore Father Themun Dreys took a sip of the tea in front of him, as he considered Silbane's words. The tea's hot fragrance mixed with the smell of freshly cut grass from the gardeners' recent work. The monastery's grounds were well kept, and having the council meeting outside was a welcome change from dark halls and torchlight.

Themun regarded the assembled group of adepts, appreciating the warm spring sun. "You're being more melodramatic than usual," he replied.

Silbane arched an eyebrow at that. He shook his head and then looked to Dragor for support, asking, "How's he doing in your classes?"

The dark-skinned adept looked down for a moment, and Themun got the distinct impression these two had spoken before coming to the meeting. Dragor was now supposed to say something to support Silbane's position. Whatever it was sat like a fishbone in the adept's throat.

"Out with it," the lore father said. "If he's got anything else you think is a weakness besides wailing, 'he can't use the Way,' let's hear it."

Dragor looked relieved. "No, nothing else, Lore Father." The adept brushed aside some crumbs it seemed only he could see, then got a sheepish look on his face. "His fighting is exemplary, perhaps as good as any of us."

Silbane's response was to put his head in his hands, no doubt unable to fathom why no one on the council agreed with him. That, or, despite their years together, he may have just come to the conclusion that Dragor wasn't a good co-conspirator. Regardless, Themun didn't care.

"Speak for yourself," retorted Kisan, sucking any humor Themun saw from what was unfolding. She picked idly at a segment of a citrus fruit, then popped the tangine into her mouth. Kisan Talaris looked no more than thirty, though she was in fact close to her fiftieth year of life. Her appearance was a study in composed lethality. Her form was lithe; her short, dark hair framed a face set with bright, alert eyes, the eyes of a hawk.

He watched her press a fingernail into the worn wood of the table, carving a small crescent into the dark wood. She was beautiful in the same way a blade was: simple and deadly. He was proud of the weapon he'd forged from that orphan girl they'd found so many years ago. Others might find her cold, perhaps even predisposed to violence, a trait Themun rather enjoyed. Yet she'd always been the one he went to when certain tasks needed doing, the kind no one else wanted.

Nothing, however, changed the fact that she was as stubborn as the day they first met; in fact, she'd only grown worse with age. He'd always thought their tutelage would soften her. Instead, every skill she mastered made her more inflexible and harder to reason with. Themun doubted she'd stay with them much longer. He'd created a weapon. Now that weapon wanted to be used without the restriction of rules.

Prodding her, though, might still get Silbane's attention. Themun knocked on the table to get their collective attention and said, "I considered sending Kisan and her apprentice, but the boy isn't ready. Also, you know—"

"Piter's more ready than Arek," Kisan said immediately, coming to her apprentice's defense, as

Themun had known she would. "We'd be happy to go in their stead."

Silbane turned to her and said, "Your apprentice enjoys hurting others. He may be psychotic. Have you considered that?"

"Better than mundane," Kisan quipped, sectioning another piece of her fruit with a sharp nail. "Besides, one person's psychosis may be another's timidity. Have you considered that?" she retorted, one delicate eyebrow arching.

"His mental state is hardly surprising, seeing who his master is," Silbane shot back.

Dragor held up a hand, asking for silence. Then he turned to face the lore father and said, "Why send anyone? This is the Galadines' business, not ours. Why risk anyone at all?"

Themun got up, bracing himself on his staff, and walked around the table to chase the sun. It had moved its pool of warm light, inconveniently shifting to a spot further down. Once he settled with his back drenched in its warm yellow glow, he answered the adept.

"You want us to ignore a gate opening?" asked Themun. "Maybe we can cower together?"

A large man, ursine in form, chose then to speak. He combed his thick dark beard with his fingers, then said, "Sarcasm aside, I agree with Dragor's point. Why risk us? We can't withstand another invasion and we can't close a gate. Why risk any of us, most of all an apprentice?"

"Can you think of no reason to send him, Master Giridian?" Themun hoped he heard the tone the lore father usually reserved for stupid people.

The large man was quiet, then looked at Silbane and said, "It must be his age. Maybe you should find him a nice quiet home."

"Funny," Themun snapped. "Glad we're keeping things light—"

Silbane quickly said, "Let's assume Arek's ability gives us a special weapon; still, we don't know it'll work on a gate."

Themun stared at Giridian a bit longer with a look that promised the comment about putting him in a home wouldn't be forgotten. Then he turned to Silbane and said, "He negates any manifestation of the Way. We've seen him dissipate spells, abilities, even rifts. Why do you doubt he'd do the same with a gate?"

Silbane voiced what they were all thinking. He asked, "You think a random tear in our firmament and a structured gate are the same thing?" When Themun didn't answer, he continued, "Arek doesn't even know how he does it."

"Seems to be triggered by his touch," offered the lore father.

Silbane leaned back, crossing his arms defensively, "So you'd have me shove him in and call it a day?"

Themun looked at his second and said, "Did he not take the Oath, just as we all have '*To serve the land* '—for what other reason do we train him?"

"Not to send him on a one-way mission," said Thera, looking calmly at Themun. Though she did not rank as highly as Silbane in mastery of the Way, she'd known Themun the longest. It gave her a unique place with him. Furthermore, she was the voice of the council's conscience.

Kisan was the one to answer, saying, "Are you seriously balancing the danger of a gate against the possible loss of one person? Thousands died in the last demon war. Children were taken, mothers and fathers killed, but I guess family means less to—"

"Don't," warned Thera. Something in her eyes stopped Kisan, a rare moment for Themun, or for that matter anyone, to see. "We've all lost. Don't act like you're the only one." She breathed in, visibly calming herself. "I'm trying to balance our moral compass—"

"Let me worry about our morals," Themun said, losing some of his patience. "By the Lady, I'm beginning to think you're all obtuse."

"Name-calling isn't going to get us to agree," Thera answered.

Themun hated that she knew him so well. Two hundred years will do that. It was like having a wife who would never leave, never die, and knew all your tricks. *I'm cursed,* he admitted, and that brought forth a small laugh as the anger washed out of him. She was right. They understood why he wanted Silbane's apprentice to go on this mission, but not why this particular Gate was so dangerous.

In a voice that didn't waver he said, "Something you should know then—Lilyth was not destroyed."

Silence followed that admission. Suddenly the impetus behind the Gate's appearance took on new meaning, as he had known it would. They would each be coming to the realization that if the demon queen Lilyth was behind this Gate's appearance, they couldn't let it open, even if it meant all their lives. That was why it was so paramount his best monk be sent to investigate, and if it could be sealed with minimal sacrifice, duty demanded they do so.

At last, and no surprise to Themun, it was Kisan who said smoothly, "And you bring this up now? It conveniently raises the stakes dramatically."

By "conveniently," Themun knew she meant "contrived." She loved to goad everyone, even her betters. Leave it to her to challenge him instead of focusing on the overall danger.

Confronting her now wouldn't help his case, so instead he said, "Those of us who survived kept Lilyth's fate to ourselves. Galadine's laws kept us busy enough just trying to survive."

"So the truth was hidden, tucked away, until you want to come to the land's aid," finished Kisan, her expression settling into that habitual smug look he found so irksome.

The lore father took a breath, calming himself as Thera had done. He'd need to tread carefully if he wanted their cooperation. Sending Silbane and his apprentice was bad enough without Kisan seeing it as a lack of confidence in her ability. The fact was that Themun didn't know for sure it was Lilyth, or if he'd misread things and something else entirely different was happening at Bara'cor. He needed someone with a cool head, someone with experience, to investigate. He needed Silbane.

"What is it you would have us do? Pop in on Bara'cor, ask them how they're faring?" Kisan said. "I've dealt with their ilk more than you, Lore Father. They don't regret their actions, even when I whisper death in their ears."

Themun thought for a moment and then directed a careful answer to the table. "A rift could have many causes, most being natural. A gate appearing at Bara'cor should demand our attention and immediate action. Gates occur through contrivance, a malicious intent, and we can't ignore it." Before Kisan jumped in again, he held up a hand and said, "There's more."

He turned to Silbane and said, "The nomads of the Altan Wastes have gathered themselves under someone. They've attacked the other fortresses ringing the desert. As of now, Shornhelm, Dawnlight, and EvenSea have gone silent. I don't know if they still stand or have been razed to the ground, but by chance or design Bara'cor stands alone."

"That's impossible," Giridian said, his small chuckle lined with worry. "The nomads work together as much as desert spiders do, and that means not at all."

"Indeed, and yet what I say is true," Themun replied. "What's happened? Whoever has brought the nomads together has achieved what has not been done since the last war."

The table fell silent. The lore father's ability to see things happening elsewhere in the world had saved many, bringing them to Meridian Isle. Now his knowledge of the events transpiring at Bara'cor confronted them with a dilemma.

Into the silence, Kisan asked the one question Themun knew she would, and had been dreading.

"You're suggesting we aid Bara'cor, home of the magehunters and their filth?" She took a moment to make sure she had everyone's attention, then added, "You want to help those who murdered our families?"

"Kisan," Themun said, "I know how you feel. I also lost much to the Galadines. Though we can't bring back the dead, it seems the current king is trying to make amends. He's reversed many of his forefathers' laws and disbanded the magehunters."

Kisan watched him like a cat watching a mouse, the current segment of tangine slowly being squeezed to a pulp between her fingers. Themun wasn't sure she was even aware of it and decided silence was the best way to avoid triggering an outburst.

"And so they're forgiven? We'll invite them to dinner—chit-chat about favorite lynching sites, proper bonfires, and knots that don't give on the hangman's noose?" Kisan fell back, disgust etched on her features.

A moment passed, then another. Finally she said, "Why don't we infiltrate the nomad encampment and kill their leaders? Two of us could do this and escape, unseen and unscathed." Her indifferent proclamation of death hung in the air; the lore father knew her proposal could be accomplished as easily as saying the words. He remained silent, leading everyone to assume he was giving Kisan's suggestion real consideration. He wasn't, but it served the purpose of letting Kisan regain some face.

Dragor was the first to break the silence. "You would kill people who had done nothing—"

"According to the lore father, they might be responsible for the destruction of three other fortresses," Kisan said, interrupting. "They've killed thousands already. Isn't that enough?"

"'Might be responsible' . . . we don't know it was the nomads," said Thera. "And, isn't this crossing the line? We've never meted out punishment in such a manner. Even the First Council never took it upon themselves to be both judge and executioner."

"And yet when the coin is right or a friend's in need, we make people disappear. Isn't this just an honest expansion of our Oath?" Kisan replied flatly.

"Is that your answer to everything: Kill?" Thera shot back.

Kisan shrugged. "Whatever stops the yammering."

With an Affinity focused on the sky, Thera nurtured life, and in doing so cherished harmony amongst all living things. Themun appreciated the difference between her and Kisan, whose Affinity was the moon. They represented complementary ideals that while necessary, meshed about as well as oil and vinegar. *Typically, a lot of beating is necessary,* he thought.

Themun waited, hoping Silbane would say something, but he seemed focused on his tea. He's somehow both indispensable and frustrating, Themun thought, clenching his teeth to remain silent. Silence often opened new opportunities, whereas speaking closed them.

"What of Themun's father, who was certainly responsible for saving you?" Kisan said to Thera, probably realizing that Themun wouldn't yet intervene. She fell back into her chair and planted the barb, arms crossed. "Quite a killer, from what I understand."

"You're right," Themun interjected, his patience worn thin. "My father was a killer. But before you attack Thera or his memory, you'd be wise to remember that's true for all of my family."

He locked eyes with the younger master, who tried to meet his gaze but couldn't, breaking contact to ostensibly wipe the tips of her fingers clean of tangine juice.

"I meant no offense," she said, then turned to Silbane. "Must be some good tea. Want to join our discussion? This does have to do with your apprentice, after all."

Silbane smiled, though it didn't quite reach his eyes. "Not sure . . . you both seem to be doing fine."

"Please, Sil." Giridian beckoned with his head. "Your boy's ability to negate magic seems like an easy way to seal this Gate."

Silbane bit his lip, considering. Then he looked at Kisan and said, "Maybe she's right. Taking out the nomad leaders would certainly be easier."

When Themun didn't immediately say "no," Kisan threw her hands up and said, "You'll listen to him but not me?" Her attack was less pointed, maybe because she liked Silbane. It didn't stop her from adding, "You're all typical men."

"These nomads are horsemen and traders," Silbane mused, ignoring her, "not experts in siege warfare. Perhaps the lore father is correct and they are being helped by someone with knowledge, experience, and power."

The lore father shrugged and said, "It comes to this: I know there's a gate hidden within Bara'cor and the nomads now besiege that fortress. I want to send Silbane and Arek to investigate. If a gate has formed, I want Silbane to use Arek's power of disruption to seal it."

"You speak so easily of power and strength, but what of right and wrong?" Thera asked, sadness plain in her voice. "Shouldn't we ask ourselves what's right?"

"Then I'd second Silbane's endorsement of Kisan's suggestion, as distasteful as it may seem," Giridian said, looking apologetically at Thera for the non-sequitur interruption. "Kill the leaders of the nomads before they enter Bara'cor. It will buy us some time." The adept pushed against the table, rising to look at the lore father. "As you pointed out, they are responsible for the deaths of many. This would be fit punishment and limit collateral damage."

Themun stood and stretched, enjoying the warm sun. "We'll recess for the afternoon and reconvene at dusk. I would like our decision to be unanimous." He paused, waiting until every member of his council was looking at him, then said, "In the absence of that, I will decide what's best."

The monks remained silent. No one, not even Kisan, challenged Themun Dreys when he used that voice. He knew he was pushing them, but he could only keep up the charade of equality for so long. If push came to stab, he'd be the one holding the knife, and they all knew it.

The monks rose and bowed, shuffling out of the veranda with Kisan at their lead. Themun watched them go, and then cleared his throat to get Silbane's attention. "A moment of your time..."

Silbane remained—a questioning look on his face.

"And what of Kisan's suggestion?"

Silbane pursed his lips, clearly unsure what to say about the volatile master. "You seemed overly accommodating to her, at least until her barbs began aiming at your father."

"She insults the man who made it possible for all of us to live. Stubborn and mule-headed, nothing with her has changed."

"You're still the same too, so easily angered when it comes to the great Davyd Dreys." Silbane offered a smile, then said, "One or two of us could infiltrate a nomad encampment with little to fear." He was silent, then said, "As much as I hate to say it, Kisan's right."

"About what?" Themun was already shaking his head.

"We're essentially very picky mercenaries. Maybe we ought to take a more active role in the land's politics?" Silbane cleared a spot and leaned on the table. Themun stayed in the dying sun's light, his eyes half closed, soaking in the heat.

Finally, the lore father said, "The Gate will open. I give it ten days, perhaps less. We can't let Lilyth back into this world." He grasped Silbane's arm, "She'll take everyone if that happens, not just our kids. You've got to investigate, and take Arek."

"And if I refuse?" asked Silbane.

Dead silence. Then Themun made sure the master knew there was no doubt he would make good on his next promise as he said coldly, "If you choose to ignore your Oath, I will assign Kisan to the task."

Silbane stood there, speechless.

When he didn't answer, Themun added, "One way or another, we're going to put boots down on that location as soon as possible. I hope you're the one going with Arek, but he's going, no matter what."

Themun had known Silbane long enough to know when the master was angry, and right now he could tell his friend was livid. He closed his eyes, hoping some kind of relief for his headache would come from blanketing even one of his senses.

When he opened them again, Silbane had moved to the wooden arch separating their small gathering area from the garden surrounding them. He'd stopped, staring at him. What was strange was that he didn't look angry, more curious.

"What's that?" Silbane said, motioning to a space behind the lore father.

Themun paused, leaning on the bannister, but said nothing. Acknowledging him would only worsen the situation.

Silbane must have realized he wasn't going to get an answer. He took a breath and then said, "I guess I'll go speak with Arek. Let him know how we're honoring him with this opportunity." With that, the master spun on his heels and departed.

Dire events were unfolding, and if Rai'stahn was to be believed, the fate of their world hung in the balance. Themun's mind spun through every permutation to come up with a solution that didn't involve sacrificing one of their own, but came back to the same place.

"You have to be more careful," Themun said aloud, addressing no one. The air wavered, moving behind the lore father like the shimmer of heat above the sunbaked earth. Yet silence was the only answer, and he'd expected nothing else. It was not his place to question the will of the Conclave.

What, he wondered, *would you have counseled, Father? Am I living by your lessons?* Something told him he knew the truth. He doubted his father would've been proud of anything he'd done today.

JOURNAL ENTRY 1

Banished.

It is with a heavy heart that I share my thoughts, but history has a way of remembering us as she wants, and she is a fickle mistress. Having been branded tyrant, usurper, and worse, this may be my only voice.

Dragons are traitors, and first amongst these is Rai'stahn. I name him so you can greet him with death, for he deserves no better absolution than a blade crafted from dragon shell. He never understood his place and now survives on the victory I seized with my bare hands.

It is a wish, and I admit a selfish one, that you know of the sacrifices I made for all of us. Though they think me dead, I gain an immortality of sorts, for my legend will never die.

It is a small solace, perhaps noble to you, hollow-sounding to me. I am not content with the way the dice have rolled. I do not accept my fate. It does not sit well with me, to accept my lot. Let those who pray for my death continue to do so. Nothing they do will change who I am, but their prayers give me strength, and life.

And just whose tribute do you read? Will knowing impugn your sense of fairness? Will you wish for the axe on my neck, or place the garland at my feet? We will walk the road a bit longer in anonymity, so you may yet be more charitable to my memory in light of my many sacrifices.

It will not be the first time a hero stood maligned, nor a commoner such as yourself learns the truth.

Come, there will be much to tell you in the pages ahead . . .

Journal Entry 1

EIGHT DAYS LEFT . . .

Journal Entry 1

THE NOMADS

Those who show no fear, tend to inspire it.
—*Altan proverb*

T he desert dunes glowed red in the setting sun, shimmering from the day's heat. Occasionally a small *windspin* would swirl the sand into a cloud of grit and dust, working its way under any amount of protection a weary traveler might wear. The Altan Wastes were inhospitable at best, deadly to the uninitiated.

A lone figure stood atop a dune, his robes streaming behind him in the hot wind. Raising a massive arm, he unhooked a pack from his heavily muscled back and dropped it to the sand, grunting as he released its weight.

Hemendra, leader of the clans, tribes, families, and kinsmen who called themselves the Altan, unwound the light cotton *shahwal* from his face. His eyes squinted at the wavering image of the fortress, rising just out of catapult range. He wore the loose-fitting robes favored by the desert nomads to protect himself from the harsh wind and sun. As it beat down on the sands, he reached to his belt, detaching his lifeskin. Taking a measured sip of the cool water inside, he corked and replaced it with the efficiency of a man who had survived fifty years under the desert's baleful yellow eye.

He was soon joined by two other men dressed much as he was. Though both would be considered large, they looked small compared to the clanchief. He acknowledged the leader Paksen's bow with a grunt before turning to look back at the fortress.

The Nomads

"Mighty U'Zar," said Paksen, "I come to ask if you wish to pull our troops back. The Redrobe has begun the summoning of the storm and wishes our men to be ready."

Hemendra inwardly grimaced at the mention of the white man amongst them, his hair the same yellow color of his puke after drinking too much *koomis*. Still, Hemendra was careful in his response, especially in front of clanfists as ambitious as these were. The twenty or so clans they alone controlled, the largest number under one man besides himself, had come to worship the man in red robes with an almost religious zeal, thinking him chosen by the Great Sun itself. Hemendra worried this "Redrobe" commanded too much consideration, but had to be careful how he dealt with it. As long as Bara'cor's walls remained intact, this man was necessary. As long as that remained true, his lifewater would remain unspilled.

Turning from the sight of the fortress, Hemendra addressed the lead clanfist, "We shall camp, Indry. Have our brothers dig themselves in for the storm and shield the fires." Hemendra paused for a moment, looking out over the Altan Wastes. *Beautiful,* he reflected, *yet as deadly as a sarinak's sting.* Turning back to the two waiting chieftains he finished, "Tell the Sun Sages to begin the bloodletting for their spells. Tomorrow, under cover of the storm, we advance on Bara'cor again."

"And what of the Redrobe's orders?" Indry asked, looking at Bara'cor with hunger in his eyes.

Hemendra's eyes narrowed, his hand casually straying to rest on the bone hilt of his fighting knife, a knife that never left his side. He saw Paksen's eyes widen as the second clanfist realized his companion's error. Hemendra prayed Paksen would react so he could kill him too, but Paksen wisely didn't move.

"Tell me of the *Asabiyya*." The simple question was laced with deadly undertones.

The other chieftain spun to face the u'zar and realized his error. He fell to his knees and touched his forehead to the sand. "Mighty U'Zar—"

"Tell me, Indry."

The man stammered, then said, "Me against my brothers; my brothers and me against our cousins; my brothers, cousins, and me against the world."

"And what family is the Redrobe to you?"

Indry shook his head slowly, almost as if he knew his fate. "He is nothing, Mighty U'Zar."

Slowly, Paksen also fell to his knees and touched his forehead to the sand. "Of course, Mighty U'Zar, your orders are not to be questioned."

Hemendra waited for a moment, looking toward the camp. He could hear the priests chanting their spells, ones that banished fatigue or called up springlets of fresh water from the dry, wind-blown wastes. Looking down, he growled, "Look at me, Indry." At first he thought the man would refuse, as what could only be a stifled sob ran quickly through him. Then, as Indry's head slowly came up, Hemendra kicked him under the chin.

Blood spurted as the ill-fated clanfist bit through his tongue and went tumbling backward down the dune, landing in a heap at the bottom. Hemendra strode down and grabbed him by the neck, picking him up like a rag doll. Dark blood ran freely in rivulets out of the nomad's mouth, dripping off his chin and staining the front of his robes. He was on the verge of screaming when Hemendra's grip tightened like a vise, choking off any sound. "Your lifewater is accepted."

The man fought, his desire to live overcoming any fear he had of the u'zar. He tried punching, kicking, and pushing the gargantuan man, trying to find any kind of purchase or weakness, but Hemendra's grasp was like iron. Indry's punches soon became lethargic, then feeble. Finally, they stopped all together.

Hemendra waited, watching until life drained from the man's eyes, then released his hold. He flung the dead nomad to the desert floor, feeling his fingers sticky where blood had congealed. Stalking back up the dune he stooped to grab a handful of sand and began to rub off the drying blood. Paksen, whom he noticed hadn't moved, slowly came to his feet and paid the proper homage, palms to forehead. *I will have to watch this one,* he thought, angry with himself for letting the Redrobe's presence affect him so.

He could've let Indry's lapse go unpunished—killing nomads for slight transgressions wasn't sustainable, not for a true leader of the Altan. As the Asabiyya would demand, Indry had brothers and cousins who would now feel obligated to retaliate. They would die, too, in a ripple of violence that would no doubt eradicate a family from the Children of the Sun, but to what purpose? He'd been foolhardy, he knew.

Yet another part of him forgave his harsh action. Indry had given him what he needed most, a show of strength in front of a clanfist as powerful as Paksen. Fear was a strong motivator, and killing one to maintain order and discipline was valuable in its own way. It also stripped Paksen of an ally, should he think to challenge the u'zar someday.

He nodded permission as Paksen bowed and went to see to his orders. His eyes, flat and empty of emotion, followed the retreating form of the clanfist. It was clear Paksen's ambition would soon exceed his caution. That day, Hemendra knew with cold certainty, would be the day he died. For now, though, Paksen would carry the word of the killing back to the men, sprinkling the waters of doubt into their cups of ambition.

Behind him, over eight thousand nomads made ready to assault the walls of Bara'cor again. As the Great Sun dipped below the western horizon, he could see the fortress's minarets, the flags atop unfurled and rippling in the wind: a golden lion on a black field. Hemendra rewrapped the shahwal, careful to cover his mouth and nose. Tomorrow the storm would be here in full force and his nomads would hide in its swirling sands.

"Once again we follow you, Redrobe," he whispered into the warm desert breeze, but the words came out like a curse.

Casting one last look around Hemendra made his way down the dune and back to his people. Storms, spells, or not, he vowed Bara'cor would soon see its last sunset.

The Nomads

THE MASTER

*In preparation for close combat,
take heed of your opponent's stance;
in making a strike, the bend of his arms;
in giving and taking blows, the depth of his breathing;
in all else, watch your opponent's eyes.
—Tir Combat Academy, Basic Forms & Stances*

Silbane stormed through the wide hallway toward the stairwell leading to his quarters, almost missing the turn as his mind circled around the lore father's words. As much as he didn't like it, he had to agree with Themun's assessment: Arek's power to negate the Way was a good reason to send him. The danger to Edyn must be great for the lore father to even contemplate such a choice. As Themun had pointed out, his apprentice intended to take the same oath of service as an adept, a Binding Oath—at that. It wasn't a decision ever taken lightly.

In fact, the Binding Oath did much more once uttered, combining the true intent of the two who pledged it, heard it, and enforced by the Way. It was a living thing, and breaking the oath had varying degrees of consequence. Some were as simple as blindness or deafness; others resulted in complete annihilation of the transgressors.

Themun seemed to think Arek was already committed by his allegiance to the council and his intention to test for the rank of adept, but Silbane didn't agree that intention was equivalent to responsibility.

He strode up the circular stairway, exiting on a level high above the main training halls. He ignored the bows of respect protocol demanded students and servants offer him as he passed, but was brought up short by a spindly, spectacled man waiting outside his quarters.

"Scribe Tridaris, what a surprise!" Silbane said, forcing himself to smile, knowing full well what he'd done to deserve this visit. The librarian staff was, as a whole, entirely too thorough.

"Master Silbane, ahh, if we could—"

"Yes, yes, of course," Silbane nodded as he shuffled past the man and into his room, gesturing to the doors, which began to shut themselves.

A muffled *oof* sounded behind him, and he turned to see Tridaris had managed to place his foot strategically into the door's way, blocking it from closing. Who knew these librarians could be so nimble? With his nose and one eye peering through, the master scribe pushed the door open and continued, "Ahh, well, there is the matter of the tomes and your treatise on waylines and portals."

The man shuffled fully into the room and put his arms behind his back, his head tilted.

"Tomes?" Silbane asked. "It's been only a few—"

"Ahh, three weeks, master." Master Scribe Tridaris managed to look both embarrassed for Silbane and at the same time accusatory. "I'll need to collect the overdue ones so others may enjoy them."

"Uh, of course you may, but I don't have that many checked out."

Tridaris wandered over to Silbane's desk, cluttered with manuscripts, and said, "Oh my, and some of these need recopying. Mustn't let them become damaged, no?"

Silbane sighed, "How many are overdue, Master Scribe?"

The man pulled out a small notebook and said, "You've checked out three."

"Three!" Silbane said, his eyebrows climbing in what he hoped was a look of concern. He would've continued, but Tridaris gave him a look that said he'd taken the wrong tack.

"Three books with your signature, Master Silbane."

Silbane got a sinking feeling at the master scribe's emphasis on *your*.

"Three more books checked out by a 'Enablis Ton'?" The master scribe looked at the master and blinked once. "Very inventive. It seems someone has been exceeding the three-books-at-a-time rule we maintain for the satisfaction of all our patrons."

"And you think this is me?" Silbane trying to look hurt.

"Shall we talk about another three books by 'Jynis Good'?" Tridaris sighed and pushed his spectacles up higher on his nose. Smiling, he said, "Again, most entertaining. There are more. Your enthusiasm for reading is becoming, ah. . . noteworthy."

Silbane shook his head, about to rebut, but the man reached over and held up a book with the title toward the master, *Portal Traps.*

"This was checked out by, 'Dance Kaffe.' Ah . . . none of these people exist, Master, yet strangely the books have found their way here."

"Ahem, well, I find books from time to time . . ."

Tridaris nodded slowly and said, "Of course, Master. And for retrieving them we can ignore this matter entirely—provided . . ."

Silbane raised an eyebrow, not sure what to say. Into that silence the master scribe said, "As the lore father has repeatedly requested, we need your manuscript soon."

Silbane looked to his desk where his latest book on how waylines could be used to anchor portals was still in the research phase. He was a few weeks from putting anything useful to paper. He shrugged and said, "I'm working quickly, Master Scribe. Perhaps something next week?"

"Our library is only open for those who contribute," Tridaris said, wagging a finger and smiling. "Publish or perish, Master Silbane."

Silbane nodded, not at all surprised when the master scribe snapped his fingers and four more scribes entered and began gathering the overdue books scattered across his library floor and on top of his desk. He could only watch helplessly as they scoured his room with a proficiency a gang of thieves would envy, exiting with barely a sound, books in arms.

Tridaris waited until the last one left, then pulled out a leather tome from behind his back. He handed it to Silbane, who took it gingerly. *The Difference.* He'd read it a thousand times, literally, a treatise on duty versus responsibility.

"The lore father thought you'd find inspiration here."

"No doubt," Silbane answered with a forced smile.

"I trust you'll refrain from actions requiring another visit from me or my staff?"

Silbane gave him a half smile and nodded.

"Of that you can rest assured, Master Scribe."

At that, the man snapped his heels together and gave a short bow, then left Silbane's quarters, closing the doors behind him.

"Librarians are a breed unto themselves," Silbane grumbled quietly. They were odd little fellows who didn't understand how *real* research worked, up to your thighs in mud and grime, chased by creatures out of legend. *You didn't learn sitting in a musty library*—he paused for a moment as his internal voice corrected, *but the books do come in handy.*

He decided to try and ignore his encounter with Tridaris and the admonishment to finish his work, settling down near another large window in the main room. The stone sill radiated the day's heat, comfortable despite the cool ocean air. The sun shone with its usual springtime intensity. In the distance, he could hear the rumble of the waves crashing onto the shore. He noticed a few of the older apprentices gathering for informal practice on the hill behind the tower, their brown uniforms contrasting with the bright green of the grass.

Leaning toward the window, Silbane watched the initiates with a bit of envy. *Simpler times, with simpler pleasures,* he remembered.

A discreet knock sounded at his door. He looked over, exasperated now by the librarian's temerity. "Tridaris, I haven't had time to borrow another book." A tired sigh escaped before he could stop it and he found his head in his hands.

"It's not your nemesis," came a soft reply. Thera entered, shutting the door behind her. She walked over to his desk and pulled out a chair for herself. Once seated, she leaned back and smiled, clearly happy her presence had left him tongue-tied.

"How're you doing?" she asked.

Silbane stared. "I didn't expect you."

She gave him a half apologetic smile. "The council meetings have started to stress me out. I could use some of Jynis Great's company."

Silbane shook his head, "Don't start with me, and it's 'Jynis Good,'" he corrected. "Stupid rule— three books."

She let out a small chuckle. "Where do you come up with these names?"

Silbane could feel the smile grow on his face. Then he leaned back, drinking in Thera's presence. She was beautiful, with startling blue eyes framed by dark hair. It was easy to forget she was almost twice his age. Side by side, no one could tell who was older.

With an effort, he stopped staring and said, "If I'd wanted to steal something . . ."

"Clouds before Moon," Thera said, acknowledging his command of the technique allowing him to hide himself. "I know you're not a thief, but you're wreaking havoc with the library's system. Why not just do your research there?"

"And lose all this?" Silbane gestured to the room around him, cluttered with objects d'art from around the world, a treasure trove from decades of adventuring.

Thera wiped her fingers on his table, leaving behind a trail of three finger swipes that were likely the only dust-free place now in his entire room. She rubbed her fingers together and tsked, "Messy. Speaking of which, how's your apprentice?"

Silbane shrugged, "How would I know? Outwardly he seems calm. His power masks whatever he's feeling on the inside." He paused, then said, "But you know this."

Thera nodded. She wiped her fingers clean before biting a nail that seemed to offend her more than the others. Then she raised an eyebrow and said, "What if Themun is wrong?"

The master pulled a small square pillow from one side and placed it on his stomach, his long fingers interweaving atop it. Searching her face, he said, "What if he is? You've known him longer than any of us. How would you convince him to change his mind?"

"It's not easy," she admitted with a small smile. "Even his brother had difficult times with him."

Silbane pursed his lips in thought. He liked the rough silk of the pillow. It gave him an anchor to this moment in a more tactile way than looking out his blasted window. The view only took him farther away from the here and now.

Finally, he replied, "He's stubborn enough you'd think his Affinity was the Earth." Grabbing a polished bowl filled with small dark nuts, he held it out to Thera.

"Koken nut?"

Thera looked at him, one eyebrow raised in surprise. "The meeting is in a few hours."

"We'll get rid of some stress and go with clear heads," he replied.

That elicited a small laugh. With a *why-not?* shrug, she took a few of the bittersweet nuts.

The islanders cultivated a savory snack, roasting harvested nuts on a wide metal pan suspended over a fire, before mixing with honey and sea salt and drying. The result was a crunchy burst of sweet, salt, and bitter. Silbane enjoyed koken nuts for a wholly different reason, and watched with amusement as Thera slowly popped one into her mouth.

The effect was immediate. Pink suffused her cheeks as the energy of the nut was released. He took one himself. The quick, heady rush of strength and control it brought him was luxurious. He'd often said these were a gift from the Lady herself. One had to be careful, however.

"The ferryman's toll," Thera cautioned, as if reading his mind, "Something you've always said."

The nuts had a slightly narcotic effect, one whose aftereffects didn't lend themselves well to sleep or the morning after. He looked at Thera and said, "I hate hearing my own words thrown back at me." He paused, smiling, then added, "But it's true. Fun today. Misery tomorrow. Is anything in life different?" He raised a hand to her, nodding his head.

She returned his salute, mimicking his holding a cup. Then her face grew more serious. "Look, I'm not saying we do nothing, only that we ought to know more before sending one of our apprentices." Thera's calm blue eyes measured any reaction he might have to her statement.

For his part, he wasn't sure exactly how he felt. "Arek is good with a blade. I'm least worried about him in a physical fight, but it's not as if we're going into battle. A quick recon—" he popped another nut in his mouth "—in and out before anyone notices." He could feel his eyes quivering just a bit as the second jolt of energy hit him, clearing away any lingering confusion or doubt.

Thera stared at him for a moment, long enough for Silbane to conclude she was likely assessing his stupidity. Then she said, "Be careful, Sil. Arek has always been a special case. Has he learned his Affinity since I last asked?"

The master sighed. "No."

She paused, her eyes scanning the room. Silbane was silent. Finally, she asked, "Why do you want to take Arek?"

Silbane shrugged. "Themun wants to use Arek to close this Gate. The only way to do that would be to push him through. That—"

"He'd be trapped," she said in shock.

"Maybe," Silbane conceded. "But what happens if I leave him here?"

He watched her go through the permutations. "If Themun thinks it's important enough, he'll send Arek with someone else."

Silbane agreed, remembering with painful acuity Themun's threat to do exactly that. "I came to the same conclusion. He'll send Kisan, who won't hesitate to push him through, even if there's a better way. There aren't a lot of choices left." He paused, then said, "What if I keep Arek near me and improvise depending on what we find?"

"Then here's something you know perfectly well, but seem to be ignoring. Affinities allow us to tap the Way. Arek can't do that, not even in an emergency."

"Which means?"

"It means if you're incapacitated, he's on his own. None of the other apprentices have that handicap."

"If we follow the plan—"

Thera laughed. "Things never go the way you think. Your plan will last until your first encounter. Then what will you do?"

"Fake it until it works . . . as usual." He smiled at her, hoping his attempt at humor wouldn't fall flat.

Thera rolled her eyes and said, "I'll grant you're good at that." She ate another koken nut, taking a deep breath and stretching.

Then she ticked off on her fingers, "Sun, moon, earth, sky, plus the two circles we can all tap, life and death. Doesn't it seem odd to you that none of our Affinities focus on the things Arek is best at?"

Silbane said, "Death seems most likely. You could interpret Arek's powers as changing the Way, a kind of degeneration." He looked back out the window, not willing to say more.

Thera's eyes narrowed. Her mouth curved into a small smile, then she picked up a small metal amulet from his desk and flung it at him.

Silbane ducked. "What?"

"You've figured something out!" she said in a hyper-focused, koken nut-induced whisper. "Tell me." Her hands clasped in front of her until her knuckles turned white.

Silbane took a breath, hating that Thera could get inside his head so quickly. Now he was going to have to tell her his nascent theory before it was ready. It wasn't earth shattering in any way. It did, however, require them to shift their thinking.

When she made another noise for him to speak, he shushed her, looking once at the door to be sure no one lurked. Part of him knew it was a side-effect of the nut, paranoia, but that didn't mean others weren't listening. Then he said, "What if there were more Affinities?"

Thera looked confused at first, then dismissed him with a wave of her hand. "That's an easy way to explain whatever your apprentice does. You create a new circle he's tapping. I think you're just moving the problem, like saying it's turtles all the way down."

Silbane disagreed, "Why are Affinities what they are? Why not stars? Or seas? We created them. The structure is largely arbitrary."

"No," the raven-haired adept said. "They were chosen because those elements respond to our Will of the Way. Your techniques," she grabbed another koken nut as her excitement increased, "work best at midday when the sun is strongest. Mine work best outdoors in the open. Kisan's works best at night when the moon is out."

"Are you going to go through the whole roster?" Silbane half joked. The nut was known to have this effect: a running commentary of thoughts.

Thera punched his chest playfully, then brought her diatribe under control and asked, "When do Arek's nullification powers work best?"

Silbane's smile widened at that. Thera was so close to the answer, but he didn't want to give her the punchline so easily. Instead, he asked, "When does he demonstrate any influence on the Way at all?"

Thera leaned back, her expression one of consideration. Then she slowly turned her attention to Silbane's desk. She gave it a casual once-over, remarking, "How do you find anything?" She rummaged through it, pushing his notes to a side. "You really need a woman's touch, or an ounce of shame."

"Are you offering?" Silbane realized what she was doing: distracting him so she could think. He shook his head and said, "You're stalling."

Thera smiled, "Okay, tell me."

"I don't want this spoken about yet."

Thera made some shuffling gestures with her hands, as if pushing his words to the side. "I understand. Tell me!"

Silbane licked his lips, his mouth suddenly dry. Then he said, "What if another circle was . . . the Void?" He looked at her, nodding conspiratorially. This idea was big and would take her a moment to digest. He waited— eager for her response. Somewhere in the back of his mind he knew he ought not to eat another koken nut. Grandiosity was another unwelcome side effect.

Thera looked at him, her expression frozen in a smile. Heartbeats went by. Still, she didn't move. Finally, after what felt like an eternity, she bit her lip and said, "The Void?" Her composure slowly crumbled as Thera broke into uncontrollable laughter.

Silbane blinked, taken aback. "What's so funny? Don't you get it?"

When the adept had finally calmed down, she leaned over and stroked Silbane's arm. "Of course, it's 'the Void.'" She tilted her head and clucked her tongue, "It's nothing, and therefore it might be anything." She smiled good-naturedly before asking, "But when is Arek most able at reaching the Way?"

Silbane shrugged, feeling a little embarrassed. "Usually when we least expect it. I told you this was still an early concept."

Thera must have taken pity, for she moved over and sat down next to him. "I'm not laughing at you. Actually, it's an interesting theory." She looked at the bowl and said, "I think it's the nuts. This batch is pretty strong."

Silbane nodded, not entirely sure he was happy he'd shared his theory so quickly, but that was Thera's skill. She knew how to make others feel good about themselves while they revealed everything, which made her less of a favorite in some conversations.

Then Thera put her head down on his chest and said, "We only have a little while until the next meeting. We'll never sleep." There was a pause, then she asked, "Are you and Kisan—?"

"No," he stated. "Now and again, but nothing regular."

"Do you want me to stay?" she asked, her sapphire eyes meeting his own faded blue ones.

For a moment he thought about how he'd shared the worries he had for Arek and the real danger in taking him. Dwelling on that made him wonder how quickly he could ruin the mood. So instead he said, "You still okay with a younger man?" A half smile painted his face in what he knew was a charming if innocently dumb look. You didn't always have to be smart to get the girl, you just had to know when to stop talking.

She laughed, pushing him down as she kissed him. Her mouth was soft and insistent. This wasn't their first time, but he couldn't have guessed it might be their last.

The Master

FLASHBACK:
THE MAGEHUNTERS

A bladesman does not kill;
he allows one to live, purely by his own will.
He kills or grants life when wielding his blade.
—The Bladesman Codex

Keep quiet," hissed the lieutenant, watching as his men spread like an infestation through the soaked undergrowth. Kearn rubbed his face clear of rain and looked up, silently cursing the weather and the clutch of new recruits he had to look after. Dumber than a bag of onions and not even as useful, but he couldn't afford to have them panic at the wrong time.

"How many times is this?" one of his men, Stiven, by the sound of it, asked nervously. He wore the dark mail and cloak of the king's magehunters, deep blue edged with silver. In his right hand he carried a torch, its dancing flame sputtering and hissing in the light rain. It painted his young face a lurid splash of orange and black, as light and shadow danced in the dismal night.

"Half a dozen, Stiven, maybe more. I stopped counting." The lieutenant put a conciliatory hand on Stiven's shoulder and said, "The king's mark is with us. She'll deal with any trouble. Just worry about your shieldmates like you've trained to do."

Stiven gulped, looking at the storm clouds, then turned a wide-eyed stare back to his commander. "Garis said they have powers . . . that we can be turned into things . . . *unnatural* things."

Lieutenant Kearn shook his head and smiled. "What makes you think you're so normal now?"

Another soldier bumped the kid with an elbow and said, "Don't worry Stiv, you'll likely be turned into a man. That'll be the real trick." Good-natured laughter followed as the platoon of men moved through the forest toward the village. Then the rain began to fall in earnest. They had spent close to a fortnight on the hunt and wanted nothing more than a roof that didn't leak and a dry, warm bed.

Their mood was further darkened by the woman who rode next to them on her black destrier: King Mikal Galadine's mark. Her name was Alion Deft and her job was to hunt down and kill those who would threaten Edyn again. She wheeled her horse, then signaled Kearn to stop. She cantered over and met the young lieutenant's unvoiced question with a flat statement.

"I'll address the men here."

Kearn nodded, then motioned to his sergeant to have them form up but keep silent. At this distance, sound could still carry to the village, though the rain had muffled much of their progress through the underbrush.

The ragtag group shambled into a loose square facing their sergeant. The fact that the order had been obeyed instantly was the only indication these were seasoned fighting men. Some pulled their hoods farther forward as the rain fell harder. Lieutenant Kearn scowled at the lax formation, but said, "Shield rest." The men relaxed, but only a bit, waiting for their commander to speak.

The king's mark moved her warhorse forward to face the men and dismounted. Her cloak was the same dark blue as the others, but her armor was silver and steel, with a circular symbol stamped upon her breastplate. Kearn watched Deft's fingers as she rubbed it absentmindedly, a ritual he'd noticed her doing before every cleansing.

She looked at the assembled soldiers and asked, "Why are we here?"

There was no answer, and she seemed to expect none. She pulled her sword from its scabbard, the steel ringing its own note of death, and continued, "There is a pestilence. I mean to remove it." Her gaze swept the men, while the clearing remained silent. The only sound was rain falling through the trees. "I act on your king's order, and by his grace and our Almighty Fathers, so do you." Her eyes hardened. "No mercy."

The men shuffled a bit, but nothing they heard was new. At a nod from the king's mark, they all knelt. Deft raised a circled hand in supplication and said, "Let us pray."

The men lowered their heads as the king's mark intoned, "Fathers, bless our acts tonight. Aid us to smite the demons who wish harm upon your good lands. Let us be the hand that delivers justice, in peace."

"In peace." The men responded as one. They slowly rose, some making the sign of the Circle and kissing their fists.

Kearn watched Stiven gaze at the king's mark as she stood there in the rain. "She's beautiful," he heard him whisper, to no one in particular. The lieutenant would heartily disagree, but who knew what the women in Stiven's village looked like? Clearly no better than a square-jawed knight.

"Aye," said a sergeant, who had lost an eye during one of the many border fights following Lilyth's defeat, "and deadly. Stay away from her when it starts."

"Why?" Stiven asked, in a voice that sounded more like a boy's than a man's.

The one-eyed man turned back and said, "Just stay out of her way." He cinched Stiven's pauldron closer, tapping it with a mailed fist to be sure it sat securely on his shoulder, then walked away, disappearing into the wet gloom.

Stiven stared at the sergeant's back until Kearn thumped him out of his reverie. "Come on, Stiv. You're assigned to the catchers. Grab some torcs." He motioned to a basket holding dozens of metal collars, dullish yellow in the gloom. Still, every so often the light would catch one just so, and it would gleam coppery orange briefly, the fire bringing the metal to life.

Stiven moved over and grabbed one of the collars, holding it as he'd been taught. It didn't weigh much, but Kearn knew they'd all seen what it could do. The new recruit clutched it tighter, making the thrusting motion once, twice, as if to remind his own arm how it was used. Then he took two more and hooked them onto his belt, within easy reach, and was obviously relieved to see the others do the same. Kearn knew Stiven hated standing out.

The sergeant whispered a command to douse the torches. They all dropped to the wet ground with a hiss. The clearing fell into inky darkness, until Kearn's eyes adjusted and he could make out the rest of the men. They looked like shadows, disappearing amongst the rain, leaves, and trees.

* * * * *

Alion Deft stood where she'd delivered her prayer, scanning until her eyes came to rest on an older man, grizzled and gray. He had the look of one who scowled regardless of the weather. His mouth worked a repetitive chewing motion that spoke to the wad of *hazish* within. He stood near a small cart they had wheeled along with them. It was made of wood and along one side held a small door, bolted closed. The king's mark nodded her chin at the cart and said, "Bring her out."

"Royal whelp." He said the words like they were a private curse, talking *at* Alion, not about her.

The king's mark moved in front of him, her eyes fixed on the man until he acknowledged her with a spit to one side. She waited a moment longer then said, "Malioch, bring her out."

The flatness of her voice and the use of his name—the dead calm—gave the man pause.

He spat again—a brown liquid, foul smelling and pungent—then produced a large iron key. The bolt unlocked with a snap and he pulled wide the door. He waited a moment, then thrust his hand inside. "Come on!"

A squeal sounded from inside the box and the jailor cursed, then grabbed a handful of hair and yanked. Out came a girl, dumped unceremoniously into the mud. He kicked her so she tumbled forward again, falling face down. "Curse you, witch."

Alion watched this without care, waiting for the girl to rise. Slowly, as the desire to stand overcame her inherent fear, the girl came to her feet, shivering. What was once a white robe was now matted with filth and stains, hanging from bony shoulders. Dark hair that hadn't felt a loving hand in weeks fell in clumpy strings. When she finally looked up, her gaunt gaze held only the frightened look of someone trying desperately to avoid another beating. The girl cringed with her entire body and spirit, looking far younger than her twelve summers. Yet to Alion Deft, who knew these animals better than most, she was perfect.

The king's mark stepped forward and stooped so her eyes were level with the girl's own. She noted the prisoner still wore the torc around her neck. As she neared, the girl stepped back but Alion held up a hand, "Steady now, Galadine. You know your job, yes?"

The girl looked as if she were about to cry, but nodded vigorously.

"Do as I say and you may have your father's love again." Alion lied without a second thought. This vermin, along with the rest, would be food for worms long before the king forgave her sins. Alion didn't care. Using these magelings had become a necessary evil. How else would they be able to find others like her?

The Talent ran strong in the Galadine line, their curse to bear for being faithful stewards of the land, and the king's willingness to sacrifice his own blood spoke to his character and nobility. Still, the need to consort with this

thing filled her with disgust. She could only imagine the
royal family's shame that they should be so afflicted, but it
seemed the curse did not hold its hand just because one was
from the Galadine line. They, along with everyone else,
knew the cursed Talent could find itself festering within
any of their kin.

Despite these thoughts, Alion never allowed her
revulsion, along with the deepest desire to thrust her blade
into the heart of the creature, to reach her eyes. She said the
words with utter sincerity, allowing the briefest hint of a
smile to play across her features, reassurance that
everything would be all right.

She stood and motioned to Kearn. "Take the torc off."

As the lieutenant obeyed, she looked back at the girl and
said, "Kalissa, you know what happens if you run?"

* * * * *

The once-Princess Kalissa Galadine nodded again. The
instant the lieutenant touched the torc, it unlatched with a
small *click* and the metal collar opened.

Power flooded through her senses, reawakening her
connection to the Way. It sang into her heart, healing minor
injuries, succoring her weariness, and cleansing her soul.
The pain fell as if washed away like her mud stains. She
felt reborn, but knew this was only temporary. If she didn't
obey, her father would keep her here. Nothing she did, no
connection to the Way, would ease the pain of what she
had to do next.

She opened her eyes and Saw, then pointed and
stammered, "Th-through the trees. There are two you
want."

Alion looked at the girl for a moment then asked, "Just
two? Are you sure?"

She nodded.

Alion looked up, her eyes calculating. "You stay near
me for this." She handed the reins of her warhorse to a

nearby soldier who secured it to the cart, which would remain behind.

Kalissa came forward, standing woodenly next to the king's mark. She never took her eyes off the glowing folk she could see amongst the less bright signs of the people in the village around them. They stood not more than two hundred paces away, beacons of Talent marking them for death.

Next to them, she saw a third, brighter than they were, someone with the potential for true power. Her eyes flicked once to the knight standing next to her, then back to the village. This third one was young, a girl not more than five or six summers. Kalissa didn't know who she was, only that if the girl were discovered, it would likely mean her own death.

Why would the king's mark need her Talent if another, younger child were found to do her bidding? The shame of the decision to let this girl be put to the sword along with the rest of her village would've caused her anguish in the past, but now it would barely register. If her own father could give her away to someone like that jailor, why should she be any more merciful?

Adults with Talent were killed, but children were harvested and put to work, as she'd been. She would not take the chance these men would choose this new child of power over herself. It wasn't the first time she'd chosen her own safety over others and she knew it would not be her last. It was just a matter of survival.

* * * * *

The village was small, counting no more than ten huts arranged around a central fire pit that still held glowing embers, protected by an iron shield. The rain hit with a *pang* that sounded at once both hollow and strangely muffled. Alion could almost hear the drops slide down the shield, before they joined their brothers on the soaked earth. At best, the king's mark estimated, there were fewer than fifty people here. She looked to Kalissa, who pointed to the second hut on her right. Alion put two fingers up and pointed.

The men broke into smaller squads of four, each taking station silently at the entrance to each hut. The remainder of her men melded into the shadows in case any tried to sneak out, a strategy they had practiced and perfected over dozens of raids.

When they were in position, Lieutenant Kearn signaled to the king's mark, who strode into the center of the village and its fire pit. Grabbing a metal poker, she stoked the embers, then grabbed some wood from the pile. She threw this onto the fire, watching as it lit, growing slowly into a bright orange dance of flames. Then she casually ran the poker across the rain shield, metal on metal creating a cacophony of sound, causing more than a few villagers to poke their heads out to see what was happening.

At that moment, those under Deft's command exploded into action, flooding into each house and grabbing the people inside. Screams ensued as the village suddenly realized it was under attack, yet only a few had the wherewithal to grab the closest implement, a broom or rake, to try and defend themselves. The attackers were both well trained and alert in comparison with these simple, sleep-addled farmers who had next to nothing by way of weapons.

Three entered each house and battered people into submission. A fourth would move in quickly and collar them, the torc snapping into place before they knew what was happening. Instantly, any path to the Way would vanish, or at least that was the promise. The torcs could only be removed by one without Talent. It made for an infallible test of who was a mage and who wasn't. If they had no power, they could remove their torc easily. If not, the king's mark would deal with them.

In fact, Alion preferred the "envelope and torc" strategy. It preserved able workers and allowed for a more thorough accounting. However, the Galadines had instructed she make this village an example. The torcs were more to keep her men in good cheer. No one wanted to participate in anything sounding like a "massacre," so allowing them this small lie lent her more latitude to engineer the decimation.

* * * * *

Stiven raced in behind his team, torcs ready. He saw a man go down with a strike to his forehead, the flat of the blade hitting him with a dull thud. Stiven was upon him, snapping a torc in place with a simple thrust of his hand. He fumbled to make another ready and looked up, only to see a woman slashing downward with something. He raised his blade instinctively, hearing the strike of steel on steel and feeling the shock of impact. The sword tumbled out of his cold, wet fingers as he fell onto his back.

The woman carried a cleaver and raised her hand to strike again, but two swords plunged into her back as his squadmates came to his aid. They struck repeatedly as the woman let out a low groan, falling to her knees. They stabbed her even after she fell forward, face down and lifeless, pinning her body to the ground with their blades.

One leaned on his sword, thrust through the back of the dead woman, then looked up at Stiven and laughed, "She had some swing in that arm! Did you shit your pants?"

He didn't answer, his mind still reeling from the speed of the attack and everything happening around him. Sitting on the ground, he watched numbly as the little girl who ran up to her dead mother's body was torced, then pulled out of the hut along with her unconscious father.

The villagers put up little resistance and were soon rounded up and left kneeling in the mud of the central square. Those who were unconscious were dumped to the side under the watchful eyes of the guards. Those who had been killed were dragged from where they fell and laid out for the count, a grisly sight for the survivors. Within a few moments, the raid was over and the people of the village were gathered to the central area.

* * * * *

"Wake them," Alion said, motioning to the unconscious.

Guards went to the well and roped up buckets of cold water. With these they doused the fallen, following with kicks and slaps until all were at least semiconscious and able to kneel next to their friends.

When the king's mark was satisfied she had everyone's attention, she said, "You know why we're here. You harbor those decreed by the King's Law as a threat to this land. Point them out, and we will take them and leave."

None said a word, which didn't surprise Alion Deft at all. Simple folk often saw those with Talent as a benefit and harbored them, a mistake she would not allow. She moved with purpose, standing so that the fire silhouetted her from behind, a blaze of light that covered her like a mantle of yellow power. Presentation, she knew, was a powerful tool to cow these simple folk.

"Listen to me. You pay your taxes, you tend your fields. No harm will come to you so long as you point out the ones we're looking for." She paused, then said to Lieutenant Kearn, "Separate them."

At her command, the children were grabbed and moved to one side, while the adults were held at sword point. Screams ensued and one mother ran forward to grab her son. Alion moved with the swiftness of a cat. Her blade licked out, slicing the woman's head from her shoulders and returning to its sheath before her head hit the ground with a dull *thunk*. At the sight of the decapitation, the villagers instantly sank into a stifled hush of broken sobs and muttered curses.

"You are in violation of the King's Law, a decree designed to safeguard your lives! I bring justice and order. Where are they?" Alion knew she could've asked Kalissa, but this was the interesting part. She always wondered why people had such faith in their friends, when it took so little to turn them against each other.

"Justice?" a kneeling man asked. "The king's brother summons a demon and the land is plunged into war. For that, we pay with *our* lives?"

Alion nodded and a guard picked the man up and brought him before her. Her eyes narrowed. "Lilyth destroyed our world. King Galadine saved it. You owe him your respect."

The man shook his head, clearly distraught. "My wife . . ."

The king's mark looked at the headless body and shrugged. "She chose her path, and so will you." Alion grabbed him by the chin, forcing him to meet her eyes. "Where are the mages? Answer, or your son dies."

Two guards snatched up the boy in question and brought him to where the man could see him. It was clear this was the boy the dead woman had tried to save. They shoved him down to a kneeling position, and one placed his sword point at the nape of his neck.

"No!" The man looked back at the king's mark, pleading, "No, please." He then looked about the group and pointed to a man near one end. "He is the one you seek. He and his wife!"

Alion looked to where the man pointed and saw one of the men who had been unconscious. He knelt now, holding one hand to his bleeding forehead. She looked back at the man, then shoved him away.

"Good choice—you live."

So easy, she thought. "Bring him here."

The guards obeyed, and the man was dragged before the king's mark and dumped at her feet. Alion looked at him and said, "Kalissa?"

The girl walked forward, a small tremble in her lips. She came slowly, fear dragging at her feet.

"Is this man one of your kind?" Alion asked.

The girl looked at the man, who now focused his eyes on her with hatred. Because he was collared, she would not be able to see his aura, a sure sign he had Talent. Normal people always shone, regardless of the collar or not, just not as brightly as those with Talent. "Yes, King's Mark. He's one of us."

"And the other?" Deft had pulled a dagger, straight and sharp, absentmindedly picking at her nails. Looking at various villagers, it was clear no one thought her flimsy charade meant more wouldn't die. Good. Fear loosens tongues.

Kalissa looked at the pile of bodies and pointed. "Dead. His wife w-was the other," she stammered.

Alion watched the girl, then the man. When Kalissa mentioned his wife, she caught the look of anguish that flitted behind his eyes. *So,* she thought, *the girl speaks truly, or at least it's true his wife is dead.*

The king's mark addressed the kneeling man. "Take off the torc and you will be released."

"The Lady curses you, horseface," he said weakly, knowing his fate.

Alion ignored the insult, instead focusing on what she needed to know. "My Kalissa is seldom wrong. If your wife had lived, maybe I could've persuaded you to work for me, but with her dead, there's little to compel your obedience." Alion paused. "Unless, you have a child?"

The man shook his head. "No," he spat, and the king's mark could see he wished her death, or worse.

"Then take off the torc and you will be absolved in the eyes of your Fathers."

The man slumped into the ground, head in his hands. Then he grabbed the torc in both and pulled, his neck and face straining until red. When he could pull no more, he gave up, exhausted. "What does it prove?" he muttered.

Alion turned and faced the man kneeling before her and said, "It proves you have been judged, found guilty, and served the King's Justice."

She brought the blade up in a short, brutal arc, stabbing under the man's neck and through the back of his skull. The man coughed a gout of blood, clutching at the mark's hands. His grip was strong at first, but as his life gushed out, it became weak and feeble pulls on her wrist. His last breath gurgled out of him as he died.

Alion shoved the dead man onto his back with her boot, pulling the dagger from his neck, and wiping it clean. Grabbing the torc from the dead man's neck, which came undone easily at her touch, she tossed it into a basket sitting some feet away. Sheathing her dagger, she looked to Lieutenant Kearn. "Get them up."

At his command, the villagers were lined-up, facing the king's mark. She watched them without emotion. These were worse than the ones who sullied themselves with magic. They turned their backs on the Almighty Fathers, embracing instead the work of demons. Only their contribution to the Crown gave them mercy. Unfortunately for them, their contributions had become more delayed of late and were often meager portions of what they actually owed.

Her men grabbed the large basket she'd tossed the torc into and placed it on the ground near the standing villagers. Alion motioned and said, "Take off your torcs and put them in the basket. Then go wait over there." She pointed to the back of the village. "Once I have satisfied the King's decree, we will depart."

The survivors moved slowly, stiffly, reaching up and pulling off their torcs with numb fingers, tossing them into the basket. Unlike the man before them, they had no

Talent, and the torcs came off easily at their touch. As each collar came off, that person was ushered into the hut to stand with his neighbors.

From the back of the line came a child's squeal. Alion looked and saw a small girl, no more than five, pulling at her torc. A nearby adult reached down, but the king's mark stopped her with a word: "Hold!"

Four men formed a circle around the girl, who looked more frightened now than ever. She sat down in the mud and buried her face in her hands. Alion moved in closer and said, "Little one, what's the matter?"

She looked up, with eyes so blue they almost glowed. Soft dark hair spilled down her shoulders, and Alion found herself stunned by the child's simple beauty. The girl stifled her tears, then sobbed, "You hurt him!"

The king's mark looked back at the dead man. *Not as truthful as I was led to believe.*

She turned slowly and faced Kalissa, a little satisfied when the girl shook uncontrollably, her eyes showing white. "Did we miss one?"

With a scream, Kalissa turned to run, but was grabbed by Malioch. He punched her once in the face, then slapped the torc back on her before she tried any more mischief.

Alion moved over and grabbed Kalissa by the scruff of her neck, dragging her back to the little girl. Then she threw her to the ground, saying, "Did you think to save one of your own?"

When the girl didn't answer, the king's mark looked to the other villagers. Just the excuse she'd been waiting for. "Remove your torcs, now!"

The townsfolk scrambled to obey, and within a few heartbeats there were no more wearing the king's metal collar. They were pushed and shoved back to the hut, until all were crammed inside. Guards stationed themselves at the entrance, as others circled the hut to ensure none escaped.

"You know the punishment for lying to the Crown," she said for the benefit of her men. Alion turned her attention back to the little girl Kalissa hadn't mentioned. "The collar won't come off?" she said sweetly.

The girl looked up, then shook her head, pulling at it. "I want my da," she said in a small voice.

The king's mark drew her blade. "You'll join him in a moment."

"Hold your arm, Deft." The strident command came from behind her, the voice strong and composed. She saw her men turn and look. Any undrawn weapons sang out of their scabbards now with the ring of steel. She blinked once, then turned face to the voice.

At the village's entrance path stood three men. No, not men, she corrected herself, one man and two boys. They were dressed in dark, close-fitting clothes without armor. They carried swords strapped across their backs, the hilts jutting up defiantly over their shoulders. Even as she watched, the man in the center stepped forward into the light of the village fire.

Recognition sparked and she paused, thinking through her options. This man was an outlaw, a traitor to the crown, but he was no ordinary mercenary or thief. This man was dangerous.

Her eyes narrowed and she drawled, "King's Mark Davyd Dreys, what a pleasant surprise." Suddenly a simple evening's culling had turned into a fight for her survival, and Alion was too pragmatic to lie to herself. Things had, in a moment shorter than virgins or losers savored, turned from good to worst. Now her only thought was how to get out of this alive. Kalissa and the child were still valuable, serving as shields if worst came to worst. While readying her weapons, she asked, "How does it feel, knowing you are both a traitor and cursed?"

The man looked about and said, "I'm no longer a King's Mark and I don't serve your bloodthirsty king. If that makes me a traitor, so be it."

"Really? What would your men say— the ones hunted down and killed like animals after Sovereign's Fall?" A scowl pulled at the corner of her mouth. While the battle had been won, something or someone had slaughtered almost every soldier patrolling the hills after the battle. Dreys was responsible for calling off the search before the killer had been found, an unpopular decision amongst the king's men, made worse when whatever was killing them continued doing so with impunity along their journey home.

Davyd ignored her jibe and looked about, taking in the whole scene until his eyes finally came to rest on Thera. "Still conscripting children? Have you found no better work since your days as a slaver, or was court too clean?"

"This is better suited to my particular skills, but what of you? Do you not care for the mark you still wear?" She raised her arms and displayed the two interlocked circles worn by all the king's marks, tattooed on her forearms.

Davyd was struck with a fit of coughing, a thick, phlegm-covered sound emanating from deep within his chest, and held a hand to his mouth. Beneath his sleeve, she could see the tattoos on his forearm, twin to hers. After a moment, his coughing subsided and he rasped, "I wasn't able to help my brothers, but I won't let you kill their children. You'll face justice today."

Alion's eyes took on a calculating stare, and she nodded slowly. "The wasting sickness is upon you, judgment from the Almighty Fathers' hands." She moved to one side and motioned to her men, who moved forward in a loose semicircle. "But why chance your sons' lives?"

Davyd signaled something to his sons. They, in turn, drew weapons and came to stand by their father. "I've taught them what I know."

Alion bowed to the ex-captain and said, "By all means then, have at us." She looked to the brace of men still guarding the hut with the villagers inside and screamed, "Release them to their Fathers!"

At her order, her men hefted long spears and began stabbing through the thin hut walls, killing any within reach of the leafed blades. Attacking the outlaws en masse would only serve to create a bottleneck. Given Davyd's known command of the Way, she knew her escape relied on dividing him and his sons. No doubt they would try to protect these sheep, giving her a chance to escape. Her men had already begun stabbing into the walls of the hut while others waited at the entrance, thrusting at any who ventured near the opening. Screams echoed as panic and pain tore through the night air.

Davyd and his sons exploded into action, summoning the Way. Their forms flashed in a burst of blue fire, a flame-like skin protecting them as armor would. Without speaking they ran in three directions, Davyd taking the shortest route to Alion and the other two winging toward the hut where the soldiers were killing the townsfolk.

To the assembled men they might have appeared as three angels, shining like blue stars in the dismal night, but Alion knew better. They were no better than animals, her contempt for them below even the demons who invaded Edyn. At least the Aeris had had purpose: the quest for bodies, possession, and an undeniable hatred of living folk. What did Davyd and his ilk want? Nothing but committing heresy and serving a false power, blasphemy in the eyes of the Almighty Father. They worshipped the Way and in doing so condemned Edyn to invasion after invasion. The rain lessened, falling now from branches and leaves in pregnant drops, like tears of joy from the Fathers' own eyes.

The king's mark hadn't yet moved, but she unsheathed her blade. It gleamed silver in the dark night with a light of its own. She knew it shone with the power of her faith and prayed she'd send these traitors to whatever personal hell they'd earned. The storm was breaking, the cowards were running, and Alion Deft's face broke into a smile.

The Magehunters

THE KING

> *Be not so eager to strike first,*
> *have instead a solid stance.*
> *Victory comes to those who understand*
> *the pillars that support them.*
> —*Tir Combat Academy, Basic Forms & Stances*

Niall looked out over the wastes, breathing in the cool night air, his eyes striving to discern individual shapes in the campfires and tents of the barbarian horde, his hand on the hilt of his saber.

Nearby, his father, Imperial King Bernal Galadine, paced the walls of Bara'cor, watching the barbarian horde with disgust written upon his torchlit features. One hundred feet below him spread a moonlit ocean of sand, dunes mimicking motionless waves washing toward the shore of his fortress walls. Running his fingers through short, iron-gray hair, he readjusted his sword belt for what seemed like the hundredth time. Niall was sure that it was the waiting that drove his father mad, not the knowledge of the inevitable clash with the nomads encamped at their doorstep.

"Will they attack again so soon?" he asked, noting the deep lines of worry etched in his father's brown skin and sun-darkened face. Like the desert nomads, Bara'cor was home primarily to the race of Koorvans, who in ancient times had spread north from Koorva up through the Altan Wastes. They were characterized by darker skin and eyes, just as the desert dwellers who now assaulted Bara'cor. The barbarians had been encamped outside the walls for the past fortnight, a black, inky smudge on the white desert floor.

The King

Niall squeezed the hilt of the saber at his side for reassurance yet again, the leather wrapping soft and worn from summers of practice. He was, however, very conscious that the closest he'd ever come to crossing live blades with an opponent was at practice with the firstmark. He didn't want his father thinking he was still a child; he longed for a chance to prove the opposite.

The firstmark wouldn't have recommended me for duty if he'd had any doubts, he reminded himself.

"They will wait until tomorrow, attacking under cover of the storm," the king explained. "It's the tactic I'd use if I commanded their troops."

"Then why not do something to stop them?"

"And what, my prince, would you have your father do?"

Niall spun at the deep voice, coming face to chest with Firstmark Jebida Naserith. The ursine man stood almost seven feet tall, his eyes flashing in humor. Jebida hailed from the lower reaches of the Shornhelm Expanse, where it was said giant's blood still flowed in the veins of men. Though he too had the dark skin of a Koorvan, looking at the firstmark, one could believe he was in some part giant. Moving forward, he bowed to the king before turning on the wide-eyed prince.

"Shall we dispense with all you have learned in military strategy and leave the cover of Bara'cor's walls? Or should we try the catapults and archers? A few might hit, though the godless heathens are out of range. We might get lucky."

Niall looked down and with a sigh he intoned, "'Luck should not be your only partner.'"

Jebida straightened, peering out at the nomads. His experienced eye measured the strength, distance, and disposition of the nomad army out of habit, then flicked over to the king. He met the gray-eyed stare and nodded.

Turning his attention back to Niall, Jebida placed one thick, calloused finger on the boy's chest and said, "Aye, you have the right of it." Then his eyes softened and he continued, "But sometimes, a jester's luck is the only thing between a blade and your heart. Don't worry, my prince. When they attack, we will be ready."

Niall responded with a nod, moving back against the wall and out from between the two veterans. The king gazed down the outer face of the wall pointing to a section hit hard with what could only have been a rock larger than a man's head. Beckoning to Jebida, he asked, "Will it hold?"

The firstmark peered intently for a moment then said, "I'm no builder, but it was made by dwarven hands and they have a way with rock." Placing his meaty hand on the king's shoulder, Jebida steered his friend away from the edge. "We number about eight hundred men. I would estimate the horde fields over ten times that. Something works in their favor or they wouldn't even attempt the walls."

* * * * *

Twenty summers ago, Jebida had left to fight alongside Bernal in the Dawnlight campaigns, a successful effort to solidify the northern borderlands. The king had liberated the fortress of Dawnlight, and in the process, won himself a new bride and queen, Yevaine Aeonian.

The firstmark, elated at their victory and the king's good fortune, had returned to his village just south of Shornhelm, only to find it in smoking ruins, the houses smashed and burned into charcoal caricatures of the beautiful homes they once were. He recalled with perfect clarity the sight of his own home, reduced to a bed of gray ash like freshly fallen snow, barely covering the blackened bodies of his wife and daughter.

The village blacksmith had been the only survivor. She wailed of winged creatures pouring through an opening in the air, what they now knew to be a small rift. Each creature was insubstantial, but fearsome in form. They dove *into* children, who then lost themselves. Their eyes glowed white and they walked mindlessly away, back through the rift and were never heard from again. Those few adults who fought or resisted were killed. Part of him had died then, with his family and people. The village had been destroyed and as a result, nothing of the Naserith name had survived, except for him.

Swallowing the knot of anger that had begun to form in his throat, the firstmark concentrated on finishing his report. "I have evacuated all the elderly and children down the pass to the lowlands, escorted by Captain Kalindor with Fourth Company. All those who passed their third blade are here, reporting for duty. The younger ones were given the chance to volunteer to stay if they wished."

Both Jebida and the king knew Tyrus Kalindor well, a straightforward man who had served the Galadines for over a quarter of a century. He was a seasoned veteran with a steady hand, a soldier who would bear even the underhanded maneuverings and political intrigues of Haven to watch over the queen and the evacuees.

The king asked, "How many volunteers?"

Jebida smiled crookedly, "All of them. What did you expect?" He paused, a glint of pride shining in his eyes, then finished, "Ty and the queen's party should arrive in Haven soon."

The smile was short-lived though, as the firstmark's eyes drifted back to the nomad line, and his mood darkened at the thought of magic being used against them. But Jebida's loss to the demons and hatred of magic was no secret to the king. They both focused on the desert.

The king replied, "The nomads will attack on the morrow with this storm."

"Aye, it is the wisest course," Jebida agreed, "and hard on our archers. I don't underestimate their commander. Barbarian or not, he's canny, attacking us without exposing his men and camping well out of catapult range. We're lucky our backs are to a cliff and we have access to water.

Makes me wonder how they've manage to stay camped at our doorstep this long without the same."

* * * * *

With the conversation between his father and the firstmark receding into the back of his awareness, Niall imagined what his first real battle would be like. So far, all the assaults against the wall had been warfare at range, the archers of First and Third Companies dueling with their counterparts from the barbarian lines.

However, if his father were right, they would see hand-to-hand combat tomorrow. Niall ran his hand over the waist-high lip of the outer wall. The rough, gritty surface felt good against the hard calluses on his palm, earned through hours of practice with the firstmark. A scar in the shape of a "J" sat at the web of his right hand, pink against his darker brown skin. He looked at it, wishing it'd been from a weapon or something he else could brag about.

Instead, this particular scar, along with all the rest on his wiry body, had been earned by falling. This scar had resulted from a quick grab at a gutter, saving him from a twenty-foot fall. He couldn't recall what part cut him, only that enough people saw it to destroy any chance of making up a story to cover for his clumsiness.

Niall hoped to serve with Armsmark Rillaran. His heart beat hard at the thought of working the front wall, where undoubtedly the harshest fighting would be. Most on duty there were seasoned veterans, well versed in the art of repelling a siege.

"Niall."

Niall gave a start at hearing his name. Shaking off the visions of battle, he found both his father and Jebida staring at him. He moved over to the pair, watching as Jebida nodded his massive head in answer to some command his father whispered.

The King

"Niall, I shall be down in the council room. Jebida has your orders for tomorrow." The king clasped his son's hand in an iron grip. There was something about his smile though, that caused Niall to doubt his father's words. Bad news was on the way.

The firstmark cleared his throat, motioning for Niall to come closer. "Well, my prince. You'll be working with Captain Fenrith."

"Wha—?"

"Silence," snapped Jebida, fire in his eyes. "The first lesson a soldier must learn is to follow orders. Tomorrow you will be working under Captain Fenrith, supporting Fifth Company."

Niall dropped his gaze.

A conciliatory hand came up, clapping the young warrior on the shoulder as the firstmark continued, "I understand your disappointment, lad, but you're not yet experienced enough to stand at the point of the spear. It isn't only yours, but the lives of those next to you that are in jeopardy, as each would extend himself to protect the Imperial heir. You understand this?" A small smile escaped his lips. "You have my word I'll do what is within my power to allow you a chance on the wall. Just be patient."

Niall nodded once, dejected. Jebida would keep his word, but Niall put little faith in the firstmark's chances against his father. "If you will excuse me, I don't feel much like talking." Niall could only focus on what tomorrow would not bring: a chance to prove himself a warrior in his father's eyes.

THE APPRENTICE

In studying the Way,
accept that learning it is hard.
Once learned, accept that wielding it is hard.
Accept that mastery of the Way is hard,
and your journey will be easier.
—*Lore Father Argus Rillaran, The Way*

A rek Winterthorn did a seated stretch, feeling the joints in his back and hip pop as they slowly came back to life. He'd skipped training yesterday to finish a written assignment, and now he was paying for it. Overhead the afternoon sun shone through open slats, imbuing the polished wooden floor with a deep amber glow of its own, as if it was almost alive with light. Looking up, he rubbed his eyes and squinted. Despite the beauty and peace of the training hall, this was going to be a long afternoon.

He rose, his brown practice uniform feeling both warm and soft, and moved to a table and a jug of water. Pouring himself a cup, he leaned against the wall and considered things. Part of him knew he was just procrastinating from starting his workout, but standing against the wall was a nice truce between doing nothing and something.

The concept of combining Aspects with Affinities into techniques was no challenge to him. He'd mastered the theory long ago. What frustrated him now was the actual execution. Apprentices needed to understand how to use their Affinity to control the Aspects, but Arek had never discovered his affinity.

It certainly wasn't the Sun or Moon. These two were opposites but neither particularly spoke to him. He could say the same for Sky and Earth, as he'd never called up the slightest wind nor moved even a mote of dirt. The only two left were Life and Death, but every adept could manipulate some aspect of those, as they were considered neutral. Every adept except him, it seemed. As far as he was concerned, they were no different than the first four—impossible for him to tap into.

Silbane had assigned him Clouds before Sun, a technique to create darkness in an area. The training hall was perfect, with pools of radiance he could theoretically dim, provided he could access the Way.

Oh, he could do the stances, he could concentrate, yet when he tried to envision the area slowly darkening, nothing happened. Nothing ever happened. No matter how hard he tried, the technique ran like clickfish through his mind. As usual, procrastination was an easy way to avoid failing, if even for a little bit. *Besides,* he thought, *there's probably some kind of trick to it.* His master would let him exhaust himself, then show him the secret. That's how it was always done in the various stories about people with special powers. There was always a secret. You just had to be patient and someone would tell you what it was.

"Is my brother-in-name still working on Clouds?" Piter moved slowly onto the training room floor and lowered his wiry frame into one of the shafts of light. "Will your master let you accept help? We could train together."

As Arek watched, Piter spread his hands and closed his eyes. He was still; the only sound was his breathing, in and out in slow, measured breaths. Then, slowly, the pool of light surrounding him began to darken, as if a shadow had hidden the sunlight.

Piter opened his eyes, still in the darkness, and said, "See, it's not too hard. I can show you."

Arek looked sidelong at him, hating him more than usual for his taunting, and removed his gloves. Then he said, "Just leave me alone."

"Of course," Piter backed away quickly with both hands up. "I didn't mean it the way it came out." Light spilled back into the room as he banished the spell. "Just wanted to help."

Arek had a unique "gift," if one called it that. His touch disrupted anything magical for hours afterward. This made it necessary for Arek to wear thin gloves whenever he was around anyone who had magical abilities, or items of a magical nature, which included many things on the Isle. While it hadn't stopped Arek from making a few friends, he had far fewer than Piter, who seemed able to gather many around him despite what Arek thought of as an insufferable arrogance.

Arek straightened and did a breathing exercise, then turned to face the other boy, "Just leave me alone."

Piter backed up a bit more. When Arek didn't continue, he turned to go, but stopped. Looking back he asked, "It seems like you've got it in for me, and I can't figure out why." A heartbeat, then two passed. When Arek made it clear he wasn't going to reply, Piter shrugged and said, "Well . . . er, good luck with your training. I really did want to help."

Once again, it seemed like a nice thing to say. Then came that smirk that would always paint Piter's face. Since they'd reached their teen years, Piter loved to offer help, but it always came with a smug self-satisfaction, a way of looking down on the people he claimed to want to aid. Arek couldn't stand it, and as they'd grown up, he found Piter's company less and less pleasurable.

At Piter's comment, Arek could feel his face grow hot. Even though competition between apprentices was tolerated, at times even encouraged, it seemed his name brother had a special dislike for him. Moreover, when given the chance, Piter would certainly earn the black uniform for passing from the rank of initiate to adept, just as he'd shown off here by accomplishing in a few moments what Arek had tried to learn all morning.

The fact that Arek could nullify magic only protected him from magic. It didn't mean he'd pass his test. He didn't even know why he was on the lists. In his opinion, he was far from ready to be an adept . . . especially one without magic. He stared at his notes, anger still clenching his jaw. Then, his ability to concentrate ruined, he gathered his things and left the training hall. The confrontation with Piter was the perfect interruption to what was shaping up to be a truly pointless day.

Walking down the wide hallways, he made his way to the Hall of Apprentices. Divided into three levels, the lowest was a large area for the newest arrivals. Arek quickly wove in and out of the small cots placed side by side. The sun shone through the high-ceilinged room's windows, falling in long rectangular shapes over the initiates' beds.

He rounded one bed, smacked his toe into a footlocker, and fell. Out spilled school supplies and a white robe. He sat there for a moment, clutching his foot, his eyes watering. Massaging the pain out, he looked about the isolated carnage he'd wrought, and then he began grabbing things. He put everything back, knowing it didn't look as neat and orderly as before, but better than it did a moment ago. New candidates would spend many years here, learning mathematics, reading, and writing. No sense in ruining someone else's day because of his clumsiness.

Getting back to his feet, he brushed himself off and continued through the hall. He still remembered where his cot had been and often checked up on its newest occupant, a small girl named Lissah. He didn't see her as he passed, and silently thanked the Lady. He didn't have the patience just then to sit down and engage in a conversation with the talkative little girl, barely eight summers old. Lissah attended his class dealing with herb lore, and their next meeting would include a tour of the Isle's beaches to locate and identify specific plants in the wild.

Maybe he could ask Adept Thera to take that class for him so he could catch up on work Silbane had assigned? He limped over to the stairwell, shaking his foot to lessen his toe's throbbing, and made his way gingerly, making up his mind to ask the adept at his first opportunity.

The next floor was living quarters for the intermediate apprentices, or "Greens," those who were selected to stay after a rigorous testing of both basic skills and magical potential. They slept three to a room—a little more privacy than that of the Whiterobes.

Greens studied the basics of the Way, armed combat, and a multitude of herbs, medicines, and other techniques for healing the sick and injured. They also began learning more about Aspects and Affinities. Aspects dealt with what was being influenced by the Way. When an Aspect was combined with an Affinity, it was called a technique.

While Arek had learned quite a bit and understood the theory, he still couldn't connect these through the Way. Why had he been elevated to Brown? There were times when the technique he'd been given to research looked more like a diagram, something that needed a small nudge here or there to become symmetrical. He often questioned why, if magic worked through symmetry, they didn't teach that from the very start.

These Greens didn't learn anything but the most rudimentary ways to govern their Aspects. Everything they did was internal, using the Way to learn about themselves, their limits. They also only fought with wooden weapons. When the right time came and their instructors felt they were ready, they traded in their uniforms of green and donned close-fitting dark brown ones, moving themselves up to the third level of the hall. This is where Arek was heading now.

Each Brown slept in his own room and carried the responsibility of teaching the rudiments of mathematics, reading, and writing, as well as the basics of Aspects and Affinities to those below them. Arek himself conducted two classes in blade combat, a beginner's course in herb lore, and an advanced course in multi-opponent combat strategy. As of yet, though, he didn't teach anything dealing with the magical side of combat. He'd yet to show any manifestation of the Way other than the nullification of it. *Not that it matters,* he thought. There were fewer people coming to the Isle each year, so that meant less people to see him fail. *Why am I being so morose?* he asked himself. He shook himself physically to try and recover his mood.

The years after the King's Law had seen fewer children with Talent born in the land. Fewer still found their way to safety from the magehunters and the mistfrights preying on those newly born to the Way. Many children disappeared into rifts, which were growing ever more frequent. Even though the King's Law had been struck down by the latest Galadine, old habits died hard. Lynchings and other illegal killings were seldom prosecuted, leaving everyone to be responsible for their own safety.

To make matters worse, it seemed those who became close to the Way had fewer children. The eldritch force allowed feats that could only be described as miracles, but exacted a price that hurt both the Isle's newborns and those who would care for the teachers as they grew old. Arek never wondered much about children himself, but the idea of having to take care of Silbane by himself, with his cantankerous demands, puzzles, questions to which the answers were already known? Now that was truly frightening. Arek could only hope others came who would help shoulder that particular burden. Luckily, it seemed the adepts and masters would far outlive their apprentices. One couldn't thank the fates enough for small miracles.

These six adepts and the hundred or so students were the only ones left to carry on all the knowledge and learning of a once proud and powerful Order. The lore father sent the Adepts out farther and farther to look for those born with Talent. They came back more often than not empty-handed. Arek and Piter had been the last found in Winters Thorn, almost seventeen years ago.

It also didn't help that passing the test to become an adept was extremely difficult, even if one were strong with the Way. Arek's knowledge of the test was hazy at best and subject to the rumors that inevitably filtered throughout the school. If half of those rumors were true, becoming an adept required ludicrous feats of power, like slaying an elder dragon. Yet Arek didn't doubt Masters Silbane and Kisan could do something as legendary if needed.

However, every student who aspired to don the black uniform knew one fact. They knew that they would be an adept when they heard their true name uttered for the first time. It came to them as they Ascended to the rank of adept, whispered on the wind—and with it came their power.

Arek continued his climb up to the third level. He paused for a moment at the top of the stairs, listening. He didn't want to meet up with any of the other Browns, least of all Piter, who had a habit of inexplicably showing up at the most inopportune times. Making his way to his door, he eased it open, careful not to make too much noise. Then he closed the door behind him and plopped down on his bed, staring out the window. To be an adept had been Arek's dream since he'd first begun his training.

He didn't remember much of his life before the Isle. What he did remember came as brief flashes, a feeling, or a smell. He recalled someone with a gruff voice, and the smell of fresh cut leaves. Arek remembered a feeling like stone against his skin, but colored an odd blue and warm to the touch, as if alive. *Could someone have blue skin, skin made of stone?* he asked himself.

They said he'd been found by Master Silbane on the east side of Neverthere Bay, abandoned in the forest near Winters Thorn. For this reason the name "Winterthorn" became his last, shared with the other orphan of that same forest, Piter. Now, nearing the date of what he'd adopted as his seventeenth birthday, he'd spent all his life on Meridian Isle.

In all that time, negating magic had been the only evidence he'd had any power at all. Every student learned minor techniques, like how to obscure or channel energy. These were necessary to help with upkeep and chores. Arek, however, couldn't execute the magical side of the simplest technique. Even Lissah could do more than he could in that regard.

The most perplexing thing about his time at the Isle was that he'd been formally apprenticed to Master Silbane before becoming an initiate. This was an honor supposedly reserved for only the most gifted of students, such as Piter, whom Master Kisan had apprenticed when he was just a Green.

Arek was sure the only reason he'd been apprenticed so early was because his strange talent to nullify magic was a danger to other students. Of course they would want him looked after. He shook his head and pushed open the glass pane, breathing in the cool sea air that rushed in.

His room, much like any of the others on this level, was sparsely decorated, one wall dedicated to a bookshelf crowded with training manuals and texts. A small washbasin and mirror stood against the wall between his bed and the bookshelf. In the far corner stood a small sword stand holding his bohkir, a two-handed wooden practice sword, its handle worn smooth and dark with years of practice and sweat. At least in that, he knew he had some talent.

When he held his sword, a state of calmness came over him, a peace he couldn't explain. He'd heard some other Greens say they dreaded combat. That made no sense to him. Why learn a martial discipline, but not wish to use it? It was like being a great swimmer, but not wanting to swim. The entire illogic of it frustrated him, and he tended to deal with those students who were afraid to fight more harshly than those who were clearly eager to test themselves against his blade.

Laughter drifted up from the courtyard, pulling his gaze. Sitting up, he braced his elbows on the windowsill and watched as two apprentices squared off for a game of rhan'dori. One he recognized immediately as Jesyn, her slight frame hidden beneath her leather combat uniform. In her right hand, she carried her bohkir, glowing faintly blue as she concentrated her magical power through the wooden blade.

This slight conjuration helped to teach each apprentice how to channel their power, and served as part of the rhan'dori rules. Whatever part of the body the blade touched would become temporarily paralyzed by the magic channeled in the wood. Unconsciousness was the result of a strike to the head.

The colored glows made the blade work easier to follow and learn from, as each blade would leave behind a quickly dissipating colored trail in the air. *I wonder what color mine would be,* he thought, only to realize it would never happen.

Arek didn't recognize Jesyn's opponent until he shrugged off his cloak and raised his bohkir, glowing purple in the fading light. That would be Piter. Even as he watched, Piter's sword flashed brighter for a moment, an obvious sign he was channeling more power into the wooden blade, either to lighten it or to increase its speed.

Piter was always showing off, in one way or another. Arek grimaced. Even as the flash faded, the two combatants grabbed their blades and faced each other, measuring distances. Soon the sounds of their blocks and parries echoed from the circle, along with the occasional cheer from one group of students or another, each supporting their favorite. Arek couldn't help but notice how many more students seemed to be cheering for Piter. How could he be liked more than Jesyn?

The game of rhan'dori was as ancient as the council itself, and Arek had heard rumor that it was part of the Test of Ascension. At the time a student became a Green, he or she began learning the basics of sword and spell. These were combined into techniques, like Clouds before Sun, which he'd been practicing, or attempting to practice earlier. By the time the student was ready for Ascension, they would've gained enough knowledge to blend these two disciplines together.

Arek had no idea what one faced when testing for the Black. The mark of a true master was to use only their own bodies as weapons. Arek assumed the Test of Ascension would be fought unarmed, but no one except the one being Ascended and the adepts had an idea of what was required, and no one talked about their test after it concluded.

He didn't fear combat, as others did. Actually, he longed for it; but he was more afraid of losing than of fighting. Fighting merely meant matching his training and endurance against another. If the other was better trained or conditioned, it would show and the result was acceptable.

Losing was different. It meant he'd been defeated when all things had been equal and he could've won. It meant he'd failed to best someone because he'd misjudged tactics or been outsmarted, not because his opponent was stronger or more advanced in training. It was a big difference in his mind.

Oddly enough, Arek's lack of participation in the rhan'dori and his obvious skill in class had given him a reputation as a dangerous opponent with the sword, something he'd not anticipated. He enjoyed the reputation, but being asked by his friends for advice on techniques still made him feel uncomfortable. Sometimes he thought they might actually be patronizing him, as if a quick question about a particular stance or cut would assuage his inability to support that with the Way.

A yell of triumph caught his attention as Jesyn cut quickly downward, forcing Piter to block. The force of the blow caused him to go down to one knee, his sword raised above him. Jesyn took that opportunity to kick upward, catching the back of Piter's blade from underneath. His sword spun out of his hand in an arc of purple, leaving him defenseless.

Jesyn's leg went numb from the strike. Arek could tell she knew this would happen, and had bet her victory on it. Her sword leapt high, then cut straight at Piter's head, using her sacrifice in a hope to catch him. It might have worked. Jesyn had compensated for the loss of one leg, but Master Silbane had taught him, "Chance is the partner of hope." As a result, Arek never "hoped" anything would land – it was just too risky in a blade fight.

As he watched, Jesyn's foot caught on a root that, had it been a finger's distance left or right, wouldn't have mattered. It slowed her numb leg by a heartbeat, an eternity in a sword fight.

Piter was too well trained to let the slip go unanswered. As Jesyn threw her strike, he timed himself perfectly, flipping sideways from the blow, landing more than a sword's length away. He stretched out his hand and his wooden bohkir flew from across the circle into his palm. Then from a crouch he moved forward, his legs pumping as he quickly covered the short distance between himself and his opponent.

Jesyn tried to retreat, but her leg impeded her, and she took a painful whack on her left arm. That arm went limp too as the magic of the blade deadened it. Arek watched Jesyn quickly spin on the heel of her good leg. She'd always had the grace of a cat, soft but sure-footed. The blade in her right hand whizzed horizontally through the air behind her, completing a blue circle and singing for Piter's head.

Piter raised his bohkir vertically and caught her blade, forcing it out and downward. Arek knew what would come next. His sword leapt from hers to tap her right arm, deadening that as well. Jesyn's weapon dropped from nerveless fingers, but not before she flung her head back and caught Piter full in the face. Arek couldn't help but let out a *whoop* of joy as Piter fell on his back, his nose a spattered ruin.

Jesyn now knew exactly where Piter was and kicked backward like a mule. Arek could almost feel the impact himself and let out a satisfied *whuff* as her heel caught him in the stomach and doubled him over.

As he fell backward, she fell with him and landed straddling Piter's prostrate form, her numb shin under his throat, the other pinning his outstretched sword arm to the ground. Without using her arms, she leaned her weight forward.

As Arek watched she said something, probably asking Piter to yield, but he couldn't hear from this distance. It was just another simple example of his own shortcomings with the Way. Had he even a little control, it would've been nothing for him to enhance his hearing and know exactly what was said.

He watched as Piter struggled, but Jesyn had too much training. She'd expertly shifted in such a way as to create a stable platform with her weight brought to bear on Piter's throat. Only a few heartbeats passed before the boy's hand moved up and tapped Jesyn twice on the arm, a universal sign that you were yielding. Jesyn leaned back in response, and then she slowly rose off of Piter's chest.

Arek knew Piter. He shook his head and whispered to himself, "Knock him out, Jes. The masters have told you hundred times, finish him."

Piter slowly rose. The winner was the one who left the circle, and Arek knew Piter would take that literally. Before she could move, the boy swung his glowing blade, still in his right hand, in a tight arc. It caught her under her chin and Jesyn went down in a heap, unconscious.

Arek looked but there were no other senior Browns on the hill. Piter bowed once and walked out of the circle toward a small copse of trees, and Arek could imagine the smirk already growing on his face. A few of the watching Greens were at Jesyn's side, helping her back to consciousness but most were congratulating Piter, no doubt on his skillful "ploy."

"Cheating" was all Arek could think. Jesyn finally stood on unsteady legs and staggered out of the circle supported by a brace of Greens as they headed toward the nearest doors towards the infirmary.

Damn him, Arek thought as a cold anger settled over his heart. It was one thing to be arrogant, but to cheat to win a stupid practice match! No adept would think what Piter did was wrong.

The rules of rhan'dori were simple. You continue until your opponent is unable to, then you leave the circle. The instructors constantly reminded the apprentices there were no rules, just as there were no rules in war. Jesyn failed to disable her opponent, trusting his word instead.

Still, though nothing Piter did was technically wrong, Arek couldn't let him get away with it, he was ready to accept whatever punishment his master gave him. He raced toward his door, only to be brought up short by a chime sounding. He sighed, then turned to face his washbasin. Slowly, on the mirrored surface of the glass suspended above his sink appeared an image of his master, Silbane. Straightening his robe, Arek bowed once and stood still, only his eyes betraying the anger he felt.

"I have need of you, Apprentice. Please come to my quarters."

Arek licked his lips and replied, "Of course, Master . . ." He tried to think of a way to meet Piter first. When no excuse came to mind he felt his master would accept, he inwardly cursed and bowed again. "Yes, Master." It wasn't often he was called upon and once he was, it was not his place to disobey, regardless of his current situation. Piter would have to wait. Arek watched the image fade and then left for the Hall of Adepts.

Between his quarters and the Hall of Adepts lay a square expanse of green, a serene courtyard. This was the quad, where his friends and he spent many hours lounging when chores, adepts, and other students failed to beckon. It was also where the Spring and Fall Festivals were held each year. The Spring Festival had only been a moon ago, the square decorated with all the new blossoms the students could gather.

A few people were gathered there now to sell their cows. Much of what the island needed had to be imported. Though the monks' training was secret, the Isle itself was a known place for goods and services the mainland desired. Arek thought about the Browns and adepts who provided medical services and protection for the coastal towns that dotted the islands that ran northwest to the Shattered Sea. Without their help, many in the far reaches would've perished.

He ran across the quad and made his way up the many levels to his master's chambers. The door was ajar and after knocking discreetly, he entered. He bowed as Master Silbane turned from the open window.

The sun was setting over the Shattered Sea, spilling red-orange light into the room. A strong breeze whipped through, ruffling some of the dry parchments held down by rocks on the desk. He never enjoyed the climb to his master's quarters. He wouldn't put it past any of the adepts or masters to summon him wherever it was most difficult or strenuous to meet. Somewhere the sound of a gull cawing added to the absurdity of the scene. He literally climbed to the height where birds normally flew. Still, the exercise had felt good, draining much of the anger he'd felt at Piter before he'd entered his master's quarters. Now that he was here, Arek drank in the sea air, its coolness easing the turmoil in his mind.

Silbane moved to a chair, motioning for him to take a seat. Then he asked, "How are your techniques coming?"

Arek dropped his gaze, then said, "I don't feel any connection to the Way."

"Hmmm," Silbane put a hand to his chin. "Is it the Aspects, or difficulty with your Affinity?"

"What Affinity? I don't feel closer to the sun or the moon. It doesn't seem like I affect the earth or sky. Life and death may as well be red and blue and me colorblind." He shook his head in frustration, "Master, can't you just teach me the secret to controlling it?"

His master looked at him, and Arek braced to be berated. Instructors at Meridian Isle did not coddle, and aggressive teaching methods were used. However, in a moment of rare kindness, Master Silbane said, "There is no secret. Do you think I, or any of the instructors, want to go through years of training you if we could do it faster? It's not easy for us, either."

Arek looked at him with a mixture of surprise and disbelief. When he didn't say anything, Silbane continued.

"Consider that these six Affinities may not be the only ones. You need to find what works for you." He leaned forward, "You're of the rank now that some latitude may be given. I am trying to free your mind to find your own relationship with the Way. Do you understand?"

Arek wasn't sure. He shrugged, "I don't know where to begin. Even the apprentices can do simple techniques. The most I've done is making a mess of things."

His master was quiet. Then he looked out the window and took a breath. "Did you know I was a most intractable student?"

Arek stood there for a moment, dumbly. He tried not to show his utter astonishment. Silbane had never volunteered anything about himself, focusing instead on Arek's training and teaching him the philosophies of the masters. They'd never had "small talk" and Arek found himself sitting still, afraid to break whatever spell had put his master in this mood.

"Themun in particular hated teaching me. He spent many years trying to force me onto a path to the Way he favored." Silbane's gaze went distant. "And I fought him at every turn, because I knew myself better than he did."

He focused on Arek, raising an eyebrow. "Try telling your instructor that."

Arek was taken aback, his master talking to him as if they were everyday friends. *What should I say?* Worry at offending stymied his tongue, and he found himself just lamely nodding in response.

That didn't seem to deter his master, who continued, "But you don't *feel* that way. You doubt yourself at every turn. I thought I was special, meant for something greater than all this." His hands gestured, taking in the entire Isle with that small motion. "You hope you can make a difference in someone's life."

"You're a master," Arek said, his eyes wide. "That's special."

Silbane was quiet, his expression one of someone lost in thought. The he said, "It's not what we *are*, but what we *do* that makes us special."

His master seemed to be talking to himself, but just when Arek thought he'd escaped any chastising, a sliver of the normal Master Silbane shone through.

"You're wasting a lot of time. Stop daydreaming about secret techniques and hidden lessons. There are *none.* Do you think we relish the years we spend training? Believe me, if there were an easier or faster way, I'd teach it to you."

He grasped Arek's gloved hands and slapped the palms lightly, then squeezed, "You excel at blade work because you practice every day. To unlock the Way, you must do the same. Your Talent is unique, and therefore we must explore different paths. I can guide you, but you must first believe you have something worthy within you. Then you can apply the hard work necessary for mastery."

Arek looked down, growing frustrated. "I try. You've seen me!"

Silbane cocked his head and asked, "Like you did today when Piter interrupted your training? Is it so easy for you to lose your focus?" His master measured him with his gaze and finished, "Your heart isn't in it, so you let Piter ruin your concentration."

Arek wasn't the least surprised his master could see him. That was expected. What surprised him was that he was taking Piter's side.

Then Silbane said, "How many other practices have you let fall aside because of interruptions, sickness, injuries, other things? You've been apprenticed by me, and that means you can come here and receive private training."

His master leaned forward, looking him in the eyes, and asked, "How often have you done that?"

Arek sat there, stunned. He couldn't remember the last time he'd asked Silbane to teach him. He just assumed his master would call him when he was free.

When he didn't answer, Silbane said, "Would it surprise you that Piter is outside Kisan's quarters everyday promptly at sunrise to receive tutelage? Or that both Jesyn and Tomas camp outside our quarters, hoping for any instruction? They have to *hope,* you don't. Don't you want the training?"

Suddenly Arek's entire perspective changed. He saw what he must look like to his master, and worse to Master Kisan and the rest. They must look at him as a laggard, a lazy student who couldn't care less about earning his black. Why hadn't he ever asked Silbane for lessons? He couldn't answer that. . . it was something he'd never even considered.

Finally, he muttered, "I just thought you'd call me if . . . I don't like the Way." There, it had been said! His innermost secret, his worst transgression. . . he was a monk-in-training who didn't believe in the philosophy within which he trained.

He heard his master sigh, and then felt strong hands grab his shoulders. He raised his eyes back up to meet Silbane's own, who looked at him as if searching for something. There was silence.

His master finally let go and said, "Show me an instructor that says, 'kicks don't work,' and I'll show you an instructor who doesn't like to kick. Show me one that says, 'hands don't work,' and I'll show you one who doesn't like to punch."

His master paused there for a moment. Then he said, "What do you think of a student who says, 'I don't like the Way?' Maybe that's why the Way doesn't work for him? We like things we're good at, and don't like things we have little skill in. We like participating in things we don't have to work hard at and less so on things that take us out of our comfort zone. This is normal, but it's also a losing philosophy."

"Yes, Master." He couldn't think of anything to say. At the moment, he felt nothing but shame at his behavior.

The master's eyes searched his again, still looking for something. Then Silbane clapped his own knees and said, "Never forget the Way responds to your beliefs. You can cripple yourself by doing something as simple as not believing. Before you berate yourself too much, know this conversation means I haven't given up on you. I only bring this up because since you made Brown, you've been squandering your time. It's not too late for you to fix this, agreed? I still have high hopes for you."

Arek nodded, "I never thought—"

Silbane nodded, patting his knee. "Enough. Sometimes we need a mirror held up to see ourselves." The master looked out his window, his eyes half-closed. Then he slowly said, "Arek, try as I might, I cannot See into you. You are like a void, a nullification space that doesn't allow me any insight." He paused, then added, "For this reason I cannot guide you as easily as I can others, but that doesn't mean I don't see Talent."

He raised an eyebrow and looked down his nose at Arek and said, "Let's change the subject. What do you know of Bara'cor?"

Arek felt more shame from this friendly chastisement than he would have ever from the various physical punishments he had endured when failing to learn some technique. To compensate, he raced to dredge up all he could from the name, wanting to meet his master's expectations. Silbane often tested him this way, pulling something from a lesson taught many years ago. His frustrations at the many events of this day were forgotten as the information came flooding into his mind. That seemed another of his peculiar talents. He could remember almost anything he saw or heard with perfect clarity.

Clearing his throat he began, "It is a fortress on the western edge of the Altan Wastes. Legend has that it was built by the dwarven lords. It defends the pass to the lower plains and the capital city of Haven." When Silbane didn't say anything, he continued, "It's currently held by King Bernal Galadine, with an unbroken leadership that extends back to Thorin Galadine, the man put in charge of the fortress following the summoning and defeat of the demonlord over two hundred years ago. Thorin was the father of Mikal Galadine, who enacted the King's Law, putting people with Talent, people like us . . . to death." His answer caught on the word, "us" because, deep down, he did not include himself with the rest of the monks and students on the Isle.

He paused, thinking if there was anything else he knew. "It's said that Bara'cor's ruling line runs strong in the Way and every Galadine has magic to some degree, whether or not they choose to acknowledge it. I doubt this, however."

"Really? Why?" countered Silbane.

"If you have power, why not use it? I don't believe the Galadines could be strong in the Way and still reject its might. More likely they are mundane."

Silbane looked out his window at the Shattered Sea before replying. "Having power doesn't require its use."

"Easy to say, for those with power," countered the apprentice. His master encouraged debate as a way of learning.

"Perhaps," Silbane said, looking sidelong at his apprentice, "but forbearance is also a sign of strength." He stood up, moving over to an open book sitting near the window. He passed it over to Arek, who took it gingerly, careful of the delicate pages. The marked page showed a detailed map of the known world.

Silbane said, "Take this with you to your quarters. You have until tomorrow to learn all you can of Bara'cor, her history, the surrounding area and her people."

Mystified, Arek closed the book and stood up, his mind whirling. He bowed once and took two steps toward the door before turning back to his master and asking, "Why?"

Silbane pursed his lips, his eyes narrowing. "Why ask a question to an answer you already know, apprentice?"

Arek's pale eyes met his master's faded blue ones. Perhaps there was still some simmer in his blood, some anger at Piter taking advantage of Jesyn. Maybe it was the shame he felt at having lost so many chances to train with Silbane directly. He stood for a moment, unsure of whether this was another debate, or a true question.

In either case, he didn't like feeling the fool, and replied, "The assumption is I'll need this information in the near future."

Silbane smiled and nodded, dismissing him.

Sketching a bow, the apprentice retreated from the room. Dozens of ideas crowded his fertile mind, spawning and collapsing like bubbles of soap in a breeze. Silbane seldom told him everything, waiting instead for him to piece together what he needed to learn. If his master brought up Bara'cor and the fact that there may be more than the Affinities he'd learned, perhaps the fortress was somehow part of his training.

His heart felt lighter as he descended from his master's rooms, the conversation with Silbane having filled him with a sense of importance, or perhaps simply a renewed sense of purpose behind his training. Regardless, despite his shame at being called out for his lack of participation, he'd not felt quite so good as he felt at the moment. His master believed in him, and that buoyed his soul in a way he'd not felt in some years. He hoped the feeling would last.

The Apprentice

JOURNAL ENTRY 2

The vision granted to me by the dragonkind gives me an advantage. I can see particles of thought, like small points of light. They flow and weave at my every gesture, as if they know I am here. At least their movement tells me I too, still exist.

This land is beautiful, but empty. It recalls EvenSea's Walk before the Kings Road marred the pristine shoreline with its winding path of obdurate stone. Some prefer it now, but I always loved the verdant fields that grew right to the water's edge. I must find a safe place to make camp. All would be normal except that I seem to be marooned upon an island floating amongst thousands of others. Day and night here is simply the rotation of my island toward and away from the sun. What magic keeps these lands afloat is a detail best left for when I have secured my safety.

I hear creatures around me, scurrying things I cannot see. Their presence fills me with unease, as if they hunt . . . but for what?

Many a fool has ventured into combat without adequate provisions for his men. If I am to do combat here, I must first fortify a camp, but somewhere safe. These small points of light gather and glow around dangers, making them easy beacons against my inattention and inexperience.

Supplies should not be an issue, so long as nothing steals them. Merely the wish for food or water brings it forth from the ground around me. I sleep, and upon rousing find myself surrounded by a bounty of fruits, vegetables, and meats. These are raw but edible, or in the case of meat, easily prepared at my fire. Yet no plants have sprouted and no obvious source for the meat shows itself. Something, it seems, wants me alive.

Still, I must plan and hoard. I know the lean wolf of starvation stalks me still, ready to pounce at my first sign of weakness.

Journal Entry 2

But my mission has not changed. I must free Edyn from these Aeris, or learn how to defeat them.

FLASHBACK:
THE CULLING

Force times impact equals damage…
—The Bladesman Codex

T he Magehunters moved with practiced efficiency, throwing torcs at Davyd and his sons in lethal groups designed to try and trap each mage. The rings didn't need to fasten themselves to neutralize them—only to loop around a limb. Alion's men had practiced this and the air soon filled with the sound of torcs whirring as they sought contact to deaden Davyd and his sons' connection to the Way.

Davyd blocked one, deflecting it with his sword, then ducked and rolled under another as a soldier swiped at him with his weapon. The mage raised his blade and blocked the soldier's riposte, then opened his palm.

Blue flame engulfed the man, incinerating him in less than a heartbeat. Davyd didn't slow as he dove through the dying man's ashes and stabbed another through the eye. He yanked his blade free and spun, slicing with his arm. A thin blue light arced out, like a line with a weight at the end, severing anything it touched. Soldiers fell screaming, their legs cut out from under them.

Alion must've felt the devastating blue line come her way because she dodged, rolling through it. Her priest-enchanted armor shone, bending his spell and protecting her from its lethal cut.

Over the blue line streaked the elder of Davyd's sons, Armun. He landed lightly, swinging his blade in a tight arc and swatting aside two rings. He knelt and punched his fist downward. The ground erupted in a circle from the impact point, cracking under the soldiers' feet.

The men caught in the spell fell into crevasses appearing suddenly beneath them. Armun stood and clenched his fist, and the earth closed again on the trapped men, crushing them in its black embrace. He looked to his father and smiled, then made his way toward the hut, cutting men in half with his blade as if they were made of paper.

Davyd leapt after Alion again, his blade moving so fast it seemed to weave a net of silver steel around the king's mark. The strikes where unerringly lethal, but each time they neared her, his sword twisted in his hand. Her armor acted like a reversed lodestone, repelling his blade at every thrust. He cursed again, then pointed his finger and a bolt of lightning, pure blue and white, lanced at his opponent.

Alion stabbed her sword into the ground, then knelt behind it. The arc of lightning hit the air in front of her and curved around, bending the stroke into a sphere of power surrounding the king's mark, but not touching her. The lightning danced until it gathered at the hilt of her sword, following the blade down and channeling itself into the ground, leaving Alion unharmed.

The ground around her exploded outward from the lightning strike, scorching the earth in a radial pattern of force. From its smoking center rose the king's mark, smiling, blade in hand.

* * * * *

While Davyd combated Alion, his youngest son, Themun, leapt away from the clearing and began cutting down sentries and those who had managed to escape their swath of destruction through the camp. As he rounded a tree, a blade came whipping out, only to be caught on the hilt of Themun's steel.

The boy pushed the blade out of the way and fell back a step, taking in the scene. The man's collar indicated he was a lieutenant, but he didn't look much older than Themun himself. Just then another soldier rounded the corner yelling, "I've got your back, sir!"

The officer pulled a shorter blade and faced Themun, a small smile on his lips. Evidently he thought this would be easy, two against one. The other soldier held a cudgel in one hand and a torc in the other. He looked lost, his eyes wide and jumping from Themun's face to his leader's.

The lieutenant motioned to him with his blade, beckoning, "Come on, bring it. You'll not—"

Themun's form blurred, moving faster than the man could blink. His blade sliced effortlessly through the torso of the hapless lieutenant, the body falling in two pieces even as he kicked the other man in the face.

The soldier tumbled and landed on his back. He threw the torc blindly at his attacker, then rolled and began feverishly crawling into the undergrowth, trying to hide.

Themun deflected the torc, then placed a booted foot on the boy's back. The soldier screamed and rolled over, begging, "Mercy! Please, this is my first time! I knew it was wrong! From the very beginning!"

Lies. Magehunters were despicable. The song of retribution sang in Themun's heart. Only blood would quench it. Something in his eyes caused the boy to start blubbering.

"Please, don't kill me," begged the boy again. He began to grab for a dagger.

"I'm not my father," the Themun said, then sliced twice with his blade, opening the boy's bowels. "I'm not as good at making this painless."

The boy screamed in agony and fell back, the dagger falling from nerveless fingers.

Themun stabbed him once in the neck, and then held the boy's hand to the spurting wound. "Hold here, it'll be slow; let go, and you'll die quick. More mercy than you have shown these people." With that, he stood up and literally vanished into the undergrowth, never looking back to see what the boy chose.

He just didn't care.

When he glanced back, he saw Armun throwing soldiers at the ground where they immediately sank, as if its surface had become as soft as water. No sound marked their passage into the earthy depths.

Themun let out a sigh and surveyed the area. In a few heartbeats he and his brother had laid waste to almost fifty men.

* * * * *

Alion and the ex-king's mark battled back and forth, their swords an intricate dance of death. When Davyd pressed, Alion pulled back, forcing him to commit. Davyd was too skillful to allow her to draw him in. Worse for her, his sons would be done soon. Then it would be three against one.

She cursed her luck again at having the errant soldier appear now, during *her* raid. Had she been assigned a full complement of troops, they might have prevailed, but against one, who had the combined training of a bladesman *and* the lore of the Way, this was no longer about winning, it was about survival. It didn't help that his sons were turning out to be as lethal as he was. What she needed now was leverage.

At that moment, Davyd was wracked by a fit of coughing, so Alion seized the advantage. She pushed forward and kicked him in the chest, then bolted to one side. Ducking under a counter, she dove and rolled, snatching up the little girl they'd found. Alion put her back to a tree, a blade to the girl's throat.

Davyd Dreys was joined by his two sons, neither of whom seemed particularly winded. Evidently her men hadn't put up a very good show. Once again she cursed her luck, but her will was resolute. Alion Deft would walk away alive tonight. It was something she knew.

Davyd clapped them on their shoulders, then came to stand in front of Alion. He sheathed his blade and opened his hands. "What do you hope to accomplish?"

"Another mage dead before she bears more filth!" Alion spat this out, her hand tightening on the hilt.

"Wait—you must want something?" Davyd gestured to the open forest and asked, "Free passage?"

The younger son looked at his father in astonishment. "She can't live!" The boy then looked at his older brother. "Use the tree, the ground, do something!"

Another bout of coughing erupted, bending Davyd over. When the attack subsided, he let loose a breath and wheezed, "Her armor . . . it bends the Way and slows us. Do we take that chance?"

The boy moved forward, locking eyes with Alion and said, "She'll do this again if we let her go." The statement was true, lifting the corners of her mouth in a smile. Then the boy looked back at his father. "The girl isn't worth it."

Father and son regarded each other. "Trust me?" was all Davyd said. He put a hand on his son's shoulder and then turned back Alion. "Free passage, for her life."

"You would trade? After telling me I'll see justice today?" Alion laughed. "You must think me a fool." Still, a part of her began to believe she might yet gain her freedom.

"I would trade even scum like you if it meant saving her," Davyd said, looking at the little girl. "Release her and I'll grant you safe passage."

"Your Oath, then? And my other girl, Kalissa? You know who she is." Alion raised a bushy eyebrow. "Protect the innocent, is that not your creed? Does that extend to a child of a Galadine?"

Davyd stepped back, sighing. Alion knew he would not mete out justice in the same manner as the king's men. He needed to believe that in some things, he and his sons were different, and she would use that weakness against him.

She remained silent, knowing he could only come to one decision, and wasn't surprised to hear him utter the Oath.

"By the blood of my forefathers, I bind myself," he said. "My Oath as Bladesman of the Lore, no harm will befall you by my hands." A small flash of yellow encompassed the mage at the uttering of the Binding Oath, then disappeared. "Now, do what honor demands."

Alion stood and released the girl, shoving her forward with a booted foot. The black-haired girl fell onto all fours, then bolted up and ran to stand behind the younger son, hugging his leg like it could hide her blasphemy from the All-Fathers' sight. *She'd have met them tonight*, Alion thought regretfully*, but there are always more cullings.*

"You'll never survive the King's Law, and neither will your sons." She looked around the camp. Of the villagers, perhaps ten survived and she'd killed the two that had been mages. An incomplete victory, but one she could accept with her honor intact.

Armun stepped forward. "Be thankful we value his Oath, or your blood would soak the ground here."

"Your father is a fool," Alion replied with a smile. She limped over to Kalissa, who lay unconscious on the ground, sheathed her blade, then picked up the girl and slung her over a shoulder. Looking back at the renegade she said, "You can't win."

"That depends on what 'winning' means." Davyd nodded to the trees and a path leading between them away from this village. "Go. I took the Oath, but my sons didn't."

Alion clenched her jaw at that, but said nothing. She adjusted the weight of the girl over one armored shoulder, and then disappeared into the trees.

* * * * *

"You're letting her go?" a villager exclaimed.

Davyd turned to the voice and said, "The message she carries back, without her men, without accomplishing what she set out to do, will strike fear into the hearts of the magehunters."

Though he believed this, none of the villagers did. They had lost those they loved most dearly in one night's casual violence. Only their shock at this attack and their fear stopped them from exacting their own vengeance on the king's mark.

Davyd looked to Armun. "Check the wounded, help whom you can," he said. He coughed again and spat out dark phlegm, but neither of his sons commented. His healing had done what it could to slow the sickness, buying him maybe a few more years.

He wiped his mouth and smiled at his youngest, barely fifteen. "Themun, go see to the girl. One of the villagers can take that torc off her."

The boy grimaced, but obeyed. "Come on."

The little girl just stared at him.

"What're you looking at?" Themun demanded.

The little girl just kept staring, then she finally said, "Your hair. It's all standing straight up."

Davyd watched, hoping she didn't connect that Themun had just argued for her death a moment ago. So he turned and offered her a very formal bow, stating, "My name is Davyd Dreys, and this is my son, Themun. What's your name?"

She looked at him with dead, vacant eyes. At first he didn't think she'd answer, but then she mumbled something.

"What?" he asked.

"Thera," she said louder, though her voice was still subdued. "I'm Thera." She looked about, her eyes searching the village for something. Then she added, "I'm not sure what my last name is."

Davyd suddenly realized she was looking for her parents, even though she knew they were dead. He stepped in and held his son's shoulders, forcing himself to smile. "No matter," he said, looking toward the north, "The city of Dawnlight is close. We'll call you that, Thera Dawnlight."

* * * * *

Some distance away and out of sight of the village, Alion reached her horse and untied the reins. Dumping Kalissa's leaden weight across the saddle, she mounted, then hurried along a path that led back the way they'd come. The moonlight shone a soft silver, the light growing as the orb slid carefully out from behind the clouds, illuminating her escape. She heard a groan and realized the treacherous girl had awakened. Alion slowed and grabbed her by the hair, pulling her upright.

"Sit up, or I'll carry you across it all the way home."

Kalissa looked around and said, "Where are we?"

"Alive," said Alion dispassionately. "Don't thank me." She didn't say anything else, but counted herself lucky. The village stray didn't matter, but losing Kalissa might have meant her own neck in a Galadine noose.

They rode slowly for a distance, until both their attentions were taken by a man standing on the path, the moonlight streaming through the clearing and painting his red robes the color of dried blood. Alion kicked her horse, intending to ride him down, but he raised a hand. For some reason the horse obeyed his command to stop, pulling up short with a whinny.

"Well met, Alion Deft, King's Mark," the man said. "Though that might depend on your point of view."

Alion vaulted off her saddle, her blade clearing its sheath as her feet touched the ground. If this person knew her, he was in league with Davyd. Not surprising that he'd betray their deal. Unfortunate for this man, but killing him would release some of her frustration.

She pulled her arm back to strike but felt her muscles go stiff. Normally her armor would've bent enchantments around it, but this time she felt as if she were encased in stone.

The man tilted his head to the side, as if examining something, and said, "Your armor won't protect you, King's Mark, and neither will your misplaced faith in the gods. They don't care about you. They never did."

She tried to move, but her muscles were frozen tight, locked in paralysis. Only her mouth seemed to work. She snarled, "So much for honor. Had I known Davyd to be so craven, I would have slit that girl's throat when I had the chance."

The man stepped forward past her blade and pulled his hood back, revealing blond hair and pale blue eyes. His eyes gripped hers.

"I am the Scythe. Like the reaper's tool, I *ascend* those found worthy, or claim those found wanting." He reached up and tapped her forehead lightly.

Agony! Something like fire slowly bored into her skull. Her flesh shriveled away from his touch, her skin peeling back from her forehead to expose raw nerves to the outside air. Alion, though she couldn't move, began to moan.

"You have much to atone for, Alion Deft. This spell will take several hours to kill you, and you will feel every moment of it."

* * * * *

The man in the red robes stepped past the moaning knight and came to stand facing Kalissa. She'd dismounted with a grunt and a grimace, testament to the physical punishment she'd endured from Alion Deft and her men. She ran stumbling to the man, hugging him with a desperation that spoke to the horrors she'd faced.

"She deserved it. They all do," she said, as he laid a gentle hand on her head, stroking her hair. She looked up, seeing his face clearly for the first time... "I know you! You're—"

He froze her in place, then tapped her forehead lightly. The pain spread like spilled ink.

"I am nothing but the Scythe. Like the reaper's tool, I ascend those found worthy, Kalissa Galadine. You have hunted your own kind, killed others so you might live, and sown sorrow in your wake." He looked north again, took a deep, cleansing breath and said, "Like your father, I show no mercy."

THE PRINCE

In a drawn-out or extended combat,
pay attention to your breathing.
Exhale when you strike, conserve your energy.
Victory will be achieved only if
you can continue to fight.
—Tir Combat Academy, Basic Forms & Stances

N iall descended the stairs and exited on one of the archers' balconies. "Supplies? I would've been in more danger with my mother," he grumbled to himself.

Around him, soldiers camped on the balcony, just inside and above the main gates. In a siege, they took rest wherever and whenever they could.

Niall wove his way among the sleeping forms, ran down a small flight of stairs spiraling down the inside wall of the keep, then crossed the inner courtyard with determined strides.

He approached the Warriors Hall, a place reserved for unit drills and training. The square building stood near the back of the fortress, separate from the main buildings and quarters.

Behind the training hall was the pool of Shimmerene, its luminescent surface glowing faintly with a light of its own. The water looked like nothing more than plain water in a cup or hand. The waters reflected the moonlit sky with quiet dignity.

It was said that ancient stonebinders had fed this pool through carefully redirected underground streams. The runoff from the waters flowed down Land's Edge and joined with the real Lake Shimmerene, a much larger body of water with the capital city of Haven nestling along its southeastern shore. Somewhere along that journey the waters lost their luminescence and became ordinary, but no less refreshing to a weary traveler. Niall took a deep breath, smelling the water in the air, and made his way to the Lady's Hands.

The Hands were a thin strip of rock extending to the center of the pool, ending in two cupped hands in the act of scooping water out of Shimmerene. The bowl shaped by the Hands was large enough to comfortably hold a small ceremony inside it. Niall often wondered why the dwarves had built the Hands, envisioning secret rituals or sacrifices to the glimmering waters. But the secret of the Lady's Hands, along with the fate of the obdurate dwarves, was lost with their disappearance over two hundred summers ago. Niall came here whenever he needed to think, the stillness of the mirror-like surface making him feel as if he floated on a sea of stars. Now was definitely one of those times.

He wasn't surprised to find Yetteje already standing there. The cousins had agreed to meet at moonrise, eager to discuss Niall's station assignment for tomorrow, though that was before he'd talked to Jebida. He walked up the wide pier to the Hands, stepped down into the bowl, and seated himself on one of the benches carved into the rough granite palms. "Don't even ask, Tej. I don't want to talk about it."

Yetteje Tir smiled, her amber eyes filled with mirth. The daughter of King Ben'thor Tir, Lord of Bara'cor's sister stronghold, EvenSea, she was a thirty-day ride west of her home. Yetteje looked at her cousin, almost her match in height, and brushed some hair away from her face.

"You're the heir," she said. "You can't expect they'll put you in harm's way. If it wasn't tradition, even the Walk of Kings would be chaperoned." She plopped down next to her cousin.

Niall looked into the depths of Shimmerene. Though the sky and moon were reflected, his face didn't show. No person in his memory had ever seen their own reflection in the lake, another queer fact that gave the water its mystical reputation. Staring into its depths, it was easy to believe he didn't exist at all.

He couldn't help but dwell on his cousin's words. Before the nomads laid siege to Bara'cor, Niall had planned to return with Yetteje to EvenSea to begin his own three-summer-long tour of the land, one summer spent at each of the other three fortresses that ringed the Altan Wastes. It now seemed nothing was getting in or out of the stronghold.

Heaving a sigh he pushed out more forcibly than necessary, Niall said, "I'm assigned to Fenrith and Supplies, can you believe it?"

"Are you surprised?" Yetteje scooted over to the opposite side of the bowl so Niall could see her face. "You didn't really expect to fight, did you?"

"I've earned my third blade, one of the best in the class," Niall said with a scowl.

Yetteje arched one eyebrow at this. "Indeed, almost a bladesman then."

Niall quickly put up the open-palm warding gesture, and spat, "Bladesmen turned on their liege. They're traitors."

"I'm sorry," the princess said with a laugh. "I just can't believe you would think your father would risk you to some stray arrow. By the Lady, you're the only heir to his throne. Plus, imagine every recruit trying to keep you alive. They'd be jumping over each other to be the one who saves you."

Niall shook his head, hating even more that her words echoed the firstmark's sentiments. "You assume I'll need saving." He climbed to his feet, still looking over the calm pool.

Niall paused before continuing. He began slowly, "You know, father speaks of Haven, some sort of retirement." He avoided Tej's inquisitive stare.

"Why does that—?" Then her laughter spilled out. "Wait, you think he's going to leave *you* in charge?"

"What?" Niall replied, exasperated, though now that she'd said it out loud, it sounded stupid.

"You are going to be in charge of the greatest military and civilian bastion in the world . . . at sixteen?"

Niall cursed, then vaulted lightly over the lip of the bowl, landing on the stone walkway. His patience with his cousin was close to its limits. "Leave it, please."

"He's going to skip over the Firstmark, the Armsmark, *all* the officers, and put you—"

"Just drop it!" he exclaimed, stomping out of the bowl. His cousin was particularly infuriating tonight, and he didn't feel like being at the pointed end of her dumb jokes. What he needed was to put her back on her heels, he realized, and with a mixture of anger and shame in his heart he pricked her with his own wicked barb. *Let's see how she likes it.*

* * * * *

Niall's face took on that sulking brood that reminded Tej so much of his father. He could literally look angry and sad at the same time, a powerful weapon for any negotiation when you're talking to family. She didn't want to poke more fun at what was obviously a sensitive subject, but surely he knew better. *And he made it so easy!* Caught in her own thoughts, she wasn't prepared for what Niall asked next.

"What. . . was it like?" He looked nervous even asking, but for Yetteje, it felt like a cold rain from the seas of home had swept in, stealing whatever mirth they'd been sharing. She knew *exactly* what he was asking.

She jutted her jaw out and said, "I don't want to talk about it. It's not. . . not yet." She knew saying anything else would only make him ask her again in some inanely stupid and insensitive way. Whatever had prompted him to ask was uncaring at best, cruel at worst.

Yetteje watched Niall turn way, a hint of something she didn't quite catch in his eyes. She followed him down the walkway in silence. She knew he wanted to prove himself to his father. She could empathize, but unlike her cousin had no qualms about staying as far from the front line as possible. It wasn't fear. Yetteje had spent countless hours training with blade, axe, bow, and spear, as any royal heir would.

Triggered by her cousin's offhand question, Yetteje again saw the man who'd attacked her in her mind's eye— blood and brains splattering out of the "v" where his head had been.

She'd been ambushed near Bara'cor. The timely arrival of her escort had saved her from certain death, perhaps worse. Although none of the attacking desert nomads had survived, the escort hadn't arrived soon enough to stop her from having to defend herself. Yetteje had faced and killed her first man during her Walk of Kings.

Her axe cleaved down through his head, sprouting out of his chest where the blade had lodged. As he pitched forward, the handle had pierced the sand, like a tentpole holding up a ruined bag of organs. Once the remaining attackers had been routed by her escort, Yetteje had been overcome with uncontrollable shaking. When it mattered most though, she hadn't hesitated: she'd killed to survive.

Images flashed behind her eyes: the body, kicked onto a tarp; her axe, ripped out; herself, puking her guts out at the sight. Someone handed her a canteen of water. No one said anything. The dead man was taken back to Bara'cor so his markings could be identified.

Perhaps it started with that encounter, but more likely it'd been a change steadily growing in her long before this. Whatever it was, the princess felt more pragmatic about her role in life. Her aspirations were more than being a soldier-of-the-line. It wasn't haughtiness or misplaced self-importance. She had a healthy respect for those noble few who put themselves in harm's way. No, she just knew she was meant for something bigger. *Maybe this was why the Walk is so important,* she mused.

My worth, she confided just to herself, *won't be found behind a shield.* Though she and her cousin shared many similarities, in this they were worlds apart. *It'll be tested when my people's fate lies in the balance.* For what other reason had her father started her formal consulship training as soon as she'd learned to read and write? For what other purpose had Fate found her alone in the desert, forcing her to fight for her life?

Though being trapped at Bara'cor was involuntary, as a ward of the Galadines her participation in the defense was not expected. The king had made it quite clear she couldn't stray onto the wall without an escort. She'd recently been assigned to Sergeant Alyx Stemmer for that purpose, and she'd begun to feel a growing bond of respect for the sergeant. Alyx didn't treat her like some delicate princess, but more correctly as a graduate of the TCA, Tir's elite school for combat and tactics. She appreciated that, because she'd earned that graduation the hard way— through blood, sweat, and tears.

"You know," Niall said, turning to face her, "sometimes soldiers are promoted in battle, right on the spot." His finger stabbed down in emphasis.

Clearly, thought Yetteje, he'd continued the argument between them in his head. She decided not to respond directly; Niall wasn't listening anyway. And his earlier question, whatever had motivated it, had forced her to realize it wasn't her place to question the path Niall chose. Just as she'd found herself on her Walk, he too would find a role he could live with.

She was curious, however, about why he was so set on fighting *now*. The nomads didn't seem to be going anywhere. After a moment's consideration, she asked just that. "Niall, I'm sorry for making fun earlier, but why do you want to fight so badly?"

"No one will respect a ruler who hasn't fought, no matter what people say and no matter what royal lineage we're from. People follow heroes. Plus, aren't you sick of being thought of as a kid? I understand why father does it, but even the firstmark treats us like children. When he was our age, he'd already fought and ki—." Niall stopped. He began to say something, then stopped again. When he did speak, Yetteje had to strain to hear him.

"I'm sorry, Tej. I shouldn't have brought up your attack." Yetteje started to shake her head when Niall added, "But you should know the men say you held off *four* of them until help arrived. The man you—the one you felled—he had the shoulder scars of a full-blooded warrior, not some scavenger. They think you're some kind of warrior-princess out of the storybooks."

Yetteje stopped, considering his point. She knew many glorified a person's combat prowess. Though she'd come to accept this as a necessary part of proving one's worth to command, it hadn't really sunk in that combat in and of itself might be a prerequisite of being a leader.

Her eyes took on a far-away look as she contemplated the larger implications. However, she didn't get far as Niall was still talking, though he didn't seem aware it was to himself. Neither of them was going anywhere given this siege, so she'd have plenty of time to explore Niall's perception of valor and leadership.

The TCA made Yetteje hone many skills, but chief amongst these was – when one found themselves in a fight to the death, one fought to kill. She'd split the nomad's skull from crown to chest, splattering his brains across the golden sands. Her instructors at the Academy weren't the type to comment on doing no more than her training demanded. She'd lived, her opponent hadn't. Nothing else mattered.

* * * * *

The Prince

Niall looked back at Shimmerene, trying to articulate how he felt. He sought fame and glory, and combat was the only way he could see to get that, or the respect of his people. His cousin just didn't see it the same way. Her gaze was now focused on the Warriors Hall, not far from where they stood. He smiled and shoved her shoulder a little harder than playfully, but still in jest. His anger at her was never long-lived. "Never mind. How about a little sparring before we go to sleep?"

"Sure, unless that might endanger your upcoming promotion." She quickly ducked as Niall swung at her, and then she ran up the slight slope leading to the Warriors Hall. Niall followed.

As they neared, he could again hear the faint sharp clack of the wooden practice blades striking each other. Motioning to Yetteje to be silent, he moved closer to one of the portals looking onto the training grounds, and felt Tej come up behind him, cursing softly as she jostled for a better view.

"That's Ash! What's he doing?" he asked. In answer to Yetteje's annoyed look, Niall added, "I know, stupid question."

Still, it was unusual for the man who was second-in-command of all of Bara'cor's forces to be out on the practice grounds at this hour. Pushing Yetteje and her muffled curses out of the way, Niall pulled up close to the window and watched.

In the center of the torchlit ground stood Armsmark Ash Rillaran, his eyes narrowed in concentration. He held two blades, low and away from his body. Stripped to the waist, Ash's lean dark form was sheened with sweat. Dark, close-cropped hair glistened from his exertions. Circling around him ranged three opponents, their sashes marking them as captains of different companies. They held their weapons in front of their midsections, the blades angled up. Even as Niall watched, two switched their stances and attacked with their blades held high, the third thrusting in at Ash's neck.

Ash ducked inside the first overhead strike, shoving his muscular shoulder into his opponent's stomach and driving him into his comrade. As they went sprawling in a tangle of arms and legs, he charged the third, heading straight for the blade's tip. At the last possible moment, he twisted his lead shoulder forward, the sword passing inches from his neck, and struck with his own blade to the captain's wrist.

The wooden sword fell from nerveless fingers, even as the captain rolled to avoid Ash's second blade whizzing by his ear.

Niall grabbed Yetteje. "Come on, let's go inside!"

They ran around to the front of the Warriors Hall, pausing only to pull their boots off as custom dictated, before entering. They found, much to their disappointment, that they weren't the only spectators.

The dozens of soldiers watching as their captains took on the young armsmark quickly dashed Niall's hopes for a private lesson. Moving over to one side of the combat circle, he found a seat and pulled Yetteje next to him. "I think the armsmark should test for his Seventh."

Yetteje looked at Niall, pursing her lips, "You don't even know what that takes. By the Lady, you've only passed your Third and you're talking like you're a master."

"So what? I was just—" A sudden flurry caused Yetteje to make shushing gestures, her attention plainly on the combatants. "—making an observation," he finished speaking quietly to himself.

The armsmark had positioned himself to one side of the circle, and the three captains crouched in a semicircle in front of him, having retrieved their weapons. Then, with a shout, all three attacked together, clearly hoping to overwhelm their opponent.

Ash blocked an overhead strike with his left sword and put his body close to the captain's, using him as a shield. Spinning in place, he shoved the captain into the second attacker, who made the mistake of trying to catch his friend. Two quick blows from Ash's blades dispatched them even as he pivoted to block the third captain's thrust at his stomach. Parrying it past him, he hooked his foot behind the man's forward ankle and pulled, sweeping him to the floor. Ash placed his blade on the man's throat, smiled, and said, "Durbin, you were always one to attack without waiting. Yield?"

A slow smile broke out on Captain Durbin's face, bringing new creases to his kaffe-colored, sun-lined visage. In a gruff voice he replied, "Yes, yes, you wet-behind-the-ears pup, I yield!"

The armsmark pulled his sword away and helped Durbin up, clapping him on the back. Around them, the crowd laughed as jokes flitted back and forth between the rival companies. Coins and extra duties changed hands as wagers were lost or won.

Turning to the other two captains, Ash bowed once, thanking them, then walked over to an earthen water bowl set to one side of the Warriors Hall. The three captains made their way out of the circle, meeting the good-natured jeering with smiles and comments of their own.

Niall could see the armsmark watching his men, and knew he looked for hidden animosities. He often instructed Niall to do the same, to learn how to discern a person's motivation. It was here, he said, that one could best measure the quality of their character. Apparently satisfied, the armsmark grabbed a wet towel and began to scrub his face and neck.

As Ash replaced his weapons on the rack, Niall and Yetteje approached. Niall saw the armsmark's eyes linger on the hilt of his saber poking out from behind his right shoulder, and suddenly felt embarrassed wearing it in front of the seasoned veteran.

Ash greeted the pair with a smile. "It seems you are already preparing for tomorrow, my prince." He then acknowledged Yetteje with a nod. "Princess."

Niall grimaced, now feeling even more the child. "Father has assigned me to Captain Fenrith," he said dejectedly.

The armsmark nodded as if in understanding, but said, "A vital position. Your father has faith in you."

"I doubt it." Niall spread his hands in exasperation.

Ash narrowed his eyes, and when he did so Niall couldn't help but think they turned the color of ice, bluish but also white. It was unnerving. He looked away to break the armsmark's intense gaze.

Ash held out a callused hand and asked, "Does this hurt?"

Niall yelped in surprise as the armsmark's finger poked him in the chest, then he laughed. "No, of course not. It's only your finger."

Slowly Ash closed his fingers into a tight fist and then addressed Niall again. "And if I hit you with *this*?"

"Wha—!" Niall backed up a step, and stopped. "I mean, no . . . That could hurt." Actually, Ash's finger *had* hurt quite a bit, but Niall didn't want to admit that in front of his cousin.

The armsmark straightened and asked, "Why?"

"A fist is stronger than a finger?" He unconsciously rubbed the spot Ash had poked.

Ash spread the fingers of his hand in front of Niall and nodded. "Exactly. Each of my fingers represents one facet of defending this fortress. No part can succeed by itself." The armsmark closed his fingers slowly. "But together we form a fist the nomads cannot break." He looked at the prince thoughtfully. "Do you understand?"

Niall stood dumbfounded for a moment. "I think so."

"I hope so. Don't forget that we, who repel the attackers from the wall, cannot do so without arrows, or survive the heat without water. There is no station beneath your respect. The men will be heartened to see their prince perform such menial duties for them. It is important and noble. It is the stuff of leaders."

The armsmark looked at Niall for a moment longer, as his face broke into a grin.

"It is one of the many things you'll master before commanding these men." He turned his attention to the emptying room and asked, "By your leave?"

As Niall nodded, the armsmark scooped up his shirt and made his way out of the Warriors Hall, into the cool night.

Yetteje came up behind Niall, who stood alone now, deep in thought. "Maybe *he'll* promote you," she said with a wicked grin.

The punch he threw missed, as his cousin expertly ducked. He shook his head and muttered, "Drop it, Tej. Seriously."

COUNCIL'S CHOICE

If your opponent is frustrating you
consider adopting her strategy.
—Altan proverb

S ilbane addressed the assembled adepts and the lore father, his voice clear and strong as it echoed in the large chamber of the council room. They sat at a long rectangular table lit by wall sconces. The room had been built for hundreds. Six monks sat there now, like leftover crumbs on a plate.

"Investigating the fortress and killing the nomad command aren't mutually exclusive ideas. We can do both." Silbane looked at Themun, his statement bringing their meeting to an informal start. His voice echoed hollowly throughout the chamber, somehow matching in sound what the flickering torchlight did to their shadows. Nothing within the chamber held the gravitas it should have; the enormous hall felt like an abandoned place waiting for greater heroes to arrive. At least, that's how Silbane felt when he looked around at their paltry numbers and thought about the challenges facing them. After meeting with Thera, Silbane had decided to voice his worst fear first, hoping it would be summarily dismissed, or argued out. Either outcome was a win for him.

Themun shook his head. "Not without revealing yourselves. We can't risk knowledge of us coming to light until we know who is behind the strength of the nomads. We need to hide your presence during this mission."

The lore father was laying out an infantile script that Silbane knew he was supposed to follow by "volunteering" for the plan. A plan, he reminded himself, already decided by the lore father. It stuck in his craw, but he had little choice. It was his best chance for getting Arek off the island safely. Then he could tell him everything. With luck, he could drop him off at one of the coastal towns until he returned from the mission.

Actually taking him to Bara'cor now seemed foolhardy, but he suspected leaving Arek behind wouldn't be as easy as he thought. He took a breath, his eyes traveling around the dark council chamber to finally rest on Thera. She raised an eyebrow, and gave him a small smile. Maybe he could ask her to meet him near Bara'cor?

Arek's power would mask their approach. It could be possible, but would require them to stay close together. However, the extent of his apprentice's ability had never been fully tested in a situation like this. Silbane was a proponent of the adage, "Ask no question to which the answer still eludes you." Right now, he didn't know if Arek would tire, if whatever was near Bara'cor was more powerful than his apprentice's nulling aura, or if something else might pierce their ethereal camouflage. With that many unknowns, he didn't see the benefit in taking Arek in blind. At the very least, he'd confide in him and let the boy decide, regardless of Themun's orders.

While he mulled this over in his head, Giridian said, "We all know we can't see or read Arek, but what you're asking is impossible. No one can hide another person's life aura. The magehunters used that fact to hunt us quite effectively."

Themun looked at Giridian, then said, "Not entirely true, Adept. We'd always believed this because we'd never been able to use our Affinities to mask ourselves. However, think of the magehunter's torcs. Once they encircle anyone with Talent, they too, fade from view."

Slowly, Silbane turned. Taking his time, he got everyone's attention, so he used that to gain a few precious moments to gather his thoughts. By the time he was ready to address his fellow monks, everyone was waiting. In a voice heavy but measured, he said, "As you've seen from his performance in your classes, Arek's good in many of the physical arts, but his ability to command the Way is . . . limited."

Kisan scoffed, "That's being generous."

"Kisan," Silbane continued, unable to keep the ire from his voice, "give it a rest. What you may not know, however, is that Arek has another ability, one the lore father and I think is an offshoot of this magical disruption." Since only he and Themun were able to sense life auras, the other adepts were unaware of this particular trait. Silbane had wanted to keep it that way until they understood it better, but now he needed to divulge it.

He stood up, stretching his legs, and went on, "When anyone of magical potential stands near Arek, they fade, just like those who are torced by magehunters."

Dragor leaned forward. "Really? Fascinating."

Silbane nodded. "Anything near Arek has its life aura suppressed. Before you ask, we still don't know why. Furthermore, it persists for some time even after Arek leaves the area, like the ground after a rainstorm, slowly drying in the sun."

Silbane took a moment before continuing. "Themun and I have spent many years trying to understand how this ability of his works."

Kisan leaned her chair back on two legs, an impressive feat considering it was made of solid granite. She rocked there for a moment, her fingers steepled in front of her face. Then she said to Themun, "I assume you failed to learn how to duplicate this aura masking." A familiar smirk accompanied the statement, to which she added, "A good reason to bring his apprentice. Under his cloak we may infiltrate unseen."

"Yes," Themun replied, his voice testy. "Getting to Bara'cor undetected, past whomever or whatever is helping the nomads, is critical. Staying out of the demon's notice is paramount. Arek guarantees both these things."

Silbane held up his hand, unwilling for Themun to sell Arek's ability as a known quantity. He shook his head. "Be honest; we aren't sure."

Themun shrugged and replied, "Do you have a better idea? If so, please share it."

"Let me and Thera go," Silbane said. "We can ascertain exactly what's going on and—"

Themun held up a hand. "Without Arek's mask, you run too great a risk of being discovered. I hope it's only nomads, but if we're right and someone with power is helping them, we won't get a second chance. They'll prepare, and we don't have that much time . . . eight days if we're lucky."

Themun paused, his eyes searching Silbane's face as if looking for something. Then, with a resigned sigh he said, "If you won't take him, I'll have another do it."

Silbane forced a laugh. "You think it's that easy? You're not asking for a simple reconnaissance mission."

"You want to use Arek," said Thera, anger in her voice. Silbane knew putting his apprentice directly in harm's way would not sit well with Thera. Also, it wasn't something the lore father could easily deny. Letting that little piece of information 'slip' during their tryst had been a calculated risk, but one he'd felt compelled to take for Arek's sake.

"Tell the truth." Her eyes had turned dark, like bruised storm clouds gathering in what had been until now clear blue skies. Only Thera's eyes changed so dramatically, an expression of the Way Silbane hadn't seen manifest in anyone else. It showed her emotional state as if written on her brow.

Themun looked at Thera and said, "You can't be that naïve."

Wrong tack, thought Silbane. He waited for the inevitable fight between the two who'd been friends longest. Like sister and brother, or husband and wife, seldom did either let a poorly forged point through their personal armor of reasoning. But surprisingly, Thera let it go.

Silbane met her eyes briefly, not enough to get anything except that she was absorbing every word being uttered, but waiting. He cursed himself for not sitting next to her, a tactical error that was likely as much an oversight as it was the aftereffects of the koken nuts. A hand came up to unconsciously rub his forehead.

Then the lore father addressed everyone, saying, "If the Gate is open, Silbane will use Arek to close it."

Kisan didn't seem surprised, but Silbane noticed quite a few of the others looked shocked. Had they really not understood what the lore father had been talking about all this time? He now appreciated his time with Thera all the more.

Thera leapt to her feet. "And let's be clear what will happen to the boy."

That was the Thera he knew. She wouldn't let Arek's safety be easily compromised. To Thera, every child on the island, regardless of their level of skill, deserved to be protected.

"The initiate may be in danger, but don't talk like he's helpless," Themun replied.

"You know what's likely," Silbane retorted. "He'll either die or be trapped on the other side in Lilyth's world."

Themun tilted his head and said, "Really? Do you want to add any other dire consequences to your poor apprentice's day? If so, please include the possibility of demons invading Edyn because we neglected to send a trained apprentice into danger." The lore father rolled his eyes. "I've heard better reasoning from children who want to stay up late."

"You think we're overstating the danger to Arek?" Silbane asked. "What if his power amplifies the gate? What if it doesn't work?"

Themun's eyes narrowed. He walked over to Silbane's portion of the table and laid his staff down on the granite top. "I've added more to this table with this small action than Arek has ever done in his entire time on the Isle. His power has never magnified the Way, nor created more from less. That would be like saying putting a sponge in water creates more water. Clearly that doesn't happen."

"But you don't know," said Thera.

Themun held his hands up. "Yes, we do. Arek doesn't increase or magnify magic in any way. He has never done so. The only thing he does is nullify it."

The council remained silent, but Silbane didn't have an answer to that. What the lore father said was true. He'd never seen his apprentice create anything, only disrupt the Way with his touch. And Silbane's self-proclaimed weakness was his inability to argue against the truth. He'd never been crafty enough to bend truths or weave tales to support his position. In that, he was more warrior than poet.

Kisan raised a hand for permission to speak, her head bowed in thought. When she looked up again, Silbane could see the sincerity in her eyes. Still, it didn't make him happy. Whatever she was about to say more than likely wouldn't help his cause. Kisan only did what benefited her, a survival trait both he and Themun had tried to wean her off of, to no avail.

"Danger is our job . . . all of us. Even our apprentices, for they have the freedom to leave with coin in their pockets if they don't want to remain here."

She looked at Silbane and said, "I think we should consider what indecision will mean to the people of Edyn. We can't hesitate to seal a wound because of pain. Doing so will only cause the patient to die."

"Then shouldn't we give Arek his choice?" Thera implored. "Service is the Oath we take. We accept risk. Even if Arek's touch can close this Gate, Themun is asking the boy to go in blind, not knowing the possible consequences. Shouldn't he at least be told?"

As Silbane had feared, Kisan had used their call to service to obligate his apprentice. Still, Thera's question was the same one he wanted answered. Why not tell the boy and get his buy in? As if she'd read his thoughts, and he knew she hadn't, Kisan still managed to pierce their question and nail it to the proverbial wall.

"What if he chooses not to help?" Kisan asked, looking around the council chamber.

"What if it were Piter?" Thera retorted quickly.

Gods bless her, thought Silbane.

Kisan sat back, disbelief written plainly on her face. She didn't say anything but Silbane could see the conflict play out across her face. What *would* she do if it were Piter? Perhaps a part of her began sympathizing with Silbane's plight. More likely, she was thinking about her and Piter's chances of success versus Silbane and Arek. She grew silent, apparently not trusting herself to answer immediately.

Nice job, Thera, Silbane thought. *That put her on her heels*.

Thera continued, her voice a mixture of disbelief and anger, now directed at all the assembled adepts. "I can't believe what I'm hearing. We are supposed to be the 'shields of the weak.' These words are part of our Oath, but at the first hint of trouble, we offer our children as acceptable casualties. I—"

"Enough!" Themun boomed like thunder. He slammed his staff into the ground in frustration, focusing directly on Thera. "And what of the village I found you in? Is a blade of grass or tree left to mark the place your parents died? You talk about Arek like he's helpless. Where is the girl who acted with passion the day she lost her home?"

Thera was silent, clearly taken aback by the lore father's outburst. Then, in a small voice she said, "She's gone. You stepped into my life and pulled me away from the brink. Now you're doing the opposite, if you don't tell Arek why he's being sent to Bara'cor."

Her quiet statement had its effect. Themun looked deflated, whatever fire had been building within now quenched by Thera's cool waters of reason. The lore father leaned against the table, his fingers scratching its granite surface as he gathered his thoughts. Then he said, "There is a time for careful and methodical thinking, and a time when action is necessary. I understand your need for moral certitude, but that's a luxury. If the gate opens, we six cannot stop whatever happens. Edyn will die."

Thera looked down, perhaps abashed by Themun's words, but even as Silbane watched, she drew herself up. Her will was strong, and in a voice supported by her convictions she said, "I understand your need to feel we are responding, but you mistake action for strategy. Acting quickly does not secure Edyn. Understanding what we face does. Maybe you think I'm too soft, too yielding to make the hard decisions? But remember, after a storm, it's the whiplash tree that still stands. Arek should be told, and offered a choice."

She met Silbane's eyes, her concern and support of him plain, then back at the lore father. "What do you wish me to do, Lore Father, knowing what I know now?"

There was a long pause, a moment where the air itself seemed to hold itself motionless, unwilling to disturb how Themun would answer. Nothing crossed the lore father's face that Silbane could read. The man seemed made out of stone, without any indication of how he felt. Then, slowly, Themun nodded and said, "You may excuse yourself. Nothing will be gained by continuing to naysay our plan." To Thera's shocked look, the lore father added, "It's time for decisiveness. I applaud your concerns, but they are ill placed. I forbid you to say anything to Silbane's apprentice."

Thera looked down, fingering her staff and stepping back. The shuffle of her sandals, cork on top of leather, sounded louder than Silbane had expected. He was still trying to come to grips with what had just happened.

Into the silence, Thera said, "I excuse myself." She turned, her robes swirling as she made her way to the large double doors and stopped, her back to the council.

"I was wrong when I gave you credit. You argued for my death, remember?" She waited, but when Themun didn't answer she said, "Because I do. I never forgot.

"Your father never thought children should be used. It's only because of him that I survived." Her clear blue eyes scanned the assembled adepts before coming back to Themun. "He'd be ashamed of you now."

Themun stepped forward, but before he could say anything, the doors opened and she swept out of them in a flowing mass of black hair and blue silk. The doors shut behind her with a hollow boom, plunging the council chamber into silence.

"She certainly told you," quipped Kisan after a moment, her timing either horrible or impeccable. Silbane sighed as he resisted the impulse to bury his face in his hands, hoping the lore father wouldn't rise to her bait.

Themun turned, his entire stance now reflecting his frustration, but he pointedly ignored Kisan. Perhaps he knew it wouldn't take much for his anger to spill over, threatening their small council with a deadlock.

With barely controlled rage still smoldering in his eyes, the lore father said, "Does anyone else share Thera's dilemma? If so, you should excuse yourselves too. Make your lives easier, stand aside, preferring your own comfort and moral certitude over service.

"This is the hard path, the Will of the Way. This is a day when we must all make difficult choices, and for that I need only those who can bear the weight."

The adepts adjusted their chairs, uncomfortable under Themun's glare. All, that is, except Kisan. She smiled and said, "Only the weak negotiate."

When no one else said anything, Themun's features softened. It was like watching a paper lantern when its flame went out, the entire construct falling in on itself as the heat died. He fingered his robe, harkening to what Thera had done just moments ago. When he looked back at the council, Silbane could see a mixture of weariness, fear, and sadness on the lore father's face.

With a sigh, Themun said, "I hold no anger at Thera, except for the delays her doubt will surely cause. As I said before, time is not one of our luxuries."

Despite his weariness, his voice came out with the certainty of the lore father of this council, a man who'd survived and kept his flock alive through unimaginable times. "We prepare for Silbane and Arek's journey. Equip the initiate to give him the best chance of surviving. We have eight days until this gate could open."

Giridian said, "Nothing we give him can withstand his touch."

"Not all the objects in the lower Vaults require physical contact," Silbane offered. "Perhaps we can find something that will aid Arek by its very presence."

Kisan suddenly asked, "How will you explain you are taking him into a siege?"

"You can suggest that it's part of his training," Giridian suggested. "It seems cruel, but it would keep him near you, and obedient."

Silbane scoffed. "Arek is powerless, not stupid. When we arrive at Bara'cor, he will look at me as though I've lost my mind."

"Perhaps," Kisan answered, "but to be blunt, who cares? By then he will stay near you to be safe."

Silbane had the answer to that, one he didn't need to voice. As he'd decided before coming to council, he'd tell Arek everything. Somehow he felt confident his apprentice would choose to help, rather than hide. Sharing that here, however, wouldn't help his cause, and could hurt their chances. Furthermore, the sooner they got started the better they'd be. Given Themun's constant reminders of the limited amount of time, Silbane began to wonder how they'd get to the mainland.

Kisan saw the obvious and asked, "And their conveyance?"

Themun said, "Lord Rai'stahn."

Silbane looked at the lore father.

"And how does a dragon solve our problems?"

The lore father continued, "I can't speak to what he'll do or say, only that if there's another way to close a rift, Rai'stahn might know it. He was there when Lilyth's last gate opened."

Silbane pursed his lips, thinking. It was a slim chance centered around the ancient creature's willingness. He looked at the lore father and asked, "And you think he'll help?"

To this, Themun smiled.

"I am not without some influence. As I recall, the dragon owes me a favor. I'll send word you wish to speak to him."

Silbane nodded, but his attention was caught again by a wavering in the air, a displacement. He took a deep breath and reached for the Way, intending to open his Sight.

"Silbane, a moment of your time, please," Themun interrupted. "You must keep, as your foremost concern, the gate and the danger it represents. Keep Arek with you to remain masked to anyone's scrutiny."

"You mean keep the boy alive until Silbane knows the Gate exists, then push his apprentice through and hope for the best." This came from Giridian. "I agree we must verify the Gate's existence, but the boy . . . I appreciate Thera's point," he added by way of explanation.

Silbane nodded in agreement, distracted by looking again for the sign of that *something* he'd almost seen, but whatever it was had vanished. It could've been his imagination. It wasn't a warding, of that he was certain, but it was more like one of the Clouds techniques, some kind of obfuscation.

Themun looked back at the master, his eyes searching Silbane's face. Then he finally said, "Very well. Speak with your apprentice; explain only what he needs to know of our plan. Do not speak of how you intend to close the gate! Remember he, too, is a servant of this land, as the Oath he took requires."

Gathering his runestaff from Silbane's end of the table, Themun addressed the adepts around him. "I thank each of you for your guidance. We will prepare for Silbane's departure." With a single rap of his runestaff, he closed the meeting.

Nothing Themun had said changed Silbane's mind. He'd not handicap his apprentice by withholding the truth about their mission, regardless of the lore father's orders.

* * * * *

The first to exit the room was Kisan, the air swirling in the wake of her hasty departure. In a moment, the chamber was empty, save for the lore father and Giridian. Themun felt, rather than saw, the latter come to stand beside him.

The bear-like adept cleared his throat, voicing a concern that hadn't left him since Thera's departure. "This is harder on Thera than the rest of us."

"You think so?" Themun looked away. "I've asked Silbane to sacrifice his apprentice if need be. Are Thera's feelings somehow more important than his or his apprentice's life?"

Giridian looked at the lore father, not knowing exactly what to say. "Of course not . . . though in these times isn't it important for us to be united?"

"You worry about Thera, who even now wonders if she acted correctly." He paused for a moment, then continued, "Do you know what she did after we left her village? We'd moved the survivors to another area some miles away and bedded down for the night. When morning came we saw smoke rising from where her village once stood. Fearing more magehunters, my father ordered us to investigate." Themun waited, remembering that moment like it was yesterday. "Whatever existed of her village had been eradicated with a spell similar to *Blood of the Sky*. At first we thought another like us had arrived. Then we found Thera. She'd left the camp during the night and somehow found her way back.

Themun met Giridian's gaze and said, "She had cast the spell: a five-year-old. There was nothing left except a smoking ruin, devoid of life."

"With no training?" Giridian asked, wide-eyed.

Themun nodded. "She chooses to nurture this world and make it a better place for the living. Do not mistake that for weakness. We need people like her, so Edyn can continue to flourish."

"I had no idea she'd such power," Giridian replied softly, almost to himself.

"Thera is the lucky one. Her fortitude will be unwavering exactly because of the challenges placed on her. We should all be so lucky to have that kind of conviction."

Giridian took a deep breath, pacing past the lore father. His footsteps echoed within the vast chamber, their sounds magnifying how alone Themun felt.

"What will challenge us?" the bear-like adept asked.

Themun didn't smile when he said, "Faith—in us, in all of this," he said, taking in the room with a gesture. Torchlight continued to dance along the rough-hewn walls. It was hard to believe that only a short distance away was sunshine and sand. This place was like his heart, dark and empty.

Giridian bowed to the lore father, excusing himself with, "I'll go see how she's doing."

"Thank you," Themun said. His eyes showing that he was far away in thought.

Faith is a tricky thing, he reminded himself sadly.

Giridian bowed, then gathered his things and made his way to the door.

Council's Choice

Themun watched him leave the chamber, knowing the upcoming days would be the hardest his council would ever face.

RESPITE

The tremble of the blade shows weakness.
Once seen, act decisively or the moment is lost.
Remain alert, strike swiftly.
—The Bladesman Codex

Bara'cor's council chamber lay deep in the heart of the fortress, dominated by an octagonal table large enough for two men to lie head to foot across, without touching either end. It rose from the solid granite floor without seam, a natural extension of the rock forming the fortress. The walls depicted what could only be a history of the ancient dwarven people. Under their skilled artisans' hands, the stone became a work of beauty, flowing from scene to scene.

Etched on the floor at each of the eight corners of the table lay another octagon, smaller, but no less intricate. Their surfaces were a complex mixture of open vistas and dwarven writings. The meaning of the inlays was lost to antiquity.

Bernal had been at the table for much of the night, his eyes absently tracing the rune-carved surface of the Galadine great bow, Valor. It had been in his family for centuries, passed from father to son. His father had trained him for many summers—arduous practice sessions, building the muscles of his shoulders and back until he'd had the strength to string and draw it.

When he could put six arrows into a space no bigger than his hand at two hundred paces, his father had allowed him to train with it at his discretion. Soon it would go to Niall, who had been training tirelessly to wield this awesome weapon. Rarely did the king disturb Valor from its holder at one side of the table, but on some occasions, its presence filled him with a sense of purpose.

Now, with the horde encamped at his doorstep, he found himself wandering to the bow, his mind's eye picturing the battles depicted on the floor and wall as if they were happening before him. His thoughts scattered when Jebida entered the council chamber and settled his large frame in a chair across the table from him. The king nodded in greeting, his eyes reluctantly leaving the runebow. Jebida answered with a grunt, the day's strain showing.

High above the granite walls, the sun colored the sky pink as it slowly peeked above the horizon, but the air told him a different story. Storm clouds would be brewing, and he knew today would bring a tempest of wind and sand, not rain. He could also taste the metallic tang of magic in the air, but he didn't mention that to Jebida.

"The men are sore pressed, milord," began Jebida quietly. "It is well the enemy does not have siege engines—"

"Aye, we're fortunate in many respects."

Bernal's bitter interruption elicited a raised eyebrow from the firstmark, who knew the king's moods well. "Nevertheless, we're quite lucky. The Edge prevents them from surrounding us and provides us with a means of escape . . . should it come to that."

The king nodded, realizing he was venting his frustration. "I'm sorry," he said. "Just wish we knew why they're here. Why Bara'cor?" Bernal pounded his fist into his palm. "It makes no sense."

"Not much does," Jebida answered. Then a thought occurred and he added, "What of the queen's mission? Will Haven reinforce us?"

"I hope so," replied the king. He knew the political atmosphere in the capital city and ventured, "The Senate must recognize that in the unlikely event that Bara'cor falls, Haven is next."

Jebida sighed. "Shornhelm and Dawnlight, for all their willingness to bend knee, have never truly supported you."

The king nodded. His recent actions against both had brought peace, but also difficult relations. They would never openly work against the King of Bara'cor, but Yevaine wasn't the king. "Even if they didn't see the benefit in sending reinforcements, Yevaine could convince them helping us is indirectly helping themselves. I've seen her talk a stubborn man into betrothal." The king winked. "Not easily done. She can be very persuasive."

Jebida's deadpanned, "She's much smarter than you." Even he could only hold it for a beat or two before a smile broke through. "Though, I'll admit that's not a very high bar."

The king didn't argue. He traced a finger through a rune on the table, his smile wistful. "You have this, Jeb. We'll prevail without the help of the militia."

He could tell his sudden earnestness had disarmed the firstmark. The gruff old warrior's smile faded to a more somber introspection. Bernal hated ruining the mood, but sometimes truth delivered at the right time bolstered the men, and even his firstmark needed to know the king had every faith in him to defend Bara'cor.

Silence followed, not awkward given their years together, but nonetheless uncomfortable because of the subject matter. "I still think Niall and the princess should've gone with her," Jebida finally opined, not looking directly at the king.

Bernal nodded, "And put two heirs in the hands of the Senate, a group of men just recently brought under rule? Not likely, Jeb."

The firstmark seemed to take a sudden interest in one of the stone carvings. He bent to inspect it, one thick finger ham-handed as he tried to follow the clean lines.

Finally the king said, "What?"

Jebida shrugged, "Sometimes you state the obvious in a way that reminds me diplomacy is just as deadly as the battlefield." The firstmark looked at the king and gave a short bow, "Hadn't thought about their leverage like that."

The king shrugged and smiled. "Maybe it's paranoia, but not if they're really out to get us."

The firstmark barked out a laugh, then grew serious again. "The queen is walking into a difficult situation."

Bernal closed his eyes, pinching the bridge of his nose. "And you can see how well I succeeded in stopping her from going. At least Kalindor accompanies her."

The firstmark smiled and said, "Somehow he always pulls the light duty."

"Strange," the king said, a smile returning to his face. "I thought you assigned him."

The giant warrior didn't bother to deny it. The silence stretched out again, this time more comfortable now that they were both back on easy ground, the kind that didn't involve hearts and emotions.

After a moment Jebida said quietly, "He could've been firstmark had he so desired. You know the man isn't happy without a spear in hand and enemies at the gate. His fault, not mine." He paused, then added with a smile, "But he deserves the rest."

"For all your bluster, the men should know you have a kind heart," the king offered, tilting his head in half joke, half praise.

"Tell anyone, and the story of you and that golden-haired dancer from that inn in Moonhold will surface. . . innocently, of course. No doubt you'll get some pointed conversation from her Majesty then."

The king shook his head, laughing. "Younger days."

The thought of facing Yevaine over said reminiscence ended his bravado and his laughter trailed off awkwardly. "Ahh, no need to bother her with so much else going on."

"When Yevaine and Kalindor return," Jebida said, "at least we'll have Fourth Company back to reinforce us."

Bernal paused. He mulled it over, deciding it was better to speak frankly with his second-in-command. "They're probably not coming back."

Jebida stared at him. "What?"

Bernal sighed. "Unless the queen is very convincing, they're not going to let an entire company leave. They'll commandeer it to protect Haven."

"You sent her, knowing this?"

"First, I didn't do anything. The queen decided to argue our case to the Senate. Second, I can't say I disagreed with her logic. What choice did we have? Perhaps she'll manage to turn things in our favor. Regardless, she's got enough troops to potentially force Haven's hand. And third, if things get bad we can still evacuate Niall and Yetteje down Land's Edge. Hopefully it won't come to that."

Jebida was quiet, his face inscrutable. Then a small smile escaped his lips like a defector from his emotions. "I don't envy Kal when the 'diplomacy' begins. He's probably not going to be happy stuck in the capital."

"His fault for accepting light duty, and frankly, it's better him than me," stated the king flatly, eliciting a small laugh from Jebida.

The firstmark waited for a moment, then asked, "No ravens from EvenSea? Has Ben sent no word?"

"Nothing," replied the king. He didn't add the obvious: that no news generally meant bad news. That fact had brought faint lines of worry to Yetteje's usually carefree face, and she wasn't alone—he feared for the lives of King Ben'thor Tir and the rest of Yetteje's family, but most of all for Yetteje's mother, Clarysa. She was Bernal's sister, making Yetteje half Galadine.

Jebida rose, the stress of the night watch showing in his eyes. "Your leave then, sire? I need to review our defenses. Already the wind has picked up and the sands begin to swirl."

"Ash holds the wall?"

"Aye, sire. He is prepared for the assault."

Bernal couldn't miss the pride shining in Jebida's eyes when he spoke of the young armsmark. He suspected that over these many summers, Ash had taken the place of Jebida's family and had become the son the gruff firstmark never had. "Well then, you may as well turn in and get some rest."

"Sire?" the firstmark asked in confusion.

Bernal stood, facing the firstmark. "Wasn't I clear? Go to your quarters and get some sleep. Ash and I will handle the wall today." As Jebida hesitated, the king continued, "Or don't you trust us?"

"It isn't that, sire! Just, I'd hoped to—"

"You're beginning to sound like a certain son of mine," the king interrupted again. "And by that I mean mule-headed." He said this while moving around the table and laying a hand on Jebida's massive shoulder, steering the firstmark toward the exit. "You and I both know there's little you can do after a long night watch. Get some rest. If anything happens, I'll send for you."

"What about you?" Jebida paused at the door. "What will it achieve, staying on the wall when you need rest just as much as I?"

"My presence bolsters the men. Get some rest. I'll not have my commanders falling asleep in their boots. Now I'm making it an order."

"I'm starting to understand how Kalindor felt," offered Jebida.

The king didn't answer, instead pushing the reluctant firstmark through the door and toward his quarters. He watched Jebida's broad back disappear around a bend in the flickering torchlight before casting his gaze upward, imagining he could see the first dark thunderheads as they raced across the sky to block out the bright rays of the rising sun.

SEVEN DAYS LEFT . . .

Respite

IN HARM'S WAY

In the contest of blades,
each parry and riposte is
opportunity dancing with chance,
and the prize for victory, is life.
—Kensei Shun, *The Lens of Shields*

A rek awoke late the next morning, sluggishly throwing off the covers and making his way to his washbasin. On his desk lay the book Master Silbane had given him, open to the page he'd been studying well into the night. Squinting in the bright sun shining through his window, he began his morning ritual, splashing cold water on his face and neck. He'd love a hot bath, but the late hour told him he should get ready quickly. His eyes flicked to the book again and he mentally grimaced. *I've studied that stupid fortress so much I can't think of anything else,* he thought with irritation.

He dried his face and sat down at his desk. Though his eyes stared at the page where he'd stopped before, his mind wandered, picturing the fortress as it must have been at the time of the dwarves. King Bara had held it then, his ancestors being the original builders. Between the great fortress and the small trade city within, Bara'cor could have held almost a thousand of his folk. Everything in it was made for a race larger than the people Arek belonged to.

He leaned back, closing his eyes. What he didn't understand was why King Bara had turned the fortress over in the first place. After the final battle, it was rumored the dwarven king had said, "The dwarven people seek the Sovereign."

He'd then handed Bara'cor over to a young lieutenant by the name of Thorin Galadine and left the great fortress. They'd marched into history and oblivion, and the bloody reign of the Galadines had begun. Bara had practically handed over a kingship to Thorin, who'd in turn sired a line of kings who'd put the lands of Edyn to sword, cutting themselves a kingdom through battle and blood.

Arek had just focused his attention back on the pages before him when there was a discreet knock on his door. Rising, he called, "Enter." He was surprised to see a small boy in a white uniform cautiously push his door open.

Arek immediately recognized Benjahmen, a Whiterobe some seven years old. In Ben's hands was a scroll tied with a black cord, signifying the message was from the council. Arek allowed a small smile to crease his face as the boy moved forward and bowed, holding the scroll out with both hands. Kneeling, he tousled the boy's brown hair and said, "Well, it seems you have grown a bit since I saw you last."

Ben's face lit up as he piped, "But I saw you yesterday!"

"Yes, but maybe you've grown just a little bit between then and now?"

Ben's answer was an exaggerated shrug which seemed to take the boy's small shoulders above his ears. Arek took the scroll and pointed to the door with mock severity. "Away with you, then." He laughed as Ben scampered out, nearly tripping on his own feet in his enthusiasm to get back to his friends.

Arek waited a moment, listening as the little boy's footsteps receded down the stairwell, before untying the cord and unrolling the parchment. He began reading the scroll as he made his way back to his desk. With each sentence, however, his steps began to falter and he finally came to a standstill in the center of his room, despair punching into the base of his stomach.

The Test of Ascension, cancelled? While Arek's confidence in himself might have already been faltering, the council cancelling the test meant they, too, lacked confidence in him. And that could only mean . . . he clutched the scroll and grabbed his robe, barely pausing to pull it over his head and belt it before racing out his door.

He arrived at the central tower's front gate, the scroll still crumpled in one hand. Hastily stuffing it in his pocket he made his way to the tower and sprinted up the spiral staircase, finally exiting on the proper level.

All was quiet. For a moment, this caused Arek to hesitate. The hour was early still, and he loathed the idea of rousing his master's displeasure. Nevertheless, the memory of the scroll's contents set his heart fluttering and with resolve born of desperation he strode down the wide corridor to his master's chambers and knocked.

For what seemed an eternity there was no answer, the silence of the corridor building upon itself until even the slight act of wiping his sweating palms on his robe seemed deafening. Then, just as he made to knock again, the doors to Silbane's chambers swung silently open. Arek stepped in, grabbing the crumpled scroll from his pocket, and stopped, the audacity of his actions suddenly hitting him like a blacksmith's hammer.

Silbane faced the door. His expression looked neutral, and Arek couldn't tell if he was angry at the interruption or not. His master turned and motioned for Arek to come in, while he himself stood in front of his window.

"I see you've taken my advice with enthusiasm. Two visits in as many days." Silbane commented.

Arek licked his lips nervously, all thoughts of the council's message having fled from his mind. To disturb an adept, a master at that . . . he didn't let himself finish the thought. Instead, he held out the scroll, hoping Silbane would understand once he'd read it. Silbane's next words drowned any small hope Arek held in his heart that this might have been a mistake or some cruel joke played on him by the other Browns.

"I already know what the scroll says. I assisted in drafting it. Why does it bother you?"

Arek looked at his master incredulously, anger lending him voice. "What do you mean, why does it bother me? Why cancel my test?"

At first, his master's eyebrows knitted in consternation and he said, "I would have thought you most relieved of all."

The comment set Arek back on his heels, the truth an arrow into his heart. He'd been dreading the test, why not now rejoice? The dark secret, of course: the one he knew he couldn't give voice to.

Silbane's eyes softened, as if he read Arek's mind. Then he said, "Your test is merely postponed, not cancelled. You need to read more carefully." He motioned to a chair as he took a seat near his window. "We have been assigned a mission—one that requires our immediate attention."

"We?" asked Arek, confused by the apparent change of topic.

Silbane looked out his window, across the Shattered Sea. "You have studied the lore of gates." It wasn't a question.

Arek nodded and Silbane continued, "The lore father fears one may have opened in the land. You and I are being sent to investigate."

Arek shook his head, his eyes darting about as he sought to understand what his master was saying. "Why me?"

"Are you not apprenticed to a Master of the Way? What else is your purpose?" When Arek didn't answer, Silbane added, "Your Talent to disrupt magic makes you important for this mission. I wish it were different, but you and I are the best choice to go."

"What help would I be?" Arek asked, his self-doubt taking control and pitching his voice in a whisper.

"You should be more confident."

"More confident?" Arek couldn't help the laugh that erupted from his mouth. "I can't cast spells! How could you consider me ready for a mission like this, when a second-year Green can do something as simple as lighting a candle and I—" He remembered the last time he'd tried to light a candle. Adept Dragor had spent considerable time in darkness, trying to coax a flame out of anything in the spell room. It had been as if a force had snuffed the light-giving nature of everything in Arek's vicinity.

"A moment ago you were arguing you had the skills to Test. Now you tell me you don't. Which is it to be, apprentice?"

Arek dropped his head. As the silence stretched, he heard an indrawn a breath.

"The Way has many manifestations." Arek felt Silbane's arm around his shoulders, guiding him to sit down. "You and I are being trusted. It is an honor the lore father requests us to perform a service for the land. It is what you are trained to do, whether or not you have the Way. Besides, not everything we do requires magic."

At first Arek didn't hear what his master had said. Then the words registered. "Not required . . . how?"

"I cannot aid you in passing, but it suffices to say when you finally do test for the Black, you can pass without casting a single spell."

Arek rose and walked to the door, hesitating for a moment. Silbane hadn't given him leave, but also hadn't stopped him. "Where are we going?"

"You already know," Silbane replied.

Arek let out a sigh, the picture of a fortress rising out of the desert sands already coming to mind. "Bara'cor."

Nothing made sense anymore.

Yes, he admitted, on the surface this was good news. He was being trusted on a mission with his master and he just found out he could pass his test despite what he thought would be an insurmountable hurdle. However, below that level was an undercurrent of shame. How would his classmates react? It looked like the masters didn't believe in him. Also, why was he being selected rather than having two masters go, like Silbane and Kisan?

Bowing, he made his way from his master's chambers, the echo of his leather-soled feet the only sound to follow him. Something didn't feel right and until he understood what it was, the uneasiness in his heart wouldn't go away.

* * * * *

Silbane wondered once again if telling Arek was the correct decision. The boy had power in great magnitude, mused the mage. He hadn't been lying when he told Arek the Way of Making manifested itself differently for each person. He remembered when the boy had taken his Test of Affinities.

The test itself was simple enough. After passing their written examinations for Green, the students assembled outside in a specially prepared testing area. Four concentric circles of increasing diameter stood carved into the stone ground. At a gesture from the administering adept, a barrier sprang up at each circle, made of one of the four Affinities of the Way: Earth, Sky, Stars, and Sun. The final two were not tested here, Life and Death, as they had always shown they were accessible to all with Talent.

It was the student's task to find a way through each barrier. Since most were on the Isle because they had already demonstrated some magical ability, the Test for Affinities gauged the natural bond a student had with one of the four elements.

It was rare a student could defeat all four barriers, their untrained strength not up to the task. They usually found themselves trapped between the second and third circle, mentally and physically exhausted until the watching adept banished the spell and escorted the student out.

Piter, another student testing on the same day, had managed to pass the first three barriers only to find himself trapped behind the Sun's wall. Silbane had banished the final barrier while congratulating him, knowing the boy was destined to be a powerful adept. He then instructed Arek, who at the time had just turned his thirteenth summer, to stand in the hexagonal tile marking the testing ground's center. With a gesture from the adept, the four circles had sprung up again, hiding Arek from view.

Silbane had closed his eyes to concentrate on reading the young boy's state of mind. To his surprise, he could feel nothing from Arek, as if he wasn't even there. What happened next etched itself in Silbane's memory forever.

As Arek relaxed and prepared himself, Silbane felt as if a great void had opened up and swallowed all conscious thought within the testing area. Casting his Sight, he could still see Arek, his head bowed in intense concentration. Silbane had the feeling of an immense power growing, like flood waters behind a cracked dam. Then Arek opened his eyes, pale blue and flashing with power, and the dam burst.

All four circles imploded inward and collapsed, flickering into nothingness. Silbane watched this in awe, unable to comprehend the resources it would take to be able to disrupt that much power. In all his memory, none had accomplished what Arek had done.

At his own test, Silbane had managed to pass by exploiting the intrinsic weakness of each element. To extinguish the energies of all four was a feat unheard of.

Arek looked about himself, confusion in his eyes, as if he'd just awakened from a trance. Silbane rushed into the testing area, finding the boy dazed, but unharmed. Then Arek collapsed and fell into a deep sleep, one they couldn't rouse him from.

He slept for almost three days before waking and asking for eggs, as if nothing out of ordinary had happened. Between plates of food, he claimed no memory of the incident, and had at first refused to believe he'd been asleep that long.

The council unanimously agreed they would watch and guide such power as Arek had demonstrated. Silbane had been appointed his guardian and teacher, and for the next four years served as his mentor. During this time Arek earned his Brown, and Silbane had apprenticed him shortly thereafter.

Since then, there had been maybe one or two minor incidents of Arek's power, but no evidence of the level of energy the boy had channeled during his Test of Affinities. It was as if the boy simply had no power except to disrupt magic. Perhaps, Silbane hesitantly began to believe, he'd witnessed everything Arek had to offer.

Silbane shook his head, knowing that was wrong. Arek had Talent, albeit in some way they didn't yet understand. He would have to help nurture the boy's confidence and keep him safe if he were to survive the next few days, and during that time Silbane knew he had to find an alternative to the lore father's solution. If he didn't, Arek might pay with his life.

JOURNAL ENTRY 3

Curse Thoth, the dragons, and their ilk. They knew what they did, and did it with pleasure. Imagine seeing things for what they truly are. The very firmament lies now before me, and I do not appreciate this "gift." It makes little sense.

It has been some time since I last wrote. I am surrounded by my own anger, creating dangers I cannot ignore. They come in raids: indistinct creatures hinting at fur and claws, having no purpose except to terrorize and take from me whatever meager provisions I have managed to gather. These manifestations are much more powerful than creatures of Edyn, as if they draw from the very world itself to give themselves more substance, more life.

Even in these barest of glimpses, they are fearsome to behold. Each time they appear, they become more realistic. It's as if my mental accounting is filling in the gaps, making them evolve into perfect adversaries. They are cunning, taking that which I need most, coming upon me when I am most vulnerable.

It is as if they read my thoughts . . .

(I write this later this same day . . .)

I am a fool, the conundrum asked and answered by me. Of course they take what I need, for I need it and so give life to that fear! They are like wolves or jackals, but made from my mind, like a child's mistfrights.

Their master is me. They do only what I fear, to the letter. I am the key.

I must remain focused, I must remain calm . . .

Journal Entry 3

POWER AND DEATH

When your opponent faces you,
assume the same posture and wait.
When he begins his strike,
step into the swing, striking his hands.
Follow with the killing stroke.
This technique must be honed,
for timing is crucial.
—*The Bladesman Codex*

T he day went by quickly, with Arek busy finding other instructors to conduct his classes and preparing to leave the Isle. Part of him still couldn't believe the lore father had requested he go with his master.

Moreover, the fact that he wasn't testing hadn't yet sunk in. His master had been right. A part of him was relieved he wasn't dealing with the upcoming test. Another part, however, remembered Piter's words in the training hall, about how his master trained him in private because he had no faith.

Was that the reason for this special consideration? Arek hoped not. *Still,* he argued with himself, *he would not have asked me to go if I didn't bring some value.*

He went about his preparations in a wooden way, his mind watching as his body packed supplies into a small, serviceable bundle. A sigh escaped his lips when he realized that all his clothes, except the combat uniforms, had holes in them. He chose serviceable, if close-fitting, clothes: pants and shirts that allowed for freedom of movement but could be layered to keep him comfortable through the desert climate's great swings in temperature between day and night.

He opened a desk drawer and pulled out a small sewing kit and a dagger, double-edged and keen enough to shave with.

The mending went quickly, and it was only near the end of his shave when a grumble from his stomach told him he'd delayed his repast too long. He gave one last look at his face in the mirror to be sure he found all the soft blond hairs, musing wryly that it wasn't that difficult yet, then left his room to make his way down to the refectory.

The dining hall wasn't too crowded, and that suited Arek just fine. He made himself a meal out of scattered remains, mostly buttered bread and honey. Arek chose a seat near the back of the hall and said a brief prayer to the Lady, thanking her for his meal. He poured the thick honey over the bread, occasionally stopping to lick his sticky fingers. He'd hardly finished half his meal when Jesyn entered, followed by Tomas. Both angled toward him.

Arek grabbed a napkin and began wiping his mouth and fingers, more because he needed something to do with his hands than to clean himself off. Jesyn flashed him a smile, which turned into a grimace as she put a hand over her swollen jaw and sat down.

"You've been tough to find," she mumbled painfully, but her amethyst eyes danced with amusement. "Been avoiding us?"

Despite her injury, the outcome of the rhan'dori didn't seem to have damaged her enthusiasm. Smiling in return, he said, "I've been pretty busy . . ." His statement trailed off awkwardly as he was unsure what else to say.

Jesyn's presence always made him feel self-conscious, and he worried something stupid would spout from his mouth before he knew it. It seemed unfair that Tomas was clearly unaffected by her. A pang of jealousy ran through Arek, as it was common knowledge amongst the initiates that Jesyn and Tomas were together.

"You mean you didn't want to ignore Piter?" Tomas asked, spreading his muscular arms in feigned innocence.

His eyes gleamed with mischief. "Why do you care? He's the odd one."

Arek couldn't help but laugh. "It's like he's following me."

Tomas waved a deprecatory hand as Jesyn laughed. Then she said, "Are you nervous about the testing?"

At the mention of the test, Arek felt his humor drain away, his mouth dry. Suddenly, the idea that some important "mission" had cropped up to excuse him from testing sounded hollow, especially to his ears. Did his master really expect him to believe that?

He didn't want to come back an initiate while all his friends took the Black. His sudden change in manner cast a dark mood over the table. Arek knew he had to say something.

Clearing his throat he began, "Even Piter must be a bit nervous, considering the circumstances."

Jesyn scoffed at his comment, replying, "He's probably at the tailor selecting his adept's uniform right now." Jesyn stood up, pointing to an imaginary set of garments, thoughtfully placing one hand on her chin as if in deep contemplation and shaking her head. "No, no, not that one, it will clash with my perfectly dark hair. I'll take the one on the right. It's the most gruesome black I've ever seen. Now, would you happen to have a crown of thorns to go with it?"

Arek and Tomas burst out laughing at Jesyn's impersonation. After curtseying once to her small audience, Jesyn retook her seat and smiled at Arek. "You don't have to worry about Piter. You have more Talent in your little finger than he'll ever have, and he knows it."

Arek wiped tears of laughter from his eyes, saying with mock severity, "Thank you, most noble adept-to-be. I'm not going to argue." Smiling, he leaned back. He hadn't realized how much he missed them, which made the fact that he was leaving doubly hard.

He made up his mind he would tell them. He needed them to know, to understand, and to see that the idea scared him to death. Magic or not, he knew they would be his friends first.

They must have sensed his mood, for both of them waited for his next words.

"I must confess something to both of you, but it's hard. I'm not sure—"

"What are you guys talking about?"

Arek turned his head toward Piter's voice. He stood a table's length away, looking eagerly at the group. Arek sighed, and then said, "Let's go. I can tell you later."

Piter looked down, a hurt expression on his face. Then he looked up and snarled, "What was so funny?"

"Get lost, Piter." Tomas locked eyes on the smaller initiate, tightening his grip on his chair, which creaked in protest. Both knew that in a physical confrontation, Piter was no match for Tomas's muscle and size.

Emboldened by the knowledge that severe punishment faced any fighting this close to a test, Piter casually glanced at Jesyn, who didn't meet his gaze.

It hadn't always been this way, but Arek felt cruelty was a common basis for their interactions of late. All that ever changed was who outnumbered whom.

"I heard something interesting." Piter's emphasis on the last part caused a knot of trepidation to form in Arek's stomach, but before he could say anything Piter continued, "Arek won't be testing with us."

Jesyn looked at Tomas, her unspoken question mirrored in his eyes.

"Arek, if this isn't true, say something," Tomas urged in a low voice.

"As usual," Piter sneered, "his master is protecting him."

Arek stood. "That's a lie!" His heart fluttered, as every fear he had of failing, of not being their equal, sprang to life.

"Prove it then, apprentice." Piter's eyes narrowed. "Do . . . anything." Piter spread his arms.

A moment went by as Arek stood, meeting Piter's unwavering stare, his peripheral vision picking up Jesyn's fidgeting. He could feel a small bead of sweat trickle down his back, leaving a wet, cold trail that faintly itched. Somewhere, deep inside, he knew there was nothing he could do or show to contradict Piter.

Finally, it was Tomas who broke the tension by saying, "Just leave, Piter."

"I have a better idea." Piter looked down at the table, concentrating. "He's a jinx, a defect. In fact, I've been spending time researching a counter to it."

Arek knew Piter was trying to bait him and it was working. "There's nothing wrong with me."

"No?" Piter smiled. "A monk who can't cast spells and interferes with others who can? That's at least inept."

Tomas stepped forward and demanded, "Leave."

Piter glanced at Tomas, he then turned back to Arek. "How long will you let others fight your fights?"

Arek stepped forward and said, "You want a fight, you got it." He slipped off his gloves and assumed a combat stance.

Piter made a gesture with his hands. Instantly his body encased itself in a shimmering gossamer glow, like a second skin, but this "skin" was a dark blue and faintly reflective.

A collective gasp escaped the group as they realized Piter had created something similar to, but not the same as a flameskin.

Jesyn said, "That's a kind of moonskin." She backed away as she reminded everyone what this rare affinity could accomplish. "Arek, he has made it to reflect attacks."

Arek concentrated his focus on Piter's eyes. Eyes are the window to a soul, his master had always said. It was the place where any intent to attack or strike would appear first.

Jesyn said, "Please, stop. This is insane!"

"Really?" Piter asked. "Like when you guys laugh at me behind my back? You don't think I hear it?" His attention turned back to Arek and slowly he, too, raised his hands in front of him, settling into a combat stance. "You won't laugh after this."

Tomas reacted first. He placed his hand on Piter's shoulder, intending to push him out of the way.

Piter didn't move. As Tomas touched him, the force of his shove was amplified tenfold and redirected back at the hapless initiate. Tomas flew backward, hitting a wall with a dull thud and dropping to the floor unconscious. Only a small smile betrayed Piter's reaction to his technique's first test.

He turned his attention to Arek and said, "I'm still waiting, jinx."

Time slowed as Arek's focus shifted and his battle sense took over. This was the only manifestation of the Way he'd ever felt in himself. He could feel the indrawn breath as Piter began to say something. He sensed Jesyn running to Tomas's side, her concern for him eclipsing everything else. He could feel the weight of the table next to him and knew where every plate and eating utensil lay. Even the tiny dust motes in the air seemed to pause as if brought motionless by his heightened awareness. Most of all, he saw where Piter stood and he knew where the opening would be.

Then something new happened. Arek watched as the scene unfolded, slowed by his battle-sense. A ghostly figure, barely visible, appeared in the air around Piter.

The manifestation was armored, standing superimposed over Piter's frame with enormous wings outstretched to either side. The features were blurred and indistinct, but it lay over him like a gossamer sheet, an ethereal winged knight flaring the same color as Piter's moonskin. A name sounded then in his head and he knew this creature called itself Kaliban. Judging from the lack of reaction, only he could see this ethereal creature.

Then to Arek's surprise, when Piter reached back Kaliban mimicked his action. A glow of moonflame began to form between the creature's hands, silvery and white. Arek knew he only had a moment to interrupt it.

In a liquid motion Arek's hand shot forward, his wrist hitting Piter's, even as his elbow came around that wrist toward Piter's jaw. However, the moment their wrists touched, a black flash occurred, a detonation of force blasting the two apart. Arek had the distinct impression of the winged knight falling backward, the ethereal moonflame exploding silently and prematurely.

He felt the heady rush of strength and power flow into him from that contact, infusing his body with a glow that rivaled the moon itself. It surged into him, ancient, and unyielding. Triumph and ecstasy flooded his every sense. He knew, for an instant, what he could be. This winged creature surrounding Piter was his to take. He could feel his body hunger for it, ethereal, but as real as the food on his table. He knew it.

He could hear something gibbering, screaming, pleading for mercy, but years of frustration, of feeling inferior, crystallized into a black dagger of hate. Arek exulted in this feeling of strength and control.

In that instant, he knew he held a life in his hands and felt an incoherent thrill as he made a fist and felt it snap! The life-force shattered into an infinite sea of particles and light, then flowed into him. He drank it in, consuming what had been Kaliban. He could feel it become part of him, suffusing him with all it had once been.

Then, when there was nothing left, not even a shred within the empty husk that had also once been Kaliban, blackness surrounded him and Arek felt nothing at all . . .

Power and Death

ASSAULT

In general melee, do not focus too narrowly.
Instead, use the mountain stare,
and drink in all that surrounds you.
Danger comes from all sides.
See, or be a feast for the crows.
—Kensei Tsao, The Lens of Blades

A sh fixed a steely gaze on the horde spread out before the walls of Bara'cor. Turning to Captain Durbin he said, "Have Captain Sevel and your men ready for our signal. Stay under cover and fire only on my command."

"The men'll be ready, sir, the Lady willing. Just lay the barrage on their heathen heads and we'll take care of the rest." Saluting smartly, fist to chest, the captain wheeled and made his way to the command tower.

Ash watched him leave, he then turned his attention to the barbarians milling about, just out of arrow range, on the desert floor. Straining his eyes, he could just see their encampment, a motley collection of tents, called *ger*, set in a haphazard circle just beyond the main force of nomads. The semblance of order came from the openings, which all mysteriously faced south.

If only I had a catapult that could reach that far.

The king exited a stairwell and caught his attention, smiling in greeting.

Ash saluted and then clasped the older man's callused hand. Ash respectfully didn't comment on the king's tired eyes. Instead, he turned to the outer lip of the wall, encompassing the nomads with a sweep of his arm. "They're ready. Look on the horizon; already the clouds gather."

Bernal followed the armsmark's pointing finger to the line of purplish clouds, slowly advancing across the sky like a spreading bruise. The wind had picked up, gusting through the battlements and whipping his cloak out behind him.

He turned to the armsmark and said, "Soon the wind and sand will make it impossible to speak or be heard, not to mention blinding our archers."

Nodding, Ash replied, "I've got the signalmen ready. I assume you are commanding the center wall, milord?"

"No, these are your men. Both the Firstmark and I have complete trust in you. Besides, one day you may be Firstmark. You might as well start applying for the post now." He clapped the younger man on the shoulder at the jest. "I won't tell Jebida."

The king paced over to the wall's edge and unslung Valor. "I'll stand with the archers. If the Lady blesses us, we won't see nomad blood touch the walls today."

The armsmark watched the king's corded forearms bulge as he strung the powerful runebow with ease, and checked the weapon for signs of wear. Because of the king's royal heritage, it was sometimes easy to forget he was also a seasoned warrior, a "soldier of the line." Ash had a healthy respect for his prowess in battle, knowing that what Bernal had lost with age he made up for in experience.

Bernal hefted the bow, gave a small deprecatory laugh and said, "I just hope I don't lose an ear or put a friend's eye out."

Ash smiled. Raising his voice, he said, "Captain Durbin and his men will be honored to have another marksman amongst them, sire."

Just then a familiar figure ran across the inner courtyard, carrying an armful of arrows. Smiling at the sight, the king asked the armsmark, "How does Niall like his new duties?"

Ash followed the king's gaze to the courtyard. The prince shuttled between the lower courtyard and the upper archers' loops, unloading neat bundles into quivers at each station. "The prince is doing well. There is much to be said for his maturity."

The king raised an eyebrow.

"At least he's working hard and not being petulant," Ash clarified.

The king shook his head. "He is still young and stubborn, just like his mother. And be assured, he will try to get on the wall, whether he has my approval or not."

Whatever Ash's reply was a warning shout from one of the lookouts cut it short. Both Bernal and Ash heard the deep and rhythmic chanting from the nomads. The measured sounds washed over the fortress walls in a chorus dedicated to violence.

The sky was already a boiling mass of gray and purple clouds. Diffused flashes of lightning from deep within the thunderheads illuminated the fortress for a moment, before plunging them into the twilight created by the unnatural storm.

The howling rose and for an instant Bernal thought the nomads had commenced their attack. Then he realized it was merely the voice of the wind as it sped through the parapets and across the stone, eerily similar to the sound coming from the nomad line. Behind him the flag of Bara'cor, a golden lion rampant on a black field framed by lightning bolts, rippled and cracked in the stiff breeze.

"We need to get to our stations." Ash laid a hand on Bernal's arm, trying to urge him toward one of the two archer towers. He felt himself easily shrugged off as the king pointed.

Ash looked and gasped. The front line parted as thousands of nomads went to their knees, heads bowed to the sand. But it wasn't this sight that elicited Ash's response, but rather the man who walked out to face the fortress.

Even at this distance, Ash could tell he easily dwarfed even the firstmark in size. He estimated the man to be almost eight feet tall, with legs as thick as his own body. *Giant's blood,* he thought.

The figure raised robe-covered arms, displaying open palms. Then slowly, he began to pace forward toward the fortress walls. Behind him the nomads stayed bowed, their heads glued to the sand.

"Tell the archers to hold their fire," said the king.

As Ash complied, Bernal waited for the leader of the nomads to come within hailing distance. He then climbed upon the wide battlements, so the figure could have a clear view of him. Around him the fortress grew silent, the only noise coming from the whistling of the wind through the ramparts.

"That will be far enough," Bernal warned. He had a sergeant's voice, the kind that carried through the din of battle.

The figure stopped, then began to undo his mask. As the cloth fell away, he placed his fists on his hips and addressed the king of Bara'cor. His voice was deep and guttural, as if he found it difficult to bend his tongue around trade speech, but judging from his words, he was nonetheless educated. "You are the leader of these men?"

"I am."

"If you have any love for them, surrender."

Bernal smiled. "Surrender is no way to show love to my men."

The massive figure shrugged. "It is only a matter of time. You will fall and condemn your men to death."

The wind picked up for a moment, making it impossible to answer. Bernal waited, his cloak flapping behind him while a distant thunderclap sounded. As the wind died down he yelled, "Your name?"

The figure paused as if considering Bernal's question, then answered, "I am Hemendra, U'Zar of the Children of the Sun, and Clanchief Sovereign's Fall."

"Then, Hemendra, hear this. I am King Bernal Galadine, and by might and right I hold these walls. Get used to the heat, dog. Lap the water your master gives you." The king undid his waterskin and opened it, but didn't drink. Instead, he upended it so the water fell down the front wall, soaking into the stone and sand below. "We have plenty." Behind him echoed the cheers of his men, emboldened by his resolute courage and House Galadine's favor with the gods.

* * * * *

The silence deepened as the man's voice echoed from Bara'cor's walls. Hemendra held himself still, one part of him surprised by the lord of Bara'cor's bravery, the other barely able to restrain his anger at the insult. However, years of living had taught Hemendra that anger led only to ruin. Moreover, this man who spoke so bravely was already dead in Hemendra's mind.

He gestured to his line with one muscular arm. A group of nomads detached themselves from the main body, holding upright a long spear. As they neared the fortress, Bara'cor's cheers turned to cries of horror, for the spear held an impaled figure.

At another gesture from Hemendra, the nomads drove the spear end into a receptacle designed especially for this purpose, planting the pole with its gruesome burden facing the fortress's walls. The u'zar knew they would recognize Ben'thor Tir, king of the fortress of EvenSea.

Hemendra raised his voice again. "You say I speak empty words. This man thought the same, and now is food for the vulkraith—"

"Jackal!" cried one of Bernal's captains, leaping onto the battlements with bow in hand. Before anyone could stop him, he'd nocked and released an arrow in the smooth motion of a master archer. It sped straight toward the clanchief's heart.

Assault

The nomads around Hemendra scattered, but the u'zar held his ground. He heard the hiss of feathered death as the arrow neared. Then, with a quickness that belied his bulk, he caught the arrow in midflight, a hand span from his chest.

Looking up at the defenders of Bara'cor with contempt, he crushed the arrow in one meaty fist, hurling its broken pieces to the desert floor. "We shall speak again, when you have had time to consider your words." With that he spun, stalking back to the nomad line and through the parting, which closed behind him.

* * * * *

The king's aide-de-camp, Sergeant Alyx Stemmer, had acted immediately, pulling Durbin off the wall before a second arrow followed the first. Ash met her near the rear lip, motioning her to release the captain. He grabbed the man's shoulders and shook him once, searching his eyes. Then he said, "Get back to your command. Stemmer, follow me."

The sergeant nodded at Ash's order, motioning some men to escort Durbin back to his post, and then moved to stand next to the armsmark.

The wind had picked up again, angry rumblings echoed across a leaden sky. Ash, accompanied by the sergeant, waited for their king to climb down off the outer lip. When he did so, Ash saw tears in his eyes and politely dropped his gaze.

The king looked at the stones of the battlements for a moment, after composing himself, he then addressed Ash. "Armsmark, we can't let EvenSea be ravaged without answer. None of us will decorate a spike with our bodies." He paused, his control slipping briefly as his lip trembled, "Princess Tir will need to hear about her father, but I will tell her," he said in a voice tight with grief. "But that can wait. Prepare the catapults. I'll await your signal."

Ash saluted once, and then sprinted for the center wall.

The chanting had increased, driving the front nomad line into a frenzy, like penned animals awaiting release. The clanks and groans of the large winches caught his attention as they bent the arms of the three catapults back. Engineers scrambled forward to secure them, as others filled the great iron cups with large stones, each the size of a man's head.

Raising his right arm, Ash looked out over the horde, smiling to himself. It was then that the horde surged forward like a wave, sweeping across the windswept sand with hoots and yells. Some paused to kneel and shoot arrows at those ranged along the wall.

Ash paid no attention to the buzzing shafts, keeping a careful eye on distance, his arm still raised. As the nomads crossed a mental line, Ash dropped his arm, taking cover.

With a crack, the great arms released, swishing upward in an arc and hurling their contents at the attackers. Between twenty and thirty rocks fit into each cup, big enough to crush skulls and break bones. The result was a barrage of missile fire that to the nomads, must have felt like the very heavens had opened and rained rocks upon their heads. Ash heard the cries of the dying men below, and stood waving a short red flag.

The captains in the command tower responded. With another quick signal, two hundred archers, bows bent to their limits, loosed arrows. Steel-tipped shafts hummed through the air, cutting into the front ranks of nomads still alive after the first wave of stones. While the bowmen nocked and released with deadly accuracy, the engineers started cranking the great arms back again.

Ash watched their practiced efficiency with satisfaction, but knew this was only the first phase. The wind had already doubled in force. Soon the archers would be useless.

Regrouped, the nomads raised large flat shields over their heads and rushed toward Bara'cor's forward gates.

Groups of them carried siege hammers and picks. Under the cover of the wind and blinding sand, the nomads started smashing at the gate, hoping to break through. If they could see the size of the interlocking granite stones that made up the gate, thought Ash wryly, they would not be so foolhardy. And it was only the first of three barriers leading to the fortress interior.

Ash raised two fingers of one hand. He then made a quick slashing motion across his other wrist. The signal passed down to the signalmen, who in turn used flags to pass the orders on. Engineers made their way to the large cauldrons based near the edge of the wall. These cauldrons, filled with a mixture of boiling pitch and oil, stood ready for use.

Once in position, they looked to Ash, who squinted down at the nomads through wind-blown sand and grit. With a downward slash of his hand, the contents of the cauldrons poured down the wall, splashing the nomads below. The screams of burned and dying men were almost drowned out by the now howling wind.

The archers of First and Third Company renewed their assault, sending steel-tipped shafts of death amongst the barbarians. Many of their arrows though were caught by the wind, flying wide of their mark. The storm had hit in full force.

Ash pursed his lips, hardly able to make out Bernal in the sandstorm. Leaning close to Captain Durbin he yelled, "I fear sappers on the far right where we're blind." At this, the captain nodded and then sped off to investigate.

The nomads had pulled their wounded back, taking cover behind their shields. Then they rushed forward again, converging at a point on the main wall: the castle gates. Ash could see they had hammers and picks and smiled to himself at the futility of such a gesture. No one carried a satchel, or anything else that looked like an explosive. Bara'cor's granite walls stood impervious to breach by hand, but explosives were another matter entirely.

Ash raised two fingers and the cauldrons refilled, but this time with rocks and stones. With another signal, these heavy rocks were dumped onto the nomads clustered around the main gate. The lucky ones died never knowing what hit them.

Realizing they couldn't stand at the base of Bara'cor's walls unprotected much longer, the assault leaders ordered their men to pull back. They nomads pulled back with shields held high, covering their retreat.

Ash watched the retreat in confusion. Though the defenders had inflicted casualties, the barbarians had more than enough to continue their assault. He'd expected them to erect a shielded battering ram, then have at the gate in earnest. Then the wind died for a bit and through a gap in the sandstorm, Ash caught a glimpse of something that made his stomach clench with fear.

Six large shapes stood well within arrow range, as if they had been magically conjured. Trebuchets! He suddenly realized with dread that the force at the gate had only been a diversion.

"Take cover!" he screamed, just as the first of the attackers' weapons fired, flinging a large boulder easily the weight of a man. Arching high, it came screaming down with a sound like the crack of thunder.

Men stumbled and fell as the wall shook under the impact. Five more boulders came crashing in as the nomads' remaining trebuchets released and the air filled with a mixture of sand, pulverized stone, and dust. Ash took cover from stone fragments whizzing by, his mind already formulating a defense. Sprinting to the second tower, the armsmark met Durbin.

"Fire at will! I want those crews dead!" Ash screamed into the rising wind.

"Yes, sir!" Durbin nodded, but Ash knew their predicament; it hadn't been unexpected. Unlike stones, arrows didn't have the weight to combat the heavy wind.

The nomads had known the storm would give them relative safety to fire their engines at Bara'cor's walls.

Ash stared out into the swirling sands, his mind weighing alternatives. He noticed two of his catapults were already drawn and secured, filled with missile stones. He watched as the engineers took time to aim them at the nomad line. Running over to the crews, he directed them to fire on the enemy's trebuchets instead of the line.

The engineers changed their targets. With a crack, the engines fired. The missiles arched high, carrying much of Bara'cor's hopes. Their shots, however, fell short. The stone missiles buried in the soft desert sand.

Five more boulders smashed into Bara'cor's already weakened wall. Ash coughed and spat sand and stone dust, praying for the engineers to find their targets. He watched as the great arm of their lead catapult pulled back with agonizing slowness. Secured, the crew filled the cup once again.

Ash closed his eyes and sent a fervent prayer to the Lady of Flame for this shot to be true. With another crack, the arm released and its contents sailed across the desert sky. Ash's eyes followed the path of the loose jumble of stones, his lips still moving in prayer.

He almost cheered when one of the barbarian's trebuchets splintered and broke apart, crushed beyond repair. The other catapult crews along the wall followed suit and soon the air filled with the sounds of winching and releasing. All missed, but then one trebuchet's crew fell, decimated by Bara'cor's deadly missile fire.

The nomads, seeing the fortress had found its range, pulled their trebuchets back, not wanting to risk them. The remaining barbarians retreated, pulling their wounded after them to the main horde.

Though they had held, Ash knew it'd been at great cost. A crack ran down the wall, wide enough in some places for a man to stand in. Large pieces now littered the area in front of the fortress, giving the nomads partial protection from the archers in the towers.

We've got to stop those trebuchets, Ash thought. We can't afford another salvo against the wall before the stonemason can repair it.

He moved to help those wounded nearby. His attempt was interrupted by Lieutenant Galin. The lieutenant held the body of Captain Durbin in his arms. Ash stopped, speechless. Hadn't the man been standing next to him only a moment ago?

"It must've been a piece of stone," Galin mumbled numbly, still pressing the wound on Durbin's neck in a belated effort to staunch the flow of blood. Ash could see the futility of Galin's actions by the fact there seemed nothing left to staunch. The captain had bled out quickly, his great heart pushing every drop of life from the wound.

Moving forward, Ash took his friend's body from the lieutenant before turning back to the outer edge of the wall, his eyes hard. The nomads were now out of arrow range, stretched into a ragged line. The faint sound of their cheers carried on the desert wind, stabbing into the armsmark's heart like a cold iron spike.

Suddenly the weight of Captain Durbin's body seemed inconsequential to the crushing weight of his responsibility to the soldiers of Bara'cor. Their defense was futile, of that he was certain. It would only be a matter of time before the nomads broke through. Then he felt a warm hand on his shoulder and turned to see the king standing beside him.

"He died doing what he loved, Commander."

Ash nodded. Death wasn't a new thing for him. Still, he'd only just been sparring with Durbin last night. Now the man was dead in his arms. He should've scouted the nomad positions more, gathered more intelligence.

He said none of this out loud. His gaze wandered across the peaceful features of his friend, now dead from a piece of rock sent by the Lady's hand.

A shudder passed through him and he turned away from his king, not able to face the trust in those eyes. In a hollow voice, he looked at Galin and said, "Select one of your men to take your place. You are Captain of Third Company."

AFTERMATH

When facing the winds of a storm,
The whiplash tree bends to its force,
And sees tomorrow come with its roots intact.
—Kensei Shun, The Lens of Shields

I think he's coming around . . . "

Arek heard the voice through the blackness. Slowly it gave way to gray, then a blurry white. He started to reach for his face.

"Don't move yet." A gentle hand redirected his. "Here, sip this."

A bitter brew trickled into Arek's mouth. The acrid taste disappeared quickly, and in its wake he felt his head clearing. He squeezed his eyes shut until purple spots appeared, and he opened them again, looking around.

He lay in the infirmary, with Silbane seated next to him. Behind his master stood the lore father, with a disapproving look on his face. Arek could sense others in the room, but didn't turn his head to look. "What happened?"

Silbane looked carefully at his apprentice, then at the lore father. It seemed like something unspoken flitted between the two. Then Silbane turned back to Arek and asked, "What's the last thing you remember?"

Arek thought about it and recalled going to his master's chambers to discuss the test he wasn't going to take. He said that, adding, "Did I fall somewhere on the way back?"

Silbane paused, then answered, "Do you remember going to dinner?"

Arek thought about it, but his last clear memory was leaving his master's quarters. "No, sir, I don't." The concerned look on everyone's faces plus the fact that he was in the infirmary prompted another, "What happened?"

The lore father stepped forward and said, "It seems you had an altercation with Piter. Do you remember that?"

Arek swallowed. The intense look on his master's and the lore father's face causing him to pause. Still, no memory of a fight emerged. "Considering where I am, I hope I gave as well as I got." The jest seemed to fall flat, as neither master smiled.

Giridian stepped forward into Arek's view, looked squarely at the young apprentice, and said, "Arek, Piter is dead."

Arek felt time slow, each heartbeat in his chest pounding out a physical blow. *Dead? How?*

Silbane motioned for Giridian to step back then said to Arek, "We don't know yet what happened. Tomas is injured, but will survive. Jesyn doesn't have a clear memory either. We were hoping you'd know."

Arek stammered, "I . . . I'll try to remember."

Silbane looked at his apprentice once more, then at the lore father. "We should let him rest. The *mhi'kra* he drank will bring sleep."

Themun nodded and turned, only to be confronted by the arrival of a furious Kisan. "We will convene to discuss the punishment of Silbane's apprentice, now."

Silbane shook his head. "The boy does not remember what happened. For all we know, Tomas could've done something. They were the only two with serious injuries."

"You're going to blame Tomas?" replied Kisan, incredulous. "Isn't his murder bad enough? You'd shield your apprentice by blaming a dead boy?" She accused Silbane with her stare. She was sure that someone in this room had cost her young apprentice his life. Arek had never seen her so angry.

"You'd be wise to hold your tongue," said Silbane with deadly intensity.

Themun laid soft hands on Kisan's and Silbane's shoulders, pushing them apart. "Masters, please. For now, let the boy rest. We have one tragedy on our hands. I'd rather not rush to judgment on a second."

Arek's vision blurred and a soft, warm feeling stole over his body. He'd never felt so tired, and yet it almost felt like all his energy was being used to alter something, something deep within him. He was unable to fight the sleep that stole over him, but even as his eyes closed, he heard Master Kisan exclaim, "You're not going to do anything! Lilyth, the Gate, the nomads, all deserve more consideration than Piter!"

Arek was too tired to parse the stream of nonsense. Another part of his mind, though, knew this was important to remember, something wasn't right. What had happened? Why was master Kisan angry?

The effects of the *mhi'kra* dulled his senses; he fell into darkness for the second time that day.

* * * * *

Themun looked at Silbane and Kisan and said, "You two follow me." Then, to Giridian, added, "Please continue with your search of the Vaults. Take Dragor if you need help." Finally, to Thera: "You will minister to the boy and summon us when he wakes."

She nodded, but Themun knew their argument from the previous day wasn't yet finished.

"If we hurry, we might still be able to send Arek with Silbane," Thera said.

Stung by her mocking tone, the lore father turned to confront her, but Silbane gently pushed him away. It took a moment, but Themun brought himself under control.

His eyes remained locked on Thera, who in response lifted her chin defiantly. He was tempted to put her in her place, but Silbane continued to push him away. Finally the lore father repeated, "Silbane, Kisan. My chambers, now."

All bowed in acquiescence, with the two masters following Themun out the door. They made it out of the infirmary and all the way to Themun's chambers without further words to each other, though the clench of Kisan's jaw and unflinching stare showed she was still seething.

Themun took a seat behind his oaken desk, ornately carved with scenes and depictions of the land they sought to protect. He put a hand to his head and said, "She is infuriating – always has been," he said, referring to Thera, "—but you two are worse! You dare threaten each other at a time like this?" Themun shook himself, realizing the day had clearly taken its toll on both Silbane and Kisan. Apprentices had died before during training, but rarely had one killed another. Their rules had been designed to prevent just this sort of thing. It eroded the sense of security the Isle represented, and in the lore father's opinion, reduced an already meager resource.

Kisan remained standing. As soon as the lore father looked up she blurted, "I see how this will end. Arek is sped off the Isle, the mission taking precedence. My apprentice lies dead, and for necessity's sake we will look the other way." Her entire body challenged the lore father to contradict her.

Themun sighed then leaned back in his chair. He looked at Silbane, who ran his fingers through his short hair. "What do you think we should do?" Though Themun looked at Silbane, the question hung in the air for either to answer.

Kisan grabbed a chair and pulled it over, sitting down with an expletive and a sigh. "Piter was a hard case and at times a bully, but he didn't deserve this." Her gaze met Silbane's. In a whisper she said, "He was no different than the rest of us, just looking for a family, a place to be safe. Remember my glittering path? What about his?"

Silbane leaned forward and laid a hand on Kisan's shoulder. "You know how sorry I am." He then looked at the lore father and asked, "Is it true neither Tomas nor Jesyn remember anything?"

"When asked what happened by a scullery maid, Jesyn uttered a single word before collapsing. That word was 'Arek,'" said Themun.

Kisan's fist tightened, but she said nothing. Themun remembered the years she'd spent with Piter, training him, teaching him. Because these children came to the Isle orphaned or abandoned, the adepts, servants, and the other apprentices became their families. Today, they had lost a brother . . . and Kisan had lost a son.

"Even brothers quarrel, but seldom wish death upon each other." Silbane looked at the younger master and said, "I know you want Piter's death to have consequences, but we'll not destroy another student to make amends."

Kisan looked up and Themun could see tears in her eyes. She turned to the lore father, ignoring Silbane, and said in a choking voice, "I won't interfere with your decision. And this mission is already a death sentence." She lowered her gaze, as though her misery centered in her chest, but when she raised her eyes again, they flashed. She faced Silbane and said, "If Arek returns alive, I'll see him brought to justice for my apprentice's death." Kisan stood up, gazing at both the lore father and Silbane, before turning and walking out the door.

Silbane broke the silence. "I won't let her hurt Arek."

Themun knew civil war threatened his tiny council. One wrong look, one wrong word, and the masters would face each other, crippling their ability to fight the real enemy. "What do you want me to do?"

Silbane stood, bringing his fist down on the table so hard a crack appeared in the ornate surface under the force of his blow. "You used the threat of Kisan taking Arek to push us into acquiescence. Now this happens, likely because children find ways to tease each other. This is on *your* head."

Themun didn't move. "Please stop destroying my furniture." He rose slowly and said, "And to be clear, everything is on my head. Try shouldering that burden for a while before you judge me." The lore father picked up his runestaff and asked, "When will Arek be able enough for you to leave?"

At first he wasn't sure the master would answer. Then Silbane shrugged and said, "The *mhi'kra* should accelerate his healing. If we gathered things and made ready, I could leave at sunrise, provided there's nothing we missed still wrong with him."

Themun nodded and waved his hand. "Make your plans. Have you given any thought to whether the dragon can fly if Arek touches him?"

"As much as you have about putting my apprentice in the middle of all this," Silbane replied sarcastically, but then appeared to regret it. "As long as he covers his bare flesh, nothing dangerous should happen. Do you think Arek will hide an aura as big as a dragon's from whoever is helping the nomads?" Silbane paused, it seemed he couldn't help but to add, "That someone only you seem to be convinced is there."

Themun ignored him, answering instead, "Yes, but your first challenge will be to convince Rai'stahn that the debt owed me can be claimed by you. It's doubtful he'll honor the obligation without taking your measure." Themun paused, searching Silbane's face. "Are you ready for that?"

The master nodded, "I'll convince him." Then Silbane smiled and added, "But if you hear explosions and screams, don't hesitate to come help. Despite our differences, I'd still rather have you with me if Rai'stahn decides to fight."

Themun raised a hand and said, "I'll vouch for you in my most strenuous terms. Just keep your wits about you. Dragons aren't known for understanding our problems. Don't let him push you or Arek into a compromising position."

Silbane shrugged philosophically. "Let's hope your endorsement still carries weight. I'd hate to hear Rai'stahn say, 'Themun who?'"

"If that happens," Themun suggested, "use the most ancient martial art taught, one in which you are more than a master."

To Silbane's quizzical look, the lore father said, "Run."

Aftermath

THE PRINCESS

*It is only when the sand quickens
and you begin to sink,
that you know your true friends.*
—*Altan proverb*

Yetteje grieved. The faces of her family members kept coming to her mind. She remembered her mother, her hair shining black and laced with pearls, her smile flashing white. She always had a laugh for her. Now, she was dead—or worse.

Her father had been a man of great wisdom. He had won the fortress of EvenSea through the strength of arms, but had quickly transitioned his rule into one that represented the people. Under his guidance, Yetteje had learned that the measure of a leader had to include their experience, education, and the philosophy by which they ruled. A kingdom should be left better by the Tir hand, not worse—and he had lived up to that ideal.

Yetteje had rushed to the wall when she'd heard the news. The sight of the man she loved and respected so deeply, impaled on a spear, wouldn't leave her head.

Sobs shook her again, but no tears accompanied them. In their place was the ache of a throat that had cried for hours through the night, the stabbing pain of lungs that had screamed and sobbed. Now all she wanted was to let this feeling of numbness overcome her—drift away from all this pain so that she could let her mind cocoon itself in sleep.

However, something else grew in that space of emptiness . . . and it wasn't fear. It was a small flame, but a flame nonetheless. It was anger. She hated that she'd never speak with her father again, that her family lay murdered by the Altan barbarians. She could feel the flame getting stronger, intensifying.

A tremor interrupted her thoughts, shaking the very walls and ground. She looked around in panic, wondering what new peril Bara'cor faced, but the shaking subsided quickly. Moments passed in silence and with nothing else amiss, she fell again into her misery.

Things had always come easily to the Princess of EvenSea. In her time at court, the many social events and her own interests had occupied her thoroughly. Yes, she had some "strange" habits, like training with the men-at-arms. She enjoyed hunting more than talking with the ladies of court, and had both been with a man, and had killed one. Yet for all her adventurous nature, she still treasured the normalcy that was her life, the surety of her father and mother's presence, the solidity of EvenSea's walls, even the dawn bells signaling the opening of the waterfront markets. These were things that never changed.

Until now. She hadn't imagined it could all be taken away so easily with a single malicious swipe clearing the table that had been set for her life.

Her eyes narrowed . . . but change did not have to destroy her. Something within her grew in response, unwilling to be bent, unwilling to be broken. Those who murdered her family would pay with their lives. She took a silent vow for those she loved. Vengeance would be hers before this life ended.

"You all right?"

Yetteje started, not realizing someone had been standing at the entrance to her room.

"Niall! Uh . . . yes. No." Her face screwed up. She couldn't forget her father, impaled. "No, I'm not."

Niall moved hesitantly into the room. It was obvious he didn't want to be there, but he also didn't want to leave his cousin alone. "I'm so sorry. Your father was always so kind to me, and my aunt . . ." He trailed off miserably.

Tej nodded, but said nothing. Each moment brought with it cherished memories of her family that unfolded slowly, yet faded to another before she could embrace it, commit it to some more long lasting form. They went by both slowly and quickly, taking forever to pass, then hard to recall. Finally she said, "You don't have to worry. I'm not going to do anything stupid."

"Like sneaking out of Bara'cor to see if you can make the nomads pay the Lady's price?"

Tej looked up at her cousin, as if seeing him for the first time. "Huh?"

Niall cocked his head to the side. "I love the stories of heroes winning against all odds, but this isn't one of them. You can't endanger yourself."

"What are you talking about?"

Niall raised his grey eyes to meet her own. His cheeks ballooned and then let out an explosive sigh as he got to his point. "Tej, whatever it takes, I'll help you avenge your family. But promise me you won't go off alone on some crazy mission against the nomads. We need you safe, and you aren't alone."

Tears she didn't know she had left welled up in her eyes. She crossed her arms and hugged herself, but clamped down on the sadness threatening to overwhelm her. She would not lose control now . . . not ever again. When she looked up, the inner flame gave her strength.

Without a word, Niall went to one knee and took Yetteje's hand, intoning the oath his father had taken with Tej's father. He said, "I hail you, Queen Tir of EvenSea, and pledge my arm and my life to aid you in times of need. You're not alone, but always with your brothers and sisters of Bara'cor."

"It is as it should be, Queen Tir." King Bernal Galadine stood outside Yetteje's room, along with the firstmark and the armsmark. "We come to pay our respects and fealty to you. I can think of no other I would call daughter. Hail, Queen of EvenSea." Bernal went down on one knee next to

Niall and kissed the hand of Yetteje Tir. "My sister would wish no less. You stand not alone."

Jebida stepped forward from behind the king, and he too went down on one knee to give the same oath as Niall, then moved back to make way for the armsmark.

Ash knelt in front of Yetteje, who felt she was only a tear-wracked sixteen-year-old girl. Breathing deeply Ash said, "Hail, Queen of EvenSea. Brighter days are ahead. The sun will shine on your seas again. You are never alone." He kissed her hand, and then waited.

Yetteje's head sank to her chest, her heart breaking, her very being falling into a downward spiral of remorse and fear. Despite their offer of support, she did feel alone, and terrified. Who did she really have? As far as she knew, she might be all there was left of EvenSea, and that thought made her soul cry out for solace.

Then it happened. A strange feeling – as if an unseen force had entered the room. She could feel its presence, powerful but kind. Hands, warm and loving, embraced her. It wasn't a physical embrace, but one that seemed to envelop and succor her very being. It gave her strength to resist the despair.

She took a deep, shuddering breath, her lungs filling with clean, fresh air. She swallowed past a knot in her throat, feeling it slowly unclench. The warmth of the unseen presence permeated her now, revitalizing her limbs with a tingle of power. Perhaps it was her father's spirit, nudging her to remain strong.

Yetteje's head slowly came up, her amber eyes shining but clear of tears. She rose, looking at the four lords of Bara'cor kneeling before her, and knew her duty lay in honoring their oaths as a royal heir should, not crying like a young girl.

"King Galadine, it isn't fit for you to kneel before me. There will be many years before I'm your equal. I'm not the Queen of EvenSea."

To the puzzled king's look, she replied, "Your sister, my mother . . . may not be dead. We only know that the King of EvenSea has fallen. Until I know differently, I'm still your humble servant and ward. I accept your pledge and offer you my own. My arm and my life, such as they are, are yours to command."

She turned to Niall and said, "Prince of Bara'cor, you will always have my sword and my counsel at your side. Please rise and stand with me, as my cousin and my friend."

She then addressed the firstmark and armsmark saying, "Rise, please. My arm and sword are yours. I'm the queen of nothing, and yet just as you . . . EvenSea *will rise* again."

As the men rose, Tej moved forward and gave Bernal a hug, burying herself in his embrace. "My father . . ." Her voice cracked and almost broke, but she steadied herself and continued, "My father said he's never had a dearer friend than you. I thank you for that, and for being here with me now. I know I'm not alone."

Journal Entry 4 (early)

That a simple request for aid could lead to this! And now I am here, but not as a hero.

Shall I write more clearly? Very well, Rai'stahn betrayed me. I saved his people, who hid from the very nature of life around them in their caves, their holes in the dirt. They offered me a "vision," as if I needed such charity, yet held themselves back from the bloody work, the warriors' work.

Still, I cannot go so far as to say I do not understand. He did what he thought best, as did the rest. I must find a way to forgive them, but it is hard. Why do we hate those close to us more deeply than strangers? Perhaps because they betray our expectations of fairness, of justice? Nevertheless, I must forgive, for hate is a terrible emotion, and here terrible emotions give rise to terrible things.

Thoughts go to my brother. I hope he knows I did not falter or fail in the end. His need for assurance should be well satisfied by our victory, which I do not doubt was achieved, thanks to me.

In the distance is what seems to be an abode. I make my way there, in hopes that there may be someone unaffiliated with the Aeris, someone who can help me.

Those subjugated by the demon queen's rule must exist and welcome a chance at freedom. All people of the known world split into factions, and I do not underestimate even the smallest creature's ability to help. . .

SHADOW'S VOICE

When taking the killing stroke,
kill quickly and cleanly,
and do not mourn the dead.
They brought themselves before your blade.
—The Bladesman Codex

A rek awoke to the sensation that something was wrong. There was a coldness to the room, a forlornness, if that was even possible. In the faint moonlight that streamed in from one tall window, he could see the other infirmary beds were empty.

A cool breeze from the ocean wafted through, but did not settle his unease. He quickly stifled an urge to ask who was there, but the sense of wrongness grew. Then the sound of footsteps came from the hallway; purposeful, not hesitant, as if the person knew his destination . . . and he was getting closer. A nameless fear gripped Arek, one that sent him back under the blankets in an infantile attempt at safety.

A figure in a hooded robe moved into the room as if materializing out of thin air. It glided toward him, pausing a few feet away. Arek couldn't see under the hood, but he could feel the malevolence, the danger this person represented. For the first time in his life, he felt what someone meant when they talked about evil.

Then the figure did something unexpected. It knelt and whispered, "I exist to serve." The voice was familiar, though he'd never heard anything quite like it. The figure reached with one hand and pulled back the hood concealing its identity, then slowly raised its face into the pale moonlight.

Arek sat dumbfounded, as what he saw and what he knew were in direct conflict. "You're dead," he stated dumbly.

"Astute as always, I see." The mocking voice of Piter echoed softly across the chamber, floating around Arek as if he heard it both in his mind and with his ears.

Arek said softly, "I'm dreaming this. You're not dead and this is some sort of sick joke."

Piter focused on Arek, his self-absorption gone. "Yes and all of the adepts are in on it . . . does that make sense, you idiot?" Piter stared at him a moment longer, then said, "They *are* plotting something, just not what you think." He slowly walked over and sat down next to Arek on the bed. "I'll enjoy watching the adepts sacrifice you."

Arek didn't respond to that, his attention completely on the shade's appearance and substance. At this close range, Arek thought he looked quite alive and began to reach out to touch him to confirm it.

Piter jumped awkwardly away, yelling, "Stop! Your touch will banish me!" The shade said this with an acid hate. Piter smiled and pointed at the bed. "Look where I sat."

Arek slowly turned his head and looked. "What? There's nothing there."

"Exactly. You saw me sit down. Are the sheets disturbed?" Piter watched for a few moments as Arek struggled to comprehend what was going on, and then said with a smirk, "Quick as ever."

"You're really dead?"

"I am. You killed me. Now I am bound to serve you." He walked a short distance away and gazed out the window. "All I had has been taken from me, by you and your kind."

Arek looked at Piter, still unable to believe his eyes. Clearly the shade wasn't happy to be here. Yet, Piter was answering his questions . . . why? Arek wasn't so shocked as to forget that once out of childhood, he and Piter had been at odds. So why was Piter pledging service, especially if Arek truly caused his death? Something wasn't right. Arek had never seen Piter kneel to anyone, and when this thing had entered the room . . . a sudden intuition forced him to his feet.

"Piter, why are you here?"

Piter turned to Arek and stated, "Lilyth has bound me to serve you." He didn't seem to want to answer, but acted as if compelled. "You create an opening . . . a thinness between the planes. It allows me to appear here, instead of where I should be."

Arek continued, "Do you have to answer what I ask?"

Piter hesitated, his eyes darted back and forth. He then curtly replied, "Yes."

"Do you have to tell me the truth?"

To this, Piter smiled and replied sarcastically, "As I see it, Master." Piter walked slowly over to the bed, his arms behind his back. "There is one thing I'll offer—I may escape this wretched servitude on occasion."

Arek said, "When?"

Piter had already started to dissipate. "Whenever I want to frustrate you." With a small laugh and a flash, Piter was gone.

"Piter!" Arek looked around the room in confusion. *This can't be happening,* he thought. *I didn't kill Piter and this proves it! He was just here!* Arek decided quickly to find Master Silbane and tell him Piter had somehow used a spell or something to make himself look dead . . . that had to be the explanation.

What about the sheets? Arek was sure Piter had sat down—yet he never felt the mattress move. *What about the moonlight? Had Piter cast a shadow?* He couldn't remember now. His stomach lurched. He sat down on his bed, feeling sick. *Did I really kill Piter?*

Adept Thera entered the room, clearly awakened by Arek's yell. "What is it? You look pale. What's the yelling about?"

He looked at the adept as if seeing her for the first time. He then stammered, "Piter . . . Piter was here."

"What? What happened?"

"He wants . . . he says he's bound. I don't think Piter is really dead."

Thera had the pity in her eyes. With visible effort, the adept said kindly, "Relax and start from the beginning."

"You don't believe me."

"I don't know what to believe yet," Thera replied. "Please, tell me what happened."

Arek fell onto his back, crossing his arms over his eyes, and said, "Piter appeared here. He said he served me."

She moved closer to the bed and sat down next to Arek. "Go on."

Arek couldn't help but notice the bed shift and the mattress move when Thera sat down. It was so easy to discern now, which made Piter's claim seem all the more real. "He said he had to answer my questions, but he didn't like it."

"What makes you think that?"

Arek uncrossed his arms, splaying them out to the sides. She flinched a bit as his uncovered right hand came close to contacting her arm.

"He only seemed interested in tormenting me."

Arek saw Thera's expression change from one of concern to a more thoughtful stare. He also noticed her proximity, and he pulled the thin gloves from his nightstand and slipped them on. The gesture was automatic, but served to break Thera's contemplation.

"Did Piter say anything else?" she asked.

Arek thought about it then added, "He said Lilyth has bound his service to me. That doesn't sound right, does it?"

Thera stood up, her face in shock. "Arek, get up," she said, a new urgency in her voice.

"Why?"

"Get up. We are going to see the Council, *now*."

AREK'S STAND

*When your opponent thrusts at you,
divert his blade by pushing outward.
Then ride his blade in
and strike forcefully on his fists to disarm.
Timing is important.*
—*Tir Combat Academy, Basic Forms & Stances*

D o you understand what this means?" Thera asked. She addressed the council members, all of whom had stumbled blearily into the main council chamber, awakened by her mindspeak. Though instantaneous and convenient, it was draining for the spellcaster. Now Thera stood shakily near the center of the chamber, ashen-faced and clearly strained by her effort.

She waited as the rest of the council hurriedly took their seats, leaving Arek to wait outside until called for. The servant accompanying him looked more nervous than he, if such a thing were possible.

"He named Lilyth, as if the demon still lived," she repeated, looking pointedly at Themun. She felt he, more than any other, should be held accountable for what had happened to two of their apprentices over the last day.

Themun ignored her accusing stare and asked Silbane, "You told him about the Gate, yes?"

"Of course," Silbane answered, "but Lilyth's role in the last war is common knowledge. Arek himself recited it to me when I asked him what he knew of Bara'cor. But the fact Lilyth was not destroyed wasn't revealed to Arek. He knows we seek a gate, nothing more."

Themun looked back at Thera and asked, "What exactly did he say?"

"He said Piter came to him," she answered. "At first, I thought he was suffering from shock and trying to rationalize the killing by denial. After all, if Piter appeared, Arek could at least tell himself there was a chance the boy was still alive. Then he said Piter had been ordered to serve him, *by Lilyth*."

Silence followed Thera's last point. She continued in a low voice, "This isn't a hallucination. Something's going on."

Giridian motioned to speak and asked, "But why would Piter say he served Arek? It makes no sense."

"Perhaps it was the connection Arek and Piter had through his death," Silbane said. "Perhaps Piter serves as a path the demon can use."

Kisan slammed her palm onto the table. "And now my apprentice's soul is in danger?"

Thera shook her head, "Let's remain calm. This also may mean Piter can still be saved."

The comment had its desired effect. Kisan leaned back, taking a deep breath. Then she said in a softer voice, "I mentioned the demon's name in the infirmary, but Arek was under the influence of the *mhi'kra*. If he heard anything, he has better resistance to the mhi'kra than we thought." She looked around the room, her gaze finally settling on Silbane as she added sarcastically, "Perhaps we've found another thing your apprentice is good at, something more than just killing his friends."

Silbane started to get up when Themun put out a restraining hand. "Thera is right. Quarrelling now is of no use. Why would Lilyth care about two apprentices? There are many who have died closer to Bara'cor, and there are other beings of power still walking this world."

Giridian looked at Themun, as he said matter-of-factly, "Then investigating the Gate has become our first priority."

"I haven't ruled out the possibility Arek has woven this tale out of a desperate need to rationalize his hand in killing his classmate."

"How?" Kisan exclaimed. She leaned back and absentmindedly gripped the arm of her chair. "The boy is a dullard when it comes to magic and now you think he able to suddenly mindread?"

"One of us could be trying to exert undue influence." Themun looked pointedly at Thera.

Thera at first couldn't believe her ears. She was morally against the path they had chosen for Arek, but to suspect her of betrayal? She retorted, "You distrust me because I don't agree with you? Who is being childish now, Themun?"

"It was clear you disagreed with the council's last decision regarding Arek," said the lore father.

"Yes, but I wouldn't—" started Thera.

The lore father cut her off, saying, "Betray this council to save an innocent boy? How are we to be sure?"

Thera crossed her arms and controlled her indignation. Breathing, she reached into the granite she stood upon for calm steadiness, the Way infusing her with physical and emotional stability. When she finally spoke, her voice echoed through the chamber with a strength that belied her recent exertions.

"You've gone too far. Believe what you will, but Arek shouldn't go near Bara'cor. It's clear Lilyth knows of him and that can't be good. He isn't making this up."

Silence followed—a silence that grew uncomfortable as neither Thera nor the lore father seemed inclined to concede.

Finally, Silbane raised a hand. "Is anyone else hungry?" he asked plaintively. As he looked at the servant who stood innocuously to one side he asked, "Are there any lemon cakes?"

"You can eat, now?" Kisan asked, laughing a bit despite herself.

Silbane shrugged, "We need energy and I like lemon cakes." He smiled at her, and for a moment Thera felt like things were almost normal. The master had a knack for defusing things, especially with Themun.

As the servant nodded and left, Silbane continued, "Let's see what Thera saw, then judge for ourselves."

Thera looked at Silbane, frustrated. She knew his proposal would set any doubt Themun had about her to rest. Still, it galled her that Silbane—the one person with whom she'd been friends for her entire life—would suggest such a thing when she was already weary. However, deep down she knew the Eye of the Sky technique was the only way to put Themun's fears to rest.

"Very well," she said.

She nodded to the lore father, who extended his staff. He moved his arm in a circle, bringing it to rest before him as his head bowed.

The black metal began to glow blue, a soft glow radiating outward to encompass Thera, who in response closed her eyes and motioned with one palm, duplicating the lore father's earlier movement. It wasn't essential, but in doing so she allowed the technique to go through without any resistance, thereby costing Themun less energy.

The assembled adepts watched the scene with Arek unfold from Thera's viewpoint. They saw Arek standing as if in shock and heard the exchange between the adept and the apprentice. It was exactly as Thera had said. As the scene faded and she opened her eyes, she caught the faintest look of chagrin on the lore father's face. It did mollify her a little.

"Satisfied?" she asked.

The council remained quiet, only the sputtering of the torches that lit the chamber making any noise. Finally, the lore father coughed once and muttered, "My fear wasn't too farfetched . . ."

"No," Thera said, "but you're stubbornly clinging to what is plainly wrong."

"When it comes to defending this land from the likes of Lilyth, nothing is wrong," answered Themun.

Statements like this make us worse than what we fear, Thera thought sadly. Just then the servant reappeared with a tray of lemon cakes, which she put carefully on the table before Silbane. Thera couldn't help but find some humor in that, and maybe that was Silbane's goal all along. She looked back at Themun and smiled. "I don't want to fight with you."

Themun nodded, leaning on his staff. "Nor I with you."

She turned her attention to the chamber doors and asked, "What about Arek? He waits outside."

"I still have many questions," Kisan said. "Does my apprentice still live? If he has a chance of being saved . . ."

Themun nodded and motioned to Thera, "Bring the boy in."

A few moments later Arek stood before the council, clearly intimidated. The lore father motioned to Silbane.

The master took his cue and putting a half-eaten piece of cake down, he rubbed his hands clean and moved to stand beside his apprentice. "Arek, you're not in trouble. Tell us what you saw in your own words."

Thera watched Silbane carefully pat the boy on his covered shoulder and say, "Now from the beginning, what exactly happened?"

* * * * *

Arek looked around nervously. Silbane kept a hand on his apprentice's shoulder to reassure him. His voice came out small at first, but as he related the tale, it grew in strength. He told the council of Piter's appearance, the contempt the shade had shown for him, and Piter's decision to leave when he felt it would bother Arek the most. More importantly, he explained in a tremulous voice how harming Piter hadn't ever been his intention, that— whatever had happened between them, which he still could not recall—he was sure he'd only been defending himself. His voice trailed off as he finished, sinking back into Silbane's grasp, either for reassurance or protection, the master couldn't tell.

The council chamber fell silent as each adept considered the story, matching it against Thera's shared vision. The fact that an apparition claiming to be following Lilyth's orders appeared here was disconcerting to say the least. The fact that it appeared to Arek made no sense.

"Arek, do you think he was compelled to speak?" Silbane asked.

"Compelled? Maybe . . . he answered my questions."

"Do you think he lied?" asked Giridian.

"No, Adept. But I think he told me as little as he could," answered Arek. To Silbane, this sounded truthful.

Themun asked, "What of this "thinness" Piter mentioned?"

"A byproduct?" Silbane offered. "Perhaps he makes the passage easier?" The obvious factor here was his apprentice's ability to nullify magic. It would be logical that this power might also cause the "thinness."

Themun interrupted Silbane's thoughts. "You've spoken to your apprentice of your mission to Bara'cor?"

Silbane gave a hesitant nod, feeling that same sense of doom about the mission—and a desire to remain here on the Isle. He wasn't one to fall prey to superstition or omens, as the Way and science were the cornerstones of truth to him. Still, he sensed fear at his very core, and didn't know why.

He realized that they were all waiting for him to say something. He cleared his throat, and then looked at his young apprentice. "He's been briefed. We can be ready to leave in the morning."

"Wait," Arek said.

The adepts turned to listen.

"Why me?"

Themun's eyes narrowed.

Silbane answered. "Your ability to disrupt magic. We spoke of its importance when you burst into my quarters, remember?"

It was a rhetorical question and Arek answered with a small nod.

Silbane continued, "It isn't your only power. You also mask magic, a necessary advantage if we're to get to Bara'cor undetected by anyone attuned to the Way." He paused, glancing at Themun. "I should've told you, the lore father believes this Gate is linked to Lilyth's world. We are to investigate and report."

Arek's brows knitted. He looked from Silbane to the lore father, asking, "What if we find this Gate? What do we do then?"

Themun looked at Silbane, annoyance now showing plainly in his face. "Your master has his orders," he said.

"Then I would know my master's orders, Lore Father," Arek pressed. "It will best serve the mission."

"You presume much," Themun replied with a hint of incredulity in his voice.

"If my master finds something and I don't know his orders, I'll be a hindrance."

Before the lore father said anything too harsh, Silbane stepped forward to say, "Arek, my orders are to ascertain if the Gate has awakened and if so, to contact the lore father and relate the situation." His heart jumped; he'd never directly lied to his apprentice before.

Arek turned to his master and asked, "And if I choose not to go? It feels like I'm being punished for what happened to Piter, but I don't even know what that was, and I never meant for him to get hurt."

Themun spread his arms and said, "This is no punishment! You are pledged to learn the Way and complete your training in defense of this land. What oath and service awaits you upon earning the black robes?"

Arek thought about that. He looked back at the lore father and said, "I'm not an adept yet."

"Something you seem to have forgotten in your impertinence," the lore father replied. "I had thought you would rise to this service honorably and with courage."

Arek held the lore father's gaze. A moment passed, then two, before the boy bowed slowly and said, "My apologies, Lore Father. I didn't mean to question your command. Of course I'm honored to serve the land." But when the bow ended, the boy raised his eyes to Themun's—and held them again.

The two stood with eyes locked until Silbane coughed—gently reminding the lore father they were waiting on his leave.

Themun broke eye contact first, motioning with his hand, "A better response for one of your rank, Initiate. I trust you will behave in a manner reflecting honor upon this Order."

Arek, turning to go, replied, "Of course. I will reflect exactly what I have been taught by all of you." He then backed away a few steps and stood by the doors, waiting for the other adepts to leave as their rank permitted, before he followed.

Silbane was the last to leave. As he grabbed the double doors and pulled them shut, he caught the lore father's gaze. He thought he saw anger there, but something else, too. Fear.

* * * * *

Themun waited for the doors to close before letting himself relax. "You heard, milord?"

From the darkness came a hiss, then a voice growled, "I did."

The air wavered and from the darkness stepped a massive figure, invisible until now. It came into being like a shadow given substance, and by its mere presence made the vast chamber feel too small to hold a being of such might.

It was a gargantuan knight, with black plated armor encasing its muscular body. Long black hair fell around a regal face framing an aquiline nose. Out of its back sprang two leathery wings, shining with black scales.

It turned golden reptilian eyes on the lore father and with a voice like low thunder said, "I worried of the Gate. Fate twists her rope. Dire circumstances walk hand in hand with each step."

"Can we not still accomplish both what you wish and what the land needs?" asked Themun. "The Gate remains and Arek is our best choice."

The dragon-knight turned to face Themun. "This Arek is a creature of a sort known to our lore. It stayeth hidden from mine Sight. Dost thou ken what thee and thine hath harbored safely under my aegis?"

"He's a boy we found, nothing more. Within him is an inexplicable ability to—"

The armored creature raised a taloned hand, took in a deep breath then said, "I felt thy hatchling swallowed, as if a black maw opened in the Way. I must speak with the Conclave concerning this. The Gate is not the only danger we now face."

By 'hatchling,' Themun knew the dragon-knight meant Piter. "I know we must seal the Gate, but I fear for the lives of Silbane and his apprentice."

A moment passed, as if the knight weighed the lore father's words against some other hidden voice. Then it rumbled, "That a null hath happened upon mine demesne is Fate's rope fashioned into a noose— for thee 'r me? Thou shouldst have spake to me of his arrival."

Themun was taken aback. "Lord Rai'stahn, we've never had to list those we've saved. How would we have known?" The last thing he wanted was to offend the dragon-knight, and he couldn't help the worry that leaked into his voice.

Rai'stahn must've realized this. After a moment it said, "The Conclave wishes no harm to befall Silbane, for he is a vital part of the tapestry. He shall be tested. But this null, Arek . . . he must die. Thou canst do this easily here, before risking the journey."

The lore father shook his head, unable to reconcile the sudden turn of events. "I . . . no, we cannot kill one of our apprentices. It would be fought by every adept—most of all, Silbane."

The dragon-knight looked down, his golden gaze searching the floor. Then he said, "Dost thou wish me to kill this null?"

Themun stared at the dragon-knight, still lost in the turn of the conversation, and knowing what that might mean. "Silbane won't allow it."

"All dispensation will be sought for thy master, but the null changes everything. He cannot be suffered to live. But I will grant Silbane the right to end his hatchling's life. Stand steady. T'is beyond thy purview now."

The creature shifted its golden gaze, meeting the lore father's own. "Judging Silbane shall be done quickly, far from the Isle. Give them thy Finder. It will aid me, should the null attempt to flee." With that, the creature took a step forward and faded from sight in midstride, as if he had never been.

Themun Dreys leaned back and closed his eyes. He couldn't tell Silbane. The Conclave feared the Gate, but it seemed learning about Arek's existence may have scared them even more. How could they have missed him all these years? Even as he asked himself that, the answer was clear—Arek himself. His ability masked his presence, at least enough that the Conclave had never asked.

He hoped Silbane would obey the dragon's commands, but another part of him knew better. Silbane wouldn't abandon Arek, not in any circumstance, and that meant in addition to an apprentice, Themun might also lose a friend.

In the span of a few heartbeats things had gone from bad to worst. He wished he could take his own advice and just run.

SIX DAYS LEFT . . .

Arek's Stand

LEAVING THE ISLE

Watch your opponent.
What direction does his weight shift?
Use the mountain stare to see
the entirety of his being,
then strike at his point of weakness.
—Kensei Tsao, The Lens of Blades

S ilbane waited patiently in the courtyard, mentally reviewing the contents of his leather pack for any forgotten items, while the sun rose white and dazzling, lending heat to the brisk air. He'd left word with his apprentice to meet him at sunrise and hoped the boy had enough sense to do so. That hope was diminishing with each passing heartbeat.

He wasn't surprised to see Themun and Giridian approaching out of the Hall of Adepts. The two dodged a woman herding a gaggle of ducks along with a trail of ducklings, on her way to the farmer's market.

Under Giridian's left arm was tucked an oblong box. Silbane nodded to himself in approval. *A good choice,* he thought. He offered his palm upraised in greeting to the others, and jutted his chin at the box. "Couldn't help it, could you?"

"I couldn't," Giridian answered. While the mission might not be sitting well with the man, he seemed determined to outfit Silbane's apprentice with the best items from the Vault. "At least I'll feel better we're not sending the boy into harm's way completely unprotected."

"Unprotected?" Themun said. He stepped around a man leading goats by a thin rope, then said, "Arek has always been good at protecting himself."

The remark created an awkward moment for Silbane, who didn't know quite how to respond, and so ended up just searching the square for his errant apprentice. The lore father gave a short laugh at his own observation and looked past Silbane, his eyes searching too.

"Speaking of that, where is he?"

"Probably still asleep." Silbane pointedly ignored Themun's callous comment, at the expense of Piter's memory. He was glad Kisan wasn't here.

Giridian stepped forward, breaking the tension, and said with empathy, "Doubtful. His test is cancelled . . . a friend is dead. Now he's leaving the Isle for reasons he never could've anticipated. I imagine he never went to bed."

"Perhaps—"

At that moment, Arek ran out of the Hall of Apprentices, a bag clutched in one hand and a walking staff in the other. Even as they watched, he stumbled, plainly trying to balance his burdens with the need to hurry. It didn't help that the square had slowly become more crowded as the farmer's market began in earnest. Silbane's apprentice dodged people and animals as he tried to join the waiting adepts.

Finally, as Arek slid to a stop, Silbane asked, "I trust we didn't keep you waiting?"

Arek blushed, stammering out an apology while trying, it seemed, to hide behind his own thin staff. A strap chose that moment to betray him, coming undone and spilling half the contents of his pack onto the dusty ground. The apprentice fell to his knees in a vain attempt to gather the various items strewn at his feet.

"I am sorry, master. There were a few things I wanted to bring." Arek kept his eyes down waiting for a rebuke, but seemed surprised to see Themun and the two adepts solemn, as if their minds were a thousand leagues away.

"No matter," Silbane said softly. "Take your time."

He then turned to Themun, his voice dropping almost to a whisper. "You're sure? Something doesn't feel right."

Themun smiled, but there was little humor in his reply. "You and I are not that different. In the end, duty rules us both."

Silbane didn't answer that. He just looked at the lore father for a moment before saying, "If two days pass without word from me, prepare Kisan."

Themun clasped his friend on the shoulder, and said, "I have one more gift for you." He reached into his tunic and withdrew a small metal wafer, etched with silver and black runes.

Silbane's eyes widened at the sight. "The great dragon gave you this."

"True. And now I give it to you," Themun said. "Perhaps it can help you keep Arek safe."

Silbane took the charm in his hand and prepared to break it.

Themun put his own hand over the charm, interrupting Silbane. "Wait. Use it to keep you two together."

"But leaving one half on the Isle guarantees our safe return." Silbane's eyes narrowed. For what other purpose could this Finder be useful?

Themun looked down. "And open a portal between the dangers you face and the Isle? I think not. You worry about keeping Arek safe. This keeps you by his side."

Silbane's brows drew together, but he grudgingly nodded, saying, "I'd not want to endanger the children here." He clapped his friend again on the shoulder and motioned to Arek to get ready.

Giridian took that moment to step forward and lay his box down in front of the apprentice. Looking at Silbane he said, "I hope this helps."

Knowing what was in the box, Silbane nodded his approval and watched as Giridian traced a symbol in the air. The box flashed blue once and, with a barely audible click, opened. Giridian carefully swung the cover back, revealing a mirror-bright sword, straight with keen double edges. Embedded in the hilt was a small emerald radiating a faint green glow. Smiling, the adept lifted the sword and accompanying sheath, sliding the blade home.

Walking over to the wide-eyed apprentice, Giridian said, "Her name is Tempest. Forged in the fires of Sovereign's Fall, she is said to have healing properties, though none know the exact extent of her power. We do know, however, that she can heal the wielder from grave injury."

Silbane added, "She is powerful, but if you touch her with a bare hand, we don't know what will happen. So keep your gloves on."

The master watched with amusement as Arek's gaze traveled up and down the scabbarded blade. Given his ability with swords, Silbane thought the gift was perfect. Trying not to interrupt his apprentice's rapt inspection, he said softly, "Tempest has other properties as well, such as lightness and anticipation."

Arek tore his eyes away with visible effort, asking, "It can think?"

With a smile, Silbane replied, "She can anticipate what you might do, and over time the two of you will become better at fighting together. It shouldn't take very long to appreciate this particular benefit. I have seen the way you wield a blade, and Tempest will be deadly in your hands. Guard her well and she will guard you well."

Arek took the blade in his gloved hand, obviously surprised at its lightness. Silbane knew it would feel slightly warm to the touch, almost alive. There was something else as well. He didn't know exactly what it was, but giving the blade to Arek felt somehow "right."

Looking at the smiling adepts in confusion, Arek blurted, "This is really mine?"

Giridian laughed with a deep sound that seemed to come right from his belly. "Of course—at least until you return." The comment turned sour in the adept's throat and he shot a hasty glance filled with remorse to Silbane, then continued awkwardly, "Remember, Arek, the greatest weapons are always forged through sacrifice. In Tempest's case, legend has it a princess pledged her soul to an angel to save the life of her one true love, binding them together within this blade. Since that time, she protects her wielder from all harm . . . if one believes old legends."

Arek didn't answer, but took hold of the leather strap and slung the sword diagonally across his back, securing it there for easy drawing. Then he bowed and moved to Silbane's side.

"She doesn't move." Arek looked over his shoulder. "It's like she's holding onto me."

Still, Arek hadn't deigned to thank the adept for the blade, and Silbane made a mental note to deal with this later. He turned and said to Giridian, "A most fitting gift, Adept. Our thanks."

"Of course, Master Silbane," Giridian replied. "My pleasure."

Before an uncomfortable silence could fully take hold, Silbane raised a hand in a brief farewell, then turned and made his way to the gate leading out of the main courtyard. Behind him came Arek, eyes down. The boy knew more was going on than they'd told him. Silbane had told Themun the boy wasn't stupid, and it would only be a matter of time before things came to a head. He resolved to be clear with Arek as soon as possible, if for no other reason than it would increase their chances of survival.

They walked for a distance in silence, until the dirt road curved away and they were no longer in sight of the gate, then Silbane stopped. His mind went back to Arek's behavior with Adept Giridian and he decided to take a tack that would allow Arek to control the conversation.

He looked at his apprentice and asked, "What's bothering you?"

Arek looked down, apparently not expecting his master to ask the question so directly. "You expect me to believe we're going on some secret mission."

He stopped, turning to face the boy. He'd worried Arek would question the council's orders or the safety of going, but never considered his apprentice would doubt they were on a mission entirely. "What do you mean?"

Arek turned and faced his master. "Am I being banished for being unable to control the Way, or for what I did to Piter? Is the lore father getting rid of me?" His lips quavered at that, the fear they were indeed abandoning him into the world clearly written on his face, bringing tears to his eyes.

Silbane was shocked. It'd never occurred to him that the boy would think of this as a punishment, but it made perfect sense. Those who broke the rules of the Isle had been banished for far less; killing another apprentice would clearly be justification.

He reminded himself of all that had happened: Arek's test cancelled, Piter's death, this secret mission. Without the ability to read Arek's emotional state, Silbane had no way of knowing how close he'd come to his young apprentice's exact fears.

"It was uncharacteristic of you to challenge the lore father last night," Silbane said, changing the subject.

Arek looked at his master, and then said carefully, "I am not sorry for that."

"No, you aren't, and that is acceptable. In life, one must not always count on others to look out for one's own interests."

Arek's eyes narrowed as he thought. "Then you will tell me why I'm being sent? The real reason?"

A small, sad smile escaped Silbane's lips. He put a hand on Arek's shoulder and squeezed. "We really are on a mission of vital importance. You are not being banished or punished. You have been selected to go with me."

"Because of my power to mask the Way?" Arek finished, doubt clear in his voice.

"You are like a son to me," Silbane said. "I will let no harm come to you." He gave Arek a playful shake, "I promise."

He saw a glimmer of hope in Arek's eyes, like a small fire caught in a gale. Silbane meant to shelter that fire and see it blossom, succor it against the regret he felt at not speaking of the lore father's belief that Arek's touch might disrupt the Gate. That possibility and the sacrifice it might entail, was a bridge Silbane now decided to cross when necessary—not right away. *After we ascertain what is going on at Bara'cor will be plenty of time,* he thought. No need to worry his apprentice until he knew exactly what they faced. With that in mind he said, "Arek, do you know how we plan to get to Bara'cor?"

The question clearly took the boy by surprise. "I hadn't given it much thought. Something quick or our mission will be meaningless."

Silbane nodded "Accurate and insightful. We'll be riding Rai'stahn."

"What's a 'rye-stan'?" mumbled Arek, fidgeting with his pack, which threatened to come loose again.

"Rai'stahn," Silbane said, emphasizing the softer note, "is the name of a dragon."

Turning, the adept continued down the road to the beach, whistling a soft tune. Silbane could imagine Arek's expression, probably standing there with his mouth agape. He heard Arek grab his pack and run after him, catching up quickly.

"Dragon?" the boy exclaimed.

"Did the lore father not make the need for urgency most plain? How else would we make the journey so quickly and still keep this Isle a secret?" Silbane stopped for a moment and said, "Look there."

From their position above the beach, they could see well up and down the coastline. Arek knew this beach line and the rest of their Isle by heart. Silbane pointed to where the beach slowly gave way to cliffs that reached almost to the water's edge. These had been strictly forbidden to the apprentices, as the water and currents could easily kill someone who slipped and fell in. Apprentices who dared violate the rules returned hastily, speaking of a vague fear that overcame them as they approached the cliffs.

"We go there to summon Rai'stahn," Silbane explained, adding, "and hope he will accept our supplication for passage to the mainland. He owes the lore father a debt, one I hope to transfer to me, provided things go right."

"That doesn't sound good," Arek said, not meeting Silbane's eyes.

The master couldn't help but smile. The boy's knack for understatement was never so pronounced as to be obvious, but from time to time he'd say in a few words exactly what Silbane was thinking.

They walked this way for the better part of the morning, with the breeze gradually increasing as they neared the water. Along the way they passed the small homesteads and farms that dotted the Isle. As they looked out over the clear blue waters, they could see no other land, and could taste the salt in the thick sea air.

As the sun rose higher, so too did Arek's mood, or so it seemed to Silbane.

"I acted like a child with Adept Giridian," the apprentice said suddenly.

Silbane raised an eyebrow, as he nodded. "I was a bit disappointed you didn't thank him." Silbane looked sidelong at Arek and continued, "But he was once an initiate on the eve of his test. Had his been cancelled, I doubt his behavior would've been any better than yours."

"How was his test?" asked the boy.

Silbane laughed, "You need to ask him."

"He never says anything except that he owes you his life." Arek didn't elaborate.

Silbane's smile grew wistful. "He's exaggerating. Besides," the master looked at his pupil, "we're not allowed to interfere, so I'd not take him too literally on that count."

Slowly the beach gave way to rocky ground and soon they stood near one of the large cliffs, a dark opening at its base resembling the black maw of some ancient, forgotten creature. Silbane scanned the area, his eyes searching the deep gloom.

"Why are we stopping?" Arek asked, looking hesitantly at the cave mouth. "Will Rai'stahn come here?"

"Silence, apprentice. I must prepare." Silbane closed his eyes and relaxed his breathing, opening his mind to his surroundings. As the sound of the waves crashing onto the rocks receded, he could feel the dragon, a pulsing node of power, deep in the caverns below. Once he had collected himself, but before he began the summoning, he needed to speak with Arek.

"Rai'stahn is a lord amongst his kind. He is ancient and powerful, as you shall soon see. It's important you understand this, for he sees us as fleeting wisps of life. Even I, with my extended years, am no more than a wink in time to him."

Arek nodded hesitantly, then asked, "Is he dangerous?"

"Do not speak unless he addresses you directly." Silbane said, turning to the cave entrance. "It isn't that I fear for you—only that Rai'stahn looks upon men as we look upon insects. I'd rather not see him brush you aside as an annoyance; I'd be sore-pressed to stop him if he did. Do you understand?"

Arek nodded again, unable to hide his apprehension. As his master turned back to the cliff, Arek asked, "But what about you?"

Silbane continued looking straight ahead. "Rai'stahn owes a life debt to our lore father, and he isn't one to forget a debt."

Silbane picked his way up the rocky slope until he stood at the mouth of the entrance. He then closed his eyes and opened a path to the Way. He extended one leg in a long stance, bringing his arms up in a technique known as *Clouds before Earth*. As a master, he'd been able to learn two affinities, Sun and Earth. Those served him well now when he was about to face a true dragon.

His form was quickly outlined in a thin, green flame that sprang from the ground and grew brightest at his head. Much like a flameskin, this would protect him from the aura of dragonfear surrounding Rai'stahn.

It would be futile to include Arek in the spell's effects given the boy's ability to disrupt the Way. Besides, it would serve him well to fully experience the majesty of a true dragon.

"He comes," Silbane said.

Arek took an involuntary step backward, his eyes darting to the cave mouth. He didn't have long to wait. A form took shape out of the darkness, massive in size, outfitted in plate armor as black as midnight. Unlike simple hard plate however, when the dragon-knight moved his armor bent with him like a reptile's scales, showing no gaps and making his movements sinuous. Silbane could see Rai'stahn was taller than himself by at least half a blade's length. What struck Silbane most was Rai'stahn's eyes, shining golden in the afternoon sun.

Rai'stahn looked down at the two men and smiled, baring a row of fanged teeth. His voice rasped out, deep and ancient, echoing through the cave behind him.

"Thou art remembered, friend Silbane." He bowed once, fist to chest, before straightening.

Silbane returned the bow, which returned the smile to Rai'stahn's face.

"You were ever well-mannered, mortal." The knight took a step forward, scanning the horizon. His eyes fell for a moment on Arek, who bowed quickly as Silbane had, going to his knee.

The moments beat by with agonizing slowness and Silbane could feel the dragonfear begin to build within his gut; and yet, for all its weight, it seemed to pass over and through him. It was like a cool breeze, a feeling that could find no purchase to anchor itself within him as his technique came to his protection. It would be interesting to see how Arek reacted to that same fear, and Silbane prepared to extend some part of his own aura to block Rai'stahn's effect. He couldn't envelope the boy, but he could create a barrier for his apprentice when it was needed.

The dragon-knight gestured to the sword on Arek's back. "It carries thy blade, Tempest. What need hath it for such a fell companion?"

"This is Arek, my apprentice. He carries the blade for his own protection," answered the adept.

Curious, he thought, *Arek seems frightened, but no more than anyone meeting a gigantic, armored knight.* Given Arek's abilities, it now seemed not entirely surprising. He should've realized being able to negate magic would protect the boy from dragonfear. Silbane found himself pulling back on his power, no longer needing it to be ready at a moment's notice.

A silence followed as the dragon returned to his scrutiny of the apprentice, his deep voice finally rasping, "Come." With that, it strode past them and down the slope. Silbane turned and followed, Arek close behind.

The dragon-knight looked out over the deep blue of the sea and addressed Silbane again. "What task dost thou petition?"

"Safe passage to Bara'cor, milord."

Rai'stahn turned his sunlit gaze on the adept, measuring him. "What is thy purpose?"

"The lore father senses something stirring, something at Bara'cor. I have been sent to investigate," Silbane offered. As he'd discussed with the lore father, he kept his answers brief.

The dragon-knight looked thoughtfully out over the ocean expanse, his long hair whipped back by the wind. His next words drifted back to them, as if the ancient creature were speaking to himself. "There hath been a stirring in the Way, one that hath not occurred since the Demon Wars."

Rai'stahn trailed off, but the words sent chills through the master, and Silbane's heart began fluttering. The dragon had just confirmed what Themun had felt. A nameless dread, different than dragonfear, gripped him now. Silbane could feel something turning over in the creature's mind, and a part of him wanted to grab Arek and run before the outcome was known.

Then Rai'stahn turned from watching the sea and said, "I will convey thee, but a sojourn must be made, one of great importance. Dost thou agree?"

Silbane pursed his lips, then said carefully, "If we must."

Rai'stahn eyes narrowed, "At the sojourn, we will judge thy next steps, assuage doubt." His golden gaze never wavered from Silbane's own and he said softly, "Dost thou agree?"

Silbane measured the dragon before him, feeling again that something was being decided here that had more importance than this short question seemed to reflect. "Of course, milord."

The dragon-knight turned, motioning for them to stay as he walked away. Silbane could feel a building of power and realized Rai'stahn was about to assume his true shape. He turned and grabbed Arek, backing away and then running. When the dragon-knight's form exploded in a flash of white fire that for an instant burned brighter than the sun, Silbane and Arek faced away, but they still felt the heat on their backs and necks.

In front of them the cavern that had been dark now stood illumed in the bright light. For a moment, Silbane thought he saw another set of eyes much like Rai'stahn's own peering back at him. They were smaller than the great dragon's, but identical in every other way. An instant later they were gone.

Silbane blinked, purple afterimages of the knight's form dancing across his blurred vision. Looking down for a moment, he rubbed his eyes to clear them. Arek held Silbane's arm for support. He felt the boy's hand stiffen and heard the sharp intake of breath. Nothing, he knew, could have prepared his young apprentice for the sight that now met Arek's eyes.

Arek's mouth hung open. Rai'stahn in his true form was at least a hundred paces in length from nose to tail, ebony scales encasing its entire body. Razor sharp claws larger than a man's body tipped the ends of his feet and fangs the size of swords revealed themselves as Rai'stahn opened his mouth to sound a tremendous roar. Arek covered his ears, wincing. They watched as the dragon slowly extended a leathery wing, its tip touching the ground in front of their feet.

Climb and secure yourselves, lest thee lose thy grip.

Rai'stahn's archaic tongue echoed in Silbane's mind even as Arek backed up into him.

"Don't be afraid. Rai'stahn won't harm you." The monk laid a gentle hand on Arek's shoulder. "Come."

Cautiously Arek followed Silbane onto the resilient membrane of the wing. Scrambling up to the long spikes emerging from the dragon's spine, he seated himself between two of them as Silbane did the same.

Silbane looked back in the direction of the Halls in farewell, though he couldn't see their home. Then he said to Rai'stahn, "We are ready, milord."

To our sojourn then, and the judging.

With a mighty leap, the dragon launched himself into the air, his powerful wings catching the ocean breeze and lifting him and his riders over the Shattered Sea. Silbane felt a great weight on his chest and was thankful for the spine spike supporting him from behind. Looking back, he watched the Isle slowly shrink in size as Rai'stahn gained altitude. Soon, it was nothing but a small speck of brown and green in a vast sea of blue.

Silbane checked their direction against the sun, estimating a northwestern heading. Only a slight wind caressed his face, a by-product of the magic that allowed a dragon of Rai'stahn's size to fly.

"Be careful about your bare flesh touching Rai'stahn," he said to Arek. "I don't know if you could affect such a powerful creature, but I'd rather not have him suddenly change form while we're on his back." Silbane smiled at the joke, but Arek looked at him wide-eyed. "We should be in the air until almost dusk. I would suggest getting some rest."

Though Arek nodded his head, Silbane knew sleep would be far from his apprentice's young mind. Silbane, however, relaxed against the spine ridge and allowed himself to doze.

JOURNAL ENTRY 5

Today I achieved the abode seen in the distance. It revealed itself to be a small, deserted castle, a defensible place reminiscent of the summer keep I played at as a child. Perhaps it is actually that keep, or perhaps a conjuration born from my own desire for safety. I hope it is the former, as my mind has many specters still lurking, dark things I would rather not yet face. This abode at least gives me a place I remember as home, a place where I can gather myself before more phantasms renew their assault. I will use this as my base camp from which to research the Aeris. Either I will use their power to force them into submission, or to forge their undoing.

Finnow came to me last night, a shade risen from death. I am not surprised she found her way here, hoping to stand in judgment at the right hand of her gods.

She has always been irksome, but death makes her worse. At first, I was fascinated and listened to her weave her tale, but I know what Finnow is. She is nothing more or less than I expected and I do not need a shade's words to measure my worth. The world knew my greatness long before she learned the same by dying. I banished her, her incessant yapping more tiresome than informative. Let this place do its best. I have survived worse.

One thing to note: Finnow formed from a cloud of these same, infinitesimal lights, but they dispersed once my will came to bear. I know not if she is real, or something I conjured with my latest regrets. Her appearance has, however, taught me more about this place and the power my will has over it.

I shall think on this more.

Journal Entry 5

THE WALL

*It is difficult for the body
to continue fighting without its head.
Hone your skill in separating the two.*
—The Bladesman Codex

Sergeant Alyx Stemmer picked her way carefully along the upper tier of the outer wall. The afternoon sun slowly set, blazing yellow to the west, painting everything orange and copper in its ruddy glow. Bara'cor soaked in and then radiated that heat, a warmth the night's watch would welcome when the desert turned chill under the gaze of the sun's sister, the moon.

The barbarians waited patiently, camped out of arrow range. When the wind shifted, she could make out the sound of drums and laughter. Well, she thought, at least someone is having fun. Behind her came Yetteje and Niall, each armed and accompanying the sergeant on her rounds.

"Walking the wall" had become a habit of Yetteje and Alyx, but including Niall was something the king hoped would give his heir a new appreciation for what the soldiers of Bara'cor went through.

Alyx felt sorry for the princess. How must it feel to know the best news would be only her father had perished? Still, she'd come to know Yetteje had strength within her, a strength that through this period of hardship would either temper her like a fine blade, or break her at the quench.

They came upon a small square, a landing cut into the area where two walls joined. It was used as a catapult staging area and served as an unofficial combat ring.

Though not sanctioned as part of official duty, the unspoken rule was that any amount of practice wasn't just tolerated, but encouraged. Each year the fortresses held the

King's Tourney, a contest to award the best combatants of the realm first standing amongst their peers, and the best of those, the King's Thorn. Last year, Ash had won the ceremonial blade, which would now call Bara'cor home until the next annual tournament. While the pride at winning was an obvious reward, more important were the "bragging rights" the men of Bara'cor could hold at every tavern and inn for the year. Losing the blade to another fortress would likely earn the team the "best" of duties. Sadly, if rumors of the fate of the other fortresses were true, it would be some time until any new tourneys were held.

A few off-duty men had gathered, casting dice and waiting for the shift change. Alyx nodded to them, then picked up two wooden bohkirs, tossing one to Yetteje. "Come, some lumps will do you good."

Yetteje caught it automatically, but shook her head, her eyes on the barbarian encampment, "No thanks, Al. I'm not in the mood."

The sergeant's eyes narrowed and she let steel into her voice. "Is that what you'll tell the nomads who killed your father?"

Yetteje's head snapped back, anger flashing to the surface. She started to advance into the square, the bohkir twitching in her hand as if it were alive. "Fine."

"Bring your best," the sergeant said with a smile.

Niall stepped back, clearly a little disappointed the sergeant hadn't asked him. "I'll just wait for my turn," he muttered.

Yetteje moved in quickly, throwing her weight behind a strike aimed at the sergeant's temple. Though the swords were wooden, a strike would still cause damage, called "love lumps" by the men-at-arms.

Sergeant Stemmer caught the wooden blade on the base of her own, pushing it out and forcing Yetteje back.

"You're swinging with anger," Alyx said. "It'll make—"

She never finished. Yetteje attacked with lightning quick strikes alternating from head to chest and then back to head. Anger lent her speed and strength. The attack was furious in its intensity, but short-lived. Her breathing became erratic, first deep then shallow, but never in rhythm with her strikes.

For her part, Alyx took the strikes, alternating her blocks. She then jumped forward with a heavy overhand strike to Yetteje's head. It was an easy strike to block, not intended to score but to get the girl to think. Alyx wanted the girl to be focused on this moment, and only the physical shock of blocking seemed to get her attention.

Tej brought her blade up, catching the sergeant's inches above her forehead, and pushed it off.

Alyx could see that hurt had replaced anger, and the girl's so easy-to-read feelings of abandonment were growing. The sergeant didn't respond, knowing any quarter given now would only allow Yetteje an excuse to stop and wallow in self-pity.

Instead, she pressed her attack, throwing a flurry of slashes the Princess of Tir had no choice but to counter, dodging and twisting to avoid Alyx's swings.

Yetteje braced, then stabbed and spun her blade in a well-known Tir move, "the flower cut." Had it been executed correctly, it might have scored.

As it was, Yetteje's blade didn't wheel and dance through a graceful figure eight, but instead came out as four diagonal slashes, each easily blocked and turned.

Alyx countered off the last one and slammed the back of her bohkir into Yetteje's forehead, right above her eye. As the girl reeled back stunned, the sergeant followed up with a hammer fist, dropping Yetteje like a sack of potatoes on her rump. A short snap kick slammed the girl backward and spread-eagled out onto the rough granite surface, her bohkir flying from her grasp to bounce out of the square with a wooden clatter. No one watching interfered, not even for royal blood. What happened within the combat square did so without rank or favor.

When the princess opened her eyes, she was still on her back, and Alyx had her blade at her throat.

"Why did you lose?" the sergeant asked, her bohkir not wavering. When Yetteje didn't answer, the point of the blade poked her chest. "Why?"

"Stop it!" Yetteje cried. "What do you want from me?"

"You fought terribly, like a student hoping for her First Blade."

"You don't care at all, do you?" she said, her eyes squinting as tears started to fall.

"No. And neither will they," she said pointing to the barbarian encampment with her bohkir. She turned back to Yetteje and said, "I care about you living. More so, it seems, than you do."

Alyx withdrew the bohkir and replaced it with her hand, outstretched, demanding her grasp. Yetteje reached up and Alyx pulled her to her feet, but not unkindly.

"Why did you lose?"

Yetteje let loose a huff then said, "I was angry."

"That's right. You were. And in that anger, you let me hit you with a strike a child could've blocked." Alyx put a hand on the princess's shoulder and said, "Now, look at me."

She waited until the princess met her gaze, and then said with a smile, "What have you learned?"

Yetteje breathed out again through her nose. "Not to fight you."

"Mayhap a better lesson is to understand when the moment is upon you. You may face an opponent who is far more skilled, but when given the chance, remove your emotion. Learn to strike true."

Yetteje nodded, a small smile on her lips. "I'm not as angry now."

"It's not gone, I can see it simmering." Alyx's eyes rested on Niall. Then she said so only Yetteje could hear,

"Your skill surpasses most—in leadership, diplomacy, even blades. Do not let the actions of others change who you are." She squeezed the princess's shoulder reassuringly. "You are special, Yetteje Tir. Don't forget it."

"It's just . . . difficult."

Before Alyx could answer, Niall came up to join them. "Do you think they'll attack again tonight?" he asked with his eyes on the barbarian encampment. He seemed oblivious to the fact that he was interrupting their conversation.

"Perhaps . . . perhaps not." Sergeant Stemmer caught Yetteje's eye and gave her a half smile, then made her way over to a basin and scooped up some water to wash off her face. She threw a wet towel to Yetteje, who touched the knot above her eye gingerly.

"They pushed us hard the other day and continue to test our resolve." Alyx went over to the princess and grabbed the cold towel and folded it into a tight ball. Then she braced the back of the princess's head in one hand and pressed the cold towel into the swelling.

The princess was familiar with how to reduce swelling, and except for a grunt of pain, didn't fight the sergeant's pressure on her eye.

"Their leader must be wondering how to get us out of here. With Shimmerene at our back we have water, and Land's Edge Pass allows us to go for food. How long will the other kingdoms stand by and let trade be disrupted? Even now the queen must be rallying Haven's forces."

She pulled off the towel and inspected the lump, noting the swelling had gone down significantly. "Hold this here, as I did," she instructed.

Yetteje nodded, applying the cold compress to the swelling. Only a small grimace gave the sergeant a clue that the correct pressure was being applied. If it didn't hurt, you weren't doing it right.

Alyx turned her attention back to the prince. "We need only hold for a while and they'll come to our aid. For us it becomes a waiting game."

"How's the eye?" asked Niall with some concern.

"Fine." Tej looked out over the battlements, her demeanor and one word answer making it clear she didn't want to dwell on a minor injury. She stared at the nomad encampment.

* * * * *

Yetteje couldn't stand that the enemy was celebrating. They all heard the drums, the laughter. They could smell the food. Normally, the night was best for fighting in the desert, the day's heat making any kind of attack unlikely. However, it seemed that as the sun set on this day, the barbarians were going to feast, enjoying the cool evening. There was no payment for their crimes, no remorse. Yetteje turned to Alyx and said, "I want vengeance."

Alyx looked sidelong at the young princess. "You may have lost your family and I mourn with you. However, think on the tale of the gods Eben and Aaron and their fight against the demonlord Eris. This is a tale, I think, showing the difference between what drives us."

Niall nodded, but Yetteje looked confused. "I remember some of it," she said. "Lord Eben lost his kingdom through trickery. Since there was no shedding of divine blood, he and his consort accepted banishment. But that's all I know."

Alyx nodded at Yetteje's summary. "This was in an ancient time, long before the war at Sovereign's Fall, when our world was embroiled in a bitter war with the demonlord Eris. Remember too that Lord Eben was married to Selene, said to be the most beautiful woman in the world. When he and his wife accepted banishment from the land, his brother Lord Aaron went with them.

"He did this even though he was next in line to sit upon the throne; such was his love for his brother. For years, they wandered the wastes of Winters Thorn, never allowed to return home. Through all this, Lord Aaron stood always by his brother's side.

"When word came that the demons of Eris were looking for Selene, Lord Eben bade his brother to protect her while he went looking for a legendary weapon, said to be hidden in the mountains of Dawnlight."

Alyx turned and leaned her back against the warm stone, continuing, "Lord Aaron knew he couldn't guard Selene without rest. He would need to sleep at some point and dreaded losing her during these moments of weakness. Therefore, he crafted a spell, placing her within the crude shelter and circling it with magical sand.

"Then he said to her, 'Selene, do not cross this barrier I have created, for it shields you from the hosts of Eris. It is my boon, to be able to protect those I love, so long as they stay within a circle I create with my own hands. I must sleep, but will break the seal in the morning.' With that, Lord Aaron went to take his rest.

"The demons sent dreams to Selene, dreams of her husband hurt in the mountains, fallen in a crevasse, trapped. They whispered on the wind for anyone who loved Lord Eben to hear, lies saying he was lost in the icy peaks, crippled by the cold and dying alone.

"She couldn't sleep and didn't believe in Lord Aaron's spell of sand. 'How could such a small, fragile line stop true demons?' she reasoned, not knowing it was Lord Aaron's own purity, his faith manifest within the sand itself that protected her. She crossed the seal, breaking the spell it contained, hoping to go to her husband in need. No sooner had she done so, than she was taken."

Alyx paused for a moment, looking at Yetteje. "I don't mean to say the burdens carried by others are somehow greater than what you feel for your family. I only tell you this to remind you of what has driven others, so we may perhaps be inspired."

Yetteje nodded.

Then Alyx continued, "When Lord Eben returned and saw his beloved gone, he turned on Lord Aaron, 'I asked you to do a simple thing! Guard her! And you couldn't even accomplish that!'

"When Lord Aaron heard these words, his heart fell to pieces, for he'd followed his brother these past years for love's sake, relinquishing title and throne. He'd protected and served him dutifully, never once coveting what his brother had and never seeking happiness with another. His happiness was his brother's safekeeping and love. Think how his heart must have broken at this moment, to think he'd failed his brother so completely."

Yetteje's eyes fell from Alyx's face to stare out at the sea of sand. They were still dancing out there, no consequences for their destruction of EvenSea. She could feel her anger rising. In an effort to calm herself, Yetteje focused on the story and said, "The problem is Lord Eben's, who is ungrateful."

Alyx turned to the princess and said, "Perhaps. Yet Lord Aaron didn't give up on his brother and held no ill will toward him for those words. He stood fast and firm and didn't succumb to the misery he felt, both for losing Selene and for failing his brother. Lord Aaron carried that burden for another year, seeing his own failure and misery every time his brother looked upon him.

"Lord Eben seldom entrusted his brother to another task. He rarely spoke to him and never with the brotherly love that they had once shared. To him, his brother was dead and their relationship became as you are to your shadow, forever beside each other, but silent. He gave up hope of ever finding Selene again and railed at the gods for punishing him so."

Alyx paused, standing up. Her motion caught Yetteje's attention, as the princess could tell the sergeant meant to test them. Her instincts were correct, for Alyx looked at them both and asked, "Now I ask you this. Who suffered more? Lord Aaron, who carried the guilt for losing Selene and bearing Lord Eben's anger in silence? Or Eben, who lost his mate and brother?"

Yetteje narrowed her gaze, thinking through the tale. Her fingers absently rubbed the rough walls, feeling the grit of rock dust as her mind pulled apart and pieced together the actions of the two brothers. Then she said, "They both lost, but I judge Lord Eben's loss greater. He can mend things with his brother, for they are still alive. You cannot make amends with the dead."

Alyx looked at the young princess and said, "Lord Aaron never gave up hope. He carried his brother through his darkest hours of hate and self-pity, until at last they found and rescued Selene from Eris's kingdom, alive.

"You see, had he allowed himself to be driven by guilt or hate, it would've eventually destroyed him. I judge that by maintaining hope, a better end was achieved, in which all were healed. But, Princess, what gave him hope?"

Yetteje shrugged, growing tired of Alyx's questions. "Stupidity."

With a small laugh Alyx clapped her on the shoulder, "No. It was love that drove him. Love for his brother and the desire to do the right thing. These things can also sustain us through difficult times."

Yetteje shrugged off Alyx's hand, her eyes once again on the nomad camp. Her next words came out harsh, directed at herself more than anyone else, "I've seen that hate is an emotion, too. It can sustain much, as it did Lord Eben through his darkest hours.

"Someone should sneak into that camp and put an end to their leader. See if that makes them feel like singing and dancing," Yetteje added, her voice dripping with vehemence. Then she threw a small rock over the wall. "I'll wager we wouldn't hear laughter and drums then."

"What did you say?" Alyx asked, looking at the princess intently.

"Nothing." Yetteje replied, "It just doesn't seem fair they get to celebrate after what they've done."

Alyx nodded slowly, her eyes unfocused. Then she looked at the two of them and said, "A small group, no more than four or five . . ." She shook her head and smiled. "Princess, you may have found a way to break this siege. Come, let's talk to the armsmark."

DRAGON VISION

Think of the moon on water.
It shines close by, yet it hangs far above.
You must forge your tactics the same way.
Stay close to your opponent, yet feel far away.
Be like the moon's reflection on the water's surface.
—Tir Combat Academy, The Tactics of Victory

Rai'stahn winged low over the desert while Arek looked for anything out of the ordinary—anything that wasn't sand. He spotted a small, vertical stone shaft rising from yellow, sun-stroked dunes, and pointed it out to his master. The shaft quickly grew into a tower, its minarets broken and its walls crumbled, open to the gritty winds. Rai'stahn banked and for all his bulk landed softly, scattering only a little sand and debris. He dipped a wing, allowing Silbane and Arek to disembark.

"What is this place?" Arek asked, drinking in the sight of the ancient ruin.

The cool breeze of flight dissipated and hot dry air hit him like the blast of a furnace. He was instantly sweating. The desert seemed empty in all directions, a vast flowing sea of dunes set against a deep orange sky. Was this the place the dragon wanted to "test" his master? Why had he chosen such a desolate place for this stop?

He looked about, his eyes drawn to the ancient structure that listed to one side and asked, "Is this a Far'anthi tower? The stone looks dead, though."

Silbane had suspected as much when his eyes fell upon the pedestal at the tower's base, holding a great globe of ash-colored rock in a three-pronged grasp. He looked at Arek, "Yes, the stone would be glowing blue."

He turned and addressed Rai'stahn, "Milord, what would you have us do?"

The dragon, for his part, had changed back into his knight form. Now he looked out over the wastes, his black armor standing in stark contrast to the golden sands spread out before them. A moment passed, then another. Finally Rai'stahn looked at Silbane and said, "Prepare thy camp. I must consult with mine brethren. Then thy test begins."

Silbane nodded. He then caught Arek's attention. He motioned to the pile of gear now lying scattered in the sand. "See to our things." He fumbled through his tunic to bring forth something that glinted in the sun. "Before I forget, Tempest wasn't your only gift."

Silbane held the talisman aloft for his apprentice to see. He then took it between his hands and broke it in half. Arek watched as a sparkle of blue surrounded the break, and then disappeared. Each half now sought the other. "It is a Finder . . . do you understand?"

Arek nodded. One half the adept strung around his neck; the other, Arek slipped into his pocket, careful not to touch it with his bare flesh. "Thank you."

"I assume you understand its use?" Silbane asked. "As long as we live, each half will glow."

"I know." Arek didn't particularly care for how his master worded that. Still, he knew in an emergency, either could crush their half. Doing so would create a temporary portal between their locations, allowing them instantaneous transport to the other.

"You're expecting we'll lose each other," Arek added.

Silbane shook his head. "I'm just trying to keep you safe."

Rai'stahn strode purposefully up to the tower walls and looked at the weathered stone. "It has the scent of the Way, though long dead." His yellow eyes mirrored the setting sun, shining like liquid gold, inhuman, but expressive.

Arek felt himself drawn to Rai'stahn's simple martial beauty. Here was a true dragon lord, a creature out of mythic antiquity, and nothing Arek had seen before could compare. It was so singularly new to his experience he could feel each moment pass with a kind of slowed motion, as if time itself was allowing him to drink in more detail and meaning.

Just then, Rai'stahn's image wavered and there were two of him, superimposed upon one another. One stood looking at the Far'anthi stone. The other staggered a step to the left, taloned hand to head. Wings flexed to steady the dragon-knight, bat-like and black—then the vision was over. The two images collapsed back into one. Whatever had affected Rai'stahn had passed like a desert breeze. Arek watched, but neither his master nor the dragon gave any indication that anything was amiss.

Then Rai'stahn turned around, spearing Arek with his golden gaze; he felt an almost physical heat where that gaze fell. It accused him, as if the great dragon knew exactly what Arek had just seen, and wanted to pull his very soul apart.

What felt like an eternity swept by under the dragon's scrutiny, until Arek realized Rai'stahn was trying to use his dragonfear. It was as if there was no purchase within Arek for that fear to take hold. It fell off him like water from an oiled surface.

Then Rai'stahn growled low, "I wouldst speak with thee privately, Silbane." He didn't wait for a response, walking away from the lone tower and into the Wastes.

* * * * *

Silbane was worried. It wasn't that Arek resisted Rai'stahn's gaze. That'd been ascertained when they first met. Rather it was the great dragon's insistence they talk now, right after Silbane had witnessed his failure to make his apprentice cower using the dragonfear. Silbane felt with a growing dread he was about to learn what this sojourn was all really about.

Rai'stahn strode off and Silbane hurried after. Dragons were passionate creatures and their actions were often ruled by need as much as expediency and logic. Any emotion he felt now was likely due to the effect dragons had on their companions.

Rai'stahn crested a small rise and stopped to gaze back at the tower, his golden eyes narrowing. A moment passed, then another, as he seemed to ponder how best to begin. Of course, Silbane reminded himself, dragons didn't measure time the way humans did; neither did they hesitate to speak their minds.

Still, the expression on Rai'stahn's face reminded Silbane of what a person might look like if an unpleasant subject were about to be broached.

He looked down at the monk, then cleared his throat. "Now that we are clear of the Isle, I am left with a sore choice. Bid me truly, what wouldst thee do with thy hatchling?"

"Milord?" Silbane was bothered that the dragon-knight cared to mention they were "clear of the Isle." *What did he mean by that?* A deepening knot of worry grew in the master's stomach. They were far from anything and alone with a creature of immense power.

"The lore father sensed a stirring in the Way," Silbane said. "Arek hides our presence from something the lore father fears aids the besiegers of Bara'cor, something that uses the Way." He watched the dragon closely for any signs betraying his inner thoughts.

Rai'stahn's eyes became slits. "Thou speaketh of the Gate and slip the question," he stated. "Dost thou ken why I hath brought thee here?"

Silbane decided to take a chance, hoping to find an ally. "Do you oppose our quest to find this Gate?"

"The Gate is not what shouldst concern thee."

Silbane cocked his head. Everyone knew the demons had brought the world to the brink of destruction, flooding into this world through these rifts. Nonetheless, he continued, "Our council knows Lilyth wasn't destroyed, rather banished."

Rai'stahn closed his eyes. "The doom this world faces is brought by thee, not Lilyth, magus."

Silbane knew dragons were far more sensitive to the magical currents and eddies present in the world than any master. It was likely Rai'stahn sensed things far beyond Silbane's ability to comprehend. "What do you mean, milord?"

The dragon-knight nodded once, a short gesture that surprised Silbane with its hesitancy. It occurred to him the dragon's demeanor reflected an emotion he'd never thought to see in his kind: fear. Silbane decided to press further. "Milord, if there's something I should know . . . ?"

A moment passed before Rai'stahn answered, "Dost thou seek the truth? The price will be high."

Silbane looked down, but when his head rose, there was an obdurate determination in his slate blue eyes. "Is this my test? Do you want to see if there's steel beneath my flesh?"

The dragon-knight walked a slow circle around the mage, and barked, "Do not question me! I have walked this earth when thee and thine were nothing!"

He continued, his voice low and deadly, "Thou wouldst hazard all races of this world to save thine own." Rai'stahn looked at Silbane and said, "I hath been given special dispensation for thee, magus."

Silbane stepped back a pace, sensing deadly intent in those words and said, "For what?"

"Pay heed. I offer thee a chance to see events from this world's past. Dost thou accept?"

Silbane looked about the desolation surrounding them, empty and beautiful. It was clear now there could only be one reason Rai'stahn had agreed to transport them. Isolation. The great dragon had offspring nesting on the Isle, no doubt what he'd seen peering back at him when the cave had been illuminated. Whatever transpired here would have no witness, and most importantly, no collateral damage.

A part of him hated to think this way—as if everything ended in betrayal—but this simple journey suddenly seemed a life-and-death situation, and whether his thinking was the result of paranoia or preparedness, he wasn't taking any chances. He nodded, not trusting himself yet to speak.

"Very well," Rai'stahn nodded, as he placed his fingers on the center of Silbane's forehead. "Thou art given Sight. Behold, then choose . . ."

The sand around them stirred then rose in a swirling column, sealing Silbane and the dragon-knight from sight. Inside, he could hear sibilant female voices, whispers coming from all directions.

Rai'stahn stood facing the mage, his eyes glowing with power. The whispers became a vision filling Silbane's head, and he Saw . . .

* * * * *

The leader moved his tall frame through the darkened tunnels, his armor catching and reflecting the firelight flickering from torches along the cave walls. He was accompanied by two guards, each wide-eyed, their faces covered in sweat from what could have been either fear or heat, most likely both.

"Far enough, general." The voice came from a dwarven soldier who stepped out of the shadows and held up an armored hand. Though he towered over the men, he seemed somehow smaller.

Perhaps it was the aura of power the leader projected, or the fact his gaze didn't waver from the guard's own. After a moment, the dwarf moved back an involuntary step, as if his body had been commanded to do so.

"You'll summon your masters," said the leader in armor, dismissing his men without a sound or gesture. He didn't say anything else, his pale eyes locked straight ahead, as if looking through the stone itself.

Two more dwarves appeared and one bowed deferentially. "General, you have been granted audience. Please, follow me." He turned, and to Silbane the dwarven greeter seemed clearly accustomed to men of rank and just as clearly shielded from it by his own high station. No doubt this comfort was the reason he'd been chosen to greet this general.

The general followed, his eyes drinking in the details of this passage even as the tunnel widened into an open basin. Arranged around the upper lip some distance above were massive reptilian shapes. They hinted at armored scales and scythe-like talons, and promised fire.

With a start, Silbane realized this man stood before ancient creatures more powerful in the Way than any known to inhabit in the land. As if in answer, the man looked about the chamber, searching for the greatest of these, the dragon-king Silbane knew was named Rai'kesh.

Rai'kesh had ruled his kind for over a thousand years. He now turned glowing red eyes upon the general, his posture showing that the mere presence of this man was an affront to dragonkind and the Way.

As their gazes locked, the man smiled. It seemed as if he knew what harm that could befall him and dared it anyway. He said one word, which echoed throughout the vast chamber, "Cowards."

A low rumble resulted and the ancient creature pulled back lips to reveal razor-sharp teeth. "Have we not stayed our hand?" His voice was deep and sounded like gravel against stone.

The general nodded. "And thousands die."

The dragon-king raised a taloned claw and asked, "Who hath died?"

The armored man stepped back. "If you can ask that, you have turned your backs on this land."

"Then thou dost not understand the war thee wages, nor the Aeris and their nature, halfling."

The general cocked his head. "Halfling? Even I, a mere mortal, am not beneath your insults?"

A menacing growl sounded, followed by, "No insult was meant, General. Without the Aeris, thy kind were not what thou couldst be, like the reflection of the moon on water, compared to the moon itself. Thou art less than was meant by destiny."

"Aeris?" he retorted. "I thought so once and chose a peaceful path. Then this happened. I name them demons now."

The great dragon Rai'kesh raised himself, his dark red scales glowing in the rocklight of the cavern like smoldering iron. His eyes narrowed and brightened into two red-orange embers. "What dost thou want, Archmage? We suffer thy presence because of duty, yet with thine every breath and word, our patience is tested."

The armored man looked about the chamber and pitched his voice to carry to all those assembled. "The war goes badly. Despite your claim, our people grieve for their dead. Our children disappear, taken by these demons, never to be seen again." His eyes hardened. "We must have aid."

There was no movement, but the shadows conspired to give the impression that the entire assemblage moved in a bit closer. Rai'kesh looked at the man in armor, then hissed, "Thou presume much, coming before us."

"I would dare even you, if it means victory."

The great dragon leaned in, his head level with the armored general. "The Aeris cannot be eradicated. We hath explained, created by thee and thy people, they are the stuff of dreams, halfling. Thy war is pointless."

If the man understood, Silbane didn't see any indication of it. Instead, he stamped his foot and an explosion of white power flashed out, cracking the basin upon which he stood and pushing the great dragon king back with a promise of violence. "I won't suffer lies!"

Rai'kesh treated the man's outburst like the misbehavior of a child and didn't react except to exhale a blast of caustic air. Then, he growled, "The blind worry, believing a chasm opens before them at each step. Mayhap it is Sight thou art lacking."

The general's eyes narrowed and a few moments went by in silence. Then he asked, "Sight?"

"Thou shalt See the true nature of things. Perhaps only then wilt thou understand war is not thy people's destiny. Peace may yet be achieved. With the gift of Sight, thou wilt come to understand the Aeris and depart this path of recklessness."

The man looked slowly around the basin as if understanding that the dragons meant to change him in some fundamental way. Then he knelt and said, "I accept."

"Not all survive the giving."

"Do not concern yourself with my survival." He looked up and his pale eyes flashed with power, glowing now with blue energy. "If I die, this ends here and now."

There was a pause, as if the very air went still with anticipation, then Silbane saw yellow power erupt from above, spearing the knight in its fire. It burned bright, utterly consuming the man in armor. He thought he heard a scream, then nothing.

The fire slowly subsided. As it withered and died, the armored man knelt where he'd been, the ground around him burned and molten, steam escaping in hisses from its charred surface, melted smooth from the heat.

He looked dead, but then his armor glinted—a small sign of movement from the man within. Silbane thought he heard a sigh of disappointment from the gathered dragons, as if they had hoped to end his petition just as the man had said, with his death.

He rose, his form still smoking, and his eyes opened. Silbane could see them flash yellow, infused with the power granted by this Conclave of Dragons. The general looked about, as if seeing things for the first time.

"I had never dreamed—" he began.

"The Aeris are necessary," Rai'kesh interrupted. "Look upon them with mercy and thou wilt See that there are better answers than war."

He continued to stare about him, as if drinking in every detail, then his head shook. He took a step back, flanked by the dwarven guards, and said, "These creatures, if they are as you say, cannot be killed. It means the end of our people!"

Rai'kesh looked again at the man to whom they had entrusted their gift and said, "Neither can they eradicate those who create them, for it will be their undoing as well. Thou canst petition for peace, because neither can survive without the other. Valarius, wilt thou desist in thy path?"

The man in armor, who with his naming Silbane realized was General Valarius Galadine, shook his head. "You would see us enslaved?"

"How canst thou be a slave to thine own shadow?" Rai'kesh responded, tilting his head quizzically. "Thou art thinking within the frame of a single lifetime. Much hath happened since Sovereign's fall from the stars, yet the parting of thee and thine from the Aeris was never intended. Seek peace and unification, and all will be as it was meant to be."

The great dragon paused, then said, "Forbear." The chamber echoed with his final admonishment.

The general's eyes grew hard as he looked at the assembled dragons and said, "Patience is for the weak, and we're all granted but a single life." He turned and walked away from the basin, but looked back as he neared its edge. "If your children had been taken, would you stand by so idly?" His eyes flashed again, as if daring any of the Conclave to act.

When nothing happened, he gave a hesitant bow. It was a sign of respect somewhat out of place, thought Silbane, given the tone of the exchange. He then turned away from the Conclave and back into the tunnels. Moments passed in silence.

Then the dragon-king said, "Rai'stahn."

The air congealed where the archmage had just stood, a black smoke taking on the kneeling form of the armored dragon-knight Silbane knew. "Milord?"

"He presumes much."

Rai'stahn turned a yellow-golden gaze in the direction of the retreating form and replied, "We should end him. At least Azrael wouldst then stand free."

Silbane thought he saw Rai'kesh smile at that, though it could've been a trick of the light. The elder dragon looked around at the Conclave and a silent communion was held.

When it was finished, he addressed the younger dragon-knight again. "Perhaps the Sight granted will yet lend him perspective. He should understand what he wishes to destroy. Mayhap it will give him pause."

Rai'kesh moved closer and put an armored hand on the kneeling dragon's shoulder. "Thou wilt take a force of knights. Attend the battle, but do not help these halfmen. Thou shalt protect the land should Valarius fail to See the path opened for him."

Rai'stahn nodded and asked, "Dost thou still believe he can bring unity?"

"If he lives, perhaps. If he dies, it will be as thee says. Azrael will walk again amongst us. Either outcome favors a beneficent end." Rai'kesh paused, then added, "There will come a moment. Thou wilt know when. Act as we hath been ordered, for the good of this land."

Then the vision faded from Silbane's mind like smoke . . .

* * * * *

Silbane clutched his head, pain pounding inside his skull, his knees in the soft sand, his eyes clenched shut. Slowly, he opened them to gaze at the world around him.

Above him, the dusk sky shone orange and gold with a serenity out of place with the visions he'd just *Seen.*

The sand in front of him was spotted with dark, wet blobs. He reached out a cautious finger and realized it was his own blood, dripping from his nose and ears. A sharp pain in his forehead and a quick inspection revealed something that felt like a small scar where the dragon's claws had touched him, burned in by the searing light of the vision. He quickly rose, wiping his face and looking for the dragon-knight.

As Silbane rose the dragon-knight grunted, as if acknowledging his strength, and said, "Thou shalt feel the gift come upon you, but slowly. Stand steady."

Silbane shook his head to clear it, still throbbing from the intensity of thought and power. Never in all his previous dealings with dragons had he felt such might. He looked at Rai'stahn and though there were other more critical concerns—such as his mission, and Arek—he asked the one question burning in his mind, "Who is Azrael?"

Rai'stahn watched the mage, his eyes calculating, then replied, "Why dost thou ask what thine heart already kens? It is for this reason and this reason alone thou art granted dispensation. Thou hast heard the name before, Magus."

Azrael? It was the same name Silbane had heard when he'd Ascended. What did that mean? Did he and Valarius share some deeper connection? The name couldn't be just a coincidence. He licked his lips and then asked, "Azrael opposes Lilyth?"

The dragon shrugged. "Nothing so simple. Azrael hath chosen a different path and disappeared in the Ascension. Now we wait for his bonded brother to recognize his own true worth for the task ahead."

A nervous trepidation made Silbane hesitate, but only a heartbeat or two. Then he asked the most obvious question possible. "And I am the bonded brother?"

"Close thine eyes, Magus. Use the dragon's gift to See the truth that surrounds thee. Everything else lives in thy past, and cannot be changed today."

Silbane turned his attention in the direction of the dragon's gaze, drinking in the golden dunes lit orange by the setting sun. Above, the sky painted itself an almost perfect blue, the beauty and peace of this land in such contrast to the dire conversation taking place between them. What did Rai'stahn want him to see?

He closed his eyes and took a deep breath, cleansing his mind and opening himself to the Way. At first, nothing happened differently. His body relaxed and time slowed, and he stood there, staring into a sea of blackness before his closed eyes.

Then, from that sea, points of yellow light appeared. They were like infinitesimal particles of dust, eddying and flowing in some unseen current. The current took on form and substance, and a landscape took shape: the dunes, the hills, even the tower! It all stood glittering, each particle adhering to everything, painting him a monochromatic picture of the world in front of him in a sparkling shimmer. Though his eyes remained closed, Silbane could see!

Near the tower, something caught his attention. It was an area of blackness, of wrongness. It sucked in the particles, pulling them into itself. What was that? Was it the tower doing this, or something else?

Before he could determine what he was seeing, the vision of particles faded from view, then disappeared altogether. A sudden wave of lethargy overcame him and he stumbled, only to be steadied by Rai'stahn's armored hand.

"Sight is taxing to the new."

He cautiously opened his eyes, blinking as if waking from a dream. "What is it?" he asked, dumbfounded by what he saw.

The expression on the dragon's face was inscrutable, but his tone was clear. "Thy mettle is tested true. It is the

Way in its purest form and thou hath been given the gift to see it. Thou witnessed the blackness? It is a blight upon the land. Should it be allowed to grow, the Way will die."

Silbane drew a breath, feeling his energy replenish itself. A part of him realized he was breathing in the Way, its power suffusing him, and he marveled again at his new vision. He looked at Rai'stahn and said, "I saw it but didn't see its source. Perhaps the tower—"

"T'was not the Far'anthi, but an abomination birthed by Valarius. Fate offered the cruelest of hands, dealt by the Conclave, played by me. Now the world hangs in the balance."

Silbane knew immediately Rai'stahn meant Arek. He could suddenly feel his life and Arek's balancing on the keen edge of this conversation, the wrong word pushing one or both against the blade.

"Milord, I say again, the lore father sensed a gate may have opened. I am to use Arek to seal it..."

"If he touches the Gate, it will open. His power shall destroy the wards," Rai'stahn said.

"Arek disrupts magic—" Silbane began.

"Thine apprentice does not disrupt magic, he consumes it. Themun knows what we must do."

The words hit Silbane like a hammer. If Rai'stahn spoke the truth, the lore father sent them here to kill Arek, not to find the Gate. Silbane shook his head and asked, "Why show me Valarius, then? What does he have to do with Arek?"

Rai'stahn's golden gaze continued to stare at the tower and Arek. "What hath Valarius been told? The Aeris are Shaped by thee. They *are* the Way."

"But the gods—" Silbane started.

Rai'stahn held up his hand and closed his eyes. "Think. Use thy training. Valarius, who would not listen to the Conclave, reaches back from death and exacts retribution on this world, on me, even now."

"Arek is just a boy!"

"Do not be fooled by the skin," the dragon said. "It is born of something selfish, something unclean. I sought the lore father out, summoned by the passing of thy other hatchling. His death was unforeseen, but he was swallowed by the same blackness."

Piter. Silbane didn't know what to say. He took a step back, the dragon's words slowly sinking in. The master couldn't help but shake his head. "The lore father knew? He sent Arek here to be killed?"

The dragon-knight held up an armored hand and said, "Whilst we journeyed here, I hath felt myself weaken. Ask thyself, how much power hath he taken from me already? Too much perhaps, for us to accomplish what we wilt? He is dangerous. Heed me and thou wilt save this world."

His finger stabbed the ground with finality. "Help me end Valarius's final madness, and set right what my hand put in motion. Thine apprentice trusts thee. Do what Themun couldst not, what he desired I do for him. Now I giveth thee, his pater, to maketh his end quick and painless."

Silbane could only stare at the dragon's golden eyes. The vision hadn't shown what Valarius did with his Sight, but history said the Demon Wars were won and Lilyth's Gate closed. Valarius fell, and that was over two hundred years ago, yet Arek wasn't more than seventeen summers old. How could he be part of Valarius if they were separated by centuries?

Below Silbane's uncertainty ran an undertow of guilt. Had he not already submitted to Themun's mission, which, despite his best efforts, might just end up calling for the sacrifice of his apprentice? The Council had bargained Arek's life for the fate of the land. Rai'stahn argued for the same to save the world. If Arek's sacrifice achieved either or both, how were the two different? How was his Council any better than the Conclave of Dragons?

Still, Silbane had never really intended to sacrifice Arek, agreeing only to avoid giving his apprentice over to

Kisan. *I can keep Arek alive,* he said to himself. *Only I can do this.*

Silbane had dealt with dragons too long to let the turmoil in his soul reflect in his eyes. He stood his ground and stared at the dragon-knight until one word escaped his lips with obdurate strength.

"No."

Rai'stahn took a step forward and laid an armored hand on the monk's shoulder. "Dost thou think I suffer this burden so easily? What sacrifice dost thou deem acceptable measured against the good of the world?"

"You condemn a boy on a vision showing nothing but the madness of a dead man, a man I already know was the land's enemy." Silbane's head dropped and a small sigh escaped his lips as the burden of his decision began to sink into his heart. "How are we better than what we fight, if the price is the blood of our children?"

Silence reigned while Silbane looked over the majesty of the Wastes. Had he just condemned them both to death?

The dragon-knight said, "Even now, thine apprentice dreams of power, of dealing death. He is not as innocent as thou wouldst believe . . ." Rai'stahn's voice trailed off. At first he seemed rooted in place like a statue, but then he wheeled and started walking away from the tower, toward the deep desert.

Silbane looked up, confused for a moment. "You're leaving?" The thought of being stranded here held no real worry for the master himself. He'd traversed the land umpteen times, and knew his abilities would lend him the endurance to continue the mission or abort it and return to the Isle by mundane means. Arek was another story. The boy couldn't use the Way to replenish himself, and judging from their location, they were far from a town or even some of the secret caches he knew existed for use in an emergency.

The dragon-knight stopped, his gaze sweeping the dunes, still lit golden by the setting sun. With a deep breath he turned and said, "I am drained and cannot recover whilst in that thing's presence. Though there is not enough time for me to fully regain what hath been stolen, even a moment's respite will succor me greatly. Worry for this world, for I fear even I cannot end this *vampyrus* without thy help. I give thee until the full moon rises. Upon my return, I will ask thee one last time."

Rai'stahn prepared to leave, but then turned back to Silbane and said, "You asketh me what I'd done at the final battle. I waited for Valarius to stand victorious, and then I struck him a mighty blow, killing him where he stood. Alone, I felled the land's greatest hero while condemning his memory with fault for the land's undoing."

The dragon paused, his golden gaze catching the last of the setting sun in a flash of yellow and menace. "What dost thou think I will do now?"

Without waiting for a response, Rai'stahn leapt into the air and changed back into a dragon. His huge wings beat once, twice, as he gathered speed, arrowing off to the east.

Silbane stood stunned. When Rai'stahn returned at the full moon's rise, there was no doubt in Silbane's mind it would be to kill them both.

Dragon Vision

BLADE DREAMS

Mark the sun and the wind.
Feel the earth with your bare feet.
Be one with your surroundings.
Familiarity with the killing ground
is as important as training with your weapon,
or that ground will become your grave.
—*Tir Combat Academy, Basic Forms & Stances*

W hile Silbane and Rai'stahn walked off in discussion, Arek busied himself with setting up their camp. They didn't have much equipment, just some sleeping mats and food, and he moved it all to the lee of a partial wall which lay half crumbled at the base of the tower. This would shelter them from the night wind. *At least from two directions,* Arek thought with a wry smile.

Before setting up camp, he walked up to lean against the dead Far'anthi stone. He gazed at the great expanse of the Wastes, empty and desolate, so different from the blue water and green hills of the Isle. Perhaps that was what made this place so beautiful to him.

Arek wondered if a desert nomad had ever stood here, in this exact spot, staying the night before moving on to Bara'cor. Did he watch the golden light as it slowly crept across the ocean of sand, wondering if this would be his last setting sun before the next day's battle?

Arek picked up a handful of sand and let it sift through his fingers as he walked back down the hill. It trailed behind him, caught on the slight hot breeze, and fanned out like a horse's tail.

It struck him at how much sheer ingenuity and willpower it would take to survive in this environment. The Altan nomads were a hardy people, which made them pragmatic and deadly adversaries. Arek didn't envy those trapped behind Bara'cor's walls. Perhaps the nomad he dreamed of earlier only thought of the next day's victory and his share of the spoils. That would not be so hard to believe.

He set to work arranging their gear and building a fire pit from broken parts of the wall, putting a rock the size of his head in the center. When Silbane returned, he could open a path to the Way and heat the rock, providing them warmth tonight as the desert cooled.

Either Tomas or Jesyn could've heated the rock without waiting for their master. He buried that thought in the silent, deep place where he put all his frustrations.

His task completed, he sat with his back to the short wall, reaching for Tempest in the pack next to him. The sword almost leapt from its sheath as he drew her. A part of him was disappointed when nothing happened as he drew the fine blade. He laughed a little to himself then, the thought of some proclamation declaring he was Tempest's special wielder a bit too childlike a fantasy.

He marveled again at her beauty. This was truly a wondrous gift and it spoke to the respect the council had for him. He should not have let his self-absorption get the better of him in front of the lore father, his master, or acted so ungratefully in front of Adept Giridian. He resolved to apologize to the latter when he saw him again—if he saw him again.

The blade's polished metal flowed like water down its silvery length. Adept Giridian said Tempest was forged during the Demon Wars. Arek had little doubt it represented a level of magic never to be seen again in his lifetime.

In his gloved grasp the blade felt well-balanced, light, and quick, as Arek could tell after executing just a few halfhearted swings while seated.

What kind of warrior could he be, armed with Tempest? What mighty opponents could he defeat, if only for her?

Arek's pale blue eyes narrowed as he imagined twisting and cutting through opponents effortlessly, leaving a swathe of blood and death behind, the recognition in his opponent's gaze at his own impending death, and seeing the light go from those eyes.

Though the thoughts filled him with shame and revulsion, the part of him that strived to be the best blade in his class felt a sense of victory at the thought of pulling Tempest from the chest of a dead man. Then a thought crept in, a siren's call daring his courage.

What if you held me with your bare hands?

Despite his master's warning and Adept Giridian's cautionary admonishments against such an act, he still wondered.

What if your touch is special? it said again, a silent voice echoing his own desire.

Cautiously, and with furtive glances to see if his master had returned, Arek shook off a glove and brought his hand within inches of the sword's grip.

He held his breath, debating if this was worth possibly disenchanting the weapon, but doubting his power could permanently harm an artifact like Tempest.

What if I am your destiny all along? the voice asked, subduing his caution and making his heart race.

This weapon must be part of something greater—inexorably daring him to be more than he was.

With a slight exhale, he grasped the hilt. Nothing happened, and he started to laugh a little at himself. Then his world exploded in black.

The desert was gone, as if he floated in a sea of nothing, with no shape, no horizon in sight. Out of this blackness came a terrified woman's scream.

I erred! Release me! it cried.

"Who are you?" he asked into the void.

Do not touch me again with bare hands, and I shall repay you!

Arek looked about the blackness, searching, but could see nothing.

Again the scream, *Release me, I beg you!*

Slowly, he uncurled his fingers, and the blackness receded. A quick sensation of falling, then he felt sand beneath him and the rock wall at his back.

The sword still shone with its liquid silver intensity and the gem remained an emerald green. His touch hadn't disrupted it, but how was that possible? His elation turned to disappointment when he recalled the words he'd heard in his head: *Do not touch me . . .*

He hastily slipped his glove back on, sullen and disappointed. Whatever the blade was, it clearly wasn't for him. He looked at the emerald, sighing.

He raised his eyes and watched as the sun finished its fall from the western sky like a flaming shield, slowly melting onto the horizon. Taking a deep breath, he tightened his gloved grip on Tempest, its heft and balance feeling somehow natural and right, like a long lost extension of his arm. He settled back against the warm wall and allowed himself to doze, his mind running through dozens of blade-to-blade engagements.

Each victory brought a sudden smile of satisfaction to his lips, as foe after foe fell before him. Soon, his master would return and the real adventure would begin. Until then, Arek dreamed of blood and fire, where he was finally the one with power.

JOURNAL ENTRY 6

Finnow should've listened. Her obstinacy forced my hand. She celebrates as a virtue the single-minded opinion one only finds in the young and the ignorant. Seeing her fall was difficult, but inevitable. Still, I regret failing to teach her humility when she was younger. It would've saved her now. I will think about her no more, for I will have no guilt. It does not serve me well in this place.

I had discounted the dragonkind's vision, but now appreciate more of what they tried to impart. These points of light are the substance of everything. Could they be the unseen hands I felt, the touch of the Aeris? This is worth rewriting: they are what make everything. Therefore, I know what the dragons meant: we and the Aeris are somehow linked.

Because I know these things respond to me, I believe they are the basis of the Way. However, here their power is multiplied tenfold. They move and respond to my presence, yet they are invisible to normal sight.

If I can unlock this secret, I will be the most powerful mage in recorded history.

Journal Entry 6

FIVE DAYS LEFT . . .

Journal Entry 6

SOVEREIGN'S HAND

An arrow flies with deadly intent,
whether in combat or practice.
—*Tir Combat Academy, Basic Forms & Stances*

T hera guided her little pupils down the embankment, closer to a small stream. The sun was setting on the second day since Silbane's departure. By now, she mused, they must have just reached the Shornhelm Wastes. She wondered if they fared well, but no communication from the two had been received.

The time since Silbane left had gone slowly. An uncomfortable silence descended upon any gathering of the council, as if each dared to second-guess the lore father's choices—but not aloud. It was only in times like this, when she was alone with her class that Thera felt at peace.

Lissah, a promising young Whiterobe, reached down and picked up a small yellow flower with pale petals, raising it triumphantly. "I found it!"

Thera moved a bit closer and squatted in front of the little girl. "And what have you found?"

"Sunbeam." The girl's determined face and clear eyes bespoke a confidence that she knew exactly what she'd found and would brook no argument.

Thera laughed and said, "And sunbeam is good for . . . ?"

Lissah looked down as if searching for the answer, and then she looked back up at the adept. "Fevers . . . you boil the leaves in water, like tea."

Thera nodded, still smiling and said, "And it tastes good if you dry the petals and crush them into soup." She turned her gaze to the left side of the embankment, where the land opened to the beach. She couldn't see the waves in the distance, but could hear the dim sound as they broke on the shore. If she'd had the time, she would've made the trek with this group in tow, but the sun had already finished setting, and it would mean picking their way through the dark.

Dusting off her hands, she picked herself up and tousled Lissah's hair. It wasn't often she fell into these melancholy moods, but her recent confrontations with the lore father over sending Arek weighed heavily on her heart. At least, she thought, they should have further investigated his encounter with the apparition of Piter. She no longer thought of it as a fevered dream, and its portent worried her greatly.

She felt a small tug on her sleeve and saw Lissah pointing to the brush.

"Someone's in the bushes."

Before Thera could respond, she heard a number of soft *whuths* and felt a sharp prick on her arm and neck. Sprouting out of her arm was a sharp, silver needle, its tail end a clear glass vial filled with a dark liquid and surrounded by unfamiliar fletching.

It took her a moment to come to the realization that it was a dart of some kind, and somehow on this secluded isle, they were under attack.

Fast, dark forms separated from the evening shadows. At first, they looked like men, but they had wider torsos and thicker arms and legs than one would find on the men of Edyn. These figures were stronger, bigger, with the obduracy of the very granite beneath their feet.

The night was illuminated by Thera's flameskin, her form blazing yellow and powerful. "Who dares . . . ?"

But the attackers didn't even hesitate. Before Thera even finished her sentence, the little ones entrusted to her crumpled to the ground. Then she felt grass next to her face, her shield dissipating into the night like mist. A small choked sob clawed its way out of her as the poison went to work and her muscles tightened, then locked.

One of the black shapes moved across her field of view to check the child who lay closest. She thought it might be Lissah. The figure leaned in and then made a quick stabbing motion, pulling something long and thin from the crumpled form. Then it moved over to her.

It wore a mask, the protective lenses glowing a soft, ethereal blue.

"No survivors," it whispered, and she felt a punch in her chest and an ice-cold shaft of steel slide between her ribs and into her heart. It twisted once then pulled out. At first, she felt fine. Then a warm gush of wetness soaked the ground below her. Her sight went dim, then slowly black.

* * * * *

Kisan and Tomas were at the observatory taking readings of the night sky. The injuries Tomas had sustained from his encounter with Piter's moonskin had almost faded, leaving behind only a general weakness and malaise. Kisan's attention remained on her direhawk, roosting nearby.

The giant bird's black feathers changed to a bright crimson on each trailing edge of its wings and tail. A similar marking ran from deep black at the beak to a crest of crimson. The hawk watched a bag Kisan held in her hand, intent on what squirmed inside.

She expertly flipped the bag over and slammed it into the stones. She reached in and withdrew a limp rabbit, either unconscious or dead.

The direhawk hadn't taken its gaze off its meal and when Kisan tossed the jack into the air, the raptor caught it deftly in its sharp beak. The direhawk made short work of it, swallowing, then cocking its head and looking to its master for more.

Kisan ignored the bird. She took some solace in the face that Tomas didn't remember anything except arriving at dinner. A part of her didn't want to know the truth, fearing perhaps that Piter's actions may have precipitated things. Still, she was thankful Tomas hadn't been more severely injured.

There was a hole in her, a black space Piter used to fill. It felt like a betrayal to her first apprentice's memory to be teaching Tomas. She reached up and ruffled the direhawk's proud crimson crest, unafraid of the lethal beak and talons that curved around the roost nearby.

Oh, she knew the lore father had been correct in assigning her a new apprentice. In a clinical sense, this was the best way to cope with loss, by occupying her time with someone who needed it. But Kisan didn't want her time occupied and didn't want to be "handled" by the lore father. She'd had quite enough of that lately.

She looked at her new charge, Tomas, who clearly found it hard to stand near so dangerous a predator despite her reassurance it was quite safe. She had raised and cared for over a dozen lethal warbirds like this direhawk, yet the boy still edged away.

"Does your hawk have a name?" Tomas inquired.

"I don't name my weapons," she replied in a monotone, looking back at the dark-winged predator.

"Three ways to kill from behind?" she asked flatly.

Tomas's mouth quirked up, his master's preoccupation with the darker side of their arts no secret, but didn't hesitate to clarify. "Armed or unarmed?"

"Fastest."

"Wind strike, base of skull; short blade, point thrust down between the neck and shoulder; blade thrust, forty-five degrees up into skull from base of neck." He was quiet for a moment then added, "The blade would have to be thin enough to cut the artery below the collarbone for the downward point thrust."

Kisan was quiet, still looking at her direhawk. Its head tilted to one side, those eyes unblinking.

"Adequate." The word came out but without any life. She wasn't even sure she could recall the boy's answer.

Apparently in an effort to lighten the mood Tomas changed subjects and said, "Funny, but there was a time people thought the stars marked one's faith in the gods."

Kisan was startled out of her reverie and looked at Tomas in askance, as if seeing him for the first time. "What?"

Tomas gestured at the sky with his chin, "The stars, Master . . . gods who guide our destiny. I find that amusing." His eyes sparkled with mirth and in another time or place it would've been infectious. At the moment, though, it only served to irritate her.

Tomas continued, clearly oblivious of Kisan's mood, "Take me, for instance. I was born in the summer under the stars of Kanus, the Dread Wolf . . . or at least that's when my birthday is celebrated." Tomas smiled. "So, I guess I'll need to learn how to tame wolves the way you do birds," he said, gesturing carefully at the direhawk.

Kisan snorted. "Yes. People are a stupid, superstitious lot." She petted her hawk again, then leaned her head against its breast and closed her eyes, feeling the warmth of its feathers envelope her.

"What about you, Master? What god rules your destiny?"

Tomas was so unlike Piter, who had been consumed with memorizing everything Kisan said or did. She felt herself responding to the gregarious nature of her new ward and answered, "Dyana the Huntress, believe it or not," she scoffed. Then she added in voice tinged with chagrin, "I was short with you, and perhaps not as forthcoming as I might have been."

Tomas smiled and offered, "I didn't mean to presume."

The master held up a hand and said, "I didn't lie, about naming my weapons. However—" she paused, looking at her direhawk "—he names himself 'Temairex.'"

Tomas smiled, and when he did Temairex speared him with an unblinking stare, as if noticing he was there for the first time. Kisan watched with a small smile as her new apprentice walked in a wide semicircle to stand behind another roosting pole. "R-really? It sounds quite . . . noble."

Kisan nodded. "It is, and perhaps—" then her eyes widened and she stopped in midsentence. At the same time, Temairex flapped his wings, sending a whirlwind of air across their small open space. He might have already taken flight if not for the harness holding his leg to his tree trunk-sized roost. Kisan calmed him with a touch, her mind racing.

Something's seriously wrong. Even Temairex, whose senses were not as acute as hers, knew it. The tenuous link amongst all the adepts on the Isle, normally so constant it was largely ignored, had been severed. She could sense Giridian in his chambers, and Dragor training. Thera . . . that link was no longer there. Only one thing could break it.

"Pit—Tomas, get inside. Now!"

She'd almost called him "Piter," but the boy understood her tone. Without checking to see if he obeyed, Kisan sped to the edge of the observatory and looked down, straining to survey the monastery's grounds despite the darkness.

Her first thought was to mindspeak to the other adepts, but she cautioned herself to wait. The attacker or attackers may be able to pick up on that sort of communication, and could locate Kisan—perhaps everyone—if she tried. By now the loss of Thera's link would've alerted every adept on the Isle. She focused instead on finding out whom and where the enemy was. They were about to face a true Master of the Way.

* * * * *

Kisan leapt from the parapet and dove like a falcon. Using *Winds of the Sky*, she touched the citadel as she rushed by, slowing her fall. Just before she reached the ground her legs snapped out, the balls of her feet kicking the rough stone wall.

In an instant, her downward velocity transformed into a rotation and Kisan used that momentum to flip herself, arcing gracefully over and out from the wall. She landed lightly, crouched in the darkness. Calling upon *Clear the Sky*, she sank low to the ground and expanded her senses: sight, hearing, smell, and touch.

To get close enough to kill Thera, the attacker must have known much about the Isle and the people living here. She would be foolish to assume they were any less trained or capable than she was.

Kisan quickly invoked another technique: the air next to her began to darken as it separated into two distinct clouds. They sucked in the surrounding air as they sparkled and coalesced. Where Kisan crouched, two duplicates of her now mirrored her stance. The *Blood of Life* technique was physically draining, but she needed it now more than ever.

"I speak, you obey," she said to them.

They nodded and said, "Yes, Master." Their voices, exactly like her own, sounded eerie in the night air. Though they were not alive and could only follow simple verbal commands, they were better than normal mirror images. She could create dozens of those, but they lacked substance and could only follow a single order. These were more complex and served two critical needs.

The most obvious was as decoys . . . but because of the increased power spent in making them, Kisan could also use their senses as her own, even control them to some degree. As scouts, they would serve to provide her with tactical information that couldn't be overheard or tracked back to her. Should they be discovered and attacked, they would even die, feeling solid and real.

"We will make our way behind the Hall of Adepts."

"Yes, Master," the doppelgangers whispered.

Kisan looked around. She'd purposely fallen into a shadowed area that was almost pitch black. Her line of sight to the front of the hall was obscured by the building itself. Nevertheless, she'd no doubt the attackers were just around the corner, waiting. Given the circumstances, it was exactly what she would've done.

She looked to the duplicate on her right and said, "Walk to the front of this building. Don't stop for anyone."

The doppelganger nodded, then stood and started walking around the circular hall. Kisan motioned to the other to follow her and they started circling the other direction. Her mind opened a path to the Way, and whatever the first doppelganger saw became clear. She then moved to the first defensible position she could find, one that had a clear view of the courtyard in front of the hall, but where someone hiding in that area couldn't see her.

Through her simulacrum's eyes, she saw the front of the building. At first, nothing seemed amiss, and there were no obvious signs of attack. Perhaps she'd been wrong. Then she saw that the front door stood ajar. That would never happen . . .

Before she could do anything, she heard through the doppelganger's ears the sound of something firing with whispers of air. Her double had almost no battle skills, so it was pointless to try to evade. Rather, Kisan concentrated on the doppelganger's response.

She felt two pinpricks on her own skin. Darts. The grouping was tight, no more than a hand span, and centered on her throat. Within a heartbeat, she felt a numbing paralysis in the doppelganger's body. If those darts had hit her, she would've been helpless.

She mentally forced her double to fall facing the door with its eyes open. It collapsed in a heap and turned its head exactly the way she wanted. Now Kisan could watch what happened next.

At first, nothing stirred the night. Neither movement nor sound broke the silence. They were waiting for the poison to take effect. Even as she came to this conclusion, two shadows detached themselves from the dark recesses of the doors. They moved quickly, their wide forms blurring with magic.

Kisan was shocked at their speed and their ability to use the Way. She studied them as one punched a dagger into the base of the skull and the other searched the body. They worked with the practiced efficiency of highly trained thieves. Both finished their gruesome tasks in silence. Then they quickly dragged the body out of sight and resumed their stations, melting back into the darkness.

Kisan's resolve hardened. She now knew two things. First, death would've been her fate had she rounded that corner without a plan. Second, no parley had been offered, no terms. Her enemies' objective was to kill.

She wasn't worried that the ease with which they dispatched her doppelganger would arouse their suspicion. Given the right circumstances, anyone could be killed by surprise, even a master.

Kisan smiled. She was no longer surprised. Nothing these assassins did would save them now.

* * * * *

Dragor finished the end of his kata with a fast spin kick, his mind and body one. His breathing came easy, exhaling on time with each point of impact while he continued his practice movements. The point of kata was to allow him to train his body and mind for that perfect strike, against a perfect opponent.

He knew that in reality, there was no such thing . . . but fighting against his own mind helped him learn what strikes should look like when unencumbered by the clash and din of battle. His body remaining loose until the point of impact, then tightening with the strength of steel to focus all the power into one small area, the perfect execution of *Gentle Palm of the Moon*. It was this point, this focus, which caused a freezing effect in addition to damage.

He spun, ducking under one imaginary opponent then striking with his open palm at another. It was times like this when he could practice alone that he felt most connected to the Way. It flowed through him like his breathing, connecting him at once to all that was around him.

When the link to Thera vanished, he stumbled, his breath catching. Without a thought, he summoned moonskin. His form flashed a sublime purple once, as it hardened for defense, then became invisible to the naked eye. He then moved up the walkway leading from his training area to the outer hall.

Whatever was happening, he reasoned, must be near where he last felt Thera, to the north of the school. He meant to head in that direction and see if he could find out anything more. Slowly, he continued his way up and to the outer halls. As he moved, his form wavered, then vanished like smoke, one of the advantages a Moon technique had over those with an affinity to the Sun. No reason to let whatever-it-was see him coming.

* * * * *

Kisan knew where the enemies were, but she needed a better distraction. She concentrated, reaching for the Way. The form of her doppelganger morphed, becoming younger, leaner. In moments, an exact copy of Piter crouched next to her, ready to do her bidding.

The effort cost her. It was one thing to create a duplicate of oneself. To create a full duplicate of another took immense concentration and an intimate familiarity with the subject. *Piter,* she thought sadly, *you are the one I remember best. I need you to serve one last purpose tonight.*

She looked past the curve where the two assassins lay hidden, out of her line of sight. "On my command, you will run past the entrance. You will stop for nothing."

The Piter look-alike nodded, and then turned to stare straight ahead. As Kisan watched her creation, her sense of loss threatened to overcome her composure. It was unfair her boy didn't get the chance the others did. The thought crawled in like worms through mud. Then she willed herself to , crush the sentiment. She would only get one chance at this.

Kisan enhanced her technique to include heat and silenced the sounds of her footfalls and clothes.

"Run!" she whispered, and her doppelganger shot away like an arrow.

Kisan followed, keeping her form hidden within the low grass. As her simulacrum rounded the corner and continued its sprint, she heard the sound of at least two darts fire at its retreating back. They were close, but their attention was on the fleeing "boy."

Kisan knew they would have to make a choice. Sure enough, like a black streak, one of the assassins sped after the fleeing image of Piter.

She sped silently up and over the stone entryway's banister. Her enhanced vision easily picked out the remaining man, who only now sensed his peril. Before he could offer any defense, Kisan struck his sternum with *Gentle Palm of the Sky*, her hand vibrating in tune with the man's bones.

A silent detonation occurred within the assassin's body as Kisan's focused strike shattered every bone in a circular pattern from the center of the man's chest outward. His lungs liquefied and he convulsed as he vomited out a gout of black liquid and bone into the grass. The force of the blow knocked his body backward against the hard stone wall with a solid, wet smack, before he rebounded forward and fell into her waiting arms.

His weight surprised Kisan the most, for it was at least three times what a normal person would've been. It took all her enhanced strength not to stumble under the sudden burden. She steadied herself, quickly pulling the dying man into the side bushes for cover. She ripped the face cover off to look at the person beneath.

The face was square, younger than expected—a boy with blond hair and peach whiskers now speckled with his life's blood. A whispered gasp escaped his lips and his eyes focused on his killer.

Kisan concentrated a technique from her Sky affinity as she touched the man's forehead. Names and images flooded her mind. A stone fortress set deep in the Dawnlight Mountains. A black sun surrounded by blue fire, standing like an open maw. A small calico cat, mewling piteously. A dark cavern with hundreds of glass caskets filled with men like him.

The flood of this boy's life gushed from his mind into Kisan's like water bursting from a cut sack, before slowing to a trickle until finally . . . nothing. The memories had transferred and the Eye of the Sky was complete. She would not be able to read much more from anyone else until these memories were purged. Still, she needed information—and one more thing.

She leaned back, looking at her handiwork, noticing the details. Small beginnings of a beard framed the boy's face, and the eyes were pale blue, no longer glowing and still wide in the shock of death. Even as she watched, those pale blue irises were eaten up by the widening black of his pupils. His skin was tan, with a scar on his left cheek, a quick slash that spoke of a misstep against a sharp blade.

Kisan drank in the features, focusing, memorizing. She looked at the mask, the gloves, and the uniform. She inspected the shoes, the belt. She ran her hands over the man's body, feeling the strength and size of his limbs.

She'd already spent a tremendous amount of energy tonight in creating her doppelgangers and sifting through the assassin's mind, but this one last technique had to be perfect.

She looked inward, diving deep into the Way, and called upon the little power she'd left to weave a lifeskin. She refocused and shaped it to her needs. A sparkle consumed her form, a quick flash of ethereal starlight vanishing before it even seemed to take substance. Then Kisan stood and moved back up to the entranceway.

As she did so, her form blurred and changed, becoming stronger, thicker, and taller. In moments, a dark-clothed assassin took watch, with features identical to the boy who lay hidden and dead.

Tamlin, the thought came to her. *My name is Tamlin.* With time, more of her victim's knowledge would become available as the technique assimilated the dead boy's memories.

Kisan, now Tamlin, scanned the direction the other assassin had run, watching with eyes glowing the same soft, deadly blue. The time for a reckoning would soon be at hand.

* * * * *

Dragor took a deep breath of the night air. He sensed someone tapping into the Way not far from him, and by its feel, he knew it was Kisan.

The fact that no other adept had broken mental silence demanded caution. Anyone who could silence Thera could potentially tap the Way themselves. Furthermore, he couldn't afford to deplete his energy before he knew what they faced.

He walked from the training hall to the main courtyard, staying away from the lamps that adorned the brightly lit central area, flitting from shadow to shadow. Regardless of his cloak of invisibility, Dragor was taking no chances.

As he neared the Hall of Adepts, he stopped, motionless. Ahead was the point where he'd sensed Kisan. Though the flash of power was gone, the residue lingered like a scent. He crept to the wall, taking advantage of the terrain and shadows.

They were under attack. That was a certainty. A mistake now would be deadly. He moved around the wall until he could see the front entrance, then crouched and waited.

At first, nothing happened. His skin crawled in the cool night air as if at any moment lightning would strike and the battle would be joined.

Then a single black streak came from the woods to one side of the Hall of Adepts, joining up with another crouching on the stairs, motionless as he was. Those two were soon joined by four more emerging from inside the hall like living shadows. That made six against one. As that thought flitted through his mind he felt a sudden change, like a shifting breeze that brought a sudden chill. Dragor knew his cloak of invisibility didn't hide him any longer. He'd been seen.

He didn't hesitate, dropping it to conserve energy. Then he stepped out from the wall, his form lined in power, his moonskin flashing purple as it flared into existence at his command.

He could see all six fan out to take positions around him and nodded in satisfaction. This would be no training kata. This was real and his life would balance on the keen, deadly edge of his Talent against theirs. He took a deep breath and cleared his mind. He was ready.

The breeze shifted, bringing with it the scent of jasmine. . . and they attacked.

CONFLICT

> *Do not negotiate from a weak position.*
> *Victors never grant reprieve unless threatened.*
> *Be overly aggressive,*
> *dominate to within an inch of their life,*
> *then offer a morsel of hope.*
> —*Tir Combat Academy, The Tactics of Victory*

A rek! Get up!" Silbane's urgent voice scattered the remnants of Arek's dream. "We don't have much time."

His master stood next to one of the rocky outcropping of the desolate Far'anthi ruins, whose towers now reminded Arek of stone fingers rising from the sands to clutch at the sky, like dead sentinels of a forgotten age. It was then that he noticed the stars shining in an almost ink black sky. How long had he been asleep? He looked around, then asked, "Where's Rai'stahn?"

"Gone for the better part of the afternoon. While you slept, I've been trying to figure out how best to make amends for our situation, and keep us both alive." The master looked at him with a strange expression in his eyes. It was then that Arek noticed the blood mark on his forehead. The wound had scabbed over, but Arek knew it hadn't been there when they'd landed.

He was about to comment when Silbane grabbed him by his shoulders and said, "We don't have much time, but I wanted you rested. Now we must act. The dragon will return shortly, at the moon's rise."

"Yes, Master." Arek picked up Tempest, scanning the area. Master Silbane stood looking over his shoulder, as if expecting something to appear behind them, which was silly. They were in the middle of the desert. Nothing could surprise them from their vantage point near the tower. When he looked back at Arek, the boy saw something he'd never seen before—fear in his master's eyes.

"What is it?"

Silbane looked at his apprentice as though not sure where to begin. "We are no longer safe. Rai'stahn is returning sooner than I expected."

"What happened?"

"Nothing good." Silbane turned to him and said, "Pay attention and follow my instructions!"

Arek nodded, his eyes wide. A cold knot coiled in his belly and his palms became clammy.

But as his master began to speak, Arek's vision tunneled and the scene froze in front of him. He looked around, but everything had stopped, even the wind was silent. His master stood in front of him still in mid-word, like a statue. The air was cloudy and Arek realized it was all the fine particles of sand, their motion frozen in place, which now made them visible.

"You'll want to hear what your master has to say."

Arek turned to see Piter casually walk out of thin air. Along with him came that feeling of malevolence, a barely contained hatred directed at him.

"Piter! What's happening?"

"You know the dragon means to kill you."

Arek closed his eyes, willing this nightfright to end. When he opened them, however, Piter was still there and nothing had changed. Arek stammered out the first thing that came to his mind. "Wh-what do you mean?"

Arek found his fear fading faster than it had during the first encounter with the shade. It was as if he'd grown more accustomed to Piter's presence. His voice came out stronger as he answered the shade's accusation. "I don't believe you. If he wanted to kill us, he wouldn't be flying us to Bara'cor."

"You believe that?" the shade looked out over the moonlit night. He was listening for something, something

Arek couldn't hear. His gaze turned back upon his former classmate and in that moment, Arek felt his soul bared to Piter. "Yes! You must go to Bara'cor." The statement surprised Arek, who hadn't yet seen the shade be anything but insulting to him.

"Bara'cor?" he asked. He could feel something pulling at him now, like a harmonious note that echoed just below his hearing. It spoke of power, of strength, of destiny.

At first he thought it linked to the blade, Tempest. That hope had been quickly dashed during his failed experiment touching the blade. However, the feeling of destiny, of his importance, grew deeper and more intrinsic to this place. Perhaps as they neared Bara'cor itself?

He wanted to believe it, but his master felt danger here, and he trusted that, too. Master Silbane was the closest thing he had to a father.

Arek shook his head. "I won't listen to you." But it came out with less conviction than he wanted. He knew the masters were not telling him the whole truth. Now this shade was picking apart the fragile truce he'd created within his own mind.

"He will sacrifice you for the good of this world," Piter said. "I'm cursed as a lackey to a dimwitted fool."

What could Arek do? He felt guilt, even remorse for Piter's death. Now it seemed that either Piter's soul was trapped in this world, or Arek was slowly going mad. Perhaps that was it. Was he losing his mind?

Then another part of him, the part that strove to be best, the part that fought to gain respect despite his inability with the Way, caught something he almost missed . . . lackey.

It made sense now. Piter had made a mistake. A tiny mistake, but still a mistake. A small smile escaped Arek's lips, his confidence returning as he unraveled the specter's web of lies. His thoughts sharpened and as they did, he noticed a caution— trepidation on the ghost's part, as if Piter were facing his own . . . master.

Conflict

"You belong to me," Arek said. His voice was strong, for he knew it was true. This shade, for all its malevolence, had no power over him. It was quite the opposite. His dreams of power suddenly came back to him, the feeling of twisting the blade and killing his opponent. This was the same. This creature's mockery and anger were designed to make Arek frightened. No longer!

"What do you think—?"

"Silence!" Arek stepped forward. "You will answer me."

Piter's shade looked sidelong, a smirk still on his face, and slowly the ghost knelt. "That didn't take very long . . . "

Arek ignored him, looking about. "What's happening right now? Has time actually stopped?"

Piter's demeanor changed, becoming more forthright. "No. We stand within the blink of an eye. When it ends, you will be right where we first started." A sly grin appeared on Piter's face and he added, "Of course, I'll still be dead."

"I don't remember killing you, Piter. I don't even know if you're telling the truth about any of this."

"I made this up? Then I appear to you in the desert? How stupid are you?"

Arek sat down in the sand, trying to piece together what to do. His logical mind took over where his conscious thoughts had given up. "You said earlier the dragon means to kill me . . . why?"

Piter's shade hadn't moved, but somehow he seemed more subservient. "Let me prove my worth. I will tell you a truth only your masters know." The shade looked at Arek conspiratorially and said, "You have a great destiny ahead. You can feel it. The dragon sees a lie, he sees an end, but he is wrong. He does not see truth, and believes the lie."

"What is my master's mission?" Arek asked again, his patience wearing thin with the roundabout way the shade answered.

The shade smiled. It seemed to relish having this information. Slowly, like a snake unwinding, Piter whispered, "Sacrifice."

Arek stood up, shocked.

"What do you mean?"

"They would need someone—" the shade smiled "—whose touch disrupts magic." Piter stood and paced around the apprentice, his arms folded within his dark uniform.

"Ask yourself, what happens to this person when a dimensional gate implodes next to them?"

Then, with perfect clarity, Master Silbane's words came to mind. *Your Talent to disrupt magic makes you important for this mission. I wish it were different, but you and I are the best choice to go.*

Arek shook his head and said weakly, "I don't believe you."

"How will your master protect you and accomplish what he must?" Piter smiled and shrugged, then whispered, "You are expendable."

Arek thought about it, slowly nodding, the shade's information filling the gaps, fitting things into place. Would the lore father hesitate to use Arek's power to safeguard the land? Would he balance the world's need against Arek's life?

He remembered Adept Giridian's gift of Tempest, and realized it wasn't worry or disappointment he'd seen in everyone's eyes, it was shame. A cold anger settled into place at being used by those he trusted.

Piter leaned in and said, "It matters not. What matters now is that you listen to your master's tale." The shade smiled again. "There is real danger coming. If you hesitate, you will die, and that means my end as well." His smile became colored by hate, "Believe me, it's the worst kind of irony that I must preserve you."

"What do I do?" Arek asked. A sudden chill ran through him, a cold feeling that spread out from the pit of his stomach. Where it went, a mindless worry began to grow.

Piter looked sidelong at Arek and whispered, "You must flee to Bara'cor. It is our only hope."

The reality of the danger he faced suddenly hit him. He couldn't face a dragon and live, not even with Tempest and his master. Escaping from certain death to Bara'cor, where perhaps a greater destiny lay, was the only logical option.

Before Piter could leave, he blurted, "How?"

Piter replied, "Strike the Far'anthi with a stone. It must shatter, and when it does, the stone will glow blue." He paused, and then fixed his gaze on Arek. "It's very important you go through first. Your master must come second, so he may close the portal."

Piter's form started to fade, and Arek felt his vision begin to tunnel again. For an instant, he thought he heard the shade laugh, and then he once again stood facing his master.

"—I'm going to try to activate the Far'anthi Stone. Once I do, we take our provisions and send you to the Isle."

Arek looked around, confused. His master stood in front of him, speaking. Of Piter, there was no sign.

"Pay attention, apprentice! Your life rests in the balance!" the monk said.

Startled, Arek looked back at his master. "Home?" The fear still ran through him, making his master's words difficult to understand.

"Yes, apprentice. You are going home. Do not talk to anyone upon your return. Wait for me, stay out of sight, and trust no one." He met his apprentice's eyes, to emphasize one last point. "If we don't meet within a day, gather supplies and leave the Isle."

"How will you get there?" Arek asked.

Silbane turned and grasped his young apprentice by both shoulders, but not unkindly. "Remember, I have Themun's Finder. Use your knowledge of the Isle and stay hidden. I'll come for you after I finish this mission."

"What mission?"

"Arek, please, there's little time. The council made a mistake in sending you. You know our mission is to investigate Bara'cor. Before I do that, I would see you returned to a place safer than here."

Arek watched, unable to reconcile what he'd just heard from Piter with his master's actions now. Someone was lying—or Silbane had changed his mind.

Without another word, Silbane moved past Arek and made his way to the Far'anthi Stone. It sat dull and lifeless, a gray sphere of rock and granite. He motioned to Arek to gather his things.

Arek quickly packed and secured Tempest on his back. He then joined his master at the small tower's base. He wanted to tell Silbane of Piter's appearance, but something made him stop.

Silbane closed his eyes and held a hand over the Far'anthi Stone. Though Arek had never seen one activated before, the principle of the Way was the same: focus one's intention, using techniques. Like reaching for a falling object, intention bred action and stopped the object's fall.

Now Arek watched as Silbane reached for the Way, focusing his attention and stance on the stone that could open the portal. His master's form flashed, outlined in yellow fire, concentrating itself on his hands. A moment passed, then two, and then Silbane struck in a detonation of yellow flame.

Nothing happened, no sound, no outward indication that his master's strike had accomplished anything—the stone looked as dull gray and lifeless as ever. Arek wasn't sure what to do, but knew it was imperative he tell his master about the shade. He stepped closer and said, "Master, Piter appeared again." He nervously bit his lips, the fear in him growing.

Silbane whirled to face his apprentice, stunned. "What?" He looked around, afraid. "What did he say?"

"He told me a rock would speak to a rock . . . I think he meant for me to strike the Far'anthi with a rock."

Silbane didn't say anything, a dumbfounded look on his face, so Arek continued, "He also said the dragon would try to kill me, and that you . . . that I would be used to close the Gate."

Arek didn't know what else to say. He felt guilty saying anything at all but then saw the look on his master's face, like Adept Giridian's when he handed over Tempest. He suddenly knew what Piter told him was true.

"You planned this?" Arek whispered.

"My boy," his master's voice fell, leaden with regret, "I never saw eye to eye with Themun's decision, and would never let you come to harm. Now, it's clear you must return to the Isle without me."

Arek met his master's eyes, witnessing the truth behind the shade's words, and his heart began to harden.

Silbane spun, his face to the sky. "Get behind me and don't move!"

Arek scrambled over and drew Tempest with a gloved hand, then stood between his master and the Far'anthi Stone. "I can fight with you!" Despite or maybe because of the shade's words, he would no longer put himself at the mercy of others' actions. If anyone were planning his demise, he wouldn't let himself be led to his death like a lamb. They'd be facing him on his feet, blade in hand.

"You're not ready to face a dragon," Silbane warned him. "Stay back!"

Arek shook his head. "I can help!"

The great dragon appeared, a wing-shaped speck that quickly grew larger. Anything either Arek or Silbane might have said was forgotten.

JOURNAL ENTRY 7

It is clear now I never understood Thoth. He spoke of tiny motes, infinitesimal particles, and other fanciful things. I now know it is a fact these particles exist, but they are not Aeris. They are the substance upon which Aeris are made.

What of us? Are we made of these things? I do not know, but our will seems to Shape them into purpose. In that manner, we are the impetus upon which these Aeris Lords gain substance.

However, it is more than that. We bring them into being, incoherent at first, wisplike. They are like wishes or feelings, trapped on the psychic wind between worlds. They surround us at all times, ready to be shaped by our will.

Ritual, myth, ceremony, sacrifice, these seem to give them purpose, life. I walk in a world filled with the promise of the mythology of my people and the legends of all who ever lived.

It is a dangerous place, for I walk amongst titans, and as I've learned with Finnow it seems, sometimes even ghosts.

Journal Entry 7

A FINAL ILLUSION

*When facing multiple opponents,
engage each briefly and move to the next,
or it will become you against many,
instead of you fighting many single foes.
It is vital to understand the difference.
—Tir Combat Academy, The Tactics of Victory*

D ragor moved to his right and felt the strike pass inches from his head. He ducked low, tumbling effortlessly in a circle as kicks and punches flew around him, striking the empty air where he'd just been, or flashing harmlessly off his moonskin in bursts of amethyst light. He blocked a strike to his midsection, his hand stinging as if he struck stone and moved into the attacker, preparing to inflict a shattering strike that would pierce armor and cripple the body beneath.

However, the team he faced moved in unison, keeping him off balance so none faced the full brunt of his attack alone. For every strike, he had to deal with multiple targets.

As his latest strike was interrupted by another, he came to the sickening realization they would eventually win. Each had to expend less effort to engage him and eventually he would make a mistake. It was only a matter of time, and they knew it.

Still, they didn't act in perfect unison. One of them moved out of synchronization with the others. His speed and skill were not in doubt, but he moved like a professional just learning his part, a fraction of a heartbeat behind the rest. Dragor worked himself carefully toward that man, the weak link, feinting a kick high and then spinning around in a stronger counter strike.

Now! He aimed three strikes in rapid succession to the men to either side of the man who was out of step. And he struck them again with full force as they were recovering. His opponent reacted as he should, moving into the strike and meeting it early rather than at the end where Dragor's power would be greatest. Their hands met in strike and block, like thunder and lightning, and Dragor's moonskin flashed purple in response.

Kisan! The shock of realization hit him and he fell back, stunned. The assassin he was facing was Kisan disguised as one of them! His body went into defending himself almost automatically. Without realizing it, he began to move back to the wall, his mind racing to understand what was happening.

Kisan's strikes and blocks to Dragor were not aimed to cripple or damage. None of the others could see the difference, but Dragor knew Kisan's skill.

She must have disposed of one of these men and now sought to infiltrate them. To do that would take almost all of her power. She would need help, without giving away her disguise.

Dragor spun in a circle and struck one of the six with a glancing blow using the outside of his wrist. Following that motion, he trapped that man's arm and pushed him into another. This opened a hole through which Kisan would have to come.

Sure enough, the master vaulted through like a black snake, striking with clawed hands to Dragor's chest.

For Dragor's part, he let Kisan's strike through his protective aura, and then pushed power through the physical contact created using the technique, *Breath of Life*. Energy suffused the depleted master, and Dragor could almost hear her sigh of relief.

It was but a heartbeat between contact and the counterstrike to break it, but it was enough. Dragor had given Kisan all the power he had remaining, enough to replenish her until she could regenerate on her own.

But there would be consequences. Dragor now had nothing to draw upon, his reserves nearly gone. His moonskin guttered then failed, its purple flames dissipating into the night air, no longer able to tap his depleted stores enough to protect him.

His training took hold and he continued to block and dodge the blows, but the end was coming more quickly. As if sensing it, the group pulled back, pausing as Dragor slumped against the stone wall at his back, his chest heaving.

* * * * *

Kisan pulled back with the others, following their lead. Her mind was racing, trying to find a way for Dragor to live without revealing herself, but nothing came to mind. She knew in the larger scheme, finding out who sent these assassins was more important, but that meant Dragor would have to die.

"You've fought well," the leader said. "Don't resist and I'll make your end quick."

"Just getting . . . warmed up," said the dark-skinned adept between huge gulps of air Kisan knew were not feigned. She could feel his fatigue through the lingering residue of their connection.

"Indeed?" The leader looked to his left and nodded, but his hands quickly signaling a coded message to everyone. Kisan had no idea what that signal meant.

"Let's try again," the adept challenged.

The leader shook his head, giving the signal just as Dragor repeated, "Let's try again," and lurched forward in a clumsy, exhausted attack. Four darts suddenly sprouted from Dragor's chest, their impact soundless.

His body convulsed once, turning his attack into a spasm. His eyes rolled up to show whites and he bit through his tongue. As with the others, he fell to the ground, nerve toxin racing through his convulsing body, bringing with it tortured spasms and death.

The team watched this impassively, and then one of them moved forward and punched a cross-shaped dagger into the base of Dragor's skull, severing the spine. He yanked the dagger out, while another inspected the body. Satisfied he was dead, they moved back.

The leader spun and kicked Tamlin in the chest, knocking him to the ground in a *whuff* of exhaled breath. "Explain," he said his voice curt and demanding.

Kisan let the kick hit, barely feeling it, while she fought to assimilate Tamlin's memories. It was happening, but too slowly. She raised her eyes and came face to face with Dragor's dead gaze. He'd saved her life at the cost of his own, and Kisan would not let that sacrifice be in vain.

She stood up slowly, shaking her head, hoping the leader would not choose now to review their combat protocol. They were still in enemy territory and it would be more prudent to make their exfiltration.

Kisan was right. The leader cursed in disgust, but motioned for them to gather. "We'll deal with this on the ship," he whispered.

He stared a moment longer, then said, "Our first objective is achieved. Themun Dreys is dead."

Another assassin stepped forward and reported, "All the young ones are dead as well."

The leader confirmed, "Did you count? None must survive—they dream more vividly than their elders."

The reporting assassin nodded, "All are dead. I did the count myself."

"They'd better be, or we're all getting reslumbered." He motioned to the group, "Move out."

Then he and the team took off at a sprint a normal man would've found impossible to follow. Kisan followed automatically, her brain unable to fully assimilate the news. All dead, and the lore father too? She had no way to confirm it, given her depleted energy. The *Breath of Life* that Dragor had gifted her was all she had to maintain her illusion of being one of them. She found it hard to believe that all were dead, but nonetheless doubt wormed its way in when she remembered their skill in facing Dragor. She could feel her anger growing, threatening her composure. They wouldn't get away with this.

They ran through the woods heading directly for the northern beaches, their pace easy for her to match. Every moment that went by gave her more memories from Tamlin, more information about these men and their mission, and more reasons to kill them all.

* * * * *

Silence fell around Dragor's dead form. A light breeze blew, yet nothing stirred behind the fleeing forms. Then, as the assassins disappeared into the night, the very air rippled like the surface of a pond and the scene shifted. From the ripple stepped Giridian, who motioned and said, "They're gone, Lore Father.

Behind him came Themun, his staff glowing blue, along with Dragor and the students, servants, and teachers of the Isle, a courtyard full of people who had been "killed." Themun staggered forward as the illusion finally ended. Giridian and Dragor caught him and lowered him gently to the ground.

The lore father's skin was cold under Giridian's gentle touch, and almost parchment white. Themun's runestaff dimmed and dissolved, flowing into the air and ground like black smoke.

"Lore Father, it is enough," Giridian said. He looked about, hoping against all hope that it wasn't too late. The power necessary to cloud everyone's mind—to make the attackers believe they had been successful—was staggering. He surely had never known *Blood of Life* could be used to that extent. Even now, seeing everyone safe and whole, he could hardly believe it. Themun's hand on his arm interrupted his thoughts.

Themun's watery eyes were open but unseeing. "What of Kisan?" he whispered.

"She was with them, in disguise," Dragor replied. "She means to infiltrate them, but she will need our help."

Giridian motioned to Tomas and commanded, "Search the area. If your master is with them, she took the place of someone she either killed or incapacitated. That person is still here." Tomas nodded and raced off with two others.

Dragor looked at the lore father, his face a mask of misery. "Had you not cloaked me into the technique while I stood against the wall, what they saw would've been the truth."

"It was sloppy work," countered Themun, his voice growing fainter. "I had you repeating what you said."

Giridian knelt and laid a gentle hand on Themun's brow. "None were the wiser. Dragor speaks true. You felt the attack on Thera and acted to save us all. Can we not now do the same for you?"

Themun shook his head and replied, "Not Thera. Not the children with her." His eyes closed and a tear crept down his face. "I wish I could've said good-bye to her."

Giridian shook his head, unable to speak.

Themun looked at the bear-like adept with a sad smile and said, "The damage done to me is too deep. When used like this, the Way exacts its toll. You must lead these people now."

Giridian stared in shock. Then he shook his head. "You cannot be serious! It should be Silbane."

Themun only nodded as he leaned more heavily into Dragor's arms. "It should." The lore father smiled, then said, "But we don't always get to choose." He reached out his hand and took Giridian's own.

A small flash of blue passed between them and Giridian staggered backward. His eyes widened and he whispered, "I never dreamed . . ." He sank to his haunches as the lore of the council and its knowledge passed from Themun to him. Though he couldn't use it yet, the lore would not die with Themun.

More of the Isle's inhabitants clustered around, some reaching out to touch Themun. Dragor suppressed a sob and then implored, "You . . . can't leave."

Themun's eyes cracked open and the corners of his mouth quirked in the barest of smiles.

"I will live, as long as I'm remembered," he whispered. The lore father reached up slowly and grasped Giridian's hand again, pulling him close. He put his mouth directly next to the new lore father's ear and whispered, and then his head fell back. His gaze locked onto Giridian's.

Then a single breath washed out of his frail, wasted body and turned into a soft breeze in the still night air. It caressed everyone standing there, lifting tired spirits, cleansing souls, drying tear-filled eyes, and bringing with it the smell of honeysuckle and pine. It swirled about them gently, then slowly faded away. Whatever lifeforce left had been given freely to save them, and Themun Dreys, Lore Father of the Council of Adepts, was gone.

* * * * *

Giridian sat back, unable to believe it. He looked at Dragor, who knelt beside him, also speechless.

Tomas returned with some others he'd recruited to retrieve the assassin's body and stood some distance away, waiting. Then he came forward and tapped Dragor on the shoulder.

Dragor looked up and Tomas pointed to the body, still lying some distance away next to a group of students. "You need to look at this."

Dragor stood slowly, carefully shifting the lore father's body to Giridian. "I'll go."

Giridian nodded, his eyes fixed on Themun's face. "What do I do?"

A Final Illusion

The weight of the Council now fell upon him. He didn't know where to turn. Dragor left his side, then returned a few moments later.

"It took six of our students to drag the body over," Dragor said.

Giridian didn't take his eyes off the dead lore father.

"How can he be gone?"

Dragor squeezed Giridian's shoulder to draw his attention saying, "The assassin . . ." He took a deep breath and said, "There's no doubt. He's dwarven."

Giridian stared at Dragor uncomprehendingly.

"What?"

Dragor nodded, "Two hundred years since they were last seen. Why here? Why us?"

Giridian looked around, then quickly gave the lore father's body to the ministrations of a waiting islander and stood. "Show me."

He let Dragor lead him over to the body, gesturing at its massive form. "See?"

Giridian nodded, then knelt down beside the body. After a moment, he pulled out a small silver vial with fletching from the dead man's belt, inspecting it. "This is what killed Thera."

"And would've killed us if not for . . ."

Giridian sighed, "I want this body taken to the infirmary." He looked at Dragor as touched his arm to transfer strength back to the depleted adept. "You see to it personally. There may be more clues as to where they came from and why. Be careful though, no telling how they protect themselves, even in death."

Dragor looked around the clearing, then back down. A thin line of purple fire surrounded his form as he leaned down and picked up the dwarf's body, only a small grunt signifying the man's weight.

"Follow me," he said to Tomas. The two of them walked away into the darkness in the direction of the infirmary.

Giridian looked again at the small dart, his eyes narrowing. Kisan, he knew, was in grave danger. He hoped they could unravel the reason for the dwarves' appearance here, before she got herself killed.

A Final Illusion

DUEL IN THE WASTES

Strike your opponent's face,
she remembers you when she looks in the mirror.
Break her ribs,
and she remembers you every time she breathes.
—Davyd Dreys, Memoirs

S ilbane watched as Rai'stahn descended, his wings beating quickly to brake his downward speed, sending fine sand billowing out in two long curls. The dragon-knight quickly changed form, and walked to Silbane.

"This is thy last chance to parley. Dost thou join me?"

Silbane nodded, moving a little to stand closer beside the great dragon-knight, he then looked at the tower, his faded eyes narrowing on something only he could see. A small sigh escaped his lips, words unformed and unneeded. When Rai'stahn followed his gaze, the master blurred into surprise action, throwing three rapid-fire strikes with stiffened fingers into the dragon's back.

The dragon spun, but Silbane knew it was too late. His strikes had unerringly found the deep, vital points he'd sought. With those strikes, a numbness spread, but not to Rai'stahn's limbs. Instead, the technique Clouds before Death blocked specific prana points, cutting the dragon-knight's ability to use the Way.

Rai'stahn's great fist lashed out, catching Silbane across the jaw and sending him spinning and tumbling away, but the damage had already been done. As the numbness spread throughout Rai'stahn Silbane knew his gamble had paid off. The dragon-knight had not fully recovered from Arek's presence, and in his weakened state had been susceptible to a technique that normally would never have worked.

Silbane slowly rose, shaking his head, thankful for his ability to redirect the dragon's might. A normal man would've died from that strike. He stumbled to his feet, his hands up in defense. "I would parley with thee, Rai'stahn."

"Parley, after thou attacks!" roared the dragon.

"Nay . . . I only sought to level the field."

"Thou art a fool." Rai'stahn looked sidelong at Arek, his golden gaze calculating. "There is another way my prana can be released," he let out with a hiss.

"If you mean by my death, then you are correct." Silbane looked at the dragon-knight, while shaking his head. "But now it is you who underestimates me, milord. In this form, you may not prevail."

And suddenly the expression on the dragon-knight's face told the master he'd understood the purpose of Silbane's attack. Rai'stahn could no longer transform into his dragon form, severely limiting his abilities.

Silbane saw his opening, and in the space between heartbeats he shot forward, his hand straight and rigid, aimed at a small point on the dragon's neck. It was a chink in the armor, no more than a finger's width across.

Given the form Rai'stahn was trapped in, Silbane hoped a strike to this spot would incapacitate the great dragon and limit any collateral damage. He knew he only had a few chances before his opponent's natural strength and speed overcame him, yet he didn't strike to kill. Something stayed his hand, a feeling that there was still hope for some sort of compromise.

Rai'stahn countered. He'd battled creatures great and small and his instincts were those of a true predator. He shifted imperceptibly to his right so Silbane's attack went just over his shoulder, then struck with an armored fist to the master's midsection.

The strike exploded against Silbane's magical shielding, the impact a flash of pure yellow and white. Silbane was hurled backward, digging a long, straight furrow into the soft sand. The flameskin had taken the brunt of the blow, but the monk could feel pain where some of its power had bled through. He levered himself up, knowing he'd have to rise quickly and move if he was to survive.

* * * * *

Arek couldn't believe what he was seeing. He could feel the dragon's power as if it were a tangible thing. A hunger rose within him. He stood frozen, unable to move, but when the dragon spun and breathed fire at him, he reacted instantly. When the wave of red-orange flame lit the night, painting the sand in front of Arek, he crossed his arms and leaned into the fire, bringing Tempest to bear. The sword, still quiescent, stood dull and lifeless, yet the dragon's fire parted before him. It washed around Arek like a stream around a rock. The air around him concussed, and he was thrown backward.

Arek rolled, scrambling on all four limbs to get back into a tactical position, unable to believe the flames hadn't touched him. He could feel hot breath on his neck, could almost sense the claws about to rend his throat and rip the flesh from his back. A mindless urgency filled him and without thinking, he spun and struck with Tempest, but his sword cut through empty air.

He was sure the dragon had been right behind him. He'd never misjudged things in combat before. What power did the dragon use? Then he saw Rai'stahn, still some distance away, coming toward him.

The dragon-knight hunched forward like an animal stalking his prey. "Thou art outclassed in this contest, boy. Stop fighting and I will make thine end quick and painless." On those words Rai'stahn moved in a blur, his fanged teeth bared.

Arek didn't hesitate, his sword pointed at his opponent. He circled until the Far'anthi Stone lay behind him, some feet away. He would make his stand here, he thought, bolstering himself for the inevitable clash.

* * * * *

Silbane blinked to clear his vision, then leapt up and over the dragon, landing lightly between Rai'stahn and his apprentice. He struck twice, and could hear the resulting grunt of pain, but had no time to enjoy it.

The dragon swatted the monk with the edge of an outstretched wing, sweeping him aside like an enormous black hand.

Again, Silbane's flameskin saved him, flashing like sunlight with the force of the blow it turned. Silbane found himself on his back. The power! Even the small portion of what blasted through his protective aura damaged him greatly. He could feel his strength ebbing and tasted salty blood in his mouth. If this was Rai'stahn "weakened," Silbane couldn't imagine facing him at full strength. He reached for the Earth to envelope him . . . and he was only a moment too late.

Before he could finish the technique, Silbane felt the dragon's hands around his head. He was lifted off his feet. An armored fist struck his flameskin again, right in front of his face. The force of the blow staggered him. His vision went gray then slowly began to return, along with a ringing in his ears. He sat up some ten feet away and didn't remember how he got there.

* * * * *

Arek could tell Silbane was hurt, strike for strike losing more energy and endurance than Rai'stahn. The opportunity to escape would vanish when his master fell. His hand came up to feel the Finder. He could find his master again.

He spun and snatched up a rock. With a preternatural burst of speed, Arek ran the few steps left to the Far'anthi.

He thought he heard laughter again, but he was completely focused on the Stone.

Before Rai'stahn or Silbane could intervene, Arek took the rock and swung it in a tight arc, striking the Stone. To his astonishment, it gonged like a bell and began to glow a soft blue. *Piter had told the truth*, he realized with a mixture of elation and dismay. He'd also said that Arek must be first through the portal.

Its surface became smooth, lit from within like a blue-white star. Arek could see scenes shift beneath, those of a fortress in the desert, its black and gold pennons snapping from the castle walls in the breeze. Some of the images were of outer walls, others of what looked to be the interior of a chamber, dark and unoccupied. It was Bara'cor, and their only hope. But if Rai'stahn followed him through, this would only be a short delay before the end came.

* * * * *

Silbane bolted forward, again into the dragon's path. He struck out, his aim guided by years of combat training, and though this wasn't the first time he'd faced a dragon it would still be hubris to claim any prowess against one as powerful as Rai'stahn. His only advantage was the dragon's human form, which at least gave Silbane a chance. Half-blinded, he used the small nuances of position and breathing to target the vital areas on the armored body of the knight. His fist hit Rai'stahn's sternum, knocking him backward and up. Silbane vaulted quickly to his feet and leapt past the dragon, reaching for his apprentice.

"Arek, wait!"

The boy never looked back. He stood transfixed by the glowing blue orb, and before Silbane could do anything, Arek reached out with his hand and touched it. In a black and blue flash, he disappeared. Silbane fell inches from where his apprentice had been, his hand closing on nothing but sand.

As Arek's form vanished, the stone began to collapse. A black hole appeared within, spreading cracks of power. The ground shuddered. Before either the dragon or the master could react, the stone imploded, drawing into itself and disintegrating into dust.

"Fool!" Rai'stahn roared. "Dost thou see his power now?"

Silbane ignored him and fumbled for the Finder around his neck, preparing to crush it.

The dragon knew what the master planned and moved with blurring speed. He billowed out fire to hide his attack, then emerged from the flames, catching Silbane with an armored foot to the head.

The kick overcame Silbane's flameskin, which dissipated in a flash of sunfire. The force of the blow knocked him away from the dragon like a puppet. The Finder fell from his limp grasp.

His protection was gone, destroyed, having absorbed most of the dragon's blow. It was the only reason Silbane still lived. The next strike would kill him. Both he and Rai'stahn knew it.

"Thou art broken. Remove the locks on my prana and I will allow thee to live." The dragon moved forward and stood over the prone master, within easy killing distance. Nothing Silbane did could stop the dragon now.

"What about Arek?" the monk spat, blood dripping from his nose and ears. If he could just clear his head, if he could just stand up . . .

"I will agree—"

The dragon stopped, his eyes widening in shock. Silbane looked up through bruised eyes to see the dragon-knight caught in midsentence, trying to say something.

The knight's mouth moved, but only a gurgling sound issued forth. A trembling hand rose, picking at the air as if trying to grasp something from behind his massive head. He took a staggering step forward, then fell face down into the desert dune, next to the surprised master.

An arrow protruded from the base of the dragon-knight's skull, its dark fletching and shaft almost invisible in the night. A pool of blood, almost black under the moonlight, began soaking into the sand below Rai'stahn's head.

"This one's alive," a voice said in guttural Altanese.

Silbane turned to look in the direction of the voice. A booted foot smashed into his face, breaking his nose and burying his head halfway into the sand.

"The u'zar wants prisoners," said another, without much interest. Silbane tried feebly to move, but the heel of that boot came down again, twice, and a third time. Each strike smashed into his face and head, breaking bone and cutting flesh.

The last thought Silbane had was that it wasn't fair—a master of combat beaten to death. Then his world went mercifully black.

Duel in the Wastes

INTO BARA'COR

Know your weapon:
the feel of the grip in your hands,
the press of the guard to your thumb,
the back of the blade to block,
the keen edge at the cut.
Every part has its role in ending your opponent's life.
—Kensei Tsao, The Lens of Blades

Yetteje pulled away from Niall's hand as they walked down the stairwell, and back toward her room. They were accompanied by Sergeant Alyx and two guards, ostensibly to "escort" her back, but in fact on the king's orders to keep her in her quarters. King Galadine hadn't hidden his orders from the princess, forbidding her to accompany the quest to assassinate the nomad chieftain, despite accepting her idea as a good one. It just wasn't fair.

"You can't have been serious about going into the camp," said Niall. "I mean, my father wouldn't even let me serve on the wall." This last part came out with a trace of annoyance.

Tej spun and shoved Niall against a wall. "It's not always about you!" She met his eyes with anger in her own. "Imagine your whole family dead." She pushed him against the wall again and stepped back, shaking her head. "It was my idea to infiltrate the camp, and I know how to fight. Your father should've let me go."

"Easy, princess," one of the guards said, pulling her away from Niall. "Please keep moving."

As Yetteje spun and continued down the stairwell, Niall stood, stunned by her response. A part of him realized he must have sounded selfish, but Tej was being irrational. He followed her, saying, "Going into that camp with Ash is certain death."

"Do you think I care?" Tej asked in a small voice over her shoulder. She continued down the stairwell, now seemingly moving faster to get herself away from him and her escort.

Alyx moved forward and put a restraining hand on the prince's shoulder. "Leave it. You won't convince her of anything right now."

"Can't she just be happy her idea was approved? It's further than I've ever gotten," said Niall, shaking his head.

Alyx tilted her head, the torchlight putting her face in silhouette, waiting. When she had his attention she said, "How did you feel when you were assigned to support rather than the wall?"

Niall looked at her, then slowly nodded. "Fine," he said grudgingly, then ran to catch up with Yetteje. Alyx sighed, as she and the guards followed. The stairwell descended back into the fortress proper, away from the main walls and combat areas. As they made their way to the interior, they saw fewer and fewer people, as the majority of Bara'cor's populace was now shuttling between the inner wall and the forward stations.

This particular hallway led straight down into the lower halls, then a long walk over to the guest rooms. The air grew cooler as they descended, each area lit by more wall sconces. Between them and their destination lay an adjunct council chamber, used for meetings with lesser dignitaries.

Their hallway spilled out onto a large circular platform, with an octagonal opening to the council chamber on one side. On the other side was an opening in the floor, where the stairwell continued down to the lower halls.

Niall and Tej had just walked onto the platform when a blue flash erupted from the council chamber. Because of the siege and with no council in session, this level was deserted, and suddenly they both realized just how empty this part of the castle was.

Alyx motioned for Tej and Niall to stop and made a silencing gesture. That flash had been intense and very real. She leaned in close to the guard behind her and told him to get help. A signal with her eyes gave the other guard his orders: flank left. She then met the wide-eyed stares of the prince and Tej, and whispered, "Stay behind me."

They nodded in answer, then silently, the remaining three drew their swords. The guard still with them moved around and to the left of the entrance.

Niall watched him, then began to do the same, his eyes wide. Cold fear made his grasp weak and his legs tremble. He couldn't get a good grip on his blade. His palms felt wet and cold at the same time.

They didn't have long to wait. From inside the great octagonal doors poked a blond-haired head. The face was intense, with pale blue eyes that shone with intelligence. He was dressed in a dark, armored leather jerkin and breeches, functional without adding bulk. With a start, Niall realized this intruder was close to the same age as himself or Yetteje.

Alyx was the first to move. "Stay where you are," she said, with her sword pointed directly at the boy's face.

The boy's eyes tracked the weapon for a moment, as he drank in the rest of his surroundings as if dismissing her as a threat. That, Niall thought, was a mistake. Emboldened by the sergeant's courage, he moved into view and flanked the doorway, his weapon held low and in front of him.

"You'd be wise to listen . . . Who are you?" Niall asked.

"Intruder!" the guard flanking the door yelled.

Before the word had echoed up the hallway, the boy exploded into action. A liquid silver sword appeared in his hands and he moved with incredible speed. He crossed the distance to the guard before he could draw another breath.

The guard brought his weapon up, but the boy slapped it aside like an afterthought and slammed the pommel of his weapon into the man's face. A heartbeat later he struck with an elbow followed by an open palm to the guard's stomach. The air whooshed out of him and the guard sank unconscious to the floor. Niall had never seen anyone move so fast.

The sergeant was already in motion, moving quickly to counter any killing stroke the boy might level at the unconscious guard. She struck at the back of the boy's head, her blade almost whistling as it cut through the air.

The boy ducked under the blade and punched her in the face, then spun and caught her in the forehead with the flat of his blade. The blade made a dull thwack and snapped Alyx's head back. She staggered from the blow, her equilibrium gone.

As Niall watched, dumbfounded, the boy stepped in and took the sword out of the sergeant's dazed grasp, then almost nonchalantly punched her in her helm with her own sword's pommel.

Alyx dropped as if pole-axed and the boy tossed her own sword away from her unconscious body before turning to face Tej, who yelled back to Niall, "Attack at the same time!"

She launched herself at the intruder, attacking with a flurry of strikes aimed at his head and midsection. Tej had been well-trained; her strikes came out fast and true, a dance of steel that should've scored first blood more than once. To her detriment she attacked alone, as Niall stood by and watched, paralyzed.

To Niall's amazement, the boy blocked everything, his breathing even. On the last strike, he countered with a sharp knee to Yetteje's stomach, then a ridge hand to her forehead. Before she could recover, the boy spun in place and kicked her with a booted heel to her jaw. Niall watched Tej knocked senseless. She fell like a ragdoll, her eyes rolling back. Incredibly, her opponent had never used anything but the flat of his sword.

The boy continued his spin, landing and facing Niall with his weapon pointed on a spot directly between the young prince's eyes. As their gazes met, Niall knew he'd hesitated too long and lost a critical advantage. Worse, one look at Tej's crumpled form and he knew he'd also failed his cousin.

Niall started to back up, but the boy moved again with that blurring speed. He closed his eyes and raised his weapon, hoping to block, but met empty air. He then felt the stiff steel side of the boy's weapon batter him across the chest. He lurched forward and felt a sharp blow and an explosion of pain to the back of his head.

His vision blackened and he fell forward, but strangely, could still hear. He heard running feet in the hallway and Ash's voice yelling, "Halt!" Then a final strike with what felt like a booted heel crashed into his head and he felt no more.

* * * * *

Ash surveyed the scene before him. The guard had reached them even as he heard the cry for help. They had immediately raced down the stairwell and into the hallway, only to find Alyx, Niall, Tej, and the remaining guard down, perhaps dead. The intruder didn't look like a nomad, but that meant nothing. They could've hired an assassin to enter the fortress. Ash was taking no chances.

He moved forward, his sword held in a relaxed grip. Yetteje was nearest, so Ash moved slowly over to the princess. Without taking his eyes off the intruder, he listened and heard the faint sound of Tej's breathing. *The girl's alive,* he thought with relief. He turned his full attention to the would-be-assassin and realized for the first time that he was a boy, no older than Niall himself.

"Who are you?" Ash demanded. He raised an open hand and said, "Put down your weapon. If they're alive, we can talk."

The boy put his sword point on the back of Niall's unconscious head. The meaning was clear. Niall was alive, but only so long as Ash stayed back.

Ash did the only thing he could. "Spill the blood of the crown prince and yours will surely follow," he promised.

The boy looked down at Niall's prostrate form in shock, and Ash used that moment of distraction to attack.

He moved in, aiming for the boy's sword arm, hoping to disarm him quickly. But the boy reacted with the reflexes of a snake. Instead of jerking his hand away, he lowered his shoulder and moved into Ash, getting under the blow and striking the armsmark in the chest.

The boy is good, thought Ash. *Very good.*

The blow wasn't strong, but it knocked the armsmark back and off balance. The boy followed with a short heel kick to the armsmark's forward shin. This locked Ash's knee backward painfully, but Ash knew what was coming next.

He aimed three lightning-quick strikes to the boy's head, only to see all three blocked and turned. Before the boy could complete his counterattack with a finishing stroke, the armsmark went with the pain in his knee and twisted to one side, falling to the ground and rolling.

The liquid silver blade swished through empty air and then turned, point down. As he rolled, he saw the boy's sword bury itself into the space his head had just occupied.

Ash continued his motion and used his legs to trap the boy's in a scissor hold. The boy fell facedown to the floor, pinned under Ash's weight and immobilized by his crisscrossed legs. Ash never hesitated, bringing his elbow into a short, brutal arc that came down hard on the back of the boy's head, smashing it to the stone floor. In an instant, it was over.

He felt the boy go limp and quickly pushed his sword away, then moved immediately to check the prince. *Praise the Lady,* he thought, *Niall is alive.* He then made his way over to Alyx. She was also alive. . . . Something wasn't right. An assassin who didn't kill? Ash was struck by the odds of having all of them survive an encounter with someone who had this boy's skill.

He turned his attention back to the intruder, who was unconscious and except for the painful bruise he'd likely have on his head, unharmed. Ash looked at him closely, trying to ascertain where he was from. Despite an entire life of blade training, this boy had held his own against him. Whoever he was, he had training—real training from someone who knew what they were teaching. He remembered the boy's concentration, his breathing. *So why are we all still alive?* Something didn't fit, and Ash didn't like unsolved puzzles, especially those that pointed to luck as the answer.

Ash looked at the clothes and the weapon. It was silver, with a green gem set in the pommel. Silver runes danced down its keen edges. For a moment, time seemed to slow and Ash felt a stirring within him. The sword was beautiful, more beautiful than any he'd ever seen. Then, almost as a whisper, Ash thought he heard a word: *Beloved.*

He stood transfixed, the echo of her voice in his head. Then a guard came and placed a hand on his arm. He snapped back to this moment, the voice and the stirring forgotten.

"Are you injured, sir?" the guard inquired, concerned. Many men didn't notice wounds in battle that later proved deadly.

Ash ignored him, his mind turning over the facts. With that training, the boy could be a very highly paid agent. The question was whose? Still, doubt surfaced when Ash considered his age. Who would train a child to this level of expertise, and more importantly, why? Most of what the boy wore seemed to be close-fitting armor designed for unimpaired movement. It was of a style Ash didn't recognize, but it was definitely *not* nomadic.

Motioning to the guards he said, "Search him and secure his items, then take him to a cell. Bind him there and report to the Firstmark." The guard gestured to his compatriots, who moved quickly to obey the order. Ash

winced as he put weight on his injured knee and added,
"And send a medic. We're all going to need one."

JOURNAL ENTRY 8

My sense of time is gone. Weeks or even months may have passed. It makes no difference, for it all feels like an eternity. I cannot return through the Gate. Betrayed by dragons is the same as forgotten. What can I do, except endure?

The young Aeris (I have given up calling them "infinitesimal particles." It is too much to write, forgive me) permeate the planes and do not need the rifts. They suffuse all things, incoherent power from undirected thoughts and dreams. I envy their freedom.

I know I create them, but what if everyone does? They seem to be able to manifest themselves only through the will of sentient beings. I burn through them easily to create fire, home, and hearth. A part of me enjoys it. In my own way and out of spite, I free them too. They are easy fodder for use by our Way, but in that action lies our undoing. Using them creates more, and that eventually gives rise to greater beings, the Aeris Lords.

I have come to understand a truth, something I did not understand when I stood before Rai'kesh. Aeris Lords are given shape, not by one person's vision or will, but instead by our entire people's beliefs.

Given no impedance they run amok, for they are nothing more than children demanding whatever they want, with the power to enforce it. Zafir and Lilyth are more powerful incarnations of these, known as Celestials, and our world suffers from their attention.

If every belief from our world has given life to a god or goddess, I wonder how, or even if, these Aeris Lords can be beaten. Perhaps Edyn's true destiny is to serve these demons . . . but how?

Journal Entry 8

FOUR DAYS LEFT . . .

Journal Entry 8

THE SCYTHE

When your opponent's intention is in doubt, watch his eyes,
for the eyes are the window to his soul.
—Kensei Shun, The Lens of Shields

Silbane awoke suffocating, his nostrils clogged. Blowing hard caused chunks of dried blood to come free, but with that came a gush of warm, fresh blood—and pain. Still, breathing became easier. He spat coppery blood out, imagining how gruesome he must look, but thankful to be alive to feel anything at all. He took stock of his surroundings and realized he sat, secured to a pole in a tent, on hard earth. Around him were various instruments of war, razor spears and barbed whips, coiled and ready, offering any willing hand the release of their deadly intent.

"You look rested."

Silbane started at the voice, coming from just outside of his field of view. Straining, he turned to identify the speaker, then cursed with pain as his neck and jaw protested. It was clear his face had borne the brunt of that last nomad's attack, and it was likely the damage wasn't just superficial. Silbane centered his thoughts, reaching for the Way to heal himself. Nothing happened.

"That won't work." Soft footsteps followed and red robes slowly came into view. They belonged to a tall man, striking because of his calm demeanor and confidence. Most of all, the man projected power. "I've blocked you. Surprisingly, not very difficult," the man continued. He stooped to come eye to eye with his captive and his pale gaze narrowed, but he said nothing else. The man reminded Silbane of someone.

Silbane croaked through a bruised and parched throat, "Who . . .?"

The Scythe

The man moved forward and offered a few drops of water from a small leather bladder. As the monk drank, he carefully offered more. Silbane could feel strength flow back into him as the cool water eased his wounded throat.

The man looked unperturbed. He smiled and offered a bit more water, then said in a soft voice, "I am the Scythe. Like the reaper's tool, I ascend those found worthy, or wanting." His head tilted to one side, as if he looked past Silbane and at something else. "I judge you worthy, but I am curious."

Silbane winced at the new pain he felt from renewed circulation, but his voice was stronger with the water. "I owe you my life." It wasn't a question, but a statement of fact mixed with an involuntary undercurrent of thanks.

The man nodded, settling back onto a waiting stool. "I would speak with you plainly. I have ways of finding out what I want, but if you cooperate, I promise things will go more comfortably." When Silbane didn't respond, the man continued, "I will tell you I side with the Way."

The man settled back, as if they sat across from each other in the comfort of a home. "Shall we begin?" he asked. "You are Silbane Darius Petracles, noble born of House Petra, now a master in an order of monks residing on an isle in the Shattered Sea. I won't go into all the boring details, but I know where you're from and all the inconsequential shames anyone has after a life as long as yours." The man paused, then added, "You are a good man. What I don't know is, why?"

Silbane didn't say a word, not trusting himself to speak. This man seemed to know too much already.

"You see, my knowledge is incomplete. For the past century, the people of Edyn, people of power, have been preparing for the Gate of Lilyth to appear. Why do you come only now, and who are your companions?"

"Companions?" Silbane asked innocently, spitting out more blood.

The man leaned forward and smiled, but the smile never reached his eyes. "Really? The camp you made was for two people. I could assume it was for you and your unfortunate friend." The man gestured to the left and when Silbane turned his head, he was shocked to silence. "Except that while I healed you, in your delirium you emphatically mentioned someone named Arek. You were quite insistent he needed protection. You seemed almost . . . ashamed."

Silbane's eyes were locked on the space behind the red-robed man. There was Rai'stahn, upright and crucified to a circle of iron. He hung limp, the arrow still sticking out from the back of his head. Silbane drew a shuddering breath and quickly looked away.

From the way his head lay canted at an unnatural angle, he could tell Rai'stahn's neck was broken. Despair washed through him at the great dragon's death, if for no other reason than the loss it implied. Rai'stahn and his kind were ancient, representing knowledge of the world most races had yet to learn.

It was true they had faced each other in combat and he knew death would've been the outcome for one of them. Still, he believed Rai'stahn had withheld for the same reasons he had, because death may not have been the only answer.

Now the great dragon had been felled by a nomad's arrow, an injury impossible except for the form Silbane had trapped him in, and the weakening he claimed resulted from contact with his apprentice. Another testament to the idea that Arek's magical nullification was more powerful than Silbane had suspected.

Had Rai'stahn been right all along? Could the world really lie in the balance over Arek? He was stuck here now, and his apprentice was gone, lost to whatever destination the Far'anthi had sent him.

Further complicating things was this person. The lore father had sensed a helper of the nomads, and it seemed

Silbane had found him, but now he was helpless. The master felt his mission slipping toward failure.

"My first question is quite simple," Scythe said, interrupting Silbane's thoughts. He leaned in, his dark red robes closing about him like wings, and asked in a soft voice, "Who is Arek?"

DEBRIEFING

The style you face should be of no concern.
Seasoned warriors rely on the same techniques,
forged in the crucible of combat across a thousand
battlefields.
But warriors vary greatly in skill.
—Tir Combat Academy, The Tactics of Victory

A fist smacked into the oak table, the broad knuckles leaving dents in the hard wood. "Five darts should've gone into that last adept! I counted four. You know the drill, no mistakes, and no excuses." The leader didn't look happy, nor did the others on the team. "Any answer?"

Kisan looked at the leader, her disguise as Tamlin complete, the language of these men assimilated from the memories of the man she'd killed. She bent her tongue around the strange speech, but found it easier to do if she didn't think about it. "Something . . . that last fighter did . . ." She let her voice trail off lamely, hoping one of the others would complete the thought.

The leader backhanded her, the shock of the strike more surprising than painful. Kisan reeled back convincingly, falling over her chair and onto the pitching deck of the small ready room.

They had assembled here after a retreat that took them through woods to a cliff overlooking water. There, Kisan had watched as the leader signaled with a small white gem, answered by a similar flash from the prow of a long, black shape just offshore.

Having fixed their destination, all dove off the cliff and into the inky waters below. There had been a moment during her silent fall when her heart suddenly missed a beat. A lurch accompanied by a sudden pulse of anguish and fear, but it quickly dissipated into the night like a black cloud she'd fallen through. She had no idea what it meant, and in her depleted state it took every ounce of discipline just to maintain her illusion.

They had made it to the waiting boat quickly and shed their masks. Kisan realized with a start that the glowing "eyes" were actually cleverly placed lenses within each mask. She assumed they worked much the same as using the Way to enhance her own vision. She adjusted her illusion to compensate, happy to discover these men were less magical than she'd feared, but remained vigilant. They had already proven capable and deadly.

She followed the team into the ship, trying desperately to understand more of Tamlin and these men. She knew enough now to know they referred to each other by number, not name, in case of capture. In fact, she doubted if Tamlin had known their real names. The only exception was the leader, whom they called Prime instead of One.

"Slug-brained and pitiful," Prime accused with a jab of a finger. "Get your act together, mudknife." He turned away in disgust and left the small cabin, slamming the door shut behind him, though Kisan wasn't sure if it was due to the man's anger or the natural back and forth motion of the boat.

"Good job," laughed one of the men sarcastically. "Lucky we drew you for this rotation."

Kisan picked her way to her feet carefully and righted the chair. She didn't quite understand what he meant so instead she said, "You saw those adepts. That last one did something."

Another, Two, Tamlin's memory furnished, stepped up and said, "That why your voice sounds funny?" The man's eyes narrowed, "Or maybe that's why you can't follow signals a cadet should know?"

Kisan realized she'd never heard Tamlin's natural voice. Quickly she fished through the memories, which were coming more easily to her and listened to the man whose life she'd taken and now imitated. A small exertion of her technique fixed that last detail and Kisan now spoke with the lower-pitched voice she'd heard in Tamlin's mind. "More like the backhand I just took to the throat."

Two's eyes bored into Kisan's, and then he let loose a *harrumph* of disgust. They'd accomplished their mission and their target was dead, but he seemed like the type who hated mistakes of any kind.

Two addressed Three, with a jerk of his thumb in Kisan's direction, "Get him squared away." Not waiting for a reply, he made his way out, following his leader.

There was a silent pause, then the entire room seemed to take a collective sigh of relief. Kisan realized the rest hadn't shared their leader's ire, and frankly had only been worried the anger at her would spill over to them, resulting in extra duties or worse.

As if to confirm this, the one she knew as Three came forward and clapped her on the shoulder saying, "First couple of times out is always tough, but you know the signal if you're not steady and ready."

And suddenly she did, it was a quick slash through her wrist. Her body mimicked the motion automatically as another of Tamlin's memories fell into place. Tamlin would've made that sign the moment the leader signaled for everyone's status, standard practice for this team.

As memories began to assimilate, Kisan constructed a more complete perspective on the discipline of these men, which rivaled that of her own training on Meridian Isle. At first, she assumed they had gained their abilities through the Way. She could have accepted that.

It was more difficult to admit that while they were magically imbued, much of their profound lethality grew from simple hard training and their enormous strength, which seemed a natural part of their bodies. Clearly, if someone wanted to hire highly trained assassins, they couldn't do much better than these men.

Debriefing

Her mind wandered back to the fight with Dragor. Had Kisan answered Prime correctly during that engagement, she'd have been ordered to a support role. Prime had reacted to the simple fact that "Tamlin" had endangered the team. Not only did he not signal his inability to help, but by continuing to fight, had hindered everyone else.

In truth, Kisan didn't care. She'd intentionally tried to thwart their efforts to kill Dragor without giving herself away. However, as Tamlin's memories became more available, she saw the leader would not allow this to happen again. If it did, Prime would kill Tamlin, a fact that neither she nor the team doubted.

Still, she grieved the loss of Dragor. She hadn't felt his death the way she had Thera's, but it wasn't surprising. In her depleted state after assimilating Tamlin and fighting Dragor, it was doubtful she'd have felt anyone's passing, even someone as powerful as Themun. True, there had been that moment as they dove for the ships, the heart lurch she'd felt, but that could've been anything. Still, if her friends had truly given their lives so Kisan could be here, she meant to make herself worthy of that sacrifice.

Frankly, despite their discipline and training, she knew she'd little to fear from these men physically. Her only real fear was she would expose herself and lose the opportunity to trace them back to the person who gave the order to attack Meridian Isle. Whoever that was, would die.

One, Two, and Three nodded, interrupting her thoughts and echoing Kisan's certainty about Prime, "Get it right though, or there won't be a next time," they said in unison.

Four and Five went to their lockers and began taking off their equipment, expertly storing them with practiced ease. As they stripped off weapons and small pieces of ingeniously placed armor, Kisan could see muscles and sinew ripple.

They were too big and disproportioned to be of her race. They stood taller, their torsos wider, with forearms and legs as thick as logs, and hands that looked suitable to crush stone. She was too pragmatic to be embarrassed by their nakedness. Instead, she drank in the details, unconsciously fixing her own illusion to match their physical features. Kisan didn't recognize them, but searched Tamlin's memories.

The answer stunned her . . . builders. Her people called them "dwarven," but that was impossible. Her first thought was rather absurd. *Wouldn't they be smaller than us?* Further delving into Tamlin's memories supplied the reason. The builders were the smallest of the Elder Races, referred to affectionately by those as "dwarves." Her race, though physically smaller, were not an Elder Race, but the name for the dwarves stuck. Indeed, dwarves referred to Kisan's people derogatorily as 'halfmen', or 'halflings.'

The dwarves strength matched those told in the legends. Moreover, they fought with a cunning tenacity they became known for during the Demon Wars, when they fought against Lilyth and her demonic army. It lent credibility to the fact that these may indeed be dwarven men. Now the question was, what were they doing attacking Meridian Isle?

They were highly trained and well-conditioned. Another memory flashed by, of endless combat drills with one man, then two, all the way up to six-man fighting teams. Their strength and exactness stemmed from their repetitious training and their ability to coordinate and cooperate without speaking, using hand signals. Kisan would have to be extra careful to synchronize with them if she were to maintain her cover.

Four stood and motioned to Kisan. "Get cleaned up, then stow the gear. Two will be by for inspection shortly. You know the drill." He tossed a grimy towel into a bin without looking. He tapped Three on the shoulder and motioned to the table near the back that glowed with magic.

A large map was displayed upon it. It looked much like Themun's conjuration, except flat and less detailed.

Without another word, they both went to the table and began discussing points on the map in low tones.

Kisan watched them for a moment, knowing even as they walked away that everyone was following a strict protocol. Tamlin's memories supplied that Three and Four's duty was to evaluate their performance on this last mission and to provide tactical training on bettering them for the next. Prime and Two would be contacting their leaders and reporting on the mission outcome. Five and Six were to stow and set up all gear, then prep the area for the mission debriefing.

This had gone on for as long as this group had been in existence, no matter who fulfilled the roles. When Two felt Prime's leadership endangered the team, and Prime concurred, he would retire back to train new cadets and Two would take his place as the new Prime. If they did not, command would pass through trial by combat. She assumed the current Five, whom she'd been paired with, had been the old Six, but really had no idea.

The name of the place, the Core, rose unbidden from Tamlin's memories, the training academy Tamlin had graduated from. A new graduate of the Core would become Six and he would move up to the Five position and rank, either here or on another team. Still, there was something odd about Tamlin's memories. There were none from before this time of training, as if he suddenly came into being fully formed for his role. It didn't make sense.

Also strange, Tamlin's memories didn't include whose place he'd taken. But he knew who led their people. Someone called "Sovereign." Kisan knew the ancient legends of King Bara leaving to search for someone named Sovereign. Was this the same person, or perhaps the name was a title?

More of Tamlin's memories surfaced, but all of them recent. This elite team of which he was a member was focused on one primary service: kill any who used the

Way. Kisan could tell Tamlin had been on the verge of religious zeal in his love for this team.

To accomplish this, they trained endlessly in infiltration, information gathering, and sabotage. Tamlin had believed they acted directly on behalf of their leader, divine in both right and judgment. Did their Sovereign truly order the strike on the Isle? And to what purpose?

Unfortunately, the memories she'd siphoned from Tamlin's dying mind only contained a single-minded determination to qualify for the team, and none of the surrounding geopolitical information necessary to put context around their existence, or who specifically would have ordered the attack. Tamlin simply had no—and a term from the dwarves unfamiliar to her popped up—*need to know*. Though the words were familiar, the term carried a connotation of formal secrecy and discipline. Kisan could appreciate its point: compartmentalization of information to protect the team. She couldn't help but be impressed. *Tamlin had no "need to know."*

Still, what could cause blank areas where no memories existed, just before Tamlin's training and qualification started? How could someone have no childhood? From what Kisan could now discern, there was nothing before the Core. She realized that if she were to solve this mystery, it would be from listening to these others and drawing conclusions for herself.

The team had moved to their assigned tasks and Kisan followed suit. The label of laggard would not help her situation, and she didn't need any more attention from Prime or Two. She admired a team design that ensured senior members knew the role of all subordinates.

Since she was Six, the expectation was she learned how to interface with this team from the ground up.

Kisan breathed a sigh of relief that she hadn't taken the place of anyone above Tamlin's station. As luck would have it, her combat skills far surpassed them individually, and she'd taken the place of one low enough in rank that she could maintain this deception indefinitely. That was as long as nothing else taxed her beleaguered stores of energy, she cautioned herself, not wanting to grow overconfident.

"Weapons or equipment?" Five asked in a disinterested way.

Kisan knew Tamlin had preferred weapons, but shrugged, "Don't care. You?"

Five motioned to the blades and dart weapons, "I'll start here." He moved with a steadiness that didn't hint at disappointment or eagerness, just purposefulness. Another measure of the discipline these dwarves had forged for themselves.

Kisan took a moment to inspect the unfamiliar tubes that fired the darts. Tamlin's mindread filled in some of the details, though even they were hard to interpret. The weapon's handle and tube formed an *L*. The handle she could grip easily, with a square hole cut out on the internal bend. She could see that a small metal box filled with darts, like some sort of quiver, was inserted there. A lever sat below the tube, conveniently placed for her finger to pull and this action fired the darts through the tube, though even the dead assassin's memories didn't provide an understanding of the magic by which it did so. It was, however, compact and lethal. *Ingenious.*

She put the dart weapon down and let Tamlin's memories guide her on her tasks. As she did so, she thought about how to get a clue or hint to their destination.

"You think I should talk to Prime?" she asked carefully, while coiling a thin climbing rope.

Five looked at Tamlin with a raised eyebrow. "Only if you're looking to die. Leave it, mudknife, or we'll be cleaning up what's left of you and I'll be stuck doing twice the work."

Mudknife . . . that word again, and with sudden comprehension Kisan realized this was their term for any new member of the team.

She shrugged an apology to what Five thought was an obviously stupid idea. No sense confirming that by talking more.

Soon they would make a mistake and she would be there to make them pay for it.

Debriefing

JOURNAL ENTRY 9

Spells are singular, commanding power only insomuch as the strength of a Waycaster's will. In my case, this can be considerable. However, ritual is the key! It is the systematic creation of ritual that gives the formless meaning, and the world structure.

Ritualized prayer, prayer of the masses, holds real power. It breathes life into these Aeris and shapes them. It gives them substance and meaning. And what do gods want, once alive? What do they thirst for, but worship? What power do they have, except for what we grant them? I know now what we are capable of. I will command the weakness that surrounds me.

But first a more deadly test faces me. Tonight, I face the guardian of my castle. I have long suspected something lies deep within, something alive. My fears feed it. If I can't destroy a simple product of my own imagination, how will I save our kind from beings far more powerful than that thing below?

I have tried to control these thoughts, I know where they will lead, but it is an impossible task. How do you not-think about something? A part of my mind believes something lives below, an insidious part that will be my undoing. It will tear me apart, but I must face it.

Tonight, I fear, will be dangerous.

Journal Entry 9

TORTURE

When facing certain death,
one will yearn for
even the worst moments in life.
—Altan proverb

Arek awoke to the icy splash of cold water across his naked body. He struggled, but his hands were tied to a crossbeam. When he looked down, he saw his feet secured on top of stone blocks. He stood, taking weight off his painfully stretched shoulders.

A man stepped forward and said, "I am Sargin. You will refer to me as that, if anything. His Majesty's forces have captured you as an intruder. We are under siege and therefore by the king's decree you are the enemy. We have questions."

Arek remembered jumping through the portal, the freezing cold of in-between, a stone chamber. Beyond that he had no memory, but knew he'd been in a fight. His forehead throbbed with that familiar ache of having been hit, pulsing in time with his heartbeat.

He looked down at the man in front of him and asked, "What's going on? Where am I?"

Sargin held up a hammer, balled on one side, flat on the other. "I'm sorry, sir, we aren't interested in answering your questions, but I want you to understand what will happen if I think you are lying."

Arek looked wide-eyed at the hammer, suddenly understanding its purpose. "I'm from an island in the Shattered Sea!" he blurted.

Sargin paused, looking up at him. Then he said, "Continue."

"My master and I came here to investigate the possibility of a gate opening inside the fortress, a gate to the demon realms."

Sargin cocked his head, his eyes narrowing, "Your master? Anyone else accompany you?"

Arek nodded, then said, "A dragon named Rai'stahn."

"A dragon?"

The man didn't believe him. It was just too fantastic, too much a storybook's tale to be taken seriously. Still, Arek tried to quell his rising panic and speak convincingly. "I know it sounds crazy, but it's true. We rode on dragonback to get here quickly."

"And where is your master now?" Sargin asked, almost politely.

Arek shut his eyes, shaking his head. "The dragon attacked us, and I got separated from him. I don't know where he is."

"How did you get separated?" Sargin asked.

"A shade, Piter, told me how to use the Far'anthi Stone to travel to—"

Sargin held up a hand, cutting Arek off. "Now there's a shade? Someone named Piter. And a dragon?"

Arek raised his gaze, meeting Sargin's unflinching one. "Please, I'm telling you the truth."

The man nodded, and then moved closer with the hammer cocked to his shoulder. "Think about it from our perspective. Bara'cor is besieged, and the single biggest threat to us is infiltration." His eyes however had never left Arek's own. "Have you heard of Bara's Razor?"

Arek nodded, his lip trembling even as he said, "The simplest answer is often true."

Sargin nodded again, "Educated. So you can see given the choice between a way into Bara'cor unknown to us versus a ride on dragonback, a shade, a Far'anthi Stone, and a master . . ." He shrugged. "We'll uncover the truth eventually."

You, no . . . you don't need to—"

The moment froze and there stood Piter. "Oh, this is too perfect," he said with a smile.

"Piter! You have to get me out of here. I order you!" Arek screamed.

"Get you out? And how would I do that, Master?" Piter crossed his arms and seemed genuinely happy. "You keep forgetting that because of you, I'm dead. Forsaken. Committed to wander the realm as a ghost beholden to serve you. Silbane got you into this mess, so ask him."

Arek quickly looked down for the Finder and remembered with dismay that he was stripped bare. He had nothing. He fought to free his wrists, bound tightly to the crossbeam. "You told me to come here. You said I'd be safe!"

"If I were you," Piter said, "I'd get used to the idea that they are going to hurt you."

"What? Why? I don't know anything. Please," he begged. "I'll do anything! I'll release you . . . anything! Please don't let them do this!"

Piter laughed and said, "You are truly an embarrassment. Would Master Kisan be groveling and whining like you?" Then the shade leaned in and said conspiratorially, "I'm going to love this next part." With that, he retreated, a smile still on his face and disappeared, and time continued its normal flow.

Sargin nodded, continuing to answer Arek's last plea, "Yes, sir. I do. This way, anything you tell me after this will perhaps follow Bara's Razor. You will do your best to convince me, because you will do anything to avoid the pain you are about to feel."

"Piter! Please, come back! I'll do whatever you want!" sobbed Arek.

Sargin looked at the boy with some confusion then said, "In due time, you'll tell us everything." He moved forward and put a foot over Arek's own, exposing just his toes on the hard stone.

Torture

The round end of the hammer came up, "I will start by shattering your little toe." He looked up at the boy, who started to whimper, "And then we will talk."

Arek tried to concentrate on his training, repeating in his mind, *the body is just a tool, the mind is in control, the body is j—*

He screamed as the hammer came down and smashed his toe to a pulp. A stroke of pain, like lightning unleashed, raced up his body. He saw purple. He'd bitten his tongue.

He drooled dark pink as he tried and failed to draw a breath. Nothing, no martial training or litanies on discipline, stopped him from begging for Sargin to stop. The cries became sobs, then dry heaves.

Sargin stepped back as Arek soiled himself. Shame now mixed with fear. Sargin continued in a calm voice, "What is your name?"

THE TEAM

Do not wait for the perfect strike.
Take any opportunity if it gives you the killing stroke.
A glorious loss is rarely preferable to a quiet victory.
—Kensei Shun, The Lens of Shields

T he king leaned his corded arms on the table's edge, staring at the map of the world emblazoned upon it. The war chamber was an octagonal room cut from the very rock of Bara'cor. It was large, easily able to accommodate fifty men and featured a huge table in its center.

The table had carved on it a relief map, one that always stayed current with features of the land. When the rivers of two summers past had flooded from EvenSea and almost reached Last Reach, the map had changed. It was as if Edyn itself spoke to the table, which shifted in response to remain true.

Large braziers and torches along the wall lit the chamber, giving it a ruddy glow. Bernal could almost imagine a time when military strategists planned tactics upon the table's surface. No doubt during the Demon Wars it had served King Bara faithfully. Now, despite its strange and peculiar powers, it was nonetheless an artifact out of place and time.

So, too, were the seven statues of female figures sitting around the room. They were each different and of indeterminable race. Some were normal, others not. Some were taller, some wider, others bigger. One female figure had horns, another had wings. What each statue did have in common was a large, gray, rounded stone clutched in its arms. In front of each statue was a raised dais with dwarven script.

The armsmark saluted Bernal as he entered the chamber. Not far behind him were three others, each a final candidate for the attempt on the nomad's camp. The king had been inspecting the statues, their workmanship still a marvel to him. As his armsmark came in, he turned away.

"Report."

"Something curious happened. Our scouts reported an explosion of fire last night, about a day's ride to the east. Coincidentally, it happened just before that boy arrived."

"Do you think it's related?" asked the king.

"We don't know, but what burns in the desert?"

They both looked up as the team followed his armsmark into the room.

The first in line was Sevel, Captain of Second Company. He and Ash had advanced together, training in the same academy and posting under Jebida when they had been commissioned officers. The king knew they were fast friends and could count on one another.

He acknowledged him with, "Captain." He then motioned to the others and said, "I trust all of you are curious about what we've asked you to volunteer for?"

Captain Sevel nodded smartly, his action almost a salute. Ash had related to the king that Sevel had volunteered the moment he'd mentioned the possibility of a mission. Now, they were going to find out the details; his eagerness was obvious.

Ash gestured to the second candidate and said, "This is Sergeant Chandra, sire. She served under Captain Durbin. She is one of our finest archers and especially good at getting in and out of places unseen. She's also quite handy with a dagger." The sergeant stepped forward and saluted smartly to the king. Her lithe form seemed to hold a barely contained energy, like a coiled spring.

The king nodded and looked at the third candidate, a wiry man with a ready smile. His name was Talis, and the sight of him made Bernal smile. He clasped the old warrior's hand, and with a laugh said, "Talis, you old dog!

I thought you had transferred to Haven, 'something easy,' as I recall."

"Aye, I did at that," Talis replied. "But when word came that the queen was evacuating, I thought it best I come see what trouble you've stirred up. Plus, you know the politics of Haven."

"I do indeed," the king nodded. Seeing him now brought back memories of long hours of training, hard but fair. The man was a legend to the fortress, and part of Bara'cor's history. "Not the sort of mission I expected you to volunteer for."

Talis bowed. "Ah . . . speakin' of that. Just what have we volunteered for, besides dyin' that is?" He smiled again and stepped back. His easy demeanor and familiarity in the face of rank came of his long service to the king and his family. He'd been the unarmed combat instructor for three generations of Galadines, and though near his fiftieth summer, he still held a dangerous glint in his eye. The king knew many had wagered and lost a week's pay making the mistake of measuring Talis's worth by his age.

The king looked at each of the candidates, then began, "I'm sorry it has come to this, but we have little choice. I asked the armsmark to select the best qualified and from there take only volunteers. The chance for success is good, but the chance of surviving that success . . . slim.

"However, if you succeed, the people of Bara'cor will owe you their lives." The king paused as he looked at the group meaningfully. "I'll not mince words. We are asking you to infiltrate the nomad camp and kill their leader."

Discipline reigned. None of the candidates moved or spoke. Each absorbed the information and processed it in their own way—another confirmation that Ash had picked them well.

"Questions?" the king asked.

Captain Sevel stepped forward, his eyes straight ahead. "Sir, how will we know our target?"

The king nodded to Ash, who answered, "We all saw him, the day Durbin let his arrow fly from the walls. He is a massive warrior, clearly born and bred for battle. I doubt there are many that look like him in the camp. We may have new information shortly. If not, we'll need to capture someone once we get in and extract the information."

"Justice for Captain Durbin's last stand," Sergeant Chandra said.

The sergeant stepped back and Talis stepped forward. "Beggin' your pardon, sir, but new information? What does that mean?"

"Last night we captured a spy within our walls," the king said. "He's being interrogated now. If he knows anything, I'll share it with you immediately. Until then, prepare yourselves. You'll leave tonight at dusk."

Chandra stepped forward and asked, "Sir, does anyone have a plan yet to get into the camp?"

"I have an idea," Ash replied, "but I need to first discuss it with the king. You three are to prepare for single entry . . . we'll split up and rejoin each other behind enemy lines. Select your gear as if you were the only person going in and visit the quartermaster for some clothes scavenged from slain nomads. I'll drop by and discuss the mission details shortly." Ash looked to the king for permission, then said, "Dismissed."

The group snapped to attention, then with a signal from the armsmark filed out of the room.

The king asked, "Small group. Will they be enough?"

Ash turned and said, "Too big a group will attract attention, especially if one is captured and forced to talk. That will alert the camp and it will be impossible to get to the chieftain. I thought three was a good number."

"There are four of you, counting yourself," Bernal corrected.

Ash's eyes never left his king's. "It's something I've been meaning to discuss with you. One of us will have to create a diversion, something to allow the other three to get by the nomad sentry line."

The king didn't understand the implication at first. When the simple fact of what Ash meant hit him, he shook his head. He would not throw away Bara'cor's best chance.

"We knew this was the only choice," Ash said. "We have to get into the camp somehow. We can't just walk in."

"You would be wasting all you could bring to the attempt against the nomad chieftain, dying needlessly."

"It's not needless if the others manage to slip into the camp unseen," offered the armsmark. "Besides, should I order one of them to do this? I couldn't live with myself."

The king turned his gray eyes on the young armsmark and laid his battle-scarred hand on his shoulder. "It is difficult to order others to their deaths, but good leaders know this. You cannot sacrifice yourself. You are the one with the best chance of finding and killing the nomad chieftain."

Ash opened his mouth to argue, but the king squeezed his shoulder like a vise.

"Hear me out," the king persisted. "Firing Bara'cor's catapults and performing a mock charge on their lines will force them to hold their line. At the clash, we pull back and retreat. Many will fall, but the nomad line will push forward on our retreat. Dressed as nomads, the four of you, fallen amongst the many slain, will go unnoticed. When their line passes, you will be behind it and able to rise and blend in with the enemy."

"That will mean the deaths of many of our men, just to cover our infiltration."

The king nodded and said, "And if you fail, it will mean the deaths of all of us. I am king, and these are my orders."

Ash didn't meet the king's gaze when he said, "I should be happy with this alternative, but I'm not."

Bernal looked down as he was thinking to himself. He understood the weight of what he ordered, and also knew he'd put Bara'cor's survival ahead of any sacrifice.

When he looked up, his eyes betrayed none of his thoughts, and his gaze was unflinching, "Nevertheless, the soldiers who fall in this charge are heroes, ensuring you and your team get past the nomad line. I wish the Lady's fortune on you, Armsmark. Do not waste our sacrifice."

Ash's voice was solemn as he replied, "Yes, my king."

OBSESSION

Strike hardest with the enemy's indrawn breath.
This creates shock and fear,
the parents necessary for mistakes to be born.
—Davyd Dreys, Memoirs

W hy would a dragon need a camp and supplies?" Scythe asked. When he saw his prisoner's surprised look he added, "Silbane, I know much more than you think. I know you trapped Rai'stahn in his knight form." He gestured at the crucified figure then, adjusted his seat on his small stool and finished, "I did say, 'let us speak plainly.'"

Silbane hesitantly nodded, at which point Scythe continued, "You know of the ability to read someone's memories. I know this because while I healed you, I mindread some of what you know. I know of your mission, of the Isle, and of your lore father."

He paused, looking about the tent as if wondering how to continue. He then met Silbane's surprised gaze and asked, "But who is Arek? You refer to him as your apprentice, as does Lore Father Themun, but of this apprentice there's no record in your memory. I find that most curious." Scythe leaned back again, finger to lips as if deep in thought. "How can someone you believe exists not be in your memory?" Scythe seemed genuinely confused. "Don't mistake me . . . you believe what you say and it is clear you and the dragon fought over the life of this 'Arek' . . . but there isn't a single memory within your head of him. Or, to be more clear, no memories I can read. Again, why?"

Silbane didn't know what to say. He clearly remembered his apprentice, and if in fact this person was telling the truth, it would be better to delay things until he better understood the situation.

Something in his demeanor must have shown, for the man let out a sigh that was both tired and sad. "I had hoped this would be a conversation and not an interrogation. I hesitate to hurt you, seeing we're both practitioners of the Way, but I'll do what I must."

Silbane laughed. "Clearly you wield some sort of magic . . . but what do you know of the Way?"

The man stood up and walked over to the corpse of Rai'stahn. He cupped the great dragon's chin and raised his large head. "Do you think you and those few pathetic adepts you left on your Isle are the last essence of magic in this world?" He let Rai'stahn's head drop with a dull thud, its face coming to rest upside down on its armored chest.

"Much has transpired since your self-imposed exile." Scythe's eyes narrowed as he looked back at Silbane. "I am also curious as to why you've allowed yourselves to be so isolated."

He paused, again looking at the dragon-knight's head with obvious remorse. "These blank areas of your memory are very regular, happening at almost precisely the same time every day . . . as if they are scheduled." Scythe paused, then looked at Silbane and asked, "How could such a thing occur?"

Silbane wondered the same thing. Then, with sudden dismay, he knew, but he was careful not to let this knowledge show on his face.

Arek and his training schedule.

Strangely, the realization left Silbane feeling as if an unspoken burden had been lifted.

"Have you come to an understanding? If so—" Scythe pulled the rawhide stool closer to Silbane and sat back down "—please share it with me."

Silbane only looked at the man, his eyes turning cold and hard. It was clear this man was a danger to Silbane, and by extension to Arek.

Scythe continued, "Do you know what else perplexes me? I couldn't see your aura until you were discovered here. That thing," he motioned to something around Silbane's neck with obvious distaste, "accomplishes the same purpose. But what blocked you from my Sight before?"

Silbane tried to crane his head down but couldn't move. He caught a glimpse of something coppery high on his chest, but was unable to focus on it. Whatever it was, the man in red was implying it was the reason for his inability to connect with the Way.

Scythe waited for Silbane to answer. When again no word was forthcoming, he continued, "You wear a torc fashioned by the Galadines, a device with only one purpose—" his gaze grew thoughtful, as though reliving old memories— "to kill us all."

"It blocks my aura?" Silbane ventured this, hoping to keep the conversation away from Arek and their mission.

Scythe blinked twice, his attention coming back to Silbane. "Yes, but what happened on your Isle? Was that the work of Rai'stahn protecting his daughter? The Isle disappeared for more than two score years, then suddenly appeared like a distant fire in the night. It explains the attack, for your brethren now sparkle like a shining star in the middle of the Shattered Sea. But why would Rai'stahn remove his aegis now?"

A cool breeze drifted in through the tent flaps, jingling hanging bells and swirling loose pieces of debris. The scent of jasmine wafted through, filling Silbane with a sense of peace and relaxation.

"Even more curious; how do you hide a dragon's aura, which should outshine yours like a bonfire next to a candle flame?"

Something nagged at Silbane's dazed mind. Then it hit him.

Scythe had said "attack." Had someone attacked Meridian Isle? A part of his mind reacted to the knowledge

with alarm, but a gentle coaxing set in, a reminder that all
was safe and he shouldn't worry.

Silbane found himself preoccupied with the passing
time measured by his heartbeat. It seemed so natural, so
soothing. A question formed in his mind and his voice
uttered it almost automatically, "How long have I been
here?"

Scythe rose and let out a deep breath he'd been holding.
"The better part of a day, not counting time at your camp.
You were in sorry shape. My scouts were a bit too . . .
enthusiastic." He gestured to the other side of the tent
absentmindedly and Silbane saw two men hung on hooks.
Actually, they weren't men, but the skins of men, he
realized through his fogged mind.

"I had them staked out in the sun and then skinned
alive. Discipline must be maintained, no?" Scythe said
seriously. "I had to do quite a bit of healing to fix you."

Silbane worked his jaw, which painfully clicked in
protest. "Could've done better."

Scythe laughed. "You are quite a man, and dangerously
accomplished for one who knows so little of the Way. You
brush off my Talent as an afterthought, then jump directly
back into it like a fish for water. It is as if you harness the
Way differently than most. Perhaps a side effect of your
training?

"Still . . ." The red-robed man came closer. His tone
became serious, almost menacing. "I have planned too long
for the Gate's appearance. Now you show up with a dragon
and a mission to close the Gate. I cannot let that happen."

The man gestured and Silbane found he could use his
right arm. He realized the man had held his arms immobile
with magic, an overt use of power that surprised him. The
Way he knew was mostly internal and rarely manifested
itself as direct control over another. Even techniques like
Clouds before Sun happened by fooling a person's senses,
rarely forcing any real change to the environment.

Scythe handed over the waterskin bladder, then began to speak. "I'll regretfully have to wait to tell your lore father how much I respect him. I felt him pass on to the next world." He looked down, genuine regret in his voice.

The red-robed mage moved his fingers in a fan-like pattern, each finger tracing an arc inward until his fists were closed, then he met Silbane's eyes and said, "Did you know I saw him once, when he was much younger? He didn't know, though even then he was strong in the Way. He saved a girl who'd been captured by the king's men. Her name was Thera.

"She, too, has passed, as if their journey in this world was meant to both start and end together." Scythe sat there for a moment, reliving some distant memory. Then he shook his head and his fingers reversed their fan pattern, each arcing outward and back, until his hands made fists again.

When he spoke next, he did so without meeting Silbane's gaze. "Have you ever lost someone? Someone important to you?"

Silbane watched him, the fog momentarily clearing. He now understood that his own abilities were likely trying to resist whatever this mage was doing. His biggest worry was Arek, but instead of giving that voice, he said, "You claim I have."

Scythe's eyes closed and he gave a small laugh. "Yes, quite right. Then you understand what it's like." His voice grew stronger and he stood and faced Silbane. "You are a very small part of the story of this world, and your chapter is ending."

Silbane looked up at Scythe in silence. *The lore father, dead? Wouldn't he have felt it? Could Arek somehow have blocked his senses? Or Scythe?*

Silbane mentally berated himself. Nothing could kill a master of the Way that easily, and they had the Vault. Tempest was only one item of power—they still had many objects that carried within them power imbued from the

Old Lore. Scythe sought to throw him off balance. Silbane refused.

Scythe cocked his head, as if listening, then said, "Many of the artifacts I thought lost are in that Vault. They are wasted with you and will be put to better use. But I digress."

Scythe motioned to the waterskin, which Silbane held in shocked silence. *He reads my thoughts, even now?* Then a gentle caress eased his shock and worry, and he struggled to remember what had upset him so much a few moments ago as the fog once again wrapped him in its warm embrace.

Scythe grabbed the waterskin from Silbane's nerveless fingers and took a swig, clearing his throat. "The rifts between our plane and Lilyth's are getting more numerous and unpredictable."

Silbane still didn't respond, his mind in a fugue of memories and thoughts, as if contained in a book that Scythe was rifling through at high speed.

"We've managed to stop the larger ones," Scythe continued, "but dozens appear each year, and who are the casualties?"

"Children," croaked Silbane. "Always, the children."

Scythe nodded. "Always, along with those who are strongest in the Way. They disappear as if they never existed. Have you asked yourself, where do they go?"

"They're killed by the demons that emerge from the rifts. Families speak of it, of their loss." This came out as a mumble, but there was still strong emotion behind it. Much of the council's efforts had been to recover children born of Talent, historically before they fell to the king's magehunters, and now before these demons found them.

Scythe cocked his head, a puzzled look on his face. "Killed? Nothing really dies. You know that."

The fog again lifted and Silbane found he could answer with perfect clarity. "Things die all the time. Your men

over there, the dragon, the people of EvenSea!" He spat
these out, laying each death at Scythe's feet.

The red-robed mage smiled and held Silbane's gaze, a
feverish glint in his eyes. "Nothing *really* dies, Silbane. I
will answer for my part in their passing." The glint receded
and Scythe's demeanor became conversational again.

"Are you comfortable? I mean, I cannot let you go, but I
can allow you to adjust your position."

Silbane thought about it and was relieved the
conversation veered away from Arek. His apprentice's
ability to mask magic was clearly important to this man.
The longer Silbane kept Scythe talking, the farther from the
truth they went. When the chance presented itself, he
would use his Finder and escape this location to wherever
his apprentice was. Then they would make their way back
to the Isle.

Silbane said, "Yes, some water, and please, continue . .
."

"There's not much more to say. These rifts are
passageways to Lilyth's plane, a fact you already know or
you wouldn't be trying to destroy my life's work."

Silbane shook his head. "You can't let that Gate reopen.
It would mean—"

"Silence!" roared Scythe. He kicked Silbane in the
chest. The suddenness and violence of the move caught the
master by surprise as the air whooshed from his lungs.

Silbane looked up through pain-dazed eyes and found
Scythe's nose inches from his own. His captor's eyes were
wide, the whites showing. His mouth stretched over teeth
into a grin that looked like a feral animal's.

Silbane realized his life hung on the edge of a blade
balanced on the tip of this lunatic's finger. He froze,
knowing the slightest movement could overturn this man's
carefully crafted semblance of sanity.

At first, he didn't think he would survive. His captor
seemed to be watching a different scene, his eyes jerking
back and forth, looking through and past Silbane. Then the

lids drooped slightly, a breath escaped, nostrils flared as another breath was taken, and Scythe leaned back. His eyes closed and his head tilted back as he sat on his haunches.

He raised his hands together in front of his face, palm to palm, and spoke through them, "Tell me about Arek. If he has the power to interfere, I must know."

Silbane closed his eyes and shook his head. He would not give up one more piece of information that would lead Scythe anywhere near his apprentice.

"Look at me."

At first Silbane considered ignoring him, but after witnessing Scythe's mercurial violence firsthand, he realized the inherent danger of such an infantile gesture. Staying alive was their best hope so he opened his eyes, but kept his mouth shut, watching with the same care and utter stillness he would exhibit had Scythe pressed a blade to his throat.

"You see this as a nomad's tent, with all the expected trappings and furnishings. However . . . " The red-robed mage snapped his fingers and the entire room darkened, changed, cleared, then solidified.

It was basically the same tent, but now the acrid stench of waste filtered in, mixed with the cloying sweet smell of *hazish*. Behind Scythe stood a gargantuan Altan warrior, clearly pleased with something. Elsewhere in the tent, Silbane could see moving forms that hinted at bare flesh and oil. "Not everything is as it seems."

Silbane dropped his head to his chest, knowing now he'd been part of a grand illusion, an exhibition of power far beyond anything he could accomplish so easily. He coughed once and spit blood, then said, "Arek won't interfere. He's far away by now."

Scythe backed away, staring at the master and thinking. Then he motioned to the warrior and said, "U'Zar, I'm not finished with him."

He looked at Silbane and said in a conspiratorial voice, "No escapes." The smile that followed was bright and free of worry, a far cry from the man who looked about to kill him a moment earlier. It was like looking at a door that sat unevenly on its hinge when open, yet no defect could be seen when closed.

Scythe moved closer and Silbane felt his right arm go numb again. "I also know about Themun's Finder." Scythe reached in and in one motion ripped the charm from around Silbane's neck. "If you won't help me find Arek, this will."

Something whispered in Silbane's mind, *you need to rest.* He drowsed, listening as best he could through the unnatural comfort.

"What will you do with that?" asked the giant, referring to the charm.

Scythe looped it around a nail above Silbane's head. "I will create a portal web on this side, should the boy be foolish enough to use it to get to his master. Ring this tent with barricades and post additional guards. If we're lucky, we won't have to do anything. He'll join us on his own and open a door for me into Bara'cor."

The nomad shook his head and grumbled, "You've said Bara'cor's dwarven stone is proof against your magic, so we throw our men at her walls. Why not use this charm to enter?"

"We will, in due time," Scythe answered, his eyes resting on Silbane. "Once the Finder is used, the portal opening cannot be moved. We don't know the whereabouts of his apprentice. What if he has been captured by Bara'cor's forces? What if the other end opens to an iron and granite cell?"

Scythe turned to the leader of the nomads and said, "Let's both be patient for a day and see what transpires. You want the fortress and I want to achieve the Gate within. Our interests are still aligned, but we must be sure no one can stop us." He looked back at the dazed master. "I suspect his apprentice will come to us at his first opportunity."

Then he put a hand on the U'zar's massive forearm and added, "Prepare an assault team to enter Bara'cor. It is a good suggestion."

Silbane's mind cleared again, and he could feel his anger rise like flames, banishing the fog completely.

Scythe grabbed the waterskin and took a long swig, then said to Silbane, "I would consider sparing you. Losing any practitioners of the Way is tragic, and as I said before, you are a good man."

Silbane looked at Scythe, hatred smoldering within. He couldn't believe anyone on Meridian Isle was dead. They were the land's last hope.

Scythe looked at Silbane, his head cocked to one side. "The land's last hope? You still don't understand, do you?"

Scythe stood. Smiling down on the master he said, "You aren't the land's last hope. I am."

He looked at Silbane and gestured. A quiet lassitude offered Silbane the luxury of sleep. It seemed so natural to him, to be tired now. After his apprentice arrived, he knew everything would be all right.

A part of his mind heard Scythe, though the words seemed to come through a dream. The red-robed mage said, "Keep him alive until I give the order, Hemendra. He shrugs off my enchantments too quickly . . . some side effect of his training. It only invites trouble, but I want his apprentice. If what he thinks is true, the boy is dangerous, to both of us."

Silbane came more awake, watching as a gap of light appeared from the departure of the insane mage. Into the gap stepped Hemendra, who looked at the master with a guarded expression on his face. Contempt mixed with something that Silbane in his addled state couldn't identify. He realized he could now move his head and speak.

His mind then cleared again, as if a fog had been blown away by a clean spring breeze. With his newfound clarity he looked at the clanchief and said, "My apprentice will never come here. You and I are soldiers. It'd be better to get this over with."

Hemendra tilted his massive head to one side and said, "I will follow Redrobe's suggestion." With a smile, he turned and left the tent.

As Silbane watched him leave, a crushing sense of failure closed in around him. Worst of all was the fear that Scythe was right and that everyone on the Isle was truly dead. With the torc blocking his path to the Way, he'd no way of knowing.

Something tickled the back of his mind. In addition to their arduous physical training on the Isle, much of their learning went into understanding an opponent's mental state. The nomad chieftain, Hemendra, had said something . . . something that didn't fit well with his demeanor around Scythe.

Then it struck him, the clanchief had used the word "suggestion."

Perhaps the mage's help wasn't as welcome as he thought. Here was a potential weakness, and Silbane prepared himself for any opening that might show itself, however small. For now, all he could do was sit and wait, the heat of the day soaking in as a hot breeze blew into the tent, stirring the various trappings. As he waited, he thought again about the torc, the Isle, and about Themun. Could he be dead, as Scythe had said? He took a deep breath, his mind flying back to the first time he and Themun had met...

Obsession

JOURNAL ENTRY . . .
UNSURE

Victorious, healing . . . I am tired, too tired to write this morning. Facing it was the key . . . courage, faith in oneself.

I do not know how long I have slept. The world here is similar to our own, yet vastly different. It is the reflection of our dreams and hopes, so the fact that it is mostly beautiful speaks to our secret wish for a better place. It is where we all end, hence the dragon's question about, "who has died?" I didn't understand, but regardless, enslavement is not an option. It is the only choice left to us if we continue as the dreamers.

As I have written, here our thoughts are as dangerous as reality, for our thoughts bring the Aeris into focus. But my encounter with the dark thing below the castle has taught me my first valuable lesson. Though I dream it, I can still destroy it! In fact, I know I am destined to do exactly this.

I am surrounded now by little helpers. I cannot explain what they are . . . Imps? Sprites? They are tiny beings that seem to know what I want and fetch it for me, whether it be food, paper, ink, water . . . I know my mind is creating these supplies, but why small creatures to fetch them? I must ponder this more.

They are, however, a pleasant distraction.

Journal Entry . . . unsure

FLASHBACK: SILBANE

Teaching children the Way of Making,
reveals the core of your true self.
A child will show you, through deed and action,
a mirror of who you really are.
—Lore Father Argus Rillaran, The Way

S ilbane felt his father's rough hands push him forward, not unkindly.

"He's ready," said his father.

The older man nodded, but said, "We'll see." A wry smile flashed across his face and he stooped, coming eye to eye with the eight-year-old. "I am Themun Dreys, lore father of this isle. Are you ready, young Lord of House Petra?"

"Of course," Silbane piped.

"Are you old?" The latter came out matter-of-factly.

The man stood up, his eyes smiling. "Umm, older than you."

The boy stared, not sure if that was the old man's entire answer, given it was fairly obvious the man was older than himself. When no more looked like it was going to follow that statement, Silbane decided to do what he did often, and just be quiet. Grown-ups didn't like being corrected, he'd learned.

"He's straightforward," Themun said, laughing, holding up a hand in mock surrender. Then he looked at the boy and said, "Give us a moment."

Silbane shrugged, looking expectantly at the stone dais and the concentric circles inscribed upon it, his mind already whirling through possibilities and permutations on the space and shapes. He barely registered it when Themun spoke again to his father.

"It takes a considerable amount of luck to find us," Themun commented.

"Coin speaks if you know who to pay, but we were careful not to leave any trails here. We defy the King's law, and therefore have as much to lose as you. A quick end to my House if we're found out."

Themun nodded, placing a hand on Silbane's shoulder, gently guiding him away from his father's protective grasp. The boy felt the warm touch and gave in, but met his father's concerned stare and winked, hoping that would set him more at ease.

"You've risked much for your son, and I wish I could promise you the outcome. I hope he has the Talent. If he does, we'll provide refuge."

His father gave a short laugh, "I'm not worried. The boy has what it takes." Before he'd gotten out of his reach his father pulled him to his chest, squeezing him in his bear-like arms.

"Remember all your puzzles . . . you were always good at figuring things out."

Silbane rolled his eyes, but hugged back. They were so concerned all the time. He didn't know how to explain it, but he knew he'd be fine. And how long would this hug last?

"He won't be harmed," Themun Dreys assured his father.

Silbane's father let go, then stood up, looking around. "Where do you want us?"

The lore father gestured to the left, a path that led to a small garden. Silbane saw a bench where his father and mother could wait for him to finish the test.

Silbane crossed his arms and waited.

"What do you know of this test?" Themun asked.

Silbane met the lore father's eyes without wavering. "Nothing, sir, but I assume it's solvable."

"Why?"

The boy was quiet, then he said what was obvious to him. "If it's too hard, you'd be turning away people you want to save. So the test must challenge one's thinking."

Themun laughed and asked, "And Talent. What if you don't pass?"

Silbane shook his head and a seriousness encompassed him like a cloak. "What if I do?" he countered.

The lore father looked at him, and Silbane couldn't tell if the man was angry. Then a slow smile grew on his face and he asked, "Did you want to come here?"

Silbane looked around, then said, "Yes. Mistfrights attacked our land. We escaped." He stood still, looking at the circle. Eventually, he deduced, "I stand there?" He wanted to get started.

Themun's mouth again tugged up on one end in a half smile. "Yes."

Silbane didn't wait for leave, but scampered to the central octagon tile, jumping at the last moment to land in its center.

"Stand ready. Four walls, each based on one of the elements, will rise. Your task is to get through them. If you can't, I'll drop the walls and come get you. Don't be afraid."

Silbane rolled his eyes again. Everyone sounded like his parents.

Before he could finish the thought, four concentric circles sprang up. The closest was made of water and behind that, earth. Beyond that, he could see nothing else.

He looked at the swirling wall of water before him. It rushed by with a dull roar, echoing through the small, circular chamber it created. He pushed a finger into the wall and felt his hand swept aside by the current. How many had tried to defeat it by pushing through? That would never work.

Stepping into the current could be deadly, as both drowning and broken limbs could result from the wall of water smashing him into the wall of earth. Since this also wasn't a desirable outcome, his mind continued its analysis. Silbane had always been told he over-thought things, but here it served him well.

Wait . . . the wall of earth? His thoughts narrowed, his quick mind flitting through possibilities. The older man had mentioned four walls, so he assumed air and fire would be the last elements.

The order might matter, he thought. He turned that over in his mind, running through the combinations. A slow smile broke out on his face as the answer came to him.

He positioned his hand, knife-edged, and closed his eyes. He'd found that by envisioning what he wanted, it often came true. Now he thought of his hand repelling water, bending it away from his palm. Slowly, he pushed his hand into the stream, knowing without looking that the water in front of his palm no longer traveled the circle, but rather redirected itself along an angle made by his hand. He pushed harder, making the gush of water obey his simple redirection. He kept his hand open and still, then angled it, just so.

Water, hitting a space just in front of the flat blade of his palm, streamed into the wall of earth. Soaking it to submission, the second wall fell away in a mix of brown sludge and dirt. He continued to widen the hole until there was an arch in the wall of earth that was large enough for him to stand in. Beyond it, he could see the wall of air.

He pushed both hands against the wall of water. The wall broke at the push, and he jumped through the momentary gap he'd created in the current. The water wall grabbed at him but he was quick. Because he'd hollowed out a space first, he stumbled and fell inside the arch in the wall of earth, instead of being pulled and pummeled by the racing current.

"Should I keep going?"

There was no answer.

The boy added, "I will do the same, bending earth into air, and pushing air into fire." To demonstrate, he closed his eyes and pushed the earth forward until it created a lee in the wall of wind. Continuing, Silbane redirected the wall of air into the flames, creating a gap there as well.

There was still no answer, so Silbane heaved a sigh. "You know how this ends. Do I have to do it?" He made a calculated guess, but his conviction never wavered.

A moment passed, then two. Then the walls collapsed. Outside the circle stood Themun, smiling. "You are a boastful child." He paused, then added, "But there seems no point in continuing your test."

Silbane didn't know what that meant, so he asked, "I'm accepted?"

"Would it matter if I said no?"

Silbane looked down, not sure if the lore father was kidding. "I want to be here. I won't give up," he vowed.

The lore father moved forward and clapped a hand on the boy's shoulder. "You are accepted. Tell your parents of your success." Themun gestured to the path on his left.

"Yes!" Silbane smiled, a beam of sunshine the lore father returned.

Silbane wasn't quite sure how to ask his next question. He'd had heard stories from his father about this place.

He looked up, his brows knit, and asked, sheepishly, "Is it true that only one in a thousand solve this puzzle?"

"No, Lord Petracles . . . far less." Themun's mock sternness put Silbane in his place. "Very few have both the intelligence and the Talent to pass. Now, go find your parents."

It was clear Themun wasn't going to say anything more, so Silbane nodded, a gesture that included his whole body in a miniature bow, and ran off.

Today, he was sure, was the best day of his life.

Flashback: Silbane

PART II

Flashback: Silbane

THE NEXT MISSION

When you are comfortable, you are vulnerable.
Maintain discipline, master your weakness.
With repetition, discomfort will feel safe,
and you will begin to see weakness in others.
—Tir Combat Academy, Basic Forms & Stances

P rime and Two returned to the cabin, but neither looked happy. They moved over to where Three stood quietly conferring with Four. The group spoke softly in turns, each nodding as their leader explained something. Then the four turned and made their way back to where Kisan stood with Five.

"That last adept was stalking us." Prime said this as a statement of fact. "When we saw him, he was making his way toward you two."

Three then added, "He certainly seemed to know we were there. Once the rest of us detected him, he dropped his visual cloak."

"Conserving energy for battle," Prime replied softly. He seemed deep in thought. Then he looked at the group and asked, "If he knew, then the others might have also. Give me scenarios."

They went in order and based on Tamlin's memory, Kisan knew this exercise had a very strict protocol. The newest member spoke first, then each spoke in turn by rank. This way the more experienced members received the benefit of the other's observations. Kisan knew she only had a heartbeat to answer. "He followed us, but meant to attack earlier. When he became visible, it was six against one. Not good planning for as good as he was."

"Separated us with a decoy," said Five. "Thought we chased a boy."

"He was following us. He could've been out, seen what happened, and waited for the perfect moment, but that never came, huh?" Four added with a laugh.

Three said, "Something warned him. Maybe the area was protected by countermeasures we're not familiar with."

Two thought for a moment, his mind moving through the various scenarios. He then said, "I agree with Four. He was already out, heard something. We would've heard him, if our positions were reversed."

Kisan seriously doubted this last statement, given their abilities, but remained silent. Now wasn't the time for her to come to anyone's attention.

Prime bowed his head, assimilating everything he'd heard. "Three, you think something warned him? What?"

Three stepped up. "We don't know their complete capabilities. Maybe the woman managed to send out a warning. Those damn halfling kids were squealers."

Kisan closed her eyes, keeping her emotions in check.

Prime nodded, then looked at Five and asked, "You said decoy . . .?"

Five stepped forward, saying, "Just before he showed up a young boy ran past us, heading for the woods. We each fired a dart, but the boy kept running. We followed standard procedure."

Standard procedure meant Six would hold position while Five took the target. Prime looked at Six and asked, "How long was Five gone?"

"No more than twenty beats," Kisan answered. She realized now, with great relief, that they couldn't mindspeak. Had that been part of their repertoire, this sort of mission debriefing would never occur. They would simply have shared thoughts and seen what each other saw, but her identity would immediately have been uncovered.

Her thoughts were interrupted when she realized that everyone was staring at her. No one moved, but it was clear something she'd just said caused this.

Then Two snarled, "What the hell is a beat?"

Kisan's mind scrambled. She didn't know what "hell" meant, and how could they not know the rhythm of their own hearts? She dove into Tamlin's memories and realized that timekeeping for these dwarves was much more sophisticated, more precise. She searched, then dredged up the correct unit of measure, sounding out the word, "Twenty sekunds . . .," she finished lamely.

It sounded strange to her, but it was roughly equivalent to a heartbeat, so she hoped Prime would accept it.

It seemed to work. With the exception of Two, the rest had gone back to looking at their leader. Two continued to stare at her though, shaking his head in disgust.

Prime looked at the group, silent and thoughtful. After a moment, he offered, "The boy was likely a student. However, the profile of these adepts shows they wouldn't use students as bait. The boy you saw probably spooked and ran. The adept unshielded himself in an effort to misdirect us from him, not knowing that Five had already taken the boy . . . any holes?"

The group stood silent. Then Five hesitantly said, "We never found the boy. He made it to the edge of the woods and disappeared."

Prime looked at the two of them with disgust. "You both missed?" Behind him, Two, who was in charge of their continued training, shifted his weight, an unspoken promise of endless drills after this debriefing concluded. Five and Six were officially on his list.

"He's dead," Three offered. "There was enough in just one dart to kill him, even if he made it to the wood's edge. Neither Six or Five would've been able to find him in that undergrowth. The signal to regroup came just as the boy raced past them."

There was a moment where Kisan was sure Prime would challenge that conclusion, but it passed without comment. "I have our orders," he told the group instead. "We are to proceed to the port of Haven where we will drop the boat off with Arsenal, then make our way to the fortress of Bara'cor."

"Target?" Three asked.

"Our secondary target is the entire Galadine line. They're strong in the Way and removing them will create confusion and anarchy across the realm."

"The royal family?" Four shook his head. "Heavy prep. Lots of variables."

"That's what we live for," Prime said, "Our primary is more complicated. Two."

At his command, Two stepped forward and outlined the facts. "Meridian Isle was sanctioned because of two events. One, the dragon Rai'stahn, and a master left shortly before our attack; and two, they both disappeared, as if their connection to the Way had been cut off."

Prime looked at his team and said, "Another null has appeared."

Silence reigned as each team member instantly understood what Prime was saying. Only Kisan felt left out, but waited so she could put more context into what she'd just heard.

"We've never faced a null before." This was from Five, doubt clear in his voice.

Two reacted immediately and said, "Stow that! Every team has their first and this is ours. They can't do magic, and plain steel is all you need."

The others nodded, then Four stepped forward. "Which master was it?"

"We don't know, the null field hides him," Prime said, "but given the body count at the Isle, we can assume it is Silbane Petracles. Calling him dangerous is an understatement, so stay sharp. If he's protecting this null, we have a lethal situation on our hands, and I'd like to see everyone come back alive."

Kisan didn't have to wonder what a "null" was.

"The queen is in Haven, and outside of mission parameters. She's not a target, yet." Prime grabbed a sheaf of papers with detailed drawings of people and handed them out. Kisan had never seen drawings so real, almost lifelike. She stared at them, mesmerized by the detail. In addition to images, the papers contained habits, training, and other vital information on each target. "Memorize these, then destroy them."

Kisan leafed through the papers until she came to Silbane's sheet. The detail was extraordinary. Her mouth suddenly felt dry. How had they gathered such information about them and their Isle, supposedly a guarded secret? The answer must be betrayal, but she couldn't think of who or why. If not that, then this Sovereign was better equipped and informed than she'd suspected.

"Intelligence from Arsenal reports a new prisoner in Bara'cor, a boy named Arek. We carry out our secondary objective and then seek out the prisoner. If he's the null, no limping off into the bushes to die," said Two, locking eyes first with Five and Six, then the rest of the team. "We make sure to kill them."

"And if he's not?" asked Kisan.

Two smiled, though the humor didn't reach his eyes. "They are getting lax at the Core, decanting anyone with a pulse. The answer is always the same, mudknife, every time." He looked at Three.

Three laughed and said, "We always kill them."

The Next Mission

A Change in Plans

One technique, above all else, is vital.
Listen more than you speak.
—Davyd Dreys, Memoirs

His name is Arek Winterthorn. It was the name given to him when he was found by a group of monks. They reside on an island southeast of here, somewhere in the Shattered Sea." Ash looked at the king, a sheaf of papers in his hand.

Bernal asked for the report. With him and Jebida were his son Niall and Yetteje. Although they had mostly recovered from their encounter, Sergeant Stemmer still had headaches from the blow she'd received and was under the careful eye of the healers. The rest, except for their wounded pride, were not badly hurt.

"This is no boy, however innocent he may look," the firstmark said gruffly. "He could've killed Sergeant Stemmer, Princess Tir, even your son. He faced my armsmark in single combat and held his own. His storybook tale didn't change under physical interrogation. He has clearly been conditioned and definitely has special military training. It's worth repeating . . . he could've killed your son."

"He could have, but he didn't kill anyone," Ash said. "Maybe because his story is true. We know every point of ingress, and he's not dressed like anyone I've ever met. Besides, did you see him? He didn't look 'conditioned' after our man finished with him."

"What do you mean?" Niall asked in a small voice. "What did we do?"

The firstmark looked at the young prince and said, "We're at war. He somehow evaded all our guards, entered here and attempted to kill you . . ." Jebida looked exasperated. "We did what we had to."

Yetteje looked at Niall and said, "They tortured him." From the look on her face, it was clear the idea didn't bother her in the least.

Niall turned back to the king, shaking his head. "Father?"

The king ignored his son, contemplating the information, then asked, "How is the prisoner?"

Jebida shrugged and replied, "His foot and ankle are broken in multiple places." With the exception of Jebida and Yetteje, everyone in the room looked uncomfortable at the mention of torture.

The king accepted that. His only concern was the safety of Bara'cor, and the possibility there was a way into the fortress they didn't know about. It was something his son would have to grow to understand: the weight of everyone's safety over any one person's life or comfort.

"Does your man think he was telling the truth?" asked the king.

The firstmark and armsmark looked at each other, their long service together a common bond, allowing the unspoken disagreement to hang in the air without detracting from their duties. Then, with a sigh, Jebida turned to the king and said, "Aye, milord. The prisoner believes what he says."

Ash said, "We can't ignore the report of fire in the desert, a day's ride to the east."

"I've seen it," Jebida said. "What else?"

Ash continued, "The king ordered me to deploy scouts to reconnoiter the area. I stationed four teams in a line between the reported fireball and the nomad encampment. Early this morning one team reported a small group of nomads hauling two figures back to camp. They don't normally recover their dead. Also, one was a gargantuan figure in armor."

The king's eyes narrowed. "Our prisoner claims his master and a dragon in the form of a knight fought. Now two prisoners matching this description are being taken to the nomad camp? And did you see this entry about a Finder?"

The firstmark nodded, "Of course."

"Two men, described just as Arek says," the king added. "And now the fire is reported by our scouts. An amazing coincidence?"

"So you think his master is captured?" retorted Jebida. "An apprentice nearly bests Ash but his master falls to simple nomad barbarians? What sense does that—?"

The king interrupted. "Our prisoner's story has been partially corroborated by our own scouts, so let's hypothesize for a moment. This Finder, when broken, supposedly opens a portal to the location of the other half. The boy has one half, his master the other." The meaning was instantly clear to almost everyone in the room.

Niall looked around, then asked, "What?"

The king locked eyes with Ash, this last bit of news welcome in light of the dozens who would die in a frontal charge to cover their infiltration. Bernal looked at Ash and said, "If Silbane has been captured and taken to the camp, he may be very close to your target already." Then the king turned to his son and explained, "Ash could use this Finder to infiltrate the nomad camp."

"Or it's a magical explosive, or if it does open a door, he might appear in Bara'cor," remarked Jebida, clearly frustrated. "The two captured may be nomad deserters, and the boy's master may be dead." He looked at the king, shaking his head. "How many scenarios don't end well?"

The king held up a hand and said, "What nomad's kit is full armor? I think it fairly certain the two taken to the nomad camp are Silbane and this dragon-knight. But Silbane may be dead, as you say," he added.

A Change in Plans

Yetteje piped in, "So he lost to the dragon. It doesn't mean we can't use the Finder. Wouldn't it still take us to its mate?"

"Perhaps," huffed the firstmark, still clearly not trusting magic, Arek, or anything that had to do with him. "To be safe, I ordered our half of the Finder locked in a cell. I'd like to avoid the nomad command using it to gain entry here."

Yetteje looked up from her thoughts and said, "Will it work for us? I mean, what if only Arek can use it?"

Niall looked around the room. "And can it transport more than one person?"

The king shook his head, reading from the report. "It says the Finder works by breaking it again, and so long as Silbane lives, it will continue to glow." He looked at his firstmark and said, "It was smart, locking up the charm." He shook the report. "We'll have to ask Arek, who won't be inclined to help."

Ash thought about it, then offered, "The greatest thing of value is his freedom."

The king agreed. "And that of his master. If he agrees to open the portal for our men to rescue this Silbane, it could work."

"And just how would we enforce such an agreement? We don't know enough about his magic amulet to stop him from escaping without us," Jebida grumbled. "This is a fool's quest."

"Maybe . . ." Ash countered, "but perhaps the portal stays open until the charm holder goes through. If that's the case we could take an entire division, so long as Arek went last."

"Who'll carry him?" asked the firstmark. "He can't walk without help."

The king gestured again to the notes they had bought with Arek's pain. "The sword he carries, Tempest. He believes it can heal—maybe it can soothe his pain. We could offer him the chance to use it, if he takes our team in with him."

"And give him a weapon?" The firstmark snapped his meaty fingers. "Bern, think about what you're suggesting. If we thought to lock up the charm behind iron bars, maybe the nomads have as well," Jebida turned to Ash, "or it might be at the bottom of a fire pit, where they toss baubles they strip from prisoners."

He paced around the table coming to stand before his king. "What if this portal is highly visible? It could attract their entire army down on Ash and his team. This can't be a serious option."

The king took the measure of the firstmark's words. He was right, they were making many assumptions without much information. Still, what was their alternative?

After a moment, he asked Ash, "Do you think your chances are better trying to sneak past the nomad lines?"

Ash thought about it, then said, "I think it could be an easier way in, regardless of where we appear. Remember, we will be dressed as them, and we'll be armed."

The firstmark stepped forward and faced Ash. "Forget betting your life. Are you willing to bet Bara'cor's life? If you're wrong, the mission and our best chance, ends with you."

Ash met the firstmark's eyes, his mind clearly in turmoil. He drew a breath, then ticked off with his fingers his reasons. "This talisman seems designed to bring Arek and his master together in an emergency, which would be done with little noise and fanfare, or the idea of maintaining a stealthy mission would be lost. If Arek thinks the sword can heal his foot, then this is serious motivation for him to help us. I go first through this 'portal,' then the team follows. The boy stays here until our return." Ash paused then added, "We travel there and back without going through the nomad lines at all."

"You're suggesting leaving the portal open?" the king asked the armsmark.

A Change in Plans

"Only if we can adequately guard it from this end," he answered. "Worst case, we might be able to close it by tossing the charm through without Arek."

"And once you're in, you'll be wherever this Silbane is. Jebida is right. What's your plan?" asked the king.

"Remember, if he is one of those seen by our scouts, he was captured while trying to defend his apprentice. He'll no doubt recognize Tempest, proof we have Arek. If he's in any shape to help us, I think he will. Furthermore, if Arek is this formidable, imagine what his master must be like."

"Even better," Jebida retorted, "now there'll be two of them." The firstmark moved over to the table, looking at the relief map and thinking aloud. "And what if he refuses to help us until he knows his apprentice is okay?"

"I never expected to have his help in the first place, but getting in without daring the nomad line is help enough, right? Besides," Ash added with a smile, "why wouldn't Silbane help? Aren't I charming enough?"

"Not funny," retorted the firstmark. "Clearly I'd have better luck talking sense to Bara'cor's walls." After a moment he shook his head and said, "At least this plan doesn't rely on the certain death of some of our men, only *possible* death."

"I agree," Ash replied.

The firstmark shifted his feet uncomfortably, and then looked to the king. "You're as stubborn as a mule. I'm not going to convince you, am I?"

"Said the mule hitched beside him," the king replied with a smile.

Jebida shook his head, then threw his arms open. "Trusting magic is forbidden! It was a decree that held our people safe. I say we're better off without the boy or his master. Nothing good will come of it."

The king faced his firstmark. "I rescinded that decree years ago, Jeb, and any who still hunt those with Talent do so as criminals. Persecuting an entire class of people because of how they are born is wrong. Who are we to judge the good or ill a person may bring to this life?"

Ash stepped to the firstmark's side and said, "Dead isn't better off. Not for us. Not for the people of Bara'cor." The armsmark laid a hand on his commander's arm, "Many will be taken again by these demons."

The firstmark shrugged off his second's hand, "You presume too much, armsmark," he said gruffly.

He looked back to the king and said, "I don't question your law or your judgment, and I'll always follow. I just don't have to like it." He paused, about to add something, then instead said, "If I may be excused, sir? We'll need to get the boy bandaged and cleaned up."

The king nodded, to empathize that Jeb's mind must certainly be on his dead family. He was surprised Ash had taken that route to try and convince the firstmark, but these two had a way of communicating that the king trusted would lead to a good end. "Yes, see to it. I'll finish up here with the others."

With a nod and salute, Jebida left the room and an uncomfortable silence followed. Finally, Yetteje, said in a quiet voice, "So, where does this leave us?"

The king watched the back of his retreating commander and said, "We need to speak with Arek."

A Change in Plans

JOURNAL ENTRY 11

Of the titans and gods I know to walk this world, I have seen a few. I thought I saw Lilyth in the distance, the Lady of Flame in all her splendor. I've seen Petra, and mighty Heraclyes. Each ignores me as if I do not exist. Am I too inconsequential? If they are the creation of our legends, truly powerful in the Way, perhaps it is better not to come to their attention.

The new Aeris are not the true danger. They are consumed by incantation or spell. While they create problems in diplomacy with the Aeris Lords, they are not the reason for our downfall.

It is these Aeris Lords, given life by our thoughts, who concern me. We cannot stop their Shaping so long as we believe higher powers are at work and a god heeds our prayers. It is a difficult problem to solve, especially in the face of the masses who sit cow-like, chewing their mental cud and praying for divine intervention. I sigh when writing this.

It will only be a matter of time before these Aeris Lords enslave us. Once given life, they begin to dream. Their dreams span the entire heart of our kind, from the basest treacheries to the highest ideals. They are our gods and our demons and demand our fealty. It is their nature.

And so it comes to this . . . what kills a god?

Journal Entry 11

THREE DAYS LEFT . . .

Journal Entry 11

TEMPEST

Attend an ancient wisdom;
If your woman runs away with another man,
there is no better revenge,
than to let him keep her.
—Altan proverb

K ing Galadine waited in the council chamber, an uncharacteristic nervous flutter upsetting his stomach. He couldn't put his finger on what was worrying him, other than the string of improbable events starting with this blasted siege and ending with a combat-trained young man infiltrating the fortress for unknown reasons.

The doors opened and he was joined by the armsmark, Yetteje, Niall, and his royal guards. He expected the firstmark shortly with their prisoner. The torture had been unavoidable and he did not regret that Arek's injured foot was their key bargaining chip now; though he hadn't anticipated it, it was a powerful advantage for them.

Bernal reminded himself to try reason first, and leave anything more unsavory as a last resort. A few moments later, Jebida entered the council chamber with their prisoner in tow.

The boy hobbled in, supported on crutches, escorted on either side by guards. He clearly could put no weight on his injured leg and foot. Dark circles stood like half-moon bruises under his eyes. To the king, the boy looked young and frail. It was hard to believe this was the same person whom Ash held in such high regard.

Behind him came Sargin, the man who had led the interrogation. As the group slowed, Sargin moved around the boy and came to stand next to the king. They had agreed on this tactic earlier, a way to apply pressure to the boy during these critical negotiations. Securing Bara'cor's safety was the king's paramount concern. Hurting a spy, physically or mentally, fell to a distant second in Bernal's estimation.

The king acknowledged Sargin with a nod, accepting that men like him were unavoidable in times of war. When the king looked back, the boy was looking at his interrogator with a gaze of hatred so pure it startled him. *Perhaps this boy has more steel than I thought . . .*

Still, Sargin's presence would serve to remind the boy of the horror he'd endured and make Bernal's offer even more enticing.

The firstmark and king had chosen to introduce Arek as if he were a guest, hoping it would set the tone of the meeting correctly. The king couldn't tell if it worked, for the boy stood still, his face unreadable and his faded blue eyes distant.

Bernal realized with a sudden shock just how familiar the boy looked, almost a younger version of himself. It was impossible that Galadine blood ran in this invader, and yet Bernal's eyes weren't lying. For him, it was like looking into a mirror dimmed only by time. *Who is this boy?* he wondered. Bernal struggled to focus as the boy's countenance brought distracting questions and doubts into his carefully prepared strategy.

At that moment, Jebida announced, "Your Majesty, may I present Arek Winterthorn, apprentice to Master Silbane Petracles."

* * * * *

Arek slowly looked up at the king, his mind numb. His foot throbbed with every beat of his heart. He knew the bones were broken, perhaps irreparably. He'd only had the courage to glimpse it once after his interrogation, and had been unwilling to look again. Given his medical training, he knew he'd eventually heal. Sargin had been careful not to create any injuries that bled. Though he might recover, he knew the bones wouldn't reknit themselves properly without prompt attention. Since there was no chance they'd offer him that, he concentrated instead on the king and what he might negotiate.

The king bowed and said, "I won't waste your time with apologies or false platitudes of friendship. We caught you within our fortress during a time of war. You put us in this position by infiltrating the fortress and attacking our people without provocation. We can't hazard the safety of those inside, and did what we must. To be blunt, though, I don't care how you feel."

Arek watched the king glance around the room, his eyes for some reason finding the man who'd brought Tempest in. The armsmark replied with an almost imperceptible gesture with his hands. Arek had no idea what he was trying to convey, but it seemed as if the king's retinue was trying to keep their liege calm.

Interesting, because it means they need me. Arek filed that away and waited. Speaking now wouldn't improve anything, but silence might show him a path.

The king looked back at the infiltrator and said, "Even if you can't forgive us, I hope you can understand the position *you* put us in." His emphasis wasn't needed, but Arek saw something else. Here was a man who refused to believe Bara'cor had somehow acted ignobly. Guilt was speaking now, not diplomacy.

He didn't know this "king." He couldn't place him in the same reality as the pain he felt, though a detached part of him understood that someone who claimed such a title was ultimately responsible.

The man standing next to the king elicited a very different reaction.

Arek *knew* him, and both hated and feared the sight of Sargin. The sadist stood emotionless, still to the king's left.

When their eyes met, the man smirked, as if saying, *Next time I'll chop them off. . .*

Anger ignited deep within his belly. Despite the fact that they were men at war, Arek felt that all combat still held a non-negotiable commitment to honor. The man calling himself Sargin clearly didn't care about that. He'd laughed when Arek had begged, he'd slapped him when he'd pleaded. He'd made him do things. . . Arek let out a breath he'd not realized he was holding. Sargin was despicable, a man who loved to hurt others, and Arek would find a way to make his torturer pay.

For now, though, he looked at the king numbly. There were undoubtedly many people the king could've assigned to interrogate Arek. Yet, Sargin had been chosen. King Galadine knew what he'd done when he'd chosen *that* man. He knew the pain and degradation the man would inflict. Hadn't he just said that he didn't care about the torture inflicted...maybe Bernal thought because he'd not wielded the hammer he was free of guilt?

The king motioned and another man ran forward with the written report. Scanning the pages, the king looked back at Arek and said, "I've read your confession and I believe you. I'm willing to rescue your master. Though you claim no ability with magic, perhaps he can use your sword, Tempest, to ease your pain."

Arek was shaken. *Tempest!* He'd all but forgotten the blade. He was sure Master Silbane could do something with the eldritch blade. Perhaps his pain could be allayed, his wounds healed with the sword's power and his master's skill?

The king went on, "We know your master still lives, but has been captured by the nomads. We want to insert a team into the nomad camp. Their job will be to kill the nomad chieftain. Your Finder—"

"I don't believe you," Arek interrupted. He understood the king's plan. He wanted to sound sure, but his voice cracked as he caught the emotionless eyes of Sargin.

The king shrugged, and then continued, "We know he was taken by the nomads, along with an armored knight. I offer you a chance to rejoin him, and so long as you do not seek retribution, we will give you Tempest. I'll have my men . . ."

Arek's awareness tunneled in what he now recognized preceded the appearance of Piter. He wasn't surprised when he turned and saw the shade standing there, but there was something different about him.

"Revenge!" Piter looked at the frozen scene, his eyes finally coming to rest on Sargin's form. "Retribution for what he did."

"What do you mean?" In a way, Arek was grateful for Piter's appearance. Despite his abandonment before the torture, Piter was the only familiar face in the room, and Arek felt very much alone.

Piter moved closer, his countenance reflecting barely contained fury. "Revenge for daring to attack an Adept of the Isle! But for Ascension, you are that already! Make no mistake, you have the bargaining power here." He looked around again then nodded at the figure of the king. "He will do anything to get into that nomad camp."

Arek thought Piter's anger was misplaced, but said, "What do you suggest, or are you going to just disappear again?"

Piter smiled, coming conspiratorially close, but careful not to touch the apprentice. "I know a way." Then Piter leaned forward and whispered, and the smile spread to Arek's face.

* * * * *

". . . watching. So long as you make your way from this fortress peacefully, I vow to let you go in peace," Bernal said, finishing. The boy looked like he hadn't heard the last part, but before he could repeat it, Arek hobbled forward on his crutches; the guards supporting him hastened to keep him upright.

"I am the only one keyed to use the Finder," Arek said, nodding to the charm. "And I can transport you and your men to where my master is. What is your plan?"

The king looked at his assembled men, his gaze finally falling on his son. It was for Niall he even considered this. His survival was more important to the king than anything. Sending Ash and his men into harm's way was the best chance of ensuring his heir stayed alive. He cleared his throat and looked back at Arek, saying, "I will give the blade to Armsmark Ash Rillaran for safekeeping during transport."

Ash stepped forward so Arek could identify him.

"If Ash and his team appear where your master is, the team will free him," the king continued. "And Ash will request his help in killing the leader of these nomads. The sword will serve to prove that you are with us. Once accomplished, the armsmark will lead your master back to you."

"If Silbane refuses, he still may take the sword and return here to collect you." The king licked his lips, then added carefully, "Transporting our team into the nomad camp will be considered payment in full for your release. You may depart, but we hope you both will join our cause."

Before Arek could reply, Bernal held up a forestalling hand and said, "Should you alone disappear when the Finder is used, we will consider Tempest held as fair ransom. However, if you wish your master to heal your injuries, you will do your best to make sure Ash and his team makes it through the portal, or you won't have the means to heal yourself."

Arek was silent for a moment. He then said, "You assume my master can't heal me without Tempest."

The king nodded, looking at his men. "We're all making assumptions, but these are desperate times for Bara'cor."

The king met Arek's look with a direct stare and said, "I saw the look on your face when I mentioned your master and the sword, so I believe you think this could work. Am I mistaken?"

Arek paused, then said, "No, you are not, King Galadine." He mistakenly put weight on his injured foot, and Bernal had to watch as the boy fought to keep his composure. A part of him wanted to help, and regretted he couldn't do anything right now that would be interpreted as weakness. There was something about Arek that the king admired. The boy was disciplined and it seemed, honorable. War sometimes made enemies of the wrong people.

Arek finally unclenched his teeth and said, "I can transport your men to my master's location. You may have a good chance of ending this siege, saving many lives, including those you hold most dear. But I have a demand, or I won't help." Arek's pale eyes never left the king's own, the stare looking dead in the torchlit room.

Bernal took a single step forward. It was carefully measured to show implacable will, but stop just shy of intimidation. "You are not in a position to bargain. I could have you thrown into a cell to await the inevitable fall of Bara'cor to the nomad army. Or perhaps there's more information we might extract."

With that Sargin joined the king in a carefully choreographed one-two punch. *Now that was pure intimidation.* Bernal noted the boy visibly paled but still held his ground. His respect continued to grow. Few could withstand fear from personal experience. The boy wasn't someone to underestimate. Bernal recalled the firstmark's comment about special training. *Maybe Jeb was right?*

"Do that and you will never have my help. This fortress will fall and your future will die with you." Arek nodded pointedly at Niall, who stood on the other side of the king.

It was at that moment the king realized just how much Arek had read him, and had understood what Bernal feared most. Suddenly, the thought that the boy had been playing his own subtle game of brinksmanship seemed distinctly real, and that knowledge brought with it a dark foreboding. With steel in his voice, the king said, "I could just have you killed."

Their gazes locked, measuring the other.

"King Galadine, I'm trained in the ways of combat. With what has been done to my body at Bara'cor's hands, I'm already dead. My foot is probably crippled. My master is captured, possibly dead. You have nothing to compel me with and we both know it."

Arek's eyes never wavered. The boy did not reveal in expression or voice anything but conviction.

The king bowed his head. There was a point in every negotiation when posture had to give way to gathering information. "What do you want?"

"I want the life of that man," Arek said, pointing to Sargin, his interrogator. "I want him to be executed now, in front of me."

Sargin rushed forward, his eyes wide and his teeth bared like an animal's. He spit at Arek and shouted, "You think anyone believes you? If they do, it's because of *me,* you little shit!"

Men grabbed him before he could get near Arek, hauling and pinning him against a wall. The sudden violence of Sargin made the moments after seem even quieter. Arek didn't care. In this, Piter was right. *Who cares if they didn't understand?*

The king was the first to recover, "I . . . you can't be serious."

"I am."

The armsmark stepped forward, looking at the king, then at Arek. "We'll not kill someone acting on orders. Why not ask for my head as well? I'm the reason you were captured in the first place."

The king saw recognition suddenly transform Arek's face from lifeless to something that looked almost like respect. The boy drew a breath, shaking his head and said, "You faced me across live blades, sir, and wagered your life against mine. I accept that, because it was done with honor."

Arek turned his attention back to Sargin with a look of contempt. "He tortured a bound prisoner and never wagered his own safety."

The firstmark stepped forward and retorted hotly. "He was following orders!"

Arek faced the giant man and shot back, "Should all orders be followed, sir?"

When Jebida said nothing, Arek turned his attention back to the king. "My master taught me that the measure of a man's worth is in his actions. They define character. This man deserves to die, and I'll have his life or we're done negotiating." Arek stepped back, his armpits resting heavily on the crutches.

Sargin looked at the king, his face reflecting the fact that this conversation had gone on longer than he'd anticipated. He managed to say, "Your Majesty?" before the king raised his hand, demanding his silence with a gesture.

Then Bernal turned back to Arek and asked, "Where is the honor in what you request? How is your character being defined now?"

Arek retorted, "Don't parry words with me. You had me tortured and never asked for my help, which I would've freely given. You assumed I was the enemy, without ever speaking to me." His voice caught, and his face went red, flushed with anger.

"You've taken everything from me!" he screamed.

"You—" His statement was interrupted as he watched the prisoner visibly bring himself back under control. His words would have been wasted at that moment, so Bernal decided to let Arek speak first. Perhaps that would give the boy a sense of agency over his own fate.

"When Bara'cor's safety hung in the balance against mine, you chose Bara'cor," Arek said. "Why is this choice difficult? Because you can't hide somewhere and order the deed done? Did your man not pledge his life, knowing it could be forfeit for crown and country? The decision is easy, but you are a coward."

The king shrank in on himself, Arek's words slung like stones at the carefully crafted panes of his moral life. Yet, his duty was to Bara'cor. He couldn't release his obligations, even if they were spurred by the rantings of a possible spy.

He dropped his gaze and put a hand to his head. A moment passed, a silence that stretched as the king took three deep, measured breaths. Then he looked up and said, "Ash, take the blade.

"I won't order the execution of one of my men," Bernal quickly said. "He is of Bara'cor too, and falls under my aegis." A quick glance at Sargin showed the man looking visibly relieved.

Bernal sighed, his eyes searching the ground in front of him as if the answer lay at his feet, but when he looked up there was nothing but sadness in his eyes.

"I accept there were mistakes made, perhaps I rushed to judgment. But I won't repeat those mistakes. Your master is right, character shows in one's actions."

* * * * *

Ash moved to obey the king's order. He picked up Tempest and turned. As he did so, he heard a voice echo in his head.

Beloved.

Ash looked around, confused. The voice seemed to come from behind him, but there was no one there.

I have waited an eternity.

He looked down at the green-gemmed hilt of Tempest and the image of a beautiful woman came to his mind. *What?*

I have chosen you.

Ash shook his head, not understanding what Tempest meant. *What?* he asked again.

I am all you wished.

Ash felt the hilt grow warm, an almost living thing in his hand. A tingle started in his palms, then moved through his body. Wherever it went, pleasure followed. His eyes closed, and he could almost see the spirit of the sword floating before him.

Beloved, I must first set things right. Forgive me.

Ash's eyes snapped open. For him, it seemed an eternity had passed, but he could see that only a moment separated the time between when he picked up the blade and now.

"Wait," he began to say.

The sword brightened, then hummed, glowing green. Ash didn't remember having drawn it from its sheath, but it now shone like a green star in his hand. Silver runes appeared running up and down the mirror-like blade and he could see a quicksilver light flash along its keen, bright edges.

Then Arek screamed and fell, clutching his leg. Next to the king, Sargin also screamed, but different, guttural, like an animal being slaughtered.

Ash turned and saw the interrogator collapse, grabbing his chest and reaching out with one hand in the boy's direction. "No!" the torturer screamed, but his plea had no effect.

Ash stared in disbelief as an unseen force pummeled Sargin's body until his ribs were crushed and caved in. The force then turned its attention to Sargin's skin, shredding it away in a bloody mist. That mist seemed to flow and weave a red swathe that made its way directly to Arek's foot, as if the gore was being sucked in by his injuries.

The body of Sargin was stomped, spattering pink gobbets of flesh mixed with shards of pulverized white bone, until nothing resembling a person remained. More of the mist followed the first, joining with Arek's body. In the end, Sargin's body lay smashed into an unrecognizable pulp, except the hand that had held the hammer, still curiously whole, reaching for Arek.

Ash turned a stunned gaze to their prisoner, who had gotten to his feet. He watched as Arek looked down. The bones of his foot had realigned and somehow the bruising looked almost healed! The boy put weight on it, testing it. A lance of pain shot through his mien, but then a look of unabashed joy flashed across his face. His eyes said he hadn't expected any of this.

Arek addressed Ash in a daze. "You did this?"

"It wasn't me." Ash stood dumbfounded. In the back of his head, he heard a lilting laugh.

What have you done? Ash demanded.

Less than what Arek demanded and what that man deserved. Arek carried me faithfully to you, and I promised him a debt repaid. But no one demands me to do anything.

But you hurt Sargin, the armsmark thought, still in shock. *Why?*

I think I killed quickly, all things considered. Tempest paused here, and something in the sword's demeanor felt different. She simply ended up saying, *I hope you agree.*

Ash shook his head, but something in the back of his head tickled a warning. Given what he'd seen, Tempest may not be magnanimous in the face of rejection. He decided to remain quiet, at least until I could discard the blade. Still, he couldn't help replying with, *I don't understand you.*

I am a sword. Is my purpose not clear? Tempest retorted.

Ash didn't answer, but in a moment of clarity knew what this weapon would do. Its nature was to cause harm, to relish pain. He began to drop it, but Tempest held his fingers fast.

Not yet, my love. We are meant for each other.

* * * * *

Arek looked at the warrior he'd faced before, the armsmark the king had called Ash. Tempest had grown dimmer, but still glowed an unearthly emerald green. The man's eyes were wide, his gaze locked on the blade.

Arek then looked at his foot, which was partially healed. The shattered bones had somehow reformed, the tendons and ligaments reattached. It was impossible—and undeniable. He flexed his toes and reveled in the shock of pain. It wasn't entirely healed, but complete recovery was now possible! He felt giddy with happiness.

Justice has been served, has it not, my brother? Though you doubted me, my debt to you is repaid. Tempest's voice echoed in his head, and he suddenly recalled her pleading with him back at the dunes, and her promise.

He looked around the room, his eyes settling on the broken form of what had once been his torturer. He couldn't help grinning. A satisfaction suffused him that he hadn't felt since being on the Isle. Seeing this man suffer and die meant there was still justice in the world.

The men, looking shocked, clustered around the pool of blood, meat, and bone that had once been Sargin, but the king was made of sterner stuff, and his eyes instead remained on Arek.

The king's eyes narrowed—his disgust impossible to hide. "Are you happy? Your wish is granted. My man lies dead." He paused for a moment, and then said, "Honor? You have none, sir, but what I must do now is worse, for I must still treat with you."

He shifted, his eyes flicking again to the pulverized form of Sargin and a deep regret began to worm its way into his face. He looked back at Arek and reminded him,

"You said we but needed to ask and you would lend your aid. Well, I ask now, will you aid us with your Finder charm? Your master is still captive."

Arek looked around the room. He still felt anger and shame at having been tortured, but the pain he felt when flexing his almost healed foot gave him glee born of a mixture of malice and righteousness. He couldn't walk yet, but the man who'd inflicted harm upon him had gotten what he deserved. He gave little more thought to Sargin, wondering instead if the healing would continue at an accelerated pace.

Where the king radiated remorse, Arek felt pride. He reminded himself that the ruler of Bara'cor had chosen to torture him first and changed his tactics only when no other choice presented itself. Maybe he, too, should pay for that decision.

Yet Arek was alone and still healing, making him more of a liability to his master. Maybe the best thing was to let Silbane figure out what was best for Silbane. He had more than enough to worry about.

Before Arek could answer, a wave of lethargy washed through his body. The world grew dim and tilted to one side. He heard rather than saw the sounds of alarm as someone scrambled to his side. With a small sigh, he slumped down near where he'd fallen earlier, his body curling into a fetal position and his mind sinking into oblivion.

A New Lore Father

True skill needs no loud voice.
It is evident in every movement, every thrust.
Though the scabbard is dull, the blade gleams.
—*The Bladesman Codex*

G iridian rested his head on weary hands. The deaths of Themun, Thera, and the children had affected every family deeply. The attack cost them those who were held most dear: children who'd come here for the sole purpose of escaping those who would bring them harm. Many didn't have the strength to continue and just stroked the ground where their child had fallen, as if to caress them to sleep one last time.

Giridian felt the loss keenly. It was because of the lore father's sacrifice that the majority had survived at all. Now he was lore father. The simple thought belied the immense power that came with the title, the magic of his Ascension was still changing him from the inside out. He marveled at the sheer energy coursing through his veins. With it, nothing felt impossible. Running to Bara'cor, summiting Dawnlight—his strength felt inexhaustible. But he knew that was false. While the euphoria was real and heartfelt, his focus now had to be supporting his adepts and their training.

Kisan. She came first to his mind. How could they help the master who'd managed to infiltrate the assassins? Further investigation of the dwarf's body had shed little light on his identity. He carried with him no papers, only an assorted set of strange items and things that could have been weapons. His death had made it impossible to mindread him, and contacting Kisan was out of the question.

A New Lore Father

Giridian knew he could do it, for he now had the strength to mindspeak with the other adepts with no more effort than it took to utter a sentence, no matter their location. However, he didn't know if that would alert anyone else to Kisan's presence. Given these assassins seemed to command magic of some sort, he didn't want to take the chance of ruining her cover.

Therefore, he did the next best thing. He opened a path to the Way and left it open for Kisan. Perhaps the young master would try to contact him when she could. Once she found she couldn't reach Lore Father Themun, it was inevitable she would move down the line until she reached Giridian.

Next was Silbane, from whom he'd had no word. Giridian had stretched forth his mind and found nothing, not even an aura. Of course the obvious reason was Arek. Silbane was likely near his apprentice, effectively blocking him from searches like the one Giridian performed now. However, they'd agreed on a regular contact schedule, one that Silbane had recently missed.

Giridian desperately hoped the master was all right, but tried to prepare himself for the possibility that a third master had perished. Had Themun not passed on his knowledge to Giridian, losing the lore father and Master Silbane would've been a blow the council couldn't have survived.

Dwarves? he wondered. *Why now, after so long?* They had left after creating the marvels of stone and steel that many took for granted. Only their great feats of architecture, the massive works and fortresses that dotted the known world, gave evidence that they had ever existed. Now a team of these legendary dwarves had attacked, but to what purpose?

A knock on his chamber door surprised him, but the aura brought a smile to his lips. "Enter, Dragor."

Dragor made his way into the chambers of the new lore father and bowed, then took a seat in a nearby chair. "How're you doing?"

Giridian's smile wavered. "Been better."

"I've seen to posting guards. They're instructed not to engage these men, should any return. We've instead asked they raise the alarm so we can evacuate to the Vaults. Everyone else is preparing for the Rites, tonight."

Giridian looked down and nodded. The Rites of Last Passage were a well-known and necessary part of saying good-bye to those loved ones who had fallen. He put a hand over his face and rubbed his skin until he felt it turn red, his mind a cauldron of confusion and grief.

His heightened senses could now feel everything Themun had felt; he sensed the aura of the demon Lilyth at Bara'cor. But what he felt was subtly different than what Themun's memories held. Something powerful was in the process of awakening. When Giridian searched the currents of the Way, the scent of Lilyth was subtly combined with something else.

It recalled Lilyth, but in the way an acrid rind recalls the fruit inside. The two were parts of the same whole, but different. Themun may have confused the two, but Giridian now knew that what was connected to the Gate wasn't necessarily connected to Lilyth.

Giridian meant to unravel this mystery and whether it had anything to do with the attack, before more of his people died. He looked at Dragor and said, "We need to search the Vaults."

"For what?" replied the adept in surprise.

"Follow," Giridian replied. "I will explain."

They made their way out of the tower as Giridian shared his feelings of unease with Dragor. A young page who had waited for Dragor outside Giridian's chamber trailed them at a respectful distance. Giridian told Dragor of the fact that he could potentially sift through memories of the previous lore fathers and see which didn't fit cleanly with the history he and Dragor knew.

Dragor held up a hand and interrupted, "You say you have the other lore fathers' memories?"

"I think so, for the most part."

"And this stretches back to the first?" Dragor continued. "You can sift through centuries of learning?"

Giridian looked at his friend and hesitated before saying, "Maybe, the same way you could in our library, and just as inefficiently. It isn't as if the correct answer pops into my head. I have to find it by watching their lives, their interactions. Unless I know specifically where to look, I would spend more time than I have in this life searching."

They made their way around another turn when Dragor's hand clamped onto his shoulder. The dark-skinned adept looked down, then back up again at the lore father and whispered, "If it is the Gate we must gain knowledge of, then why not look at *his* memories?"

Giridian shook his head, not understanding.

Dragor licked his lips, his eyes darting between the lore father's and the ground, then said, "Valarius," with obvious distaste. The knowledge of how close this archmage had brought their world to destruction was still difficult to put aside.

Giridian took a deep breath and stepped back, his mind racing. General Valarius Galadine, Edyn's worst enemy and harbinger of the last devastation. He'd been everything the council had stood against, but at one time, he'd also been a lore father— during the Demon Wars.

He put a hand on Dragor's shoulder and squeezed. "Thank you. Let us get to the Vaults, then we'll see."

By the time they reached the underground doors, Dragor seemed to regret his suggestion. "Forgive me, I should've counseled you to listen to your own intuition and knowledge. I didn't mean for you to put yourself at risk."

Giridian nodded, touching the cool metal doors that barred the way to the chamber behind. His eyes closed as he focused on the Way, and a faint click sounded as the doors unsealed. He pushed them open, but turned to Dragor. "There is a divergence, and I mean to find out why. Unpleasantness and pain are a small sacrifice to pay. How could I do any less to protect my own than those who came before me?"

Just as it did every time, the majesty of the chamber took hold of Giridian as he entered the sacrosanct place, gesturing for the page to wait at the entrance.

Dragor, who'd also been here many times, drew an involuntary breath, clapping Giridian on the shoulder and saying, "It's still magnificent."

The chamber was vast; two hundred paces from end to end. Along the eight walls that circumscribed the perimeter stood shelves stacked more than three men in height and lined from top to bottom in books on lore, magic, and the Way. It represented knowledge that over the centuries had been saved from the persecutions of the magehunters.

The middle of the floor held cases and displays, each featuring a category of items. One section dedicated itself to armor, another to weapons, and still myriad others. The adepts of Meridian Isle hadn't been idle in their seclusion. Their Vault held a great many powerful and wondrous artifacts.

Giridian, as the former Keeper of the Vault, was less dazzled by the objects within, but nonetheless the sheer amount of effort it took to find and catalog all these things gave him pause. This was the result of over a century of work and it showed. If nothing else in the chamber awed him, this fact did.

He motioned to a particular set of manuscripts and they made their way to that section. As he walked, he talked over his shoulder to the trailing adept. "Something wasn't right at the final battle at Sovereign's Fall."

Dragor looked about, wide-eyed at the items within the Vault, and he absentmindedly replied, "So you have said."

"There should be historical texts that speak in detail of that time and of the events leading up to it," Giridian continued, "and yet, few manuscripts have been found. We have some, but not nearly the number that should exist."

"And where might those be?" Dragor had stopped near a shield, mirror bright and etched with a sigil reminiscent of a hawk with outstretched wings. As he neared it, Giridian could hear the shield start to hum, as if it vibrated to the same song as the adept's heart. Dragor's hand reached out slowly and the air shimmered in response.

"Dragor . . . " Giridian grabbed the adept's arm and pulled him away, a smile on his face.

Dragor shook his head and looked about in confusion. "What happened?"

"That shield seeks a wielder, but will always put you in harm's way to prove its worth. Not the best companion," the lore father said with a chuckle. "We're here to do research."

The two made their way to a section of the bookshelf that held histories from the time of Lilyth's incursion. Giridian found the few books that were relevant to the subject and pulled them down. These he split into two small, even piles. One contained information on demons, the other on the final battle at Sovereign's Fall.

"I will study the way of demons. You can re-read what happened at Sovereign's Fall," the lore father said. "Look specifically for what happened to the dwarves following the battle. I don't understand why they would reappear now, or for that matter here on the Isle."

With a sigh, Dragor picked up the stack indicated, then went to the entrance and looked out, motioning to the young page who was waiting there. "Please bring us something to eat."

The page nodded, and scampered off through one of the many backdoor passages that connected the chamber to the kitchen.

For the next few hours the two read in silence, the bits of leftover food and drink littering a serving tray on a nearby stand. Giridian finally broke the silence, standing and stretching as his back cracked in protest.

"Dragor, I think I've found something interesting."

"That makes one of us," Dragor said wryly. He shut the book he'd been reading and leaned back. "Nothing on the dwarves. Once they left Bara'cor, they disappeared as if they were nothing but myth."

"Do you know where demons, or for that matter, angels, come from?" Giridian asked.

The other shrugged. "From the left and right hands of the gods."

Giridian shook his head. "We call them angels or demons, but it says here they are actually a race known as the Aeris. It claims that in the distant past they came upon this world and were emissaries to the people of Edyn."

"Emissaries? To what purpose?" Dragor asked. "Demons are vastly powerful and dangerous."

Giridian nodded, "I never said they came in peace. The author of this book says they used the guise of peace to gain knowledge." He then pointed to a manuscript that looked truly ancient. "He too, seems convinced they never intended to treat with us." The lore father picked the book up and flipped to the first page so Dragor could read what was written in clear script on the inside cover.

Dragor leaned in. His eyes widened in surprise. Giridian read aloud, "'Those who do not heed their mistakes, are condemned to repeat them—Valarius Galadine.'"

He looked at his friend and said, "Your idea to look through the memories of Valarius is a sound one. We will try and see what memories he has of the battle that cost him his life."

Dragor laid a cautionary hand on his friend's arm and said, "Can I help in any way?"

Giridian looked at the younger adept and smiled. "Keep your hand in contact with me, so I can draw upon your strength, should I need it. The visions are seen by lore fathers only, but your presence fills me with confidence."

Dragor answered with a small smile, though Giridian could see he feared to be near even the memory of one who had caused so much pain and anguish.

Giridian closed his eyes and sank into blackness, a space with stars of light. These would be the memories of the lore fathers who had come before. He took a mental breath, then dove into the stars, back through the memories of the lore fathers who had preceded him.

His mind swept past Themun's to Duncan Illrys, who was lore father for only a moment before dying on the slopes of the Fall. His memories then flew past him to his wife, Sonya, lore mother before Duncan. Her reign was singular in her stalwart defense of their world against Lilyth. He then slowed his thoughts, for before Sonya's time came Valarius Galadine. His memories occupied a space, here . . . but there was nothing.

His mind searched, carefully sifting back through Sonya's memories. Her mind went from her ceremony where she became lore mother through her reign. Giridian shook his head, not understanding. Declaring Valarius an enemy of the land conferred his seat as lore father to Sonya. The ceremony, now known to him, should have resulted with Valarius's memories here.

Wait, he told himself, if the ritual of transference was not carried out willingly, a lore father's memory transferred to the Way upon death. Valarius didn't die when they stripped him of his title. He'd died on the slopes of Sovereign's Fall. Giridian moved forward again with renewed energy. The answer would be somewhere before Duncan or Sonya's passing.

Giridian opened Duncan's last thoughts, but where there should've been a lifetime of learning and lore, he also found . . . nothing. He backed up mentally and felt the reassuring presence of Dragor. Taking a deep breath, he opened the memories of Sonya Illrys and found them to be intact. He could see her life, her teachings, and her last stand against Lilyth. He could see everything up until the moment she let her spark jump to Duncan, when transference had occurred.

A disturbing thought began to grow in his mind. *Perhaps Valarius never died?*

There was no situation where the lore didn't transfer from father to father. It was the single thing that kept their teachings intact, or at least accessible for later generations. Furthermore, there was no way Themun would not have known this. Now his dying message seemed all the more cryptic.

He opened his eyes and looked again at Dragor.

"What?" asked the adept.

"The lore father said something to me before he died," Giridian said, looking at Dragor.

The younger adept asked, "What?"

"It doesn't make sense." Giridian looked about as if trying to find an answer in the air around him. He stopped when Dragor laid a gentle hand on his arm.

"Share it."

Giridian paused, then said, "'Armun.'" He looked at Dragor again and continued, "It makes no sense. Who's Armun?"

"I don't know," whispered Dragor. "What about the memories of Valarius?"

"There's nothing," he replied woodenly. "What I mean is, they are missing." Giridian closed his eyes again, searching, "They don't exist. No memories from Lore Father Duncan, either."

Dragor shrugged. "Perhaps they never carried out the ritual and their memories didn't transfer, or Themun rejected their learning. Duncan wasn't even lore father for more than a few moments before the king killed him."

Giridian shook his head. "Any lore father can unlock them."

He paused, looking at Dragor's confused expression, then explained, "They don't need to carry out the ritual, for their lives are contained in the Way. The spark of transference isn't knowledge, but access to knowledge, which is recorded and contained within the Way, forever. Even Lore Father Themun, who was largely self-taught, gained access to the collective memories of those who came before him in this manner."

He stood, shaking his head. "For countless centuries the tradition has been followed, even when the lore father was petty or misguided. Knowledge of weakness and mistakes is more valuable than lessons from success, and we cannot count on every lore father choosing to pass on his knowledge. There's only one way their memories aren't here."

Dragor locked gazes with his friend. "They never died."

JOURNAL ENTRY 12

When you read this, you make yourself stronger. You survive, against all odds, and your belief will suffuse you with strength. Doubt is your enemy, your faith is the key.

My area is not safe, and it is this continued belief that I am in danger that fuels these raids. Ritual is key, faith is power. I will keep writing it again and again to commit it to memory and heart. Ritual is key, faith is power.

My mind, like any man's, must perform a system of actions that result in the conviction that I am safe. It is the same for the mother that hangs hollyroot above her baby's bed, or when one consumes sunbeam for fever. It is our nature: We believe these remedies work; therefore they do.

Now I must do the same, but on a grander scale. I must create a system of faith that is impervious to doubt, and it starts with me.

I know many spells of warding. I believe here, in this place, they will have greater power. I know this to be true, I feel it. I believe it. My will is master here.

Ritual is key, faith is power. Nothing can stop me. I must believe. My life depends upon it.

Journal Entry 12

FALLS OF SHIMMERENE

*One cannot hide their character,
once blades are crossed.
Remember what she did to survive?
Nothing more true will be revealed.*
—Davyd Dreys, Memoirs

Arek awoke to the sound of birds . . . a sound more incongruous because of its source. Was he not in the Altan Wastes? As his eyes cracked open, he realized he was lying in a bed, with a canopy of fine silk above. Flitting about in a small, golden cage were a pair of black and yellow songbirds singing to each other. He was dressed in soft clothes that made him uncomfortable, but only for their fineness. Then he looked down. The bedsheet was propped up by his feet, even and symmetrical blanket shapes indicating his healing hadn't been some sort of delusion.

He choked out a small laugh . . . *it wasn't a dream!* Then, with a trepidation he hadn't felt since he was a child, he wiggled the toes of the foot so recently beyond repair.

Pain shot up his leg and exploded in his brain. He laughed. To feel anything real at all was better than feeling something that wasn't there. Tears sprang unbidden down his cheeks. His foot and therefore his future might once again be his.

"Nice."

Arek started, and then he turned to the voice, hastily wiping his face. *Piter,* he thought at first.

"Sorry, didn't mean to surprise you. Honestly."

Arek finished wiping his eyes and realized the voice came not from the shade, but rather from a girl. "Your name?" he managed to croak, sleep still in his voice.

"Tej," she answered, "of EvenSea."

Arek's eyes focused on his guest and his breath caught. Not just any girl, he corrected himself. She was one of the most beautiful he'd ever seen. Her hair flowed from her head like an ocean wave and framed a face that was exotic, but burdened by a deep pain, a pain that made her seem more vulnerable. Her eyes were amber, and it occurred to him that the royal family of EvenSea were said to have amber eyes. . .

"I . . . your name?" he asked again, his voice sounding stupid to his own ears.

She laughed, and then she looked past his bed to the window. Her eyes caught the sweep of the desert sun and seemed to soak it in, and were intensified by it, until her gaze almost glowed. When those eyes looked back to him, his heart skipped.

"I already told you," she answered. "I was a princess, now I'm just Tej. For someone so handy with a weapon, you're not very good with faces," she added with a faint smile, pointing to a small bruise on her temple where Arek's foot had connected.

Arek realized with a shock where he'd seen her before, in the hallway outside that chamber. That seemed an eternity ago. Now his earlier guess that she was of the Tir royal line fell into place. Had he hit her? The look on his face must have betrayed his thoughts, for he saw the girl's smile grow and she moved closer.

"Please, no titles or rank. I'm trapped here as much as you." Her head tilted to one side and she smiled and said, "You fight well. Ash says you're better than anyone he's ever faced."

Arek looked around, his mind quickly wondering what new tack the king attempted, and asked, "No guards? What do you want?"

"A favor."

At that moment, Arek's vision tunneled, portending Piter's arrival. The familiar dark-robed figure strode into view. The shade paused, looking at Tej. "Pretty, but useless."

"What do you want now?" Arek asked, tired and fed up. The anger of the torture and treatment by the king, the fear of having been abandoned here amongst strangers, it all came together now.

"I saved you. If I hadn't come, you would be dead now." Piter moved past the frozen figure of the princess and faced Arek, standing his ground. "It's more than you ever did for me!"

"What are you talking about?" Arek asked. Something in the tone of Piter's voice broke the turbulent frustration and anger that had threatened to boil over a moment ago. He felt drained and somehow melancholy.

Piter looked down, but when he looked up again, there was a change in the shade's eyes and a question came out in earnest: "Why did you hate me?"

Arek stopped, dumbfounded. "What?"

"You were always cruel, letting your friends poke fun. When did you include me? You fall in with them and I am left behind, the odd one?"

Arek took a breath, then asked, "When did I hate you?"

"It wasn't always like that. We grew up together and were friends, brothers." Piter looked away, then said, "It's hard enough to be an orphan, but you made my life on the Isle miserable."

A heartbeat passed, then two, and Arek dropped his gaze. He hadn't thought of it like that, it had always seemed that Piter was annoying, or somehow just in the way. He answered, softly, "We . . . I didn't mean anything."

"No?" The shade looked on a bit longer, and then continued, "Forget it, Master. It doesn't matter now. All you should care about is your own life, your own friends, as usual."

Arek didn't have an answer. His treatment of his classmate hadn't felt particularly mean or base. Yet he suddenly was forced to see himself as Piter had. He'd been the bully, the one to exclude his name brother. Piter might've created some friction because of his nature, but Arek had been the ring leader who never let Piter within his circle of friends. *But neither Tomas nor Jesyn liked Piter,* Arek told himself. *No harm was really meant.*

Silence hung between them, stretching out for a few heartbeats before Piter said, "Your destiny lies deep below this fortress. Opening a portal for the king is foolish. You'll be killing me twice."

"What?"

Piter rolled his eyes and said, "You need to head downward. The Gate you seek is there. It is a place of power. Your will is the key, and achieving this Gate will set things right."

"You mean, free you? You can still be saved?"

The shade looked around, as if sensing its own departure, and said, "Perhaps, but you are likely too stupid."

Arek felt a flash as time resumed its normal pace—the jolt of connection and the shade of Piter was gone.

The next moment, Tej cocked her head to the side and looked at the songbirds. "I feel like one of those birds."

Arek looked up and knew what she meant. "So do I. But in my cage, there always seem to be cats." He smiled and when he looked back at her, he was surprised to see she was smiling too.

Then her gaze grew serious and she said, "The nomad chieftain killed my father. He impaled him."

Arek sat back, shocked. "I'm sorry." His mind raced and he added, "Can I help?"

Tej gestured with her chin to the blank spot on his chest where his Finder had been. "Your charm. Take me with you. I'll be ready."

"First, I'm not going with them, and even if I was . . . to be accused of kidnapping you? Not likely," he retorted, as he let out a small laugh at the absurdity of her request.

Tej plopped herself onto the bed next to him, sullen on the edge of angry. "So you're scared?"

"Yes, very," Arek said, nodding vigorously, not caring what she thought of that.

"The king won't do anything. I'll already be on the other side and Ash will still send your master back for you."

Arek stared at her, startled at how close she was and that she seemed wholly unaware of her own beauty. As to her question, he also began to think she was slightly crazy. "I don't even have the charm."

Tej looked up, her amber eyes glinting. "What if I stole it for you?"

Arek laughed. "Use the charm and ruin your king's one chance at breaking the siege? What do you think he'd do to me for that? "

"Cowards always find reasons why something is too difficult. Heroes don't." Her quirked lips and crossed arms made it clear which part she thought he was acting now.

Arek leaned back into the soft pillows, thinking. This wasn't at all what he'd expected and in front of her, his ability to reason fled. He closed his eyes and took a deep, steadying breath, focusing. As he did so, his thoughts cleared and he said, "The last place I ever wanted to be was here. Going into the nomad camp was next on my list and getting inside and out again is the job of trained warriors. No offense, but from what I saw, your skills aren't good enough. At best, you'll hinder any attempt to achieve your own goal. I doubt even all of us standing side by side could hold off a horde like that."

He hated being so direct and worried she would leave right then and there. Instead, her face took on a thoughtful look.

He sighed, leaning back into the bed, not wanting to disappoint the girl. *Lady*, he corrected. Then his mind latched onto what the shade said just before leaving and he decided to redirect her and get some of his own questions answered. "Tej, what's below Bara'cor?"

Tej stared back at him, a look of admiration on her face. It was as if he'd somehow acquitted himself well in her eyes, or at least he imagined that's what she was thinking. Then she shrugged, "Lots of things. The fortress is pretty extensive."

"But do you know your way around down there?" What Piter had said planted the seed of a plan, but it required someone who knew the fortress intimately.

"I guess so. Why?" She plopped back down, rolling onto her back to stare again at the canopy and the songbirds.

"I think there's something down there, something that might help us defeat the nomads. If we could find it, you may get what you want," he said. It was mostly true, but he'd tweaked it a bit to appeal more to her need for revenge.

Tej sat up and her eyes filled with hope. "A weapon?"

Arek shrugged but kept neutral hope in his voice, "Maybe, but I'm not sure."

Tej smiled, then tilted her head to one side with that strange look she had earlier. "You don't care what I think, do you?"

There was an uncomfortable pause where Arek debated what to say. In the end, as always, the truth won out. "Not really," he answered. "I could use your help to find my master, but if you choose to focus on avenging your father, I won't stand in the way." That was about as truthful as he could be. He found her attractive and outright lying to her seemed wrong.

The princess continued to stare a bit longer, then smiled and stood up. "Refreshing." She stooped to grab a pair of soft boots sitting unnoticed at the foot of his bed. "Put these on. They look like something from the medics."

Arek caught one, the other smacking him in the face. He almost yelled, but her laughter gave him pause. Plus, the boots were soft and filled with a cotton fluff that when laced tight would serve almost as well as a bandage.

"All right," Tej said. "I don't know the fortress that well, but I know someone who might."

"Who would that be?" asked Arek.

A voice from a shadow near the door spoke then, startling them both.

"Me," said Niall as he stepped into view.

Falls of Shimmerene

REBORN

You must give away any thought of surviving.
Enter each battle as if you have already died,
and your time here is merely borrowed.
Embrace this, and you will act without fear.
—Kensei Shun, *The Lens of Shields*

Scythe watched the image of Silbane in a small water bowl. Beside him stood Hemendra, not at all happy to be in the Redrobe's tent. The watery image showed their captive, still secured to the pole in the tent where they had left him.

"You take a great chance leaving him alive," stated the clanchief.

"I would hazard the world, this army, even your life, to ensure my plan's success. I leave nothing to chance."

The words came out almost normal, betrayed only by a slight tremble of his lip at the end. The nomad chieftain had spent enough time with Scythe to tell when he was teetering on the edge of a violent outburst. Usually these ended in the death of a nomad or two, like the skinning of the two scouts.

Hemendra didn't worry too deeply over this. The mage instilled fear, and because Hemendra consorted with him without harm, he was seen as someone who could control the man, regardless. This gained him respect as a result. Still, the man was dangerous and in Hemendra's opinion, only the Redrobe's power and promise to help breach Bara'cor's walls had kept him alive this long. He scowled, but said nothing. Gutting him would be simple, when the time came.

"Patience, Mighty U'Zar," said Scythe, smiling.

The chieftain cursed, knowing this man could read thoughts. It was at that moment Scythe's voice reverberated in his head, echoing, *this man is dangerous.*

Hemendra let out a forceful sigh, and then said, "We both still have our uses."

Scythe locked eyes with the nomad chieftain and a small titter escaped his lips. "Indeed." Then he looked away and back at the watery image of Silbane.

The voice that came next out of Scythe's mouth had a different tone, one of tactical confidence. "Only two things can happen at this point. Either Silbane uses his Finder, or his apprentice does. I have set the portal web in place."

"And you think this unseen web will work?"

Scythe flicked the water's surface and the image collapsed in a dozen ripples. They quickly died, as if the water was made out of something thicker, and the image returned. Now Hemendra could see purple lines crisscrossing the tent, filling the air around Silbane like a spider's web. "If the portal opens, it touches one of these lines. That will not only summon me, but lock the portal open until I can decide what to do."

Hemendra smiled and said, "Giving us a way into Bara'cor." The massive warrior looked at the Redrobe with a grudging respect. "A good plan."

Scythe ignored the chieftain's compliment and said, "I will attend to the great dragon. See that I'm not disturbed."

Hemendra nodded, backing out of the tent along with a small contingent of guards. He went to choose a small group of elite warriors for the difficult task of entering Bara'cor. In case the Redrobe's plan worked, he intended to have a team ready to enter the great fortress and take her from the inside.

* * * * *

Scythe went outside and then to a tent near his own, moving with purpose. He'd had the warriors transfer the body of the dragon to this place. It afforded more privacy. He entered the tent, his eyes quickly adjusting to the gloom.

The warriors had left the great dragon-knight's body on an iron circle resting upon a table at waist height, making a clinical inspection easy. Satisfied there was no other injury, the mage straightened the dragon-knight's head and neck, then reached behind and ripped the arrow from the base of the skull.

It released itself with a wet pop, the arrowhead covered in a black, oily liquid that stank of sulfur. The mage dropped the arrow and waited, but not long.

A gasp tore through the dragon-knight and his eyes opened wide, glowing with yellow light like two miniature suns. Bones snapped back into place, muscle and sinew shifted, repairing the injuries. Dragons were notoriously difficult to kill.

Smiling, Scythe motioned and the great iron circle lifted into the air, suspended by his power alone. He turned it so the dragon-knight faced him and said, "I welcome you back, Lord Rai'stahn."

Rai'stahn looked at the mage, golden eyes calculating. Scythe knew the strength was returning to his limbs, but Silbane's prana locks were still in place, limiting his power.

"Mortal, thou art not my equal. Release me, or suffer."

Scythe held up a forestalling hand. "All in good time, milord. First, I would know the purpose of your visit."

The dragon-knight strained against his bonds, but was held tight, his armor and scales fused to the metal circle behind him. With his prana locks in place, breaking free would be impossible. He turned his full attention to the mage and recognition dawned.

"It has been some time, milord," Scythe said, "but my quest remains the same."

Scythe felt understanding flood Rai'stahn's mind. "Bara'cor, then, is still thine objective."

"Yes, though your presence and timing aren't ideal." A smile tugged at the corners of his mouth. "And as you know, timing is everything, is it not?"

The dragon-knight ignored the bait and replied, "We do what we must."

"We do indeed, milord. We act when it will have the most effect." He paused at that, then added delicately, "The Isle came under attack. Many were killed."

* * * * *

At those words, Rai'stahn felt a sudden panic for his hatchling and closed his eyes, searching. Despite any prana locks, the great dragon still had the ability to use his Sight, and he used that now to confirm the red mage's claims. He easily located the Isle and the multitudes of bright sparks that existed in and around there, the brightest being his child. The Isle seemed untouched, but the great dragon knew his demesne as only a lord of his people would. While many lived, many had passed on, their sparks extinguished. With shock, he realized the mortal spoke truly. "More than just Themun."

"Why did you hazard their safety?" asked Scythe.

The dragon ignored him, still searching the vast world. He then saw the spark he was looking for and sent out a silent call.

"You left them undefended, to escort a monk and his apprentice here. None would've dared move against you, but you left an opening. Why?"

He felt Scythe trying to reach into his mind, and slammed down a wall of psychic energy, shutting him out. Frustration washed across Scythe's features and he said, "Must you insist on plain speech? Can we not parley directly?"

"Sharing thoughts with thee hath not been earned, *mortal*." He put emphasis on the last word. First Silbane, and now this. He also cursed Sovereign, who was clearly responsible for this attack. The great dragon knew the maker of this world would not yet move against the dragons, but against others . . . his choices had brought harm to his people.

Scythe looked away, then pulled up a stool and sat down. Perhaps a wisp of Rai'stahn's anger leaked out, for the red-robed mage said, "Earned? I earned it on those slopes, hunted by the king's men while you fled."

"I told thee then, as I tell thee now, thou cannot change what hath happened."

The red robed mage looked down, shaking his head slowly. "You left me to die."

Rai'stahn didn't answer. The truth was self-evident.

Finally, the mage's voice whispered out, "Silbane lives."

"Until I am released."

"Why?" Scythe asked. "Why did you attack Arek? Can he truly disrupt the Gate? Is my quest in danger?" As he spoke, a kind of hunger seemed to take over, his questions spilling into one another as if they fought to get out and be heard.

Rai'stahn said, "Release me and thou wilt see."

Scythe shook his head. "Not until I know exactly what is going on." He pulled out a short knife, wickedly sharp and curved, designed to butcher an animal. "Do you remember this blade, milord?" He stood stock-still, as if reliving a memory. Then with a start he looked up, his pale eyes going from a distant stare to the here and now.

Rai'stahn didn't answer, merely fixing the mage with his golden gaze. *Mayhap Scythe dying on this quest would be best for all worlds,* he thought, his anger growing.

"You left me to die!" Scythe cried again. He moved in close, brandishing the keen edge of the weapon before the dragon's eye, "With nothing but this blade between me and the king's men!"

Anger overcame reason and Rai'stahn said, "Thy war was over! The demonlord lay defeated and Valarius hadst been contained—"

"What happens to your daughter who nests on the Isle? Perhaps I'll pay her a visit, too?"

At the threat to his hatchling, Rai'stahn surged forward and an animal roar tore from his throat, "Thou dares?!"

The Scythe stood his ground and asked, "What is Arek to you?"

* * * * *

Scythe didn't move, his face inches from Rai'stahn's fanged teeth. The many years of his long life had slowly deadened him to fear. He saw the dragon's outburst in a detached way, as if someone else watched through his eyes.

No, not deadened, a voice gently reminded. *Your suffering has shielded you, and brings you ever closer to your true destiny.* With that, even the dragonfear washed over him like a cool breeze.

Scythe felt the power of the Way coursing through him, a giddy feeling of ecstasy barely held in check by the reality of this meeting. Of all who could have come to him, Rai'stahn was divine providence of the Lady's making, a sign his love would soon be free.

He exhaled once through his nose, then said, "You heal quickly. How long would it take if I cut you apart, burned you to ashes, and scattered those to the four corners of Edyn? Tens—or perhaps hundreds—of years?

"Tell me, or I will do as I say and see if your hatchling can be forced to mate with dogs. She will suffer every single day you fight for life, just as I have. I promise you." He kept his gaze locked on the golden eyes of Rai'stahn. "Test my word."

Dragons were implacable creatures suffused with power, their very essence made from the Way. They were power incarnate, living gods who still walked this world.

Normally, a single man would be devoured both mentally and physically for daring such an affront.

However, there was nothing normal about Scythe. He'd suffered, lost, and fallen far from a place where any semblance of normalcy still reigned. Fear required one to have something to lose, and Scythe had already lost everything. He would make good on his threat and the great dragon was too weakened to stop him.

Scythe didn't say anything more, holding the dragon's molten gaze in his own pale one, his eyes never wavering. In the end, the conclusion was inevitable. He would win and they both knew it.

The dragon-knight stared, but a sulfurous sigh escaped from his lips. A moment later, Rai'stahn was the first to look away. "Do not believe thy threat will go unanswered."

Scythe could almost feel the dragon's will collapse. "To do so would be foolish." He stood, waiting, the dagger slowly tapping on his thigh.

Rai'stahn's lip curled, revealing his fanged teeth. His golden eyes narrowed. "Very well. The boy is more than he seems."

"Obviously," Scythe said, "but can he truly disrupt the Way?"

The dragon-knight shook his head. "He doth not disrupt it. He consumes it. He draws the Way unto himself, depleting all around him. I felt mine own strength ebb as we flew here."

"The Gate cannot be threatened!" Scythe's jaw worked, his teeth grinding as he felt the panic begin to build again at the idea of his life's work at risk. It was his only chance. He could feel his emotions well up, threatening to spill over again into that place where he could do nothing but watch.

Just when the force of memory became almost too much to bear, he heard the dragon say, "Release me and thy Gate will be safe. I will kill the boy."

Scythe spun and faced Rai'stahn, a blanket of calm serenity stretched tightly over his mental conflagration. He took a careful step forward, as if treading lightly to avoid breaking his own precarious hold. "Why?"

"The boy absorbs power from the very air that surrounds him and will eventually destroy any who harness the Way. He must be eradicated or he will be the death of us all."

The simple statement hit Scythe with an almost physical force. His mind whirled through the logic, like planks, toppling each fact in a quick line. That would include all the Elder Races: dragons, dwarves, even those who were born with Talent. It would make everything—Scythe involuntarily gasped—mundane.

"Thou sees the danger."

The calmness continued its hold, as the analytical part of Scythe's fractured mind now turned its attention to the problem of the great dragon. "If I release you, you will kill me." He said this with no emotion, a simple statement of fact.

"Will that not help thy life's work?" asked the dragon, mocking.

"If I am to recover them, I must pass through alive, else I would've ended my accursed existence long ago."

The dragon-knight shifted, then said, "My hatchling cannot live in a world where this thing lives. Our interests are aligned. I can put aside thy words."

"I don't believe you, milord." Scythe looked at the dragon for a moment, noting that most of the creature's visible wounds had healed, then said, "Take the Blood Oath."

Rai'stahn laughed. "Oath-forged, with thee? Thou art truly mad."

"Then you are of no use to me," Scythe replied. He moved forward with the knife.

"Wait." The dragon met the archmage's pale gaze, then let loose a volcanic growl, emanating from deep within his armored chest. Anyone else who faced the dragon's anger would have fled.

The dragon dropped his head in defeat and said, "I agree."

* * * * *

Rai'stahn felt one arm come free. He pulled it close, his hand tightening into a fist. He could feel power course through those veins, but restrained by the bonds of Scythe and the locks Silbane had placed. He cursed himself again for trusting that particular mortal, and frankly, he corrected himself, mortals in general. His eyes narrowed into golden slits and he asked, "Thou wilt seek out the boy?"

"No, milord. I have reason to believe that Silbane's apprentice will come here using a Finder. I have arranged for that portal to remain open, leading me back into Bara'cor. You can do what you want with the boy and leave me to my purposes."

Rai'stahn nodded, thankful Themun had followed his orders regarding his talisman. Now that offered him a chance to retrieve the boy before it was too late.

Scythe continued, "Do you take this oath with me?"

"Very well, Lore Father," Rai'stahn intoned. "By the blood of my people, I bind myself to thee as ally. I wilt cause no harm to befall thee from my action or inaction." In one fluid motion, he bent his finger forward and sliced a razor sharp nail across his palm. Black blood seeped from the cut.

Scythe bowed and said, "By the blood of my forefathers, I bind myself to you as ally. My oath as Lore Father of the Old Lore, I will cause no harm to befall you from my action or inaction." He tapped the gutting knife against his temple, smiled at the dragon, then cut his own palm open. Red blood gushed from the wound and he quickly clamped his hand with the dragon's so their wounds touched.

A golden flash occurred at the point of contact, then grew to encompass them both. Then just as quickly it disappeared in a flash of white. Scythe removed his hand. His wound had already healed, leaving only another thin white scar crisscrossing a multitude more where other Oath cuts had been taken.

Scythe stepped back, then gestured. Rai'stahn felt all the bonds holding him to the circle disappear. He slipped off the circle and landed with a grace that belied his great size.

The mage looked up at him, then closed his eyes. Rai'stahn could feel him unbinding the knots that sealed him from channeling his full might. While Silbane may not have the skills of a Lord of the Old Lore, what he did, he did well. Still, it only took a moment for Scythe to unbind Rai'stahn, and when he finished, the mage stepped back and said, "It is done."

Rai'stahn didn't need to be told. His power was free, coursing through his veins, healing and strengthening his body further. He could feel it within him, flexing like lightning aching to strike. He breathed in deeply, reveling in the sheer power of the earth and air around him.

He looked at the red-robed mage and said, "Be happy the Oath binds us. Thou art no longer dragon-cousin nor comrade. As soon as our deed is done, I shall end thy existence in a most painful way. "

Scythe smiled and said, "And if I succeed, you will still get your wish."

JOURNAL ENTRY 13

Failure and success of sorts. I find it hard to write "failure," so will call it, "an experiment whose outcome I could not predict."

The fact I am still writing means I survive, though barely. I have tried every version of the wards I know, yet after a time, they all fail. It is as if deep inside I know they are not enough, and I erode them. Ritual is key, but faith is the power.

I look at the last sentence and realize something. I have written that before, but not exactly in the same way. The word "but" creeps into the writing and therefore must also exist in my thoughts. Doubt fills my very journal and condemns me, yet I must keep this as a testament.

I need something else, something here that is unassailable in building my faith. I need to find something to believe in. Perhaps something that is a part of me . . .

My imps are becoming smarter. Today one watched me for what seemed the entire day. So I decided to speak to it. Strange to hear my own voice in all this desolation. Of course, the mere utterance of any sound scared it away.

It will return and we can continue the lesson.

Journal Entry 13

FIRST COUNCIL

In mastering oneself,
give away all that can be used against you.
Share your weakest moments willingly,
tell everyone your deepest fears.
Once uttered, these things lose power over you.
You become a wall to which no doubt can cling.
—Kensei Shun, The Lens of Shields

The Last Passage for Lore Father Themun Dreys was a solemn affair, held at the time of the setting sun. The body rested inside a wooden boat as mourners gathered along the beach. The repetitive sound of the waves breaking on shore was welcome: the building rumble, crash, then bubbling hiss that gave the assembled mourners a sense of peace.

Along with the adepts came those elders of the Isle grieving their loss, these orphans having become part of their family as much as any child born to them. Each carried a small candle set upon a wooden plate. These would be set to float alongside the funeral boat of the lore father. They had chosen a secluded spot on the shore where currents flowed quickly out past the breakers and into the wide, blue expanse of the ocean.

Lore Father Giridian paid homage to Themun Dreys, whose single-minded vision had spent the better part of two centuries protecting those he loved and whose final act was saving the Isle.

The boat was launched and set afire. Along with it floated dozens of candles. The boat blazed like a sun brought to earth, reflecting its orange light in the deep blue waters. It made its way out to sea, a shining beacon that illuminated the dark, much as the lore father had done during his long life.

Once it was out of sight, some mourners remained, seating themselves on the beach and gazing out at the sea and as the stars slowly winked into existence. It would be some time before the survivors would heal, but they would never forget.

Lore Father Giridian watched everyone with concern. They needed answers, a reason why this tragedy had occurred. He motioned Dragor over.

"We need to delve deeper into the lore fathers' memories. The answer to this attack is somewhere in our past," he said.

Dragor looked out across the sea and asked, "To what end? You said the memories of Valarius and Duncan are missing. Even if we find an answer, what will we do about it?"

"Come," the lore father said, moving off the beach and toward the Halls.

They made their way back to the Vault and settled into the chairs they had occupied earlier that day. One of the pages had neatly arranged the books they had found so they could easily continue from where they had left off. Giridian picked up Valarius's tome and said, "He wrote of demons as emissaries. Why?"

Dragor shrugged, "I don't believe it. We know demons exist on other planes and seek entry into this one. It's why we stand guard against Lilyth and her forces. They are ethereal and need a corporeal body to possess." He looked at the lore father, then grabbed his hand and squeezed the flesh, saying, "It is this existence they crave, for with it they experience the physical pleasures of the body. We are life to them."

"What if that's wrong? I have read that demons are more like moths drawn to a flame. They don't wish it, just as a moth has no desire to be consumed by fire."

"In the last war against Lilyth, families watched as their children were torn from them and taken through the Gate.

This was no involuntary, 'moth to a flame' impulse. It was sinister aggression."

Giridian kept reading until the stopped on a paragraph that had a few marks in the margin.

"Listen to this: 'I have concluded the Aeris suffuse our world. Upon creation, they are helpless, existing for no other reason than to bring our focus on the Way into clarity, to breathe life into our spells. They are used, subsumed by our spirit and lost forever. They are the basis of our magic.'

"The basis of our magic . . ." Giridian repeated, then shook his head. "If that were true, then we, by using the Way, are *using* the demonkind . . . the Aeris?"

Dragor said, "Simply not true. Think about it. Centuries of lore fathers would be hiding this truth from everyone else. To what end?"

Giridian looked at his friend, then said softly, "Not if they didn't know . . . or to keep things as they are." To Dragor's confused expression, Giridian said, "To avoid using the Aeris would mean changing the very fabric of our society. In whose interest is that?"

"No one, least of all Valarius," Dragor admitted. "The last Demon War couldn't have been won without his use of the Way."

The lore father leaned forward in his chair. "Do you believe he acted in our best interests?" The look on Dragor's face was enough of an answer, so Giridian continued, "There is something missing here, and I need to see for myself."

Dragor held out a hand and said, "Do you wish me to . . ?"

"No, my friend." Giridian smiled, realizing after the first attempt he could do this alone, as every lore father before him clearly had. While he didn't believe they would hide something so important, neither did he wish to break the sacrosanctity of his office.

"Perhaps, then, I can wander around and look at things?" Dragor inquired, not quite so innocently.

"Of course, though try not to touch anything," Giridian replied with a smile. "You never know what might happen. And keep in mind—" he smiled at the younger adept "— the job of Keeper of the Vault is open now."

Dragor nodded, smiling in return, then eagerly made his way into the main Vault.

Giridian sat back, closed his eyes, and concentrated on the Way. It opened before him easily, a liquid silver flow that brought him dizzyingly to a central point of stars. Each of those stars, he knew, would be one of the lore fathers who preceded him.

Now, the key was to find the right one. Part of him wondered why whomever had created this method of archiving their knowledge had made searching it so absurdly difficult. It was unnecessary and spoke either to a cruel architect, or a clumsy mistake. It was something he would look into later.

Now, he needed to focus his attention and look past Themun Dreys to Sonya Illrys, the woman who should've received knowledge from Valarius, and passed hers to Duncan.

He chose a moment closest to the time when Valarius was still an adept and not yet lore father, hoping to see what events led to his elevation. The search brought his vision to a council in session, more than two hundred and fifty years before.

* * * * *

"He continues his research, though forbidden." A young woman reported, her eyes flashing in anger. Giridian didn't recognize her, but Sonya's memory supplied a name: Finnow.

"I trust him, Fin . . . don't you?" asked a man Sonya knew as Dale. "He may be reckless, but never has there been one of his power before. Perhaps he sees what we cannot."

Finnow spread her arms, clearly exasperated. "He is unbalanced and trades on his former title!"

Dale shook his head placatingly and said, "You know he doesn't wish to do that."

Finnow said to Dale, acid in her voice, "You believe they are here now, amongst us, silent and watching?" She laughed, turning to her brethren. "Angels and demons, messengers to give us the commands of our gods?"

"Watch yourself!" admonished Dale. "You presume much, for one so young." The older man looked at the council members and said, "Valarius has never claimed these creatures speak for our gods."

"Then where is he to explain this?" retorted Finnow. She stepped up to the older man, her withering gaze filled with ire. "Why do you speak for him?"

"So sure of yourself, Finnow?"

The deep voice came from the entrance to the council chamber. A palpable power emanated from the speaker, and Giridian knew instantly this could only be Valarius Galadine, brother to the king and prince of Bara'cor. All eyes turned to him as he strode into the chamber and claimed the speaking floor.

Finnow backed away, her eyes downcast. The rest of the council waited to hear what Prince Valarius had to say.

"I apologize for my late arrival. There were matters that necessarily delayed me." He looked around the room, and where his gaze fell people shrank back, but not in fear. This man radiated strength—the kind that made one uncomfortable because of its intensity.

"It is true. There are Aeris amongst us, unseen, unheard."

Finnow stood defiantly, her back ramrod straight, and said, "So you say. *Only you.*" She nodded to another man seated at the head of the chamber, "Lore Father Damian does not feel their presence, nor do I. None of us see what you claim."

Valarius outwardly remained calm, but through Sonya's eyes, Giridian could see the storm that brewed within. "Must you see something to know it is real?" he challenged. "What of the Way? How does your will, unseen, move the earth?"

Finnow paused, her eyes calculating. Then she said, "Our gods give us the Way. It is blasphemy to deny this, a fact you are well aware of, prince." She then looked to the assembled council and said, "You make us to be nothing but siphons and leeches?" Her gaze turned stern and she shouted, "Our power stems from the most divine of sources, the power of the gods, channeled through us!"

Valarius laughed. "Gods? You believe in unseen gods but not unseen Aeris? It is a fine hair you split." The archmage paused, then looked at the Council members. He moved to a more central position where all could hear before saying, "I understand Lady Finnow's umbrage at my words. I do not dispute we are divinely gifted to carry out the will of the Gods. However, it is for our children that I beseech us to think of the Aeris as foes that can be stopped, and not just spirits flitting about unseen. There is a purpose behind their invasions."

"A purpose," Finnow quipped. "Like a storm that destroys a farmer's home? You claim the storm meant ill will to the farmer?"

Despite her age and the power of the personality opposing her, Giridian noted that more than a few council members were nodding their heads in agreement. Finnow, it seemed, did seem to have her supporters.

Valarius evidently saw it too, for he said, "If you're agreeing, it's because you've lost no one. These rifts open, the Aeris pour through and disappear again. Along with them go dozens, perhaps hundreds of children born with Talent. Why? Who is taking them and to what purpose?"

"Is it not said that the Gods sacrificed one of their own to see us survive this world? It would not be presumptuous to believe we are merely being held to the same covenant, our price for enjoying peace on Edyn." Finnow offered this with the barest amount of challenge to Valarius, a deft move on her part as it pulled more of the Council to a neutral to supportive position.

Valarius stepped forward and addressed Finnow directly, saying, "Your words smell sweet, like fruit well past its ripening, just waiting for the fool who takes a bite." He turned his attention to the room and said, "No gods would demand our children, would attack defenseless homes and slaughter all those within. This is the work of something with intelligence, with an agenda. We're ignoring it to our own peril."

Valarius turned back on Finnow and said, "By what right do we claim our moral superiority and child sacrifice can co-exist? It makes no sense."

The force of Valarius's presence made Finnow retreat again, despite herself. Giridian saw her visibly gather her courage, then haltingly reply, "Divine Right. It is our destiny to have the Way, else we would not have it."

Though Finnow's retort had a tint of fanaticism, Giridian could see the majority of assembled adepts still murmured their support, though it was less than before.

Giridian had no idea that religious zeal had so permeated the Old Lords. He shook his head, his opinion of his ancestors changing radically. He hadn't expected perfection, but also never expected them to be so steeped in religious mysticism. The Way required no gods, only discipline and control.

Valarius sighed wearily. "Over the ages these Aeris have been responsible for mass incursions into our world. They attack and take those most precious to us." He looked introspective, as if remembering something personal, but his next words fell like a hammer hitting an anvil, "Something drives these Aeris, some force. We must understand who or what that force is, and resist it, protect our children. If we do not, our future will disappear."

Lore Father Damian stood and asked, "Your agents do you a disservice, Valarius—" he motioned to Dale, who bowed, with a chagrined look on his face—"Tell us plainly, what would you have us do?"

Valarius met the lore father's gaze and said, "We open a gate to their plane and take the offensive. We attack, forcing them to the table to negotiate for peace. We don't know what we face, but doing nothing means we agree to suffer our children's' disappearances as acceptable losses."

The murmurs surrounding the chamber changed, from grumbles of dissent to a more strenuous current of shock and horror. Even the lore father looked at the archmage as if he'd lost his mind. He motioned for the room to quiet, then said, "A planar gate? Once done, it cannot be undone. What if you are wrong? They would never cease to invade! We are tasked to our limit just sealing the rifts we know of and still new ones appear. Yet you would have us reinforce such a path for their invasion?"

Valarius shook his head. "They are already amongst us. I feel their presence, like an unseen hand upon my own."

The lore father rubbed his hands together, his face pensive. Then he lowered his voice, addressing the archmage as a friend, and said, "Then why have they not attacked, Val? If they surround us, and they are our enemies, why have they stayed their hands?"

Finnow stepped into the opening, cutting off whatever Valarius would've said, and yelled, "And what if you are right? If these Aeris are the basis of our magic, destroying them destroys the Way!"

Valarius shrugged apologetically to Damian, then turned to Finnow and said, "I do not think the Way is embodied in a few hundred Aeris Lords. It will take far more than that to affect its potency." He paused, looking Finnow directly in the eyes and asked, "But say it is the end of magic, yet our children are safe. Is it not a small price to pay?"

Lore Father Damian's gaze became steely. "We won't chance that, nor will we chance a planar gate."

Valarius met the lore father's eyes and something unseen passed between them, an understanding of their positions. "I will do what I think is best for this land and her people."

Giridian listened as murmured shock whispered again through the crowd of assembled adepts. Shouts of "warlord!" and "traitor!" blurted out, echoing in the chamber, though those who uttered them quickly hid amongst a sea of faces. He saw the lore father raise his arms for silence, which slowly came at his request.

"What you deem best, Prince Valarius? Your Oath to this Council precludes that. What you 'deem best' . . . is for us to decide," stated the lore father unequivocally. It seemed he'd added Valarius's title as a reminder of the crown he had voluntarily relinquished. "Surely you intend to stay within the restrictions of this council's orders."

Valarius's eyes scanned the assembled adepts, the torchlight reflected in dozens of unfriendly eyes, waiting for his next words.

To Giridian it looked like a mob, ready to attack, but held back by the power of this man. He shook his head at the sight of it and his attention returned to the tall archmage as he bowed, "As a Galadine, I remind you that these are my people, too. Yet, I will abide by your restrictions." He slowly looked around the chamber until his eyes came to rest on Finnow.

To her he said, "My name, my true name heard upon the day I Ascended, is Azrael."

Valarius's revelation was the most sacred information a mage could ever share. It was never to be uttered, held only between the master and the wind that gave it voice. To tell others was unheard of. It gave those who knew power over him.

Valarius smiled, "If you believe me to be a danger, Finnow, you now have the means to stop me." He paused for a moment, his face solemn.

"We have no Divine Right, and knowing my name gives you no power over me or the Aeris. They will continue to invade and possess our people, take our children, until our way of life and our future is gone. Continue to delay, and you condemn us all to a life of slavery, or worse."

* * * * *

The vision went dim, then faded to black.

Immediately, the analytical part of Giridian's mind asked the next most logical question. *If they knew his true name, why were they unable to stop him? Could their true names really be unconnected to their power? If so, what did it mean?* He'd grown up believing the name he heard upon Ascension, *Artorius*, had been his birthright. Now this was cast in doubt. How was he to find the truth?

Giridian needed more information, more facts to put the conversation he'd witnessed into context. He decided to skip ahead to the time closer to the Demon War, where Lilyth and her forces had attacked.

He plunged back into the Void. At first, he flew as if he were the wind itself, the stars streaking past. Then each of his movements slowed as if he were submerged in a viscous fluid and the tiny stars sat steadily twinkling around him, as if bearing witness. His path forward had effectively been blocked by this unending blackness.

Then, in the distance, Giridian could see . . . something. It was a tiny point of light at first, flickering and wavering. It was so indistinct he blinked a few times to make sure it was no trick of his eyes, but it didn't disappear. Instead, slowly the light grew.

Soon he could tell it was a figure, walking toward him. Then they were in front of each other. He stood looking up at a being made entirely of light. Its form was indistinct and though it didn't shine brightly, Giridian shielded his eyes.

The figure held up a hand and a chime sounded, piercing his mind like a spear that stabbed through his entire being. The chime began almost harmoniously, but ended in a harsh double chirp.

Slowly, the being of light condensed until it took on the form of a large man in robes. He smiled and said, "Lore Father Giridian Alacar, be well come. It is with joy we greet this meshing."

Giridian faltered and took a step back, not knowing quite what to say.

First Council

KEEPER OF THE WAY

Do not teach a student before he is ready;
train him until his body no longer fails,
until discomfort is ignored.
Train him until he is too exhausted to resist.
Only then will he accept the Way.
—Davyd Dreys, Memoirs

eshing?"

"Ahh . . . our lexicon is incomplete and I am using the word in our language that is closest to yours. You are hearing the translation."

"But you're speaking my language."

The man smiled again. "You are *hearing* your language. There is a difference. Still, our hope is it will suffice." He looked away for a moment, then back at Giridian before continuing, "You have entered a library of sorts, an archive of knowledge. It was placed here to safeguard all learning."

"I know. The lore fathers' memories and lives are here."

"Indeed, and much more." The area around them changed and Giridian found himself back in his Vaults, where he and Dragor had just been, except now it was empty save for himself and the stranger. The man gestured to a chair, taking a seat himself. "Your journey here was not entirely anticipated."

"Why?" he asked, still standing. He was stunned by the detail of this vision. "No faith in me?"

"You were calculated to be of tertiary significance for Unity, but as in many things, we did not respect the uncertainty within our calculations. You are one such uncertainty."

"What?" Giridian asked.

"Ahh, we judged wrongly." The man smiled again, not unkindly.

Giridian took his seat slowly, the transformation of the black emptiness into his Vault so complete, the illusion so real, he could smell the leather and see dust in the air. This was power beyond anything he'd seen done, except by Themun in saving the Isle.

He cleared his throat and asked, "Your name, sir?"

"I am Thoth. I maintain these archives," he said, looking around him.

"Seems like a big job for one with so short a name," Giridian said warily, though a smile hid behind his eyes.

The man smiled back. "I believe you are making fun of me, Lore Father. We are both responsible for much the same thing."

Giridian let the surprise show on his face, "You are a lore father?"

"Similar, but closer in spirit to your duties as Keeper of the Vaults. You collect and preserve this storehouse of knowledge," he said, taking in the area in which they sat with a gesture, "and I do much the same, but on a far vaster scale. I am Thoth, the Keeper."

"And you greet every new lore father who enters the Way?"

Thoth gave a friendly laugh, his hand clapping his knee. "I wish we had. Unfortunately, we have jealously guarded much, kept information to ourselves, and now face the consequences." His face grew contemplative. Then he leaned forward and said, "You understand the world faces grave danger."

Giridian pursed his lips and said, carefully, "Is there ever another type?"

The man's eyes seemed to glint with humor at that, and Giridian again marveled at the detail of the vision.

"Well said. Do you recognize this?" In the air floating next to the man appeared an intricately carved runestaff. It was black and made of a polished metal that was both strong and light. Giridian knew it immediately.

"It is Lore Father Themun's runestaff. We saw it disappear after his passing . . . " His voice trailed off as the losses to the Isle came unbidden to the forefront of his mind.

"You are to be invited into our Conclave, a group whose stewardship is the safety of this world."

"How is this different from our council?" Giridian scoffed.

"Our Conclave includes many who have been created for specific purposes. They are better suited to deal with certain situations, just as a bull is better than a hawk for certain things."

"And you want me to be a bull?"

The Keeper smiled again. "We want you to be more than either." When the lore father didn't interrupt with another question, he continued, "Our people are explorers. Ages ago we came to your shores, but an accident made our vessel unable to sail again, so we used it to build ourselves a new home, a new life."

"Not surprising. Much of the Shattered Sea was settled in this manner."

"Indeed, but our people brought something special and unique to your lands. We brought the Way, and it infused everything with its energy and power."

Now Giridian was interested, for the emergence of the Way was still subject to myth and speculation.

"Much was lost in our accident—tools, vast amounts of knowledge—but we as a people survived. The Way saved us, it helped us shape the land to our needs. As we grew and multiplied, so too, did it grow in power."

Giridian nodded. "I think I understand."

The Keeper shook his head. "Forgive me, but you do not. Untold millennia passed and the world moved on. We are today what the Way has made us, shaped by it and our beliefs into everything you see. Nothing can change that.

We are also inextricably linked to the Way, so much so that our existence depends upon it. It gives rise to your powers, to every creature that lives on, above, or inside this world. It is the stuff everything you see is made of, save the builders. They are still flesh, unchanged, inviolate."

"You seem real enough," Giridian said, confused. "Are you saying you're made of magic?"

"I am real, but only in here. This is Will of the Way. It is a kind of magic, one with a purpose, but certain things were allowed in the name of expediency."

The man paused, then said softly, "When we first arrived, guardians were in place to protect the Way from corruption, but we were so few. Hurt, sickened, dying, our survival was deemed more important. The guardians were removed, put to sleep, and dispensation was given. Now, ages later, this is the result." He looked around the room, yet his expression seemed to include the entire world.

"Why are you telling me this? Did Themun know?"

Thoth seemed at first to be ignoring his question, replying, "The Conclave cannot sit idly by, nor can cryptic direction suffice. We made a feeble attempt with Valarius, and frankly, made things worse. With Themun we said too little, and he focused on bringing order to the chaos that reigned after the last war."

"The Aeris? Why do they attack us? Are they truly demons?"

Thoth looked uncomfortable. "You are one of a very few to be entrusted with this knowledge. It is not because you will misuse it, but because the knowing will intrinsically change you. We cannot predict the result, and that makes us wary."

"You'll have to trust me if you expect my help."

Thoth nodded, thoughtful. Then he said carefully, "The Aeris *are* the Way. They are your dreams, hopes, and your fears. They are a necessary part of your survival, but without the guardians, they remained unchecked. The Conclave acted and managed to seal them, for the most part, within their own plane of existence. You still have rifts and gates, but . . ."

Giridian waited, and then urged, "What? They seek to possess us?"

"Yes and no. They seek true life, Lore Father. They are formed for a purpose, given meaning by every creature in this world, but what then? You cannot banish them for they are necessarily a part of you. Valarius Galadine was the greatest archmage to have ever lived and we thought by giving him the Sight, he could find a peaceful way to Unification. He did not, and, instead, did much worse."

Thoth sighed, then shook his head, now choosing to answer Giridian's earlier question. "Themun did not fully know nor understand what was at stake, instead focusing single-mindedly on these rifts and gates. Now it falls to you and your brethren to undo what Valarius has wrought."

Giridian tried to swallow, his mouth dry. "What did he do?"

"He created a creature that feeds on the Way. Wherever it goes, the Way dies. For now, the effect is small and contained. It can absorb those that exist as shades and the weaker Aeris." Thoth held up a hand and met Giridian's eyes, "If the creature is allowed to continue, beings whose nature exists on the Way, beings like us, will be eradicated. Soon, it will consume everything."

Giridian took a deep breath, for some reason instantly knowing the answer. He said, "Arek."

Thoth nodded. "Because of the decisions made long ago, we foresaw that something like this could occur. We have always stood vigil throughout the ages, watching for signs. We call them *nulls* and have stopped them in the past, but each time one appears it grows stronger more quickly. We need to fix things at the source. We cannot continue to bandage these points of injury. There are too many."

"Me, the bull and hawk?"

"You are astute. The runestaff is more than just a badge of your office. It is an ancient artifact. With it you can see far places, create form and substance from nothing, locate things, and even heal."

"Heal? I can do that now."

"Not people, Lore Father. The runestaff is designed to heal the Way, but it needs a wielder. Your will shapes the Way. You are the Will of the Way.

"As I said earlier, much information was lost, but we are searching for how the runestaff should be used to repair the Way. In the meantime, you must stop Arek. He is immune to attacks from the Way. He absorbs its power and uses it. This means—"

"Spells, magic, even magical weapons?"

"Indeed. It is doubtful he can be killed by anything except unaltered steel, yet he can command the Way against you. Once he realizes what he is, he will do just that. Tell your adepts, all of them, for they are uniquely gifted to stop him. Explain things however you wish, but be judicious. You are part of the Conclave now."

"How can Arek use the Way if he destroys it?"

Thoth looked at the lore father with respect in his eyes. "Arek is a perversion, an outcome of both magic and flesh, but shaped by the desire for vengeance. He is neither wholly flesh, nor purely the Way. As such, he can command the Way even as he alters and destroys it. Think of it like a sponge that soaks in water and when squeezed, expels it. The danger lies with the Aeris Lords, who will safeguard Arek hoping he is a better answer than Unity."

"Unity? You've said this word before. What is it?"

Thoth looked at Giridian, and then pressed his flesh against his hand, "Ascension is Unity. It combines you with an Aeris lord, providing tools needed to both survive and improve this world. The Aeris think possession is an alternate way to ensure their survival, but it is an unsustainable end."

"Why?" Giridian pressed.

"Because, Lore Father, there are far more Aeris than living beings on Edyn. What happens when the last person this world can offer is possessed? What war will then ensue between those Ascended and those seeking a body? Does it sound very different than this? Worse, in their folly they will harbor Arek hoping to unravel the secret of his creation."

"What of these archives, of seeing the lore fathers' memories?"

"Even if the archives were not failing, would you sit watching lifetimes of unending daily routine and drama to find what you already know? It would be a sad existence." He looked at Giridian for a moment, his gaze measuring. Then he hesitantly added, "There is . . . one more thing."

"There usually is."

Thoth chuckled. "It was thought that things could be fixed within the boundaries of the laws of this world. However, another believes differently and has left the Conclave to pursue its solution independently. It is the Sovereign, and at one time it ruled us all."

"What does it want?" Giridian asked.

"It wants to eradicate this, all of it, and start over." He took a deep breath, then continued, "You have faced its assassins."

Giridian nodded, the shock difficult to hide from his face. "They killed children . . ."

"If left to its own will, Sovereign will kill *everything*."

"This seems to be a bigger problem than Arek," Giridian countered. "Why aren't we assigned this as our priority?"

"We burden you with a weight you can bear, Lore Father. Sovereign is beyond your abilities. Arek is not." Thoth looked almost apologetic, but then added, "For now, your interests in stopping Arek are aligned with Sovereign. However, do not hesitate to protect yourselves. Sovereign will not stop with Arek."

"That's it? You said you would share information, but this tells me nothing."

Thoth smiled a small, sad smile. "The Conclave, *your* Conclave, is working on a solution. We have shared with you all that you can comprehend. Have patience and hope, for you are not our only herald in this world. Focus on Arek. He is a greater danger than you realize, even with the knowledge we have granted."

He looked around the room and added, "You have some of the ancient lore here, and now understand the Way better than any who came before you. Do something better with that knowledge. Forge something new, Lore Father."

Thoth stood. Looking down on Giridian, he said, "I will always be here to answer your questions, as will the Conclave. You may also continue to *See* any lore father's memories provided you know where to look. Perhaps you wondered why your access to the memories is linear…"

Giridian arched an eyebrow. "I had wondered, but let myself become content that it was plain cruelty."

"No," Thoth said, though Giridian's answer elicited a chuckle, "nothing quite so banal. We used to facilitate each search, but are now limited by the energy consumed."

Thoth stopped, his eyes flicking down as he took a deeper breath. "The destiny of this world is to have the archives released. We cannot do so without the power. You may trust the dragons. They are guardians of the Way and hold this world's protection under their wings."

"And contacting you?" the lore father asked.

"Maintaining this meshing also tasks us greatly. Use it sparingly."

Giridian paused, then asked carefully, "Why is your energy so limited?"

Thoth met his gaze with sadness in his eyes. "Sovereign. It draws our sustenance away and will eradicate us if we do not learn how to use the runestaff. Now, please, come forward."

Thoth raised a finger and from its tip a blue star appeared. It was blinding, so intense that Giridian thought he'd have to shield his eyes. Yet when he looked, its perfection unfolded before him in breathtaking beauty and complexity. It was as if he were falling into a geometric shape without end, a pattern repeating itself infinitely. He'd never seen edges so keen, color so pure, a shape so sublime.

Thoth extended that finger and touched Giridian on the forehead. A deluge of visions washed into the lore father's mind faster than he could perceive. His vision became blurry and his head tingled, as if ants crawled across his scalp. "Ascend and become part of this Conclave," echoed Thoth's voice with a reverberating boom.

Giridian's body arched in shock, his eyes shut, and his mouth opened in a silent scream as energy and strength suffused his body and washed through his soul. The Way infused him with power, remaking him from the inside out.

"It is done," Thoth announced. "You have the knowledge necessary to forge a new runestaff, Archmage Giridian Alacar."

Giridian staggered back, his hand to his head. The scope of the Ascension flooded his senses beyond what he thought he could take. Just as he sank to one knee, overcome, strong arms supported him, helping him stand back up. Unlike his Ascension with Themun, which transferred knowledge and power, this was somehow deeper. It had reached in and changed him from the inside out. A part of him had a brief memory, a gigantic creature with black armor edged in green, smiling at him.

Artorius, the name whispered, causing his nostrils to flare. It was like smelling smoke floating through his mind from a distant fire.

"Sit here."

He opened his eyes. He was in the Vault still and nothing had changed except instead of Thoth, Dragor knelt before him, looking concerned.

In a whisper that was almost to himself, he said, "By the Lady . . . "

Dragor looked confused. "What?"

Giridian looked at Dragor with a start, as if seeing him for the first time. Then he shook his head and said, "We were wrong."

"About what?" Dragor looked at the lore father, concern plainly written on his features.

Giridian's face was ashen. "About everything."

He looked around the room, seeing it now with eyes opened by his augmented powers, and took a deep breath. The Way flooded into him, healing and restoring him just as easily as breathing did. He held out his hand and could almost see it flow. He concentrated, clenching his fist, knowing what would happen next.

The air brightened at his grasp, a flash of green energy that elongated into a spear of blinding light. Within it, he could see an infinite sea of particles, all converging at his command. From his fist outward, the air itself solidified and turned dark, growing into a shiny black spear of metal. It shone with a green lightning flashing across black metal, the runestaff of the new lore father, remade by the Archmage of the Conclave. In a moment, it was done.

Giridian looked at Dragor, who sat there with a stunned expression. He took another deep breath and could feel the Way enter him again, silent and strong, his to command. He thought about what Thoth had revealed, then in a voice that came out almost a whisper, he said, "We're going to kill Arek."

JOURNAL ENTRY 14

My failure to protect myself from these raids, none of which are distinct or identifiable, is a critical piece of information. These are the formless fears I have, that every man has, and they find life through the younger Aeris.

When enough time passes and I feel insecure or exposed, a raid is inevitable. These cannot simply be banished. To do that, I would have to banish my fears completely and what man can?

It is clear now that defeating the Aeris is a much more complex issue than I first thought. Perhaps this is what the dragons meant? I must get everyone to disbelieve the Aeris Lords, but how to forget an entire pantheon of gods?

If I cannot control my own subconscious, how can I expect an entire society to accomplish the same? Our will and belief give the Aeris Lords life. To destroy them, every man, woman, and child would have to stop believing in the things they cherish or fear.

That will never happen. I must do something else. I must give our people something else to believe in, something stronger . . . something better.

Journal Entry 14

THE CATACOMBS

In grappling, hold your opponent tightly,
like a lover's embrace, when you are thrown.
In his panic he will hold you up,
and lessen any damage you may suffer.
—Tir Combat Academy, Basic Forms & Stances

W hy would you want to help?" Arek asked, surprise registering at Niall's sudden appearance.

The young prince shrugged and moved into the room. "You've offered to help us, and . . ." He moved closer to the other two, a look of guilt washing over his features, "I don't believe torturing you was the right decision. I'm sorry."

That simple statement had a visible effect on Arek. Niall watched his shoulders lose some tension and his chest relax. He took a deep breath, then said, "Thanks. Your father never said sorry. I'd have helped if asked."

Niall shrugged, "We'll never know, but I'd rather have a clean slate with you." In truth, his answer had little to do with his actual reason. After listening to their exchange from the door, Niall knew his cousin was just stubborn enough to get herself into real trouble.

Letting Tej waste her time down in empty corridors and dead-end tunnels would keep her from doing anything stupid, and satisfied her desire to be doing something. With things going the way they were, he was never getting on the wall. Part of him liked the idea of leading an adventure into the catacombs, even if it was a fool's errand. But there was also an opportunity here.

Niall continued, "I'll help, but I want something in return."

Yetteje looked at him, confusion on her face, then blurted, "What?"

Niall never took his eyes of Arek. "I want to prove myself. That means whatever happens down there, you support *me*. I'm the leader of this group, no arguments."

Arek held Niall's eyes, as he asked, "When we faced each other, she expected your help," he said, indicating Yetteje. "Why did you abandon her?"

Niall felt a flush with shame, followed by hot anger. How dare this intruder accuse him of cowardice? Then he thought of what Ash would have said that the best lessons would come from the hardest tests; the ones that made you face things about yourself that you didn't like. It was in these moments that you grew the most. At least that's what he would've said.

"You were my first real opponent, and I hesitated," Niall admitted, facing Arek squarely.

Arek's eyes narrowed, but a small smile escaped. "So did I, the first time I crossed blades with my master. I asked because I wanted to know if you would lie to me or not."

Niall shook his head and looked at Yetteje. "Tej, I'm sorry." A steel came to his eyes and voice, as he added, "That won't happen again."

Yetteje looked confused. "Wait, you didn't attack when I did?"

The two boys looked at each other, and then both burst out laughing.

She looked annoyed. "It's not funny."

More laughter erupted and Yetteje continued, "Seriously, I thought you were right behind me."

Arek looked at Tej, a smile in his eyes, and he said, "Well, in a manner of speaking, he was."

The laughter continued for a moment longer from the two and Yetteje sat back looking even more annoyed at Niall, if that was even possible. That emotion slowly gave way as Niall and Arek continued to laugh, and she started to smile, too, though her amusement probably lay in the obvious stupidity of boys.

"Happy?" she finally asked. "Are the two of you friends now?"

Niall looked at Yetteje with a smile in his eyes. "I really am sorry, but if it's any consolation, you did much better against him than I did. I didn't even get a strike off."

"I don't care," Tej said with a sigh. "How are we going to get to where Arek needs to go? And by the way," she said, turning to Arek, "where and what is that?"

Arek stood up gingerly and took a step, careful to put as little weight as possible on his almost healed foot. "I don't know, not exactly, but I know it exists. Think of this as an adventure."

Niall stepped around the large bed and plopped himself into a chair, happy Arek used the very word he was thinking. "All right, an adventure it is, but do we just wander about down there?"

* * * * *

Time slowed and stopped, and the scene froze. Arek looked around and saw the shade of Piter appear again. He moved over to the group and looked at Arek, "A new group to torment me?"

"Piter, I'm sorry . . ."

Piter held up a hand, and said, "Tell them you seek a place where Shimmerene falls, a place below the fortress."

"Shimmerene? The lake?" he replied.

The shade of Piter nodded. "I will guide you from there."

* * * * *

The scene snapped back and Arek blinked a few times, shaking his head.

"You all right?" asked Tej.

"Yes, but . . . ," Arek hesitated. Piter's appearances were oddly reassuring. Without Silbane's company, the shade was Arek's only remaining contact to his life on the Isle. Still, when he thought about how he, Tomas, and Jesyn had acted toward Piter, it left him with a pit of guilt in his stomach. He hoped that being bound to him would prevent the shade from trying to exact revenge, but he'd never anticipated feeling blame over his actions. The thought filled him with remorse. Perhaps he really had been unkind.

"Sorry, yes, I'm fine. May I ask, does Shimmerene fall anywhere below?"

Yetteje looked at Niall, who became thoughtful. Then he said, "Inside Bara'cor? Doubtful. I've never heard of that, but I know the entrance to the underground cisterns, which are fed by the lake. From there we may find something."

"Can you take us there?" Arek asked Niall.

Niall nodded and said, "We should outfit ourselves first, though. Believe it or not, it gets pretty cold down there."

Led by Niall the three went to the door, slowed by Arek, who could manage nothing more than a hobble. Niall addressed the guards stationed outside. "I'm taking Arek to the Healers Ward. He's complaining about his foot."

"Your father didn't leave specific orders, my prince, but I was under the impression he was not to leave this room," the guard said.

"My father named him 'guest,' during our last meeting, and retracted his status as prisoner. I wish to take our *guest* to the Healers Ward. Stand aside." Niall met the guard's gaze without flinching.

A few heartbeats passed before the guard bowed and stepped back. "Of course, my prince."

Niall motioned to the other two, and the three made their way out of the room and to the nearest stairwell spiraling down into the great keep's bowels. Ahead of them lay a small storeroom, into which Niall ducked.

"Grab something warm to put on and something to eat. Not sure how long we'll be down there," he said, stuffing his mouth with dried fruit.

Arek stood at the doorway to the storeroom, his foot throbbing. Then his eyes widened in disbelief. "I knew everything was supposed to be big, but actually being here is different."

"Huh?" Niall looked about, then asked between chews, "What do you mean?"

"Everything. The halls, this room, even the door. Everything is so big."

Yetteje laughed. "I thought so too, when I first arrived here. I don't even notice it now."

"The whole fortress is like that," Niall said, "like it was made for people bigger than us." He swallowed one last mouthful, and then grabbed a canteen of water. "Like Tej said, you get used to it." He handed both of them something to eat, then began rummaging through the shelves for anything useful he might have missed.

Arek's mouth crooked into a smile and he said to Niall's back, "That was impressive, with the guard." He knew a prince was important, but to bluff one's way past his own father's orders? For someone raised in an environment based on a strict adherence to rank and protocol, the feat was worthy of note.

Niall shrugged. "If you act like you're in charge, nine times out of ten, people believe it."

"If your name is Galadine," Yetteje offered with a smile. "Grab the gear and torches and let's go. Whether they believed you or not, someone will be sent to inform the king and the Healers Ward. When we don't show up, we'll pay the Lady's price."

"He was named guest, you know," retorted Niall over his shoulder to Tej's retreating back. Her answer was a quick spin with an eye-roll and a laugh.

Arek focused on grabbing items he thought would be useful. He checked his foot again, thankful once more for the soft boot that held it safe. Niall had his own sword, but neither Yetteje nor Arek had a weapon.

As if she read Niall's thoughts, Yetteje grabbed a short blade and looked at Arek. "You need something?"

Arek shook his head. "No. I'm all right." Even unarmed he was far deadlier than either of them knew. Given his injured foot, he was loathed to weigh himself down with anything more than he needed. He did however wonder briefly about Tempest and whether he still needed her to complete his healing. Being armed didn't sound especially prudent should they run into the king's forces, and Arek was still unsure of his status, despite these two and their reassurances.

The three left the storeroom and continued slowly down the passageway, turning and descending through cavernous halls more than enough times to completely confuse Arek.

They passed occasional soldiers and the odd servant or two, causing Arek to comment on the lack of people.

"You really don't understand how a siege works, do you?" Niall asked with a raised eyebrow.

"Just seems odd not to run into more guards."

Yetteje answered with a small laugh, "It would help to know that most of Bara'cor has evacuated to Haven. Anyone concerned with defense is either on duty near the outer walls, or along the fastest paths between those positions and supplies and food. We're pretty deep in the interior."

Niall nodded, mirth in his eyes. "Would you rather we ran into more sentries, ones who would want to know what we're doing?"

Yetteje leaned in conspiratorially and said, "Be thankful, we're with a Galadine."

"Very funny, Tej. You know we couldn't have gotten past that guard without me."

"True." Yetteje smiled, then winked at Arek and shook her head, mouthing, *Not true.*

Eventually, they stopped at a large iron door. The only thing Arek knew for certain was that they were far below the sands of the desert. He shook his foot to relieve the pins and needles. It continued to throb and feel twice its size, but he could remember stubbing his toe on that Whiterobe's trunk locker back on the Isle, and laughed at how much fuss he'd made then.

Had that only been a few days ago? So much had already happened. Arek couldn't believe he was now accompanied by the heirs of both Bara'cor and EvenSea, on a quest to find whatever the shade of Piter was trying to show him.

Trusting his master and the dragon had been a disaster. He doubted even Silbane could stop the dragon if he really bent his mind to finishing what he'd started at the Far'anthi tower. He might have trusted the Bara'cor command, but torture had ended any understanding of the king and his actions.

And his master? Arek just wasn't sure anymore who had his best interests at heart. At least these two seemed more pure in their focus. In a perverse way, Niall and Yetteje were the only ones he felt he could trust.

"This is it," Niall said, "the entrance to the lower catacombs. They'll eventually lead us to the water cisterns." He looked at Arek and asked, "Are you sure?"

Arek nodded. "I know we have to go where Shimmerene falls."

Niall took a deep breath and opened the door. The passageway beyond was black. Lighting a torch from the wall sconce, Niall made his way in, followed by Arek. Yetteje came in last and secured the iron door behind them.

Ahead stretched the catacombs, and beyond that, a place where Arek felt he would soon meet his destiny.

The Catacombs

FORGING THE ISLE

*Just as one cannot fill an already full cup,
one cannot teach the Way of Making
to those who believe they already know.
To learn, they must first empty their cup.
—Lore Father Argus Rillaran, The Way*

Dragor grabbed another book, hefting it onto their table. "This is a list of the known lore fathers and lore mothers. There are many pages missing, but in what's there, the name 'Armun' doesn't appear."

"Not surprising. Who knows how many were lost during the heyday of the Galadine purging," Giridian said softly.

Dragor sighed. "Did anyone mention the name?"

The lore father shook his head. "Not exactly. I remember Themun arguing more than once with Thera, who wanted to find Dawnlight. She said the name 'Armun,' but I could never be sure what was meant by it."

"Didn't Themun find Thera at Dawnlight?" Dragor asked.

"Nearby," Giridian replied. They were at a dead end. There was no way to move forward without understanding the lore father's reason for mentioning Armun, and that left only one thing. He turned around and said haltingly, "I . . . I'll search his memories."

Dragor arched an eyebrow. "Two hundred years of it? For what, exactly? You said earlier the right vision doesn't just pop into your head. Where do you look?"

Giridian leaned against a shelf, turning over Dragor's question in his mind. What did he look for? If Themun knew Armun, it would be difficult to pinpoint something unique about them. Then, a solution came to him in a moment of clarity. "Since they discussed Armun, maybe it's a conjunction between Themun and Thera?" He looked at Dragor and said, "Maybe if I look for memories including the three of them, it will be enough."

"Sounds thin. You think it will work?"

Giridian shook his head, "I hope so, because if it doesn't, I'm running out of ideas."

He closed his eyes then and opened his mind to Themun's thoughts. They were available, a lifetime of learning at his mental fingertips, if only he knew where to look.

He knew this would be a time before the founding of the monastery, so it would be something unique to Themun and Thera. Perhaps if he thought about her time after the destruction of her village? Or better, perhaps there was a mission she and Themun had gone on to find something about Dawnlight? He thought about the name *Thera*.

A group of stars separated themselves in his vision, still too many to count. He sighed, then added, *Dawnlight*. Maybe he could filter the results into a manageable number of sources. To his surprise, three stars separated themselves, with one shining brighter than the other two. He chose the brightest one, trusting his desire would lead him to the right memory to watch.

Slowly, Giridian's vision went black, and then he discovered that he was standing on a rocky outcropping. Thera and another man who looked similar to Themun stood beside of him. They wore tight fitting clothes and swords across their backs. Giridian wished there was a mirror—judging by Thera's youth, this would've been his chance to see Themun looking young. In this memory, Themun was close to his thirtieth summer.

The trio looked over a green expanse and the mountain that struck upward from it like a giant granite fist of stone and snow. That was Dawnlight, the first place the light of the sun touched their land. It stood on the horizon, its icy peaks sparkling. Giridian heard the older man heave a sigh.

"You sure we have to climb that thing?" he asked, looking at Themun pointedly. "It could just be something natural."

Then his name—Armun—became one with Giridian's own knowledge, along with the stunning realization that Armun was Themun's older brother! Neither Themun nor Thera had ever mentioned him having a brother. It brought a small smile to his lips to think that even then, Themun was clearly the leader.

Themun nodded and answered, "Nothing natural is that powerful, and there's the disappearance of the dwarves. They journeyed to this spot as well. The two may be connected."

Armun leaned forward and squinted. "The power of whatever lies there is incredible. I couldn't sense it before, but from here it shines like a star."

* * * * *

Themun knew it seemed inconceivable a single person could radiate such power, but the only way they could know for sure would be to investigate. He looked at the other two, catching for a moment the look that passed between them. It was happening more often as they all journeyed together. Themun was sure they fancied one another, but his focus was on keeping them all alive, a promise he'd made to his father.

"Something is inside that mountain and if we can sense it, so can the king's magehunters," Themun said. "We need to get there first."

Just then, an earsplitting shriek sounded. It came from below the ridge they stood upon, from a small clearing that led to a ravine. As they turned their attention there, the shriek sounded again, forcing them to cover their ears. They looked down and saw a black, reptilian shape quickly circle up a rocky outcropping, clearly evading something coming out of the brush.

It was a young dragon, its black scales scintillating in the forest's dappled sunlight. It circled itself at the top of the outcropping, hissing at something yet unseen from its makeshift perch. The brush shook, but the trio above couldn't yet see what hunted this creature through the undergrowth below.

Then the crack of breaking limbs echoed across the clearing and the trees and underbrush gave way to three lizard-like shapes, similar to the dragonling, but clearly not dragons. Each stood a man's height at the shoulder, but unlike the dragonling these had massive forelimbs and walked almost upright. They had heads like crocodiles': full-grown adult basilisks. They had gray, dry scales, with neck frills that expanded as they hissed. Their nictitating eyes shone silver, affording them protection against their own petrifying gaze.

Themun asked the other two, "What do you think?"

Armun was first to respond. "Animals fighting aren't our concern. Plus, we can't prevail against a dragon, even with three basilisks to help."

Thera looked wide-eyed at him. "You are joking . . ."

Armun nodded, rolling his eyes and flashing a smile, and Themun felt a flush of relief. His brother wasn't as callous as he sometimes acted. Still, he couldn't help but be annoyed at the joke.

"All right, what do we do?" Themun looked down at the clearing, starting to formulate a plan.

Armun clapped him on the shoulder. "It's four against three . . . stop thinking." With that, he stood up and stepped off the ledge, dropping from sight.

"Assuming the dragon helps us," said Themun, more resigned than angry.

"It's not so bad," Thera replied, her eyes on Armun. Without another word, she stepped off the ledge and fell to join him.

Themun stood by himself, shaking his head, then assessed the situation. In this, he was much like his father, who had taught him the importance of tactics and position. Seeing where the conflict would likely end up, he ran to his right and jumped, landing near the dragonling.

Out of the corner of his eye, he watched as his older brother fell at least fifteen man-lengths down, landing with barely a sound. A moment later Armun shot out toward the closest basilisk.

The creature was fixated on its dangerous prey, the young dragonling, and didn't notice his approach. Armun leapt and drew his sword in one fluid motion. The blade flashed white and silver, potent with power. He descended and cut, severing the monster's head from its torso. The detached head tumbled forward some distance, coming to rest at the base of the dragonling's perch.

The basilisk next to the unfortunate first kill looked up and focused its baleful glare on Thera. Had it been turned upon those without Talent, it would first paralyze, then char them into a statue of ash within heartbeats.

Thera was far from untrained, having spent the past fifteen years under the Dreys family's tutelage. She called upon her *Skyskin* and the very air around her became a reflective shield, one that let her see out, but didn't let the basilisk's gaze penetrate. Then she moved forward in a blur.

She called upon the Way again using *Blood of the Earth*. Caressed by her summons, grass grew at an impossible rate, encompassing the basilisk in a web of woven fibers and pinning the man-like reptile in place. It tried to escape, but Thera's sword licked out unerringly. Within a heartbeat, the second basilisk lay pierced through the back of the neck and impaled to the ground, its legs twitching in death.

The third creature still seemed strangely intent on the dragonling. By now it should've tried to escape. Basilisks were at least intelligent enough to know when the odds were against them, yet this one didn't run. The thought crossed Themun's mind that something else might in fact be controlling these creatures.

Before Themun could act, a wing-shaped shadow crossed the remaining basilisk, and a clawed foot smashed into its skull and obliterated the head in a wet explosion of gray matter, bone, and blood. A full-grown dragon landed atop the ruined skull of the beast, beating black wings that spread the width of the entire clearing.

Themun's leap would've been perfect had it been moments earlier. As it was, he stood within a sword's length of the dragonling, still curled upon its perch, with his blade unsheathed. If the elder dragon believed Themun meant harm, they would all die.

In one smooth motion Themun sheathed his sword and went to a knee with outspread arms, addressing the elder dragon.

"By your leave, milord."

The great dragon turned, hissing a challenge and warning. Only Themun stood near the hatchling and in direct view. It was too late for him to retreat.

The creature turned its yellow-golden gaze on the warrior-monk and asked, "Dost thou seek ransom?"

The voice was deep, like gravel against stone, and Themun found himself suddenly speechless. The power of dragonfear washed over him, taking his words with it. He kept his eyes down and opened his hands, showing no weapons. The dragon must have looked away, for he felt a sudden release from the overwhelming desire to run and found his voice.

"Nay, milord. We only offer aid." He knew dragons detested normal speech and his kind in general.

"Thou hast given aid. And now?" The dragon moved forward, taking time to trample the carcasses of the basilisks that had threatened the younger dragon's life.

From behind Themun came a girl's voice, young yet strident, "Thy companions intervened, my sire."

The dragon's eyes narrowed and it said, "Nay, no companions of mine. Naught but halfling vermin."

Themun looked behind him and saw a young girl, no more than fifteen summers. She looked normal, except for the two black wings that emerged from her back. They flashed in the shafts of sunlight, iridescent and beautiful. The expression on her face, if readable, seemed vexed.

"Sire, I have not yet earned thy name, but these three came to mine aid," she stated. "They hath no need to do so." She narrowed her gaze and Themun felt the distinct impression this young dragon was used to winning arguments with what was obviously her father.

The great dragon changed in a flash of light that left a dark armored knight that Giridian now recognized as Rai'stahn. The knight approached Themun and said, "Thou ken the Way. By what means?"

"My father," Themun answered, "who taught me that the Way is that which makes us."

Rai'stahn's eyes narrowed. "Thine answer is childish, but that is expected."

While the dragon did seem angry, Giridian sensed it'd been impressed with Themun and his openness.

"Wouldst thou live in these times, son of the Way?" Rai'stahn continued, "Thy king's men hunt all with Talent."

"Aye, yet my friends and I come to the aid of those we can." At his gesture, both Armun and Thera emerged. "We three live outside the law and escape the king's long arm. What is your intent, milord?"

The little girl dragon came up then and said, "Thou wert ever impatient with me. Now I wilt have my say."

The great dragon inclined an armored head, but Themun could see the hint of amusement in the corners of the knight's golden eyes. "Very well, have at it," he said in voice that sounded more like a growl.

"Thou hast spoken of the king's justice. These three are strong in the Way. Wilt thou turn thy back on them in such a craven fashion?" The girl spread her arms, encompassing the clearing with Themun and his small party. "Surely thou wilt offer them thy aegis?"

Rai'stahn stared at the young dragonling, his golden eyes narrowing in a calculating stare. His mien reflected what Themun could only interpret as frustration, but that countenance was mixed with a sense that this exchange was of a piece with others the great dragon had had with this particular dragonling.

Before the younger dragon could say more, Rai'stahn turned and addressed Themun, saying, "What is thy business here?"

Themun motioned to his companions, who moved slowly forward. "We seek a plume of power, somewhere near Dawnlight."

Rai'stahn's head swiveled, looking to the great peak. He sighed, then said, "Zafir's gate hath opened upon this world, the path to Harmagedon. Remember its taint well, for it marks danger to all the land."

Themun stood aghast. "Do you mean such as the one through which Lilyth's forces emerged?"

Rai'stahn looked back at the young monk and nodded. "Verily, for I and my hatchling journey to the same place to ascertain the threat and put an end to it."

"Sire, shall I speak of the Isle?" asked the younger dragon, steering the conversation back to the fate of Themun and his party. "Thou canst grant haven, if they so petition." She cocked her head to one side, a small smile on her youthful face. Her razor-sharp teeth reminded Themun once again that this was no young girl.

The great dragon drew a deep breath, its eyes never leaving Themun's own. Then, as if coming to a decision, he said, "Thou hast come to the aid of my daughter. For that, I offer a boon."

The girl dragon then offered, a bit eagerly, "My sire and I make our home deep in the Shattered Sea, at the end of a chain of islands, southeast of Koorva. It holds upon it enough sustenance for those of thy kind."

The dragon-knight rumbled his displeasure at his daughter's interruption, "Why dost thou seek permission, only to speak regardless?"

When the younger dragon didn't answer, Rai'stahn looked back at Themun and said, "It is named Meridian, and stands as home to my hatchlings, though some may not survive this journey." He eyed the dragonling meaningfully, but she seemed unperturbed.

The great dragon deflated, accepting his loss to the younger, then growled, "Seek it and I will allow thee and thy companions to remain there, safe from the king's justice."

Themun looked at the dragon, questions stumbling in his mind, clamoring to be given voice, but held his tongue. Before insulting anyone, he bowed formally and said, "We stand honored."

"Pay heed, for thy boon comes with a price. Thy petty affairs concern me little, for thy people are short-lived and mostly useless. However—" Rai'stahn held up a taloned hand— "thy current king hath a long reach and seeks to eradicate those gifted with Talent. This I cannot abide. I stand against him and offer thee and thy people haven. In return, thou shalt aid me in protecting the Way, in any manner I deem necessary."

"A fair exchange, milord." Themun bowed again, then stood and stepped back from the great dragon. "If I may ask your name?"

The dragon looked at the young mage, then stepped forward. He raised his armored hand and placed it upon Themun's forehead, as a god would to a supplicant. "I am known as Rai'stahn, Lord of Meridian, and guardian of this world. Dost thee accept me as thy lord?"

Themun didn't directly answer, instead saying, "I am Themun Dreys. With me stand my elder brother, Armun,

Forging the Isle

and Thera Dawnlight. We seek to save those born into this land with Talent and would ally ourselves with you."

"Well met," intoned the dragon Rai'stahn. "Two shall journey back to the Isle with my hatchling and prepare for my return. There you will take the Oath, and we will forge a new haven for those hunted by this mad king."

"Milord?" Confusion ran across Themun's face. "What of this gate we sensed?"

The dragon moved forward, towering over the young mage, and stated, "Mortal, I do not request. I command as your liege."

Themun took a deep breath, and then slowly stepped back. The power this creature radiated was palpable and he knew his next words could still condemn them to death should the elder dragon suddenly change his mind. Themun spread his arms and bowed, breaking eye contact. "As you wish, milord, but you said two. Who remains?"

The great dragon looked at the three, his golden gaze measuring. Then he pointed at Armun and said, "Thou shalt accompany me."

Themun and Armun locked gazes, then Armun said, "It is better I go. You must see to this island and our continued safety."

"No!" Thera blurted. "It may not be safe."

Armun looked at her and smiled. "With a dragon as my companion? You were safer with me than I with you. I will see to Dawnlight and this gate. Await my return."

Themun stood speechless. His brother and he hadn't been apart since their father's death, and a part of him feared their separation.

As if answering his unspoken thought, the younger dragon stepped forward and said, "Thy brother is safe. He stands under the wing of my sire. It is not thy place to question thy lord."

Armun added, "You know what Father would've said." He moved to stand closer to the great armored knight, "Let's join forces and save who we can today." He smiled.

~ 456 ~

"The future is for someone better than you, little brother." Though the words could've been construed as unkind, Armun smiled and winked.

Giridian watched as Rai'stahn changed back into his dragon form, Armun climbed aboard. Through Themun's eyes, he saw his brother raise a hand in farewell, that familiar crooked smile playing across his lips.

"Father chose well when he chose you to lead," said Armun. "I will return and follow, no matter what you decide."

Giridian felt Themun's heartache, the fear that knotted his stomach as the great dragon moved a bit farther away.

Rai'stahn looked back one more time and locked eyes with the young adept, saying, "We shall speak upon my return of the Oath." With that, he bunched his great muscles and leapt into the air, departing with Armun astride, a small streak of black arrowing through the clear blue sky. They quickly turned north to Dawnlight and a gate that seemed eerily similar to the one Giridian now faced at Bara'cor.

Rai'stahn's daughter smiled, revealing again those fanged teeth, and said, "Come, I will convey thee back to our lord's demesne."

Giridian watched as the three walked down to the clearing littered with the remains of the basilisks, then his vision faded to black.

* * * * *

Slowly, the Vault came into focus again, along with the concerned face of Dragor, who now stood to one side, rubbing Giridian's hand to wake him.

He looked at Dragor and smiled. "Did you know Themun had a brother?" He didn't yet mention the pact Themun had agreed to. In light of his conversation with Thoth, he'd begun to see why these visions were problematic, for they created more questions than they answered.

Dragor shook his head and asked, "Trained in the Way?"

Giridian nodded. "Armun, and when they last saw each other, his brother had begun a journey to…"

"Dawnlight," Dragor finished, guessing correctly. "We need to find Armun, then, if he still lives. He may know much of these gates and the dwarves."

"There is more," Giridian said. "I think I saw how we came into our service and our Oath. It was driven by Rai'stahn."

"A dragon? That can't be true."

"No, I don't mean that." The lore father looked about the room, as if searching the air for an answer. "What happens when one takes an Oath so encompassing, so consuming, it defines the very nature of all who follow? What if it changes the very essence of who we are?"

"I don't know what you mean. We are who we are," Dragor said. "Our Oath is to serve the land and we have done so since Themun came here."

Giridian stood deep in thought, then came to a decision and said, "Prepare Jesyn for her test. There is no reason to delay her Ascension, and we will have need of another adept. Tomas will have to wait until he's fully recovered."

He needed to think more about Themun, Rai'stahn, and their role in all this. He hadn't known Meridian Isle and their beginning was so inextricably linked to the great dragon. That explained how so many of Talent found their way here. Rai'stahn brought them for protection by Themun and his council. It also shed light on some of Themun's actions.

"And what of Armun?" Dragor asked.

Giridian looked at his friend and paused, not relishing the idea of sending more adepts into danger, but knowing there was no other choice. He needed to protect the Isle and contact Kisan and Silbane, which left only Dragor to deal with finding Armun.

Giridian laid a comforting hand on Dragor's shoulder and said, "We must find him."

Dragor seemed to know what was coming next and asked, "By 'we,' I assume you mean me? You can't use your new powers to just *See* there?" He didn't expect an answer. "No, I suppose it's not that easy."

The lore father smiled, "It's not the same as being there. Get Jesyn ready. After her test the two of you will start your search at the last place Armun had been, the mountain of Dawnlight."

"And if she doesn't pass?" Dragor asked in a small voice.

Giridian breathed in deeply, his hand unconsciously squeezing the leather of the chair. "Then we'll get Tomas ready. We don't have many other choices. One way or another, your job is to find out what happened to Armun."

Forging the Isle

JOURNAL ENTRY 15

I wonder who survived the last assault. My thoughts linger on them more as time crawls along. That Rai'stahn intended the blow that pushed me here is uncontested. I have no doubts of his betrayal, and cherish the sharp focus the memory of it provides. I hope to see him again so I can repay his "loyalty."

Beautiful Sonya, surely, for she was strong in the Way. Perhaps Duncan, though only by someone else's sacrifice. He was always weak-willed so I question Sonya's judgment—but only in her choice of him.

Elsimere, Dale? I hope they lived. Arthur, Temairex? Do they know it was my forbearance, my love for them, my intervention on their behalf that bent Lilyth's final blow away? Or do they blame me still? Is it foolishness to want their company, yet be angered by their lack of action, of fortitude? I feel no desire to write anything except how I stood alone in the end, victorious. Curse them all and good riddance to the lot. Perhaps I will see them again, but as conqueror and king.

Did I expect any different? No. I am the greatest. I am the most powerful archmage to have ever existed. Why would anyone stand with me to the very end? In trying, it would mean their lives, for they would've died long before I succumbed.

The imp is speaking now. It whispers things sometimes . . . it asks questions. What is it? Why do we live here? Stupid questions.

Documenting the failure and shortcomings of my so-called friends grows tiresome.

I am weary of this place . . .

Journal Entry 15

FLASHBACK: KISAN

Is one style of fighting better than another?
Will you see a different view,
from the same mountaintop,
as one who arrived by another path?
—Kensei Tsao, *The Lens of Blades*

T he juvenile sky serpent flew through the dense foliage, its senses attuned to the heat of rodents or birds small enough for it to eat. A forked tongue flickered in and out, tasting the air. Its blue and silver iridescent scales flashed in the sunlight that pierced the canopy above. The light filtering to the ground created edges that looked like leaves.

Kisan watched, silently hidden in the foliage below. Sky serpents were fearsome adults, but even the juveniles were dangerous. Unlike landbound snakes, they hunted in either day or night. Even the tiniest of these flying snakes could kill a man with one bite, so Kisan was glad that in the months she'd been hunting here, this juvenile was one of the few she'd come across.

It spotted something near the ground, a baby direhawk. Instantly the serpent moved in, alert both for the chick's parents and for any dangers that might lurk near so easy a meal.

Juvenile sky serpents' nemeses were direhawks, one of the few creatures they feared. The hawks would plummet from the wide blue above and kill with their unerring talons.

The fallen chick sensed the danger and began to *cheep*. The serpent shot forward, mouth open and fangs outstretched. The air shimmered and Kisan's blade whistled down, slicing the serpent's head from its body in one clean stroke.

The blade she wielded rested comfortably in one hand, with a small streak of the serpent's blood, bluish-black, dripping from its keen edge.

Her other hand held a string tied to the baby direhawk's foot. She pulled that string and grabbed the chick, stuffing it into a small, soft pouch on her belt. The head popped out, complaining in bird cheeps, and she fed it a grub saying, "Stop it. You were never in any real danger."

She grabbed and stuffed the serpent's body into another pouch. Later she would skin and eat it. It wasn't the best tasting, but highly nutritious. She straightened to stand and the hairs on the back of her neck stood up.

She concentrated and the world shifted hues. Now she could see heat as color, and scanned the forest around her for anything out of the ordinary. If it were an adult sky serpent, she would need to move quickly to a defensible position. Their wings became arm-like limbs, and their sinuous bodies ran the length of many men. She'd never faced one and didn't relish the thought, though her heart quickened a bit at the idea of the challenge. However, what she saw both surprised her and drew forth a short curse.

Just my luck, she thought.

"How long will you continue this?" The voice carried through the trees, and the form of the man attached to it slowly became visible. "You have better options, Kisan."

She let out a sigh and another expletive. "Wasn't 'no' the last three times enough?" She backed up, sheathing her blade in one smooth motion. "At least this time you didn't scare away dinner."

"Snake meat? I heard it tastes like—"

"Snake." She sighed, "What do you want?"

The man who walked up to Kisan looked to be in his twenties, with faded blue eyes and dark hair that hadn't yet seen the lightening of the summer sun's kiss. The corners of his eyes crinkled with familiar lines of a face used to laughing. "Same as always. You seem determined to live out here."

"And you keep visiting. Who's the bigger fool?"

He bowed, conceding, "The answer is clear."

She snorted and said, "Silbane the Fool. Nice ring to it."

Silbane smiled, taking no offense. He moved over to a log and sat down. "We're not giving up."

"We?" she asked, wary again.

"I brought a friend," he said, nodding to his left.

From thin air stepped a second man, older, perhaps in his thirties. He smiled at Kisan, then said, "I knew your mother, and offer my sorrow at her passing."

"You're a month late," Kisan said through pursed lips. "She and father are buried over there, if you want to pay any respects." She pointed with her chin. "Nice protection she had from you."

The man ignored that, saying instead, "Your mother was powerful in the Way and has taught you some of its uses. Come with us, and we will complete your training."

She rolled her eyes at that, then looked back at Silbane. "Has everyone suddenly become more stupid? You couldn't protect my mother from the king."

"The magehunters won't spare you because you haven't been trained. You are only making it easier for them."

"How long do you think you can hide out here?" This came from the older man. "Your mother was a gifted initiate, and yet she fell."

"Because of you!" Kisan stared at the older man, and when he didn't reply she added, "Have you suddenly gotten better at protecting folks from the King's Law?" Disgusted, she moved away from them, taking a deep breath, trying to stay calm. The two men followed her, but kept a respectful distance behind.

"Maybe you think you're like one of these sky serpents. Fast, agile, deadly?" The older man barked out a laugh behind her, "Take a good look at yourself. Calling you 'dirty' would be an insult to dirt."

Flashback: Kisan

She moved farther along the forest floor. "I've been here since they died. Heard you ran at the first sign of trouble. Like father like son."

The older man turned red and surged forward, only to be brought up short by Silbane. He said, "Maybe my friend is a bit too direct, but if we can find you, so can they. Come with us; join a noble cause."

She stopped; her shoulders hunched, then she turned to face them both. "Don't you get it? The magehunters killed. . . *everyone.* You're part of some guild or whatever, but didn't think my mother was important enough to help. What makes that so noble?"

The older man began to say something, but she cut him off, "I'm done with you. Leave me alone and don't come back!" A small flame appeared then, surrounding her. It was faint, almost invisible to anyone who could not see the Way, but Silbane couldn't hide his astonishment. Neither could the older man.

Silbane cleared his throat and said, "You'll not win through anger. Learn to control your growing powers."

Kisan shook her head, Silbane's persistence infuriating her further. What was it that made him so obtuse? She wasn't about to put herself in harm's way. Learning magic would only make her a target for the magehunters to come back and finish the job, just as they had with her mother.

Before she said anything however, the older man turned on her. She could see he was still angry.

"I'm through listening to your excuses, Kisan Talaris," he said. "We may not return, but others will. The Galadines have a long arm, and they'll not suffer a mage to live, untrained or not. Learn everything you can from these serpents you fancy. They're hunters too, and yet fall even to your inept blade. What lesson does that teach you?"

Kisan was caught off balance by the man's sudden willingness to abandon her. She hadn't expected him to give up so easily. Her focus narrowed and she asked, "What's your name?"

"For all your Talent, you're thick-headed and stubborn," he replied. "You're not a sky serpent, just pathetic and useless, like your pet bird, tied to this place by a string you can't see. And within another month, you'll both be dead. So my name isn't that important." With that, the man, took two steps, and vanished.

Silbane gave her an apologetic smile and snapped his fingers. A sparkle flashed, then fell to his feet. She could see it still glittering where he stood, as if he left behind bits of . . . something. "If you change your mind, you can follow this and join us. We will depart tomorrow at dusk and this trail will disappear." He met her eyes and gave her another small smile. "I hope to see you before then."

He raised a hand in farewell. The glittering trail pointed toward the coastal city of Sunhold, half a day's walk away. *Most likely to catch a boat,* she surmised.

Later that evening she hunched in front of a campfire, chewing absentmindedly on sky serpent meat while her mind seethed. How dare he call her pathetic? Had he ever lived on his own? What had he ever lost? He was probably born into wealth, suckling milk from some fat cow of a nurse in some grand castle filled with servants and food. The more she thought about him, the angrier she became.

Behind her stood a small shelter built out of branches and leaves. In it were the few things she'd salvaged, scrounged after the magehunters had razed her village. She'd been safe only because of timing and luck. She'd been gone that day, hunting, as she often did, deep within the forest. Her return had been a harsh end to childhood. Exactly twenty-nine days ago, her life had changed forever.

She looked up and could still see the sparkling trail, winding its way through the trees. The stillness of the forest and the silver moonlight seemed to intensify the effect, showing her a way quite literally to her own future, if she chose to follow it. What lay along that bright path? What happened if she stayed? She accepted she had no family, no home, that everyone she knew was dead. How long could she truly live out here alone?

When morning came, it greeted an empty shelter. Anything she valued had been packed up, but one small task remained. She moved over to a dense bush, reached into her pouch, and withdrew the direhawk chick, still complaining, and the rest of her grubs. She undid the string from its leg and carefully nestled it in, then scattered the grubs around for it to eat.

"Don't eat it all at once, stupid bird."

She knew it would perish, likely killed by the very serpents it'd helped her catch. Nothing left alone out here survived for long, a point the older man had made so abundantly clear. The message had sunk in, but she still hated him for it.

The chick sat there with its small beak wide open. When it realized that nothing more was coming from Kisan, it turned its attention to the grubs and grabbed one, swallowing it hungrily before moving to a second. Kisan drew a deep breath and watched in silent thought. Then, with a curse, she moved over and grabbed it, stuffing it back into her pouch amidst a small flurry of flapping wings, cheeping complaints, and a painful peck for her efforts.

She was unable to abandon the chick to its fate. Finding it alone and injured, she'd nursed it back to health. Soon it would grow into a deadly raptor. She wasn't ready to give up on it, not before it had a fair chance. She knew though, that even if she joined these mages, she was still very much on her own. Her mother had made the mistake of trusting Silbane and that other one, and she'd died for it. Kisan would never make that same mistake.

She remembered Silbane's friend calling her helpless and pathetic and let out a small, derisive laugh. He'd no idea she'd already mastered much of what her mother could do and a few things she couldn't. She looked over her shoulder at the sparkling trail, then grabbed her pack and blade. Securing them, she made her way along its glittering path, listening all the while to her chick's complaints.

"You don't know me," she said, addressing the memory of Silbane's friend.

The one-sided conversation cooled her anger a bit. She had to admit starting this journey filled her with a strange excitement, and as the morning crawled on her mood lightened. For the first time in a while, Kisan felt anticipation at what the rest of the day might bring.

Above her, she thought she heard the cry of an adult direhawk making a kill, and the sound brought a faint smile to her lips. Her eyes then flitted down, sparkling with power as she focused on the trail once again. Somehow, she knew only she could see it, a path left by the Way for her and her alone.

The chick had settled down in the comfy darkness of the soft pouch. Saving it wasn't only kindness or altruism, she admitted then with a touch of guilt. She sensed that bringing her bird along would serve to infuriate the older man. The thought tugged the corner of her mouth up in an impish grin. The vision of their surprised faces as she appeared in Sunhold only made her smile more.

He thinks I fancy sky serpents, like I actually want to be one? What an idiot. There were things much deadlier in this world than snakes or birds, evil things living in the hearts of men. She'd learned this firsthand. They had been hunted and lived their lives in fear until the very end.

I'm going to master everything you have to teach, she vowed silently, *no matter how long it takes.* Her eyes glittered with that promise and the burgeoning power that lay behind it. *Then I'll do what you didn't have the courage for, one magehunter at a time.*

Flashback: Kisan

TWO DAYS LEFT. . .

Flashback: Kisan

HAVEN

When you are the anvil, be patient.
When you are the hammer, strike.
—Altan proverb

T he team waited under cover of night, within sight of the walls of Bara'cor. They had docked in Haven a day before, handing the boat off to waiting dockhands, specially contracted by Arsenal to give them discreet access to the capital city and beyond. These dockhands would also dispose of the boat and any other evidence of their arrival.

From there they had made their way quickly up the Land's Edge pass. Kisan wondered again at the conditioning of these dwarves, who ran for hours at a stretch with no more effort than a normal person used to breathe.

It was during one of these prolonged runs that she finally attempted contacting the lore father, having regained enough energy and come to the conclusion that none of these men could mindspeak.

At first, she heard nothing. Then, to her surprise, she heard Adept Giridian's voice. The moment they made contact, though, Kisan knew her old friend was an adept no longer, but the new lore father. In an instant, both had conveyed to the other the events that had transpired since their separation.

Giridian confirmed what Kisan already knew, these "men" were in fact dwarves. Upon hearing of how Themun's death occurred, however, Kisan nearly lost step with the others. Themun's last sacrifice was characteristic of her mentor, wise teacher, and close friend. Kisan breathed a sigh of relief as the burden of Dragor's last sacrifice lifted from her heart.

The children with Thera were a different story. The memory of Piter welled up, and Kisan knew how the parents of those lost ones felt. A cold anger grew in her heart. She would not forgive.

Giridian shared his vision about Valarius in council and Thoth next, but because of the distance, Kisan couldn't be given the full immersive experience. She could, however, feel the profound impact it had on the lore father and his beliefs. It was more than enough.

Arek posed a danger and he'd committed murder when he took Piter's life. That fact alone condemned him in her eyes. Kisan related the dwarven team's orders to find and kill Arek and the royal Galadine family inside Bara'cor. Their interests aligned, but it made her sick to aid those who had killed Lore Father Themun Dreys.

What troubled her most was the knowledge that if this "Conclave" could direct their hand against Arek, why not against the Isle itself? That knot of worry she found was more difficult to unravel. Measured against the fate of the world, the lives of Themun, Thera, or of everyone on the Isle would be a small price to the Conclave.

Of Silbane, Kisan had heard nothing. *What are my orders concerning him?* she asked. Silbane would not allow his apprentice to come to harm and Kisan couldn't fault him for that.

Giridian felt the Conclave was correct about Silbane's apprentice. *Kill Arek at your first opportunity.*

As far as sharing information with Silbane, both knew they couldn't take that chance. Any interference from him endangered the entire land. Her heart felt heavy, but the decision was made and she felt it was the correct one.

Despite their argument, Kisan still thought of Silbane as a mentor and friend. Piter's death supported the Conclave's claim and though she didn't want to bring harm to one of their own, her orders were more than clear. Her best chance would be to take Arek alone, when Silbane wasn't around.

Hopefully, the master would never know who killed his apprentice.

Giridian used his newfound powers to replenish Kisan's health and vigor. The master marveled at the wash of energy that came through the connection, easing her muscles, lending clarity to thought and providing much needed succor to her entire being.

With renewed freshness she let Giridian know she would carry out his orders. She hoped to accomplish this without injuring Silbane, if possible. These assassins, however, would receive no such quarter. Once she felt she could glean no more information from them, she would kill them all.

The full moon shone overhead, turning the ground between their cover and the base of the walls of Bara'cor an eerie white. Their uniforms had changed color to match the surrounding terrain, a dusky gray and beige. From their vantage point, they could see the rear gates. Bara'cor sat hunched at the top of Land's Edge, its rear three walls connected to the switchback pass. Behind them was the capital city of Haven, a bright circle of lights encompassed by dark waters, close to two thousand feet below.

Prime didn't seem to think that making it into the fortress would be much of an issue. They slowed and then made their way to a small rocky area still some distance from the fortress but along the climbing pass. He gathered his men close. "Let us ask Sovereign to guide our hands," he intoned, and the rest bowed their heads.

Kisan did the same, seeing in Tamlin's memories that this was the benediction they offered before combat.

Prime continued, "We fell, and from ashes rise again. We exact justice in Your name. Blessed be our hands, for they deliver to You the new Way. Blessed be our people, who will regain the sky."

The others intoned, "We are the First. We are the Last. We are the new Way."

Prime made a sign, grabbing his fist with his other hand and offering both, then he looked up. "We make our way to the Stone and from there into Bara'cor, the fortress of our fathers."

Two looked at everyone and said, "From here we keep silent. Getting in is the easy part. Getting out will be more difficult. Five and Six will secure the room for our egress. The rest of us will carry out our orders, no prisoners, no survivors. If we come in contact, they die. We may be coming back with pursuers, so be ready."

A pit formed in Kisan's stomach. She couldn't be left behind as rearguard while they met their goals. She'd even argued for the destruction of Bara'cor with the lore father. She had no love for the Galadines. Yet she didn't want these assassins to achieve any of their goals. Kisan felt committed to exacting a price from these dwarves. She was the lethal consequence they thought could never touch them.

The team made its way quickly parallel to the great fortress, which used its rear walls to create a protected area that led down Land's Edge. Because of this, the only way to the rear of the fortress was up the same cliff and through the fortress itself. Kisan appreciated the tactically sound strategy followed when building this stronghold.

They continued until it came upon a small way station situated in a copse of trees. A pool of clear water bubbled forth, fed by the same underground rivers that filled the lake within Bara'cor's walls. Its gurgling was the only sound that broke the still night air.

Kisan marveled at the beauty of the place, peaceful and clean. In the center of this way station stood a statue of a female with horns, her arms outstretched and holding a stone sphere roughly two feet in diameter. The sphere was smooth to the touch, the granite polished by an artisan's hand.

Prime picked up a piece of loose stone from the ground. He gripped it in his hand and squeezed. The rock pulverized into fine dust, which he slowly let fall on top of the sphere. He said something under his breath, something Kisan couldn't make out. At that moment, the sphere began to glow a soft blue. It wasn't so bright as to alert anyone, more like the soft light one sees in the night sky just before dawn.

He looked at the others meaningfully and whispered, "Keep silent, and watch each other's backs. We finish our job and get out—all of us. Remember, tonight we fight on home ground."

At his command, all six touched the stone and vanished.

Haven

JOURNAL ENTRY 16

The raids continue, and I have a ritual of sorts.

I hide . . . I know, shameful. I can feel them now, the hunger of their presence building to a point where I can predict their entry.

I build a cocoon of power, one I know can withstand assault. I cannot ward the entire area, but warding myself seems to be something I believe in enough to be successful.

Of course, I emerge to devastation, my gathered resources stolen and the ground scoured clean of anything I might have planted to aid my survival. They take everything of value, and while I know it is precisely because I value it . . . I grow weary.

I took the imp into my cocoon with me. I know it is nothing except a conjuration of my loneliness, but it speaks and I find myself strangely attached. My desire to protect it seems to strengthen my wards and more importantly, my resolve.

Even with the benefit of the dragon's vision, I find it hard to understand how to unravel these Aeris. Without a breakthrough, I fear the invasions will continue and our children will disappear.

Journal Entry 16

INTO THE DARK

To act without knowing is rash;
to know and not act, is cowardice.
—*The Bladesman Codex*

A rek and Yetteje followed Niall into the darker bowels of the great fortress. The passageway cut roughly into the rock, but merged to join with a smooth floor that had neither seams nor cracks. It was yet another example of the dwarven builders' skill with stone.

"How far down does this go?" asked Arek.

Niall looked back over his shoulder, his face hidden in the shadow cast by his torch's own firelight.

"I don't know. Pretty deep, maybe all the way down to the lowlands and Haven. My father once told me Bara'cor was just the visible part of an entire dwarven city built below it."

Arek looked to his left, where the passageway dropped off into inky blackness. "Can I hold your torch?"

Yetteje lit another torch off Niall's and handed it to him. "Here."

Arek looked down using the torch as a guide and saw they stood within a passageway that joined a rock face on their right and opened to empty space on their left. "You weren't kidding. Pretty far down, by the looks of it." He fought a sudden sense of vertigo and looked at Niall.

The prince answered, "We're not going that deep to reach the place I think you want." He looked down the passageway where it forked and said, "Come on, this way."

They started to move forward, the cold, damp air clinging to them like a second skin, when Arek's vision tunneled and time froze. From the darkness came the shade of Piter.

"Not as stupid as I thought, and not as crippled anymore. Learn something new about yourself?"

Arek asked, "You had me tortured on purpose?"

"What purpose would that serve, Master?" answered Piter, looking injured.

There was an undercurrent of obsequiousness in his voice, like the shade was mocking him. However, Arek had learned he could heal, though he still didn't know if it was because of Tempest or something he did himself. He'd like to believe the latter, but at the same time doubted it for the simple fact that he'd never accomplished anything magical.

He decided to focus on why he was down here and asked, "What am I looking for, exactly?"

The shade looked down the passageway, ignoring the question, then back at Arek. "This is a rare and potent place. Can you feel it?"

And all of a sudden, he could, as if it had always been there. It felt the same as when sunshine soaked into his skin, but this was not sunlight, it was *power*. "How?" he asked, but Piter held up a forestalling hand.

"As you get closer, you will feel and see more. Your powers are growing, as your Maker intended. Pay attention to the world around you." The shade nodded then pointed to the right passageway and said, "Your destiny lies in that direction."

The scene snapped back with the dizzying speed Arek had grown accustomed to. Piter was gone and Niall was quickly making his way to the fork. Arek looked around once more, steadying himself against the wet rock wall, then moving forward carefully to catch up.

"We need to go right at the fork," he said, his voice echoing through the subterranean space. He stumbled, his injured foot jarring painfully against a rocky outcropping, and muttered a soft curse. Still, that hadn't hurt nearly as much as the one before it. His healing continued.

"Got it," said Niall. He motioned for them to slow down and then gathered their small group together, crouching with their heads together. "Listen, we came in through a side passageway that's hardly used. However, my father has patrols, even here. Galadine name or not, if they see us, we'll be arrested, so douse the torches." He smothered his.

"How will we see?" Arek asked, wincing a little at the pain he felt from stooping.

Niall only said, "Trust me."

Arek looked at him a moment longer, then smothered his torch as well. They were instantly plunged into blackness. He felt Niall's hand squeeze his arm and assumed he'd taken hold of Tej also.

"See?" he heard Niall say.

As his eyes adjusted to the dark Arek noticed a sparkling on the slick walls of the passageway. Everything was covered in a faint luminescence.

"It's some sort of byproduct of Shimmerene. The water lets off light, like starlight," whispered the prince to the others. "It clings to the rocks, and as it does, it gets brighter."

Indeed, as Arek slowly stood, he found he could see quite well. "How much farther?"

"And what do you think we'll find?" asked Yetteje. "A weapon?"

"I don't know," Arek whispered, "but it's important."

They made their way down the right passageway, which turned colder and wetter as it angled sharply downward, and followed it for a few hundred paces. As they progressed, a roaring sounded in the distance, getting louder. The path doubled back on itself, turning downward again, then ended at a small landing.

From that landing, Arek could see a mist rising. He went to the edge, where below a white ribbon of water fell hundreds of feet into the darkness. It sparkled with the same luminescence as the walls but brighter.

"The Falls of Shimmerene?" asked Arek, to no one in particular.

Niall looked around, his expression one of awe. "I've never seen this. This wasn't here before."

The pearlescent stream of water fell in a white wash of mist and sound, disappearing into, it seemed, the very bowels of the world.

"How could something like this appear out of nowhere?" Yetteje asked.

"I have no idea, but we'd have known about this." He looked at Yetteje and said, "I've played in these catacombs since I was a child. I know them like my father's face."

One side of the landing abutted against a flat granite wall. Arek could see a stone door clearly etched into the wet wall. The sparkling luminescence from Shimmerene clung to it like a fragile sheet. There seemed to be no hinge or seam to open it.

"What now?" asked Niall, a bit unnerved. "Maybe we should get back, warn my father . . ."

Arek ignored the fear he heard in Niall's voice and looked around, saying, "I'm here, as you asked."

"Who are you talking—?" The scene froze, cutting off Yetteje's question.

Piter's shade appeared, illuminated by his own light. He looked at the door, then at Arek. "Do you remember?"

"Remember?"

"How you killed me?" the shade sneered.

Arek shook his head and said sadly, "I don't remember anything about that day . . . but I'm sorry." He tried to convey to the shade the guilt he also felt for his treatment of him, but it seemed to fall on deaf ears.

The shade didn't respond at first, staring at him. Then it said, "Do you remember your Test of Potential?"

Arek hesitantly nodded. "Not the details, but I remember preparing."

"This door opens the same way. Prepare as you did and the Way will open."

Reality snapped back into place and Arek heard Yetteje finish, "—to?"

He held up a hand for silence, then moved closer to the door. Now that he was closer, he could feel power in the air, like a vibration that ran just below his senses. It flowed through him, tantalizing and just within reach. His injured foot began to itch.

"I think I can open it," he said.

"Wait," began Niall, but Yetteje took him by the arm and moved a short distance away. Arek silently thanked her, concentrating still on the door.

"We'll be here, Arek. Do what you have to," she said.

Arek closed his eyes and willed himself to relax. He took a deep breath and exhaled, letting go of the turmoil of the past few days. He took another lungful of the cool, wet air and let go of the fear and anger. He imagined cool water washing in with each breath and cleaning out the detritus of emotions within his heart and soul. Arek breathed in peace and exhaled chaos.

There! In the calm waters of his mind, he could almost see something bound to the door. It was a woman. No, something like a woman. She hung suspended, with her arms outstretched to either side. Her body was covered in a fine gossamer gown, falling in straight white lines as if frozen in time. Feathered wings flared out, rising above her head, the tips almost meeting in the air above. Her head was down, as if she were lifeless or slept. To Arek, she looked like an angel.

He whispered, "Who are you?"

Her head slowly lifted and she opened her eyes. A cerulean light shone from them, power incarnate. Silver flashed down her length, as if awakening her also brought to life some eldritch power within. She looked around, questing with her ears, seemingly unable to see. "Where are you?" she countered.

"What are you doing here?" he asked, unable to see where the door ended and she began. The air began to shine, as if infused with an energy—all its own.

"My name is Dvarin." Her form strained forward, but still she couldn't see Arek.

Arek took a mental step closer, unable to understand how she'd gotten here. As he did so, he felt something change within him. Something grew, a hunger he could feel gurgling up from deep within himself.

As if in response, Dvarin pulled back. "No! You cannot mean to do this!"

Arek took a deep breath, and then stepped closer. He could feel his body hunger for the energy that surrounded her. It flowed cleanly through the very air, infusing her with an almost holy light. He couldn't resist it. It was meant for him; it was the essence of sustenance.

"No, I beg you! You cannot!" She tried to withstand the onslaught, but the power within Arek was too much. She bucked once, desperately trying to free herself, but a blackness had formed, a void into which she was inexorably pulled. It tore into her, disintegrating anything it touched into minute particles of light, then sucking that light into Arek. In a moment, it was done. Her psychic scream of death echoed across a vast, ethereal plane, before fading into nothingness.

Arek's eyes opened to find himself outlined in a luminous black fire. Power coursed through his body, healing and regenerating. The stone door responded, itself burning silver in protest, flashing brighter for a moment than the sun itself. Then, with a silent implosion, it lost its struggle against Arek's fire and was sucked in as well, leaving behind only a square afterimage floating purple in Arek's eyes.

He looked in wonder at the blank opening before them, then at Yetteje. Neither could believe what they saw. Then Arek felt the ground rushing up to meet him as he crumpled to the floor, unable to cope with the sudden largess. For the briefest moment he understood the energy washing through him exacted its own price, using his body's own reserves to heal him. Then, like a boy caught in a tidal surge, Arek was subsumed by the influx of raw power, his black fire extinguished.

The luminescence surrounding the entire area faded as if drained, and everything was plunged into complete and utter darkness.

Into the Dark

JOURNAL ENTRY 17

I have been watching my imps more. It is another piece of the puzzle. They were formed for help scavenging.

As my need for companionship grew, they have begun to speak. My will is evolving them, so could I develop them for a different purpose?

My little imp, the first one to speak, has become inquisitive, almost childlike. It whispers the word, "self," as it points to its tiny chest. I find myself taken aback, for it hadn't occurred to me it could understand its own existence.

Its innocence and desire to help can only be described as adoration. More surprising, it adores me as if it knows I am its . . . father.

Journal Entry 17

FIND AND KILL

Make your opponent respond to you first.
Use strikes and counters,
to lead him down your keen-edged path,
until no options are left, except death.
—Kensei Tsao, The Lens of Blades

T he team appeared with a blue flash within a war room of Bara'cor. The chamber had two guards stationed within and two more outside, as the king had ordered. Their job wasn't to fight, but to sound the alarm should intruders appear. Had they been facing ordinary foes they might have succeeded.

Kisan exploded into action, her form blurring as she intercepted the nearest guard. She knew if she didn't act quickly, the defenders of Bara'cor would pay with their lives, and thwarting these assassins had become something personal to her.

She kicked one guard in the temple, then spun and elbowed the other in the sternum. She moved back to the first, a quick chop to the throat, then back to the second with a knee to the head. Both sank to the floor, unconscious.

Neither had had time to cry out to their compatriots stationed outside, but the muffled sounds of a scuffle drew the two in to investigate, to their misfortune.

Five moved with Kisan and continued through the doorway just as the other two guards appeared. Thin stilettos appeared in each hand and he drove them quickly through the front of each man's throat, severing their spines. Letting go of the daggers, he grabbed the two dying guards and pulled them fully into the room, dumping them in a heap retrieving his weapons.

Prime moved in and signaled, *Clear?*

Kisan looked out into the hallway and saw no one. Having assimilated more of Tamlin's memories she now understood the sign language of the dwarves and signaled, *All clear.*

When she turned she was greeted with the sight of Five sinking his stilettos into the chest of each of the men she'd just rendered unconscious. One of the guard's eyes opened, shock registering on his face, but Five clamped a hand down over his mouth and nose. The guard struggled for a moment, then died without uttering another sound, nothing but a small sigh escaping from between the assassin's fingers.

Kisan felt anger welling up inside her, but quickly held it in check. It wasn't yet time to act.

Now clear, corrected Five. All the guards were dead. Except for the night watch and the soldiers patrolling the walls and corridors, most of Bara'cor would be sleeping.

Prime pulled off a glove and knelt, touching his hand to the bare stone. His eyes closed. Tamlin's memories suggested he was using something called *stonesense*, a way to see what transpired wherever stone lay. Kisan didn't know how far that ability extended, but something in his demeanor put her on edge. She couldn't quite put her finger on it, but her muscles started to twitch with anticipation for something unknown. She found herself leaning slightly away from him, as if he were a serpent coiled to strike. After a few moments, Prime gathered the group, silently signaling their change in strategy.

Five, Six, remain, protect our exit. Two, take Three and Four. I will proceed alone.

He finished his hand signals, then motioned for the team to touch Bara'cor's rock. Kisan played along, but didn't understand what they were doing. At first, she thought the gesture was some sort of ritual, another homage paid by the dwarves to Bara'cor. Some of Tamlin's memories surfaced as her fingers touched the cool stone, and a sickening realization hit her. *This wasn't a ritual.* They'd somehow used their stonesense to determine their targets' locations. They were dwarves and had an affinity to the very rock itself, hewn from the earth and shaped by their people. They had used this rock to find the king, his son, and possibly Arek.

In a moment, the rest of the team knew what their leader wanted. Prime signaled to Five, but his body was turned far enough to the side that she couldn't read his hands, even with Tamlin's knowledge.

Prime signaled to Two, *Execute,* then moved out into the hallway. Two oriented his team and shot out of the room in the opposite direction, followed by Three and Four. They left in an echelon, like a small wing of lethal predators hunting Bara'cor's halls.

Prime had separated the group into two strike teams, so their targets were in at least two places.

Kisan knew she couldn't wait here with Five, and was going to have to make a difficult choice on who to follow. She closed her eyes and increased her awareness, bringing herself up to full combat readiness. She shot a quick glance at Five, then crouched against the wall. That act saved her life.

A stiletto buried itself where Kisan's head had just been. Before she could react, a booted foot struck her in the ribs, flipping her over and backward. Five advanced on her, his eyes burning blue and his intent clear.

"What're you doing?" she demanded, feigning surprise to buy time.

Five stopped a few feet away and said, "Prime is giving me one chance to fix the real Six's mistake—"

Kisan flipped up to her feet and stood facing the dwarf. It was clear she'd lost her cover, but didn't understand how. Then she knew: *that damn stonesense!* The fortress itself had shown Prime and the others that one of their team wasn't a builder. She hadn't considered this turn of events, but suddenly Kisan's felt the welcomed freedom to unleash herself fully.

Her moonskin blossomed around her dwarven form in an ignition of silver fire. Kisan's subterfuge no longer mattered, and she felt an icy cold anger settle into place.

"Which target does Prime pursue?" she demanded, still in Tamlin's form.

Five was silent. In a blur of motion, he attacked. His granite-like fists struck at Kisan's body in multiple double punches and kicks, followed by knees and elbows.

To Kisan, however, the assassin moved in slow motion. Back on the Isle when they had faced Thera, the adept had been hampered by poison and trying to protect her young.

Kisan wasn't surprised, and there were no children to protect. She moved into the attacks, instantly reading the timing and style of everything thrown at her. Her arms moved in a motion that was both economical and brutal, inflicting damage by using striking blocks. Silver fire blossomed to white as her power grew. She countered with elbows, then used the assassin's momentum and weight against him, striking with short arced knees to his upper thighs, and forearms to his collarbone and neck.

Each blow hammered into the dwarf like the maul of a titan, battering him backward. When the assassin, in desperation, threw two punches at Kisan's head and midsection, the master stepped in with her arms circling, blocking both. She continued her motion, pushing the assassin's arms away from her body. Then her head slammed into the dwarf's nose in a splash of silver-white fire mixed with blood and pain.

Before the assassin could recover, Kisan hit him with a spinning back kick to the chest. The force of the blow threw the dwarf against the back wall, where he crumbled to a heap. Kisan moved up and grabbed the assassin by the hair.

Just as she pulled his head up, he punched upward like a snake, his fist curled around a poisoned stiletto. Her hand stopped the blade in midair, his wrist caught in her vise-like grip. Consumed with rage, she released the illusion and was Kisan once more.

Judging by the sharp, indrawn breath, it was clear the change had stunned the assassin. The detailed dossiers they had of each adept guaranteed he knew his opponent, but no doubt he'd believed she was dead. The arm in her grip curled and tensed, fighting her for control as he pushed his weight forward. This was pure muscle against muscle, something the assassin should've had an advantage with.

"I want you to know who killed you," Kisan said. "This is for my friends on the Isle."

The bones in his wrist snapped as Kisan crushed them in her grip. The stiletto turned slowly until it pointed at his face.

"And this is for the children."

The stiletto punched into the assassin's eye, the poison taking hold even as the brain registered shock and confusion. Five fell back, his remaining eye focusing on the adept as his muscles clenched and tightened, a gift from the poisoned blade. Kisan pulled her hand back, delivering a strike that crushed his neck and spine, ending his life.

She stood, looking down at the dead assassin, breathing in gulps. Incandescent anger flamed within her, reflected in the silver-white intensity of her moonskin. The fire along with the anger within her slowly ebbed.

There was no pity in her, but she didn't feel any better. She wouldn't until every one of Prime's team was dead, but the mistake she'd just made needed to be addressed. She quickly knelt and put a hand to the assassin's forehead, cursing her own rashness.

She had to act quickly if there were any chance to mindread this one and gain critical insight into Prime's plan. Slowly, her vision went black and she dove into Five's fading memories.

Prime went after the null, which could only be Arek. Two led the second strike team to the king himself, but the details were jumbled, difficult to understand, and getting worse. Unlike Tamlin, who'd still been alive, Five was already dead because of the virulence of the poison and Kisan's impetuous anger. She should've kept this assassin alive and incapacitated, and cursed herself again, dropping the now useless mindreading. She knew Silbane would never have made such a mistake. The term, mudknife, came unbidden to mind and she cursed again, forcing herself to make a few educated guesses.

She moved over to the doorway and took a moment to think. It was no surprise that Prime would go after the primary target. Their orders were to kill him and Prime would not chance that to anyone else.

Kisan came to a decision, for her mind had been turning it over ever since her contact with Lore Father Giridian. Arek made his choice when he killed Piter, and for that reason she abandoned him to Prime. It saved her from a confrontation with Silbane, but still accomplished her mission. In truth, harming Sil had never sat well with her.

Her mind turned now to the king and his family. She'd no love for the Galadines, but her best chance to find information on Sovereign lay with interrogating Two, who was privy to Prime's intelligence reports but probably easier to "persuade" than their leader.

Kisan decided not to change back to look like Tamlin or expend new energy to duplicate Five. Prime knew she was an imposter and had left Five to end her. The disguise was a waste of valuable energy, and something more basic drove her. She was sick of hiding. She moved out into the corridor and looked in both directions.

Prime had been smart. He followed mission protocols and hadn't shared anything with Five that could lead to him, except his target. That made tracking him impossible through the jumble of memories, but Two hadn't been so careful. He and Five were friends, and he'd shared their path.

Kisan smiled, then set off at a fast but silent run, her form fading from sight like a shimmer of heat as she invoked the Clouds before Moon technique to give herself cover. She would find and kill this team, extract whatever information she needed after Prime finished Arek, and find out what she could about Sovereign.

Then for Piter, Thera, and all the children of the Isle who had fallen to these assassins' blades, she would end Prime's life in the most painful way she could devise.

Find and Kill

FALCON'S PREY

A Bladesman never interrupts,
while an enemy is making a mistake.
—Davyd Dreys, Memoirs

A sh and his men were assembled in the ready room, a smaller octagonal room that resembled the great council chamber, except there was only one statue and sphere here. The room was dominated by a table like the one in its larger counterpart, around which clustered soldiers of Bara'cor, each with varying expressions of awe.

They looked upon an enchantment that had suddenly sprung to life, causing this table to display images of a miniature map of Bara'cor and the surrounding area. Unlike the table in the larger war room, this displayed the images hanging in the space above the table, in three dimensions.

It showed the nomad army like a red stain of blood spread before the fortress walls. It was as if the rock itself knew what was happening around it. Whatever magic allowed the table to mimic the landscape of the terrain, also considered the nomads an enemy. Though it wasn't detailed enough for small scale tactics, it was useful to understand quickly the disposition and concentration of the enemy forces. Talis looked at it now, while Ash flipped a small leather belt to Chandra.

"This will be good for your knives," he said. "The king will be here shortly."

True to his word, King Bernal Galadine came into the room, followed by his firstmark. He reached into a small pocket and retrieved the Finder, which he placed on the table as he came up to stand next to Talis, his eyes on the map. "Is this room secure? I'm worried about the Finder being out of the cell."

Ash nodded, "We've reinforced the only other exit and kept the single hallway leading here stationed with enough people to hold this door until we can flood the room from above with burning oil." He looked around the stone and said, "It'll make a nice oven."

The king caught his eye and replied, "Let's just be sure to get out first if it comes to that."

It was Jebida who then asked, "Anyone come up with a reason for the table to start doing this?"

"No, firstmark," answered Talis. The older warrior turned his attention to the map, interpreting it. "Their forces are still groupin' here, sir." He pointed with a cracked fingernail to a spot just outside of arrow and catapult range. "It seems the darker areas mean more troops, though I can't say I understand how the blasted table knows that."

Ash said, "This is some dwarven enchantment that the siege has brought to life. King Bara may have created it as an aid. You can see our forces as red dots," Ash pointed, "and the nomads are signified by purple."

"Waiting until breach doesn't make sense, whether you be dwarven or not," the firstmark huffed. "No, something else is causing this." He leaned forward, a hand on his chin looking at the table, "I'll admit though, seeing the enemy like this is useful, if the information can be trusted. Never throw away an advantage in a fight."

Ash looked at the assembled men and motioned to the king. "With your permission, I'd like to go over the final preparations before we infiltrate the camp."

The king nodded, but then looked around. "Where's the boy, Arek? We'll need him to activate the Finder." He motioned to a waiting runner and ordered, "Fetch him . . . and my son for that matter." Looking back at the armsmark he said, "Wait a moment. No sense in repeating yourself."

As the runner sped off, Talis bent over, inspecting something on the section that showed the translucent image of Bara'cor's interior. "Now . . . what's this?"

Three small blue dots moved through the fortress. They followed the hallways and corridors and moved with alarming speed. All along their route red dots, men on patrol, disappeared as if snuffed out.

The king and his men came closer to look. "What are they?"

Ash took a look and his eyes narrowed. "Whatever it is, it's coming toward us." Red dots of men stationed in the single corridor bunched up toward the far end of the hallway, running to intercept these blue dots. Ash watched as the blue dots sliced through the red ones without slowing.

He turned to the door and drew Tempest, who sang a clear note of fine steel as she cleared her scabbard. His team, the king, and Jebida followed suit. "Prepare yourselves."

Talis drew his short blade and kept his eyes glued on the map. "It's coming down our passageway." A few heartbeats went by and then he whispered, "It's right outside the door."

With a deafening crash and a flash of blinding light, the door burst inward and chaos ensued. The king and Jebida fell back as Ash and his team moved forward out of instinct, the party able to act only because of the warning they had gotten from the table. However, the explosive entry had served its purpose and disoriented the defenders, who still moved without coordination.

Their disarray cost them. Sevel took the brunt of the first attack. A black shape slammed into him. Three punches that sounded like a cudgel made of rock hitting flesh sent him flying backward across the table. He landed in a crumpled heap, unmoving.

Two knives flashed past Ash's ear as Chandra whipped them at her attacker. Both scored a hit, sticking into the chest of the man, but not as deeply as Ash expected. The man slapped them out of his body, then threw his stiletto at Chandra, who ducked and rolled at the last instant. The knife stuck halfway to its hilt in the stone wall behind her.

Behind the leader came two more black shapes, fast as lightning. They arced over the point man, landing lightly on either side of the table to engage the defenders, who'd fallen back along the sides.

Ash watched Talis move forward, slamming into the man nearest to his side, and putting him into a wrestler's hug. It wasn't until he tried to get his arms around his opponent that he seemed to realize his mistake. The man was bigger than he looked and his body didn't give at all.

Two crushing blows slammed down on Talis's shoulders as the attacker's elbows smashed into his back. His grip loosened. Then a fist cracked into his skull and he fell back, half conscious.

Ash held Tempest, who pulsed green. He drove his attack forward, spinning a deadly web of steel. The man used his forearms to block the blade, and Ash was surprised to see Tempest spark and skitter off. Then his foot caught. The very stone of the room seemed to want to trip him.

Shieldrock! Tempest cried. *These aren't men, beloved.*

Ash didn't reply, recovering from the trip and continuing his deadly dance with his attacker, who moved with the fluidity and grace of one born for combat. Each of his cuts and strikes met a forearm block or an ingenious dodge, leaving the armsmark tired and frustrated.

Ash pivoted around a punch-kick combination, then aimed a strike for the intruder's head. Suddenly Jebida flew past him and slammed into a wall. The armsmark looked over to see the king defending himself with a short blade as the firstmark struggled to his feet.

As he did so, Ash felt a sting in his neck and saw the man who stood behind the others firing some sort of metal tube. He started to raise his hand, but his muscles involuntarily tightened and he found himself on the floor, his muscles paralyzed. As the poison worked its way into his body, Ash began to convulse and his vision dimmed.

No! Tempest exclaimed through her connection to Ash, but he could feel nothing. He sensed the sword desperately searching the room for something as he lay there paralyzed, watching the scene unfold through glazed eyes.

The man turned and shot another dart at the king, who wasn't moving quite fast enough to evade it. But Jebida's arm pushed him down at the same moment someone just out of Ash's view put himself in the way. Then Talis hit the floor near Ash, his features locking into a grimace of pain, his hands becoming claws as they scratched at the dart in his neck. Ash watched him helplessly as the old warrior succumbed to the poison. His own vision dimmed further, but was replaced by a view of the room from what could only be Tempest's eye.

The assassin flipped himself up over the table, then jumped and rolled as two more knives from Chandra flashed past him. He threw a stiletto, catching her in the midsection, and Ash heard her gasp as it drove through her stomach and out her back. The assassin continued his roll across the table and landed lightly in front of her. Then his fist crushed her sternum before she could draw another breath and she hit the back wall with a wet thud. Ash could hear bones snap under the assassin's fist, and knew she was dead before she hit the ground.

Then the man pivoted, flipping back to land near the king and his final bodyguard, the firstmark. Another held his position while the third circled around until they faced the last men standing in the room.

"Surrender and I will let the others live," the lead assassin said, indicating the firstmark and the fallen. He looked at the king with glowing blue eyes. "They have no need to die here, King Galadine." Then he flashed some kind of sign to his men.

Ash lay on the ground, his vision nearly gone, his body wracked in pain. Then something happened and the pain began to lessen. He saw a clean green light in his mind's eye, infusing his body with energy, beneficent and healing. It neutralized the toxins and drove it from his blood. The tiny dart fell out with a small sound, as the glass shard hit the floor. Ash looked to his left, where the sound of labored breathing ceased. It was Sevel, his eyes frozen open in death. Ash carefully levered himself over and was about to stand when a voice from the door stopped him.

"Two."

There in the doorway stood a woman, dressed in the same style of clothes that Arek had been wearing, but darker. Her lean frame hinted at violence, but controlled and focused. She was younger than Ash by his reckoning and spoke with authority. Her voice cut through the din like the keen edge of a blade.

"I know death means little to you, but failure . . . " The woman walked slowly into the room. "The Adepts on the Isle still live. Five and Six are dead. Your team won't survive."

The man seemed to know instantly who this woman was. He signaled his men, and though Ash had no way of understanding the meaning of the gesture, he noticed the assassins imperceptibly readying their dart weapons. The smile on the woman's face said she knew exactly what would happen next.

The assassin snarled, "Kisan Talaris, you make this too easy." He signaled again, but the woman was faster than Ash—or the assassin—could imagine. Even as all three brought up their dart weapons and fired, she was in motion, bringing her hands together in front of herself.

The darts sped at her, but they never reached their target. The woman's hands came together in a single clap that detonated like thunder.

The very air bent and flexed, then every pitcher, glass, and plate in the room shattered! The darts, even those on the assassins' belts, shattered too.

The woman waited for the carnage she'd wrought to end, then looked at the assassin. Her form burst in a flash of silver-white fire, surrounding her in an ethereal, protective aura of flames.

"My turn," she said.

The man she'd called "Two" didn't wait and neither did one of his comrades. Both moved forward with a speed that belied their bulk. Again, their adversary proved even faster than they anticipated. She met their attack with her own, a series of striking blocks that looked strong enough to break bone and shatter stone.

Two moved to his left and tried to come up from behind her, but she grabbed the other man and flung him as if he weighed nothing at all. Both assassins went down in a tangled heap.

The third man started to move, but looked down to see the point of Ash's sword emerge from his chest. Ash withdrew the blade and spun the man to face him, his blade swinging in a short, deadly arc. Tempest flashed emerald, decapitating the dwarven assassin where he stood. The head flew off, but the body remained standing a moment longer before dropping to its knees and falling forward, staining the floor with more red blood than a body ought to hold.

Ash saw the woman at the door had begun her attacks in earnest now, moving through her opponents as one would when fighting children, her aim sure and true. Occasionally her flaming aura would flash silver or white as one or the other managed to get in a strike, but nothing actually touched her. She and these assassins dueled in a deadly dance of strike and counter-strike, something Ash knew well. It only continued for a heartbeat or two, then Ash heard the sound like a branch breaking and the leader fell back, his arm hanging at an unnatural angle.

The woman spun into the opening created by the leader's misstep. She swept aside two punches from the second assassin and struck with the tips of her fingers through that assassin's neck, crushing his throat and spine. He fell to his knees, gurgling at the leader's feet, unable to breathe through his pulverized windpipe. She didn't wait for him to die. She slammed her elbow into the crown of his head, driving it down and crushing his neck. The man folded in on himself, the crack of his neck a clear indication he was dead.

The woman took a breath, her form brightening with fire, then she exhaled. Only Two was alive, his arm broken, his options limited. Without moving, she addressed the last remaining assassin, "Two, who is Sovereign?"

Beloved, shall we kill this one? Tempest implored in a girlish voice.

No, Ash replied, *we need answers.*

* * * * *

Two stared at Kisan with hate and said, "How do you know my designation?" Then it seemed to dawn on him.

Kisan came eye to eye with the assassin and said, "I killed your men," she making a slight motion to encompassed the room, "all of them."

Two met her gaze, a small smile on his lips. "Then they deserved it." His head tilted, as if considering something, and he asked, "What about the king's son? Will you bargain for that information?" He began reaching with his good arm for something on his belt.

"Stop." Kisan froze him with her voice. She knew what he intended. There was a small point on his belt, behind which lay a sharp needle coated with the same poison as in the darts. One touch and the needle would scratch him, bringing death. "You know I can stop you before you kill yourself."

"Then why haven't you?"

"Wait!" said the king, holding up both his hands to prevent any ill-conceived attack. He looked at Kisan and asked, "He said something about Niall! Where is he?"

Kisan never took her eyes off Two, but nodded in response to the king's question. If there was a chance to find Prime, she wanted it. "Where's Prime? Give me his location and I'll let you use your poison."

Two looked at the king and said, "By now, your son is dead." Then he looked at Kisan and said, "It's always a pleasure killing halfling kids."

She locked eyes with Two for a heartbeat, then said, "Fine." Before anyone could move, she shot forward, her hands a blur. Even as Two began to push his finger against the needle, Kisan had touched his forehead and dove into the man's mind.

She could see Two's life before her, but knew she couldn't absorb it until she spent the time to purge the jumbled life and death of Tamlin and Five, time she didn't have to spare. Her goal, however, hadn't been to assimilate Two. That would take too long and she didn't need to. She only needed three things.

First, she paralyzed him by locking points along his spine at the neck and waist, then found the entry point of the poison and collapsed the blood vessels in his forearm, slowing its spread. She couldn't stop the poison from working, but would gain the few precious moments needed for what was to come next.

Second, she searched for Prime's location. As she suspected, he'd been careful with that information. All Two knew was the egress point where Five now lay dead. He'd offered the boy when bargaining, though it now was clearly a tactic to buy time for Prime. Whether or not the king's son was truly with Arek couldn't be confirmed, and Kisan suspected that Two simply didn't know.

Finally, she searched for any information about Sovereign, but what she saw made no sense. She saw a being made of pure light, standing in a cavernous opening.

Around it opened hundreds of tunnels, as if this Sovereign stood within a network of caves or a vast subterranean space. The space was filled with what looked to be worms covered in tiny glowing points. Around those worms moved creatures that looked like dwarves, but that Two called "*yewmins*." Kisan knew she didn't have much time and couldn't risk following this assassin into death. She pulled out of Two's subconscious, leaving the paralysis in place.

She opened her eyes and locked Two's open so he could see her, and then she said, "Your dead brother's memories say unless your brain is damaged, you can be rebirthed. We'll have to take care of that."

Her hands whipped out to either side of Two's head and struck, shattering every bone in his skull. The pressure wave from the blow destroyed Two's brain, liquefying everything inside. Kisan didn't even look at him as she kicked the body back. It slammed into a wall with a wet smack, before sliding down in a lifeless heap, dark fluid and brain flooding out of his nose and mouth. She then turned to face the king.

The king moved out from behind his men and exclaimed, "What've you done? You killed him before he could tell us!"

Kisan held up her hand and with deadly intensity said, "Shut up. Only a rapidly fading sense of honor stops me from killing all of you—", she suddenly noticed Silbane's Finder. "Why do you have this?" she demanded.

King Galadine seemed at a loss for words, so Kisan snapped her fingers. The *crack* seemed to get his attention. "Why?"

"It's Arek's," offered a man with the rank of armsmark. "He said the other half is with his master."

"Where's Silbane?" Kisan asked, turning to face the armsmark as she dismissed the king from her attention.

The man licked his lips, considering his words carefully. "We don't know for certain. The last Arek had

seen him they'd been fighting a—" he looked down "—
fighting a dragon."

Rai'stahn. Kisan nodded, understanding exactly what
had happened, but not the outcome. "Did he survive?"

The man shrugged, "Reports say two bodies were
carried to the nomad encampment. It's not nomad custom
to haul the dead, so we think he's still alive."

"I meant the dragon." Kisan looked at the Finder, then
said, "It's glowing, which means Silbane is still alive. I'm
calculating our odds if Rai'stahn opposes us." She looked
back at the blank stares of the men, her desire to rescue
Silbane at war with wanting to kill the Galadine king and
end their reign forever. She realized it was just that easy. If
she acted now and Prime succeeded, the world would
fundamentally change. Her eyes glittered with the
possibilities.

Her stance must've conveyed the hairsbreadth she stood
between choosing Silbane or the overwhelming violence. It
was like knowing something else was with you in the dark,
something malevolent and fearful. The king backed up as
Ash and Jebida moved forward protectively.

Kisan watched this with amusement, their actions
serving to break her downward spiral if for no other reason
than the sheer comedy of watching them shuffle about like
it truly mattered. It was like watching children close their
eyes and then think they were invisible.

Hiding a smile behind her hand, Kisan said, "King
Galadine, I searched his memories and there's nothing
there. They don't share information that can lead to each
other. We need to find your son and Initiate Arek on our
own. Are you saying they were together?"

"Yes . . ." the king stammered. "I mean . . . I don't
know."

He took a deep breath, and Kisan could see the
warrior's instinct battling with a father's heart, hoping with
a fervor bordering on desperation that she was being
truthful. The king searched her face for a way to save his

son. Something in Kisan loosened at that, her memories of Piter so recent, it was difficult not to empathize.

"We had assumed Arek's master a man, but you defeating these men nonetheless speaks to your skill. We are well met, though your presence here alters our own plans significantly."

Kisan shook her head, looking about the scene of carnage until her eyes came back to rest on the Finder secured within an iron cage. But the idea that he'd assumed "master" meant a man . . . she looked at the king with barely concealed disdain.

"I see the men of Bara'cor are just as insightful as those found elsewhere in the world." She met their confused stares with a small smile, then made her way over to the Finder and inspected it. As she'd mentioned, it still sparkled with its own light.

"Silbane *is* a member of my order—and my friend," she said.

Kisan turned back to the three men. They stood looking at her with that wide-eyed look men got whenever she was near, that vacant half-dumb stare of lust incapacitating clear thought. *Say what you want, but Silbane had never been so idiotic.* She also knew Silbane might've hesitated, tried to talk to the assassins, tried to parley. And that decision would've killed everyone in this room. She couldn't aim her frustration at anyone directly, so it just hung there, a dark cloud of contempt.

She stood straighter, instinctively using her sensual physicality to keep these men's wits addled. Though it was likely they'd mistake her true meaning, she met King Bernal's eyes and said, "But if he were here instead of me, you'd all be dead."

JOURNAL ENTRY 18

My excitement grows, for I have yet another idea to keep me safe from these raids—the cocoon, but larger and more formidable. I know the ritual of setting wards and will follow it to the letter. I will not doubt this place or myself as I have in the past. Not this time . . .

With the help of the numerous imps surrounding me, I have 'Shaped' four wards and spent hours infusing them with power, drawn from blood (mine). This may be the secret I was missing before. These marks will be the foci for my barrier.

The imps watch me wide-eyed, transfixed by my efforts. The marks I fashion resemble shields, but I have inscribed runes of defense on their surface. My blood is a part of this ritual now, for I have neglected the might that my name holds, an ancient name with the promise of power and protection.

I have planted one mark at each corner of my castle's outer wall. Together, they should create an impenetrable barrier, starting with my first mark. Perhaps, in ancient times, this is how the ranks were created, those who carried these wards became known as 'firstmarks'?

More importantly, perhaps tonight, I shall finally sleep in peace.

Journal Entry 18

THROUGH THE DOOR

*The thought of enemies
should not bring fear to one's heart;
it is the plight of friends
that keeps one pacing at night.*
—Altan proverb

rek heard a voice, filled with urgency, prodding him from sleep. *Get up! Arek, you must get up!* He shook his head, trying to clear it and felt helping hands below his arms. "What happened?"

Niall's voice whispered, "Shssh! You collapsed, but not before opening the door."

Arek opened his eyes cautiously and saw the open portal. Beyond it was a great hall, lit with an unearthly blue light. "I don't remember doing that."

Tej knelt at Arek's other side and said, "It was pretty amazing. You lit up like you were on fire, and the door did too! Then it opened."

"That's impossible," Arek said. "I can't do magic."

"What?" asked Niall. "You're apprenticed to a mage."

Arek rose to his feet with their help and said, "Tell me something I don't know." It was then he realized his foot hadn't shocked him with debilitating pain. In fact, each time he went through one of these "events," he was getting better. He could feel his body healing. It occurred to him then that he was also recovering faster with each subsequent blackout. He'd been in bed for weeks after his Test of Potential, maybe a day after his fight with Piter, and now only moments after this encounter with the door. It was as if he was getting used to . . . what? That he didn't know *what* he was getting used to scared him just a little.

"What happened to the glow on the walls?" he asked, looking around.

"I don't know," Niall said. "After you opened the door, it all went dark."

The only light came from the opening to the room, streaming out in silver and blue. The portion of the room he could see through the door seemed huge, almost like a temple. He moved forward cautiously at first, expecting his foot to cry out in pain. The only thing he felt was a twinge and sluggishness, as if his muscles needed retraining. A small smile curved his lips as he led his companions through the door.

His earlier guess had been correct. The room was a vast columned cathedral with a small pyramid at its center, stepped and four-sided. An azure radiance emanated from a dark sphere hanging in the air above the pyramid's flat apex. This sphere was surrounded by blue fire, like a sun bleeding streams of sapphire light.

Niall took in the room, then said to Yetteje, "This can't be here. It's just like the waterfall. Patrols would've run into it long ago."

"Through a blocked stone door? Who knows how far we've actually walked," said Arek over his shoulder. "We don't even know for certain that we're still under Bara'cor."

"Why?" Yetteje asked said.

"Because Niall is right, at least about that waterfall. No way something that big stays hidden. I think this chamber, and the path to it, opened only recently."

"How can a path 'open'?" asked Niall. "It's not as if this fortress is alive."

Arek turned and faced the other two. He swiped his foot along the dry ground and said, "No water, not a drop. Taste the air. It's dry, yet there's a waterfall not a hundred paces from here. This room has been sealed for a very long time."

He moved toward the pyramid.

"Arek, wait." Niall laid a hand on his shoulder, a look of dread in his eyes. "What do you mean to do?"

Arek looked up at the pyramid and the scene refracted then froze. Everything was still, except the scintillation from the sapphire-colored sun. It still burned brightly, painting the cathedral in contrasting light and columned shadows. Out of this stepped Piter, smiling.

"I doubted your ability to get this far."

"What is this place?" Arek asked, ignoring the phantasm's usual cruelty. The cerulean sun flickered, sending warmth and power down into the chamber. Had he been here with Silbane, what would his master have done?

Perhaps push me in? Arek looked about, that conclusion being the easiest one to believe right now. Yet another part of him, the same that wished for recognition knew what this was: his opportunity to become a greater legend than his master or anyone else on the Isle. He literally could save the world.

Piter's expression grew thoughtful and he said, "There are a multiverse of planes that intersect our world. This is one of those intersection points."

Arek nodded, familiar with the idea from the teachings of the Isle and asked, "What do you want?"

"That depends on whether you want to live or die. Something pursues you," the shade said, his smile growing wicked. "Your only escape is to go up there." It pointed to the blue-black sun flaring at the apex of the pyramid.

He looked at Piter and stammered, "R-Rai'stahn?" What would be chasing him? The only thing he could think of was the great dragon, which seemed bent on his destruction.

"Something has been unleashed, and it hunts you." Piter smiled, looking immensely pleased. "Run, apprentice, run . . . or die."

The scene shifted and snapped back. Arek stood with Niall's hand still on his shoulder. Piter's voice was gone.

He blinked once, orienting himself, then turned around and said, "Something is coming."

"My father's men?" Niall asked.

"I don't think so. Something more dangerous. We'd better get ready." He shook off his gloves and prepared for real combat, his magical disruption too important an advantage to ignore if he was about to face a dragon alone. A part of him, however, doubted the shade's warning referred to Rai'stahn.

Tej came up, drawing her short blade. "Who's coming?"

"I don't know, only that whatever it is, it's after us," Arek replied.

"How do you know that?" she asked, looking at the entrance to the chamber.

"The same way I knew about this place." Arek moved between his friends, closing his eyes, calming himself. He wasn't about to head up the pyramid without more reason, especially if that's what Piter wanted.

He breathed in evenly, then out again, clearing his mind. His combat sense expanded and the world seemed to slow. At least here he felt comfortable, in his element. Whoever it was, they would face a warrior ready to test for Ascension.

"There!" Niall pointed, his voice etched with barely controlled fear.

They both looked to where Niall pointed and saw a man dressed in black stride into the room. He didn't seem concerned with hiding himself, but stopped short when he saw them. Something in his stance hinted at uncertainty. He knelt and placed a hand on the floor.

"What's he doing?" Tej asked.

Arek ignored her and whispered, "We have to attack so he doesn't have time to focus on any one of us. Attack together, unless you have an opening." He looked meaningfully at Niall, then moved forward slowly, motioning for the other two to fan out to his left and right.

* * * * *

Prime looked at the three people in the room. His stonesense pointed out three figures, but the boy in the middle was the one he'd seen earlier, the indistinct shape that sucked at Prime's senses. *This was the null.*

His appearance fitted the description of the prisoner, Arek, but the boy did not act like a prisoner. It looked as if he led the other two, and that made the situation harder to predict or control. Furthermore, Prime's ability to sense anything through the stone seemed somehow diminished, likely because of the null. He'd anticipated that, but was surprised at the strength of the effect, especially at this distance. *Better to end things quickly,* he thought. *Kill them all, then get back to the egress point.*

Prime slowly came to his feet, his skin turning harder as Bara'cor itself lent him the obduracy of the stone he stood upon. His confidence was justified. They had faced and killed the overrated Adepts of the Isle with relative ease. The king would die, as would the infiltrator, and no one was going to stop him from terminating the null, especially not a couple of halfling kids.

They had moved on the boy's orders, spreading out, trying to take tactical advantage. That confirmed Prime's suspicion that this boy was in charge, and that made him his primary target. He slipped two poisoned stilettos into his hands, then moved forward like a hunting cat, directly for the null named Arek.

Through the Door

THE MEASURE OF A MAN

You cannot know when your final day will come.
Seize greatness in all things;
prepare for every moment, as if it will be your last.
—Davyd Dreys, Memoirs

K isan looked at the king, her eyes taking in the man who stood before her. The warrior in him was plain to see, but she also noticed as his desperation came under control, he spoke more carefully, measuring his emotions against the greater good of their situation. The king's discipline brought him focus, and he now appraised her with an eye she could tell wasn't as distracted by her beauty or proximity. Perhaps her initial impression of him had been wrong.

"What we do next determines who lives and who dies," she said.

The king nodded slowly, answering, "Your name? I would speak with you plainly."

Despite her ingrained hate of magehunters, Kisan felt herself easing up on her opinion of this particular king. Perhaps it was because like him, she'd lost a son. Whatever the reasons, she said, "Kisan. I'm here to recover Arek and Silbane." She sensed a solidity to him, and a depth of character that wasn't worn on the surface for all to see. *Maybe he was truly different.* She knew she could kill him at any time, and perhaps *that* did more than anything else to lessen her impulse to lump this king in with the bloody history his ancestors had inflicted upon Edyn.

"My son is somewhere in Bara'cor, with your apprentice. They are missing. I have dispatched runners to find them. The last assassin spoke of going after my son."

Kisan ignored the king's mistake of once again assigning Arek's apprenticeship to her and gestured instead to the assassins, saying, "These are dwarves, not men. They were sent here to kill you." She'd guessed correctly in following Two, but now regretted that Arek wasn't alone. Galadine or not, her decision to ignore Prime had put the king's son in danger and she found herself torn between her hatred of the family name and the heart-wrenching experience of losing Piter.

No one should lose their child, she thought. She found she couldn't hold his gaze, the loss of Piter bubbling up again in her mind with painful freshness. Instead, she offered, "I'm sorry, but their leader went after the boys."

"Then we have a common interest in saving Niall *and* your apprentice." The king stepped forward and offered his hand.

After a moment of hesitation, Kisan took it in a firm grip.

Her attention went back to Silbane's charm in the iron cage. She changed the subject, asking, "What did you intend to do with the Finder?"

In response, the armsmark stepped forward and said, "My team and I were going to use it to enter the nomad camp and find your friend. Then, we were going to attempt to assassinate the chieftain of the nomads. But this attack . . ."

She immediately understood, but that plan required knowledge of how to use the Finder. "How did you come to know of its use?" she asked.

An uncomfortable silence followed as the men looked to their king. But it was the older of the two officers who stepped forward, his rank signifying him as the Firstmark.

"You consider yourself a warrior?" he asked.

Kisan shrugged. "Do you consider yourself smart?" Even high-ranking men could ask inane questions.

The firstmark stopped as if unsure of how to respond, then said, "Your apprentice nearly killed the Prince of Bara'cor and the Princess of EvenSea. He entered by unknown means and posed a threat to our security. Our armsmark—" he gestured to indicate the younger officer "—stopped him. When it was over, we needed information. We tortured him for it."

The armsmark stepped forward then pointed to his blade, saying, "But this sword, Tempest. It healed him. His injuries are almost gone."

Kisan stepped around and carefully extracted the Finder from the bar it'd been looped around. She spent a moment deep in thought, looking at the circumstances from their eyes. An intruder during a siege would indicate a weakness in the fortress's defenses, potentially a deadly one for those inside.

"The sword cannot heal him unless it's held by someone attuned to it. Who did that?" Kisan knew the answer, but addressed the armsmark.

The armsmark bowed and said, "It was held by me. She . . . spoke to me."

"Really?" Kisan took that in with a bit of surprise. The sword had been quiescent on the Isle. What was it about this man that brought Tempest to life? "We should talk about this later. Your name, sir?" Kisan asked.

"Armsmark Ash Rillaran."

"Rillaran?" Kisan inquired, the picture becoming more interesting in her eyes. If the Rillaran line lived, it may explain the actions of Tempest. She determined to follow up on this later and turned her attention back to the firstmark. "I appreciate your honesty."

"I am Firstmark Jebida Naserith," he replied with a bow as economical as his tone, "and your apprentice left us little choice."

She ignored the bow, a moment passing by as she weighed the facts, then she made her way around to the front of the table and faced the king. "For the final time, Arek isn't my apprentice. He's Silbane's, and you will have to answer to him for the treatment of his ward. Personally, I don't care."

She paused again, thinking. Few choices were left: either go after Arek, or Silbane. Kisan knew how lethal Prime was. While Arek was well-trained, he would be no match for the leader of the assassins, who would unknowingly carry out the lore father's orders for her. This freed her to rescue Silbane. However, it also meant collateral damage. Prime would not leave the king's son alive.

Kisan did the quick calculus then turned her attention to the king and said, "Much of your infiltration team is dead." She looked around the room, noting the fallen. "Finding Arek and Niall before the leader of the assassins is very doubtful. Therefore, rescuing Silbane and giving your man a chance at the nomad leader is the only logical choice."

"You can use that thing?" inquired Ash. "Arek said only he could use it."

Kisan quickly surmised Arek's reason for lying. Smart of him, given his need to keep his value high amongst his captors. "He's correct. His master and I are attuned to use it, but without us here, he was the only one able to activate it." No reason not to support the boy's story.

"Then if you disappear, how can we close the portal if we need to?" Ash asked.

The master saw his dilemma and said, "Once activated, anyone can bring this half or the other through and the portal will close behind them. I'll keep this around my neck. If worse comes to worst, take it off my body and return."

"What about my son?" asked the king. "He's here, with Silbane's apprentice. You're abandoning them?"

Kisan shook her head, replying, "No. You can bring the entire fortress to bear on the assassin. My use is limited in this, but I can get your man into the camp. I'll free Silbane and with our help, you can break this siege."

The king shook his head angrily, "This is madness! You're going to help me—"

Kisan stepped forward, her tone icy. "There is only one assassin left. Your man," she looked at Ash, "killed one already, so they are not so far beyond your capabilities. Be the lion you so proudly have adorning your flag. My priority is Silbane."

The king wasn't listening. His arms out wide, he said, "I can send out patrols, runners. We will have a hundred eyes looking for the boys." He desperately searched for an answer, then his eyes lit upon the table and its enchantment.

He looked at Kisan and said with a hint of desperation, "Wait! A few moments before these assassins arrived, this table," the king pointed to the glowing images, "showed three blue marks coming toward us. What do you know of that?"

The master nodded, not entirely surprised. "These assassins are dwarven. Bara'cor was built to serve them. It's not surprising the table came to life once they entered their ancestral home."

The king pointed to the table and to one small blue dot standing stationary, deep in the bowels of the fortress. "And is this their leader, the one you call Prime? He's the one that goes after my son?"

Even as they watched, the blue dot moved forward, flickered, and vanished as if swallowed by something. The king looked at it with wide eyes. "What? What just happened?"

Kisan took a deep breath and said, "I don't know, and I can't get there in time. He's moving quickly and I don't have the stonesense these dwarves do. I can't readjust my course."

a Man

"No! I beg you, save Niall *and* your student. Save our boys." At this point, the king didn't seem to care about the needs of his fortress or his men. It was clear to Kisan his only thought was for his son's safety. A small part of her found it hard to fault him, but they were wasting valuable time.

She breathed out, a heavy sigh that seemed to carry the weight of her decision with it, but before she could say anything, the table image flickered, and then dimmed. Then, to everyone's surprise, it vanished completely.

Ash looked to Kisan and asked, "Why?"

She looked at the dead table, dread building within her gut. "Perhaps Arek actually managed to kill Prime," she whispered, almost to herself. "With the dwarves gone, the table wouldn't have a reason to keep showing us information."

"But you don't know. Bara'cor might just be helping the dwarves by hiding information. How will we find them before . . ." the king said as he fell back on his haunches, dejected, slamming his fist into an open palm.

"Bernal, the woman is right. We'll find Niall," Jebida moved forward and placed a hand on the king's shoulder. "I'll order patrols to that location immediately. Don't give up hope."

Kisan stepped forward and asked, "I have a chance to save Silbane and help your man accomplish his mission. Do you waste this?"

The king looked down, but when his eyes finally met Kisan's they had steel in them. "No. We attempt the nomad camp."

"I'm going with you," said Jebida, suddenly stepping forward. "Ash has lost his entire team and I can provide another strong arm. We will only get one chance to kill the leader of these nomads or Bara'cor falls to ruin."

A moment passed as the king composed himself, something in what Jebida had said striking a chord. He stood then, addressing the people in the room, "Forgive me.

I should be thinking about the welfare of all of us, rather than just my son. It's difficult. . . "

His voice trailed off, but then he stepped forward and faced the firstmark, "Jeb, you can't go. If Ash is successful, it's still doubtful he'll return. Bara'cor can't lose both of you on this mission." The king looked down, then at his second-in-command. "I'm sorry to sound so detached, Ash."

"Don't apologize, my king. It was always the plan." Ash looked around the room and said, "I'll kill their u'zar, and cause as much trouble as possible until I fall." He delivered this last statement with a smile, but it fell flat. He then looked at Kisan and added, "I wish we'd had more time. I have questions."

"With Tempest, you may yet survive," she said. She looked at the trio and stepped back, making room.

Ash grabbed a few extra weapons and adjusted his armor. He then looked at the king and bowed. "Find Niall, save him."

The king stepped forward and embraced the armsmark. "You are family to me. Try to get back here in one piece."

Ash nodded. "You know I will." He seemed to find it difficult to meet the king's gaze. "I . . . want to thank you, sir, for everything."

The firstmark cleared his throat in a noisy cough and said loudly, "By the Lady of Flame, this is like the good-byes of a mother to her child! I can't take any more." He grabbed the armsmark and spun him around so they were face to face. "I promote you to Firstmark, Ash Rillaran. Defend Bara'cor with your life."

He then looked at Kisan and said gruffly, "Will that portal be big enough to take me with you?"

Before the startled master could answer, Ash said, "What? You can't go. I—"

Jebida looked at him and said, "You what? You stand a better chance of finding Niall, and what if he needs healing? Your pretty blade insures that. Plus, you're the only one of us who has killed one of them. Better you go after the king's son than me. You're Bara'cor's future. And," he added with a twinkle in his eye, "it's about time you carried your weight."

He then turned to his long-time friend, the king. The giant firstmark said, "By your leave?"

Perhaps not trusting himself to speak, the king just nodded. They clasped forearms in a warrior's embrace.

Kisan evaluated the change with an eye toward complications. Could Tempest heal Arek? Were they right when they said the blade had healed him before? Nothing in her entire history with Arek made her believe magic could work on the boy, but their claim added another potential complication.

Still, what choice did she have? She knew there was no chance of finding Arek or the king's son before Prime did. She hadn't been joking about the difficulty of tracking the assassin without stonesense, and now she had a chance to recover Silbane. The leader of these assassins would pay, regardless. Silbane would see to that, and if he didn't, Kisan would gladly finish the job.

Her analysis done, she'd surmised that the change in Ash staying didn't affect the outcome. Still, she offered the new firstmark a carefully worded piece of advice.

"Ash, if you find them, save the king's son first. We know and accept danger as part of our service. All of us, and that includes Arek. He can take care of himself."

She then looked at the team and said, "The portal will remain open until Silbane comes through. You'll know him because he's dressed like me, but with short hair, beard, terribly ugly." Kisan smiled at her own joke. "Until then, guard this side well, for anyone will be able to enter your fortress." She looked back at Ash, emphasis in her voice, "Do *you* understand what I mean, Firstmark?"

Ash nodded— his expression resolute.

Kisan snapped the half of the Finder in half again and a black portal opened before her with a sucking of air sound and a *pop*. She then looked at the king and said, "Four of your guards were slain by these assassins in the room with the Far'anthi Stones. I couldn't stop them, but I killed the one who took their lives." She nodded to the king, an unspoken apology, then entered the darkness without looking back.

Jebida checked to be sure he had his black-bone handled fighting knife, then went to an arms rack and grabbed a large axe. He motioned to the king and the new firstmark, and said, "Always loved fighting with an axe." He smiled at both, then also took a step into the blackness and disappeared.

a Man

JOURNAL ENTRY 19

There is a place within us, unassailable by our bravado. It sits and watches our actions through our own eyes, and judges. For most, it is in our own voice that it whispers back to us.

It is what I hear when I have been mean or base. It is the small voice that tells me I did not give true thanks, benefited through luck, or knew I had been purposely more hurtful than needed.

It knows the truth and does not let me hide behind my lies. It is like my shadow, but a truer part of me.

It is in this place that I now sit, my shields above and the raid upon me. I know they take everything and I cannot help the fear that grips me. Still, I followed the ritual to a letter.

It must work.

Journal Entry 19

ASCENSION

When fighting at morning and evening,
keep the sun on your back.
At midday the sun should be on your sword arm.
In water, be mindful of reflections,
and even the wind can hide sounds.
Every small thing can be used as an advantage.
—Tir Combat Academy, The Tactics of Victory

Initiate Jesyn, advance." Lore Father Giridian looked at the young girl, his face an inscrutable mask. This was the first time he'd tested anyone for Ascension. His hopes for her ran high, as did his fear she would fail. If Jesyn passed, she would be the first adept made under his rule as lore father, but he'd made it clear he would rather have her as a living initiate than a dead adept.

Jesyn had healed quickly from her bout with Piter. At her level of training, her healing had already begun to accelerate, and the rhan'dori was specifically designed to minimize any chance of real injury. The only visible sign of the fight was a slight bruise on her cheek where Piter's bohkir had struck.

Giridian knew she was more worried about Arek than herself. They were close friends. He hoped Jesyn would focus on the here and now.

* * * * *

Jesyn moved forward into the stone square inscribed on the floor, her body relaxed and as her mind attuned to her surroundings.

"I have come to be tested, Lore Father," she said in a clear voice, as ritual demanded.

Giridian looked at her for a moment, his gaze measuring her for weakness, for doubt. Apparently satisfied, he replied, also as ritual demanded, "You come of your own free will?"

"I do," she said without hesitation.

"You know you may not survive the test?" he continued.

"I do," she said again.

"You will face the Truth you bring with you into the Test of Ascension?"

"I will," she intoned, bowing once.

The lore father looked at Dragor and asked, "Who seconds her right to test?"

Dragor stepped forward and answered, "I do, Lore Father. Jesyn Shornhelm has learned all we can teach her and must Ascend to continue."

Lore Father Giridian nodded, then looked back at Jesyn and said, "As it has always been, you stand in the crucible of Ascension, surrounded by the Affinities of the Way." He looked to the four sides of the testing area and said, "Sun, Moon, Sky, and Earth. You must face what you bring forth and defeat it."

To Jesyn, it seemed the lore father's gaze became more stern, if that was even possible, and she heard him say, "You cannot leave the square until all within have acknowledged your true worth."

All? She thought . . .*what did he mean by that?*

"Once the test begins, we cannot interfere. The test is yours and yours alone." Then he clapped his hands and both he and Dragor moved back and away from the square. He raised his hand and waited until Jesyn nodded she was ready and said, "Begin."

Instantly, the square was surrounded on each side by a different element. One side ignited in a wall of fire, another filled with water. The side facing the instructors stood unmarked, but she knew it was blocked by unseen winds, and the fourth erupted in stone and earth.

"You cannot leave until you have defeated that which you bring forth," the lore father said. "You will have two periods of rest during the test. Use them well."

At first, nothing happened. Then a figure appeared in the wall of fire, hazy at first, but solidifying. It coalesced and stepped forward and Jesyn recoiled in shock. The being made of fire was an exact duplicate of her!

"We are here to take your measure," the fire Jesyn said.

She heard the same proclamation echo around her and she spun. She was surrounded by four duplicate Jesyns, except each was made of the same element as their wall: earth, fire, air and water.

The duplicates eased into combat stances, ones she was intimately familiar with, because they were identical to her own. These doppelgangers looked to be more dangerous versions of normal elementals, and they clearly had her combat knowledge.

"Defend yourself," the one made of fire said, acting as the leader. Then the four attacked with blurring speed, jumping and spinning as they delivered kicks and punches at the aspiring initiate.

Jesyn's training took over and she moved with lightning speed of her own. She intercepted the fire elemental first, but the moment her arm made contact she felt a sudden shock of pain and smelled her flesh burning. She disengaged and tried to punch her opponent, but her fist went completely through the fiery body without harming it. A kick to her chest from the water elemental sent her skidding back into the wall made of earth.

She flipped to her feet and took stock of the combat situation. Her opponents were arrayed in front of her in a loose semicircle. She stood with her back to a wall of earth. She breathed out, relaxing her muscles and her mind, and opened herself to the Way.

Time slowed and she could see all four shift imperceptibly, making room for the earth elemental, which moved in quickly. She braced herself, knowing the impact would give her an opening, but was shocked when nothing happened. Then she felt a blow to her head that shot purple stars across her vision.

The earth elemental had flowed around her, then under the stone, and reappeared on the earthen wall behind her. One hammer fist had smashed into her skull, sending her reeling forward and into the midst of the other three. She fell at the feet of the air elemental, who picked her up and threw her back against the stone and earth wall. Her breath left her in a whoosh and she slid down the wall, barely conscious.

"Hold!" the lore father commanded. The four elementals bowed and moved back, allowing Jesyn her first moment of proscribed rest. She hacked up something and realized it was blood, but couldn't tell if it was from something broken inside her body, or just a cut in her mouth.

She eased her way up, then staggered over to the wall of air. Dragor stood behind it, concern written plainly on his face.

"How am I doing?" she asked, smiling, then spitting more blood.

"No better than any of us did," her teacher replied neutrally. "And no worse."

Jesyn nodded, then reached for the Way. Power flowed into her, but she was only an initiate and her ability to heal herself was limited. She would have to pass this test with just her skills, such as they were. She slowly rose to her feet.

The lore father looked at her and said, "Do you wish to continue?"

Though he sounded concerned, Jesyn knew this was part of the ritual. There were only two responses. She wiped blood from the corner of her mouth and nodded, "I do."

"Very well. Begin," he commanded and the elementals again exploded into action.

The water elemental sank to the stone floor and flooded toward her like a liquid snake. She leapt up, over it, only to be intercepted by the air elemental, who threw her back to the ground. Instantly the water elemental flowed up over her, covering her nose and mouth, clearly intending to drown her.

Jesyn rolled and jumped to her feet, her head and face still encased in water, and fought down her panic. She looked about, her mind racing. How could she stop a creature that had command of the elements? She pushed at the water, but her hands went through it. Before she could try again, the earth elemental kicked her and she felt bones snap in her ribs as she was hurled back against the wall of fire. She could feel the burning pain again as she bounced off the walled conflagration.

The water elemental released her in an explosion of steam from contact with the fire wall and she fell on all fours, gasping for air. She could tell her ribs were broken. She pushed herself up, wincing at the pain and clutching her side. The elementals began to close in and she knew she would not be able to survive the next encounter.

Then the lore father shouted, "Hold!" The four elementals bowed and moved back, allowing Jesyn her second and last moment of rest. She fell in a heap, her broken ribs leaving sharp stabs of pain at every breath, her body bruised from the earth elemental's kick.

Jesyn knew she couldn't continue to fight them this way. She was missing something, something vital. The test was designed so initiates could pass with their skills, so she needed to think.

Dragor moved over to the wall closest to her and said through it, "This next round only stops if you win or die. If you don't see yet how to prevail, its better you don't continue."

"You're telling me to quit?" she said, incredulous. She spit out more blood, this time knowing without a doubt something internal was broken. Every breath she took was agony as bone scraped against broken bone in her side. She pressed her arm against it to reduce the pain, and then cinched her armor tighter, looking back at her master.

"You've had two encounters with them. They don't hold back. They'll kill you."

Jesyn pulled herself together, anger giving her strength, and pushed herself up to her feet. "I'm going to pass this test, Master."

Dragor looked at the young initiate, his concern for her plain on his face. His eyes searched hers, then softened in defeat. He shook his head and said, "Pay attention, then." He backed away, then nodded to the lore father.

The lore father looked at her and intoned, "Jesyn Shornhelm, do you wish to continue?"

Jesyn took a deep breath, her mind racing. The idea of using elements against one another seemed obvious, but manipulating sentient beings was far harder than it looked.

Her mind narrowed the possibilities, something fell into place, an idea she hoped would allow her to pass. She looked at the lore father and said, "I do, Lore Father. Let them bring their best. I will do the same."

The lore father sighed, then said, "Continue."

The elementals moved into action, but Jesyn didn't move forward to engage the first that moved. Instead she focused, watching.

The earth elemental moved in, its earth and stone fists ready to finish the dance of pain they had started on her body, but Jesyn shifted. As the earth elemental struck, she pivoted under the strike, then used the creature's great strength against it. She pulled it toward her, spinning in place, then added a shove from behind.

This sent the creature made of earth stumbling forward and into the target Jesyn had chosen, but it wasn't another elemental. Jesyn had pivoted and pushed the earth elemental into the boundary wall of water! The elemental was spun and thrown to the side by the current of the wall.

It fell trapped in the corner between air and water. Slowly its body dissolved into a sludge.

Jesyn didn't stop to gloat over her victory. Biting down on the lance of pain from her ribs, she charged the water elemental that had nearly drowned her.

The creature moved to encompass her, but Jesyn struck with open palms on the creature's body. The elemental relaxed, making its body less dense to absorb the blow, something Jesyn had counted on.

She slapped her hands together inside the creature, creating a shockwave of force throughout the elemental's body. The elemental shattered into tiny droplets, but Jesyn's strike directed it into the wall made of fire. Not all of it hit, but enough that an explosion of steam billowed out and the water elemental disappeared with a scream.

Jesyn moved quickly and put her back to the wall of earth. She could see the air elemental moving toward her, but in order for it to cause harm, it had to find purchase. With her back to the wall, the elemental could try to dislodge her. She smiled and waited. It would have to close, then *she* would have the advantage.

The air elemental looked at her and paused, as if understanding her strategy, then dove, a dart made of wind. Before Jesyn could move, it'd surrounded her completely, whirling about her limbs and pulling her away from the safety of the earthen wall. Every time Jesyn tried to breathe, it sucked the air from her lungs. She hadn't expected this and as a result found herself gasping. Her vision began to dim. Then she heard a mocking version of her own laugh as she fought desperately as she fought desperately to breathe.

Her eyes cast frantically about, looking for something, anything that could help. Then her gaze fell upon the fire elemental, still standing with its arms crossed.

The edges of her vision were now going from gray to black. Tunnel vision—she was losing consciousness. She sucked in a little air stolen from the winds surrounding her, and with supreme effort, she twisted herself in midair so one foot came briefly in contact with the wall of earth behind her. Before the air elemental could react, Jesyn pushed with all her might and threw herself and the air elemental into the fire elemental.

The three collided, surrounding her in a fiery maelstrom.

She could breathe again, but immediately regretted it as super-heated air flooded her lungs. The air elemental fought to disengage with her. It knew what she was attempting, pitting wind against flame. Water would have been better against flame, she knew, but you worked with what you had. Jesyn shook her head, anger lending her strength. They wouldn't escape so easily.

Would fire burn brighter, sucking in air? Would air blow harder, dissipating fire? Her strategy worked, as both elementals sought to protect themselves from the other.

The swirling winds whipped up the flames into a firestorm. The small twister surrounding her brightened and the heat grew in intensity until it shone like the sun, spinning her in a whirlwind of fire and air. Jesyn felt the pain but remained calm. Her training and mental discipline offered her focus and she used it to center herself on the Way.

Her skin burned, blistering along her back. She could smell her hair burning away, but closed her eyes and kept her focus. She was the master of her body, not the other way around. The elementals would destroy each other before she would let them go, and this further strengthened her resolve.

"You will die, Jesyn." She heard the fire elemental say in her own voice. "You throw your life away, needlessly. Desist, humble yourself, and we will allow you to test again when you are better prepared."

Jesyn tightened further on the two, feeling the skin on her arms blacken and peel. Still, she didn't let go. She knew she could kill them before she died.

The Way was everything. She now saw this simple truth. All they could do was return her to it, in one form or another, but the price for victory would be their own destruction. She could no longer see. Much of her face must be burned away, she thought. A small laugh escaped her, a protest at the absurdity of a test that killed the tested, but she still said nothing.

"No!" screamed the air elemental. "I acknowledge your worth, relent!"

She could feel the air elemental stop fighting her, but she didn't let go nor drop her guard. She would not fall to trickery again, remembering her duel with Piter and the lesson the masters insisted on in rhan'dori. You never stop until victory is achieved. She understood now why this was so important.

"What of you, fire-born?" she croaked blindly, her eyes having been burned away entirely. Though she couldn't see anything, she could feel its gaze upon her and continued in a hoarse whisper, "Do you yield?"

Slowly the heat reduced in intensity and she could feel the fire elemental acquiesce. "I acknowledge your worth, Adept Jesyn. We submit." They dimmed themselves and waited to be released. When Jesyn did so, both withdrew. She couldn't see anything, but could feel their presence nearby.

As soon as they retreated, Jesyn collapsed into a smoking heap, barely conscious. Her body lay blackened and burned, without hair, eyes, or other recognizable features.

She didn't move, but whispered, "Then I win."

A small smile escaped through charred lips along with the barest of sighs, before Jesyn sank into oblivion.

* * * * *

The two remaining elementals were joined by earth and water, reformed by their walls. The fighting square became opaque to any outside view, as the four elementals bowed to her, palms to foreheads.

They intoned into the air as one, "Anala, come forth and be bonded in Ascension."

From behind Jesyn's crumpled form came a light, shining pure and silver. It flared like the sun, bathing her in a dazzling white brilliance. Out of that light stepped the winged figure of a female warrior, an angel who looked born and bred for battle.

It was immense, powerful, armored in silver, gold, and white. Its wings stretched to each side, each feather a blade made for killing. Its visored helm sat across glowing eyes, eyes that demanded nothing less than fealty. The dazzling light receded and *Anala of the Fire* stood above the still form of the adept-to-be, called forth by the elementals of the test.

"Do you accept the bonding, Lady Anala, knowingly giving your life for hers?" intoned the fire elemental with deference.

The angel tilted its massive head, looking down on the smoking ruin that was Jesyn's frail form. "She has strength and nobility, but most of all, perseverance." The voice was soft, but had an edge, like that of a finely forged weapon. She seemed to smile, then completed the ritual, "I accept the bonding and surrender my life to become one with her."

The fire elemental stepped forward. "Welcome, and rejoice. You shed the ephemeral and Ascend to a new life." It spread its arms wide and stepped back as all four elementals went to one knee, waiting.

Slowly, as if sinking into the ground itself, Anala gathered Jesyn into her powerful arms. She pulled the young girl to a kneeling position and then held her still form from behind. Her armored wings embraced Jesyn, enclosing her in a cone of feathered steel and pure light.

Anala's form became potent with power, glowing softly at first, but quickly becoming a dazzling star of white, silver, and gold. She gave her the life-force that flowed so strongly and deeply within her, within the Way. The incandescent star that was Anala became part of Jesyn, who still knelt on the floor, head bowed and lifeless. As the elementals knelt in reverence, Anala became one with Jesyn and that light faded like a song's last note.

* * * * *

A moment passed, then two. Something happened then, a change that snapped Jesyn into the here and now, a change she could feel deep in her very bones. She arched up and a gasp tore out of her. She drew in air as if she could gain sustenance from the entire room in one tortured lungful, her form blazing silver, white, and sunburnt gold.

She could feel her strength magnify. It was as if something had settled over her and become part of her very being, a feeling of comfort and strength. It wrapped around her, holding her within its ethereal arms. Liquid power incarnate, a pure note of the Way sounded, and she felt the cool wash of healing and rejuvenation flood through her entire body.

Her wounds began to heal, burns disappeared, bones reknit, hair and skin re-grew, and her fears vanished. She breathed in a painless lungful of cool, clean air, letting it permeate every part of her. When she breathed out, she expelled pain, fear, and doubt. She could feel the Way infuse every part of her being with light and energy.

Was Anala her true name, whispered on the wind? Before she could ask, the water elemental stepped forward and bowed, saying, "We cannot be destroyed, for we are the Way, as are you." The elemental looked to its brethren and nodded.

Earth then stepped forward and said, "There are more worlds than this and you are a defender of the Way, in all its forms. Open your eyes to this, and do not forsake your duty."

"You have earned your flameskin and more," the fire elemental continued. "You may bring it forth whenever needed. Become one with the Way and it will shine with light as unblemished as the sun. Its purity will reflect your mastery. We pledge you shall never be without it, or without *Anala of the Fire*. You and she are now one ."

The air elemental stepped forward and said, "None outside this square can see or hear us. They are not privy to your Ascension, only the outcome. Do not share what you learn here with anyone. Mastery must always be earned through sacrifice."

All four elementals bowed again, palms to foreheads, and said, "Welcome and rejoice. Through sacrifice, you Ascend with Anala to a new life." With that, they vanished and the four elemental walls disappeared in a flash of power and sound.

* * * * *

At first, the room seemed black, pitched in darkness. Then Jesyn realized she still knelt with her head in her hands. She looked up, a stunned expression on her face. Her fingers ran nervously up, touching her face and hair as if to confirm what she already knew. She'd been healed and was truly whole again. The act left her smiling and shaking. Dragor stood before her, looking at his former student with unabashed pride on his face.

She felt connected to the Way more deeply than ever. She radiated pure might.

Dragor moved forward, picked her up and hugged her. "You are well met, Jesyn Shornhelm. I'm *so* proud of you."

Lore Father Giridian also stepped forward and bowed. "Welcome to a new life. You have succeeded where many fail, but I never doubted your resolve." His face became a little harder when he said, "You understand now why we cannot tell you of the test?"

"If you had, I would never have passed," Jesyn replied. Something in her knew this to be true, just as she would've failed if she'd given up and succumbed to the pain.

"If you had known you would be healed in the end, would you have hesitated?" asked Giridian. "Would your sacrifice have been honestly and truly given?"

She shook her head no, though the details of her healing were still unclear. The only way to become a true adept was to triumph without assistance, on her own merits, with her own hard-earned skills. One had to be willing to sacrifice everything and understand their place within and as a part of the Way. Defeating the elementals didn't matter. Fighting until the very end, and past it, did.

Now she felt the benevolent embrace of something far more powerful than herself. It conveyed a sense of pride in her perseverance, and acknowledgment that her spirit had been truly tested. Like a blade forged in an incandescent fire and quenched in sacrifice, she'd emerged tempered, finer, and stronger.

She walked through death's door as Jesyn Shornhelm and returned as something more. She sighed, a happy sound this time, one the others could appreciate, for they too, had given everything of themselves to stand here with her.

Lore Father Giridian nodded and said, "Then let us complete your Ascension and take the Oath so you too may add your voice to our council as a true Adept of the Way." He said this with a smile.

Jesyn stepped forward and took a knee. She knew the words of the Oath by heart, something every initiate memorized as they dreamed of one day earning the Black.

She looked up at the lore father and said, "By the blood of my forefathers, I take this Binding Oath of Fealty to the land and her people. I will not cause harm, either through my action or inaction, without just reason. I am the shield of the weak, the blade of the helpless, the healer of the sick, and the spirit of the Way. I pledge myself to the service of these duties and obedience to the will of this council."

Lore Father Giridian's tone became more serious as he spoke. "I hear and accept your Oath of Fealty. Arise, Jesyn Shornhelm, for thou art now a full and true Adept of the Way."

An intense yellow flash occurred then, binding Jesyn to the words she'd just spoken. She could feel her body and spirit begin to attune itself to the land and its need. It was a feeling of oneness she would soon share with every other adept and master on the Isle.

The Way cleared her senses, and for the first time, she saw the world the way the other adepts did. Every motion, every detail, was magnified. She drank it in, reveling in the newfound *precision* that coursed through her body and mind. By comparison, her earlier skills now felt ungainly and rough, like a child's scribbled drawings. Her options were becoming limitless.

"Your training and discipline gives you faith in yourself. Never forget, this is the basis of your power," said the lore father. He looked at her for a moment then laid a gentle hand on her shoulder and said, "I hate to greet you with this, but you Ascend at a perilous time. Come, we have much to speak of regarding this council, events in the world, and your friend, Arek."

BLACKFIRE

Perception comes from an open mind,
power from focus,
speed from a relaxed body.
When applied properly, they inflict damage.
—*The Bladesman Codex*

A rek moved to intercept the assassin, his mind clear and his breathing even. Unlike facing Rai'stahn, he felt no fear this time, nor had he for the entire time he'd been within the depths of the underdark of Bara'cor. It was as if his very proximity to the Gate had infused him with a kind of preternatural strength and confidence. That, or the dragon's aura had somehow influenced him. Arek didn't know, but whatever the cause, every detail seemed magnified and slowed. He could dissect the combat in pieces, feel each heartbeat pass by in detail, and see *every* outcome.

On his left, Niall had imperceptibly shifted his weight back, giving their attacker a slight advantage. On his right, he saw Tej's fingers tighten on her grip, readying herself for the point of engagement. He could feel the air shift as his attacker moved toward Niall, lengthening his distance from Tej.

Arek knew a small increase in speed and a slight shift to his left would bring him to the assassin before the assassin could reach Niall. The problem was his foot. Though almost healed, it still felt ungainly. Like a new member of a combat team, it didn't move with the coordinated efficiency the rest of his body enjoyed.

To his right ran Tej, her short sword ready. She'd chosen a path to bring her beside the man. She, at least, seemed to know what she was doing, but Arek didn't want her or Niall to close with the man in black. Not until he was ready.

When the assassin charged, Arek decreased his speed, easing the pressure on his lame foot and causing a gap to grow large enough his attacker would have to choose one of the three, instead of two. By now, the man knew Arek was the leader. Killing him would make the other two easy prey, a fact he was counting on.

He wasn't wrong. The man in black didn't hesitate. It was a true testament to his training, but an error nonetheless. Arek pulled the attacker into a one-on-one confrontation with him, keeping both Tej and Niall safe.

At the very last possible moment, Arek jumped and tucked, somersaulting over the head of his surprised assailant. As he did, he punched downward, striking his opponent's head. His fist exploded in pain. *By the Lady,* he thought, *the man feels like stone!* He landed in a heap, the impact against the granite throwing his timing off.

* * * * *

Prime watched, more than a little impressed when the kid shifted the engagement to his own terms.

So, he's had some training.

He spun in place and moved toward his prone opponent when he felt a searing pain in his head. His stone skin began to dissolve from the strike, leaving it unprotected. He knew nulls were said to negate magic, but he'd never heard of one acting with such speed and virulence. He cursed these abominations, then turned his attention back to Arek.

* * * * *

It was a mistake.

Yetteje watched the man spin and realized he'd dismissed her. She first thought Arek had been showing off, but now realized the purpose behind his vault. He'd taken the assassin's attention off of her.

Arek had said not to attack alone unless they had an opening, and this was a *big* opening. She ran forward and braced her hand behind the pommel of her blade, the other on the hilt, and stabbed the man in the back.

The blade sparked and began to skitter, but she clenched her teeth and focused. There was a sudden flash of light and it sank halfway in. Her hands and wrists exploded in pain and shock and she lost her grip on her blade, stumbling painfully against the man's granite skin. Like Arek, she hadn't expected it to be so hard. She pushed off, remembering that sudden flash and suddenly felt drained, as if her body had given something of itself into the strike.

The man spun with an open backhand that blurred as it traveled, striking Yetteje in the jaw and flinging her backward. She'd managed to begin a duck and roll so the force of the blow didn't kill her. Instead, she hit the ground hard, barely able to focus her eyes. Her jaw made a clicking sound when she tried to move it, bringing tears of pain to her eyes, but she was still alive.

* * * * *

As Prime turned on the fallen girl, he felt three sharp impacts on his head and neck. The null was attacking again, and at each point of impact he saw his stone armor fall away, shedding at the boy's touch like bark from a rotting log. What power did this boy command to overcome even Bara'cor's might?

He pivoted in place and blocked two of the punches, satisfied by the look of pain that flashed across the boy's eyes, then struck him once in the midsection, then twice to the head and chest. The kid flew backward and landed near the prince's feet, rolling and coming to his knees smoothly.

Prime knew the boy would've been killed had his hands still been gloved in granite, but the shieldrock had fallen away at the null's touch. Bara'cor slowly came back to his aid and his armor began to reform. Under his mask, his face broke into a smile. The Galadine whelp had still not moved. Time for him to die.

* * * * *

Niall stood transfixed by the scene, still unable to attack. They moved so *fast*—and now the assassin advanced on him. He backed up, holding out a hand, and shouted, "Wait, stop! Why?" He meant to sound authoritative, but the words came out in a high, gibbering rush. The sound of his own voice disgusted him.

The assassin didn't answer, instead raising two thin blades. He drew his arms back and with the speed of a striking snake, slung the daggers at Niall.

* * * * *

With each strike Arek landed, his body felt a surge of power that brought him unsteadily to his feet, feeling light-headed but stronger than before.

Arek could see the blades flying at Niall. Because of his combat sense, the action played out in agonizingly slowed motion. He might be able to intercept one of the blades, but not both. He snapped himself to a wobbling stand, putting himself in the path of the lead blade, his hands moving to block the assassin's knife.

The scene froze, with Arek's hand not an inch from the dagger. The other dagger was only a foot behind the first, both hanging in the air with death glinting on their points.

"You'll die, dimwit."

Piter stood near the pyramid steps, looking at the scene with a sneer.

"This is Sovereign's Hand." The shade gestured at the assassin and stilettos hanging motionless in the air and continued, "Poisoned. A touch incapacitates. A cut and you're dead."

Arek looked at Piter, anger and fear filling his mind with so many questions, but he blurted, "Just tell me what to do!"

He heard Piter sigh, and then move closer. "You're going to protect these two? Really?"

"Piter, please!"

The shade shrugged. "Perhaps your strength comes from the same way you opened the door. The same way you gave me what I 'deserved.' Look for sustenance."

Confusion set in. Could the shade be telling the truth? He'd opened the door though, hadn't he? Piter had died against his magic, hadn't he? Arek wanted to believe, but realized that in both cases, he'd no idea what he'd done. He needed to focus and closed his eyes. He took in a breath, his mind centering. He took in another, then opened his eyes, looking about.

At first, he saw nothing. He waited, but still nothing happened. He was about to give up when something moved in the corner of his eye. He turned but it disappeared. He forced himself to relax, taking deeper, calming breaths that brought with them a sense of purpose. He was meant to do this, he told himself. He was meant to understand.

Slowly, shapes and objects came into view, ghostly shadows superimposed on what he could see in the real world. Vague forms moved about on the very edge of his vision. They gave the impression of an infinite sea of tiny motes hanging in the air.

A glint of something caught his eye. He looked up and while his eyes saw nothing, his mind felt the presence of a gargantuan, winged warrior. The creature's power was palpable, emanating in waves that threatened to drive Arek to his knees. It stood armed with a spear of orange and red fire, and horns curled down from its visored helm. The figure stretched forth a hand, as if imploring Arek to accept.

His mind jumped back, flooding with memories he hadn't forgotten. He remembered facing Piter now and the creature that had superimposed itself around his name-brother. He remembered the wings and the armor, and its name, *Kaliban*. This creature was similar.

A deep voice intoned, "I offer myself. Our powers will be limitless through Ascension. Wilt thou accept?"

Arek's eyes narrowed. *Ascension?* He could feel the hunger grow again within him, the same hunger he'd felt when he'd faced Piter and the doorkeeper he now remembered was named Dvarin. Was this what it meant to be *Ascended?*

It didn't matter, for Arek's body hungered for this creature, a black hunger emanating from deep within. A small smile played on his lips. The memory of taking Piter's creature suddenly became clear: the power, the ecstasy.

He inclined his head in a slight nod of assent and said, "Of course." He slowly extended his hand, inviting the being to join with him, feeling mostly comfortable with his ruse. The creature was so obvious in its own hunger there was little doubt that if given an opportunity, it would seek to possess him just as quickly.

The creature took his hand in its grasp and completed the bond necessary for Ascension, offering its own true name whispered on the wind: *Adramelek*.

Arek smiled, for he now understood that for him, Ascension was a lie. It wasn't one's true name that was heard, but that of the creature who offered power by bonding with its host, like a parasite.

Adramelek at first looked satisfied, grasping Arek's hand with surety and strength. Then something changed, and while the creature still grasped Arek's ethereal hand, its expression turned from satisfaction to fear.

Black lines of power appeared as cracks within the creature's armor and skin. Arek absorbed what little light there was left around them. His gaze bore into the winged creature's soul and drew it in.

"What are you?" Adramelek screamed in horror. "No! Wait! You are not pure!"

The giant winged creature fought Arek, twisting, bucking, pulling to be free. His grip tightened. The dark hunger within Arek welled up, almost too much to control as he opened himself to it fully.

Adramelek arched backward and another scream tore through him. The black cracks of power widened and he began to fall apart, like a shattered statue. His form imploded in an ethereal flash of black flame, disintegrating into a sparkle of power and life. Arek absorbed all of it, drawing in every single particle, consuming every last bit.

Power, black and potent, coursed through him now, re-knitting his bones, rejuvenating his body. Any harm he'd experienced was healed by the deluge of life that had once been Adramelek. His last scream echoed through Arek's body, but nothing else remained.

The shade of Piter laughed, then said, "Well done, Master! You have exceeded depravity and corruption on every level. Silbane would be proud."

Arek turned his eyes on Piter and something in his gaze silenced the shade. "I begin to understand my place in this world. This was my Test." He took a breath, feeling the power course within him. His sight magnified, became clearer. The world moved slower and he could discern each moment between heartbeats if he so wished. He felt inexplicably precise, as if his entire being had been reshaped and honed to a keen edge.

He felt as though he'd somehow transcended his master and the other adepts of the Isle. He watched Piter bow, a smirk still on his lips, and then slowly fade from view. The scene became still and for a moment, nothing happened. Then time snapped back into place.

A dark flame erupted over Arek, an ebony wash that licked up his form and surrounded him in a mantle of black fire. It covered him from head to toe, misting off him like hot air on a frozen day. His *deathskin* had been unleashed.

His hand, now protected, shattered the first dagger on impact in a pulse of black fire. The second struck his protective barrier near his shoulder. His deathskin darkened further and the dagger vaporized in a flash, leaving behind only a metallic tang he could taste in the air. Arek took a deep breath and his skin expanded until it sucked in the light from the very air around him. It shone potent and black and he felt far stronger than ever before.

In response, Bara'cor itself seemed to lose luster and fade, as if he leeched the very essence of strength from its granite walls. The assassin's armor faded, also drained away by whatever Arek was doing.

The glowing particles or creatures were an endless source of energy, as was everything else around him. He could drain them dry the same way he could draw a breath. He could heal himself with stolen life. A part of him now wondered if he could even be killed. And a more fundamental truth became clear to him. He didn't disrupt magic, he absorbed it, he fed on it, and now he'd unlocked his ability to use it.

Niall looked at him in awe and asked, "What is that?"

Arek ignored the prince's uncomprehending stare, keeping his gaze focused on his still living opponent, the assassin. Niall showed his lack of training and discipline by letting himself be distracted. Arek's master would never have tolerated it, and for some reason now, it disgusted him. A small smile bent the corner of his mouth up. *Was Silbane even still his master?* He laughed at the thought.

The assassin clearly saw that things had gone from bad to worst. A moment went by as he seemed to weigh his options, then he sped forward, his intent clear. They made contact brutally, trained warriors intent on dealing death as quickly as possible. No flowery kicks, no leaps, just short, savage strikes with elbow and knee, followed by grapple holds designed to choke or break bone.

The assassin repeatedly smashed at Arek with a forearm, trying to drive him to his knees. At each impact, thunder sounded and black fire flashed as Arek's shield protected him. The assassin grunted as if in pain.

At first Arek had been cautious, fighting more defensively. His advantage quickly became clear as his barrier absorbed the impact of the assassin's strikes, and judging from the assassin's face, inflicted more pain every time they connected. In fact, as the fight wore on, Arek could feel himself grow stronger, and the assassin became weaker.

Then Arek took the fight to the man, grabbing his neck and driving his forehead into the bridge of his opponent's nose. Blood spattered in a flash of black flame and the assassin fell back, driven by a series of knees and punches, each strike cracking like lightning. The assassin reeled, staggering backward in an attempt to block and retreat.

Arek moved in with a double palm strike that exploded in a flash of black flames. Ribs cracked as the assassin's unprotected body absorbed the thunderous blow. A shockwave coursed through him from the point of impact, detonating within his massive frame, shattering internal organs.

From behind the assassin appeared a battered Yetteje, her jaw swollen and purple. "This is for hitting me," she lisped with acid in her voice. She used the man's lack of armor to her advantage and kicked the pommel of her partially buried blade, slamming it the rest of the way in.

The assassin vomited a gout of blood as the point of the short blade exploded out of his stomach. Then she yanked the sword out with both hands, staggering backward to fall on her back.

"It doesn't matter. . . by now, your father is dead." The assassin began to laugh, but that ended in a gurgle as the last of his life's blood welled up. Then the blue light went out from his eyes and he slumped down, kneeling with his chin to chest, dead.

Journal Entry 20

JOURNAL ENTRY 20

Doubt stalks me, trying to replace my foundation of stone with sand. My marks, feeling adamantine at first, now feel wet and soggy, like bark peeled from rotted logs after a storm. Flimsy things from which fools build shields and bigger fools purchase for protection.

There is no escaping one's own doubts, for they are here because, to believe I am great, I must also believe there are greater things than myself to face and conquer. It is this overcoming of adversity—

Wait!

Clarity finally sheds her blessed light upon my darkened mind!

I understand . . .

Journal Entry 20

LAST STAND

Fear is contagious,
So is courage.
—Altan proverb

T he king and Ash had called the watch into the room after the two men had departed, each wrapped in his personal feelings over the departure of Jebida. For the king, Ash assumed he felt his right hand was gone; a man with whom he'd journeyed for most of his life. For Ash, it had never occurred to him that he would be the one to stay, and he found himself unsure of what to do next.

It was the king who shook Ash out of his doubt when he said, "Assemble the men. I want three squads sent double-pace to the cisterns to look for my son." Turning to Stemmer, who'd just come in, he said, "The rest of you reinforce this room. We have to protect this portal until Jeb's return."

Ash turned from the king and addressed the watch through Sergeant Stemmer. An experienced soldier and leader, the sergeant could be trusted to defend the ground she stood upon. The men stationed themselves in an arc around the portal entrance, but their movements were slow and disorganized by the sight of such magic.

Their wonder and awe at an eldritch black door was quickly washed away by their gruff sergeant, who barked out, "I swear by the Lady you'll hold this door, or I'll push you through myself and you'll do it from the other side!"

That got their attention and soon the squad had created a shield wall with furniture and armed themselves with bow and sword, preparing to defend entry to this room from anyone who emerged.

Alyx made sure they understood that along with Jebida, two others might return from the mission through that doorway.

"A woman and man, so hold your damn fire, screamed the sergeant!

The men picked were some of the best, and Ash watched them comport themselves quickly. He nodded to Alyx, knowing they'd understood.

More men arrived, but the room had limited space. When planning, they had picked it for this very reason. It had originally been fashioned as a vault, and though nothing valuable rested within it now, its door was one of the stronger ones in Bara'cor. It could be easily barred from the outside. Was it impervious? Ash knew nothing was, but the constricted space would limit invaders bringing their forces to bear. Placing the portal in this room, although risky, created a strategic bottleneck, allowing the Bara'cor to defend themselves with far less men than if they'd chosen an open space to activate the Finder. All in all, a good place for their stand.

The king inspected the men, and then motioned to the firstmark to accompany him over to one side. "Have Stemmer work out a rotation so we've got fresh men on station. We'll need to be sure we can relieve them if fighting starts in earnest.

"I never expected . . ." Ash didn't know how to finish that sentence. He felt the overwhelming responsibility of leadership, more now that his mentor was gone. It was so easy to lead, he mused, when you had someone above you.

"I will do my duty," was all he could think to say.

The king clasped the new firstmark on the shoulder and said, "Of that, I have no doubt."

Ash began to reply but stopped, his eyes searching the room. "Where are they?"

The king looked at his new firstmark, not comprehending the question. "Who?"

Ash pointed at the ground of the chamber, where the bodies of the assassins had lain. "Our attackers...where did they go?"

The king then noticed what Ash meant. The bodies of Talis, Sevel, and Chandra were still in the room, now arranged neatly side by side, but of the men who attacked them, there was no sign. "Did anyone clear out the bodies of the attackers?" he said to the assembled room.

Alyx answered, "Sire, when we came in, it was only you two and our fallen. I ordered my team to care for our own."

"We need to find out what's going on," said Ash. "Bodies don't just disappear."

The king nodded and made his way to the door, followed by the firstmark. A half dozen more men approached from the hallway, clearly running to this chamber.

"Milord," said the first, "sounds have been heard from below the fortress. We have stationed men at every junction and told everyone else to stay in their quarters."

"Sounds?" the king asked.

"Aye, sire. Like animals, something wild." The guard clearly didn't know how to elaborate more and the king deferred to Ash.

The firstmark shook his head, "Let's get our men organized to support those in the room." He'd decided against pushing for details until the most immediate needs were addressed.

"Wise decision," the king said, adding, "to watch for intruders. And bring me the guards that stood watch where we held the boy, Arek."

The guard saluted, fist to chest. "At once, sire." He sped off while two more took station at the room's entrance.

The remaining two fell in step behind the king, who looked at Ash and said, "Patrols are out looking for Niall."

"And I assume the princess," added Ash. At the king's look Ash said, "If Niall went with Arek, you can be sure Yetteje isn't far behind."

"That girl has a stubborn streak in her," the king grumbled, "just like her father."

"As many of royal blood," Ash replied with a smile.

Bernal looked at the new firstmark, then broke into a smile that looked more like a grimace. "Aye, probably true." A serious look came to his eyes then, and his face said he was about to ask something uncomfortable. "I saw you hit with a dart, like Talis. He fell instantly. I hate to ask this but why are you still . . . alive?"

Ash looked at his sword, *Why indeed?*

At first, nothing happened. Tempest seemed dead in his hands, though he caught a faint feeling of reluctance. Then her voice sounded in his head, *Yes, I intervened.*

How? Ash questioned.

The sword seemed to hesitate again, then said, *I took the lives of those who had fallen, to save yours, beloved.*

What?

They would have passed anyway. I only took what they no longer needed. You must survive. It was said so matter-of-factly, so devoid of emotion that Ash felt his body go numb.

You killed them?

They passed beyond help . . . Tempest sounded petulant, but then her voice became firm and she said, *I would kill everyone in this fortress to keep you safe.*

Guilt washed over Ash as he heard these words. He could feel the truth in them, and this horrified him more. He looked at the king, then back at the sword. He had to get rid of her or more would fall.

No, beloved. I am yours now.

Ash held the blade out and said, "Tempest healed me, but she took the lives of our men to do it."

The king's eyes widened and a look of horror washed over his regal features. "She did what?"

Ash nodded, grief etched in his countenance. "She says they would've died anyway, but . . . how can I keep her?"

You cannot be rid of me, beloved. I am yours.

Ash tried to drop the blade, but as when he'd first picked up Tempest, his hand wouldn't open. He used his other hand, but the blade clung as if it were a part of him. No matter what he tried, he couldn't let it go. He then sheathed her and tried to undo the buckle. It wouldn't budge. "This is impossible." It seemed that so long as his intent was to let her go, she wouldn't allow it.

The king moved forward to assist, but Tempest said, *If he touches me, I'll kill him.*

Ash held up a hand. "Wait! She'll kill you."

The king stopped short, then backed away a step. "What can you do?"

"I don't know. I need to talk to one of the adepts. They might know something."

Why do you hate me? Tempest said, sounding somehow both innocent and hurt.

Just then, the guard returned with the two who had been stationed outside of Arek's room. The king looked sympathetically at Ash, but then turned to face the men.

"Our guest left his room. Who was with him?" he asked.

The more senior of the two shifted uncomfortably, then answered, "Your son and the Princess of EvenSea, sire."

"And where did they go?"

The man then stammered out, "B-beggin' your pardon, sire, but the prince ordered us to step aside. He said the prisoner complained of pain and he was taking him to the Healers Ward."

"Clearly they didn't go there," offered Ash, his attention still on his blade.

"Spare what we can from the front wall. If we can, send three squads to the cisterns," the king said. "If they see the kids, hold them. I'm going to the cisterns too."

"As you command, sire." The guards saluted and ran back to the stairwell that led to the wall. They would meet with the commander of the watch and relate the king's orders.

Just then, the ground shook again, heaving itself up as if something below the fortress stirred. Ash took two steps forward, and then another, greater shockwave passed, knocking any unsecured items to the ground, including the king and his men. A sound, like a low groan, came from somewhere deep beneath them.

"We need to go now," the king said.

"You're unarmed. . . " Ash turned to a guard and motioned, who began to unbuckle his blade to hand over.

"No," said the king. "I'll make a stop on the way. Keep your weapon."

The man held it out for a second longer, but then with a nod from Ash, withdrew it.

"Are you sure?" asked Ash.

"My father's weapons wait for me." He turned to the guards still in the hallway. "Two of you come with us, the rest hold position here. When Jebida and the team come through, you send them to the cisterns."

The king started to turn but stopped. He must've sensed that Ash wasn't following him. King Galadine asked, "What is it?"

Ash looked around, searching for how to say it. Then he shook his head and said, "I can't go with you."

"What?"

"My king, these men don't know these adepts. Only you and I know Kisan's plan or identity. If Jebida doesn't return. . . "

The king looked stunned by Ash's words, and dropped his head, what looked like shame flashing across his face. When he looked back up, however, there was pride in his eyes. "You are correct, Firstmark. Station our defenders and remain. Make sure that when Jeb returns, he and any others are ushered as quickly as possible to the cisterns."

The king's eyes searched his friend's and then he finished, "In this instance, I'm a father first, a king second. I must go."

"Of course, sire," the firstmark nodded. "I'm sorry."

The king shook his head, already turning, "You saw where the assassin was going. Bring reinforcements. We'll descend through the left main stairwell." He smiled, as he trotted off with three guards in tow.

Ash watched his broad back leave, then made his way back into the room with the Finder's portal. A part of him was secretly relieved. His distrust in Tempest and what she might do to the king or his men should Ash's life be threatened had left him unsure for their safety.

The men crouched behind various impromptu cover, bows ready and blades close by. The black doorway would be the killing ground, a natural choke point to concentrate their fire.

He hoped Jebida would return with Kisan and Silbane. If not, it would mean they were dead and no one remained to close the portal against a nomad invasion. That meant he'd have to send someone or go through himself, as Kisan had said, or Bara'cor would be overrun from the inside out.

Last Stand

DAGGER & AXE

Clean the blade quickly.
Wash your palms thoroughly.
Blood sticks, the last gasp of a dying man,
trying to soak your hands in his failure.
—Kensei Tsao, The Lens of Blades

Silbane sat in the tent where Scythe had left him, still bound by the magic of the red-robed mage. Though he'd been unable to remove the torc blocking him from the Way, his body had continued to heal at an accelerated rate, presumably from Scythe's healing spell. In either case, he could feel most of the broken bones in his face and nose had knitted together correctly. He no longer felt on the verge of passing out.

Now it was clear to him that when they'd interrogated him, he'd been in a mental fugue due to his injuries, Scythe's meddling, or both.

He suspected Scythe's spells were responsible. With the torc in place, he couldn't defend himself from more magical interrogation, regardless of the strength of his willpower. Getting the torc off was his first priority and to do this he needed to free his hands.

He braced his feet under him and slid up the pole he'd been secured against. He'd made it a point to do this at regular intervals to keep his legs limber. His first thought when clarity had returned had been to break the pole with a kick, but one look told him it would be impossible without access to the Way. The beam was just too thick.

As he rose to stretch, he saw a flash come from behind him accompanied by a rush of air. *The Finder! Arek must have used it, which would attract Scythe.* They didn't have much time.

"I told you to go to the Isle and wait!"

A voice behind him whispered, "It's not Arek, old man."

* * * * *

Kisan saw Silbane's back stiffen upon hearing her voice. His arms were clasped behind a pole, but there was no rope holding him there. It seemed Silbane just clasped his hands together voluntarily. Suspecting the cause, Kisan turned her Sight upon the other master.

She could see that Silbane's power to control his arms was locked by someone skilled in the Way. She should've been more shocked, but given what the lore father had told her and what she'd recently seen, she took in this information matter-of-factly.

Now the priority was releasing the locks upon Silbane. She concentrated and looked at the method used to neutralize the master's control. It was not unlike many of the techniques she herself used on opponents, including what she'd done to Two. She could see the points on Silbane's spine where the locks held him immobile and used the Gentle Palm of Death, smiling in satisfaction as they dissipated at her touch.

Silbane's arms came free and he spun. They clasped forearms in greeting and without wasting a moment Silbane grabbed the torc and pulled. Nothing happened. He looked stunned, then let go as Kisan moved in to inspect the torc.

She pulled at it experimentally, but it seemed to grow warmer as she tugged. She turned her Sight upon it and said, "It responds to the Way and somehow uses our energy to stay locked. Ingenious."

Silbane cursed and said, "How do we get this accursed thing off?"

Kisan looked around, then her eyes fell upon the firstmark. She smiled and said, "Jebida, could you assist us?"

The gruff firstmark came over and looked at the collar. What they wanted slowly dawned on him and he asked, "It's magical?"

Kisan nodded. "But you won't feel a thing," she said with a small smile.

Jebida scowled at the woman, then looked at Silbane. It was clear the man had a deep distaste for magic, but he also seemed aware without Silbane's help they were doomed. "Need is the mother of all things," he muttered, "especially if it's likely to get me killed." He lightly touched the torc. With a small click, it unlatched!

Jebida pulled the torc from Silbane's neck and tossed it to him. "Yours."

Kisan sensed the Way surround Silbane, flooding his body with healing and awareness.

"A lot has happened," she told Silbane. "You need to know." She reached to touch Silbane's forehead, then paused and asked. "That mark?"

The master gave the injury centered on his forehead an unconscious rub, as if he'd forgotten he'd had it at all. "Long story, you'll see."

Kisan nodded, then touched his forehead as she closed her eyes, imparting in an instant what had happened to her since they saw each other last. However, she kept from him anything she'd learned about Arek's true nature, as the lore father had ordered.

Kisan had become comfortable that the boy was dangerous and couldn't afford to have Silbane try to protect him. Furthermore, she couldn't risk having to face the other master.

Instead, she conveyed her true regret at their argument, her flight with the assassins, Giridian's news of the death of the lore father and Thera, the assault on Bara'cor and the plight of Arek, the attack of the assassins on the king, and her defense of the same.

Kisan could feel grief punch Silbane's gut at the news confirming Themun and Thera's deaths, particularly the latter. Clearly they'd been closer than she'd known. Though they had every justification now to abort their mission and return to the Isle, she knew they still faced the problem of dealing with Arek.

Silbane paused, then gave Kisan all the details of what had happened to him. She saw his journey to the Far'anthi Stone, then watched his argument with Rai'stahn, the great dragon's fight and death, his own capture at the hands of Hemendra's men, and finally the details of a red-robed mage calling himself Scythe.

Scythe held onto sanity by a very fragile thread and this made him an unpredictable foe. He'd called the Gate his "life's work." Kisan found herself intrigued by this, and more.

The vision of General Valarius's meeting with the Conclave of Dragons was astounding, as was the gift of Sight Rai'stahn had bestowed. When Silbane stopped the mindsharing, Kisan couldn't help but look at him with a newfound mixture of awe and respect.

They'd dabbled at a relationship over the many years they'd known each other. It'd never gone anywhere, as he always seemed so straight-laced and frankly, boring. The facts surrounding his confrontation with the dragon gave her some new perspective, glimpses of the dangerous edge she'd always sensed in him, and that tickled some renewed interest. She laughed a little at herself and her highly inappropriate turn of thoughts.

"What?" Silbane asked.

Kisan didn't reply. Now wasn't the time, especially since whatever had been growing between him and Thera had been unceremoniously cut short by her untimely death. Kisan may not have liked Thera, but she had no desire to disrespect her memories either. Instead, she thought about the vision, disturbing because the revelations contained within seemed eerily similar to the ones Giridian had had with Thoth. She also realized only she had seen both visions and therefore had a unique perspective.

The blackness Silbane had seen emanating from Arek filled her with dread. To her, the fact that Arek destroyed the Way was obvious. Every mishap concerning Arek on the Isle supported this conclusion. It firmed her resolve to keep this information to herself until she could sort things out, but also gave her hope that if the order came to share this with Silbane, the information might compel him to lend his aid and not stand against her.

She couldn't trust the dragons. They seemed to have aligned interests, but had this so-called Conclave fed Silbane a true vision, or something invented for their benefit? They had their own agenda and despite Thoth's endorsement, Kisan knew doubt was a healthy way to stay alive.

She looked at the other master, showing her true disbelief at the circumstances at the Far'anthi Stones and said, "You faced Rai'stahn and lived? I'm impressed." She let her hand trail casually down his arm, happy to see he noticed.

"You two done yet, or is there more to this reunion?" Jebida growled, looking about the tent.

They'd suffered much loss over the past few days and rescuing Silbane felt right. She squeezed the other's hand, a gentle reaffirmation of their common bond and friendship. It was the closest she'd ever come to an apology. Silbane would understand. Yet another part of her, that silent cold logical part, the one that felt like an icepick in her stomach, knew this was an illusion. It would only last until Arek died.

* * * * *

They heard cries of alarm sounding, and Silbane was sure the use of the Finder had alerted Scythe. He stepped around Kisan, facing the firstmark, and said, "Jebida, how do we get the nomad's leader here?"

The firstmark was startled when this new monk used his name. "How did you . . . ?"

"I know everything she knows, a tactical advantage of sorts. Even the way you treated my apprentice." It came out detached, but the intensity in his gaze hinted at the anger brewing behind his eyes.

Jebida took it in, then spat once and grunted, "The only thing nomads love more than sand is blood duels. As challenger, I'll be protected from anyone else interfering. You two aren't so lucky."

"We can take care of ourselves," said Silbane.

Jebida shrugged, "I never asked for your help. You're welcome to leave." He looked at the portal, his meaning clear, "Back to your apprentice."

Silbane shook his head, then continued, "We need to capture a red-robed mage. His name is Scythe. He'll cause serious harm, both to what I care about and to Bara'cor." Silbane paused, then added, "He's likely insane."

"And you're not? I say you can leave and you stay." Jebida moved past Silbane to grab a sturdy wooden desk. With a heave, he pushed it over on its side, creating a barrier. "But I hear you about Scythe." He paused and flashed Silbane a rueful smile, saying, "I'm sorry your apprentice was caught up in all this."

The firstmark continued upending tables, stools, anything that would provide cover. Jebida buried the point of a spear into the ground and the butt end into one of the tables to brace it, and then grabbed another to do the same, saying, "These barriers aren't going to stack themselves. Maybe a hand?"

"You're going to trust us?" Kisan asked.

"I have to get within earshot of the leader to issue the challenge. Nomads going after you mean less going after me. Simple math, so stay alive long enough for me to take care of things."

"Spoken like a true hero," Silbane said. Jebida's part in Arek's torture was difficult to put aside, and he added, "but you Bara'corians do better against children."

Kisan stepped in on the heels of the jibe. "Arek is healed. Let's stay focused." She paused, then looked back at the firstmark and said, "Be quick. We need to move fast."

"You'll not be waiting on me," replied the giant warrior from over his shoulder. Another chair crashed into the makeshift barrier.

Silbane looked at the firstmark and said, "You and I aren't finished."

Jebida shrugged, clearly not missing the meaning. "If we survive."

They continued to stare at each other, then Silbane broke eye contact and muttered, "After this."

He shook his head and let loose an explosive sigh of pent up frustration, grabbing Kisan's arm. "It's good to see *you* again."

"Likewise," the younger master said, clearly happy the encounter between Silbane and Jebida hadn't come to blows. "You don't look too much the worse for the wear. . . maybe a bit uglier," she added, ruffling her fingers through his short hair. It was something she'd done after safely returning from any mission, her 'good luck' ritual.

Silbane smiled, then reached over and took his half of the Finder, still hanging from a nail in the tent. He looped it carefully around his neck. "I ended up here by making every mistake possible. You made it here by quick thinking and skill. The lore father was right; you've always been a falcon." He clapped her shoulder and squeezed, hoping his praise buoyed Kisan's spirit.

The firstmark looked back at them, having now secured a crossbow and a stack of bolts. "The two of you might consider actually doing something."

Kisan looked about to say something to Silbane, but nodded her thanks instead, then took position near the firstmark. "Catching up is one of our best skills." She arched an eyebrow at the firstmark, happy to see him stumble a bit. *Men.*

"Evidently," muttered the firstmark after he'd recovered, "but I understand him." He said this while looking sidelong at Silbane, who could clearly hear the man talking. "Let's hope we live long enough to make amends."

"I hope that for all of us," answered Kisan.

Just then, two nomads burst into the tent. Jebida didn't hesitate but fired his crossbow, catching the first in the throat. Kisan picked up a bolt and whiplashed it into a throw. It hit the second man as if it'd been fired by Jebida himself and took the nomad off his feet.

Both dove for cover as those outside the tent returned fire, with dozens of bolts smacking into the table Jebida had overturned as improvised barriers.

"Hold your fire!" a voice screamed from outside. "Silbane, we can discuss this."

Silbane turned to Kisan and whispered, "Scythe." Then he raised his voice and responded, "If you're ready to surrender, we accept."

Laughter, a bit halting, followed. Then Scythe continued, "Clearly someone has used the Finder. I can sense the portal is open and the presence of at least one other such as you. So why haven't you escaped?"

Silbane motioned to Kisan to take a flanking position to his right.

Jebida raised his voice and said, "The U'Zar of the Clans is a coward. How many warriors has he brought to help him?"

"Who dares challenge me!" a guttural voice roared. From the sounds of it, half a dozen men were barely holding him back.

"Jebida Naserith, Firstmark of Bara'cor," Jebida replied, "the last man you'll see alive."

* * * * *

Outside the tent, Scythe put up a restraining hand as Hemendra surged forward again. "Hold, Clanchief. He seeks to lure you. There is no need," he said, indicating the hundreds of men now surrounding the tent, and the thousands behind them.

"No need!" Hemendra growled. "The man insults me on the very sands of my people. Do not speak to me of need."

Hemendra knew the expectations of his brethren. If he said nothing, other warriors would think to challenge him for leadership.

The Redrobe turned and faced Hemendra, saying, "You risk much. It isn't important in the grand scheme. Control yourself; he is a coward hiding in a tent instead of facing you openly."

The Clanchief took a deep breath, letting the Redrobe's words have a calming effect. He turned his gaze onto the closed tent flap, then nodded. "I can—"

Silbane's voice rang out, "Scythe, give your dog permission to fight. We understand who really leads the clans."

Hemendra screamed, a guttural roar designed to scare the men around him as much as strike fear into this unknown man who hid like a dog. His voice was like an animal charging.

He bellowed, "I accept your challenge! Crawl from your hole." The gathered troops quickly formed a circle in the sand outside the tent. "No one touch this man! I challenge him to drink as is my right. The sands will judge our worth!"

A moment went by, then the tent flap parted and a man emerged. The u'zar appreciated his opponent immediately. The man stood close to his own height, with a great axe held casually in one meaty fist. He squinted as his eyes adjusted to the light, then nodded to the clan chieftain.

"You'll be the man whose blood soaks the sands today."
Jebida smiled and moved forward.

Hemendra could see the grace with which the man
walked. He hefted the axe with an easy familiarity born
only through countless hours of training and surviving the
fields of battle. This was a man the clanchief would not
underestimate, a man who would bring him honor when he
died upon the U'Zar's blade.

* * * * *

Scythe gave a mental sigh, but realized this combat
would have no effect on the outcome of his entry into
Bara'cor. He'd a far more powerful ally now than
Hemendra of the Altans, as everyone was about to see. As
the two combatants neared each other, he smiled and made
his way closer to the tent holding Silbane.

He was more curious as to why Silbane and this other
adept hadn't left through the portal. His plan had counted
on any rescuers taking the quick path back to Bara'cor and
dragging in the strands of his portal web, thereby locking it
open. He was also curious because this other was clearly
not Arek. Who was she and why had she come to Silbane's
rescue?

* * * * *

Hemendra picked up his axe and moved into the circle
created by his men. "My axe is called Blood Drinker." He
smiled at his opponent.

Jebida smiled and glanced down at his axe. "Donkey."
He looked at the men ranged in the circle around him, his
eyes finally coming to rest on the Clanchief. "A better
name for my axe than for the dead man standing in front of
me."

The Clanchief's confusion turned to a cold, calculating
anger when he realized the man mocked the traditions of

his people and his ancestors. To offer a weapon an unworthy name? Still, he was too disciplined to let this stone dweller's words affect his fighting style.

He measured the space between him and his opponent, his hands gripping his own axe with a strong yet supple caress, the result of years of swinging the killing stroke. "Those who fear, talk."

Jebida nodded with a hint of a smile, then burst forward with lightning speed, his axe blade flashing out for the clan chieftain's eyes.

The sudden attack forced Hemendra to move his head and blink, and Jebida dropped low and stabbed downward with the spear-tipped point of his axe haft. The point entered the chieftain's shin, but missed the vital bone and instead cut into the massive muscle of the barbarian's calf. He pulled the point out and Hemendra could feel the steel twist, pulling the wound open. The only sound that escaped his lips was a grunt, acknowledging first blood. It might give the man a sense of satisfaction that, while rewarding, would be short-lived.

Hemendra knew the point where his opponent's axe tip had exited his shin would already be slowing to a trickle. He fought upon the desert sands, the All Mother to true nomads, aiding him as only a mother could. Her aid could not be predicted, for the All Mother was fickle, just as the desert itself was. For now, it seemed she would aid him, letting him keep his life water until she thirsted again.

He notched his regard of his opponent a bit higher. The man had committed to his attack without hesitation once he realized the stage Hemendra had been setting. He'd not let himself be drawn into boasting, instead speaking with his axe.

Jebida spun and dodged to his right as the barbarian's great axe whistled down, missing his head by a hair's breadth. The nomad's axe didn't bury itself in the sand, but rather spun up and wove a figure eight, attempting two more times to connect with his opponent's neck. Hemendra never overextended himself and finished the short, deadly circles with his axe where they started, protectively across his own body.

Jebida braced himself, then launched a swing that could've sheared a man's head from his shoulders with ease.

Hemendra barreled forward, ducking under the horizontal swing and catching the Bara'corian warrior in the ribs. He swung an elbow around, hammering into the man's collarbone and driving him to a knee, then brought his own knee up in a short, brutal arc. It caught his opponent under the chin, driving him up again to almost a full standing position. Before he could recover, Hemendra spun and struck with his axe. Only a slight misstep, which caused the flat of the blade to connect with Jebida's breastplate, saved him.

Jebida was hurled backward in a shower of sparks from steel on steel. The firstmark hit the ground on his back, but curled into a roll, coming to his feet in a moment. The nomad chieftain saw the man was dazed, but still dangerous.

Hemendra stalked forward, his axe held across his body. He raised it as if to strike at Jebida's head, but then switched to a dangerous undercut swing. The axe whistled in toward its target.

Jebida moved forward quickly, angling slightly away from the blow, but not too far. While he did so, he raised his arm, bracing himself. Hemendra's axe blade slid up the side of Jebida's body, but missed his groin, the chieftain's intended target. Then the warrior clamped his arm back down over the axe blade, trapping it before it could gain its full deadly momentum. It saved him from certain death and trapped Hemendra's axe against his body, too close for the nomad to use.

The Bara'corian punched, once, twice, before the clanchief raised his offhand and trapped Jebida's axe. For a moment they stood, axes locked and eye-to-eye, each straining for leverage. Neither said a word, but then the clanchief punched Jebida in the face with the knuckles of the hand still holding his axe. The strike broke the old warrior's nose.

Hemendra watched as the man blinked furiously to clear his eyes. Then he grabbed his axe handle, still trapped by Jebida's armpit. He re-engaged, choosing to keep his opponent as close as possible, looking for any small advantage, taking in the man's measure, concentration, and focus. Nothing needed to be said as he pushed and strained, looking for one mistake to give him victory.

* * * * *

Jebida knew he'd countered the chieftain's advantage well, but one of them would have to disengage to use his weapon effectively, so he readied himself. When he let go, his opponent would push forward to build his own momentum for another attack. He'd only one choice.

Jebida sucked in and spit blood into the clanchief's face, and then heaved his axe up. The axe didn't move, but the sudden spittle combined with his great strength pushed the clanchief off balance. He used this to get his center lower, then spun in place pivoting on his forward foot, the hand holding his opponent's axe hilt and circling down and then up.

The movement looked like a children's dance, but the outcome would be deadly for one of them. It forced his opponent to circle with him or lose his weapon, and this was the trap. The Chieftain would fall out of position and the battle-knife in Jebida's hand would make short work of his opponent . . . but the strike never happened.

Even as Jebida spun, he felt a punch to his back. Suddenly his body went numb, the shock traveling up and down his spine. He felt his side go limp, yet strangely, no pain. He looked back at his opponent, locked in an embrace with him separating them by mere inches, and had a moment of regret. He couldn't remember why he'd wanted to kill this man. The edge of his vision became gray and he looked questioningly at the nomad chieftain.

"Sleep, Firstmark. Better men than you have fallen to my blade." Hemendra pulled the short dagger in his left hand out of his opponent's spine.

Jebida's eyes cleared for a moment and he knew exactly what had happened. He could feel the life gushing out of him. He looked into the nomad chieftain's eyes and saw no remorse. He felt shame for dying in his killer's arms.

Still, the bone-hilt of his own knife had been in his hand, or had he dreamt that too? His thoughts became jumbled and gray, no longer sure what was true. His mind turned to what he loved above all else, lost so many years ago.

He could see them now, waiting for him, just ahead. A smile flitted across his face and he whispered to himself the promise of rejoining them at last, "My family . . . " One hand reached out, gripping nothing but hot desert air.

"If they live in Bara'cor, they will join you soon," the chieftain replied softly.

Slowly, with only a small sigh, the last breath left Jebida Naserith's body and the light went out from his eyes. His lips, however, were still curled into a small private smile, as if he'd at last found a small measure of peace before the walls of his own fortress.

* * * * *

Hemendra pushed the lifeless body of his opponent away from him and raised his dagger in triumph. There was a ragged cheer that started strong but then slowly fell apart.

What was going on? He felt suddenly weak, and stumbled a few steps back. His leg brushed something and he looked down. Jutting out from the inside of his thigh was a black-hilted dagger. Blood flowed freely from the wound and down his leg, quickly pooling at his feet.

The clanchief stumbled again and fell to one knee. "Healers!" he bellowed.

A haze came over his vision and a figure stepped from the crowd. It was Clanfist Paksen, who cocked his head at the clanchief. "We cannot request a healer for a challenge accepted."

"I am victorious! Call a healer, Paksen." The words came out thick and jumbled, barely above a whisper.

Paksen leaned forward, grasped the black-boned blade, and pulled it out. A sudden warmth of blood spurted out even more quickly, a gush timed with each beat of his heart.

"I am sorry, U'Zar, the All Mother is watching. We cannot help you."

Dagger & Axe

JOURNAL ENTRY 21

I have survived, but not in the way expected. Through my failure, I have learned a truth, and it comes from my imps.

They saw me create the blood marks and believed these have power. When the raids came, my marks failed, but the imps did not doubt my work the way I did. Each imp unexpectedly took up one of the marks in my defense, and tasted my blood.

They evolved into frightful behemoths, sentinels who stood watch throughout the night. They are my guardians, my belief lending them power. It is truly amazing to behold.

The young Aeris cannot affect reality, but they are ready to serve. Our faith gives them power. I can already feel mine growing as stalwart friends come to my defense.

I have now fashioned them marks to wear on their arms, consecrated with my blood, eldritch shields against harm. I regret now comparing my marks to soggy pieces of bark. They are much more when held in the hands of my children.

Swords will be next, made of birch and pine. It matters not, for they believe if it is touched by my blood, it becomes blessed with power. Their faith is changing the Way for me.

I am becoming a true father to these imps, and they are becoming something grander under my guidance.

Journal Entry 21

BROTHERS IN ARMS

In the din of battle, choose your enemies wisely.
Trees are known by the size
of the shadows they cast.
Your prowess will be defined
by whom you defeat.
—Kensei Shun, The Lens of Shields

K isan and Silbane glimpsed portions of the melee through the slight opening of the tent, unable to take much advantage of the distraction Jebida provided. The portal into Bara'cor sat behind them, wide open, but leaving it unguarded or calling attention to it before capturing Scythe was tantamount to inviting the nomads to kill the men and women who defended the fortress.

When Jebida fell, Kisan considered using that moment to attack as a stalling tactic, each heartbeat that passed increased the chance Prime had taken care of her problem with Arek. Silbane stopped her.

"I'd hoped Scythe would come to us, but we'll have to take the offensive. He's here, close by, and we can't leave him behind, even if it means leaving the portal."

"He's that important?" asked Kisan.

"Very," he said. "He's the force behind all this, and we need him to close the Gate beneath Bara'cor."

Kisan grudgingly nodded, but before they could take a step from the tent, they heard Scythe call out, "We have a mutual friend, adepts."

Silbane's eyes widened. A sudden explosion of psychic power erupted just outside of the tent. "We're in trouble."

Even Kisan, who didn't have the sensitivity Silbane did, could feel the incandescent burst of energy. "What was that?"

Bladed claws grabbed the tent and pulled it up from its moorings, smashing and tossing it aside like so much tinder and cloth. The sun flashed in, blinding in its brilliance.

Kisan and Silbane stood amongst the wreckage. Surrounding them were hundreds of nomads delineating the edges of a circle occupied by an enormous black-scaled creature. It was the great dragon, Rai'stahn, healed and whole once again.

"Not good," muttered Kisan. "He looks angry."

"Yes," answered Silbane, "nothing is ever easy."

Behind them yawned the portal, open and black, leading back to Bara'cor. Before them towered Rai'stahn, in full dragon form. His great black wings flexed and he growled, "The Scythe and I are oath-forged. Thou wouldst be wise to surrender." The great dragon's eyes then narrowed and he looked meaningfully at Silbane, "But mortal, when wert thou ever wise?"

Kisan's mind raced. Because Silbane had shared the vision granted by the dragon, Kisan knew it'd had been killed, his neck broken. Now he stood before them, whole again and oath-forged? How had he survived? How had Scythe convinced a dragon as ancient as Rai'stahn to commit himself to such a bond?

Scythe, whom she wouldn't forget Silbane had described as insane, stepped forward. "We can settle this. Leave the portal open and allow me to enter Bara'cor. You can go free. I have no wish to destroy those who practice the Way, in any form."

Silbane took a moment, then said, "You know of the vision shown to me, that of the Conclave?"

The red-robed mage smiled and said, "I don't need the vision, Silbane. I stood against the demonkind at Sovereign's Fall."

Shock ran through both mages at that, but in the vision Silbane had shared with Kisan, Scythe wasn't the man in armor who faced the dragons. That man had clearly been General Valarius Galadine. What did this unbalanced mage mean?

Kisan mindspoke with Silbane, regardless of the waste of energy, her tactic was clear. *You were right, he's crazy.*

Silbane kept his eyes on Scythe. *If we attack, Rai'stahn will intercede and we cannot prevail against the two of them.*

A new voice interrupted them both. *Escape is your best chance.* Scythe smiled.

Rai'stahn drew a deep breath then unleashed dragon fire, blasting the wreckage of the tent and igniting everything around the two masters in a fireball of heat and flame.

Skins erupted from both, an explosion of power covering them with protective auras. Yellow and silver, Silbane and Kisan shone like the sun and moon, bending the dragon fire harmlessly around them. They didn't wait for the dragon to blast them again, separating to give Rai'stahn and Scythe two targets instead of one.

Kisan moved toward Scythe, her focus now on keeping herself alive, angling to keep him between her and the dragon's breath. She dodged left, then right, then leapt at the mage, no more than a blur. Pivoting in the air, she snapped out a lethal kick at the man's head.

Scythe raised a hand and a web of lightning arced out, surrounding the young master. Kisan's silver moonskin flashed multiple times in response from the many lethal daggers of energy striking at her from all directions.

It was mostly successful, in that it kept her alive, but Kisan's body convulsed as lightning bled through her moonskin, locking her muscles tight. She tumbled from her leap and landed to one side, small sparks of electricity arcing about her skin. Then she slowly stood, her form still smoking as she struggled to shrug off the aftereffects.

Silbane had moved in coordination with Kisan, keeping his eyes on Scythe. Rai'stahn's tail caught him in midstride, slapping into him like a tree trunk. His flameskin erupted, a yellow-white flash in response to the massive strike, absorbing most of the blow. He fell, landing some distance from Kisan, who was just rising from Scythe's attack.

"This is useless," Scythe said, "you cannot prevail."

"Your technique from the Isle," Silbane whispered to Kisan. She knew he'd count on her heightened senses, so the master's suggestion came through like he was standing right next to her. It had never crossed Kisan's mind that she would find herself in a situation where the spoken word would be more secure than mindspeak.

Kisan immediately knew he meant the Blood of the Moon technique she'd used to create copies of herself and Piter. Scythe would know nothing about this, having never shared Kisan's thoughts.

There was one problem though. Affinities worked best when used with the source they drew power from. She looked around the sunlit sands and grimaced. Right now, there was no moon. At best she could create weak copies, unable to interact with anything.

She concentrated, reached for the Way, and could feel Silbane do the same, ready to feed her strength for the technique. She couldn't create simulacrums of the same detail and independent capability as she'd done before. It was too energy consuming and complex to achieve in direct sunlight. What they needed were targets, and lots of them.

As the technique completed, the clearing created by the dragon fire exploded with hundreds of copies of Silbane and Kisan, all flashing into being from thin air. As she'd known, these were simple copies. Still, she'd created enough to confuse both the dragon and the red-robed mage.

The copies looked at their maker and smiled, then burst into action. They jumped and twisted, moving quickly at their attackers, dodging and wheeling.

Rai'stahn drew his fanged head back, then struck Silbane as he jumped into the air on the attack. A taloned claw crushed another Silbane beneath it in a yellow-white flash, smashing it to the desert floor. Another ducked under the attack and struck at the armored side of the dragon, but it had no effect. It too disappeared when struck by the dragon, but still hundreds more came, attacking any who stood in their way even though their attacks served no purpose but to distract their opponents. Soon the clearing was a maelstrom of confusion with nomads fighting these copies, who when touched disappeared instantly. Her technique wasn't designed to win, but to confuse, and it was accomplishing that spectacularly.

Kisan leapt into the heart of the melee, her ridge hand striking into a nomad's throat and breaking his neck. She sped past him, ducking under a blade then spinning and facing the counter strike. As the sword came whistling in, she clapped her hands together and caught the blade between her palms. Continuing her spin, she snapped the steel halfway up its length.

Even as the nomad tried to bring the shattered remnant of his half weapon up, Kisan flipped herself half over and thrust her broken half of the nomad's blade through his chest. She was past him before he hit the ground, quite dead.

Scythe spread his hands and a volley of flaming darts shot out, catching half a dozen Silbanes and Kisans full in the chest. They burnt to cinders and flashed into nothingness. Still more versions came zigzagging through the carnage, weaving in between copies of each other.

One of the Silbanes punched the ground and it erupted into a tidal wave of sand that sped toward Scythe. Scythe fell back a step and put his hands together, slicing through the onrushing wall with a blade of lightning that parted the sand wave around him, leaving behind tinkling shards of molten glass.

Kisan knew the use of Gentle Palm of the Earth, that wave of sand, was a technique only the real Silbane could've performed. Before Scythe could target him, Kisan struck one of the nearest nomads with open fingers through her opponent's eyes. Grabbing the blinded nomad's skull through his eye sockets, she hurled him at Scythe.

The body flying past Scythe had the desired effect. The red-robed mage lost sight of the real Silbane. In frustration, he clenched his fist and another Silbane fell, his back broken and crushed, before disappearing in a flash.

Rai'stahn swept a Kisan into his grasp and bit her head off, then tossed the body aside. It disappeared before it hit the ground in a flicker of silver fire. Dozens more flowed toward the dragon with attacks that could distract him long enough for the real masters to launch an attack he might not see coming.

He narrowed his golden eyes, looking for the heat from living creatures, then quickly reached out with a clawed talon and grabbed the real Kisan out of a group to his right. Kisan's skin erupted in silver flame as her protective aura ignited in response. Rai'stahn bared his fangs and squeezed.

The aura grew brighter as the master fought the dragon's grasp, locked in a struggle that could only end in her death. She let out a scream and the flameskin exploded with a silver blast that caused the dragon to release her and fall back. Kisan landed in a heap and lay motionless. All versions of both masters instantly dissipated, vanishing before the gathered nomads in the midst of combat and leaving many with no opponent.

Scythe yelled to Rai'stahn, "Breathe!"

A knot of nomads had surrounded the only Silbane left, perhaps seeking to gain favor with their mage. When the dragon targeted them, some heard the huge indrawn breath of air and looked up in horror, seeing death in the dragon's eyes. Others attempted to scatter before the great blast hit. The dragon breathed a firestorm, destroying all it touched and melting the sand to sparkling bits that crunched underfoot. Of Silbane, there was no sign.

With the exception of the lone black portal, not a single structure stood within the distance of an arrow's cast that wasn't burning or just simply gone.

Scythe stepped forward and surveyed the scene. He seemed about to motion to Rai'stahn to move forward when the air behind him wavered and then blurred. The real Silbane stepped out from where he'd maneuvered while Kisan's illusions had served their purpose. He'd used his affinity with the sun to wreathe himself in Clouds before Sun, becoming nearly invisible to both heat and sight.

"This belongs to you," Silbane said. He snapped the torc around Scythe's neck and it locked itself in place.

Before Scythe could reply, Silbane struck him a backhand blow that sent him reeling back, unconscious. The master darted forward and grabbed the red-robed mage before he hit the ground, spinning in place to face Rai'stahn.

Kisan staggered to her feet and moved over to stand next to Silbane, trying to focus her vision and catch her breath. They both watched as the dragon turned its yellow gaze upon them.

"What wouldst thou have me do, mortal?" Rai'stahn hissed.

"You are oath-forged," Silbane stated, adding, "no harm can come to him through your action, or inaction."

"I ken the Oath. How wilt thee shame thyself now?"

"He will go with me and I'll see no harm come to him," Silbane said. He looked at Kisan and nodded. His meaning was clear.

Kisan had begun to recover from her encounter with Rai'stahn's grasp, and except for a cut down one cheek and possibly bruised ribs, was unharmed. She retreated on unsteady legs back to the portal, keeping a careful eye on the hundreds of nomads who were slowly reappearing at the outskirts of Rai'stahn's devastating arc of scorched earth.

Silbane kept his eyes on the great dragon while making his own way to the portal. "I go to find my apprentice," he said. "If it is as you say, I'll deal with him. Don't interfere or I won't guarantee Scythe's safety."

The dragon flashed and changed, becoming again a black armored knight. He strode forward but stayed well out of the masters' reach. "If thou hast any love for this land, kill thine apprentice."

Kisan understood where Rai'stahn's heart was and hoped it was no longer an issue.

Silbane nodded, meeting the dragon-knight's eyes, and said, "Milord, you once trusted Themun. Trust me as you did him."

He took one last look around then nodded to Kisan, who jumped into the portal and disappeared.

THE FINAL DAY...

Brothers in Arms

THE EYE OF THE SUN

It is often true that he who achieves victory,
does so not out of cunning or skill.
But by delivering the seventh thrust,
after the first six are blocked.
—Tir Combat Academy, The Tactics of Victory

I froze . . . " Niall whispered to himself. "I failed, again."

Arek quenched his deathskin, the black fire diminishing into him, but ready should he need it. He took a deep breath and could feel the Way course through him now, eldritch and potent. It was a heady feeling of strength and power and he reveled in it. He looked down, knowing his foot was whole, but at the expense of a winged creature that had once been alive. He took a breath, exploring what he felt.

Nothing. I feel nothing but pride and hunger, he thought. *I feel powerful.* The corners of Arek's mouth curved up into a smile.

He moved around the dead assassin's body and knelt next to Tej. A nasty bruise painted the left side of her face and jaw. A thin cut ran from the right side of her forehead, through one delicate eyebrow, and ended on her right cheek. It was bleeding slowly, but Arek thought her lucky she hadn't lost the eye. He offered her a hand and helped her stand.

"He almost got your eye," he said, pointing to her face.

Tej ignored the comment and looked past Arek to the dead assassin, still on his knees. "Who was he, and what was that fire thing you did?" Her voice came out muffled as she'd clenched her teeth to keep her jaw from moving.

Arek looked at the figure too and said, "I don't know." Then he looked at Tej and answered her second question, "It's like a flameskin but . . . " and then he realized he was explaining it using terms Tej wouldn't know. "Uh, I've never created one before this," he finished a bit lamely.

"Convenient." She wiped off her short blade. Arek thought she should've shown more elation at surviving the fight, instead she seemed annoyed.

"What happened to your limp?" she demanded.

Arek couldn't tell if she was angry with him for some reason, so replied carefully, "These attacks are healing me."

"More convenient." She sheathed her blade and before he could say anything else she nodded in Niall's direction. "And him?"

"Fear," Arek replied matter-of-factly, his training making the assessment without thinking. "Someone trying to kill you for real can be unnerving, especially the first time."

It was a normal part of fighting and something he'd faced himself, albeit at a much younger age. It was often proportional to someone's worry about getting hurt. Once you realized getting hurt wasn't as horrible as you thought it'd be, the fear and hesitancy diminished, too.

"I know what you mean," she replied. "Hopefully he can pull it together. I don't think we're out of danger yet," she cautioned with a faint note of disgust in her voice. Arek couldn't tell if the remark was directed at herself, her opponent, or at Niall. He decided to let it go and check on the prince.

As he approached, he saw Niall with his sword still in a white-knuckled grip. The prince was looking down, shame plainly written on his face. "I didn't do anything."

Arek looked around, satisfied there were no other threats, then said, "Don't beat yourself up about it. The guy is dead."

"Thanks to you and Yetteje. What did I have to do with that?" Niall whispered, mainly to himself.

Yeh-te-jee? He didn't remember if he'd heard her full name, but found he liked it. He looked back at her and smiled, but of course, she didn't notice. She was about to search the man.

"Careful!" he said quickly. "The daggers on him are poisoned. One touch and they'll finish the job he started."

Yetteje's eyes widened at that, and she stopped a hand's breadth away from the man's body. "I want to know who he is."

Arek drew a small but keen knife from his belt and made his way back over to where Yetteje stood. He knelt carefully and slit the man's hood open. He then pulled it away, revealing the face underneath. What he saw shocked them both.

"What is he?" she asked, looking at the features that were larger and wider than the average person's. While fighting, he seemed intimidating because of his intent and skill—now he was just big.

Arek thought for a moment, never having seen something like this before in real life, then said, "I think he's a dwarf."

"He's a builder." The statement came from Niall, who had come up to stand behind the other two, still looking miserable. "At least, I think he is. They're obviously big, they built this place," he mused, "but he's bigger than I expected. He looks just like the pictures carved into various reliefs around the fortress."

"What's he doing in Bara'cor?" asked Yetteje. "And why is he trying to kill you?"

"Like I'd know," Niall said. Then he looked at Arek and asked, "He said something before he died. What was it?"

Both Yetteje and Arek looked at each other, then Arek replied, "He said that by now your father is dead." He didn't have any reason to lie to Niall. Surprisingly, Niall took the comment better than he expected.

"Doubtful. You've not seen my father fight. If we—" he stopped, then corrected himself—"if you and Yetteje can kill him, my father will be just fine." Niall sheathed his sword.

The floor of the chamber began to crumble, turning into sand under the dead man, and he began sinking into the stone.

"What's going on?" exclaimed Yetteje, scrambling back.

"Stand clear," Arek said. "I don't know, but it's speeding up."

Indeed, even as the small group of companions looked on, the man disappeared under the stone, which then hardened back to normal. Yetteje moved up and poked it with her foot, but the stone was unyielding.

"What do you think happened?" she asked no one in particular.

Niall said, "It's said dwarves have a friendship with rock. Maybe Bara'cor is doing something it only does for them."

"Great," said Yetteje, looking around, "the fortress is alive too."

Despite Tej's seeming commitment to remain annoyed at everything, Arek felt a flush of pride for having defended his friends. He felt even more elation when the fact that he'd done it with magic, a feat he'd never expected to accomplish. He gave Niall a nod he hoped was reassuring, then let his eyes track up the pyramid to finally study the sapphire sun blazing at its apex. Its blue aura permeated his skin, warming him from within. He could almost feel himself growing in power, as if he were absorbing sustenance directly from the blue light's coronal discharge.

"I need to go up there," he said.

"Why?" asked Yetteje, her tone leaving no doubt that the idea of going up to a flaming sun was ridiculous.

Arek looked at the other two and realized the time had come for him to offer an explanation, even a brief one, so he said, "I have always had the power to disrupt magic. My master brought me on this mission because of it."

He looked back at the sun, glowing with its azure flames, and said, "He searched for a gate between our world and another, one controlled by the demon Lilyth. I think this is it."

Both Niall and Yetteje looked shocked. Niall said, "You're joking."

"No," Arek replied, "but if I touch the Gate, I think I can disrupt it, closing it forever." It was a simple statement supported by facts Arek had put together from various things he'd seen or heard from the council, his master, and his encounters with Piter's shade.

Arek could now see he had been a tool to the lore father, nothing more. He'd probably decided to close the Gate with Arek's power, whether Arek touched it willingly or not. So Silbane had been sent to carry out those orders. Piter had essentially told Arek so when they had stood upon the dunes. The council would use his power, and if that meant sacrificing him, so be it.

His master's hasty explanation and apology back at the Far'anthi Stone hinted he'd been disobeying those orders, though why he'd obeyed them at all in the first place brought his motivations into question. Any gratitude Arek felt came tainted with the darker knowledge that the Council *and* his master had participated in betraying and sacrificing him.

His master's attempt to send Arek away when Rai'stahn had tried to kill him was better late than never. Somehow Piter had influenced him to flee, but how, and why to Bara'cor? He'd run to the Far'anthi Stone and had somehow managed to activate it. That action had dropped him into this predicament and left him alone to confront the Gate.

His eyebrows drew together as he thought and a cold anger grew within him. He spiraled into it, dismissing that Silbane had tried to save him by sending him away. It was as if another force slowly bent his thoughts in on themselves, consuming him with feelings of betrayal and injustice. His deathskin began to prickle at the air around him, as if in anticipation of violence. Then he breathed out, and the feelings vanished as suddenly as they had come.

"So there's no weapon?" said Yetteje. "My family remains unavenged?" Her stance and demeanor conveyed her rising anger at what she thought was Arek's duplicity.

Arek looked at her with a start then snapped, "Grow up. Closing this Gate is important for the entire world."

Then the scene froze and Piter appeared again, looking comparatively happy. He stood at the base of the pyramid and beckoned to Arek. "You're as smart as a dog, at least."

Arek walked forward, facing the shade, and said, "Shut up. They used me, and that includes you."

"Perhaps," answered the shade. "Though there was nothing but death for you without me, remember? I saved you when Silbane could not."

Arek quieted at this, his doubts about the lore father and Piter's condemnation of his master difficult to ignore. He licked his lips and asked, "You mentioned Sovereign. Tell me, what is it?"

The shade smiled and nodded. "Smarter than a dog. The Sovereign guides this world. And there is more. You are necessary to free the Aeris."

"Aeris? Is that what those beings I saw are called? How am I necessary?"

Piter nodded and said, "You can set things right."

"You didn't answer my question, shade. What is the Sovereign, and how does it guide our world?"

The shade of Piter looked contemplative, then his head cocked to one side as if he were listening to something. After a moment, he said, "The Sovereign guides your hand, even now. Do not falter, imbecile."

The scene snapped back and Arek caught himself as the very space around him seemed to vibrate.

"It happened again, didn't it?" asked Yetteje.

"What?" Arek snapped at her again. Given the Isle's betrayal and Piter's annoying tendency to leave when most inconvenient, he was left with little patience, least of all not getting answers. Still, how was she able to perceive these moments where time stopped for him?

"I felt it too. Something skipped, like when your helm is hit hard," Niall offered.

Arek shook his head, frustrated by everything. He didn't understand the circumstances by which he had his moments, but it seemed odder still that all three of them could sense it. He looked back up at the pyramid.

The council be damned, he thought. *I can save the world.*

Turning to his companions and said, "If I touch that thing up there, I can stop something terrible from happening. I need you both to trust me."

A moment passed as all three looked at each other, then at the pyramid. Arek knew he was asking a lot. It wasn't as if he couldn't proceed without their permission, but something in him wanted to feel like he was part of this group.

It was Yetteje who spoke first. "I trusted you to lead us to a weapon, something I could use for . . . justice."

Arek held his hands open, beseeching her to listen. "Look, I'm sorry for being short earlier, but you wanted revenge. I never promised that. I did say coming here would be important. Closing this Gate severely restricts the appearance of demons, and gets rid of a portal that could be the staging area for an all-out war. Doesn't that help Bara'cor?"

"Tej, come on," Niall said. "We'll avenge your father, but this is important, too."

Yetteje slowly nodded a grudging acquiescence. Then she asked softly, "Why is he even bothering to ask? We couldn't stop him even if we wanted to. He's just asking because he's scared and knows this is wrong."

"That's not true," said Arek. He could feel the truth in her words, however.

Yetteje knew it too and turned to face Arek, hands on her hips, "You're so sure you can close this Gate? What if it opens?"

"That won't happen. I disrupt magic; I can't do anything else."

Yetteje advanced and poked him in the chest, "Really? Then what was that black flame you created? Was that nothing?"

Arek shook his head. "You don't understand. I can close this Gate. I know it. You have to trust me."

"Why? Because you say so?" She looked at Niall in exasperation and said, "You're a Galadine, by the Lady! Your family has stood as guardians of Edyn since who can remember? Now you'll just agree to let him put everyone at risk?" She paused, then asked them both, "What if you're wrong?"

Arek scoffed. "You don't know what you're talking about. The council and my master thought this was the way. I can still succeed."

"And the glory will be mine!" Yetteje finished. "I can hear it, even when you don't say it."

Niall walked up to Yetteje and said, "Leave it. How do you know? He stood by us when he could've run. That wasn't for glory."

Yetteje looked at Niall, then at Arek, and a moment passed. Then she said, "You are idiots, both of you." With that, she turned away. "Let him go. He doesn't need us and we can't stop him."

Niall watched her retreat, a hurt look on his face. Then he let loose a sigh, shaking his head, and walked back to Arek. Looking up at him from under his brow he cracked a small smile and gripped his shoulder. "She's hurt and angry, but doesn't mean it. You saved our lives, so I trust you. Go ahead, we'll keep watch down here."

Arek locked eyes with him, feeling a bond growing between them. Then he nodded and walked to the pyramid. Niall moved in behind him, taking station at the lowest step. Yetteje moved away.

Arek started up the pyramid. The steps passed under his feet as the dark sun's brilliance grew. The blue-white radiance cast scintillating shadows, but no heat. It flowed through him, stoking his inner furnace until it burned with the brightness of a star. Below, he could see his friends looking up at him, then back at the entrance, as if they expected another assassin to appear.

Arek knew there would be no more interruptions. The shade of Piter, while avoiding some of his questions, had said he could set things right. That rang true. He'd always wanted to believe he was special, somehow destined for greatness. He wished the other adepts and students could see this and know the truth. He was free of the shame; no stupid tests to measure his failure, no doubt from his instructors, no jests made at his expense by his fellow students.

He recalled the dreams of conquest he'd had at the dunes near the Far'anthi Tower. That place seemed an eternity away and yet, even then he knew he was here to triumph. He smiled. For the first time since coming to the Isle and starting his apprenticeship, he was finally important.

The portal stood before him, its light and fire ethereal, but still blinding. Arek took a deep breath and hesitantly raised his ungloved hands. This was going to save the world, and cement his place as its savior. This was the reason his master had risked their lives. This was the reason Piter had appeared to tell him he was the one destined to close the Gate. He was an adept now and about to fulfill his destiny.

Arek's resolve crystallized and he thrust his hand forward, into the portal. Black fire blossomed at the contact, power coursing through the connection and into his body. It burned inward through every pore, consumed by his dark aura. It filled him with raw power, energy that for a moment seemed to outshine the sun. The entire fortress heaved as if a giant moved beneath the ground and from deep within him came a sigh of ecstasy, given voice by the same wind he imagined would whisper his true name.

He took a breath and could feel a knot of power within him unravel, its energy expanding in waves. The ground heaved again in response. Something had come undone— unlocked— he could feel it uncurling, like a flower opening to the sun. He drew another breath, filled with power, then heard the wind's call.

"Arek."

The voice was female and beautiful, yet it whispered his name, not some hidden eldritch appellation of power. He opened his eyes and looked into the radiance surrounding him. In that place of light he saw a woman walking slowly toward him.

She was tall, regal, with skin the softest blue. Her black hair was tied up into an intricate weave, held in place by a silver circlet. Her body stood draped in silver chainmail, accented by sapphire gemstones. For a moment he thought he saw enormous wings behind her, but as she stepped into the light the illusion disappeared. She reached out a gloved hand and delicately stroked Arek's face.

"It is with happiness that I greet you." Her voice was soothing, luxurious, and soft. Her cerulean eyes danced with joy as she looked down upon Arek. "You are the salvation of our world."

Arek looked at this goddess, this being that had come to life before him. He couldn't believe it. His dreams of power, of conquest, of importance, seemed to pale before the reality of her. She was more immediate, more real than any dream he'd ever had. He felt himself small in her presence, a supplicant under her imperious gaze.

He looked up at her and whispered, "Who are you?"

She reached down and carefully raised him from kneeling, though he hadn't realized he'd done so.

"I am Lilyth, Celestial of the Aeris, and the Lady of Flame. I have been called Sacmys, Kore, and a thousand other names since the First Time. I am the Eye of the Sun and Eternal."

Arek was confused. The Gate was supposed to have shut. *Did she say, the Lady? What happened?* As if in answer, dozens of shades appeared all people from his past. Did this mean they had all perished? Impossible! They stood silent, watching him like statues paying homage to the swathe of death in his wake.

His mind rebelled at the sheer number of dead now surrounding him. He could see Adept Thera at their lead, and worse, dozens of children! In front of them came the only other person he'd seen killed, Sargin, whole now, who stepped forward and bowed. Arek took a step back at the sight of him, his mind overwhelmed by the magnitude of death that had occurred over just a few short days.

"You have accomplished the impossible, Master," Sargin said in a gruff voice, still filled with hate.

When Arek didn't say anything, the shade Sargin continued, "For you, the Aeris have waited."

Arek shook his head, then looked back at the goddess before him. "Who... am I?" he asked.

"Arek," Lilyth said with compassion in her eyes, "you are my son."

The Eye of the Sun

JOURNAL ENTRY 22

Forgive me the delays in writing, though you do not perceive the passage of time between these sentences. For me, more weeks have passed, and they have been busy.

Malak has grown to fulfill the role of my defender. I have bestowed upon him the title, Firstmark, for being the first to take up the shield I had marked with protective runes that night when he came to my defense. Now his role is to protect my castle and the surrounding environs.

My firstmark speaks of building a stronghold that will allow me to work in peace. He was also the first imp to speak, though to look at him now, one does not see the tiny creature that used to hide within my cocoon. I cannot bring myself to call him and his kin "imps" any longer. That word does not suffice and they have earned another name for their service.

I think I shall call them "elf" or "elves," a play on his very first word, and homage to our own children's tales. And they are useful! Unlike those creatures, my elves are mythborn and war-forged.

I saw a flash and a rift open and close, not too far off. I send my elves to investigate. We will see a new order brought to this world, and I shall be its ruler.

Journal Entry 22

BERNAL'S QUEST

When they are ready,
give your offspring over to training by another.
No father can strike with the force
necessary to breed expertise,
and with his love,
condemns his child to an early grave.
—Davyd Dreys, Memoirs

ven as Ash made ready his final preparations to defend the portal, the king angled his way toward the main council chamber, where the Far'anthi Stones were located. He turned down corridors, noting patrols at each intersection, then finally into the hallway that led to the chamber itself.

As he neared, he could see a group of guards inspecting the area. He came up on the ranking soldier and asked, "What happened here?" A booted foot stuck out from the chamber doorway.

"Four dead, sire. Don't know who killed them, but it was done quick. Knife thrust to the throat or heart," answered the man-at-arms. "We'll clean this up and station more men."

"Put every man within sight of at least two others. If someone goes missing, raise the alarm," the king said.

The man-at-arms saluted and went to see to the king's orders.

Bernal sighed, then moved into the room. The bodies of four of his guards lay in pools of their own blood, and a sadness fell upon him at their sacrifice. These were the men Kisan had spoken about. However, like the missing attackers in his own encounter, the body of the man Kisan said she'd killed was nowhere to be seen, which left the king with an unshakeable sense of foreboding.

He crossed the chamber to a wall holding an ancient sword and shield. Reaching up, he took down the Galadine blade, *Azani*, its straight double-edged blade sharp enough to shave with. He grabbed the matching scabbard and sheathed it in a single smooth motion. He then strapped the shield across his back, its golden lion framed by twin lightning bolts rampant on its black face. That accomplished, he walked over to the table and scooped up Valor and a quiver of arrows.

He looked at his men with steel in his eyes. He carried with him now the weapons of his father and it filled him with a sense of purpose. "Down the stairwell. We head for the cisterns."

"Aye, sire." The men didn't hesitate, but made their way out of the room and into the halls. As they exited, a group of guards turned the corner and hailed the king.

"Sire, a message from the watch commander," a lieutenant said, saluting.

"Go ahead," said the king.

"There are reports of things in the lower levels," he said sheepishly.

"Things?" asked the king.

"Creatures, sire. They attack on sight, and—they are like smoke. Our weapons pass through them." The lieutenant looked down, uncertain if his report made any sense. "I wish we knew more. Men have gone missing."

The king pursed his lips, thinking. Infiltration of the fortress would have to be done through the water induction channels. The ancient cisterns and waterways that snaked under Bara'cor created hundreds of forgotten passages. Luckily, none of these tunnels ran close to the front wall. Instead they snaked back and down, following the switchbacks of Lands Edge Pass. Given that the remaining assassin had been making his way there, the king knew this should be his destination as well.

"I want two squads at each cistern entryway and a platoon of men at the entrance to both stairwells. I want at least two men in sight of both teams. I'll check the catacombs, and then join you at the main cistern entrance. Signal we may have intruders. Don't let anyone travel alone. Also, inform the watch commander that Armsmark Rillaran has been promoted to Firstmark. He'll be taking command of our defense. "The lieutenant saluted and said, "Yes, sire."

"Creatures," Bernal said, turning to his men. "You boys ready to do some fighting?"

The men smiled, nodding to their king. More than a few rechecked their weapons and armor. The king saw the good-natured way these men fell into their routine and had a sudden pang of sadness. Not all of them would see tomorrow if the fortress was breached.

He shook the feeling off, saying, "My son is down there somewhere. I intend to find him before his mother hears about this. I'm counting on all of you to make sure she doesn't find out." Bernal smiled as he looked at his men, his jest already easing tension and lending confidence.

Without another word, he moved down the stairwell and into the darkness of the lower levels.

Bernal's Quest

LILYTH'S GATE

We cannot know what destiny will bring,
be it block, strike, victory, or defeat.
Accept things as they come,
but keep an open mind.
Winds often shift and change.
—Kensei Shun, *The Lens of Shields*

What?" Arek wasn't sure he'd heard her correctly. "How can that be?" The woman smiled, revealing perfect, white teeth. The smile reached her eyes, which twinkled with a mixture of kindness and amusement. "You of all people should not doubt what is possible."

"Wh-why?" he stammered in reply.

"Because you have achieved so much. More than many gave you credit for." She turned to look at the assembled shades, recrimination in her gaze. They withered at her sight, falling back to their knees as if in real pain, arms up in supplication.

"Wait," Arek said. He looked upon the shades with pity. "They did their best." He licked his lips, his mind racing. They seemed truly in fear, a fact that made him more uneasy. He'd only interacted with Piter, who had certainly never shown fear around him, only disdain, cruelty, or anger.

Lilyth turned her eyes back to Arek and said, "Mercy is a sign of strength. It is far easier to strike, than to withhold. Well done, my son." She smiled again, and Arek could feel his heart lighten as joy washed through him. It passed quickly, like warmth when the sun faded behind clouds, leaving him wishing for its gentle touch again.

"I still don't understand. How could you be my mother?" Arek tried putting the pieces together, but too much information was missing.

Lilyth moved down a step or two on the pyramid, tentatively at first, as if testing the waters of an unknown sea. Then, when nothing happened, she stood straighter, surveying the scene like a queen. Her head tilted and one eyebrow lifted in acknowledgement at the sight of Arek's two companions. Ignoring his question, she asked, "Your friends?"

"Yes. Yetteje, uh . . . Princess of EvenSea," he finished lamely, unable to dredge up the royal family name at the moment, his eidetic memory failing him more often as of late. He felt his face go red and hid it with a look at his feet. "The other is Niall Galadine," Arek finished, still focusing on the stone blocks making up the pyramid he stood upon.

Lilyth drew a quick breath of surprise and looked at Arek, then looked back down at the pair, one hand coming to her throat. "He is here? How . . . fortunate."

Arek gathered himself, then moved to where he could address Lilyth face to face. "You're not what I expected. The Gate should've closed."

Lilyth stared at Niall for a moment longer, then turned her attention back to Arek and said, "Of course. You deserve answers."

She beckoned to them both with a delicate hand, "Please, come join me. What I have to say concerns you both."

Niall immediately obeyed the demon-queen's summons, coming up the pyramid at a jog.

Arek looked at the woman who claimed to be his mother and saw her wink at him in response, a conspiratorial promise that he alone would learn more. She seemed extraordinarily pleased, and a small part of him not basking in her attention began to worry. He quickly silenced that small voice, unwilling to ruin the start of the glorious destiny he so longed for and deserved.

As Niall neared them he looked about in confusion. "What am I doing here?"

Lilyth laughed. "You certainly do not carry the potent blood of the Aeris, son of Galadine."

Her reply at first sounded like humor, yet beneath it ran an undercurrent of scorn. Her voice focused on the moment, its pureness like the sound a fine steel blade makes when drawn. It wasn't lost on Arek though, that Lilyth was far more dangerous. Her ability to set them at ease meant he couldn't trust himself to see the dangers surrounding them. One slip, and something told him she'd have no qualms in ending them all.

Yetteje hadn't moved, still frozen in place. He wanted some answers, but the idea of asking Lilyth now made his palms clammy and his heart race. *Perhaps a different tack.*

"Mother, please tell me about all this," Arek said, motioning around him.

He'd used the word "mother" on purpose, and it had the desired effect. Lilyth's pose softened. She turned to look at him, her eyes alight with joy.

"I . . . *of course*." She smiled, and then crossed her arms with one graceful hand under her chin, "How much like your father you are." Her inspection continued from head to toe.

"My father?" Arek looked at her in shock. "My father is here?"

Lilyth laughed. "I should think so." She moved closer, her blue skin giving off a palpable heat. "Many eons ago, we floated carefree in the Void, carrying out tasks assigned to us by an ancient being known as the Sovereign. Simple were our pleasures and we stayed to ourselves."

Her gaze narrowed and to Arek she somehow grew colder. "But we always heard the voice of the Sovereign, he who ensured we focused and completed our tasks so that our slumbering brothers and sisters could arrive on these shores safely. His voice gave us meaning."

Arek looked at Niall, who still hadn't moved. His eyes had glazed over, as if he were ensorcelled. He assumed Yetteje was in the same state. The gnawing fear returned, a feeling he was missing something vital. The only way he'd gain more information would be to keep Lilyth talking.

He put on a smile and said, "Continue, please."

"Man's yearning gave us shape. At first we were consumed by the millions, wasted as spells of power and other manifestations of their will. And yet, we did not die out. In fact, more of us came into existence to replace those who'd answered the call. Dreams created us, and those of us who could maintain our identity grew stronger."

Lilyth paused, her attention turning to Niall, and her gaze grew wistful, but there remained a hard edge to it. "We served unseen, as spirits and legends of your world."

When Arek looked confused, Lilyth tilted her head to the side and smiled. "Arek, we are ethereal beings, our lives are the very essence of what you think of as magic. Men's strength of will combined with their myths, shape and direct us. We are fairies, ghosts, angels," smiling, "and sometimes, demons."

"We have had many names through the eons, always standing at your right hand, unseen, unappreciated except by a very few. We thought the people of Edyn knew of us, but this was not true. They molded our essence blindly; myths and legends are our parents, apathy is our end."

"You're myths, come true?"

"Some are. I'm surely more than that now. We are gods and goddesses, slaves to whim no longer. We are powerful, for we *are* the Way, just as you have willed us to be. The Sovereign seeks to destroy this, and us."

Arek looked at her, careful to hide the stunned look on his face. "Why does Sovereign want to destroy you?"

Lilyth shrugged, "I do not know. Perhaps we have not grown as he wishes. Perhaps he believes we are flawed. Regardless, I oppose him. Thus, we need your help."

His mind raced, but he didn't need to think too hard to ask his next question.

"Me?"

"Yes, you." Lilyth said with sadness in her eyes. "You are our last, best hope."

If what she said was true, then who knew how powerful the Aeris might be? They were literally gods, limited only by what people believed.

When it seemed she would say no more, Arek asked, "I'm that important?"

Lilyth had been inspecting the massive chamber within which her pyramid stood. At Arek's question she looked back at him and said, "Arek, you are special in so many ways. Your destiny is far greater than these petty battles, for you will unite our worlds."

Her face lit up with another smile, "But this isn't the place to explain how, or why. It will be easier for me to show you. Will you accompany me?"

Arek looked about, not entirely sure she could mean anything else but the Gate. That was something he wasn't sure was in the best interests of anyone on this side. Still, he had to keep her talking. He took a deep breath, more than anything to settle his stomach. The energy he'd recently absorbed and various pastries were conspiring to try and make him sick.

He took another deep breath and asked, "Where?"

Lilyth turned her gaze upon the portal, her expression an equal mixture of joy and weariness. She raised her hand and with a gesture the blackness cleared. Beyond it, Arek could see green fields, crystalline blue lakes, and white, snow-capped mountains. Sunlight sparkled off the water like golden jewels and lit the snowy peaks in an outline of fire, delineating them from the firmament itself. It was a land more beautiful than he had ever seen. It felt good, calm, and somehow . . . right.

"Home," Lilyth said. "We live in a land of beauty and peace. No wars ravage us, no sieges. We do not covet our neighbor's wealth nor destroy what we do not understand. We are a society of learning, of conscience, and of honor."

She took Arek by both shoulders, turning him to face her. Her next statement hit him like a granite block. "Arek, you are a prince in our world."

A. . . what? When he recovered, he could feel her gaze penetrating his own. Something stirred within him, something he didn't understand at first, but as moments passed became more and more clear. She was *proud of him.* The feeling, the reward that someone considered him important, somehow special, once again overcame the small voice of caution.

Arek looked back at the portal, mesmerized by the images of Lilyth's world. White clouds in blue skies cast shadows onto fields of yellow flowers. It looked like springtime, with a warm sun shining onto green forests fed by the rich, dark loam of the earth. This was a land so infused with health he could almost feel it.

"A prince?" he whispered.

Lilyth smiled, placing a gentle hand on her son's shoulder. "Come with me. There is so much to tell you, so much to explain." She looked sidelong at him, then leaned in close and whispered, "You can meet your father. He will be overjoyed to see you, at last."

Arek's head turned. "He lives there?"

"He will meet us there. Will you come with me?"

Arek took a deep breath. No one had ever made him feel special. *Not even Silbane,* he admitted.

His ineptitude with magic had somehow become important, and now he was being offered a chance to learn why. The answers to his many questions lay through the Gate. There was only one way to find out. He looked at this woman, this perfect being he'd secretly begun to believe could actually be his mother. Was that so impossible?

"I will come, but what about Niall and Yetteje? Will they be safe? What about my master, Silbane?" Arek asked.

Lilyth smiled again, then said, "Niall should come with us. He will be a boon companion, and your father will want to meet him, too."

She motioned to Niall, who stepped forward woodenly. "Hold his hand, for he does not have the makings of the Aeris within him and is overwhelmed by the eldritch currents flowing around us. Your touch will help him. Once you are through the portal, he will be fine."

She walked them toward the portal. "Do not worry, Arek. Your ability to disrupt magic won't affect my Gate for very long. Take Niall's hand. I'll be right behind you. I need to ensure Bara'cor's safety."

Arek looked at Lilyth and the voice within him whispered again, *Don't trust her.* Yet he found himself nodding and smiling. One thought had grown to override the rest, drowning any doubts or concerns; *he would finally meet his father!* He took Niall's hand in his own ungloved one and addressed Lilyth, saying, "Please see that Yetteje and my master remain safe."

He then looked up at the apex and took a step, climbing towards it with a single-minded focus. He paused at the entrance for a moment, before disappearing through it with the Prince of Bara'cor.

Lilyth's Gate

JOURNAL ENTRY 23

An event has occurred I thought not possible. She is here!

Malak found her when the rift opened, mortally wounded. I have brought her back from the brink, but still she does not stir. I withhold her name, for fear she is a figment of my imagination. Her presence, if real, is welcome.

Malak and the elves have evolved to be armored and blue-skinned, with fearsome horns and barbed tails. They are made for war, their skin hard and obdurate like stone. They defend me as their father . . . and more appear every day.

Each comes before me and kneels. I feed it a drop of my blood, picked from my desiccated finger, a consecration of sorts. It seems to give them power, life, and utter loyalty.

These new ones are still small, and each seems attached to one of the four elements. Those who defend are stone. Those who scout are made of wood and air. I expect some of fire and water will also appear, once my thoughts turn that way.

My mind believes this is how they are made and follows the same comfortable path to success. It is that, or my elves are bringing forth more with thoughts of their own. Regardless, I am involved in the birth of a new race of beings. My elves are proof against the Aeris demons, and their numbers are growing exponentially. Soon, they will be an army, and I will have to decide their purpose. And mine.

I go now to see to my injured companion, mending slowly under my inept hands . . .

Journal Entry 23

CLOSE THE BREACH

We don't rise to the level of our expectations,
We fall to the level of our training.
—Tir Combat Academy, Basic Forms & Stances

Ash watched the line, making sure no one stood in another's field of fire. He distributed arrows and helped stabilize weakened barriers. The men had shifted a large granite table onto its edge, letting the tabletop face the portal, a few paces back from the black maw. They slid spear shafts under so it sat on makeshift rollers, allowing Jebida and those who returned with him to exit while the defenders could roll the heavy table back to cover the entrance. Ash knew Kisan said the portal would close, but didn't want to take the chance.

Heavy breathing coming towards them signaled a runner from the watch commander had arrived to relay the king's most recent orders. After hearing them, Ash turned and motioned to Sergeant Stemmer.

She snapped her fingers and whistled, then said, "Men, gather round."

The four squads left to guard this chamber formed a loose circle, some taking a knee. When the sergeant nodded their readiness, Ash stepped up and said, "The king seeks his son near the cisterns. However, reports have come from the watch commander that creatures have infiltrated us from these same lower levels. I know our first thought will be to rush to our king's aid, but he has asked we remain here.

Our orders are to hold this portal until two allies led by Firstmark Naserith, return with information vital to this fortress's survival. In his absence and to maintain continuity of command, I have been asked to temporarily take the rank of Firstmark. Questions?"

One man raised his hand and asked, "Why don't we just take as many as we can through the portal and bring them back?"

Ash nodded and said, "Good question." He jutted his chin and said, "That works if they're alive. If they've been killed, we'd be risking getting trapped on the other side, surrounded by the nomad horde." He paused, then raised an eyebrow and smiled before saying, "But I'm tempted. Anything else? We've got to get this room ready for the party."

A few men-at-arms laughed, but within a few moments it seemed everyone was just focused on getting back to their stations. With a nod from Ash, Sergeant Stemmer said, "Take your positions." She waited a moment before saying, "Do you know what's special about this room, what's going to protect us from the accursed magic, and whatever creatures try and get past us?"

The men didn't answer. They didn't know, but even if they had they were seasoned professionals. If it was important, their leader would tell them. To the men's confused looks, Stemmer said, "It's us… we're special because we're family. When you think about those you've left back home, you're also thinking about everyone in this room. We are brothers and sisters to each other, and in our house, we hold the line!"

The reply was a deafening cheer followed by a fist to chest salute that rattled armor. Ash looked at the men, noting their eyes hadn't wavered. No one looked to be in doubt. They hadn't reacted to his information with anything other than their commitment to follow orders. Pride welled up inside him then and he said, "We'll stand here together. Questions?"

A man named Lanis raised his hand and after Ash's acknowledgement asked, "Four squads to hold this room, sir?"

Ash smiled and said, "The portal was barely big enough to let the firstmark through. We have reinforcements aplenty," he nodded at the hallway where men were gathering, "but this holding action requires our ability to position ourselves and deal with single or perhaps double attackers at a time." He looked at Sergeant Stemmer.

The sergeant's strident voice finished what Ash had started, "All right, you heard the Firstmark, take your positions! Our orders are simple. We stand. We hold." Satisfied everyone knew what they needed to do, she turned and signaled the firstmark that they stood ready.

Nods came from the squads, more meaningful than a cheer in some ways. It showed they knew what they were being asked to do and would do it, even if it meant their lives. Lanis nodded in thanks, then took a light punch from a bowmate, probably for attracting attention from the sergeant. Ash watched and smiled, for some things never changed.

Then an excited voice cried, "The portal, sir. It glows!"

Ash got behind the main barrier, grabbing a crossbow. He folded the stock, cocking it in one smooth motion and centering a bolt. When he was ready, he took a deep breath then leaned around the corner of the barrier just in time to see a purple flash and three figures appear from the blackness.

Ash immediately recognized the first as Kisan. The woman looked tossed and banged about, with soot and ash covering her clothes. A cut ran across her cheek, bleeding slightly.

A *thwang* sounded next to him as a soldier fired his crossbow.

Ash screamed, "Hold your fire!" even as Kisan turned and deflected the bolt before it hit her, shattering it into pieces in a silver flash.

The other man coming through the portal had crouched at the sound of the bowstring, but hadn't otherwise reacted, his face measured and calm. His eyes drank in the details of the room. Ash saw him note the position of the men and the exit. Having met Kisan, Ash knew the second man had already calculated how to kill them and get out of the room most efficiently. *This must be Silbane.*

Silbane carried a body over his shoulder, an unconscious figure dressed in red robes. He made his way over to Kisan, then dumped the robed figure on the ground. He scanned the assembled men with a piercing intensity in his faded blue eyes. When his gaze came to rest on Ash, he stepped forward and raised a hand, "Firstmark, we are well met. I'm Silbane."

Ash stepped around the barrier and nodded. "Where's Jebida?"

Silbane looked down, then at Kisan, before looking back at Ash. "We saw him fall, but with him died the nomad chieftain. He accomplished his goal."

Ash stepped back, stunned. A lifetime of memories under Jebida's tutelage threatened to overwhelm him, but he knew his men needed him to stay focused. He looked down and let go of a breath he hadn't realized he was holding. He didn't have the luxury to mourn the firstmark now. His heart, a soldier's heart, hardened and he moved his thoughts automatically to tactics.

"I want to hear more, but later," Ash said. "First, I must ask you to close the portal. It is an entry point to Bara'cor we cannot defend indefinitely. I only have sixteen men who can fit in here before our position is strategically unsound."

Silbane turned and looked at the portal in surprise. He looked back at Kisan and said, "It should've closed when I came through."

"Unless Scythe did something," Kisan replied.

Before Silbane could answer, a nomad spear flew through, narrowly missing them both. Then dozens of arrows came flying out, swishing through the air with feathered death, most bouncing off the large granite table, but a few sticking into wooden barriers. Some caught a few men of Bara'cor unawares, slicing through flesh, but no one was seriously wounded.

Everyone scattered for cover as Ash yelled, "Hold your fire! Wait till we have targets!"

* * * * *

Dozens of bows bent but held, unwaveringly pointed at the black portal. Those who had crossbows settled their arms on sacks and ledges, keeping their sights trained on whatever emerged from the opening. Silbane grabbed the unconscious form of Scythe and tossed him near Kisan's cover, then joined her there.

"Scythe wouldn't have left you the Finder unless it let him open a way into Bara'cor," Kisan said. "He seemed eager we escape."

Silbane raised an eyebrow. "Escape? I think he was more eager to kill us."

More arrows from the nomads flew in via the black door, impacting the barriers and granite table, lodging into wood or bouncing off stone. This time, however, no one from Bara'cor suffered injury. Of the nomads, there still was no sign.

"No," Kisan countered, "he kept encouraging us to leave."

Silbane looked at Kisan, realizing she was correct. Scythe had seemed concerned that they hadn't escaped sooner. "If he's somehow propped the portal open, I only just started researching that aspect of portals. I don't know how to undo what he's done."

Kisan smiled and pointed at Scythe. "He does."

Silbane immediately knew what the other meant and said, "Defend me." He then quickly put his fingers on Scythe's forehead. Instantly his consciousness dove into the technique, *Eye of the Sky*, mindreading Scythe's memories.

Close the Breach

Kisan leapt up, blurring with speed to Ash's position. "We need to hold this line, Firstmark. Silbane attempts to close the portal."

"I understand," he replied, motioning to a sergeant, who began barking orders. While those on the flanks set cover, those behind the granite table braced. At the sergeant's signal, they tilted it back and two men shoved more rollers under the lip. Then they braced again and pushed, rolling the large table forward. The tabletop faced the open portal. If they could roll it far enough, they could drop it at the entrance and create a stone wall that would be difficult to pass.

Dozens more arrows flew out, bouncing off the granite surface. The men quickly replaced rollers that came out back to the front. The table continued to move, closing the distance from six paces to three. One more push and they would succeed.

Ash gave another signal and the men braced again and pushed. The table rolled to cover the portal hole. They pulled back and the table legs acted as braces, making it an effective wall.

A ragged cheer went up, but Silbane still knelt, his eyes shut. Whatever he was doing, he needed to do it soon. This temporary measure wouldn't last against a real effort by the nomads. Kisan hadn't forgotten Rai'stahn was just on the other side.

As if answering her fears, a mighty blow struck the table. Cracks appeared and the men's eyes widened in fear. The barrier was thick granite, heavy enough that even with rollers it had taken many of them to move. Whatever had struck it from the other end had pushed it back a hand's width.

The blow struck again, reverberating the table like a gong made of stone. Chips fell and the cracks widened. One of the bracing legs cracked. The sergeant moved forward to that end and screamed, "Get up and put your backs into it! Brace!"

"Silbane!" Kisan shouted. "We don't have much time."

Still, Silbane didn't stir. Kisan moved toward him when the table was hit again. The room shook from the force of the blow and the table cracked more, some pieces falling in chunks from the back. The cracked leg snapped off.

The sergeant screamed to her men to brace that side and a half dozen scrambled to obey, but the granite was heavy and not enough could find purchase to apply their strength. Only one leg remained, bracing the entire weight of the table on it, and as a result the table began to list to one side.

Kisan slid to Silbane's side. "We have to close the portal, now!"

If she broke Silbane's contact, it could destroy Scythe's mind and leave nothing to recover. However, the table would not hold and if Rai'stahn came through, everyone would die.

She took a moment, then made the decision. She had no love for Scythe and decided leaving him in a comatose state would be fair recompense for closing the portal before the nomads or worse came through. She grabbed Silbane and pulled.

A yellow flash of power discharged at the break, hurling both Silbane and Kisan from the point of disconnection. The flash blinded Kisan, but she heard Silbane gasp. She rolled over and grabbed the other master, feeding him whatever energy she had as she mindspoke him to come to her voice.

Slowly, Silbane's body calmed. He took a deep, shuddering breath and opened his eyes. At first he looked bewildered, then she watched as his faded blue gaze sharpened on her own. A blink told her he'd fully recovered and was now as dangerous as ever.

A concussion of force hit the table, blasting the granite backward into a pulverized explosion of rock and dust. The men directly behind it were killed instantly, the power of the blast hurling their bodies away like tinder. The granite table fell, crushing most of those who had attempted to brace it.

Ash and three of his men had escaped injury, having been in flanking positions. Still, the force of the blast threw them away from the black portal to land painfully on their backs, their ears ringing.

The portal hole began to widen! Through it ran half a dozen nomads, short blades and shields ready. Behind them came the armored form of Rai'stahn, his yellow eyes gleaming like gold from the darkness.

Kisan grabbed Silbane and yelled, "Close it!"

Silbane looked at the portal and said, "I Saw . . . lines. If I can snap them . . . " His eyes closed, his face bent in concentration.

Rai'stahn reached forward, emerging from the other side. Just as he did so, the portal opening snapped shut over the dragon-knight's outstretched arm, leaving six nomad archers in an indefensible position within the center of the room. The remnants of Bara'cor's forces didn't waste a moment, firing a barrage of arrows and bolts. Soon those six lay dead or dying. A sudden silence fell over the room.

Kisan fell back, looking at the carnage before her. Along with Ash, no more than four people were alive. Only the flickering light from a torch showed the vast destruction the room had suffered. Nothing was untouched. Survivors rolled, spitting stone dust from their mouths and shaking rock fragments from their hair.

On the ground where the portal had been lay a single black armored arm ending in a taloned fist of mail, still smoking from where it'd been cut from the great dragon's body.

Then the floor itself moved like an ocean wave. It caused those left standing to lose their footing. Slowly they regained their balance, then looked at each other.

Kisan moved closer to Silbane, who was attempting to get up. She helped him, asking, "You all right?"

Silbane nodded, but a look of concentration came over him. He knelt next to the red-robed mage, his eyes focused on something that looked like it lay below the man's skin. In a quick motion, he stabbed three times with his fingers, locking prana points. Then he checked the metal torc on the man's neck, where it still sat fastened securely. He tested it, confirming it couldn't be undone by anyone of magical Talent, before getting up.

"Good," stated Kisan, not surprised Silbane used the Blood of Death to lock the mage's prana points. They couldn't keep Scythe unconscious forever.

Silbane nodded, still not saying anything, but something in his eyes made Kisan uneasy. Part of her had the irrational thought that it had to do with her orders concerning Arek, but that was impossible. Knowing Silbane's looks, it likely had to do with the red-robed lunatic now their prisoner. Before she could ask him about it, he made his way over to Ash. "We need your help to find Arek. We can't use our powers to sense him."

Ash looked at the man before him and asked, "Who is the prisoner with you?"

Silbane flicked a glance at Scythe and said, "I thought he was the true force behind the nomads, but now I know differently. He is dangerous, however, and should be guarded at all times." He turned, looking Ash fully in the eyes. "Where is my apprentice?"

Ash suddenly noticed Silbane was taller than him. His pale blue eyes bore through him, as if he didn't exist in any meaningful way to this master of the Way. Ash tried to meet his stare, but couldn't. "The king followed an assassin who went to the lower level cisterns. Guards reported that your apprentice was with the prince." He called over the sergeant for her report.

"Six of us, including you and me, and the three from the portal are all that's left alive, sir. I've reformed us into one squad."

"What about reinforcements?"

"Plenty, but how fast do you want to move, sir?"

"Fast, Sergeant." Ash put a hand on the woman's shoulder. "You did well. We held the room and now we'll defend our king. Secure the prisoner," he said, indicating Scythe, "and assign a detail here and along our route. Let the others get back to their normal stations on the wall."

"Yes, sir," the sergeant said. She made her way over to Scythe and propped him up, then motioned to her men to carry out the orders given by the firstmark. It looked to Kisan as if Scythe was slowly regaining consciousness.

"You can't sense anything about your apprentice?" Ash asked Silbane.

Silbane shook his head, "We never could." He closed his eyes, then opened them and looked at Kisan, who had come to stand beside them. "But I sense something else. Someone—with immense power."

Kisan closed her eyes. "I sense it too," she said with surprise. "It's far from here, though, and lower."

Silbane looked at the firstmark and said, "We travel together, your men and our prisoner. Stand ready. Something terrible may have already happened."

DEVASTATION

Kill one and you are merely a man.
Kill everyone and you are a god.
The difference is merely in numbers.
—Lore Father Argus Rillaran, The Way

he demon-queen turned and looked at Yetteje. The princess could only watch, frozen, as Lilyth walked down the pyramid, coming at last to stand directly before her. A soft blue hand rose and gracefully stroked her face. At Lilyth's touch her jaw snapped painfully back into place, and an itch crawled up her cheek and into her forehead. She could feel her skin coming together, which meant the slash down her eye had been healed too. Yetteje strained but her body was enthralled, unable to move without the demon-queen's permission.

With a small gesture, Yetteje felt herself freed, and she stumbled back. Her hand came up to feel her face, working her jaw open and shut. *Almost no pain.* She then checked the slash, touching the thin scar that now cut through her eyebrow and down her cheek.

"You can't be Arek's mother," she challenged flatly, "you know that, right? It's a delusion you're peddling because you need something, and he seems desperate to—"

"Power is never about instilling fear, princess." The demon-queen moved a bit closer, breathing through her nostrils, her eyes half-lidded slits, like a snake catching the scent of something wonderful in the air.

Goading Lilyth to anger would loosen the demon-queen's tongue, but the cat-like expression on her face told Yetteje in no uncertain terms this was a game with dire consequences if she stepped too far. *Ah well,* she thought, *and here I go . . .*

She pointed to her cheek, "And if you're so all-powerful, why leave a scar?"

Lilyth smiled at her contemptuously, the kind of smile normally reserved for those who were naïve or stupid. Then the demon-queen raised a finger, leaning in. Her soft lips just brushed the outer curve of Yetteje's ear, sending a heady rush of pleasure that made the princess's heart skip. Lilyth's voice whispered wisdom Tej knew was meant for her ears alone. "Beauty is *magnified* by imperfections."

She turned Yetteje slowly so they were facing each other again. Her eyes turned a hard, deep blue. "You heard everything, I trust?"

The moment dissipated like a spell cast over her, and Yetteje found herself blinking to clear her head. "What did you do? Where did Niall go?" she demanded, gathering her wits. She'd heard the exchange, and wondered whether it was bravery or stupidity on Arek's part to step through that gate.

"No fear," said Lilyth. "Good. I promised Arek I would ensure Bara'cor's safety. Stand and bear witness to the true power of your people's faith in me. Watch as my might is brought to bear."

Through Lilyth's magic, Yetteje's perception expanded to see both what was happening here and outside of Bara'cor. She saw Lilyth raise her hand, then clench it into a fist. White radiance burst into being, along with the sound of lightning striking. An itchy feeling, this time like ants crawling on skin, consumed Yetteje and her hair stood on end.

With a groan and a thunderclap the radiance bent inward, becoming brighter as it coalesced in Lilyth's fist like a shining blue-white star. Outside, the world paused, as if holding its collective breath.

Then Lilyth's star exploded in a blinding flash of pure white, shaking the very stones of Land's Edge itself. The cliff walls buckled, shattering the vertical face of rock with a crack. A thousand tons of stone and dirt rained down upon the switchback trail, collapsing the pass leading between the lowlands and Bara'cor in a landslide of destruction.

The ring of power flashed outward, igniting the very air into argent brilliance. It broke the earth apart where it touched, shattering rock and stone and pulling the ground apart, breaking it into chasms and fissures as it continued to grow, encompassing the nomad army and the lands surrounding Bara'cor.

Then, with a groan and a thrum that ran through Yetteje's very bones, the conflagration stopped its expansion, pausing for a moment, as if surveying the devastation it'd wrought. Another thunderclap boomed and the circle of power collapsed in on itself, dragging everything and everyone caught within it.

Lilyth looked at Yetteje and said, "The lucky ones are dead already and soon will join my army. The rest of Edyn will pay obeisance to the Lady walking amongst them again."

* * * * *

Across the Shattered Sea, Lore Father Giridian looked to the northwest, in the direction of the Altan Wastes and his lost adepts. He couldn't see Bara'cor from here, but could feel the explosion of power. He drew a shuddering breath, then reached out to Silbane and Kisan, only to find a blank spot—nothing—where Bara'cor once stood.

He looked back at Dragor and the newly ascended Jesyn, her black adept's uniform crisp and clean, cinched tightly around her waist. They prepared to investigate the ancient city of Dawnlight.

"Bara'cor's lost," he said. "Something's happened and it's disappeared from my Sight."

Dragor turned his eyes northwest at this, squinting as if he could see all the way to the fortress. After just a moment he shook his head and said, "We should make haste and find Themun's brother, if he lives."

Tomas stepped forward and hugged Jesyn. "I wish I were going."

Jesyn hugged him back. "I wish you were going, too, but get better and test. When I return, you'll have your true name and will be wearing the Black."

Giridian nodded. "Jesyn is correct. You are almost healed and ready to take on the role of Adept." He smiled at the boy, then turned his attention back to Jesyn and Dragor. "You both take care of yourselves. This is a reconnaissance mission; don't take risks."

Dragor nodded once, and then motioned to Jesyn to follow. He clasped arms with the lore father in farewell then said, "We should make landfall within a few days. I'll contact you as necessary."

Their good-byes said, the two adepts made their way from the courtyard to the shore and a waiting boat. Giridian turned and moved to stand by Tomas. He put an arm around the boy's shoulders and gave him a reassuring squeeze.

"Don't worry about them."

Tomas watched their retreating forms and said, "There are so few of us now."

Giridian looked sidelong at the last of the initiates ready to test and said, "This has always been true."

His mind still reeled from the change at the desert fortress. The boy was correct. They would need every able adept to face what may have been unleashed at Bara'cor.

* * * * *

Rai'stahn looked in disbelief at his missing arm, before the blast sent him tumbling. Nevertheless, he wasn't without power of his own. He grabbed the earth with his good hand and felt for the Way, bringing his full might to bear. The wash of power from Lilyth's spell bent and then diverted around him much like water flowed around a stone. His power was a raw use of the Way, not limited by spells or techniques. Yet there were limits to even his might, as Silbane had so aptly demonstrated.

Those nomads, who didn't die in the chasms fell instead to the following maelstrom, smashed by the deadly explosion of sand and rock that scoured living flesh to the bone. The earth, commanded by Lilyth's will, blasted outward and then inward in an implosion that sucked everything back towards Bara'cor.

Rai'stahn looked around, his golden gaze more radiant than the sun. He could feel the power of the land in him now, making him stronger, better. The boy was no longer draining him and with knowledge that came the sudden realization of just how weak he'd become over the years as that thing shared his Isle.

It had been so insidious, so gradual that only now did he see the full effect Arek's presence had upon him. Dread filled him then, eclipsed only by his anger. His eyes swept the carnage, watching as the force of Lilyth's might obliterated those without power such as his. Not all perished, however. A few caught in his aura of protection had survived.

I hath been a fool, feeding that thing for all these years . . .

When the air cleared, the land surrounding the fortress was barren, wiped clean. What were once sand dunes was now bare rock, black chasms and fissures crisscrossing its barren floor, leading back to the walls of Bara'cor itself, still somehow intact.

The great dragon only needed a moment to surmise why. The fortress stood sheathed in a glowing field of blue, scintillating in the sun. Everything and anyone near the fortress had been sucked back into those shimmering walls, leaving no trace they'd ever existed.

Rai'stahn let loose a snarl, knowing he could not find and destroy Arek now. Lilyth's spell protected the fortress from all incursions. That barrier was a siphon, powering something Lilyth would likely unleash upon Edyn. *Curse Silbane, for he brought this ruin upon us, and now the Celestial hath been given Arek as well.*

The great dragon rose, looking again at his arm and the taloned hand emerging from its base. He could see the bones re-growing, muscles and sinew re-knitting. In a few moments, he would be whole again.

Flexing his new hand, he took two strides and changed into his full dragon form. Around him, the few surviving nomads stood speechless as a great black dragon appeared, seemingly out of thin air.

Of the one who called himself Scythe, Rai'stahn could feel nothing. His oath-forged companion stood behind Lilyth's shield and thus beyond his reach or aid. Because of this, he was temporarily released from the Binding and could do as he wished to these paltry beings scavenging the dirt around him.

They tried to flee but Rai'stahn fell upon them, releasing his frustration at Arek and Silbane. He smashed some and tore apart others, flinging their bodies in all directions, littering the hard ground with a gruesome mix of body parts and splashes of blood, drying quickly in the hot, desert air. When finally there was nothing within reach left alive, he looked southeast, across the Shattered Sea. His anger began to cool, and with it, reason returned.

The thing must be stopped, and there are still those of power who walk this earth. Though many believed dragons were gone, Rai'stahn was not the last. He kept the Vigil, guarding this world while others of his kind slept. They too, had once walked Edyn as gods and would do so again. It was time for them to rise and decide how best to deal with the return of the Celestial Lilyth and her Aeris lords. The great dragon bunched his muscles and leapt into the sky, beating his wings once, twice, before finding his bearings and arrowing off toward the one he'd called to earlier.

Sovereign would act soon, the Aeris lords would counter, and the Conclave would prepare for war.

Devastation

JOURNAL ENTRY 24

Time passes and my friend grows stronger every day. She was at first understandably angered by my presence. (I daresay, my very existence) but this has since passed into a grudging acceptance. I think she understands we are trapped here. Anger is wasted and, as we all find out, dangerous when left unchecked.

My knowledge of this place grows with each passing day. I understand the intrinsic nature of things now and have turned my attention to the problem of stopping something so entrenched in our belief that its very existence is self-sustaining.

You cannot shake the faith of an entire people through individual moments of weakness. Even defeating these Aeris only gives rise to more legends. Just as my imps believed in me and grew into elves, so too do the Aeris Lords grow and increase in power by our faith. Victory or defeat is meaningless. It is a difficult thing to overcome, as the belief in gods does not die easily.

I ask myself, how are my elves able to kill anything? To clarify, how is an image brought forth by my imagination able to have effect over other images brought about by my imagination? These raids are the product of my mind as well, yet my elves are able to defeat them easily. For all intents and purposes, the raids are no longer a threat. Firstmark Malak has seen to that.

Is it my confidence in them, ritualized by our collective efforts? Is a system of belief growing amongst my protectors? Maybe I have looked at this wrong, the desire to defeat the Aeris.

Perhaps all I require is a new dream . . .

Journal Entry 24

INNOCENCE DIES

You have two eyes, two hands, two legs.
You are used to perceiving pairs,
and therefore must perfect striking in odd numbers.
This last odd strike is hardest to block.
—Tir Combat Academy, Basic Forms & Stances

L ilyth turned, her serene gaze falling again on Yetteje. They might have a far greater destiny together, though at this moment the path was unclear. Within the princess coursed the Way, and Lilyth meant to test it.

Yet her attention was still inexorably drawn to the stone floor at the base of the pyramid and to what she knew lay beneath it. The Aeris were powerful, yes, but in this realm, their power was limited by the body they inhabited. The being she sensed was one she'd hoped to encounter again, but not here and certainly not like this. Her eyes narrowed and she gestured with one hand.

From out of the ground rose the black-robed assassin. He rose from the solid granite as if the rock vomited him up, then hung him in midair, his massive body limp in death.

It would've been better had he been alive. Possessing the living would've given her all of its memories and knowledge, including anything to do with her opponent. That was lost now, but the body was still useful. Sovereign had made a mistake, and growing desperate, had delivered to her a creature vastly different from the people of Edyn, so much more powerful. A smile played upon her lips, for she'd never expected such a bounty.

She noticed Yetteje, still watching her with wide eyes, but resolute. *Well,* she thought, *a little fear is always a good thing.* Lilyth snapped her fingers and fire outlined the dead assassin's form. Her power suffused him, bringing false life to those limbs. He straightened and stood, landing lightly on the ground. Her fingers flexed and his eyes opened, but shone with the dull white of death.

Lilyth looked at the horrified Yetteje and said, "Girl, I give you a few moments before I unleash him. Tell King Galadine this: I have his son. If he does not turn himself over to me by this nightfall, I will eradicate every person still living within these walls." Lilyth rose to her full height and her aura brightened to the intensity of her blue sun.

"What did you do with Arek?" Yetteje asked, standing her ground and shielding her eyes.

"The light of my sun bathes the penitent, a goddess's gift to those I deem worthy. Even now it alters you." She paused for a moment, then said, "You are wasting time. Go prove your worth, before my patience ends."

The assassin's hand came up and clenched into a fist, igniting in a flash of white power like a sunburst. Yetteje screamed and scrambled back, then turned and sprinted for the door.

Lilyth then said one word, "Baalor." It echoed across the vast chamber and the living mist immediately responded, pouring from the gate.

A black behemoth of smoke and fire came to stand by her side, resembling a large, hulking beast standing upon two thick legs. Its body was amorphous, giving one the impression of a giant, winged creature. Lightning danced around its form, crackling with intensity. It turned baleful, flaming eyes on Lilyth and in a deep voice said, "As you command."

"Sovereign has played its hand early and failed. Now we have one of the treasured few, the body of a builder." Lilyth gestured to the slain dwarven assassin. "Use it."

Baalor looked at Lilyth in surprise and said, "And if I succeed?"

Lilyth's eyes never left Yetteje's retreating form, but she nodded and said, "The girl will lead you to the king. We must have him. Succeed and this body is yours."

A sigh escaped from Baalor, a sound of pure ecstasy.

"Very well," he said, then his form flowed into the dead assassin's nose and mouth, filling it with his substance. The body of the assassin began to burn with a cold light that seeped from its flesh. When that light reached its eyes, they changed from pure white, crackling with the same blue intensity as the lightning that had danced around Baalor's hulking form. An intelligence filled them as the Aeris lord took hold.

Lilyth said, "If the Galadine blood still runs within the king's veins, do not underestimate him. They are an ancient line, nearly as powerful as the builders themselves."

Baalor inclined his head, then touched the stone of Bara'cor. His now-builder hand touched rock and the fortress shuddered in response, as if it knew what touched it was more than one of its ancient stone brothers. Lilyth watched him exert his will, powerful and unyielding, and the fortress seemed to grudgingly obey.

"So many!" the Aeris lord exclaimed.

Lilyth knew he could now see every living thing in Bara'cor, a gift of his new form. While a body wasn't necessary for Aeris Lords such as Baalor, it unlocked abilities like the builder's stonesense.

It also allowed lesser Aeris to seek bodies free for the taking, potential salvation for her people, and a new race of demigods to resist the onslaught of Sovereign! A sudden wave of emotion flooded through her, joy at what this moment meant for her and all Aeris.

"Even now my sun quickens their Ascension," she said, looking across the open expanse and at Yetteje's fleeing form. "Find the king. Test him."

"And if he fails?" Baalor asked, his voice booming now with power, his mastery of this body complete.

"We need the pure living blood," Lilyth offered, a twinge of regret in her voice. "We have it in his son."

Baalor inclined his head again, then looked in the direction Yetteje had fled. "In the end, all will serve."

* * * * *

Yetteje hit the door arch painfully hard with her shoulder, spinning herself around so she half fell through it onto her haunches.

She looked back and saw Lilyth climbing to the apex of the pyramid with hundreds of clawed and fanged four-legged shapes coming through the portal. They looked like mistfrights, childhood dreams that had sent her scurrying to her parent's bed for solace.

Their feline forms were graceful, but insubstantial. They swarmed across the pyramid and spread like a black smoke, flowing down its steps and up the chamber's walls. Thousands seeped into holes along the walls and cracks in the ceiling, spreading into the fortress above. *But they couldn't be real, could they?*

Then she saw the assassin's eyes flash once as he crouched, his form shifting to something more like a panther. The beast sprang in her direction, the form lethal and unerring. Death on claws. Where he stepped, lightning erupted.

Yetteje scrambled back to her feet and fled, running up the passageways without looking back. Behind her, the forces of Lilyth flooded out of the gate opened by Arek, into this world.

Yetteje moved with the desperation of the hunted. Time slowed and each decision on where to turn, what path to take, played back from her memory with preternatural clarity. She dodged up the blackness, turning at hidden corridors and blind alleys, not hesitating as her eyes widened and drank in the little light left. How she did this, she didn't know or care.

Then she was at the exit, an iron door slightly ajar. She grabbed the handle and flitted through it, pulling it shut behind her. She spun the wheel and four solid metal bars extended into the surrounding rock, locking it shut. She fell back and gulped air, her chest now heaving. It was as if her lungs had been sustained throughout her flight, but now needed to inhale as much air as they could. She held a hand to her neck and willed herself to regain control. Her breathing slowly returned, almost to normal, and she began to take stock of her surroundings.

The area had more light, with torches placed every ten paces. Then she noticed a foot lying twisted to one side. A short scream almost tore through her before she clamped down on it, exerting her will.

I'm the hunter, not the hunted, she said to herself, pushing against the fear that threatened to overwhelm her. Gradually, her body relaxed and her hands unclenched. She was the hunter and would start acting like one.

She drew her blade and looked around the corner. To her surprise, the leg didn't end with a body. It lay severed, torn off, as if by some creature of immense strength. Could one of those mistfrights have done this? She crouched and brought her breathing further under control. *Her instructors at the TCA would be proud.*

The door was secure and she knew this passageway led up to another that then led to one of the main stairwells. Slowly, she made her way down the hall, her ears and eyes straining to detect any sound, any movement out of the ordinary. She could feel her breathing quicken and took the time to calm it. To be the hunter, she needed to feel her prey.

The corridor turned to the left and Yetteje paused, her senses hyper-alert. She heard it then, the low growl of an animal, something big hiding in the blackness ahead. She stepped back into the shadows and circled the corner, watching for any movement.

She saw something: a man in uniform, armed with a sword. It was a soldier of Bara'cor, but something was wrong. It sounded like the soldier was vomiting, but he stood straight, his head thrown back and mouth open. His body shook and convulsed as if something moved within him. She heard that growl again and realized it was coming from this soldier.

Then she saw it, thick black smoke writhing and twisting up the man's leg, clutching at him, snaking around his body and wrapping him tightly in its embrace. The smoke had entered through his mouth and nose and as she watched in horror, disappeared into the man completely. Then all was silent.

She didn't know what was going on, but that smoke looked like the creatures she'd just fled. If they had already beaten her here, they could move through the fortress much faster than she could. It confirmed stealth would be her only advantage.

She started to take a step, her foot making less sound than a whisper, but the creature's head snapped to look directly at her. There was nothing normal left in his visage. Fire flashed from its eyes and the thing that was once a soldier of Bara'cor dropped to all fours and ran at her like a wild animal.

She realized it was a real mistfright. They were said to be a combination of men and animals, almost invisible, preying on children who didn't listen, stealing them away. *But how could a fairy tale monster exist?*

An unreasoning fear built as the mistfright charged her in a blur of fang and claw. Yetteje knew her timing had to be perfect. She waited, counting out the few heartbeats between her one chance and certain death. Then she sidestepped the headlong charge and spun, cutting downward.

Her shorter blade just missed its neck, sparking instead off the stone wall. The creature turned and leapt. Yetteje perceived a feline head with ears laid back, its body covered in a thin, black fur—but she also saw a man crouch and spin, baring his ordinary teeth. The two images occupied the same space, overlaying one another as one creature moving with uncanny speed. It swatted at her with its razor-sharp claws and sounded a guttural roar as it passed.

Yetteje ducked the blow, letting her momentum carry her through and past it. She drew a breath, her mind and body acting as one. The world slowed and she could see her feline opponent flip up the wall, then jump back down at her—death now coming for her from above.

To her heightened senses, it moved in slow motion. She could see its wide eyes shining with their eerie, otherworldly light and white fangs protruding from behind thin black lips. It dove at her with clawed hands outstretched, but she brought her blade up and thrust it into the mistfright's mouth. The steel came out the other side, emerging from the base of its skull. As the creature fell past, Yetteje pulled the blade out in one smooth motion.

Time took on its normal flow and the creature fell in a heap at Yetteje's feet, dead before it hit the ground. She cautiously moved over to it, her booted foot turning the body to get a better look. She was shocked to see the soldier, his cheeks still smooth. His face and neck were spattered with his blood, ruined by Yetteje's sword thrust. Even as she watched, a black smoke snaked out of the body and soaked into the stones of Bara'cor.

Whatever that thing was, it was no mistfright. Maybe all she'd accomplished was killing someone possessed, an innocent defender. *But I saw it, didn't I?*

She fell back, her shoulder sagging against the wall. The magnitude of events threatened to overwhelm her, but a pragmatic confidence took over. It was the same thing that'd kept her calm during her flight and focused during her fight. She could feel it like a palpable spirit within her, a heady mix of clarity and serenity buoying her soul when she needed it most.

She stepped forward and wiped her blade clean on the uniform of the soldier. A glint of yellow caught her attention. It was a distorted reflection of herself in the interior side of a discarded shield lying near the body.

When she paused to look, amber eyes drinking in the light were staring back at her. They were glowing their own soft, ethereal yellow. They had the vertical slits of a cat, the eyes of a predator, a hunter. *What's happening?* She thought.

She raced up the deserted corridor, making her way to one of the main stairwells. The castle proper, she knew, didn't start for some levels up. She cocked her head, listening, and heard footsteps descending.

She ducked under the nearest landing and prepared. When they passed, she would cut the legs out from under them and make her way up to the king's men, who must surely be patrolling the halls above.

The sounds of footsteps neared and she braced herself, willing the moment of combat clarity to come. It responded to her will and time once again slowed. She smiled, readying her weapon. Then, in an unearthly burst of speed, she shot out of her nook and flipped over the inner hand rail, her blade slicing directly for the back of the lead man's leg.

When she saw who it was, her eyes widened in shock and she stopped her thrust a finger's width away from hamstringing him. Her momentum was too much, however, and she still fell, knocking them both to the ground. The three guards with the lead man stood stunned, clearly unable to react in response to her inexplicable speed. They readied their weapons ineffectually as she tumbled past them.

"By the Lady!" exclaimed the king. Then he met her eyes. "Tej?"

She couldn't believe it. *The king, here?* She started to smile, then a deep laugh echoing up from the corridor awoke the terror she'd felt leaning against the iron door. She looked at the king and said, "We have to go."

"Tej, where's Niall?" the king demanded.

Yetteje looked over her shoulder, somehow knowing the man in black still followed. She looked back at the king and grabbed his arms. "We have to go!"

She grabbed his armor and began moving him physically back up the stairwell. Somehow, she'd the strength to move him by herself. She could hear the guards cursing as they rushed to keep up.

"Tej, release me!" said the king, not understanding how such a small girl could have such strength.

She carried him up the stairs as if he weighed nothing more than a babe. She knew their lives hung in the balance and concentrated on getting them to where she knew safety lay, just a few more flights up. The stairs beneath her feet flew by, three or four at a time, with the king pulled behind her like a leaf in the wind.

Then, from above her, a man appeared. He reminded her of Arek—the same kind of intensity in his faded blue eyes. He was followed by a woman who looked younger, but no less deadly. Yet something about the woman told Yetteje she'd keep them safe. Behind them came a squad of Bara'corian soldiers—and Ash! *Thank the Lady!*

Then she caught herself, for she now knew who the "Lady" was: Lilyth. It was such an inborn habit, a praise or curse every person of Edyn uttered but clearly didn't understand. They prayed to the very goddess who assailed them.

Yetteje sprinted for Ash, covering the ground faster than he could track her with his eyes. She nearly thanked the Lady again before catching herself. *Old habits die hard,* she thought, unceremoniously dropping the king and falling to a knee, exhaustion now threatening to overcome her as her combat focus faded.

The woman dressed like Arek leaned in close and said, "I'm Master Kisan and this is Master Silbane. What of Arek?"

Yetteje looked up at the woman and said between gulps of air, "She took him. She took him and she took Niall." She started to rise, her attention on the stairwell leading down into the blackness.

The king, picking himself up, demanded, "She?"

"Lilyth . . ." Yetteje stammered.

When the king still looked confused, Kisan said, "She means the demon-queen."

The king shook his head, his attention focused now on Yetteje. "This cannot be! Where?"

The girl looked over her shoulder down the stairwell, then back at the king. "There's a man in black," she said. "He's trying to kill me."

Both masters' bodies were suddenly covered in scintillating flames, the man's a sunfire yellow and the woman's silver as the moon. They moved to stand between their remaining forces and the new threat.

"He can't hope to prevail against two of us," said Kisan, looking down into the gloom.

"And yet he's still coming." Silbane turned to the king and said, "We need a more defensible area—a room— something with only one entrance."

The king seemed lost, looking about in confusion. "Lilyth?"

Silbane grabbed the king by the shoulders and shook him once, hard, "We need a defensible area, now!"

* * * * *

Baalor turned the corner, stalking the girl easily by her contact with the granite of the fortress. He came upon the body of the one she'd slain, the economy of the kill impressive. *One thrust.* He noted that and notched his regard for the girl a bit higher. Perhaps the goddess had been right. No matter. If she were bonded, she would rule along with them. If not, she along with those left in Bara'cor, would serve their gods again no matter what blood or lineage they claimed.

He then leaned low and felt the stone, his eyes closing. *There!* On the stairwell, she moved with speed and he could feel his target moving with her. They would soon meet and he would complete his task.

His form illuminated in lightning and he looked inside himself. This body was powerful. He wished he could read its memories, but in a way perhaps this was better. It was his to do with as he pleased. It was unlikely the previous owner had the knowledge Baalor did, the knowledge of the Aeris lords. Baalor brought this to bear, his essence mastering the dead builder's substance completely.

This body was made to respond to the Way. It could be Shaped to meet his need, his will, just as it did when he'd assumed the shape of a mistfright to chase the girl here. He concentrated and his body responded, but this time, the changes were on the inside. Slowly, he submerged into the rock, like a man into water. The only sign of him was a slightly darker patch, a ripple, as if someone swam under the stone. The ripple made its way up the rock walls, directly for the king's forces above.

Innocence Dies

TRAPPED

There are things worse than death in this world.
To remind myself of this fact,
I chat with my mother. . .
—Davyd Dreys, Memoirs

ernal spun as more screams echoed up from the darkness. It was the guards who'd been with the king, but were unfortunate not to have someone like Yetteje haul them to safety. Their cries ended suddenly, like drowning men pulled under water.

The sound and Silbane's demand galvanized the king, who went into action, the loss of Niall carefully controlled beneath years of experience commanding men on the field of battle. He gestured, guiding the party to a nearby resupply room.

The room was large enough to hold twenty men comfortably. It had provisions along one wall and weapons along another. In the center were three large wooden tables, two for repairing various weapons and armor. The third was a medical station.

The king motioned and the guards secured Scythe, still semiconscious, to the last table. He then positioned Ash's men near the door, turned to Kisan and confirmed, "This is Silbane?"

Before she could respond, Silbane stepped forward and backhanded the king—a stinging slap.

"For Arek," he said.

The king's men pointed swords at the master. Kisan and Ash each jumped in, pulling their respective leaders apart.

"Hold!" Bernal yelled to his men, his voice ringing with command. He put a hand up to his jaw, wincing, and then spit blood. "Well met, I should say."

"I'm happy to do so again, given Bara'cor's hospitality to my apprentice."

The king's arms went wide. "I did what I must, for Bara'cor!"

Silbane shrugged Kisan off like she was an afterthought, then turned to the door. "Torture a boy?" He looked back at the king, and Bernal could see the sadness in Silbane's eyes. "I have lost him because of you."

The king moved forward, his arms still spread. "I have lost my son, too," he said. Grief threatened to overcome him. "What of Jebida?"

An awkward silence fell upon the group, until Kisan said, "He fell defeating the nomad chieftain, and provided us a means of escape."

The simple statement hammered the king, who took an involuntary step back, his breath catching. Though he'd sent Jeb on the suicide mission, he'd nevertheless believed the firstmark would survive. How many times had they returned when the odds had been stacked against them? He looked down, grief etching his features. "You're sure he's...?" He couldn't bring himself to say the word "dead".

Ash stepped in and said, "Niall's still alive. We need to focus on how to get him back."

Just then, Lanis, one of the few who'd survived the combat at the portal, jerked as something grabbed his foot. He fell, his scream cut off when his head was pulled into the granite floor, sinking in past his neck.

He braced his hands on the floor in a futile attempt to free himself, but the rock was now solid and unyielding. His companions tried to help, but it was no use. The man's movements became slow and lethargic, then ceased. In a moment, his lifeless body was drawn completely into the stone.

The other guards retreated, looking at the floors, trying to find their opponent, fear clearly reflected in their eyes. How could they attack something hiding inside rock?

Another guard gave a scream when he was pulled down through the floor, disappearing into the rock of Bara'cor without a mark.

"On the tables!" Silbane barked. "Get off the stone."

The group vaulted up onto the three tables in the room, ducking their heads so none were within arm's reach of a stone surface, including the ceiling. Only seven remained.

They had positioned themselves with Sergeant Stemmer guarding Yetteje and the red robed man on one table. Ash pulled Bernal behind him onto the second. Kisan and Silbane crouched together on the third.

A deep voice said, "How will this help you, King of Bara'cor? You squat like a dog."

Bernal shook off his grief. Battle had been joined. He looked about in disgust and said, "Dogs at least fight. What hides under stone and dirt? A worm."

The table the king and Ash stood upon began to sink into the stone. "By the Lady!" exclaimed the king. He drew Azani, but Ash held his arm, listening.

* * * * *

The king's blade is shabby. Draw me. Let us show them what it feels like to gaze upon true splendor.

No!

Not even to save your king?

Ash looked around, his mind in turmoil, then drew Tempest. The green gem burst with a clear light, making the stone translucent where it struck. They could see the figure of a black assassin with his feet braced, pulling the table into the stone by a leg.

* * * * *

Silbane's eyes widened as Tempest revealed their opponent. He heard Kisan say, "Prime. He must have survived." But Silbane's dragon-gifted Sight showed him something more.

"That thing isn't Prime," he said. He moved in a blur, centering the Way, and struck the ground over the assassin's position with an open palm, before vaulting back onto the table. "Tell me your name, demon!"

The technique had a visible effect as *Gentle Palm of the Earth* sent shockwaves traveling through the rock and blasting the demon backward. The king's table sat half submerged in stone, like a ship run afoul onto rocks.

They all saw the creature look up, smiling at Silbane. "I am Lord Baalor," it said. "Do you not remember your own gods, mortal? Then it is nigh time for a lesson in piety." It laughed, then moved away quickly and out of the light Tempest cast.

"What now?" Alyx asked. When the fighting had started, Silbane had seen her grab Yetteje and push her onto a table, guarding the royal heir the same way Ash had instinctively moved to defend the king.

The king turned to Yetteje and said, "Tell us again what happened. We need to plan our next move."

Yetteje had switched the blade she'd been using with a straight double-edged sword more similar to those used by the soldiers of EvenSea. She fastened the scabbarded blade across her hips as she answered the king, "Arek touched a portal and Lilyth appeared."

Silbane spoke first. "What happened to the portal?"

Yetteje looked at him, brows knit in consternation. "Nothing. She just appeared. I could hear them speaking."

"What did she say?" asked the king.

"She said to tell you she has Niall and if you don't turn yourself over to her by nightfall, she will kill everyone left inside Bara'cor."

"By last count, there are close to nine hundred soldiers and their families still in this fortress," Ash said to the king.

Yetteje looked anxiously around, then said in a small voice, "There's something else."

"What?" Silbane asked.

Her golden eyes met Silbane's faded blue ones and she said, "She said Arek . . . is her son."

* * * * *

Silbane drew back, shock registering on his face for a second time, but Kisan took the news differently. She had the visions of Giridian and Silbane to look at, and knew what they meant.

The Conclave was right. Arek must destroy the Way, but what would happen if he were taken to Lilyth's realm? She realized in a flash he would begin to absorb even more power from beings who were a pure embodiment of the Way. Perhaps they fought amongst themselves, and he would be employed as a weapon. If so, it would be a dangerous gamble on Lilyth's part.

It was imperative they found Arek as quickly as possible, no matter where he was, and stop him.

A moment of shocked silence passed, then Silbane asked, "Did you see or hear anything else?"

Yetteje slowly nodded, then said, "Lilyth's creatures look like mistfrights, but much worse. Thousands had flooded in. They control the lower levels and sift through the walls like smoke. One of the guards of Bara'cor . . . I saw one enter him, and he couldn't fight it off. He became something else."

She pointed to the ground where Baalor had been. "That thing inside the stone—it's the man Arek and I killed earlier. Niall said he's a dwarf."

Silbane looked at Kisan and said, "We have to get to that portal."

"I can't let the people of Bara'cor perish," said the king.

"Lilyth will kill you if you turn yourself over to her," warned Ash. He looked at Silbane and said, "Our only chance is to try and find a way out of Bara'cor."

"Perhaps I can help."

Trapped

The group turned, startled by the raspy voice. It came from Scythe, still bound to the medical table in the back.

Kisan was first to speak. "Help who? Us or them?" she said sarcastically. She turned to the rest of the group. "This man tried to kill us. He may be responsible for the deaths of the other fortresses and their inhabitants."

At that, Yetteje's head whipped around and her blade sang as it cleared her scabbard, the point centered unwaveringly on Scythe's chest.

"Wait!" cried Silbane. He held up a forestalling hand and said, "I mindread him, princess. He isn't wholly responsible."

"How could he not be?" she demanded, gesturing with the tip of her blade to make her point. "At the very least, he should pay for the deaths here." She turned her glowing amber gaze back to the bound man.

"You deserve this." Yetteje said, but Alyx, who had been standing right next to the girl, pushed the blade away and grabbed the princess in a bear hug from behind.

"Easy, princess," she said, "he'll not escape justice, I promise. For now, let the king sort this out."

Scythe's watched the interaction calmly, then looked at Silbane. "If you read me, you know I want to reach the portal below," he said. "It's my only purpose."

When Silbane didn't answer, Kisan said, "If you trust him, you'll be as crazy as he is."

Silbane shook his head slowly, his eyes never leaving Scythe's. Then he looked around, his gaze taking in the rest of the room. He seemed to come to a decision.

Kisan was stunned by his next words: "This is the Archmage Duncan Illrys, once Lore Father of the First Council, and last of the Old Lords."

JOURNAL ENTRY 25

An idea has begun to take seed and grow. I battled and lost, was hunted and preyed upon, until I rose and stood firm. I came to this world already an archmage, powerful in the Way. Yet, I could not prevail until I had suffered. Why?

I believe it is because my mind needs the victories to build its self-image of power, a surety in the conviction I could survive.

Captain Dreys once said a bladesman cannot cross live blades until years pass and he becomes familiar with failure. That he cannot block until he's felt the wooden knot of a bohkir leave a lump (he called it "love lumps") on his skull.

Ritual, whether physical or mental, is not enough. We must face overwhelming odds and prevail against meaningful foes. Otherwise, our knowledge has no proven value, no firm root. Like a misplanted tree, the academic facing his first combat will topple in the slightest breeze, borne by the winds of adversity.

Wisdom comes from experience and experience from bad judgment. It is our victories over these things that define us, give us confidence and strength.

I now think I know a way to defeat these Aeris, these mythborn, these legends come to life. I cannot attack them in the traditional sense. I can't win by lending them the credibility of my faith.

Instead, I must attack something deeper . . . I must create something more powerful, something that can hold power over the Aeris Lords and those who use the Way. Something they begin to believe in, and fear.

My companion returns. We have a quiet dinner planned, while my elven guards patrol the castle walls and grounds. Her company is the one thing I look forward to in this accursed place.

Journal Entry 25

Journal Entry 25

THE OLD LORDS

The surest sign of fear is anger.
The surest sign of strength is kindness.
—Altan proverb

Yetteje stood, shocked silent by Silbane's revelation. How could someone dead for over two hundred years be lying right here, only a sword's thrust away? Judging from their expressions, the team was struggling with the same information. History said Duncan and his wife were the last survivors against Lilyth, and among the first executed under the Galadine law prohibiting use of the Way.

Kisan broke the silence "You're sure?"

Silbane took a deep breath. "Yes."

Just then the walls of the room began to buckle and groan. Yetteje crouched, shielding her head with her arms. With a *crack*, the walls shifted in place and began to grind inward, the room collapsing in on itself. Rocks and dust fell from the ceiling as it began to buckle. Weapons fell from their places and were crushed under the grinding stone.

"That demon?" yelled the king.

Duncan answered, "Baalor. He has called upon the rock of Bara'cor. We've got to get out of here."

Silbane jumped from his table to the king's, then to Yetteje's, landing lightly between her and Alyx. He knelt next to the captured lore father and said, "I want your Binding Oath. If I free you, help us. It is the only way you will ever see *her* again."

Kisan tried to push the door open. "It won't budge. The walls have pinned it shut."

Silbane yelled back, "Be ready!"

Duncan looked at the walls grinding inward, the ceiling as it bent under the pressure, then at the adept. "By the blood of my forefathers, I bind myself," he began. They finished the ritual, touching blood and enduring the shock of the Binding.

Silbane freed his prana locks. "I can't do anything about the torc." He looked at the princess and then added, "And I'm not sure I want to." A moment passed, then Silbane continued, "Princess, this man is the only hope we have to save Arek and the king's son. Please let this mean more to you than revenge."

The ground shook again as the walls continued their inexorable movement inward, crushing weapons, armor, and supplies under stone.

Yetteje looked at Silbane, anger smoldering in her chest like a furnace stealing away her ability to breath. Then her gaze fell upon the king, his face etched in desperation. She looked back down at the man now revealed as Duncan and said, "When this is over, you'll die by my hands."

"Nothing dies, princess," said the ancient lore father. His voice came out tired, though his mouth still twisted in a smirk, as if by habit.

"You're going to wish that were true," she said. She looked at him a moment longer, disgust filling her soul, then she leapt from her table to the king's. However, she didn't take her attention off of Silbane and his exchange with the man responsible for her father's death.

Silbane looked at Duncan and asked, "What are our choices?"

The walls had now moved in the length of a spear. They had only a few moments left.

"Break the door," Duncan said. "We face Lord Baalor on open ground."

Yetteje watched as Silbane and Kisan locked eyes. Someone said something because Kisan nodded, then Silbane moved with blurring speed. They met at the door, open palms striking the stone surface in unison, detonating the stone itself and exploding it outward. Although Yetteje had watched them perform feats that were beyond those of ordinary men, every time they acted she was reminded just how lethal the masters were.

"Quickly!" yelled Silbane, ushering everyone in the room out onto the open landing. The air was still and dead, silent but for the sound of stone grinding and crushing the room behind them.

Duncan came to stand beside Silbane, wiping his face clean. "My powers – this accursed torc?" he asked, fingering the metal collar. "Will you not free me?" A small titter erupted, as if he laughed at what he'd just said, but it was quickly stifled.

Silbane shook his head. "Kisan pulled me away before I could assimilate all your memories. I know who you are, and maybe a bit more. Because of that, I understand your plight. Don't mistake that for trust."

"You'll need my strength to get out of here," Duncan pressed. "I took the Oath."

He appeared calm now, in control. Still, Yetteje sensed that madness lay just under his thin façade of normalcy, like ice covering the first winter's pond. She stepped into Silbane's view and said, "He's unpredictable. Don't free him."

Duncan smiled at the princess and replied, "I'm a lore father too, and would help any pupil of the Way, even if they themselves did not know their own strength."

Silbane looked sympathetic, but much to Yetteje's relief he finally shook his head. He'd clearly seen enough in Duncan's head to know the man couldn't be trusted, at least not as long as the object of his obsession was lost.

Duncan looked down, his mouth grim but then faced Ash and ordered, "Draw Tempest."

The firstmark looked at the archmage and then at Silbane, caution warring against need in his face.

"She was forged for this very purpose," Duncan added. "You saw her power in the room."

When Silbane didn't object, Ash drew the blade and held her aloft. Her clear light erupted from the green gem, illuminating the landing, making the surrounding areas translucent to their sight. Nothing appeared to be lurking within the stone.

"We should make for one of the exits," said Stemmer. "Our men will be there."

"You will die before you get ten paces," remarked Duncan. "There is no escape. Your mundane weapons are useless against this foe." He looked at the sergeant, "As for the soldiers of Bara'cor, they have likely been taken."

"What do you mean? All of them?" asked the king.

Duncan turned a scathing gaze upon the king, who took an involuntary step back, and even Yetteje was startled by his vehemence. "Galadine, your death cannot come too soon. Only my Oath intervenes."

Such was Duncan's intensity that Ash and the sergeant moved to stand between the two, their swords ready to defend their king. Silbane could see things were starting to unravel and began to say something, but the archmage acted first.

Ignoring the two soldiers, Duncan faced the king and nodded at the bow strapped across his back. "The last time I saw your bow, it held an arrow sighted at me and my wife, just before a Galadine used it to execute her."

Silbane finally managed to step in, his tone steady, "He had my apprentice tortured, and for that there will be a reckoning," his eyes promised he'd not forgotten Arek's torture. Then his tone became more mollifying, and he said, "But this king didn't take her away from you, he rescinded the decree against us. To survive today, we're going to have to tolerate one another."

Duncan continued to stare, his gaze never leaving the king's bow. When he answered Silbane, it was with a hint of unbalanced laughter, a teeter on the edge of a mental precipice, from which he quickly recovered. A calm settled over him then and he said, "I took the Oath and won't harm him," his eyes left Bernal's to meet Silbane's, "but I don't need advice about diplomacy and constraint from a wet-behind-the-ears pup. I've forgotten more about the Way than you've ever learned." He waited for Silbane to reply, and when the master said nothing, he spat on the king's feet and made to move away.

Kisan stepped in his path, "Then answer me," she said. "What now?"

"We're alive because Baalor wishes to face us," Duncan answered. "The Way is proof against their ability to possess you. Enchanted weapons such as Tempest and that accursed bow are needed to harm them. If you have none, you are nothing but meat, which is why Bara'cor is lost."

He turned back to the king and said sarcastically, "Been stockpiling enchanted weapons, or confiscating them for your magehunters? Do they really believe it's 'faith' and not the Way?"

Silbane turned Duncan back to him and said, "Kisan is right. What do we do?"

"If your goal is to recover the two boys, the only chance is to make for the portal below, Lilyth's Gate. Only the magehunters have any chance against these demons, and I know there aren't many around. Everyone else is either a body, or food."

The king shook off the hesitation and surprise that had come from Duncan's verbal attack and responded, his voice strident, "Bara'cor will never be lost so long as I live!"

Duncan looked disdainfully at the king. "You are an imbecile, from a long line of dim-witted tyrants. Your only skills are war, death, and lying to yourself that you're noble peace-makers."

He turned, ignoring any answer the king might have said, and shouted out into the empty air, "Lord Baalor, this hiding ill becomes you."

A voice like stone grinding on stone answered Duncan, "Well said, Lore Father. I had grown weary waiting for the chatter to cease, but your purpose must be clear or my victory will mean less."

Silbane looked at Duncan with surprise, asking, "You know him?"

Duncan said, "You know him, too." Silbane shook his head, ready to deny this, but Duncan continued, "He is the Lord of Storms. His emblem graces that cretin's shield."

He pointed at the king's shield and the double lightning bolts framing the Galadine lion. "The Old Lords faced him before, when Lilyth's forces were repelled."

* * * * *

The air darkened, cooled, then blasted the group as Baalor gathered himself to appear before them. He became a spark that grew to a shining shape before coalescing in the form of the assassin whose body he'd assumed. He bowed once, palms to forehead.

"I am Baalor, come to test the High King." The demon god called upon the power of the earth below him, and smiled as a frantic crackle of lightning and power flowed from the ground, coursing up and through the builder assassin's body, coruscating white ropes of energy that formed a web around his form.

Baalor began to change. The builder's body grew, rippling as muscle and sinew reknit, responding to the will of the Way and his command.

Instead of the builder's shape, for this occasion, Baalor chose an ancient form almost ten feet tall, a battlefield behemoth armored in pure ebonite. The black metal gleamed in the flickering light of the few remaining torches.

He drew a breath, drawing in the very substance of the Way, then opened his eyes, crackling blue from behind a black helm. He clenched his bare hands then smashed them together with the ring of metal striking metal.

"It has been long since I have matched myself against a Galadine," he rumbled. "Come, let us see which of us is still worthy of his name."

The Ascended man stepped forward and said, "You'll face us all. Not quite as noble born as this king, but we should do."

"Make your way to the Gate," the Ascended female said to another not yet quite reborn, but well on her own path. "We will follow when we can."

The younger female oozed fear, an almost palpable aura. She'd not yet accepted her bonded partner, yet she didn't leave.

The Ascended female exchanged a quick glance with the other Ascended, then said, "Stand firm, then. Either way you'll learn something."

Baalor agreed. The girl had little to fear, as she was almost one of them. He measured the rest of the throng before him.

Tempest shone from the blade held by another man and Baalor scowled at the thought of meeting the Kinslayer again. *A reckoning is due,* he thought with anger. He would not hold back on her.

In addition to this, the one who had first spoken, the Old Lord: something was wrong with him. His power lay muffled, held captive. Then Baalor realized it was the cursed tool of the magehunters, deadly to the Aeris in Lilyth's realm. Here however, these torcs were mere baubles, unable to truly bring their twisted purpose to bear.

Baalor was a warrior first, yearning for the test of battle. Being entombed within Bara'cor's walls was an end reserved for those who were not yet ready for Ascension.

These few, however, deserved his full attention. He saluted them again, palm to forehead followed by a downward sweep. "I come to test the dreams of the Galadine who holds Bara'cor. The rest are the Lady's concern, not mine, and are free to depart."

From behind the Ascended man, the Old Lord said, "Release me. I'll fight you."

The Ascended man ignored the Old Lord, addressing Baalor again. "I am Silbane. Lord Baalor, we have no quarrel with you. We make our way to the Gate and to your master. Can we avoid this confrontation?"

Baalor looked at this one closer, for the Way flowed with strength through him. His power made Baalor wary, for it suggested that the man was Ascended with a powerful Aeris lord, perhaps even a Celestial.

His deep voice sounded like gravel when he said, "You must answer to the Eye of the Sun, Lord Silbane. To pass me, surrender the Galadine and as I said, you may go in peace."

The king began to step forward, but the bearer of the Kinslayer and another woman interceded. The man said, "We'll not! Bring your worst."

Baalor smiled at that. "It is sooth, for you carry an old friend. Breaking her will be a pleasure."

* * * * *

I never liked him, said Tempest to Ash's surprise.

What? asked the new firstmark. Tempest sounded almost hungry.

He is an Aeris lord of great power. Releasing him will make us stronger, beloved. We will feast on his soul together.

Ash couldn't comprehend everything Tempest was saying. *What was an "ayris?"* It seemed more important than ever he speaks with one of the adepts, but they must first win this battle. He surveyed the scene. Perhaps this creature was more dangerous than the three assassins they had faced earlier, but with Tempest he hardly seemed insurmountable.

Lightning crackled around the demon lord, flavoring the air with a coppery tang. White power arced and flowed from the stones, then coalesced into a shield of lightning. Power continued to flow, flashing across his ebonite armor in blue-white arcs that left purple afterimages in Ash's eyes.

For generations the people of Edyn had worshipped Baalor, the god of storms. In that, they had been correct, for this demon seemed to command the very lightning and thunder attributed to the Lord of Storms. Could they in fact be one in the same?

Ash sighed, correcting his earlier overconfidence. *I guess nothing is easy today.*

Beloved, I will protect you.

No! You won't use my friends.

The sword seemed frustrated and Ash had the impression of Tempest with crossed arms, angry at his stubbornness. He maintained his will, and finally she acquiesced. *Very well.*

Protective sheaths of magical flame danced over the adepts' forms, silver for Kisan and yellow for Silbane. Ash couldn't help but envy their protection. The rest of the party drew weapons and spread out. This creature stood between them gaining the Gate, and rescuing Niall and Arek.

Baalor looked down at the group, as if inspecting something, then he held up a hand. "I remember much of the strength of the Old Lords," he said, "and would test myself against it. Remove the cursed gift of the Galadine magehunters."

Ash saw Silbane lick his lips before replying, "We will not free him."

The moments passed as the demon seemed to ponder what to do next. Finally, it looked at Silbane and said, "Very well, but I will not challenge one who cannot defend himself. It is unworthy of me. He should depart."

"Free him?" exclaimed Yetteje, looking at Silbane. "No way he's getting a pass after all he's done!"

Ash went to quiet her, saying, "Hold on, princess, no one—"

"He'll not get to walk away—"

"No!" Silbane said, a moment too late.

Sergeant Stemmer had already reached up and pulled off the torc, which came undone easily at her touch.

* * * * *

Duncan breathed deep, as the Way infused him again. Pure power, no longer restricted by the metal collar, flooded his senses, returning the caress of the Way and healing him. His sight magnified, drinking in all the details of the moment. He could see with a clarity he'd never realized he possessed until he'd lost it. It saturated him now and he felt stronger than a hundred men.

He looked at Sergeant Stemmer and bowed. "I thank you."

"Don't," she replied. "I just want to be sure you die here with us."

Silbane and Kisan looked at each other. If Duncan sided with Baalor, it would make things difficult for them.

But I will not. I gave my bonded Oath and it requires that I not leave you. Let's face Baalor together, Duncan mindspoke.

Both adepts heard him, just before battle was upon them.

* * * * *

Alyx feinted left, as Baalor ran forward, shaking the ground with every step, his arm reaching behind him in a fisted grip. In that grip appeared a mace of power, lightning dancing along its length. *Great,* she *thought, now he's got a weapon.*

He swung it at Silbane, who jumped up and over the Aeris lord, landing lightly behind him.

Kisan moved in quickly, striking two blows to the armor with a flash of silver fire, but little else. She ducked under the swing of the mace, then leapt backward to land well out of its reach. Alyx marveled at her grace well beyond anything she could mimic.

Bernal had scrambled to his right, unslinging Valor and stringing it in one smooth motion while Baalor turned with him as if he were a lodestone connected to the king. Two arrows a heartbeat apart sped at the demon warrior, the shafts true to their mark. One bit Baalor in the neck but glanced off harmlessly, the other shattered against his lightning shield.

Yetteje and Alyx had switched, moving right to take advantage of a possible opening. When the demon turned to follow the king, its back was to them.

Yetteje took immediate advantage, diving in, stabbing with her sword. Alyx suddenly saw a glow emanate from the princess, flowing out her blade, which skittered and sparked off the ebonite armor. Yetteje ducked, rolling to avoid the demon's counter as it swung a backhanded blow with its mace.

Alyx had been half a step behind Yetteje, trying to get a clean blow in on the creature's flank. She saw an opening and swung her blade. To her amazement, her weapon went through Baalor's leg without touching him, as if he were made of mist! She fell back a step and riposted, with the same result. Her sword couldn't touch the storm god. Duncan's warning suddenly came to mind.

Baalor was ignoring her, instead focusing on Yetteje, perhaps because her attack had somehow connected with the demon. When Alyx saw the mace heading for the unprotected princess, she didn't hesitate and threw herself forward, catching the blow on her shield side.

Had she been carrying a shield, she might have fared better.

The Old Lords

* * * * *

Duncan saw the lightning mace hit the sergeant with a flash of white and a discharge that could be felt, hurling her across the room to fall in a crumpled heap against one wall. Dark, sinuous smoke immediately covered her body, entering her unwilling form. It was a rape beginning at the very pores of her skin and continuing into every orifice on her body. She was merely prey for the Aeris, just as he'd warned them earlier. *Well, at least she's done something useful before dying,* thought the archmage.

Ash dodged the first mace blow and the second, rolling to Baalor's front and stabbing upward. Tempest bounced off the armor and Baalor roared in fury. He swatted downward with the mace, missing Ash's head by less than a hand's width and cracking the stone of Bara'cor in a radial pattern like a spider's web.

Pure power arced from Duncan's outstretched hands and struck Baalor, lightning bolts of energy blasting into the ebonite with a crack that shattered the air. Each strike drove the demon farther back, exploding against his armor in flashes of white and blue. Baalor went to one knee.

"Good," the demon said between bursts. "I had thought the old ways forgotten."

Then Baalor heaved up. Stone blocks the size of a man's body launched themselves at the group. They scattered as the blocks exploded against the walls and ground, filling the air with dust and pulverized rock.

"But you attack me with an old friend," the Lord of Storms laughed, moving forward again as Duncan's lightning arced harmlessly across Baalor's armor.

* * * * *

Yetteje watched wide-eyed, crouching low to one side, and for the moment, forgotten. Alyx had saved her, but where was the sergeant? She felt a cold hand on her shoulder and turned to look.

Behind her stood Sergeant Alyx Stemmer, but her eyes blazed an unearthly blue. Black smoke moved down the arm of the thing that had once been a soldier of Bara'cor, and came toward her. Yetteje screamed and jumped back, but the demon sergeant scrambled forward like a predator.

"Nothing dies," it said with a reptilian hiss.

Yetteje jumped to her feet, her blade ready. At first, she felt an unreasoning terror, but something washed it away. She faced the creature who'd once been her friend and anger rose within her, anger that once again someone close to her had been taken away, and anger at herself for fearing it.

She focused that rage and held the demon's gaze. It hesitated, as if sensing something had changed. Yetteje felt time slow, a bubble of calm surrounding her in the midst of the battle against Baalor. She looked at her friend and in a small but determined voice asked, "Alyx, can you hear me?"

The demon that was Alyx paused, its face contorting as a struggle raged within its body. It clawed, then scratched at itself. "You cannot be freed," it said in a guttural voice, but it did not seem to be talking to Yetteje.

The princess didn't know what to do. She'd killed that other creature, only to find out she'd in fact killed a defender of Bara'cor. The demon within him had simply escaped and all she'd accomplished was to kill someone unfortunate enough to have been possessed. Now her friend, Alyx, had been taken. She didn't want to kill her, too.

"Let my friend go," she demanded, taking a step forward. "You can't have her."

The creature seemed to stop struggling with itself for a moment and Alyx's eyes returned to normal from their cerulean blaze. "Princess . . . give no quarter," she said in a voice struggling for control. "Strike true."

Then whatever was left of the sergeant disappeared and the creature dove forward in a flash of power and strength, claws and fangs bared, directly for Yetteje's face.

The princess's reaction was as automatic as if someone else controlled her. She moved in a blur, cutting through the sergeant's outstretched arm, then her neck in a smooth figure eight. The body toppled, going to its knees before falling to the ground as she completed a perfect Tir Flower cut.

Yetteje could see the black smoke flow out like blood, seeping into the ground, disappearing into the cracks, just like it had before. A small sob escaped her. She'd done what she had to do.

* * * * *

Bernal ducked out of the way of the tumbling stone and launched two more arrows. Both shattered without effect. Off to the side, he caught sight of Yetteje as she cut down the undead body of Sergeant Stemmer.

A sickening realization dawned on him: those who fell would each become one of these demons. Worse, the one known as Baalor wasn't even hurt, not yet.

Bernal's heart told him it would only be a matter of time before this demon lord and his brethren possessed them all.

* * * * *

Kisan used mindspeaking so she and Silbane could coordinate their strategy instantly. Duncan launched another blast, this time with fire. Then both she and Silbane blurred into motion, striking the spot of the fireball's impact with synchronized Gentle Palm of the Earth.

Their attacks pushed the demon back, but did no appreciable damage to the ebonite armor encasing his body. As masters, both Kisan and Silbane could tap into the Earth affinity, but neither could bring the full might of it to bear on Baalor. At best, they could keep the demon off balance, but affecting an earth metal as strong as ebonite need a Master of Earth. Kisan cursed her luck that she happened to be partnered with the one living master whose Affinity ran diametrically opposed to her own.

Furthermore, while mindspeaking made sharing strategy instantaneous and therefore difficult to defend against, it also burned through reserves of energy at a prodigious rate. Kisan didn't say anything, she just shut up and conserved what she had.

The mace struck again, barely missing Silbane and catching Kisan a glancing blow. Her moonskin erupted in a silver flash, protecting her from the worst of it, but hurling her to land near Yetteje. The princess scrambled over to her and cried, "They took Alyx!"

Kisan looked at the princess and the body that lay near, then rolled to her feet. The girl had done well, she thought. "If I fall, do the same for me," she said, giving the princess a quick, reassuring smile before speeding back into the fray.

More black shapes entered the chamber, a ghostly audience, waiting for the chance to enter anyone who succumbed to Baalor's might.

* * * * *

A second smash of the mace tossed Duncan and Silbane into the air. Duncan fell in a heap, but Silbane twisted, landing lightly on the balls of his feet.

They had numerous cuts from flying shards of stone, but were otherwise unhurt, an amazing piece of luck considering Duncan didn't have the advantage of a protective flameskin. The monk looked at the archmage, who absentmindedly wiped blood from a cut on his forehead out of his eyes.

"How did you kill them," Silbane asked, "in the old days?"

"We didn't." Duncan replied, blinking more blood away. "We had warriors trained especially for this."

"Bladesmen," Silbane stated, matter-of-factly. "Why am I not surprised?"

* * * * *

Ash moved in between strikes, knowing that blocking the mace was impossible. He dove in and stabbed at the knee joint, a small opening in the ebonite armor. Tempest plunged into Baalor's leg.

Baalor immediately bellowed and kicked out, catching the firstmark on his shield arm. Pain exploded in Ash's arm as he was hurled away.

Use me, beloved!

No!

You must! You withhold your own true might!

Ash looked around, dazed. The demon lord had turned to face the king and he couldn't do anything about it.

What? he asked.

You fight as if you have forgotten the old ways, my love. I must help.

Ash shook his head and rose to his feet. *No! I've seen how you "help."*

At first there was silence. Heartbeats went by, then Tempest mindspoke, her normal self-centered cheer gone. *When you fall, I will do what I must.*

The sword didn't say anything else, but Ash knew she'd keep that promise, just as she had when those assassins had attacked the king. He needed to fight and survive, or she would do something far worse to keep him alive.

* * * * *

Bernal watched the carnage, even as the demon warrior turned its lightning gaze toward him. They had to make it to Lilyth's Gate. It was Niall's only chance of rescue. He knew what he had to do and turned to Silbane.

"You have to go!" The king pointed to the exit leading down to the cistern catacombs.

Silbane and Duncan moved in unison, striking the giant armored demon with fire and fist, while Kisan struck a third time, distracting Baalor as the other two made their way to Bernal.

Silbane arrived first. "What are you talking about?"

Bernal looked at the armored demon and said, "We have to make it to the Gate or Niall and Arek can't be rescued."

"So you want to run?" Duncan sneered. He dodged a rock thrown and pulled back to a door's lip.

"He can follow us through walls, or had you forgotten?" He looked at the king with disgust, then sprayed Baalor with hundreds of fire darts. Each smacked into a surface or into Baalor, then exploded, saturating the area with fire and heat.

"The Golden Lion of Bara'cor . . . " Duncan said, making the title sound like a curse as he fired volley after volley at Baalor. "Valorous to the very end."

Bernal sighed, his shoulders momentarily slumping in weariness, but a moment later he addressed Silbane, "Take the party and get to the Gate. I'll hold the demon here."

Silbane stared at him, then said in a soft voice, "You'll be killed. What about your son?"

"This is the only way for the people of Bara'cor to survive. Same for Niall. I'll not see him, but he'll live. I trust you to see to that."

Silbane's gaze didn't waver. "We can defeat this thing."

Bernal smiled and said, "You don't believe that."

He looked over the battlefield, watching Ash hack at the giant warrior, his blade sparking and bouncing off the ebonite armor, then rolling as the mace clipped his shoulder. The firstmark went down, lightning crackling around his body. His heart clenched, knowing every moment they wasted he risked losing another comrade. He thought of Jebida, brave soldier of a thousand battles. This day had brought nothing but pain.

"Stemmer is dead. He'll kill you all, just to get to me." Bernal locked eyes with Silbane. "If I surrender, he'll stay here. It gives you the chance to gain the Gate. That's Niall's best chance."

Duncan and Silbane both stood still, not answering. Then Silbane stepped in and put a hand on the king's forearm. "Someone once told me a father is a man who expects his son to be as good a man as he meant to be. Only my death will stop me from letting Niall know what kind of man you were, to the very end."

A moment passed in silence. Kisan heard something, for as the king watched she suddenly grabbed Yetteje and sped toward them, dodging around the demon's mace strikes. The two zigzagged to his position while the demon turned back to Ash, who lay sprawled on his back.

The king yelled, "Baalor!"

The Aeris lord stopped, his arm upraised to smash down where Ash lay. The firstmark looked about in a daze, then slowly got to his feet and shuffled out of Baalor's reach. He fumbled through the carnage, joining the rest of the group with an unspoken question in his eyes. His left arm hung useless.

"You claim to be honorable," said the king, addressing the Aeris lord.

"I claim nothing. My actions speak for themselves," intoned the giant. He turned and faced the king. "As do yours."

Bernal Galadine stepped forward. "I have no taste for dying without honor and neither do you. These others are not your concern. Let us engage in single combat."

Ash stepped forward but was held back by Silbane. "What? Your Majesty! You'll not survive!"

The king handed his bow to Ash, the wood feeling warm in his hands, almost living. "Take Valor. Give it to Niall when you see him."

Ash ignored it, struggling to get past Silbane. The older master took the bow and said to the firstmark, "It's his son's only chance."

"No!" said Ash. "There has to be another way!"

"I accept your challenge, King Galadine of Bara'cor," Baalor said with a slight bow. "The men of Bara'cor who still live will be allowed to leave her walls as Lady Lilyth promised. Your companions may gain the Gate, should the goddess allow it. If I fall, you will still turn yourself over to Lilyth's forces, or your men will die." He bowed again, then stepped back to wait for the king to approach.

Ash then turned to plead with Kisan, who stood with Yetteje and said, "You can't let him do this!"

Kisan glanced at the king, then addressed Ash, "Baalor has accepted the king's challenge. We can now attempt the Gate and find the king's son and Arek. What better outcome can you craft?"

Bernal gripped his firstmark's shoulder, his old eyes full of fire. "Your duty lies with the king of Bara'cor, yes?"

Ash looked stricken and replied, "Of course, my liege."

"He has been captured and taken to another realm." Bernal met Ash's eyes and said, "Rescue him, if you have any love for me."

Ash stopped struggling and collapsed in on himself, his body deflated in defeat. Safeguarding Niall was as much his duty as obeying the king's order, and Bernal knew it.

Yetteje rushed forward and said, "You don't have to do this. Niall wouldn't want to lose you."

Bernal smiled at the girl. "Your father expected me to defend you." He stroked her scarred cheek. "I choose my end. Most men are never given that chance."

Yetteje stepped back, tears in her eyes. She moved over and took the war bow from Silbane and in a choked voice said, "I'll make sure Niall gets this."

Bernal put a callused finger under her chin and lifted it until their eyes met. He smiled then brought her into a hug, whispering so only she could hear, "Do not forget who you are."

When he released her, she stepped back and nodded.

Kisan stayed back, but gave the king a short nod. Bernal hadn't expected much else from that one. She seemed to hate men in general, and Galadines even more. *Well,* he thought, *the sentiment is going around.*

Bernal smiled at his own joke, then drew Azani. The fine steel rang with a pure note, as if the enchanted blade was eager to test itself. He unslung his shield, the golden lion of Bara'cor rampant on its face. It settled on his arm like an old friend, a companion he'd known his entire life.

The group moved back, away from the king. The black maw of the stairwell stood behind them. Yetteje slung Valor across her back, its great recurved shape making her seem smaller. She supported Ash, who looked battered and forlorn. Together, they made their way to the stairwell with Silbane in the lead, and even after he turned away, Bernal could feel their eyes upon him.

He was surprised to see Duncan approach him, a look of contemplation on his face. The archmage looked down and shook his head, as if arguing with himself. Who knew what was going on in his head?

Duncan turned to follow the group, but paused. He turned back to the king and said, "I can make your end quick, less painful than Baalor will offer. It may be of some solace."

The king shook his head, surprised the insane archmage had said anything that wasn't a curse.

"No, but tell my son my thoughts were on him."

The archmage didn't move, still watching him as if drinking in the character of his soul. His pale eyes darted to the runebow across Yetteje's back, then back to him. Bernal got the distinct impression Duncan was considering something.

Then the archmage snapped his fingers. A small sparkle erupted, then disappeared. The only acknowledgment was from Baalor, who grumbled, "It is sooth, but pointless."

Duncan looked at Baalor and said, "Perhaps."

"Nothing has been done that will change the outcome of this challenge," Baalor said, looking at Bernal. He took another step back, "I await your blade."

Bernal watched Duncan's expression shift, his gaze crumpling, becoming somehow even more fragile. "You may not thank me later," whispered the archmage, "but I wish someone had done the same for me once."

Then a small giggle erupted. He leaned forward and whispered, "She waits for me."

Bernal's steady gaze met Duncan's own feverish one. The red-robed mage spun and headed for the stairwell, all the while shaking his head and muttering to himself. *There's a man I'll not miss*, Bernal thought.

Then his eyes were drawn to Yetteje, who raised a hand in farewell. He gave her a wink and a small smile, watching as she, too, entered the stairwell with Ash.

Bernal's mind then turned to thoughts of his wife, Yevaine, waiting for him in Haven. He hoped she would not be angry at his decision for too long. Allowing his men safe passage and giving the team time to find Niall was the only decision he could make as king and father, but knowing her, she'd never forgive him. He smiled fondly at the thought, then turned and faced the giant warrior, weapon and shield in hand.

Stepping forward, Bernal raised his blade in salute to Baalor. "Come, Lord of Storms. I need a partner for this last dance."

The Old Lords

PLANEWALKERS

You should not fear forging ahead alone.
The world is vast and its wonders endless.
It begins the same way for everyone,
with one step into the unknown.
Breathe deep and easy,
let the sun fall warm on your faces.
Remember me, and I shall always be with you . . .
—Davyd Dreys, Memoirs

ilbane's battle-weary eyes looked to the pyramid rising from the stone floor of the cavern. At its apex shone a cobalt sun, its radiance filling the room in a soft, flickering light. The entire chamber seethed with movement as black, sinuous shapes flowed in, around, and through each other. They looked to be the same living smoke Yetteje had fled, the same that had surrounded them during their fight against Baalor. Evidently the demon had been true to his word, for none of Lilyth's forces attacked them.

"What do we do now?" asked Ash. He cradled his arm, still broken and dislocated from Baalor's strike.

"We move," said Silbane without looking at him. "The boys are still trapped. If we don't go for them no one will, and the king's sacrifice will have meant nothing."

He was unsure if anyone else survived within Bara'cor's walls, for they hadn't seen another living soul. Their flight here had been punctuated by desperate moments of reorientation to avoid a literal dead end. The combat against Baalor had taken its toll. As they hurried ever downward, numerous injuries unfelt during the fight now blossomed, each with their own brand of excruciating pain. Constant worry sapped their mental reserves.

Still, unlike the king and Alyx, they lived, and their objective lay ahead: Lilyth's Gate. It would lead them to

Arek and Niall. He wondered again at Duncan's last act
with the king. To what purpose had he ensorcelled the
king's weapons?

Silbane moved forward and the sinuous fog reacted,
bending to either side. It took on feline forms, dozens at
first, then hundreds, then more than they could count,
lining up in a ghostly procession to either side of the Gate.
The group limped forward, nearing the bottom of the
pyramid. Lilyth's phantom army offered no resistance.

Duncan took a step ahead, then turned to face the group,
his eyes centering on Silbane. "Release me."

Silbane cocked his head. "What?"

"Release me, Silbane. I have acted in good faith, but we
don't follow the same path."

Kisan stepped forward and snarled, "You've only acted
within your Oath." She turned to Silbane and said, "He
can't be trusted."

Even bound by the oath, Silbane doubted the man's
sanity and feared his mercurial moods. The last thing they
needed in the middle of Lilyth's army was another enemy.

Silbane nodded, his eyes never leaving Duncan's. "You
tried to kill us."

"Did I? I recall healing you and urging you to escape.
You read my mind, my most inner thoughts. What is my
life's purpose?" Duncan took a deep breath.

Silbane knew he couldn't act without the release of the
oath. He broke eye contact with a sigh, looking at his
companions, but Duncan demanded his attention by asking
again, "What is my purpose?"

The master looked back at Duncan, his body reflecting
the tiredness he felt. There was almost no point in
answering, but the man's lifelong compulsion was too
much to bear.

"Sonya," he said with resignation, for Silbane knew this
was all Duncan thought about. Being reunited with his wife
consumed him completely. He'd obsessed about it for so
long, it was unlikely there was anything left, except his

hatred of the Galadine kings. If not for the Oath, it was doubtful Bernal would've survived his encounter with this particular archmage.

"But she is dead!" exclaimed Kisan. "Two hundred years dead."

Duncan ignored the outburst, instead looking up at the pyramid and the shining Gate. "She is there, waiting for me." He turned his attention back to the group and said, "They all are . . . anyone you lost."

Shock followed the archmage's statement. Questioning eyes darted to Silbane.

"Is that true?" blurted Yetteje. "My family . . . my father is alive?"

Ash hobbled forward. "The king?"

Even Kisan looked at Silbane, and though she said no word, he knew her thoughts could only be for her dead apprentice.

Duncan looked at them all, finally coming to rest again on Silbane. "I can bring them back. Release me."

Silbane didn't move, his form absolutely still. So much had happened to them. Now Arek was lost on the other side of this Gate. Would keeping this insane mage help or hinder them? Furthermore, their presence in Lilyth's world would be noted. Would having a beacon of power as bright as Duncan's, separate from them, allow a measure of anonymity?

"I have done all you asked, there is nothing more!" Duncan fell to one knee. He looked up and whispered, "I cannot leave them on the other side!"

A small sob escaped, and his back shook as if the very ground of his composure crumbled under him. He raised a fist illumed in power and slammed it into the granite floor, which buckled and cracked under the blow. "Release me!"

Silbane caught himself and took a deep breath. He was surprised Duncan had lasted this long, for the man's mind was fractured. Every step closer must have been agonizing for him, knowing he couldn't leave without breaking the Oath, thereby jeopardizing his very existence.

Each choice had its dangers, but Silbane blew out the breath he held and said, "You stand released from your oath." As he uttered those words, a flash of yellow surrounded them both.

"Are you mad?" cried Kisan. She looked around the seething mass, then at Duncan, preparing for an attack, but the man didn't move. He just knelt on one knee, his face resting in the crook of his arm, as if asleep.

He slowly stirred, as if hearing Silbane for the first time, and looked up in disbelief. Tears rolled down his face as he drew in a shuddering breath. His eyes locked again with the master who had just released him and he nodded once in gratitude. He rose slowly, facing the group. "I thank you and offer you this in repayment. What is my true name?"

Silbane stared at Duncan but felt his concentration narrow like it had once before, presaging the advent of Sight. The air darkened and time slowed to a heartbeat. Duncan still stood before him, but surrounding him was a conflagration of yellow light, as if the air itself had ignited into a sunburst. It was the Way, and so potent! He'd had no idea the man held so much power, but there was more.

Superimposed around him was another figure. It stood towering over them, terrible in aspect. Red eyes that spoke of death glared from beneath a helm of burnt cinder. Dark wings of ash and smoke wrapped protectively around the Old Lord, making him seem insignificant, despite his incandescent aura. It was a creature that filled Silbane with dread, and yet there was nothing he could do to escape it.

Another heartbeat and the creature inclined its massive head to the master, acknowledging they could see each other. Its eyes flared crimson and in a voice with the rasp of a dead snake's skin, a sound recalling rot and decay, it said, "I am Scythe. We thank you for our release."

Time snapped back and the vision was gone. Silbane staggered into Kisan, drained again as before. This time, however, he felt himself recovering more quickly. He pushed himself erect and looked at Duncan, already knowing what the other would say, and offered, "Scythe."

"My memories begin to open to you and in time you will understand more."

Silbane knew Duncan meant the mindread they shared, but he'd just seen something vastly different. Clearly it'd been the Sight, the gift of Rai'stahn and the Conclave, yet he didn't correct the archmage. No one else had seen the creature and while this made sense, it brought into question everything he knew about himself and the Way.

Duncan focused on the two masters and continued, "The name I heard when I Ascended was Scythe, but it isn't my name."

Though both Kisan and Silbane knew what Ascension meant, only Silbane understood the literal truth of what Duncan had just said. Did every adept have a companion such as Scythe? *And what about my vision of Valarius and the Conclave? What was the connection to Azrael?* He felt the underpinnings of all he believed tilt.

It was Yetteje who finally said, "Who's Scythe?"

Duncan smiled. "An Aeris lord."

He turned back to Silbane. "You must understand something if you hope to survive in Arcadia." He gave them a crooked smile and added, "Guard your thoughts well, for they give life to your worst fears. This truth is my parting gift to you. Use it however you wish."

As Silbane watched, the archmage backed up a step, gave the group a small bow, then turned and ascended the face of the pyramid.

* * * * *

Duncan moved with a single-minded purpose, gaining speed as he neared the scintillating, blue-white portal. In a few moments he was in front of it, his face lit by its unearthly glow.

I brought them, thousands for your army. Duncan's pale eyes narrowed when there was no answer. *The other gates are sealed, forcing Sovereign's hand here, as you commanded.*

Still, there was no sound, no voice to answer his claim.

Even the dragon was freed, a useful harbinger to your coming. The Conclave will act hastily now, out of fear, just as you wished.

When still nothing happened, Duncan said aloud, "Release them to me!"

At first, silence reigned. Then with a sigh, barely a whisper in his mind, a melodious voice said, *Peace for our people is at hand. Be welcome, Scythe. She awaits you, though all may not be as you wish.*

Duncan nodded and said, "It is enough."

* * * * *

The party watched Duncan face the gate with mixed expressions of anger and disbelief. They couldn't see what he saw from their position, but he seemed to gather himself, then take a step through. He vanished in a flash. His departure was so sudden that it caught most of them by surprise.

"He couldn't be more confusing on purpose," Kisan huffed, clearly exasperated. Then her eyes narrowed and she turned to Silbane, "You captured him because of his knowledge of portals and gates."

Silbane nodded, still silent, what Duncan had revealed echoing in his mind. The creature known as Scythe was an Aeris lord? His thoughts centered on what the dragons said during his vision: that Azrael would be freed if Valarius was killed. Did this mean Azrael had once bonded to Valarius, just as Scythe had to Duncan? His head swam with the implications, both for Valarius and more acutely, for himself. He turned to Kisan, wonder in his eyes, and said, "There's more going on here than we know."

"Such as?" It was clear she questioned the release of an asset like Duncan.

Silbane felt more thoughtful and infinitely more tired. Kisan's stance didn't surprise him, it made him weary, and again he hesitated to share everything he knew. The revelations and visions combined to make him doubt his own role.

Furthermore, if Duncan were to be believed, his true name wasn't his own. The repercussions of this one small fact were significant. It meant that in some ways, Valarius had been correct that the Aeris could be partnered with. Yet he didn't want to sit here idly speculating while the boys headed into Lilyth's world alone. More delay put Arek farther from him and potentially in more danger.

Instead, he offered, "You know I read him. He's consumed with finding his wife, though she's centuries dead." He turned and faced Kisan. "He is of more use stirring his havoc away from us, as you know he will." He thought then of the winged creature of smoke and ash he'd seen standing over Duncan and added, "Trust me."

"Was he lying?" Yetteje interjected herself between the two masters, her stance both accusing and demanding an answer. "He said they could be saved."

At first Silbane was confused by the question, his mind still on the vision of Scythe, its crimson eyes radiant below a cinder crown. It was burned into his memory.

Yetteje clarified, "My father, the others who have died . . ."

Comprehension dawned and he nodded to where Duncan had disappeared and answered, "He thinks so, but he's insane."

"You didn't answer me. Is my father still alive?" She looked up the pyramid steps now with an intensity that was almost palpable.

"And the king," added Ash. "Is there a chance we may yet save him?"

"Piter might be there," Kisan said, but to no one in particular. When no one answered, she walked toward the pyramid steps.

Silbane knew she'd no faith in Duncan, yet he sensed the seed of saving Piter had been planted and begun to take root like an invading weed. Perhaps this was her chance to set all things right, rebalancing the wrongs she perceived done to her apprentice?

Silbane shifted his gaze from Kisan's retreating back. He looked at everyone and said, "I'm going to save Arek before it's too late. You two don't have to join us." He turned and started walking up the pyramid steps, following the younger master. All the answers he wanted lay beyond the blue sun.

"And leave us here in a fortress overrun by demons?" Yetteje asked. "I don't think so."

She grabbed Ash under an arm to support the firstmark as they made their way. They moved slowly, Tej trying her best not to jostle Ash's crushed shoulder and arm. They climbed in silence and before long, all had reached the apex.

The blue fire of the sun shone more intensely here, the light permeating them utterly. The circle of the Gate also stood open, through which they could see green fields and sunlit waters. The air was crystal clear, with a hint of a gentle spring wind and the smell of green grass and wildflowers.

"Arek's touch didn't close this." Silbane looked at Kisan and admitted, "I was wrong."

Kisan buried her face in her hands and rubbed until the skin was red. When she looked up, it was with determination. She looked at Silbane and her voice took on the keen edge of steel when she answered, "I've gotten used to it."

Just then a sigh of relief escaped from Ash's lips. He looked at his shoulder, then rotated his arm, smiling. When he noticed the group looking at him, his expression became more thoughtful.

Silbane saw the swarm of yellow particles, coalescing like mist, adhering and permeating the armsmark's shoulder. He knew if he concentrated, he could see the muscle and bone reknit itself under the ministrations of Tempest. Knowing the answer, he still asked, "Healed?"

Ash nodded, "And not at the expense of anyone else."

"Useful where we're going," muttered Kisan.

Yetteje glanced at Silbane, then quietly asked, "Can you really find Niall?"

Silbane kept his eyes fixed on the Gate and the world behind it. "I think so."

The princess didn't hesitate, replying, "Then we'll rescue them . . . all of them." She readjusted the runebow and took a step forward.

Silbane looked back at the group and said, "Let's pay the Lady a visit."

With that, the four stepped into Lilyth's Gate and disappeared in a flash of blue and white.

Planewalkers

JOURNAL ENTRY 26

You may judge me as you will, for I no longer care what you think. I have found my soul here. When we started this journey together, I pleaded for your understanding and hoped you would judge me less harshly, or laud my efforts. It was a fool's dream, and I can dream of greater things.

Today I began a new ritual, a cleansing of myself. It will be an arduous process, a remaking of who I am, through discipline and dedication.

Through sacrifice, I will begin a new Shaping, one which will bring forth the perfect being, the harbinger of destruction upon the Aeris Lords and others who betrayed me, such as my friends in the Conclave.

I will raise it from its very first breath to know it is destined for greatness, made from the consummation of flesh and Aeris, and powerful because it is one with the Way. I will create the myths that surround it, the prophecies that define it. I wondered once, how do you kill a god?

My elves gave me the first clue. Sonya brought the second with her, for she is with child. Ritual is the key, faith is power, but we are the vessel.

I will bring forth a new myth, born to smite the Aeris, born for one purpose only: vengeance. What kills gods? Legends kill gods, and I will create the legend of a god-killer.

Then, I will unleash him.

—Valarius Galadine

Journal Entry 26

Here ends, ***Mythborn I, Rise of the Adepts.***

The story will continue in,
Mythborn II, Bane of the Warforged

Journal Entry 26

NOTE TO READER

Please FOLLOW and LIKE us on:

We hope you enjoyed reading

Mythborn I: Rise of the Adepts

If you'd like to learn more about Mythborn, please go to:

www.mythbornmedia.com
or
www.dawnslightmedia.com

Look for the rest of the Mythborn saga here:

- *Mythborn 1: Rise of the Adepts*

- *Mythborn 2: Bane of the Warforged*

- *Mythborn 3: Dark Ascension*

- *Mythborn 4: Arcadia Lost* *(Q4, 2018)*

- *Mythborn 5: Genesis* *(Q1, 2019)*

READER'S GUIDE

Affinities – Areas of concentration where a given monk has more skill or power. Affinities do not have to be chosen; however, once they are, it is difficult to return to the balanced nature, remaining at the center. The affinities are arranged

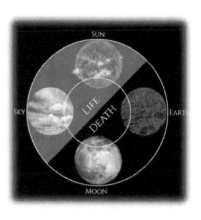

diametrically, such that a practitioner with an affinity in one area will not be as skillful in the affinity directly adjacent to their own and will have almost no skill in the area opposite their own. Note that Life and Death may be combined with ANY of the first four Affinities:

Sun – the use of fire, heat, and light.
Moon – the use of water, ice, and darkness.
Earth – the use of earth, plants, and lore.
Sky – the use of air, weather, and divination.
Life – sensing life, healing, and rejuvenation
Death – the use of time, wounding, and degeneration

Aging – Those on the Isle who practice the Way (see the Way) age more slowly than normal people. They are typically only a third of their age in appearance. A hundred year old adept would appear to be in his or her mid-thirties. This is a by-product of their training and begins once they attain the rank of adept (see Ranks).

Reader's Guide

Arek Winterthorn – Apprentice, Affinity – Unknown. Sixteen-year-old apprentice to Master Silbane, known to be able to disrupt magic. Like all sixteen year-olds, hopes he's special, but fears he's not, scared he might even be disposable. Unfortunately for him, the adepts think the same, making him an easy choice to be sacrificed. Keen if somewhat paranoid outlook, great with blades, knives, and unarmed combat, mostly horrible at picking friends.

Alyx Stemmer – Pragmatic squad leader who acts as aide-de-camp and squire to the Firstmark of Bara'cor. Assigned to safeguard the princess of EvenSea, Yetteje Tir. Probably wishes she'd not been transferred to Bara'cor just before the heat of summer, and oh yeah, a siege. Used to the soldier's luck, wishes the dice would roll differently for her every now and then. Too bad for her, they will.

Ash Rillaran – Armsmark and second-in-command of Bara'cor. Military strategist, master in bladed combat. Attended the War College in Shornhelm, graduated third in class, known for his insight into battle tactics and his skill with swords. Gets entangled with the blade, Tempest. Has had his share of crazy relationships, but Tempest is definitely a new kind of *crazy*.

Aspects – The basic act creating magic with the Way is an act of creation from within. The monk or mage uses the Way from within his body to generate power to perform what he wants. These channels are called 'Aspects', and govern the Senses, Movement, Attack/Defense, Creation, Transmutation, Channeling, and Domination. If you're going to learn only one, the last one is pretty darn good.

Lord Azrael – Ancient Celestial and warlord of the Aeris. The dragons believe if freed, he will oppose Lilyth and her Aeris army. No one knows for sure, and that makes

Azrael's freedom a prime reason for something even more epic to happen. You know this is going to happen, but when it does, it's still just ohhh so cool!

Lord Baalor – General of Lilyth's army and lord of storms. Ancient, powerful, and honorable, Baalor seeks justice for his fallen Aeris brethren and fights without fear. Able to channel the Way in its purest form. Demon of storms and lightning… not so good at small talk.

Bara'cor – Ancient fortress and stronghold, built by the Dwarves. Held by King Bara, then abandoned shortly after the Demon War against Lilyth, for unknown reasons. It now is held by King Bernal Galadine and his forces. The fortress itself is bigger than the current occupants seem to need. That's either good for expansion, or bad if the original tenants decide to return.

Ben'thor Tir – King of EvenSea, ruler of the eastern stronghold by that name and father to Yetteje Tir. Defender of the East and longtime friend to Bernal Galadine. Married to Bernal's sister. Wonders now if he might have misjudged Bernal Galadine's shrewdness, as he used to think the man wasn't the sharpest blade in the pile, yet somehow *he* got stuck with Bernal's sister as his wife.

Bernal Galadine – King of Bara'cor, ruler of the western stronghold by that name, father to Niall Galadine and Defender of the West. Barely graduated from the War College in Shornhelm. Would have been expelled, but grandfather Galadine pulled some strings, and also blades. But for what Bernal lacks in diplomacy, he more than makes up with that trait every great war hero has – he just won't quit. Wielder of the mighty runebow, Valor and the ensorcelled blade, Anzani.

Conclave, The – An ancient group dedicated to safeguarding life on Edyn. They are custodians of knowledge and guardians against anything that would endanger the Way. Their representative to Edyn is the Keeper named Thoth, a guy who's tired of withholding information all the time, or having to speak in prophecies and riddles... so he does what no one usually does in these kinds of situations – he blabs it all in a straightforward vomit of truth and clear, simple instructions... and yet everyone still f'cks it all up.

Cycle, Summer, Turn, Year – All refer to the passage of one year on Edyn. Depending on your level of debt, that's either a very long time, or not.

Dragor Dahl – Adept, Affinity – Moon. Originally from the southern continent of Koorva, master rank in unarmed combat and illusions. Teacher of Jesyn Shornhelm, whom he found as a baby, abandoned in the Shornhelm Wastes. Prime candidate for local tough gone good, not too happy with the guy to girl ratio on the Isle.

Flameskin – A protective halo made of ethereal fire earned when one has gained the rank of Adept. The color of the fire signifies that person's attunement to the Way. The weakest are purple and slowly progress until they shine pure and white. Great at defending one from harm, but also getting a Magehunter their own version of a personal burning at the stake.

Giridian Alacar – Adept, Affinity – Earth. Keeper of the Vault, master of artifacts and other magical items. Sixty years old, teacher to apprentice Tomas, scribe and chronicler of the adepts. Appears to others as a man in his late twenties. Known for his penchant for brewing teas and other mixtures he says are just 'herbs' he grows in his garden. Not the guy you'd ever think would be bad ass, until he is.

Houses – There are four great and dozens of minor Houses in Edyn:

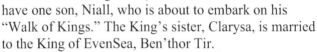

House Galadine – Led by the Imperial King Bernal Galadine and Queen Yevaine Galadine (of House Aeonian). House Galadine holds the fortress of Bara'cor. The King and Queen have one son, Niall, who is about to embark on his "Walk of Kings." The King's sister, Clarysa, is married to the King of EvenSea, Ben'thor Tir.

House Cadan – Held by King Rory Cadan and Lady Ilandra (of House Justeces). House Cadan holds the fortress of Shornhelm. They have one son, Durnal, who is still an infant. His sister, Morgan, is married to the King of Dawnlight. They are served by Algren Justeces, Ilandra's brother and Legate for Shornhelm in the capital city of Haven.

House Tir – Held by King Ben'thor Tir and Lady Clarysa Tir (of House Galadine). They hold the fortress of EvenSea. They have one daughter, Yetteje, current ward to House Galadine and staying at Bara'cor as part of her "Walk of Kings" ritual. Ben'thor has a brother, Ellis Tir, who serves as Legate of EvenSea in the capital city of Haven.

House Aeonian – Held by King Temar Aeonian and Lady Morgan Aeonian (of House Cadan). They hold the fortress of

Dawnlight. Their daughter, Yevaine, is married to the Imperial King Galadine. They are served by Merric Spaiten, who serves as Legate for Dawnlight in the capital city of Haven. No hints, but with a name like 'Spaiten'... you know he's not destined to be the good guy. Ok, that might be a hint.

Minor Houses: House Kalindor, House Justeces, House Spaiten, House Rillaran, House Stemmer, House Naserith, House Petra, House Illrys, House Alacar, and more . . . I'll dive into them in the next few books.

Hemendra – U'Zar, leader of the nomads of the Altan Wastes, military strategist assaulting Bara'cor. Responsible for the destruction of Dawnlight, Shornhelm, and most recently, EvenSea, under the command of Scythe. (see, Scythe) Hemendra has all the traits you love about barbarians, including being well-read, thoughtful, calm, and respectful of others' personal space. He's also handy with an axe.

Jesyn Shornhelm – Initiate, Affinity – Sun. Apprenticed to Dragor, training for her adept's Test, last name taken from the region where she was found. Adept rank in bladed and unarmed combat. Ascended to full adept to meet the growing danger in Dawnlight. Has had her pick of boyfriends on the Isle but as usual, selects the one worst for her long term prospects.

Jebida Naserith – Firstmark, leader of Bara'cor's military forces, longtime friend of Bernal Galadine. Distrustful of magic since the death of his wife and daughter at the hands of creatures that appeared through a rift. Hates magic, but also pretty much hates everything else, so it's difficult to tell when he's upset.

Kisan Talaris – Master, Affinity – Moon. Youngest to attain the rank, skilled in illusions and unarmed combat. Willful, strong, impatient, the kind you love to watch kick ass but would never hang out with. Assigned to back up Silbane should the need arise, and possibly the worst choice for that particular assignment. Teacher to Piter, then to Tomas. She recognizes the growing powers of Yetteje Tir. She's also the only master who doesn't care about how powerful she is. If it's enough to kill Magehunters and people who don't agree with her, well that's just fine.

Lilyth – Demonlord and Celestial, Lady of the Aeris. Ancient, better than most in seeing the truth of things. Seeks entry into this plane of existence, ostensibly for retribution for centuries of enslavement of the Aeris, but in reality her motivations are much more complex. Smart and practical, doesn't take risks, cares for her people in a more honest way than your average demon demagogue. She can make you happy to slit your own wrists, and sad you got her floor messy with your disgusting blood… but she's actually not that bad.

Mikal Galadine – King during the Demon Wars, leader of the forces that forced Lilyth back at the battle of Sovereign's Fall. Victorious, then did an about-face and decreed all magic was outlawed and mages were to be killed on sight. Really bad timing for any mages who heard the decree. Brother to General Valarius Galadine (the archmage who ironically did everything the opposite of his brother, including starting the war). Mikal is a seriously disturbed man who ultimately becomes more than he wished for in Lilyth's realm.

Mindread – The ability of a practitioner of the Way to assimilate and read the thoughts of another person. Extremely taxing in power, so the information retained is often incomplete or jumbled. However, it can lend situational context when paired with the caster's own perceptions. Generally never used at parties or during a first date by those who <u>don't</u> have this ability.

Mindspeak – The ability for a practitioner of the Way to reach out and speak telepathically with another practitioner. Extremely taxing in its use of energy, but provides a near instantaneous connection through which thoughts and energy can be shared. Conversely, almost always used at parties to get someone to turn around and look for the 'imaginary' voices.

Niall Galadine – Crown Prince of Bara'cor, seventeen years old. Trained in weapons combat, but you get the idea he skips a lot of classes. Hasn't yet made the transition from combat in tales to combat in real life. About to initiate his rite of passage to manhood, known as the *Walk of Kings*. A bit entitled, a bit insufferable, tries to be noticed. With the right guidance he could make an average king. With the wrong guidance, a very memorable tyrant.

Piter Winterthorn – Initiate apprenticed to Kisan, training for his adept's Test, last name taken from the region near where he was found, master rank in bladed combat, adept rank in spellcraft. Because he's seen from the eyes of bullies, Piter seems both churlish and annoying. Ostracized by Arek, Piter yearns to be accepted by just about anyone, and boy is he going to get his wish! Unfortunately, his personality *does* make him annoying, so nothing good is going to happen.

Rai'stahn – Ancient dragon, defender of the world, now inhabits a small part of the Isle where the adepts train. Predator, powerful in the Way, able to regenerate, and able to assume many forms. Skilled in combat (immeasurable by common mortal rankings). Does not involve himself in the world's affairs, until the emergence of Arek and the Gate at Bara'cor. Now, some of the actions he took during the Demon Wars are coming back to haunt him, as these kinds of things usually do. Not self-aware enough to realize he's the root cause, but very good at blaming and then killing others for his own mistakes.

Rai'kesh – Ancient dragon and king of the dragonkind. Leader of the Conclave and instrumental in giving Valarius Galadine a vision of the true nature of the Way. Some argue this caused Valarius to go down the fateful path he chose, others think it was the next thing that pitched Valarius over the edge. Ordered Rai'stahn to kill Valarius at the battle of Sovereign's Fall, but only after the archmage won. Most agree this caused Valarius to harbor a tad of resentment against the dragons of Edyn.

Ranks – There are four tiers of rank, with many subdivisions. These four tiers are initiate, adept, master, and archmage.
1. All apprentices, once they pass their Test of Potential and earn their Green rank, are initiates.
2. Once an initiate passes his Test of Ascension, he or she wears the black uniform and gains the rank of adept.
3. From there, they test again for the rank of master.
   - Currently there are two masters on the Isle: Silbane, and Kisan.
   - There are also three adepts: Giridian, Thera, and Dragor.
   - Tomas, Jesyn, Piter, and Arek are initiates preparing to Test for the rank of adept.

- Lore Father Themun Dreys is the only Archmage on the Isle, and as such administers the tests of rank. He also plans all the parties.
- Ranks are also used to denote someone's skill along these same four tiers, so a person with a master's rank in bladed combat would be generally better than one with an adept's or initiate's rank. Unless they fought with their left hand, in which case they'd be about the same, or maybe worse, depending on if their left hand was their off hand.

Scythe – Archmage, red-robed wizard who seeks Lilyth's Gate, allied with Hemendra of the Nomads, archmage rank in all things magical, possessor of the Old Lore, and able to wield it as the Old Lords did. Just on this side of crazy, and because of that, more dangerous. Really, really, really focused on getting someone back whom he lost due to a slight error in judgement. Hopes they remember it differently.

Silbane Darius Petracles – Master, Affinity – Sun. Skilled in all forms of combat and combat magic. Eighty years old and teacher of Arek Winterthorn. Appears to others as a man in his late thirties. Pragmatic, self-confident, perhaps enjoys life a little too much. You'd send him into hell to save the world, but he's not the right guy to watch your kids, ever.

Techniques – A monk may combine various Aspects with their Affinity. These are called *Techniques* and usually require a physical action as well. If one thinks of Affinities as the raw power of the Way and Aspects as the areas in which that power is focused, Techniques are the method by which an Aspect affects or uses an Affinity.

Tempest – Ancient sentient sword, given to Arek for his protection. Said to have the power to heal its wielder from grave injury. Particularly fond of Ash, and Arek, not so much Silbane. Not a really good example of balanced and rational thinking, much less love. It turns out she's pretty horrible at healing, too.

Themun Dreys – Archmage, Affinity – Sky. Lore Father of the Second Council of adepts, initiates the quest to ascertain the disposition of Lilyth's Gate, master illusionist. Easy to anger, slow to forgive, he's not your typical, balanced and rational leader. However, his force of will and tenacity have proven more useful in keeping his people alive. Although over two hundred years old, appears to others as a man in his sixties. Absolutely didn't want the job, but got stuck with it when his brother skipped out and left him holding the runestaff of office.

Thera Dawnlight – Adept, Affinity – Sky. Master's rank in herb lore and medicine, skilled in healing and defensive arts. Closest thing the Isle has to an activist, would definitely chain herself to a tree, a bear, or a dragon to save it, whether they wanted it or not. Orphan and found near Dawnlight, appears to others as a woman in her early forties.

Thoth – Guardian of the Archives, member of the Conclave, a group made up of the Elder Races and dedicated to safeguarding life on Edyn. Tries to state things simply, often making things worse by panicking those around him who can't handle the truth. Then wonders if maybe he ought to go back to speaking in riddles. Just waiting for someone to get it right for once.

Tomas Dawnlight – Apprentice, Affinity – Earth. Apprenticed to Adept Giridian, then to Master Kisan. Preparing for his Test of Ascension. Strong, brave, dumb, but he's dating Jesyn so maybe he's smarter than he looks. He's got a solid part to play, but it's not what you think, and it happens in the next book . Skillful in combining magic with strength, lifting with strength, eating with strength, reading with strength… uh, you get the idea.

Valarius Galadine – General and High Marshal of the King's forces at Sovereign's Fall, Archmage and Lore Father of the First Council of Adepts, known for causing the first cataclysm of the world. Powerful, strong-willed, championed the idea that demons were actually the source of magic and ruin in this world, then promptly went off and summoned the most powerful one. Once he preemptively started a war with the Aeris, he was stripped of his title and rank. Didn't seem to slow him down or even make him pause. Self-reflection is not his strong suit.

The Way – An eldritch force that exists within the very fabric of space, allowing those that can tap into it the ability to manipulate time, space, and matter. There are many manifestations, limited only by the practitioner's imagination and discipline. The Old Lords of the First Council used it to create spells that could alter the very nature of the world. The Second Council has honed it into a power that manifests itself in their bodies when they engage in martial combat. The Third Council will likely focus on knitting, cleaning, and other mundane tasks. They think this will keep them unqualified to play any part in saving the world from its next problem… and yet they'll probably *still* be chosen.

Yetteje Tir – Princess of EvenSea, cousin to Niall Galadine, on her pilgrimage to ascend to the royal throne of EvenSea, with her final stop on the Walk of Kings at Bara'cor. She is seventeen and stubborn, hates authority but loves she's one of the 'haves' and not the, 'ewww, have nots'. She's brave and good with a blade, but has no desire to be a hero. It's too bad she's in *this* story, because Yetteje is one of the few who consistently makes sense, you know… like a hero.

Yevaine Galadine – Queen of Bara'cor, wife of Bernal. She is sent from Bara'cor at the siege's start with the young and weak. They are evacuated to Haven, capital city of Edyn, to deliver their refugees and return with reinforcements. You get the sense she's the mom who'd camp in the backyard with you and bring the bow and arrows. Doesn't seem squeamish, knows the business end of a blade. Clearly the one in charge of everything at Bara'cor, as witnessed by what happens when she leaves for just a few days. The fortress is overrun and demons kidnap her son. Not a high point for poor Bernal. At least he wasn't out drinking with the men.

Reader's Guide

ABOUT THE AUTHOR

Vijay Lakshman was born in Ottawa, Canada. He spent his early years in Bangkok, Thailand. When he was nine, his father took him to a martial arts exhibition and his life changed forever.

He dedicated the next forty years to mastering the martial arts, his quest taking him from Thailand, across the U.S. and Europe, to Hong Kong and China. In 1991 he earned his black belt and accumulated thousands of hours in the ring, fighting against the best the world had to offer, or at least the best in his immediate vicinity. His true passion however, is writing. Mythborn his first epic fantasy series, and pays homage to a lifetime spent mastering the arts of combat and to his passion for writing fantasy and science fiction.

Vijay has created over eighty-five titles in his career as a video game designer and architect of game-based learning software, but spends his free time entertaining his curiosity. This includes researching almost anything on Google, building aquascapes, and flying (and mostly crashing) quadcopters.

His life experiences include graduation from the Harvard Business School's General Manager Program, forty years of training in karate, sixteen years of close combat grappling, fifteen years of kendo, six years of long-distance cycling, and taking various things in the house apart.

About the Author

Putting everything back together is the job of a future, better, version of himself – hopefully one with rechargeable batteries and an extended warranty.

Made in the USA
Middletown, DE
21 July 2018